CHILDREN OF THE NIGHT

CHILDREN OF THE NIGHT

THE BEST SHORT STORIES BY BLACK WRITERS, 1967 TO THE PRESENT

Edited by
GLORIA NAYLOR

Little, Brown and Company
BOSTON   NEW YORK   TORONTO   LONDON

First Edition

Permissions acknowledgments appear on page 571.

Library of Congress Cataloging-in-Publication Data

Children of the night : the best short stories by Black writers, 1967 to
the present / edited by Gloria Naylor. — 1st ed.
    p.   cm.
  ISBN 0-316-59926-3 (hc)
   1. Short stories, American–Afro-American authors. 2. Afro-
Americans—Social life and customs—Fiction. 3. American
fiction—20th century. I. Naylor, Gloria.
PS647.A35C5 1995
813'.018896073—dc20   95-16356

10 9 8 7 6 5 4 3 2

MV-NY

*Published simultaneously in Canada
by Little, Brown & Company (Canada) Limited*

Printed in the United States of America

For My People

Let a new earth rise. Let another world be born. Let a bloody peace be written in the sky. Let a second generation full of courage issue forth; let a people loving freedom come to growth. Let a beauty full of healing and strength of final clenching be the pulsing in our spirits and our blood. Let the martial songs be written, let the dirges disappear. Let a race of men now rise and take control.

— Margaret Walker

Contents

Editor's Note

THE STORIES collected here are not in chronological order because they aren't offered as documents of the changes in this society since the Civil Rights Movement; they are too recent, we are still within them. Compiling an anthology purporting to be "the best" of anything begs several questions; the most obvious — By what standard? These stories were selected as the best to demonstrate, either thematically or structurally, mechanisms for surviving constant assaults against one's mind and spirit.

Aside from that, I had two criteria for these short stories: First, that they be just that and not excerpts from novels; although some of these pieces were later incorporated into a novel or in one case a play by the author, they were originally published as short stories and did stand on their own. Second, the authors were to be African-American, with the Americas limited here to North America. But even with such circumscriptions, the diversity among these writers was astounding.

As this volume began to take shape, it was fascinating for me to watch how varied writers' takes might be on the exact same subject — depending upon when they were born, where they were born, what gender they were born, or what gender they chose to love. So while this anthology earmarks 1967 to the present, it is arranged to allow the reader to follow the course of a particular subject matter — slavery, for example — in the hands of different writers over a span of time and experience. Too often we think that there is something called *the* black experience; so stories are thrown together in an anthology with some all-encompassing title and left at that. We are not a monolithic people; in this anthology you will find several black experiences. And I wanted to give those who had no choice but to read this particular one (a beleaguered college student, no doubt) something interesting and different. Something to provoke thought.

Acknowledgments

WHEN IT'S OFTEN BEEN SAID in acknowledgments, "I couldn't have done it without . . . ," it was always my suspicion that a bit of hyperbole was at play. Yes, of course, I could have completed this anthology without the assistance of a single soul; but it would have taken me a long, long time. Long enough to have made undertaking the whole enterprise impractical, if not akin to insanity. So for saving my sanity and uncountable years of my life, my thanks go out to everyone at the colleges, universities, creative writing programs, and state arts agencies across the country; as well as Al Young and Madison Smartt Bell, who so generously answered my solicitations for the names of promising African-American writers.

The New York Public Library, the Schomburg Center for Research in Black Culture, Mooreland-Spingarn, and the Library of Congress were invaluable resources as were many small independent bookstores including Vertigo Books in Washington, D.C., Nkiru, and Community Bookstore in Brooklyn, New York.

And I was also fortunate enough to have a team of human resources for this project: Kathy Anderson, Veronica Mitchell, Andrea Wade, Gwynn MacDonald, Stephanie Jones, Grigsby Morgan-Hubbard, and Debbie Morris. To you all I give my sincere gratitude. And a special note of thanks to my assistant, Caledonia Kearns, for her outstanding and continual effort on behalf of this historic anthology.

Children of the Night

The great mystery is not that we should have been thrown down here at random between the profusion of matter and that of the stars; it is that from our very prison we should draw, from our own selves, images powerful enough to deny our nothingness.

— André Malraux: *Man's Fate*

In THE BEGINNING was the word. Yet in the fertile grasslands of Tanzania for eons there had been sound. Volcanic eruptions. The groans of splitting continents. The grinding of receding glaciers. The hissing of hot springs. The skittering of sea creatures gaining leg and speed on firm ground; air creatures whishing through the trees — the cry of birth. No longer beasts, but not yet men, *Homo erectus* hulked across the primeval landscape: broad flat feet, elongated forelimbs with prehensile fingers, they negated hunger by grubbing for roots and seeds; negated cold by worshipping fire; negated fear of mutilation and death by honing sharp stones against the claws and teeth of predators waiting to leap from the darkness of the forests. Procreation, the suckling of young, the banding up with kind, done with the instincts of their fellow scavengers, the hyena. Grunts. Spitting. Whistles. Keens. And perhaps the forming of a guttural sound for "no," since it was a survival that depended upon negation. A constant struggle against the overwhelming odds for extinction. Life could have continued in this vein for eternity. An eternity of waiting for that first small step away from the instincts of an animal, for the beginning to dawn. How it happened, no one knows, but somewhere in this vast plain of time, on those plains of Africa, the dwarfed brain of the man/beast, *Homo erec-*

tus, evolved to conceptualize *the* word. I like to think, because of my love for the poetic, that it was, indeed, at dawn. After a night a bit colder than others, in a hungry season with the grubbing scarcer than others, she feels the first warmth of the sun creeping over the horizon; untangles her arms and legs from the spooned bodies of the band; shakes the lice from her matted hair; digs the clotted mucus from her eyes, and crawling out from their low rock shelter, she sees streaks of early light revealing a fresh upcropping of seed grass. As she reaches a clawed hand for the nearest shoots, a droplet of dew on another patch — just beyond her reach — begins to turn from dark red to gold. Her eyes dart between the immediate and the far, between negating hunger and seeking light, as her clawed hand stills just a fraction of a second. And in that stillness civilization awaits. The word: *Yes.* The first reach beyond. A fist clutching dirt and tender shoots. A fetid arm raised to the blazing horizon. *Yes.*

We have come, in evolutionary time of a minute a millennium, roughly six hours from that propitious moment. The first awakening of reason. The ultimate evolution of these creatures into *Homo sapiens* that then branched into Negroid, Mongoloid, Caucasoid, Australoid, Amerindian, and Polynesian happened only half an hour ago. And in our present stage of development, we are still utilizing only two languages: one of survival and one of affirmation. One reactive, the other active. One the foundation of all commerce and wars, the other the foundation of science and the arts. One, in spite of the embellishments of technology to warfare and business, does not elevate us beyond our primal concerns of base existence and territoriality; while the other, in spite of the commerce that now surrounds creativity, is all that separates us from the beasts of the forest and the beast within.

To see the arts as a bulwark against evolutionary regression is hardly a novel idea, but neither is it an extreme one when we realize that the Sumerians invented writing only five minutes ago. And from that time the "classics" marking all of Western literature from *The Iliad* and *The Odyssey*, and all of Eastern from the *Shih Ching* and *Bhagavata*, have yet to evolve beyond themes that deal with the base instincts of men making love or making war among themselves or the gods they created in their image. And so what an artist must do today is what artists started out doing with the cave markings and drawings in Dordogne — reach beyond the base machinations of their respective societies, in toward the space that sits apart from the bestial and testify to that space; document the existence of a core humanity; and with the documentation give witness to the same. It is not done for pleasure or profit. It is done because it cannot *not* be done. And that it is done at all is one of life's minor miracles.

And where does one place this anthology of writers in all of this? Dead center. Ours is an identity, with its peculiar formation in America, that mates the best — and worse — impulses springing from the human condition. Survival and self-interest have always been the driving force of human nature. While using the language of affirmation as impetus or ideology, governments came to power, national identities were established, territories were staked out, protected, and expanded by conquest of the weaker. America was born for no other reason than that, and eventually stretched from sea to shining sea for no other. At the bottom line the English colonists arriving here had to eat; at the top line this continent held the potential for some to get rich with farming, mining, and commercial enterprises. Voluntary immigration during the eighteenth century wasn't providing enough manpower to fuel that top line; neither was the enslaved European or enslaved Native American. So enter the African.

Slave labor was not a new concept for the Western or non-Western world — *paid* labor was, having come into full force with the rise of factories during the Industrial Revolution. But prior to that, each of the seven wonders of the world; the glory that was Greece and the grandeur that was Rome — and all of the resultant European empires — had been built with slave labor. Some prefer to call the European agrarian system "serfdom"; I prefer to call it what it was. So while the practice was common and the tradition long, the complicating factor with Europeans enslaving Africans in America was the difficulty of reconciling the ideology of this newly formed nation with economic necessity. So enter the myth.

A myth is more powerful — and lasting — than reality. Because it is born of the need to ward off our fear of the irreconcilable around us or within us. Those things that go bump in the night of our primal beginnings. The Revolutionary War, or any war fought in the eighteenth century, was bloody business. Poor velocity of the bullets meant getting within ten feet of a man to blow a hole in his chest. The admonition not to shoot "till you see the whites of their eyes" meant that when you did shoot, the gore splattered back into your face. One bullet. Then reload. And if another man was coming too quickly to allow the reload, the butt of the gun was used as a club to smash his head in. This is how that war was fought; and such brutality *had* to be against tyranny — to be free, as it was every man's right to be. And so the Africans they needed to enslave to ensure their continued survival could not be men. And, oh, there were such a host of things that made them less than human: the gods they worshipped, the language they spoke, the music they made, the shelters they built, the loincloths they wore — the color of their skin.

And since it took only one generation in America to remove most of the visible cultural traits from Africans but the color of their skin, that became the sole foundation for the myth of their subhumanity, as well as the demarcation for continued enslavement. And their contin- ued enslavement automatically relegated them to a status inferior to that of free laborers who worked side by side with them. So a tauto- logical situation was set up from the first generation of Africans in America: They are slaves because they're inferior; and they're inferior because they are slaves. Lost in all this was a simple truth — to be the descendant of a Senegalese, Gambian, Ivorian, or Nigerian is to hold a national identity as much as to be the descendant of an Englishman, Dutchman, Scot, or German. But when a society legislated that a skin color defined an inferior social status, then it necessitated that a skin color must also define a superior one. While there were excep- tions to the rule, the rule of the land held firm that you knew a slave (inferior being) by the color of the skin; as you knew a nonslave (su- perior being) by the color of the skin. And we moved slowly, inextri- cably, from a political definition into *personal identification*.

A negation of the color of the African's skin was an affirmation of freedom and all that America stood for: the inalienable right to be free from political or religious persecution; to profit from backbreaking la- bor and personal sacrifice; to have a chance to build a better life for oneself and one's children as part of a growing and thriving democracy. The clarion call was loud and other European immigrants streamed in: the Irish and Italian, the Poles and Slavs, the Greeks and Scandi- navians. Their living conditions often abominable, their hunger ex- ploited, their spirits broken; often gaining little profit as they "worked like slaves" — but once they lost the visible cultural traits of the language they spoke, the music they made, the shelters they built, the clothing they wore — they painfully but inextricably gained the right for their children to benefit and — much more important — to be known by the color of their skin. A White American. An identity born from the negation of all it meant to be a slave. The negation of all it meant to be Black. And like a mangrove tree, the branches becoming roots, the roots becoming branches — able to live without the original life source, to grow solid and impermeable enough to create whole land masses — the myth lived on; long after the political reality of slavery died. Because the myth had gained an independent life: fed by the need of slave owners to protect their belief in their own humanity; fed by the need of the masses of immigrants to finally thrive where they'd been denied; and fed by the acculturated slaves who didn't take up the ultimatum to live free or die, thus escaping the extermination visited upon the Native American. There was no *need* for all concerned that was strong enough to uproot a myth that spoke to the survival instincts of all concerned. And there was hardly a need for the government to change laws or fight a war — civil or any other kind — over issues that weren't threatening the survival of the nation.

Slavery, in truth, was never damaging to the economic survival of America. It would have, as an inefficient form of labor in an increasingly industrialized society, slowly disappeared on its own. And, the moral protestations of nineteenth-century abolitionists and twentieth-century liberals aside, it wasn't even damaging to the psychic survival of America. My point is to the contrary — its existence helped to shape a cohesive national identity for the majority of Americans. Lip service is paid to it having been a horrible institution, but our cultural reality belies such protestations as we renovate and beautify slave plantations; build tourist industries and mythologies surrounding the grandeur and glamour of the lifestyles of slave owners; turn an apologia like *Gone With the Wind* into a cultural icon. Because no one really cared, except the slaves and their descendants, that there was slavery in America. Its existence had threatened nothing that was meaningful — meaning: the survival of them and theirs.

And so the myth grew and grew — no longer needing the presence of slavery or the compliance of slaves; the presence of mandated inferiority under constitutional law; or even the evidence of a skin color. Black. The idea of it could live alone. Black. Could live to root itself deeper than politics. Black. Deeper than reason. In that place where the elements of survival and affirmation tremble in balance to constitute — and preserve — a humanity against the bestial; the idea of Black lurks to threaten that balance. Because Black is what White is not. It is naïve to think that anyone who calls himself or herself a "white" American can totally uproot these feelings, because they have been given no other way to be them. And concomitantly, anyone who calls himself or herself a "black" American has been given no other way either.

With this backdrop the Civil Rights Movement lived up to its name. The rights of American citizens who were of African descent were moved into the political forum with resultant federal laws to protect those rights in voting, employment, education, and housing through the courts. A political movement spawned a social movement that spawned a cultural movement. In the last forty years this has changed the *face* of America while the heart of America remains the same. It has changed the way white Americans talk about or to black Americans; not the way they think. And there will be more change. More visibility for the talented and gifted and driven. More power in the political and economic arena for those same talented and gifted and driven. This is irrefutable. And for none of the above, there will be bitterness and desperation and bewilderment. There will be segregated schools. Segregated neighborhoods. A segregated death row. And Los Angeles will burn — again and again. For the lifetime of this anthology, fear will wear a black face in America. This is irrefutable. Yes, at a minute a millennium, we haven't got a prayer that *twelve seconds* of paper and ink — the sum total of all American literature — could witness a true evolution.

The tradition of letters on which this anthology stands is as old as this country. Before literacy was even legal for the majority of African-Americans, in 1773 Phillis Wheatley, a Boston slave, published *Poems on Various Subjects: Religious and Moral,* making her the first woman in America — of any race — to compile a collection of poetry. And what we can trace over the next two hundred years is that while some early African-American writers also utilized the literary stereotypes prevalent in white American literature: the tragic mulatto in the nineteenth century, and the free-hearted primitive during the Harlem Renaissance in the early twentieth; central to their work is a struggle for self-identity. Who am I? "I yam what I yam," Ralph Ellison said in *Invisible Man* — the classic prototype for the social and literary journey the African-American as citizen and artist has taken. Ellison's unnamed, faceless protagonist makes the odyssey from the South to the urban North searching for a meaning — a language of affirmation. It is not found within the larger society after he goes from confrontation to confrontation. And so he ends up in a dark basement, ruminating on the musical forms and words of his own unique culture — creating his own light.

Modern African-American literature has taken this same path as exemplified by the two volumes of this anthology. In the first volume, covering the first seventy years of the twentieth century, with many of the older writers there is little ironic distance between narrator and event when the subject is racial oppression; it is there as a central metaphor, immediate and burning. Images of victimization pile up, one behind another, as their protagonists confront the oppressive symbols of southern bigots, northern bigots, educated bigots, uneducated bigots, young bigots, old bigots. . . . This gives way under the pen of the younger writers to a different type of confrontation: political militants or cultural militants against oppressive symbols of assimilation. But always fighting something outside. A need to be known as a contender — as Ellison's inexperienced protagonist — to be seen. The earlier stories in this volume also exemplify the vestiges of militancy as metaphor, as narrative strategy; but they give way to a preponderance of work that turns inward — a contemplation of our personal self and communal self. There is a maturing consciousness here of language as language; of human nature as the true enemy of us all. It is as Langston Hughes, the former editor of this anthology, stated in "The Negro Artist and the Racial Mountain": "We Negro artists who create now intend to express our individual dark-skinned selves without fear or shame. If white people are pleased, we are glad. If they are not, it doesn't matter. We know we are beautiful. And ugly too. The tom-tom cries and the tom-tom laughs. If colored people are pleased, we are glad. If they are not, their displeasure doesn't matter either. We build our temples for tomorrow, strong as we know how, and we stand on top of the mountain free within ourselves."

And the present editor of this anthology states that as artists we also stand on a continuum of what writers have been documenting since the Sumerians invented the form: that while we have spent a consummate amount of energy making love or making war, there is *more* to what we are. We can no longer survive just surviving. With the small distance it has brought us, evolution has brought us that far. So these stories are collected here as examples of affirmation: of memory, of history, of family: of being. They are the work of artists attempting to make sense of language and form; to make sense of the times in which they lived and the times over which they witnessed change; and with the science-fiction writers, of the times even yet to be.

But we are still at the beginning: of mankind as a species; of America as a nation; of the African-American as a full citizen. A lot of beginnings. Much uncertainty. Still children of the night. Except there is the fact that we have come, at least, to this place because we are survivors. And if we ever evolve past this stage, we will need to keep reinforcing the language of affirmation within ourselves. Although it is not as ancient or powerful as the language of survival, without it we become empty vessels. And the human soul howling empty into the wind is a chilling sound. But the impulse to create any music, any splash of color; to feel the rhythm of the body through space or words on a line; is to hold us here — timorous at best — on this level of development while we await the next epiphany, for the clock to tick us, hopefully, another minute out of this dark and toward another dawn.

CHILDREN OF THE NIGHT

PART I

REMEMBERING . . .

SLAVERY

The Tale of Gorgik

by Samuel Delany

Because we must deal with the unknown, whose nature is by definition speculative and outside the flowing chain of language, whatever we make of it will be no more than probability and no less than error. The awareness of possible error in speculation and of a continued speculation regardless of error is an event in the history of modern rationalism whose importance, I think, cannot be overemphasized . . . Nevertheless, the subject of how and when we become certain that what we are doing is quite possibly wrong *but at least a beginning* has to be studied in its full historical and intellectual richness.

— Edward Said,
Beginnings, Intention and Method

1

HIS MOTHER from time to time claimed eastern connections with one of the great families of fisherwomen in the Ulvayn Islands: she had the eyes, but not the hair. His father was a sailor who, after a hip injury at sea, had fixed himself to the port of Kolhari, where he worked as a waterfront dispatcher for a wealthier importer. So Gorgik grew up in the greatest of Nevèrÿon ports, his youth along the docks substantially rougher than his parents would have liked and peppered with more trouble than they thought they could bear — though not so rough or troubled as some of his friends: he was neither killed by accidental deviltry nor arrested.

Childhood in Kolhari? Somehow, soldiers and sailors from the breadth of Nevèrÿon ambled and shouted all through it, up and down the Old Pavē; merchants and merchants' wives strolled on Black Avenue, so called for its topping that, on hot days, softened under the sandals; travelers and tradesmen met to chat in front of dockside inns — the Sump, the Kraken, the Dive; and among them all slipped the male and female slaves, those of aristocratic masters dressed more elegantly than many merchants, while others were so ragged and dirty their sex was indistinguishable, yet all with the hinged iron collars above fine or frayed shirt necks or bony shoulders, loose or tight around stringy or fleshy necks, and sometimes even hidden under jeweled pieces of damasked cloth set with beryls and tourmalines. Frequently this double memory returned to Gorgik: leaving a room where a lot of coins, some stacked, some scattered, lay on sheets of written-over parchment, to enter the storage room at the back of the warehouse his father worked in — but instead of bolts of hide and bales of hemp, he saw some two dozen, cross-legged on the gritty flooring, a few leaning against the earthen wall, three asleep in the corner, and one making water astraddle the trough that grooved the room's center. All were sullen, silent, naked — save the iron at their throats. As he walked through, none even looked at him. An hour, or two hours, or four hours later, he walked into that storage room again: empty. About the floor lay two dozen collars hinged open. From each a chain coiled the pitted grit to hang from a plank set in the wall to which the last, oversized links were pegged. The air was cool and fetid. In another room coins clinked. Had he been six? Or seven? or five . . . ? On the street behind the dockside warehouses women made jewelry and men made baskets; for oiled iron boys sold baked sweet potatoes that in winter were flaky and cold on the outside with just a trace of warmth in the center and, in summer, hot on the first bite with a hard wet knot in the middle; and mothers harangued their girls from raffia-curtained windows: "Get in the house, get in the house, get in the house this instant! There's work to do!"

With spring came the red and unmentionable ships from the south. And the balls. (Most things dubbed unmentionable have usually been mentioned quite fully in certain back alleys, at certain low dives, beside certain cisterns, by low men — and women — who do not shun low language. There have always been some phenomena, however, which are so baffling that neither high language nor low seems able to deal with them. The primitive response to such phenomena is terror and the sophisticated one, ignoral. These ships produced their share of both, sold their cargo, and were not talked of.) The balls were small enough for a man to hide one in his fist and made of some barely pliable blackish matter that juvenile dissection revealed hid a knuckle-sized bubble. With the balls came the rhyme that you bounced to on the stone flags around the neighborhood cistern:

> I went out to Babàra's Pit
> At the crescent moon's first dawning.
> But the Thanes of Garth had covered it,
> And no one found a place to sit,
> And Belham's key no longer fit,
> And all the soldiers fought a bit,
> And neither general cared a whit
> If any man of his was hit . . .

The rhyme went on as long as you could keep the little ball going, usually with a few repetitions, as many improvisations; and when you wanted to stop, you concluded:

> . . . And the eagle sighed and the serpent cried
> For all my lady's warning!

On *warning!* you slammed the ball hard as you could into the cistern's salt-stained wall. The black ball soared in sunlight. Boys and girls ran, pranced, squinted . . . Whoever caught it got next bounce.

Sometimes it was ". . . for all the Mad witch's warning . . ." which didn't fit the rhythm; sometimes it was ". . . for all Mad Olin's warning . . ." which did, but no one was sure what that meant. And anyone with an amphibrachic name was always in for ribbing. For one thing was certain: whoever'd done the warning had meant no good by it.

A number of balls went into cisterns. A number simply went wherever lost toys go. By autumn all were gone. (He was sad for that, too, because by many days' practice on the abandoned cistern down at the alley end behind the grain warehouse, he'd gotten so he could bounce the ball higher than any but the children half again his age.) The rhyme lingered in the heaped-over corners of memory's store, turned up, at longer and longer intervals, perhaps a moment before sleep on a winter evening, in a run along the walled bank of the Big Khora on some next-summer's afternoon.

A run in the streets of Kolhari? Those streets were loud with the profanity of a dozen languages. At the edges of the Spur, Gorgik learned that *voldreg* meant "excrement-caked privates of a female camel," which seemed to be the most common epithet in the glottal-rich speech of the dark-robed northern men, but if you used the word *ini*, which meant "a white gilley-flower," with these same men, you could get a smack for it. In the Alley of Gulls, inhabited mostly by southern folk, he heard the women, as they lugged their daubed baskets of water, dripping over the green-gray flags, talk of *nivu* this and *nivu* that, in their sibilant, lisping way and usually with a laugh. But when he asked Miese, the southern barbarian girl who carried vegetables and fish to the back door of the Kraken, what it meant, she told him — laughing — that it was not a word a man would want to know.

"Then it must have something to do with that happens to women every month, yes?" he'd asked with all the city-bred candor and sophistication of his (by now) fourteen years.

Miese tugged her basket higher on her hip: "I should think a man would want to know about *that!*" She stepped up the stairs to shoulder through the leather curtain that, when the boards were removed for the day, became the Kraken's back door. "No, it has nothing to do with a woman's monthly blood. You city people have the strangest ideas." And she was gone inside.

He never did learn the meaning.

The lower end of New Pavē (so called somewhere between ten and ten thousand years) was one with the dockside. Along the upper end, where the road dipped down again to cross the Bridge of Lost Desire, male and female prostitutes loitered or drank in the streets or solicited along the bridge's walkways, many come from exotic places and many spawned by old Kolhari herself, most of them brown by birth and darkened more by summer, like the fine, respectable folk of the city (indeed, like himself), though here were a few with yellow hair, pale skin, gray eyes, and their own lisping language (like Miese) bespeaking barbaric origins.

And weren't there more of them up this year than last?

Some stood about all but naked, squinting in the sun, while some wore elaborate skirts and belts and necklaces, most of the women and half the men with dark wings of paint laid about their eyes, some sleepy and slow-moving, some with quick smiles and inquisitive comments to every passerby, with sudden laughter and as-sudden anger (when the words for women's genitals, men's excreta, and cooking implements, all combined in truly novel ways, would howl across the bridge: the curses of the day). Yet all of them had, once they began to talk to you, astonishingly similar stories, as if one tale of pain, impoverishment, and privation (or a single, dull, if over-violent, life) had been passed from one to the other, belonging really to none of them, but only held by each the length of time it took to tell it, the only variation, as this one or that one recounted it, in the name of this small town or that abusive relative, or perhaps the particular betrayal, theft, or outrage that meant they could not go home.

By the dusty yards and stone-walled warehouses where the great commercial caravans pulled up after their months out in the land, with their mules and horses and covered carriages and open carts and provision wagons, once Gorgik stopped to talk to a caravan guard who stood a bit away from some others — who were squatting at the corner over a game of bones.

Rubbing his sweating hands against his leather kilt, the man began to speak to Gorgik of bandits in the mountains and brigands in the deserts — till, in a swirl of dark brocade, with street dust rising about his sandals, a merchant with cheeks as wrinkled as prunes, long teeth stained brown and black, and a beard like little tufts of wool stuck all over his dark jaw, rushed forward waving both his fists about his shoulders. "You . . . ! You . . . ! You'll never work for me again! The steward has told me all, all about your thievery and your lies! Oh, no — you'll not endanger *my* carriages with your cowardice and your conniving! Here —" From among his robes the old man pulled out a handful of coins and flung them so that gold and iron struck the guard's neck, chest, and hip. (As if the disks were hot from the smithy across the street, the guard flinched away.) "That's half your pay! Take it and be happy for it — when you're not worth a single bit of iron!" And though the guard wore a knife at his hip (and that must have been *his* spear leaning on the wall behind them) and was younger, bigger, and certainly stronger than the enraged merchant, he went scrabbling for his coins in the street and, with only a snarl and a glare — not even a fully articulated curse — snatched up his spear and hurried off. Only when he was a block away did he look back. Once. That's when Gorgik saw that the other guards had stopped their gambling to stand and move a step nearer. Still muttering, the old man turned back among them (who, Gorgik realized, were still very much expecting their own full salaries). They followed the merchant back to the warehouse, leaving Gorgik in the street with half an adventure in his head, a tale yearning for completion.

Another time when he and some friends were playing near the docks, from beside a mound of barrels a woman called to them: "Come here . . . you children!" She had a hard, lined face, was taller than his father, and her hair was shorter than his mother's. Walking up to her, they could see her hands and feet both were callused and cracked about their lighter edges. "Where . . . ," she asked, quiet, tentative, "tell me . . . where do they hire the women to wash the clothes?"

He and his friends just looked.

"Where do they . . . hire the washerwomen?" Her speech was accented; her skin was that deep, deep brown, a shade or two darker than his own, so often called black. "They hire women . . . somewhere near here, to wash the clothes. I heard it. Where is it? I need work. Where . . . where should I go?"

And he realized what halted and held back her words was fear — which is always difficult for children to understand in adults; especially in an adult as tall and as strong as this hard, handsome woman.

One of the older girls said: "You don't want to do that. They only hire barbarian women to do that, up in the Spur."

"But I need work," she said. "I need it . . . the Spur — where is that?"

One of the younger boys started to point. But, as if in an excess of nervousness or just high spirits, another suddenly shouted and at the same time flung his ball into the air. A moment later all of them were running and yelling to each other, now leaping across a coil of rope, now dodging around an overturned dinghy. He looked back to see the woman calling after them — though, for the shouting, he could not hear — and turned, as a friend tagged him, around a corner into another alley, all the time wondering what she was crying, what more she wanted to tell, what else she wanted to ask . . . The rest of the afternoon, in the dockloaders' calls, just below his friends' shrieks between the warehouses, behind the echoes of his own shouts across the yard where he ran after the others, he seemed to hear her, hear the fragments of some endless want, fear, hope, and harassment . . .

And still another time, when he wandered into the yard, he saw the boy (a few years older than himself? an old-looking sixteen? a young-looking eighteen?) sitting on the abandoned cistern wall.

Thin.

That's the first thing he thought, looking at those knobbly shoulders, those sharp knees. Gorgik walked nearer. The boy's skin had begun the same brown as his own. But it was as if some black wash of street dirt and gutter water had been splashed over him, heels to ears. The boy was not looking at him but stared at some spot on the flagstones a little ahead, so that it was easy to walk by and look at him more closely —

When he saw the iron collar around the boy's neck, Gorgik stopped — walking, thinking, breathing. There was a thud, thud, thud in his chest. For moments, he was dizzy. The shock was as intense as heat or cold.

When his vision cleared, the next thing Gorgik saw were the scars.

They were thick as his fingers and wormed around the boy's soiled flanks. Here the welts were brown, there darker than the surrounding skin — he knew what they were, though he had never seen anyone bearing them before. At least not from this close. They were from a flogging. In provincial villages, he knew whipping was used to punish criminals. And, of course, slaves.

Wanting desperately to move away, he stood staring for seconds, minutes, hours at the boy — who still did not look at him. No. *Only* seconds, he realized when, a breath later, he was walking on. Reaching the other alley, he stopped. He took three more breaths. And a fourth. Then he looked back.

Under his matted hair, the slave still had not looked up.

Stepping close to the wall, Gorgik stood there a long time. Soon he had framed ten, twenty, fifty questions he wanted to ask. But each time he pictured himself going up to speak to the collared boy, his breath grew short and his heart pounded. Finally, after trying three times, he managed to saunter again across the yard — first behind the cistern: the boy's back was webbed with six welts that, even as Gorgik counted them with held breath, seemed like a hundred in their irruptions and intersections. After waiting almost three minutes, he crossed the yard again, walking in front of the boy this time — then crossed twice more, once in front and again in back. Then, all at once, he left hurriedly, fearing, even though the boy *still* had not looked, someone passing by one of the alley openings might have seen — though the slave himself (newly escaped? a mad one who'd wandered off from, or been abandoned by, his master?), immobile on the cistern wall, gazed only at the ground.

Half an hour later, Gorgik was back.

The boy sat on the flags now, eyes closed, head back against the cistern wall. What had begun as a series of silent questions had turned for Gorgik into an entire dialogue, with a hundred answers the boy had begun to give him, a hundred stories the boy had begun to tell him. Gorgik walked past, his own feet only inches from the foul toenails. He gazed at the iron collar, till, again, he was moving away. He left by the Alley of No Name, telling himself that, really, he'd spied enough on this pathetic creature.

The dialogue, however, did not end.

When he returned in the lowering light an hour on, the boy was gone from the wall. Seconds later, Gorgik saw him, on the other side of the yard, by one of the buildings, curled up with his back against the sandstone, asleep. Again Gorgik walked past him, at several distances, several times — one minute or five between each passage. But finally he settled himself against the far alley entrance to watch, while the tale the boy told him went on and on, stopping and starting, repeating and revising, sometimes whispered so faintly he could not catch the words, sometimes crisp and vivid as life or dream, so that the square before him, with its circular cistern and the few pots, mostly broken, beside it, grew indistinct beneath a sky whose deepening blue was paled by an ivory wash above the far building, as the moon's gibbous arc slid over it —

The slave stretched out a leg, pulled it back, then rubbed at his cheek with one hand.

And the tale halted, again hammered to silence by Gorgik's heart. While Gorgik had been talking to himself, he'd been thinking, really, how easy it would be, once the boy woke, to go up to him, to speak, to ask him where he was from, where he was going, to offer sympathy, maybe a promise to return with food or a coin, to inquire after the particulars of his servitude, to proffer friendship, interest, advice . . .

Across the yard the slave stretched out his other hand, made a fist. Then, not suddenly but over a period of ten or fifteen seconds, he rocked a few times and pushed himself up on one arm. Contending fear and fascination bound Gorgik as strongly as they had the moment he'd first glimpsed the dirty fellow's collar. Gorgik pulled back into the doorway, then peered out again.

With a child between, two women ambled by and into the yard. Again Gorgik froze — though they paid no more attention to the boy lingering in the doorway than they did to the slave lounging by the wall. As the three of them strolled across the dust, the dirty youth stood, very slowly. He swayed. When he took a step, Gorgik saw that he limped — and a dozen tales in his head were catastrophically revised to accommodate it.

Walk out now and nod at him, smile at him, say something . . .

The two women and their child turned out of the yard down the Street of Small Fish.

The slave limped toward the cistern.

Gorgik stood paralyzed in the alley door.

When the scarred youth reached the cistern's waist-high wall, he stopped, not really looking into it. Hair stuck out about his head, sharp in the moonlight. After a few moments, he lifted his face, as though the single thread of cloud across the indigo sky attracted him. He raised his hands to his neck, to hook his fingers over the collar. He tugged —

What occurred next was, in the moment it happened, wholly unclear to Gorgik, for the tale he was just then telling himself was of an escaped slave who, with his criminal markings and limping toward an abandoned cistern, had raised his face to the moon and, in a moment of rebellion, grasped his collar to yank futilely and hopelessly at the iron locked on his neck — the collar that forever and irrevocably marked him as a fugitive for the slavers who patrolled the land, searching out new laborers in the villages, mostly these days (so he'd heard) in the south . . .

The semicircles of metal, hinged at the back, came apart in the boy's fists, as though the lock had not been set, or was broken. Now the boy raised the metal to the moon, its curved jaws open in his hand like black mandibles on some fabled dragon or even some unknown sign Gorgik's father might mark down in the dockside warehouse.

The boy tossed the collar over the wall.

Only when the iron vanished below the stone (the splash was very soft — and a beat after he expected it) did Gorgik realize that the collar, broken, or not locked in the first place, had truly been removed. With no comprehension as to why, he was overcome by chills. They rolled over him, flank, thigh, and shoulder. His fingers against the doorway corner were sweaty on the stone. After five breaths with his mouth wide so as not to make a sound, questions began to pour through his mind: Was this some criminal only pretending to be a slave? Or was it a slave who, now that he'd freed himself from the iron, would pretend to be a criminal? Or was it just a young madman, whose tale in its broken, inarticulate complexities he could never hope to know? Or was there some limpid and logical answer to it that only seemed so complex because, till now, he'd never thought to ask the proper questions?

The boy turned and lowered himself to sit again on the stone.

Gorgik moved his hand, just a little, on the jamb.

Go, he thought. Speak to him. He may be older, but I'm still bigger than he, and stronger. What harm could it do me, if I just went up and asked him to tell me who he is, to give me whatever bit of his story . . . ? Chills irrupted again, while he searched among the tales he'd been telling himself for any right reason to fear — in the middle of what had every aspect of terror about it, save motivation.

For some reason he remembered the woman on the docks. Had her fear, in all its irrationality, been anything like this . . . ?

Five minutes later, he walked into the yard again — as he had already done half a dozen times that day. The boy sat there, still not looking. Gorgik's own eyes fixed on the thin neck, below ear and black, spiking hair, where the collar had been. In the moonlight, now and again as he neared, with this step and with that, he could almost see the iron against the dirty brown, where a neck ligament was crossed by an irregular vein . . .

No, the collar was gone.

But even absent, it plummeted Gorgik into as much confusion as it had before, so that, as he passed, it was all he could do not to flinch away, like the guard before the merchant's coins, ears blocked by his own loud blood, all speech denied — and he was walking on, to the other side of the yard, down the alley, unable to remember the actual moment he'd passed the boy, who, he was sure, still had not looked up.

Gorgik was back at the yard with the sunrise.

The flogged boy was gone.

But as he wandered about, now glancing into the nearly empty cistern (he could make out nothing among the flashes on the black), now ambling off to examine this corner or that alley entrance, while dawn light slanted the western wall, all Gorgik was left with was a kind of hunger, a groping after some tale, some knowledge, some warm and material feeling against his body of what had escaped through silence.

Soon he returned to his house, where the dock water glittered down between the porch planks.

Kolhari was home to any and every adventurer — and to any and every adventure they were often so eager to tell. As Gorgik listened to this one and that, now from a tarry-armed sailor packing grain sacks at the docks, now from a heavy young market woman taking a break at the edge of the Spur, now to a tale of lust and loyalty, now to one of love and power, it was as if the ones he heard combined with the hunger left from the ones he'd missed, so that, in a week or a month, when he found himself reviewing them, he was not sure if the stories he had were dreams of his own or of the lives of others. Still, for all the tales, for all the dreaming, an adolescence spent roaming the city's boisterous back streets, its bustling avenues, taught Gorgik the double lesson that is, finally, all civilization can know:

The breadth of the world is vast and wide; nevertheless movement from place to place in it is possible; the ways of humanity are various and complex — but nevertheless negotiable.

Five weeks before Gorgik turned sixteen, the Child Empress Ynelgo, whose coming was just and generous, seized power. On that blustery afternoon in the month of the Rat, soldiers shouted from every street corner that the city's name was now, in fact, Kolhari — as every beggar woman and ship's boy and tavern maid and grain vendor had been calling it time out of memory. (It was no longer Neveryóna — which is what the last, dragon-bred residents of the High Court of Eagles had officially, but ineffectually, renamed it twenty years before.) That night several wealthy importers were assassinated, their homes sacked, their employees murdered — among them Gorgik's father. The employees' families were taken as slaves.

While in another room his mother's sobbing turned suddenly to a scream, then abruptly ceased, Gorgik was dragged naked into the chilly street. He spent his next five years in a Nevèrÿon obsidian mine thirty miles inland at the foot of the Faltha Mountains.

Gorgik was tall, strong, big-boned, friendly, and clever. Cleverness and friendliness had kept him from death and arrest on the docks. In the mines, along with the fact that he had been taught enough rudiments of writing to put down names and record workloads, they eventually secured the slave a work-gang foremanship: which meant that, with only a little stealing, he could get enough food so that instead of the wiry muscles that tightened along the bony frames of most miners, his arms and thighs and neck and chest swelled, high-veined and heavy, on his already heavy bones. At twenty-one he was a towering, black-haired gorilla of a youth, eyes permanently reddened from rock-dust, a scar from a pickax flung in a barracks brawl spilling one brown cheekbone. His hands were huge and rough-palmed, his foot soles like cracked leather.

He did not look a day more than fifteen years above his actual age.

2

The caravan of the Handmaid and Vizerine Myrgot, of the tan skin and tawny eyes, returning from the mountain hold of fabled Ellamon to the High Court of Eagles at Kolhari, made camp half a mile from the mines, beneath the Falthas' ragged and piney escarpments. In her youth, Myrgot had been called "an interesting-looking girl"; today she was known as a bottomless well of cunning and vice.

It was spring and the Vizerine was bored.

She had volunteered for the Ellamon mission because life at the High Court, under the Child Empress Ynelgo, whose reign was peaceful and productive, had of late been also damnably dull. The journey itself had refreshed her. But within Ellamon's fabled walls, once she had spent the obligatory afternoon out at the dragon corrals in the mountain sun, squinting up to watch the swoopings and turnings of the great, winged creatures (about which had gathered all the fables), she found herself, in the midst of her politicking with the mountain lairds and burghers, having to suffer the attentions of provincial bores — who were worse, she decided after a week, than their cosmopolitan counterparts.

But the mission was done. She sighed.

Myrgot stood in her tent door; she looked up at the black Falthas clawing through evening clouds and wondered if she might see any of the dark and fabled beasts arch the sunset. But no, for when all the fables were done, dragons were pretty well restricted to a few hundred yards of soaring and at a loss for launching from anywhere other than their craggy ledges. She watched the women in red scarves go off among other tents. "Jahor . . . ?"

The eunuch with the large nose stepped from behind her, turbaned and breeched in blue wool.

"I have dismissed my maids for the night. The mines are not far from here . . ." The Vizerine, known for her high-handed manners and low-minded pleasures, put her forearm across her breasts and kneaded her bare, bony elbow. "Go to the mines, Jahor. Bring me back the foulest, filthiest, wretchedest pit slave from the deepest darkest hole. I wish to slake my passion in some vile, low way." Her tongue, only a pink bud, moved along the tight line of her lips.

The eunuch touched the back of his fist to his forehead, nodded, bowed, backed away the required steps, turned, and departed.

An hour later, the Vizerine was looking out through the seam in the canvas at the tent's corner.

The boy whom Jahor guided before him into the clearing limped a few steps forward, then turned his face up in the light drizzle, that had begun minutes back, opening and closing his mouth as if around a recently forgotten word. The pit slave's name was Noyeed. He was fourteen. He had lost an eye three months ago: the wound had never been dressed and had not really healed. He had a fever. He was shivering. Bleeding gums had left his mouth scabby. Dirt had made his flesh scaly. He had been at the mines one month and was not expected to last another. Seeing this as a reasonable excuse, seven men at the mines two nights before had abused the boy cruelly and repeatedly — hence his limp.

Jahor let him stand there, mouthing tiny drops that glittered on his crusted lips, and went into the tent. "Madame, I —"

The Vizerine turned in the tent corner. "I have changed my mind." She frowned beneath the black hair (dyed now) braided in many loops across her forehead. From a tiny taboret, she picked up a thin-necked copper cruet and reached up between the brass chains to pour out half a cup more oil. The lamp flared. She replaced the cruet on the low table. "Oh, Jahor, there must be *someone* there . . . you know what I like. Really, our tastes are not that different. Try again. Bring someone else."

Jahor touched the back of his fist to his forehead, nodded his blue-bound head, and withdrew.

After returning Noyeed to his barracks, Jahor had no trouble with his next selection. When he had first come rattling the barred door of the guards' building, he had been testily sent on in among the slat-walled barracks, with a sleepy guard for guide, to seek out one of the gang foremen. In the foul sleeping quarters, the burly slave whom Jahor had shaken awake first cursed the eunuch like a dog; then, when he heard the Vizerine's request, laughed. The tall fellow had gotten up, taken Jahor to another, even fouler barracks, found Noyeed for him, and all in all seemed a congenial sort. With his scarred and puggish face and dirt-stiffened hair he was no one's handsome. But he was animally strong, of a piece, and had enough pit dirt ground into him to satisfy anyone's *nostalgie de la boue*, thought Jahor as the foreman lumbered off back to his own sleeping quarters.

When, for the second time that night, the guard unlocked the double catch at each side of the plank across the barrack entrance, Jahor pushed inside, stepping from the rain and across the sill to flooring as muddy within as without. The guard stepped in behind, holding up the spitting pine torch: smoke licked the damp beams; vermin scurried in the light or dropped down, glittering, to the dirt. Jahor picked his way across muddy straw, went to the first heap curled away from him in thatch and shadow. He stopped, pulled aside frayed canvas.

The great head rolled up; red eyes blinked over a heavy arm. "Oh . . . ," the slave grunted. "You again?"

"Come with me," Jahor said. "She wants *you* now."

The reddened eyes narrowed; the slave pushed up on one great arm. His dark face crinkled around its scar. With his free hand he rubbed his great neck, the skin stretched between thick thumb and horny forefinger cracked and gray. "She wants *me* to . . . ?" Again he frowned. Suddenly he went scrabbling in the straw beside him and a moment later turned back with the metal collar, hinged open, a semicircle of it in each huge hand. Once he shook his head, as if to rid it of sleep. Straw

fell from his hair, slid across his bunched shoulder. Then he bent forward, raised the collar, and clacked it closed. Matted hair caught in the
clasp at the back of his neck. Digging with one thick finger, he pulled
it loose. "There . . ." He rose from his pallet to stand among the sleeping
slaves, looking twice his size in the barracks shadow. His eyes caught
the big-nosed eunuch's. He grinned, rubbed the metal ring with three
fingers. "Now they'll let me back in. Come on, then."

So Gorgik came, with Jahor, to the Vizerine's tent.

And passed the night with Myrgot — who was forty-five and, in the
narrowly restricted area she allowed for personal life, rather a romantic. The most passionate, not to say the most perverse, lovemaking (we
are not speaking of foreplay), though it run the night's course, seldom
takes more than twenty minutes from the hour. As boredom was Myrgot's problem and lust only its emblem, here and there through the
morning hours the pit slave found himself disposed in conversation
with the Vizerine. Since there is very little entertainment for pit slaves
in an obsidian mine *except* conversation and tall-tale telling, when Gorgik began to see her true dilemma, he obliged her with stories of his life
before, and at, the mines — a few of which tales were lies appropriated
from other slaves, a few of which were embroideries on his own childhood experiences. But since entertainment was the desired effect, and
temporariness seemed the evening's hallmark, there was no reason to
shun prevarication. Five times during the night, he made jokes the
Vizerine thought wickedly funny. Three times he made observations
on the working of the human heart she thought profound. For the rest,
he was deferential, anecdotal, as honest about his feelings as someone
might be who sees no hope in his situation. Gorgik's main interest in
the encounter was the story it would make at the next night's supper
of gruel and cold pig fat, though that interest was somewhat tempered
by the prospect of the ten-hour workday with no sleep to come. Without illusion that more gain than the tale would accrue, lying on his
back on sweaty silk his own body had soiled, staring up at the dead
lamps swaying under the striped canvas, sometimes dozing in the
midst of his own ponderings while the Vizerine beside him gave her
own opinions on this, that, or the other, he only hoped there would be
no higher price.

When the slits between the tent lacings grew luminous, the Vizerine
suddenly sat up in a rustle of silks and a whisper of furs whose splendor

had by now become part of the glister of Gorgik's fatigue. She called sharply for Jahor, then bade Gorgik rise and stand outside.

Outside Gorgik stood, tired, lightheaded, and naked in the moist grass, already worn here and there to the earth with the previous goings and comings of the caravan personnel. He looked at the tents, at the black mountains beyond them, at the cloudless sky already coppered one side along the pinetops: I could run, he thought; and if I ran, yes, I would stumble into slavers' hands within the day; and I'm too tired anyway. But I *could* run. I . . .

Inside, Myrgot, with sweaty silk bunched in her fists beneath her chin, head bent and rocking slowly, considered. "You know, Jahor," she said, her voice quiet, because it was morning and if you have lived most of your life in a castle with many other people you are quiet in the morning; "that man is wasted in the mines." The voice had been roughened by excess. "I say man; he looks like a man; but he's really just a boy — oh, I don't mean he's a genius or anything. But he can speak two languages passably, and can practically read in one of them. For him to be sunk in an obsidian pit is ridiculous! And do you know . . . I'm the only woman he's ever had?"

Outside, Gorgik, still standing, eyes half closed, was still thinking: yes, *perhaps* I could . . . when Jahor came for him.

"Come with me."

"Back to the pit?" Gorgik snorted something that general good nature made come out half a laugh.

"No," Jahor said briskly and quietly in a way that made the slave frown. "To my tent."

Gorgik stayed in the large-nosed eunuch's tent all morning, on sheets and coverlets not so fine as the Vizerine's but fine enough; and the tent's furnishings — little chairs, low tables, shelves, compartmented chests, and numberless bronze and ceramic figurines set all over — were far more opulent than Myrgot's austere appointments. With forty minutes this hour and forty minutes that, Jahor found the slave gruff, friendly — and about as pleasant as an exhausted miner can be at four, five, or six in the morning. He corroborated the Vizerine's assessment — and Jahor had done things very much like this many, many times. At one point the eunuch rose from the bed, bound himself about with blue wool, turned to excuse himself a moment —

unnecessarily, because Gorgik had fallen immediately to sleep — and went back to the Vizerine's tent.

Exactly what transpired there, Gorgik never learned. One subject, from time to time in the discussion, however, would no doubt have surprised, if not shocked him. When the Vizerine had been much younger, she herself had been taken a slave for three weeks and forced to perform services arduous and demeaning for a provincial potentate — who bore such a resemblance to her present cook at Court that it all but kept her out of the kitchen. She had been a slave *only* for three weeks: an army had come, fire-arrows had lanced through the narrow stone windows, and the potentate's ill-shaven head was hacked off and tossed in the firelight from spear to spear by several incredibly dirty, incredibly tattooed soldiers so vicious and shrill that she finally decided (from what they later did to two women of the potentate's entourage in front of everyone) they were insane. The soldiers' chief, however, was in alliance with her uncle; and she had been returned to him comparatively unharmed. Still, the whole experience had been enough to make her decide that the institution of slavery was totally distasteful and so was the institution of war — that, indeed, the only excuse for the latter was the termination of the former. Such experiences, among an aristocracy deposed by the dragon for twenty years and only recently returned to power, were actually rather common, even if the ideas taken from them were not. The present government did not as an official policy oppose slavery, but it did not go out of its way to support it either, and the Child Empress herself, whose reign was proud and prudent, had set a tradition that no slaves were used at Court.

From dreams of hunger and pains in his gut and groin, where a boy with clotted mouth, scaly hands, half his face in darkness, and his flank wrapped round with whip welts tried to tell him something he could not understand, but which seemed desperately important that he know, Gorgik woke with the sun in his face. The tent was being taken down from over him. A blue-turbaned head blocked the light. "Oh, you *are* awake . . . ! Then you'd better come with me." With the noise of the decamping caravan around them Jahor took Gorgik to see the Vizerine. Bluntly she informed him, while ox drivers, yellow-turbaned secretaries, red-scarved maids, and harnessed porters came in and out of the tent, lifting, carrying, unlacing throughout the interview, that she was taking him to Kolhari under her protection. He had been purchased from the mines — take off that collar and put it somewhere. At least by day. She would trust him never to speak to her unless she spoke to him first: he was to understand that if she suspected her decision were a mistake, she could and would make his life far more miserable than it had ever been in the mines. Gorgik was at first not so much astonished as uncomprehending. Then, when astonishment, with comprehension, formed, he began to babble his inarticulate thanks — till, of a sudden, he became confused again and disbelieving and so, as suddenly, stopped. (Myrgot merely assumed he had realized that even gratitude is best displayed in moderation, which she took as another sign of his high character and her right choice.) Then men were taking the tent down from around them, too. With narrowed eyes, Gorgik looked at the thin woman in the green shift and sudden sun, sitting at a table from which women in red scarves were already removing caskets, things rolled and tied in ribbons, instruments of glass and bronze. Was she suddenly smaller? The thin braids, looped bright black about her head, looked artificial, almost like a wig. (He knew they weren't.) Her dress seemed made for a woman fleshier, broader. She looked at him, the skin near her eyes wrinkled in the bright morning, her neck a little loose, the veins on the backs of her hands as high from age as those on his from labor. What he did realize, as she blinked in the full sunlight, was that he must suddenly look as different to her as she now looked to him.

Jahor touched Gorgik's arm, led him away.

Gorgik had at least ascertained that his new and precarious position meant keeping silent. The caravan steward put him to work grooming oxen by day — which he liked. The next night he spent in the Vizerine's tent. And dreams of the mutilated child woke him with blocked throat and wide eyes only half a dozen times. And Noyeed was probably dead by now anyway, as Gorgik had watched dozens of other slaves die in those suddenly fading years.

Once Myrgot was sure that, during the day, Gorgik could keep himself to himself, she became quite lavish with gifts and clothing, jewels, and trinkets. (Though she herself never wore ornaments when traveling, she carried trunks of the things in her train.) Jahor — in whose tent from time to time Gorgik spent a morning or afternoon — advised

him of the Vizerine's moods, of when he should come to her smelling
of oxen and wearing the grimy leather-belted rag — with his slave collar — that was all he had taken from the mines. Or when, as happened
quite soon, he should do better to arrive freshly washed, his beard
shaved, disporting her various gifts. More important, he was advised
when he should be prepared to make love, and when he should be
ready simply to tell tales or, as it soon came, just to listen. And Gorgik
learned that most valuable of lessons without which no social progress
is possible: if you are to stay in the good graces of the powerful, you
had best, however unobtrusively, please the servants of the powerful.

Next morning the talk through the whole caravan was "Kolhari
by noon!"

By nine, winding off between fields and cypress glades, a silver
thread had widened into a reed-bordered river down below the bank of
the caravan road. The Kohra, one groom told him, which made Gorgik
start. He had known the Big Kohra and the Kohra Spur as two walled
and garbage-clotted canals, moving sluggishly into the harbor from
beneath a big and a little rock-walled bridge at the upper end of New
Pavē. The hovels and filthy alleys in the city between (also called the
Spur) were home to thieves, pickpockets, murderers and worse, he'd
always been told.

Here, on this stretch of the river, were great, high houses, of two
and even three stories, widely spaced and frequently gated. Where
were they now? Why, this *was* Kolhari — at least the precinct. They
were passing through the suburb of Neveryóna (which so recently had
named the entire port) where the oldest and richest of the city's aristocracy dwelt. Not far in that direction was the suburb of Sallese, where
the rich merchants and importers had their homes: though with less
land and no prospect on the river, many of the actual houses were far
more elegant. This last was in conversation with a stocky woman —
one of the red-scarved maids — who frequently took off her sandals,
hiked up her skirts, and walked among the ox drivers, joking with
them in the roughest language. In the midst of her description, Gorgik
was surprised by a sudden and startling memory: playing at the edge
of a statue-ringed rock pool in the garden of his father's employer on
some rare trip to Sallese as a child. With the memory came the realiza-
tion that he had not the faintest idea how to get from these wealthy
environs to the waterfront neighborhood that was *his* Kolhari. Minutes

later, as the logical solution (follow the Khora) came, the caravan began to swing off the river road.

First in an overheard conversation among the caravan steward and some grooms, then in another between the chief porter and the matron of attendant women, Gorgik heard: "... the High Court ...," "... the Court ...," and "... the High Court of Eagles ...," and one black and sweaty-armed driver, whose beast was halted on the road with a cartwheel run into a ditch, wrestled and cursed his heavy-lidded charge as Gorgik walked past. "By the Child Empress, whose reign is good and gracious, I'll break your fleabitten neck! So close to home, and you run off the path!"

An hour on the new road, which wound back and forth between the glades of cypress, and Gorgik was not sure if the Khora was to his right or left. But ahead was a wall, with guard houses left and right of a gate over which a chipped and rough-carved eagle spread her man-length wings. Soldiers pulled away the massive planks (with their dozen barred insets), then stood back, joking with one another, as the carts rolled through.

Was *that* great building beside the lake the High Court?

No, merely one of the outbuildings. Look there, above that hedge of trees —

"*There ... ?*"

He hadn't seen it because it was too big. And when he did — rising and rising above the evergreens — for a dozen seconds he tried to shake loose from his mind the idea that he was looking at some natural object, like the Falthas themselves. Oh, yes, cut into here, leveled off there — but building upon building, wing upon wing, more a city than a single edifice, that great pile (he kept trying to separate it into different buildings, but it all seemed, despite its many levels, and its outcroppings, and its abutments, one) could not have been *built ... ?*

He kept wishing the caravan would halt so he could look at it all. But the road was carpeted with needles now, and evergreens swatted half-bare branches across the towers, the clouds, the sky. Then, for a few moments, a gray wall was coming toward him, was towering over him, was about to fall on him in some infinitely delayed topple —

Jahor was calling.

Gorgik looked down from the parapet.

The eunuch motioned him to follow the dozen women who had

separated from the caravan — among them the Vizerine: a tiny door swallowed them one and another. Gorgik had to duck.

As conversation babbled along the corridor, past more soldiers standing in their separate niches (". . . home at last . . . ," ". . . what an exhausting trip . . . ," ". . . here at home in Kolhari . . . ," ". . . when one returns home to the High Court . . . ," ". . . only in Kolhari . . ."), Gorgik realized that, somehow, all along he had been expecting to come to his childhood home; and that, rather than coming home at all, he had no idea *where* he was.

Gorgik spent five months at the High Court of the Child Empress Ynelgo. The Vizerine put him in a small, low-ceilinged room, with a slit window, just behind her own chambers. The stones of the floor and walls were out of line and missing mortar, as though pressure from the rock above, below, and around it had compacted the little space all out of shape. By the end of the first month, both the Vizerine and her steward had almost lost interest in him. But several times before her interested waned, she had presented him at various private suppers of seven to fourteen guests in the several dining rooms of her suite, all with beamed ceilings and tapestried walls, some with wide windows opening out on sections of roof, some windowless with whole walls of numberless lamps and ingenious flues to suck off the fumes. Here he met some of her court friends, a number of whom found him interesting, and three of whom actually befriended him. At one such supper he talked too much. At two more he was too silent. At the other six, however, he acquitted himself well, for seven to fourteen is the number a mine slave usually dines with, and he was comfortable with the basic structures of communication by which such a group (whether seated on logs and rocks, or cushions and couches) comports itself at meals, if not with the forms of politeness this particular group's expression of those structures had settled on.

But those could be learned.

He learned them.

Gorgik had immediately seen there was no way to compete with the aristocrats in sophistication: he intuited that they would only be offended or, worse, bored if he tried. What interested them in him was his difference from them. And to their credit (or the credit of the Vizerine's wise selection of supper guests) for the sake of this interest and affection for the Vizerine they made allowances, in ways he was only to appreciate years later, when he drank too much, or expressed like or dislike for one of their number not present a little too freely, or when his language became too hot on whatever topic was about — most of the time to accuse them of nonsense or of playing with him, coupled with good-natured but firm threats of what he would do to them were they on his territory rather than he on theirs. *Their* language, polished and mellifluous, flowed, between bouts of laughter in which his indelicacies were generously absorbed and forgiven (if not forgotten), over subjects ranging from the scandalous to the scabrous: when Gorgik could follow it, it often made his mouth drop, or at least his teeth open behind his lips. *His* language, blunt and blistered with scatalogs that frequently upped the odd aristocratic eyebrow, adhered finally to a very narrow range: the fights, feuds, and scrabblings for tiny honors, petty dignities, and minuscule assertions of rights among slaves and thieves, dock-beggars and prostitutes, sailors and barmaids and more slaves — people, in short, with no power beyond their voices, fingers, or feet — a subject rendered acceptable to the fine folk of the court only by his basic anecdotal talent and the topic's novelty in a setting where boredom was the greatest affliction.

Gorgik did not find the social strictures on his relations with the Vizerine demeaning. The Vizerine worked — the sort of work only those in art or government can know, where the hours were seldom defined and real tasks were seldom put in simple terms (while false tasks *always* were). Conferences and consultations made up her day. At least two meals out of every three were spent with some ambassador, governor, or petitioner, if not at some affair of state. To do her credit, in that first month, we can thus account for all twenty-two evening meals Myrgot did not share with her slave.

Had her slave, indeed, spent his past five years as, say, a free, clever, and curious apprentice to a well-off potter down in the port, he might have harbored some image of a totally leisured and totally capricious aristocracy, for which there were certainly enough emblems around him now, but which emblems, had he proceeded on them, as certainly would have gotten him into trouble. Gorgik, however, had passed so much of his life at drudgeries he knew would, foreman or no, probably kill him in another decade and certainly in two, he was too dazzled by his own, unexpected freedom from such drudgeries to question how others drudged. To pass the Vizerine's open door and see Myrgot at her desk, head bent over a map, a pair of compasses in one hand and a straight edge in the other (which, to that clever, curious, and ambitious apprentice, would have signed work), and then to pass the same door later and see her standing beside her desk, looking vacantly toward some cloud passing by the high, beveled window (which, to the same apprentice, would have signed a leisure that could reasonably be intruded upon, thus making her order never to intrude appear, for a lover at any rate, patently unreasonable), were states he simply did not distinguish: their textures were both so rich, so complex, and so unusual to him that he read no structure of meaning in either, much less did he reading the meaning of those structures somehow as opposition. In obeying the Vizerine's restriction, and not intruding on either situation, his reasons were closer to something aesthetic than practical. Gorgik was acting on that disposition for which the apprentice would have despised him as the slave he was: he knew his place. Yet that apprentice's valuation would have been too coarse, for the truth is that in such society, Gorgik — no more than a potter's boy — *had* no place . . . if we use 'to have' other than in that mythical and mystifying sense in which both a slave *has* a master and good people *have* certain rights, but rather in the sense of possession that implies some way (either through power or convention) of enforcing that possession, if not to the necessary extent, at least to a visible one. Had Gorgik suddenly developed a disposition to intrude, from some rage grown either in whim or reason, he *would* have intruded on either situation — a disposition that his aristocratic supper companions would have found more sympathetic than the apprentice's presumptions, assumptions, and distinctions all to no use. Our potter's boy would no doubt have gotten himself turned out of the castle, thrown into one of the High Court's lower dungeons, or killed — for these were brutal and barbaric times, and the Vizerine was frequently known to be both violent and vicious. Had Gorgik intruded, yes, the aristocrats would have been in far greater sympathy with him — as they turned him out, threw him into a dungeon, or killed him. No doubt this means the distinction is of little use. But we are trying to map the borders of the disposition that was, indeed, the case. Gorgik, who had survived on the waterfront and survived in the mine, survived at the High Court of Eagles. To do it, he had to learn a great deal.

Not allowed to approach the Vizerine and constrained to wait till she approached him, he learned, among the first lessons, that there was hardly one person at court who was not, practically speaking, in a similar position with at least one other person — if not whole groups. Thus Lord Vanar (who shared Jahor's tastes and gave Gorgik several large rocks with gems embedded in them that lay in the corners of his room, gathering dust) and the Baron Inige (who did not, but who once took him hunting in the royal preserves and talked endlessly about flowers throughout the breadth of Nevèrÿon — and from whom Gorgik now learned that an *ini*, which brought back a torrent of memories from his dockside adolescence, was deadly poison) would never attend the same function, though both must always be invited. The Thane of Sallese could be invited to the same gathering as Lord Ekoris *unless* the Countess Esulla was to be present — however, in such cases Curly (the Baron Inige's nickname) would be excused. No one known as a friend of Lord Aldamir (who had not been at Court now for many years, though everyone seemed to remember him with fondness) should be seated next to, or across from any relative, unto the second cousins, of the Baronine Jeu-Forsi . . . Ah, but with perhaps half a dozen insistently minor exceptions, commented the elderly Princess Grutn, putting one arm back over the tasseled cushion and moving nuts about on her palm with her heavily ringed thumb.

But they were not minor at *all*, laughed Curly, sitting forward on his couch, joining his hands with a smile as excited as if he had just discovered a new toadstool.

But they *were* minor, insisted the Princess, letting the nuts fall back to the silver tray and picking up her chased-silver goblet to brood moodily on its wine. Why, several people had commented to her only within the last month that perhaps the Baron had regrettably lost sight of *just* how minor those exceptions were.

"Sometimes I wonder if the main sign of the power of our most charming cousin, whose reign is courteous and courageous, is that, for her sake, all these amenities, both minor and major, are forgotten for a gathering she will attend!" Inige laughed.

And Gorgik, sitting on the floor, picked his teeth with a silver knife whose blade was shorter than his little finger and listened — not with the avidity of a social adventurer storing information for future dealings with the great, but with the relaxed attention of an aesthete hear-

ing for the first time a difficult poem, which he already knows from
the artist's previous work will require many exposures before its meanings clear.

Our young potter's boy would have brought with him to these same
suppers a ready-made image of the pyramid of power, and no doubt in
the light of these arcane informations tried to map the whole volume
of that pyramid on to a single line, with every thane and duchess in
place, each above this one and below that one, the whole forming a
cord that could be negotiated knot by knot, a path that presumably
ended at some *one* — perhaps the Child Empress Ynelgo herself. Gorgik, because he brought to the supper rooms no such preconceptions,
soon learned, between evenings with the Vizerine, dawn rides with the
Baron, afternoon gatherings in the Old Hall, arranged by the young
earls Jue-Grutn (not to be confused with the two older men who bore
the same title, the bearded one of which was said to be either insane, a
sorcerer, or both), or simply from gatherings overseen and overheard
in his wanderings through the chains of rooms which formed the
Middle Style of the castle, that the hierarchy of prestige branched; that
the branches interwove; and that the interweavings in several places
formed perfectly closed, if inexplicable, loops; as well, he observed that
the presence of this earl or that thane (not to mention this steward or
that attendant maid) could throw a whole subsection of the system
into a different linking altogether.

Jahor, especially during the first weeks, took many walks with Gorgik through the castle. The eunuch steward was hugely rich in information about the architecture itself. The building still mystified the
ex-miner. The oldest wings, like the Old Hall, were vast, cavernous
spaces, with open roofs and water conduits grooved into the floor. Dozens of small, lightless cells opened off them, the upper ones reached
by wooden ladders, stone steps, or sometimes mere mounds of earth
heaped against the wall. Years ago, Jahor explained, these dusty, dank
cavelets, smaller even than Gorgik's present room, had actually been
the dwelling places of great kings, queens, and courtiers. From time to
time they had housed officers of the army — and, during the several
occupations, common soldiers. That little door up there, sealed over
with stone and no steps to it? Why, that was where Mad Queen Olin
had been walled up after she had presided at a banquet in this very

hall, at which she served her own twin sons, their flesh roasted, their organs pickled. Halfway through the meal, a storm had burst over the castle, and rain had poured through the broad roof opening, while lightning fluttered and flickered its pale whips; but Olin forbade her guests to rise from the table before the feast was consumed. It's still debatable, quipped the eunuch, whether they entombed her because of the supper or the soaking. (*Olin*, thought Gorgik. *Olin's warning . . . ?* But Jahor was both talking and walking on.) Today, except for the Old Hall that was kept in some use, these ancient echoing wells were deserted, the cells were empty, or at best used to store objects that had grown useless, if not meaningless, with rust, dust, and time. About fifteen or fifty years ago, some particularly clever artisan — the same who laid out the New Pavē down in the port, Jahor explained, waking Gorgik's wandering attention again — had come up with the idea of the corridor (as well as the coinpress). At least half the castle had been built since then (and most of Nevèrÿon's money minted); for at least half the castle had its meeting rooms and storerooms, its kitchens and its living quarters, laid out along corridors. There were six whole many-storied wings of them. In the third floor of one of the newest, the Vizerine had her suite; in the second and third floor of one of the oldest, most business of state was carried on around the throne room of the Child Empress. For the rest, the castle was built in that strange and disconcerting method known as the Middle Style, in which rooms, on two sides, three sides, four sides, and sometimes with steps going up or down, opened on to other rooms; which opened on to others — big rooms, little rooms, some empty, some lavishly appointed, many without windows, some incredibly musty, and frequently two or three perfectly dark ones, which had to be traversed with torch and taper, lying between two that were in current, active use, a vast and hopeless hive.

Did Jahor actually know his way around the entire edifice?

No one knew his way around the *entire* court. Indeed, though his mistress went occasionally, Jahor had never been anywhere near the Empress's suite or the throne room. He knew the location of the wing only by report.

What about the Child Empress herself? Did she know all of it?

Oh, especially not the Child Empress herself, Jahor explained, an irony that our potter's boy might have questioned, but which was just another strangeness to the ex-pit slave.

But it was after this conversation that Jahor's company too began to fall off.

Gorgik's aristocratic friends had a particularly upsetting habit: one day they would be perfectly friendly, if not downright intimate; the next afternoon, if they were walking with some companion unknown to Gorgik, they would pass him in some rocky corridor and not even deign recognition — even if he smiled, raised his hand, or started to speak. Such snubs and slights would have provoked our potter, however stoically he forebore, to who-knows-what final outburst, ultimate indelicacy, or denouncement of the whole, undemocratic sham. But though Gorgik saw quite well he was the butt of such behavior more than they, he saw too that they treated him thus not because he was different so much as because that was the way they treated each other. The social hierarchy and patterns of deference to be learned here were as complex as those that had to be mastered — even by a foreman — on moving into a new slave barracks in the mine. (Poor potter! With all his simplistic assumptions about the lives of aristocrats, he would have just as many about the lives of slaves.) Indeed, among slaves Gorgik knew what generated such complexity: servitude itself. The only question he could not answer here was: what were all *these* elegant lords and ladies slaves to? In this, of course, the potter would have had the advantage of knowledge. The answer was simple: power, pure, raw and obsessive. But in his ignorance, young Gorgik was again closer to the lords and ladies around him than an equally young potter's boy would have been. For it is precisely at its center that one loses the clear vision of what surrounds, what controls and contours every utterance, decides and develops every action, as the bird has no clear concept of air, though it support her every turn, or the fish no true vision of water, though it blur all she sees. A goodly, if not frightening, number of these same lords and ladies dwelling at the Court had as little idea of what shaped their every willed decision, conventional observance, and sheer, unthinking habit as did Gorgik — whereas the potter's boy Gorgik might have been, had the play of power five years before gone differently in these same halls and hives, would not even have had to ask.

For all the temperamental similarities we have drawn, Gorgik was not (nor should we be) under any illusion that either the lords, or their servants, accepted him as one of their own. But he had conversation;

he had companionship — for some periods extremely warm companionship — from women and men who valued him for much the same reason as the Vizerine had. He was given frequent gifts. From time to time people in rooms he was not in and never visited suggested to one another that they look out for the gruff youngster in the little room on the third floor, see that he was fed, or that he was not left too much alone. (And certainly a few times when such conversations might have helped, they never occurred.) But, stripped to nothing but his history, Gorgik began to learn that even such a history — on the docks and in the mines — as it set him apart in experience from these others, was in some small way the equivalent of an aristocracy in itself: those who met him here at Court either did not bother him about it, or they respected it and made allowances for his eccentricities because of it — which is, after all, all their own aristocratic privileges gained them from one another.

Once he went five days in the castle without eating. When Gorgik did not have an invitation to some countess's or prince's dinner or luncheon, he went to the Vizerine's kitchen — Jahor had left standing instructions there that he was to be fed. But the Vizerine, with most of her suite, was away on another mission. And since the Vizerine's cooks had gone with the caravan, her kitchen had been shut down.

One evening the little Princess Elyne took both Gorgik's great dark hands in her small, brown ones and exclaimed as the other guests departed around them: "But I have had to cancel the little get-together that I'd asked you to tomorrow. It's too terrible! I must go visit my uncle, the count, who will not be put off another —" Here she stopped, pulled one of her hands away and put it over her mouth. "But I *am* too terrible. For I'm lying dreadfully, and you probably know it! Tomorrow I must go home to my own horrid old castle, and I loathe it, loathe it there! Ah, you *did* know it, but you're too polite to say anything." Gorgik, who'd known no such thing, laughed. "So," went on the little Princess, "that is why I must cancel the party. You see, I have reasons. You *do* understand . . . ?" Gorgik, who was vaguely drunk, laughed again, shook his head, raised his hand when the Princess began to make more excuses, and, still laughing, turned, and found his way back to his room.

The next day, as had happened before, no other invitations came; and because the Vizerine's kitchen was closed, he did not eat. The day after, there were still no invitations. He scoured as much of the castle as he dared for Curly; and became suddenly aware how little of the castle he felt comfortable wandering in. The third day? Well, the first two days of a fast are the most difficult — though Gorgik had no thoughts of fasting. He was not above begging, but he could not see how to beg here from someone he hadn't been introduced to. Steal? Yes, there were other suites, other kitchens. (Ah, it was now the fourth day; and other than a little lightheaded, his actual appetite seemed to have died somewhere inside him.) Steal food . . . ? He sat on the edge of his raised pallet, his fists a great, horny knot of interlocked knuckle and thickened nail, pendant between his knees. How many times had these lords and ladies praised his straightforwardness, his honesty? He had been stripped to nothing but his history, and now that history included their evaluations of him. Though, both on the docks and in the mines, no month had gone by since age six when he had not pilfered *something*, he'd stolen nothing here, and somehow he knew that to steal — here — meant losing part of this new history: and, in this mildly euphoric state, that new history seemed much too valuable — because it was associated with real learning (rather than with ill-applied judgments, which is what it would have meant for our young potter; and our young potter, though he had never stolen more than the odd cup from his master's shelf of seconds, would certainly have stolen now).

Gorgik had no idea how long it took to starve to death. But he had seen ill-fed men, worked fourteen hours a day, thrown into solitary confinement without food for three days, only to die within a week after their release. (And had once, in his first six months at the mines, been so confined himself, and had survived.) That a well-fed woman or man of total leisure (and leisure is all Gorgik had known now for close to half a year) might go more than a month with astonishing ease on nothing but water never occurred to him. On the fifth day he was still lightheaded, not hungry, and extremely worried over the possibility that this sensation itself was the beginning of starvation.

In his sandals with the brass buckles, and a red smock which hung to mid-thigh (it should have been worn with an ornamental collar he did not bother to put on, and should have been belted with a woven sash of scarlet and gold, wrapped three times around the waist with the tassels hanging to the floor; but absently he had wrapped round it the old leather strap he'd used to girdle his loin rag in the mines), he left his room on the evening of the fifth day and again began to wander the castle. This time, perhaps because of the lightheadedness, he entered a hallway he had never entered before — and immediately found himself in a circular stone stairwell. On a whim, he went up instead of down. After two circuits the stairwell opened on another hallway — no, it was a roofed colonnade: through the arches, the further crenellations and parapets of the castle interrupted a night misted by moonlight while the moon itself was somewhere out of sight.

At the colonnade's end, another stairwell took him back down among cool rocks. About to leave the stair at one exit because there was a faint glimmer of lamps somewhere off in the distance, he realized that what he'd taken for a buzzing in his own ears was really — blurred by echoing stones — conversation and music from below. Wondering if perhaps some catered gathering large enough to absorb him were going on, with one hand on the wall, he descended the spiral of stone.

In the vestibule at the bottom hung a bronze lamp. But the vestibule's hangings were so drear the tiny chamber still looked black. The attention of the guard in the archway was all on the sumptuous bright crowds within. When, after half a dozen heartbeats' hesitation, Gorgik walked out into the hall, he was not detained.

Were there a hundred people in this brilliant room? Passing among them, he saw the Baron Curly, and the Countess Esulla; and over there the elderly Princess Grutn was talking with a dour, older gentleman (the Earl Jue-Grutn); and that was Lord Vanar! On the great table running the whole side of the room sat tall decanters of wine, wide bowls of fruit, platters of jellied welkin, circular loaves of hard bread and rounds of soft cheese. Gorgik knew that if he gorged he would be ill; and that, even if he ate prudently, within an hour of his first bite, his bowels would void themselves of five days' bile — in short, he knew what a man who had lived near hunger for five years needed to know of hunger to survive. Nevertheless, he made slow circuit after slow circuit of the hall. Each time he passed the table, he took a fruit or a piece of bread. On the seventh round, because the food whipped up an astonishing thirst, he poured himself a goblet of cider: three sips and it went to his head like a torrent reversing itself to crash back up the rocks. He wondered if he would be sick. The music was reeds and drums. The musicians, in great headdresses of gilded feathers and little else, wandered through the crowd, somehow managing to keep their insistent rhythms and reedy whines together. It was on the ninth round, with the goblet still in his hand and his belly like a small, swollen bag swinging back and forth uneasily inside him, that a thin girl with a brown, wide face and a sleeveless white shift, high on her neck and down to the floor, said: "Sir, you are not dressed for this party!" Which was true.

Her rough hair was braided around her head, so tight you could see her scalp between the spiralling tiers.

Gorgik smiled and dropped his head just a little, because that was usually the way to talk to aristocrats. "I'm not really a guest. I am a most presumptuous interloper here — a hungry man." While he kept his smile, his stomach suddenly cramped, then, very slowly, unknotted.

The girl's sleeves, high off her bare, brown shoulders, were circled with tiny diamonds. Around her forehead ran the thinnest of silver wires, set every inch with small, bright stones. "You are from the mines, aren't you — the Vizerine's favorite and the pet of Lord Aldamir's circle."

"I have never met Lord Aldamir," Gorgik said. "Though everyone I have known here at Court speak of him with regard."

To which the girl looked absolutely blank for another moment. Then she laughed — a high and childish laugh that had in it an hysteric edge he had not heard before in any of his courtier acquaintances' merriment. "The Empress Ynelgo would certainly not have you put out just because your clothes are poor. Though, really, if you were going to come, you might have shown *some* consideration."

"The Empress's reign is just and generous," Gorgik said, because that's what people always said at any mention of the Empress. "This will probably sound strange to such a wellbred little slip of a thing like yourself, but do you know that for the last five days I have not —" Someone touched his arm.

He glanced back to see Curly beside him.

"Your Highness," said the Baron, "have you been introduced to Gorgik yet? May I have the honor of presenting him to you? Gorgik, I present you to Her Majesty, the Child Empress Ynelgo."

Gorgik just remembered to press the back of his fist to his forehead. "Your Highness, I didn't know —"

"Curly," the Child Empress said, "really, we've already met. But then, I can't really call you Curly in front of him, now, can I?"

"You might as well, Your Highness. He does."

"Ah, I see. Of course, I've heard a great deal about Gorgik already. Is it presumptuous to assume that you —" Her large eyes, close to the surface of her dark brown face (like so many of the Nevèrÿon aristocrats), came to Gorgik's — "have heard a great deal about me?" Then she laughed again, emerging from it with: "Curly . . . !" The sharpness clearly surprised the Baron as well.

"Your Highness." The Baron touched his fist to his forehead and, to Gorgik's distress, backed away.

The Empress looked again at Gorgik with an expression intense enough to make him start back. She said: "Let me tell you what the most beautiful and distressing section of Nevèrÿon's empire is, Gorgik. It is the province of Garth — especially the forests around the Vygernangx Monastery. I was kept there as a child, before I was made Empress. They say the elder gods dwell somewhere in the ruins on which it was built — and they are much older than the monastery." She began to talk of Nevèrÿon's craftsmenlike gods and general religion, a conversation which need not be recounted, both because Gorgik did not understand the fine points of such theological distinctions, and also because the true religion, or metaphysics, of a culture is another surround, both of that culture's slaves and of its lords: to specify it, even here, as different from our own would be to suggest, however much we tried to avoid it, that it occupied a different relation to its culture from that which ours does to ours — if only by those specified differences. (We are never out of metaphysics, even when we think we are critiquing someone else's.) Therefore it is a topic about which, by and large, we may be silent. After a while of such talk, she said: "The lands there in the Garth are lush and lovely. I long to visit them again. But our nameless gods prevent me. Still, even today, there is more trouble from that little spit of land than any corner of the empire."

"I will remember what you have told me, Your Highness," Gorgik said, because he could think of no other rejoinder.

"It would be very well if you did." The Child Empress blinked. Suddenly she looked left, then right, bit her lip in a most unimperial way, and walked quickly across the room. Threads of silver in the white shift glimmered.

"Isn't the Empress charming," Curly said, at Gorgik's shoulder once more; with his hand on Gorgik's arm, he was leading him away.

"Eh . . . yes. She . . . the Empress is charming," Gorgik said, because he had learned in the last months that when something must be said to fill the silence, but no one knows what, repetition of something said before will usually at least effect a delay.

"The Empress is perfectly charming," Curly went on as they walked. "The Empress is more charming than I've ever seen her before. Really, she is the most charming person in the entire court . . ."

Somewhere in the middle of this, Gorgik realized the Baron had no more idea what to say than he did. They reached the door. The Baron lowered his voice and his largish larynx rose behind his embroidered collar. "You have received the Empress's favor. Anything else the evening might offer you would undoubtedly be an anticlimax. Gorgik, you would be wise to retire from the party . . ." Then, in an even lower voice: "When I tell you, look to your left. You will see a gentleman in red look away from you just as you look at him . . . All right: now."

Gorgik looked. Across the hall, talking to a glittering group, an older man with a brown, bony face, grizzled white hair, a red cloak, and a heavy copper chestpiece over his tunic, turned back to his conversation with two jeweled women.

"Do you know who that is?"

Gorgik shook his head.

"That is Krodar. Please. Look away from him now. I should not need to tell you that Nevèrÿon is *his* Empire; his soldiers put the Empress on the throne; his forces have kept her there. More to the point, his forces threw down the previous and unmentionable residents of the High Court of Eagles. The power of the Child Empress Ynelgo is Krodar's power. While the Child Empress favored you with a smile and a moment's conversation, Krodar cast in your direction a frown which few in this company failed to notice." The Baron sighed. "So you see, your position here is completely changed."

"But how — ? Of course I shall leave, but . . ." Feeling a sudden ominousness, Gorgik frowned, lightheaded and bewildered. "I mean, I don't want anything from the Empress."

"There is no one in this room who does not want *some*thing from the Empress — including myself. For that reason alone, no one here would believe you — including myself."

"But —"

"You came to court with the favor of the Vizerine. Everyone knows — or thinks they know — that such favor from Myrgot is only favor of the flesh, which they can gossip about, find amusing, and therefore tolerate. Most do not realize that Myrgot decides when to let such news of her favor enter the circuit of gossip — and that, in your case, such decision was made well after your flesh ceased to interest her, and in such ways the rumor can be, and has been, put to use." The Baron's larynx bounded in his neck. "But no one ever knows precisely what the Empress's favor means. No one is ever quite sure what use either she or you will make of it. Therefore, it is much more dangerous to have. And there is Krodar's disfavor to consider. For Krodar is the Empress's minister — her chief steward if you will. Can you imagine how difficult your life would have been here at court if you had, say, the Vizerine's favor but Jahor's enmity?"

Gorgik nodded, now lightheaded and ill. "Should I go to Krodar then and show him he has nothing to fear from —"

"Krodar holds all the power of this Empire in his hands. He is not 'afraid' of anyone. My friend —" the Baron put his pale hand up on Gorgik's thick shoulder and leaned close — "when you entered this game, you entered on the next-to-the-highest level possible and under the tutelage of one of its best players. You know that the Vizerine is not at court and is not expected till tomorrow. Remember: so do the people who planned this party. There are many individual men and women in this very room, wearing enough jewelry tonight to buy a year's produce of the mine you once worked in, who have struggled half their lives or more to arrive at a level in the play far below the one you began at. You were allowed to stay on that level because you had nothing and convinced those of us who met you that you wanted nothing. Indeed, for us, you were a relief from such murderous games."

"I was a miner, working sixteen hours a day in a pit that would have killed me in ten years. I'm now . . . favored at the High Court of Eagles. What else *would* I want?"

"But you see, you have just moved from the next-to-highest level of play to the *very* highest. You come into a party to which you — and your protectress — were specifically *not* invited, dressed like a barbarian; and in five minutes you won a word from the Empress herself. Do you know that by fifteen minutes' proper conversation with the proper people, who are here tonight, you could parley that into a governorship of a fairly valuable, if outlying, province — more, if you were skillful. I do not intend to introduce you to those people, because just as easily you could win your death from someone both desperate for, and deserving of, the same position who merely lacked that all-important credential: a word from Her Majesty. The Empress knows all this. So does Krodar. That indeed may be why he frowned."

"But *you* spoke with —"

"Friend, I may speak with the Empress any time I wish. She is my second cousin once removed. When she was nine and I was twenty-three we spent eight months together in the same dungeon cell, while our execution was put off day by day by day — but that was when she was still a princess. The Empress may *not* speak to me any time she wishes, or she risks endangering the subtle balance of power between my forces at Yenla'h and hers at Vinelet — should the wrong thane or princeling misconstrue her friendliness as a sign of military weakness and move his forces accordingly. My approaches to her, you see, are only considered nepotistic fawning. Hers to me are considered something else again. Gorgik, you have amused me. You have even tolerated my enthusiasm for botany. I don't want to hear that your corpse was pulled out of a sewage trough or, worse, was found floating somewhere in the Khora down at the port. And the excuse for such an outrage need easily be no more than Krodar's frown — if not the Empress's smile."

Gorgik stepped back, because his gut suddenly knotted. He began to sweat. But the Baron's thin fingers dug his shoulder, pulling him forward:

"Do you understand? Do you understand that, minutes ago, you had nothing anyone here *could* have wanted? Do you understand that now you have what a third of us in this room have at least once committed murder for and the other two-thirds done far worse to obtain — an unsolicited word from the Empress?"

— Gorgik swayed. "Curly, I'm sick. I want a loaf of bread and a bottle of —"

"There is a decanter." The Baron frowned. "There is a loaf." He looked around. They were standing by the table end. "And there is the door." The Baron shrugged. "Take the first two and use the last."

Gorgik took a breath which made the cloth of his tunic slide on his wet back. With a lurching motion, he picked up a loaf in one hand and a decanter in the other and lumbered through the arch.

A young duchess, who had been standing only a few feet away, turned to Inige. "Do you know, if I'm not mistaken, I believe I just saw your inelegantly dressed companion, who, only a moment ago, was conferring with Her Highness, do the *strangest* thing —"

"And do *you* know," said the Baron, taking her arm, "that two months by, when I was in the Zenari provinces, I saw the most remarkable species of schist moss with a most uncharacteristic blossom. Let me tell you . . ." and he led her across the room.

Gorgik lurched through the drear vestibule, once more unhindered by the guard; once he stopped to grasp the hangings, which released dust dragons to coil down about the decanter hooked to his thumb and his dribbling arm; he plunged into the stairwell.

He climbed.

Each time he came around the narrow circle, a sharp breeze caught him on the right side. Suddenly he stopped, dropped his head, and, still holding the decanter by his thumb, leaned his forearm high on the wall (the decanter clicked the stone) and vomited. And vomited again. And once again. Then, while his belly clamped once more, suddenly and surprisingly, his gut gave up its runny freight, which slid down both legs to puddle under his heels. Splattered and befouled, his inner thighs wet, his chin dripping, he began to shiver; the breeze scoured his right flank. Bread and bottle away from his sides, he climbed, pausing now and again to scrape off his sandal soles on the bowed steps' edges, his skin crinkling with gooseflesh, teeth clattering.

The wide brass basin clattered and clinked in its ring. He finished washing himself, let the rag drop on the basin edge (weighted on one side, it ceased its tinny rocking), turned on the wet stones, stepped to his pallet, and stretched out naked. The fur throw dampened beneath his hair, his cheek, his heavy legs, his shoulders. Each knob of bone on each other knob felt awash at his body's joints. Belly and gut were still liquefactious. Any movement might start the shivering and the teeth chattering for ten, twenty seconds, a minute, or more. He turned on his back.

And shivered awhile.

From time to time he reached from the bed to tear off a small piece from the loaf on the floor, sometimes dipping its edge in the chased silver beaker that, with every third dip, threatened to overturn on the tiles. While he lay, listening to the nighthawks cooing beyond the hangings at his narrow window, he thought: about where he'd first learned what happened to the body during days without food. After the fight that had gained him his scar, he'd been put in the solitary cell, foodless, for three days. Afterward, an old slave whose name for the life of him he could not remember had taken him back to the barracks, told him the symptoms to expect, and snored by his side for three nights. Only a rich man who'd had no experience of prison at all could have seriously considered his current situation at the palace its equal. Still, minutes at a time, Gorgik could entertain the notion that the only difference between then and now was that — now — he was a little sicker, a little lonelier, and was in a situation where he had been forced, for reasons that baffled him, to pretend to be well and happy. Also, for five years he had done ten to eighteen hours a day hard labor. For almost five months now he had done nothing. In some ways his present illness merely seemed an extension of a feeling he'd had frequently of late: that his entire body was in a singular state of confusion about how to react to anything and that this confusion had nothing to do with his mind. And yet his mind found the situation confusing enough. For a while Gorgik thought about his parents. His father was dead — he'd watched that murder happen. His mother was . . . dead. He had heard enough to know any other assumption was as improbable as his arrival here at the High Court. These crimes had been committed at the ascent of the Child Empress, and her entourage, including the Vizerine, Curly, the princesses Elyne and Grutn, and Jahor. That was why he, Gorgik, had been taken a slave. Perhaps, here at court, he had even met the person who had given the order that, in the carrying out, had caused Gorgik's own life to veer as sharply from waterfront dock rat as it had recently veered away from pit slave.

Gorgik — he had not shivered for the last few minutes now — smiled wryly in the dark. Curly? The Vizerine? Krodar? It was not a new thought. Had he been insensitive enough never to have entertained it before, it might have infused him, in his weakness, with a new sense of power or purpose. He might even have experienced in his sickness an urge to revenge. But months ago he had, for good or bad, dismissed it as useless one. Now, when it might, in its awkward way, have been some bitter solace, he found he could not keep it in the foreground of consciousness. It simply coiled away till it fragmented, the fragments dissolving into myriad flickers. But he was, for all his unfocused thought, learning — still learning. He was learning that power — the great power that shattered lives and twisted the course of the nation — was like a fog over a meadow at evening. From any distance, it seemed to have a shape, a substance, a color, an edge. Yet, as you approached it, it seemed to recede before you. Finally, when common sense said you were at its very center, it still seemed just as far away; only by this time it was on all sides, obscuring any vision of the world beyond it. He lay on damp fur and remembered walking through such a foggy field in a line with other slaves, chains heavy from his neck before and behind. Wet grass had whipped his legs. Twigs and pebbles had bitten through the mud caking his feet. Then the vision flickered, fragmented, drifted. Lord Aldamir . . . ? Surfacing among all the names and titles with which his last months had been filled, this one now: was this phenomenon he had noted the reason why such men, who were truly concerned with the workings of power, chose to stay away from its center, so that they might never lose sight of power's contours? Then that thought fragmented in a sudden bout of chills.

Toward dawn, footsteps in the corridor outside woke him. There, people were grunting with heavy trunks. People were passing, were talking less quietly than they might. He lay, feeling much better than when he had drifted to sleep, listening to the return of the Vizerine's suite. To date Gorgik had not violated the Vizerine's stricture on their intercourse. But shortly he rose, dressed, and went to Jahor's rooms to request an audience. Why? the eunuch asked, looking stern.

Gorgik told him, and told him also his plan.

The large-nosed eunuch nodded. Yes, that was probably very wise. But why didn't Gorgik go first to the Vizerine's kitchen and take a reasonable breakfast?

Gorgik was sitting on the corner of a large wood table, eating a bowl of gruel from the fat cook, whose hairy belly pushed over the top of his stained apron (already sweatblotched at the thighs from stoking the week-cold hearth), and joking with the sleepy kitchen girl, when Jahor stepped through the door. "The Vizerine will see you now."

"So, said Myrgot, one elbow on the parchment-strewn desk, running a thumb, on which she had replaced the heavy rings of court, over her forehead — a gesture Gorgik knew meant she was tired, "you had a word last night with our most grave and gracious Empress."

Which took Gorgik aback. He had not even mentioned that to Jahor. "Curly left a message that greeted me at the door," the Vizerine explained. "Tell me what she said: everything. If you can remember it word for word, so much the better."

"She said she had heard of me. And that she would not have me put out of the party because my clothes were poor —"

Myrgot grunted. "Well, it's true. I have not been as munificent with you of late as I might have been —"

"My Lady, I make no accusation. I only tell you what she —"

The Vizerine reached across the desk, took Gorgik's great wrist. "I know you don't." She stood, still holding his arm, and came around to the side, where, as he had done in the kitchen a little while before, she sat down on the desk's corner. "Though any six of my former lovers — not to mention the present one — would have meant it as an accusation in the same situation. No, the accusation comes from our just and generous ruler herself." She patted his hand, then dropped it. "Go on."

"She nodded Curly — the Baron Inige, I mean — away. She spoke of religion. Then she said that the most beautiful and distressing section of Nevèrÿon's empire is the province of Garth, especially the forests around some monastery —"

"The Vygernangx."

"Yes. She said she was kept there as a girl before she was Empress. Curly told me later about when the two of them were in prison —"

"I know all about that time. I was in a cell only two away from theirs. Go on with what she said."

"She said that the elder gods dwell there, and that they are even older than the monastery. She spoke of our nameless gods. She said that the lands were lush and lovely and that she longed to revisit them. But that even today there was more trouble from that little bit of land than from any other place in Nevèrÿon."

"And while she spoke with you thus, Krodar cast you a dark

look . . . ?" The Vizerine dropped both hands to the desk. She sighed. "Do you know the Garth Peninsula?"

Gorgik shook his head.

"A brutish, uncivilized place — though the scenery is pretty enough. Every other old hovel one comes across houses a witch or a wizard; not to mention the occasional mad priest. And then, a few miles to the south, it is no longer forest but jungle; and there are nothing but barbarian tribes. And the amount of worry it causes is absolutely staggering!" She sighed again. "Of course, you know, Gorgik, that the Empress associates you with me. So any word spoken to you — or even a look cast your way — may be read in some way as a message intended for Myrgot."

"Then I hope I have not brought Myrgot an unhappy one."

"It's not a good one." The Vizerine sighed, leaned back a little on the desk, placing one fingertip on the shale of parchment. "For the Empress to declare the elder gods are older than the monastery is to concede me a theological point that I support and that, till now, she has opposed. Over this point, many people have died. For her to say she wishes to go there is tantamount to declaring war on Lord Aldamir, in whose circle you and I both move, and who keeps his center of power there. For her to choose *you* to deliver this message is . . . But I shouldn't trouble you with the details of that meaning."

"Yes, My Lady. There is no need. My Lady —"

The Vizerine raised her eyebrow.

"I *asked* to come and speak to you. Because I cannot stay here at Court any longer. What can I do to help you in the outside world? Can I be a messenger for you? Can I work some bit of your land? Within the castle here there is nothing for me."

The Vizerine was silent long enough for Gorgik to suspect she disapproved of his request. "Of course you're right," she said at last, so that he was surprised and relieved. "No, you can't stay on here. Especially after last night. I suppose I could always return you to the mines . . . no, that is a tasteless joke. Forgive me."

"There is nothing to forgive, My Lady," though Gorgik's heart had suddenly started. While it slowed, he ventured: "Any post you can put me to, I would happily fill."

After another few moments, the Vizerine said: "Go now. I will send for you in an hour. By then we shall have decided what to do with you."

"You know, Jahor —" The Vizerine stood by the window, looking between the bars at the rain, at further battlements beyond the veils of water, the dripping mansards and streaming crenellations — "he really is an exceptional man. After five months, he wishes to leave the castle. Think how many of the finest sons and daughters of provincial noblemen who, once presented here, become parasites and hangers-on for five *years* or more — before they finally reach such a propitious decision as he has." Rain gathered on the bars and dripped, wetting inches of the beveled sill.

Jahor sat in the Vizerine's great curved-back chair, rather slump-shouldered and, for all his greater bulk, filling it noticeably less well than she. "He was wasted in the mines, My Lady. He is wasted at the castle. Only consider, My Lady, what *is* such a man fit for? First, childhood as a portside ragamuffin, then his youth as a mine slave, followed by a few months skulking in the shadows at the Court of Eagles — where, apparently, he still has not been able to keep out of sight. That is an erratic education to say the least. I can think of no place where he could put it to use. Return him to the mines now, My Lady. Not as a slave, if that troubles you. Free him and make him a guard. That's still more than he might ever have hoped for six months back."

The bars dripped.

Myrgot pondered.

Jahor picked up a carefully crafted astrolabe from the desk, ran a long forenail over its calibrations, then rubbed his thumb across the curlicues of the rhet.

The Vizerine said: "No. I do not think that I will do that, Jahor. It is too close to slavery." She turned from the window and thought about her cook. "I shall do something else with him."

"I would put him back in the mines without his freedom," Jahor said sullenly. "But then, My Lady is almost as generous as the Empress herself. And as just."

The Vizerine raised an eyebrow at what she considered an ill-put compliment. But then, of course, Jahor did not know the Empress's most recent message that Gorgik had so dutifully delivered. "No. I have another idea for him . . ."

"To the mines with him, My Lady, and you will save yourself much trouble, if not grief."

Had Gorgik known of the argument that was progressing in the Vizerine's chamber, he would most probably have misassigned the positions of the respective advocates — perhaps the strongest sign of his unfitness for court life.

Though it does not explain the actual assignment of the positions themselves, there was a simple reason for the tones of voice in which the respective positions were argued: for the last three weeks the Vizerine's lover had been a lithe seventeen-year-old barbarian with bitten nails and mad blue eyes, who would, someday, inherit the title of Suzeraine of Strethi — though the land his parents owned, near the marshy Avila, was little more than a sizable farm. And the youth, for all his coming title, was — in his manners and bearing — little more than a barbarian farmer's son. His passion was for horses, which he rode superbly. Indeed, he had careered, naked, on a black mount, about the Vizerine's caravan for an hour one moonlit night when, two months before, she had been to visit the Avila province to meet with its reigning families anent taxes. She had sent Jahor to ascertain how she might meet this yellow-haired youth. A guest of his parents one evening, she discovered that they were quite anxious for him to go to Court and that for one so young he had an impressive list of illegitimate children throughout the surrounding neighborhoods and was something of a bane to his kin. She had agreed to take him with her, and had kept her agreement. But the relationship was of a volatile and explosive sort that made her, from time to time, look back with fondness on the weeks with Gorgik. Four times now the suzeraine-apparent had run up atrocious debts gambling with the servants; twice he had tried to blackmail her, and he had been unfaithful to her with at least three palace serving women, and what's more they were *not* of Lord Aldamir's circle. The night before the Vizerine had departed on this her most recent mission — to get away from the child? but no — they had gotten into an incredible argument over a white gold chain which had ended with his declaring he would never let her withered lips and wrinkled paws defile his strong, bronzed body again. But just last night, however, hours before her return, he had ridden out to meet her caravan, charged into her tent, and declared he could not live without her caress another moment. In short, that small sector of Myrgot's life she set aside for personal involvement was currently full to overflowing. (Jahor, currently, had no lover at all, nor was he overfond of the Vizerine's.)

The Vizerine, in deference to the vaguest of promises to his barbaric parents, had been desultorily attempting to secure a small commission for the blond boy with some garrison in a safer part of the Empire. She knew he was too young for such a post, and of an impossible temperament to fill it, even were he half a dozen years older; also, there was really no way, in those days, to ascertain if any part of the Empire would remain safe. In any open combat, the little fool — for he was a fool, she did not delude herself about that — would probably be killed, and more than likely get any man under him killed as well — if his men did not turn and kill him first. (She had known such things to happen. Barbarians in positions of power were not popular with the people.) This young, unlettered chief's son was the sort who, for all his barbaric good looks, fiery temperament, and coming inheritance, one either loved or despised. And she had discovered, upon making inquiries into the gambling affair, much to her surprise, that *no* one in Court other than herself seemed to love him. Well, she still did not want him to leave the Court . . . not just now. She had only put any effort toward obtaining his commission at those moments when she had been most aware that soon she must want him as far away as possible.

The commission had arrived while she had been away; it was on her desk now.

No, after his marvelous ride last night to meet her, she did *not* want him to leave . . . *just* yet. But she was experienced enough to know the wishes that he would, with such as he, must come again. As would other commissions.

"Gorgik," she said, when Jahor had led him in and retired, "I am going to put you for six weeks with Master Narbu. He trains all of Curly's personal guards and has instructed many of the finest generals of this Empire in the arts of war. Most of the young men there will be two or three years younger than you, but that may easily, at your age, be as much an advantage as a hindrance. At the end of that time, you will be put in charge of a small garrison near the edge of K'haki desert — north of the Falthas. At the termination of your commission you will have the freedom in fact that, as of this morning, you now have on paper. I hope you will distinguish yourself in the name of the Empress, whose reign is wise and wondrous." She smiled. "Will you agree that this now terminates any and all of our mutual obligations?"

"You are very generous, My Lady," Gorgik said, almost as flabbergasted as when he'd discovered himself purchased from the mines.

"Our Empress is just and generous," the Vizerine said, almost as if correcting him. "I am merely soft-hearted." Her hand had strayed to the astrolabe. Suddenly she picked up the verdigrised disk, turned it over, frowned at it. "Here, take this. Go on. Take it, keep it; and take with it one final piece of advice. It's heartfelt advice, my young friend. I want you always to remember the Empress's words to you last night. *Do* you promise? Good — and as you value your freedom and your life, never set foot on the Garth Peninsula. And if the Vygernangx Monastery ever thrusts so much as the tiny tip of one tower over the treetops within the circle of your vision, you will turn yourself directly around and ride, run, crawl away as fast and as far as you can go. Now take it — take it, go on. And go."

With the Vizerine's astrolabe in hand, Gorgik touched his forehead and backed, frowning from the chamber.

"My Lady, his education is already erratic enough. By making him an officer, you do not bring it to heel. It will only give him presumptions, which will bring him grief and you embarrassment."

"Perhaps, Jahor. Then again, perhaps not. We shall see."

Outside the window, the rains, after having let up for the space of an hour's sunlight, blew violently again, clouding the far towers and splattering all the way into the edge of the stone sill, running down the inner wall to the floor.

"My Lady, wasn't there an astrolabe here on your desk earlier this morning . . . ?"

"Was there now . . . ? Ah yes. My pesky little blue-eyed devil was in here only moments ago, picking at it. No doubt he pocketed it on his way down to the stables. Really, Jahor, I *must* do something about that gold-haired little tyrant. He is a true barbarian and has become the bane of my life."

Six weeks is long enough for a man to learn to enjoy himself on a horse; it is not long enough to learn to ride.

Six weeks is long enough for a man to learn the rules and forms of fencing; it is not long enough to become a swordsman.

Master Narbu, born a slave himself to a high household in the foothills of the Falthas not far from fabled Ellamon, had as a child shown some animal grace that his baronial owner thought best turned to weapon wielding — from a sort of retrograde, baronial caprice. Naturally slaves were not encouraged to excel in arms. Narbu had taken the opportunity to practice — from a retrograde despair at servitude — constantly, continuously, dawn, noon, night, and any spare moment between. At first the hope had been, naturally and secretly and obviously to any but such a capricious master, for escape. Skill had become craft and craft had become art; and developing along was an impassioned love for weaponry itself. The Baron displayed the young slave's skill to friends; mock contests were arranged; then real contests — with other slaves, with freemen. Lords of the realm proud of their own skills challenged him; two lords of the realm died. And Narbu found himself in this paradoxical position: his license to sink sword blade into an aristocratic gut was only vouchsafed by the protection of an aristocrat. During several provincial skirmishes, Narbu fought valiantly beside his master. In several others, his master rented him out as a mercenary — by now his reputation (though he was not out of his twenties) was such that he was being urged, pressed, forced to learn the larger organizational skills and strategies that make war possible. One cannot truly trace the course of a life in a thousand pages. Let us have the reticence here not to attempt it in a thousand words. Twenty years later, during one of the many battles that resulted in the ascension of the present Child Empress Ynelgo to the Throne of Eagles, Narbu (now forty-four) and his master had been lucky enough to be on the winning side — though his master had been killed. But Narbu had distinguished himself. As a reward — for the Empress was brave and benevolent — Narbu was given his freedom and offered a position as instructor of the Empress's own guard, a job which involved training the sons of favored aristocrats in the finer (and grosser) points of battle. (Two of Narbu's earliest instructors had been daughters of the mysterious Western Crevasse, and much of his early finesse had been gained from these masked women with their strange and strangely sinister blades. Twice he had fought with such women; and once against them. But they did not usually venture in large groups too far from their own lands. Still, he had always suspected that Nevèrÿon, with its strictly male armies, was over-compensating for something.) In his position as royal master at arms, he found himself developing a rich and ritual tirade against his new pupils: they were soft, or when they were hard they had no discipline, had no heart. What training they'd gotten must all be undone before they could really begin; aristocrats could never make good soldiers anyway; what was needed was good common stock. Though Master Narbu *was* common stock, had fought common stock, and been taught by common stock, Gorgik was the first man of common stock Master Narbu, in six years, had ever been paid to teach. And the good master now discovered that, as a teacher, somehow he had never developed a language to instruct any other than aristocrats — however badly trained, undisciplined, or heartless they were. As well, he found himself actually resenting this great-muscled, affable, quiet, giant of a youth. First, Gorgik's physique was not the sort (as Narbu was quick to point out to him) that naturally lent itself to horsemanship or any but gross combative skills. Besides, the rumor had gone the rounds that the youth had been put under Narbu's tutelage not even because of his exceptional strength, but because he was some high Court lady's catamite. But one morning Master Narbu woke, frowned at some sound outside, and sat up on his pallet. Through the bars on his window, he looked out across the yard where the training dummies and exercise forms stood in moonlight — it was over an hour to sunup. On the porch of the student barracks, beneath the frayed thatch, a great form, naked and crossed with shadow from the nearest porch poles, moved and turned and moved.

The new pupil was practicing. First he would try a few swings with the light wooden sword to develop form, moving slowly, returning to starting position, hefting the blade again. And going through the swing, parry, recover . . . a little too self-consciously; and the arm not fully extended at the peak of the swing, the blade a little too high . . . Narbu frowned. The new student put down the wooden blade against the barracks wall, picked up the treble-weight iron blade used to improve strength: swing, parry, recovery; again, swing, parry — the student halted, stepped back, began again. Good. He'd remembered the extension this time. Better, Narbu reflected. Better . . . but not excellent. Of course, for the weighted blade, it was better than most of the youths — with those great sacks of muscle about his bones, really not so surprising . . . No, he didn't let the blade sag. But what was he doing up this early anyway . . . ?

Then Narbu saw something.

Narbu squinted a little to make sure he saw it.

What he saw was something he could not have named himself, either to baron or commoner. Indeed, we may have trouble describing it: he saw a concentration in this extremely strong, naked young man's practicing that, by so many little twists and sets of the body, flicks of the eye, bearings of the arms and hips, signed its origins in inspiration. He saw something that much resembled not a younger Narbu, but something that had been part of the younger Narbu and which, when he recognized it now, he realized was all-important. The others, Narbu thought (and his lips, set about with gray stubble, shaped the words), were too pampered, too soft . . . *how* many hours before sunrise? Not those others, no, not on your . . . that one, yes, *was* good common stock.

Narbu lay back down.

No, this common, one-time mercenary slave still did not know how to speak to a common, one-time pit slave as a teacher, and no, six weeks were not enough. But now, in the practice sessions, and sometimes in the rest periods during and after them, Narbu began to say things to the tall, scar-faced youth: "In rocky terrain, look for a rider who holds one rein up near his beast's ear, with his thumb tucked well down; he'll be a Narnisman and the one to show you how to coax most from your mount in the mountains. Stick by him and watch him fast . . ." And: "The best men with throwing weapons I've ever seen are the desert Adami: shy men, with little brass wires sewn up around the backs of their ears. You'll be lucky if you have a few in your garrison. Get one of them to practice with you, and you might learn something . . ." Or: "When you requisition cart oxen in the Avila swamplands, if you get them from the Men of the Hide Shields, you must get one of them to drive, for it will be a good beast, but nervous.

If you get a beast from the Men of the Palm Fiber Shields, then anyone in your garrison can drive it — they train them differently, but just how I am not sure." Narbu said these things and many others. His saws cut through to where and how and what one might need to learn beyond those six weeks. They came out in no organized manner. But there were many of them. Gorgik remembered many; and he forgot many. Some of those he forgot would have saved him much time and trouble in the coming years. Some that he remembered he never got an opportunity to use. But even more than the practice and the instruction (and because Gorgik practiced most, at the end of the six weeks he was easily the best in his class), this was the education he took with him. And Myrgot was away from the castle when his commission began . . .

3

There was an oxcart ride along a narrow road with mountains looking over the trees to the left. With six other young officers, he forded an icy stream, up to his waist in foam; a horse ride over bare rocks, around steep slopes of slate . . . ahead were the little tongues of army campfires, a lick on the blue, with the desert below white as milk in a quarter light.

Gorgik took on his garrison with an advantage over most: five years' experience in the mines as a foreman over fifty slaves.

His garrison contained only twenty-nine.

Nor were they despairing, unskilled, and purchased for life — though, over the next few years, from time to time Gorgik wondered just how much difference that made in the daily texture of their lives, for guards' lives were rough in those days. Over those same years, Gorgik became a good officer. He gained the affection of his men, mainly by keeping them alive in an epoch in which one of the horrors of war was that every time more than ten garrisons were brought together, twenty percent were lost through communicable diseases having nothing to do with battle (and much of the knowledge for this could be traced back to some of Master Narbu's more eccentric saws concerning various herbs, moldy fruit rinds, and moss — and not a few of Baron Curly's observations on botany that Gorgik found himself now and again recalling to great effect). As regards the army itself, Gorgik was a man recently enough blessed with an unexpected hope of life that all the human energy expended to create an institution solely bent on smashing that hope seemed arbitrary and absurd enough to marshal all his intelligence toward surviving it. He saw battle as a test to be endured, with true freedom as prize. He had experienced leading of a sort before, and he led well. But the personalities of his men — both their blustering camaraderie (which seemed a pale and farcical shadow of the brutal and destructive mayhem that, from time to time, had broken out in the slave quarters at the mines, always leaving one or two dead) and the constant resignation to danger and death (that any sane slave would have been trying his utmost to avoid) — confused him (and confusion he had traditionally dealt with by silence) and depressed him (and depression, frankly, he had never really had time to deal with, nor did he really here, so that its effects, finally, were basically just more anecdotes for later years on the stupidity of the military mind).

He knew all his men, and had a far easier relationship with them than most officers of that day. But only a very few did he ever consider friends, and then not for long. A frequent occurrence: some young recruit would take the easiness of some late-night campfire talk, or the revelations that occurred on a foggy morning hike, as a sign of lasting intimacy, only to find himself reprimanded — and, in three cases over the two years, struck to the ground for the presumption: for these were basic and brutal times — in a manner that recalled nothing so much (at least to Gorgik, eternally frustrated by having to give out these reprimands) as the snubs he had received in the halls of the High Court of Eagles the mornings after some particularly revelatory exchange with some count or princess.

Couldn't these imbeciles learn?

He had.

The ones who stayed in his garrison did. And respected him for the lesson — loved him, some of them would even have said in the drunken evenings that, during some lax period that, now at a village tavern, now at a mountain campsite where rum had been impounded from a passing caravan, still punctuated a guard's life. Gorgik laughed at this. His own silent appraisal of the situation had been, from the beginning: I may die; they may die; but if there is any way their death can delay mine, let theirs come down.

Yet within this strictly selfish ethical matrix, he was able to display enough lineaments both of reason and bravery to satisfy those above him in rank and those below — till, from time to time, especially in the face of rank cowardice (which he always tried to construe — and usually succeeded — as rank stupidity) in others, he could convince himself there might be something to the whole idea. "Might" — for survival's sake he never allowed it to go any further.

He survived.

But such survival was a lonely business. After six months, out of loneliness, he hired a scribe to help him with some of the newer writing methods that had recently come to the land and composed a long letter to the Vizerine: inelegant, rambling, uncomfortable with its own discourse, wisely it touched neither on his affection for her nor his debt to her, but rather turned about what he had learned, had seen, had felt: the oddly depressed atmosphere of the marketplace in the town they had passed through the day before; the hectic nature of the smuggling in that small port where, for two weeks now, they had been garrisoned; the anxious gossip of the soldiers and prostitutes about the proposed public building scheduled to replace a section of slumlike huts in a city to the north; the brazen look to the sky from a southern mountain path that he and his men had wandered on for two hours in the evening before stopping to camp.

At the High Court the Vizerine read his letter — several times, and with a fondness that, now all pretense at the erotic was gone, grew, rather than diminished, in directions it would have been hard for grosser souls to follow, much less appreciate. His letter contained this paragraph:

"Rumors came down among the lieutenants last week that all the garrisons hereabout were to go south for the Garth in a month. I drank beer with the Major, diced him for his bone-handled knives and won. Two garrisons were to go to the Able-aini, in the swamps west of the Falthas — a thankless position, putting down small squabbles for ungrateful lords, he assured me, more dangerous and less interesting than the south. I gave him back his knives. He scratched his gray beard in which one or two rough, rusty hairs still twist, and gave me his promise of the swamp post, thinking me mad."

The Vizerine read it, at dawn, standing by the barred windows (dripping with light rain as they had dripped on the morning of her last interview with Gorgik, half a year before), remembered him, looked back toward her desk where once a bronze astrolabe had lain among the parchments. A lamp flame wavered, threatened to go out, and steadied. She smiled.

Toward the end of Gorgik's three years (the occasional, unmistakably royal messenger who would come to his tent to deliver Myrgot's brief and very formal acknowledgments did not hurt his reputation among his troops), when his garrison was moving back and forth at bi-weekly intervals from the desert skirmishes near the Venarra Canyon to the comparatively calm hold of fabled Ellamon high in the Faltha range (where, like all tourists, Gorgik and his men went out to observe, from the white lime slopes, across the crags to the far corrals, the fabled, flying beasts that scarred the evening with their exercises), he discovered that some of his men had been smuggling purses of salt from the desert to the mountains. He made no great issue of it; but he called in the man whom he suspected to be second in charge of the smuggling operation and told him he wished a share — a modest share — of the profits. With that share, many miles to the south, he purchased three extra carts, and four extra oxen to pull them; and with a daring that astonished his men (for the Empress's customs inspectors were neither easy nor forgiving) on his last trek, a week before his discharge, he brought three whole cartfuls of contraband salt, which he got through by turning off the main road, whereupon they were shortly met by what was obviously a ragged, private guard at the edge of private lands.

"Common soldiers may not trespass on the Hold of the Princess Elyne — !"

"Conduct me to her Highness!" Gorgik announced, holding his hand up to halt his men.

After dark, he returned to them (with a memory of high fires in the dank, roofless hall; and the happy Princess with her heavy, jeweled robes and her hair greasy and her fingers thin and grubbier than his own, taking his hard, cracked hands in hers and saying: "Oh, but you see what I've come home to? A bunch of hereditary heathens who think I am a goddess, and cannot make proper conversation for five minutes! No, no, tell me again of the Vizerine's last letter. I don't care if you've told me twice before. Tell me *again*, for it's been over a year since

I've heard anything at all from Court. And I long for their company; I long for it. All my stay there taught me was to be dissatisfied with *this* ancient, moldy pile. No, sit there, on that bench, and I will sit beside you and have them bring us more bread and cider and meat. And you shall simply tell me again, friend Gorgik . . .") with leave for his men and his carts to pass through her lands; and thus he avoided the inspectors.

A month after he left the army, some friendlier men of an intricately tattooed and scarred desert tribe gave him some exquisitely worked copper vases. Provincial burghers in the Argini bought them from him for a price five times what he recalled, from his youth in the port, such work was worth in civilized cities. From the mountain women of Ka'hesh (well below Ellamon) he purchased a load of the brown berry leaves that, when smoked, put one in a state more relaxed than beer — he was now almost a year beyond his release from the army — and transported it all the way to the Port of Sarness, where, in small quantities, he sold it to sailors on outgoing merchant ships. While he was there, a man whom he had paid to help him told him of a warehouse whose back window was loose in which were stored great numbers of . . . But we could fill pages; let us compress both time and the word.

The basic education of Gorgik had been laid. All that followed — the months he reentered a private service as a mercenary officer again, then as a gamekeeper to a provincial count's lands, then as paid slave-overseer to the same count's treecutters, then as bargeman on the river that ran through that count's land, again as a smuggler in Vinelet, the port at the estuary of that river, then as a mercenary again, then as a private caravan guard — all of these merely developed motifs we have already sounded. Gorgik, at thirty-six, was tall and great-muscled, with rough, thinning hair and a face (with its great scar) that looked no more than half a dozen years older than it had at twenty-one, a man comfortable with horse and sword, at home with slaves, thieves, soldiers, prostitutes, merchants, counts, and princesses; a man who was — in his way and for his epoch — the optimum product of his civilization. The slave mine, the Court, the army, the great ports and mountain holds, desert, field, and forest: each of his civilization's institutions had contributed to creating this scar-faced giant, who wore thick furs in cold weather and in the heat went naked (save for a layered disk of metal, with arcane etchings and cut-outs upon it — an astrolabe — chained around his veined and heavy neck, whatever the month), an easy man in company yet able to hold his silence. Often, at dawn in the mountains or in evenings on the desert, he wondered what terribly important aspects there were to his civilization in excess of a proper ability, at the proper time, to tell the proper tale. But for the civilization in which he lived, this dark giant, soldier, and adventurer, with desires we've not yet named and dreams we've hardly mentioned, who could speak equally of and to barbarian tavern maids and High Court ladies, flogged slaves lost in the cities and provincial nobles at ease on their country estates, he was a civilized man.

— New York, October 1976

Meditations on History

by Sherley Anne Williams

The myth [of the black matriarchy and the castrating black female] must be consciously repudiated as myth and the black woman in her true historical contours must be resurrected. We, the black women of today, must accept the full weight of a legacy wrought in blood by our mothers in chains . . . as heirs to a tradition of supreme perseverance and heroic resistance, we must hasten to take our place wherever our people are forging on towards freedom.

> — from "Reflections on the Black
> Woman's Role in the Community
> of Slaves" by Angela Davis, to
> whom this story is respectfully,
> affectionately dedicated.

SHO WAS HOT out there today."

"Yeah, look like it fixin to be a hot, hot summer."

"Hope it don't git too hot."

"Naw, dry up the crop, it do."

The desultory conversation eddied around her but she took no part in it. The day's heat still hung in the air even though the sun was only a few minutes from setting. The sweaty dust that clung to her skin was reminder — and omen — enough of how hot it could get in the fields. It was enough to feel it; she didn't have to talk about it, too. Even the ones talking, Petey and Brady and them, didn't seem very interested in what they were saying. She smiled. Talkin bout "the weather" and "the crop" — knowin they jes puttin on fo Ta'va.

"I see ol crazy Monroe been ova Mas Jeff'son place agin."

She listened more carefully now. Monroe had been trying for the longest time to get Master's permission to be with some girl over at the Jefferson plantation. But Young Mistress had said all the girl was good for was housework and they didn't need another wench up to the House. And that should have been that, but Monroe kept sneaking over to see her every chance he got — which was no more than saying he made chances. As much as Boss Smith worked people in the fields, there was no way any of them were just going to *find* a chance to wander off and go "visiting." All this was common knowledge among them, though none of them ever said anything about when Monroe left or when Monroe returned unless Boss Smith learned on his own that Monroe had gone visiting before the visit was over.

"What *did* they do him?" she asked when it seemed that no one would answer — had it been Brud who asked the first time? No matter; she knew they didn't want to talk about Monroe in front of Tarver. But talk couldn't hurt Monroe now and Harriet — that had been her talking — shouldn't have brought it up if she didn't want to continue with it. It was too hot to start thinking about something and then have to stop just because Harriet didn't know the difference between "talkin" and "talkin smart." "What they do him?" she asked again.

"Mas jes chain him out to one-a the barns; say he gon sell him," Santee, who walked a couple of feet ahead of her, said over his shoulder.

"Lawd, why won't these chi'ren learn."

Sara was always making as if she were so old, so experienced in dealing with the world. She started to reply but someone else spoke.

"Can't learn a nigga nothin."

The laugh Petey's quick answer brought took away most of the evil Sara's statement and Harriet's reluctance to answer had made her feel.

"Well," Brady said, breaking in on their laughter. "I sho wished I knowed what that lil gal — what her name is?"

"Thank it Alberta," someone supplied.

"Yeah, that's it."

"Well, whatever it is, I sho wished I knowed what she got to make a nigga walk fifteen miles a night and jes be *da'in* a beatin when he get back."

"Don't know," Santee said loudly, "but it sho *gots* to be gooood."

"This one nigga won't never find out." Charlie was laughing with the others even as he said it.

"Now you talkin some sense." She hated it when Tarver broke in on their conversations. Since Boss Smith had made him driver, he thought he knew everything and was better than everybody else. She waited, her lips poked out, knowing whatever he said would make her angry. "Much give-away stuff as it is around here, ain't no way in the world I'd chance what Boss Smith put behind them licks jes to get some mo somewhere else."

Only way *you* get any, at all, is cause if a woman don't, you see Boss Smith or Mas hear bout it. But she didn't say it. Tarver wouldn't even have to run to Boss Smith or Master with that. He'd just slap her in the mouth and no one there would go against the skinny driver. That would mean that two — or however many more helped her — would get whipped instead of just one. But she couldn't resist cutting her eyes knowingly at the women who walked on either side of her. Polly looked as though she wasn't listening but Martha's lips were pushed forward in a taut line that flattened their fullness. Martha was the only lone woman Tarver never passed sly remarks with, and that was saying something. Since he had been made driver, Tarver wasn't even above trying to pat on women who already had men. But Tarver hadn't so much as looked at Martha for some time, now, and if he did say something to her it was only an order about what work she should do.

Martha put her hand on her hip, pulling the shapeless overblouse she wore tight against her heavy breasts, emphasizing the smallness of her waist, and she swung her hips in an exaggerated arc. Even dirty and with that old sweaty head rag on her head, she looked good. "Yeah, I give it away — to some; othas got to take it."

There was a choked kind of laughter from the men and the other women hid their smiles behind their hands. Go on, girl, she thought and then, looking over at Tarver, she saw the muscle along his neck jump.

"Too bad you ain't gived Monroe none; if it all that good he might woulda stayed home," she laughed as she said it and pushed Martha lightly on the shoulder.

"Naw, Monroe was one that'd had to take it," Martha said with a sigh that caused even more laughter.

And she relaxed. Tarver was laughing too.

"I jes meant, I don't want to *love* . . ." She liked to watch the older man shake his head like that when he talked; no matter what he said after he did his head like that, it was bound to be funny. "No, I'm a nigga," and again the shake of his head, "what can't *love* where he don't *live*."

"Listen to Charlie talk!"

She didn't join in their laughter this time. Someone was coming down the quarters. It was him. She knew that even before he raised his hand or opened his mouth — who else could still move like that at the end of the day, like he'd just started out fresh not two minutes ago; even without the banjo banging against his back, she would have known him — and she quickened her steps.

"Somebody sho is walkin fas all a sudden."

She heard the voice behind her as she pushed past the people in front of her but she paid no attention; already, and almost of their own will, her lips were stretched wide in a grin. She could see him clearly now though he was still some distance away, see the big head of nappy hair and the pants hiked up around his waist so that his dusty ankles showed. She stayed in front of the others, but now used the hoe like a cane, swinging it high in pretended nonchalance.

> *Hey, hey, sweet mamma*

His voice, high and sweet and clear as running water in a settled stream, always made her feel so good, so like dancing just for the joy of moving and all the moving would be straight to him.

> *Say, hey now, hey now, sweet mamma*
> *Don't you hear me callin you?*

"Seem like they been wid each otha long enough now fo them to stop all that foolishness."

Huh; you jes mad cause you ain't got nobody to be foolish wid. But she didn't say it aloud. That had been Jean Wee's voice and Jean Wee's man, Tucker, had been sold to Charleston not three months ago. She simply quickened her steps.

Hey, hey, sweet mamma, this Kaine Poppa

His arms were outstretched and though she couldn't hear them, she knew his fingers were snapping to the same rhythm that moved his body.

Kaine Poppa callin his woman's name

Behind her, they were laughing. Kaine could always give you something to laugh about. He made jokes on the banjo, came out with a song made up of old sayings and words that had just popped into his head a second before he opened his mouth, traded words with the men or teased her and the other women. But she never more than half heard the laughter he created. By then she'd thrown the hoe aside and was running, running . . .

He caught her and lifted her off the ground and the banjo banged against her hands as she threw her arms around him. "What you doin down here so early?" She was scared. After that first spurt of joy seeing him always brought, she would get frightened. Lawd, if Boss Smith saw him — And that no-good Ta'va was still behind them — Why he want *do* crazy thangs like this.

"They thank I'm still up there at that ol piece-a greenhouse trying to make strawberries grow all year round." This was said into her neck and as they turned to walk on. Then he laughed aloud. "Why I jes got hungry fo my woman," he said with a glance back over his shoulder.

There was appreciative laughter from behind, but neither the laughter nor his words eased her fear. There must have been something for him to do back at the Big House. Either Childer could have found him a closet to turn out, some piece of furniture to move so the girls could clean behind it, or Aunt Lefonia might have had some spoons or some such to polish in the kitchen. And she knew Emmalina would have wanted him to help serve supper if there was nothing else he had to do. Master was always complaining about how they couldn't afford to have a nigger sitting around eating his head off while he waited for some flowers to grow. But Young Mistress would cry and say how the gardens at the House had always been the showplace of the county. Then, so Aunt Lefonia said — and Aunt Lefonia always knew — Old Mistress would get a pinched look around her mouth and her nose would turn up like she'd just smelled the assfidity bag Merry-Day wore around her neck when she had a cold in her chest, and start talking about how Master was forever trying to drag the Reeves down in the mud where he and the rest of the Vaunghams had come from. And Master would really get mad then and say the Reeves had finally arrived at their true place in life and since it was his money that kept the House a showplace, that nigger, meaning Kaine, better turn his hand to whatever needed doing. That would be the end of it until the next time Master got peeved about something and he would start again. Kaine wouldn't tell her about it, but Aunt Lefonia and Emma-lina did and she was afraid that someday Master wouldn't care about Young Mistress' tears or Old Mistress throwing his family up in his face and would sell Kaine to Charleston or the next coffle that passed their way.

"You jes askin fo trouble, comin down here like this."

"Baby, I'm all *ready* in trouble."

The quarters were filling up now, people coming in from other parts of the plantation, the children who were too small to work coming back from Mamma Hattie's cabin where she kept an eye on them during the day. A few fires had already been lighted and she could smell frying fat-back and wood smoke. Her breath caught at his words.

"What you mean?"

"Mean a nigga ain't born to nothin *but* trouble." Lee Tower, who headed the gang that worked the rice fields, stopped as he spoke, "and if a nigga don't *cou't* pleasure, he ain't likely to git none."

He was the best driver on the plantation, getting work out of his people with as much kindness as he could show, not with the whip like Luke, who headed the gang that Master hired out to cut timber, or Tarver who drove the group she worked with. But she couldn't return Lee Tower's smile or laugh when Carrie Mae, who had come up behind him carrying her baby on her hip, said, "Naw, Mas done sent his butt down here to git it *out* o' trouble; takin care that breedin bidness he been let slide."

"Now yo'all know I be tryin." Kaine was laughing too. "But I got somethin here guaran*teed* to ease a troublin mind." And he patted her shoulder and pinched her lightly in her ribs.

Lee Tower and Carrie Mae laughed and passed on.

"Kaine — "

"Lefonia gived me — "

"Afta how much talkin?"

"Didn't take much."

The laugh was choked out of her; she had looked into his eyes. They were alive, gleaming with dancing lights (no matter what mamma-nem said; his eyes did sparkle) that danced only for her. And when they danced, she would love him so much that she had to touch him or smile. She smiled and he grinned down at her. "Don't neva take much — you got the right word, and you know when it come to eatin beef, I *steal* the right word if it ain't hidin somewheres round my own self tongue," he said as he pulled her in their doorway. She laughed despite herself; he could talk and wheedle just about anything he wanted. "And I pulled some new greens from out the patch and seasoned em wid jes a touch o' fat-back."

"A touch was all we had. Kaine, what —"

"Hmmmm mmmmm. But that ain't all I wants a touch of," he said holding her closer and pulling the dirty, sweaty rag from her head. "Touch ain't neva jes satisfied me."

She laughed and relaxed against him. They were inside, the rickety door shut against the gathering dusk. "Us greens gon get cold."

"But us ain't." He stood with one leg pressed lightly between her thighs, his lips nibbling the curve of her neck.

"I got to clean up a little." She said it more to tease, to prolong this little moment, than because she really felt the need to wash. Sometimes he got mad — not because she was dirty, but because the dirt reminded him that she worked the fields all day. She couldn't say why his being angry about this pleased her so, but it did. Or, sometimes, he would start a small tussle: she trying to get to the washbasin, he holding her back, saying she wasn't that dirty and even dirty she was better than most men got when their women were clean. And that response pleased her, too. She liked the little popping sound "men" made as it came from his mouth.

He ran the tip of his tongue down the side of her neck. "Ain no wine they got up to the House good as this." His fingers caught in her short kinky hair, his palms rested gently on her high cheekbones. "Ain't no way I'm eva gon let you get away from me, girl. Where else I gon find eyes like this?" He kissed her closed lids, his hands sliding down her neck to her shoulders and back, his fingers kneading the flesh under her tow sack dress, and she wanted him to touch all of her, trembled as she thought of his lips on her breasts, his hands on her stomach, or his legs between her own. "Mmmmmm mmmm." He pulled up her dress and his hands were inside her long drawers. "I sho like this behind." His hands cupped her buttocks. "Tell me all this goodness ain't mine," he dared her. "Whoa! and when it git to movin," and he moved, "and I git to movin and we git to movin — Lawd, I knowed it was gon be sweet but not this doggone *good!*"

This was love talk that made her feel almost as beautiful as the way he touched her. She shivered and pulled at the coarse material of his shirt, not needing the anger or the other words, now, because his hands and mouth made her feel so loved. His skin was warm and dry under her hands and even though she could barely wait to feel all of him against all of her, she leaned a little away from him. "Sho you want to be wid this ol dirty woman? Sho you want —"

His lips were on hers nibbling and pulling, and the sentence ended in a groan. Her thighs spread for him, her hips moved for him. Lawd, this man sho know how to love . . .

It was gone as suddenly as it had come, the memory so strong, so clear it was like being with him all over again. Muscles contracted painfully deep inside her and she could feel the warm moistness oozing between her thighs. There was only the thin cotton coverlet that provided no weight and little warmth, the noise the corn husk pallet made each time she moved. It was moonlight that shined in her eyes, not his eyes that had been the color of lemon-tea and honey. She lay still but she could not conjure the visions again, and finally she turned her back to the tiny window where the moonlight entered, pulled the coverlet up around her breasts and closed her eyes.

Hey, hey, sweet mamma

(She knew the words; it was his voice that had been the music.)

> *Hey, sweet mamma, this Kaine Poppa*
> *Kaine Poppa callin his woman's name.*
> *He can pop his poppa so good*
> *Make his sweet woman take to a cane.*

MEDITATIONS ON HISTORY

The Hughes Farm
Near Linden
Marengo County, Alabama.

June 9, 1829.

I must admit to a slight yearning for the comfort of the Linden House (comfort that is quite remarkable, considering Linden's out-of-the-way location), but Sheriff Hughes' generous offer of hospitality enables me to be close at hand for the questioning of the negress and this circumstance must outweigh the paucity of creature comforts which his gable room provides.

The negress is housed here in a little-used root cellar until such time as sentencing can be carried out. Hughes told me at dinner tonight the amusing story of how the negress came to be housed in his cellar. It seems that the town drunk, a rather harmless fellow who usually spends some portion of each week in housing provided at public expense, protested the idea of having to share quarters with the negress over an extended period of time. The other blacks involved in the uprising had, of course, been given a speedy trial and the sentences were carried out with equal dispatch, so the drunk — I cannot recall his name — had not been too inconvenienced. He drew the line, however, at protracted living with the wench in the close quarters which the smallness of the jail necessitates. In this he was supported by his wife, a papist from New Orleans but otherwise a good woman and normally a very meek one. She was convinced that the girl had the "evil eye" and was also possessed of a knowledge of the black arts — for how else, she asked at one point, could the negress have supplied the members of the coffle with the files which freed them when there were none to be had (a provocative question, but Hughes says that it was never proved that it was the negress who supplied the files). The woman demanded of Hughes, and later, when Hughes could give her no satisfaction, of the judge, the mayor and several of the large landowners in the vicinity, that the girl be moved or her husband be provided with separate quarters. She raised such a rumpus, invoking saints and all manner of idols, and pestered the gentlemen so repeatedly that Hughes in desperation offered his root cellar and, as his farm is also only a short distance from town, the village fathers jumped at his offer. Calmer reflection showed them the wisdom of this hasty decision: Jemina (a singularly inappropriate name for one of her size), the house servant here, is a noted midwife and excellent care is thus close at hand when the negress's time comes.

There is, however, some uncertainty about when that time will be. The Court, at Wilson's request, has postponed the hanging until after the birth of the child, which, according to Wilson's coffle manifest, should be two to three months hence. Hughes, however, says that it will be sooner. Jemina declares that the wench is eight months gone now and the entire district swears by the woman's prognostications. It is all in one to me, for, however far gone she proves to be, there is ample time for me to conclude my investigation of this incident before the law extracts the final punishment for her crimes. And the price will be paid. She will hang from the same gallows where her confederates forfeited their lives for the part they played in that perfidious and, fortunately, unsuccessful uprising.

It is late and the branches of the huge oak which commands the back yard brush softly at the shutters. It is a restful sound and the sense of urgency which had driven me since first I heard of this latest instance of negro savagery has finally eased. The retelling of this misadventure will make a splendid opening for the book and I am properly elated that I managed to reach Linden before the last of the culprits had come by their just deserts. It will be a curious, an interesting process to delve into the mind of one of the instigators of this dreadful plot. Is it merely the untamed, perhaps even *untamable* savagery of their natures which causes them to rise up so treacherously and repudiate the natural order of the universe which has already decreed their place, or is it something more amenable to human manipulation, the lack of some disciplinary measure or restraining word which brought Wilson and countless others to such tragic consequences? Useless to ponder now, for if I do not discover the answer with this one negress, I have every confidence that I shall find an answer in the other investigation I shall make.

June 10, 1829.

I have seen her: the virago, the she-devil who even now haunts the nightmares of Wilson. I had not thought it possible that one of his calling could be so womanish, for surely slave-trading is a more hazardous profession than that of doctor, lawyer, or *writer*. Yet, this wench, scarcely more than a pickaninny — and the coffle manifest puts her age somewhere in the neighborhood of fifteen or sixteen — and one of such diminutive size at that is the self-same wench whom Wilson called a "raging nigger bitch." In recollecting the uprising, it is the thought of *this* darky which even now, weeks after the events, brings a sweat to his brow and a tremble to his hand. Why, her belly is bigger than she is and birthing the child she carries — a strong, lusty one if the size of her stomach is any indication — will no doubt kill her long before the hangman has a chance at her throat. Oh, she may be sullen and stubbornly silent. Although, in this initial visit, she appeared more like a wild and timorous animal finally brought to bay, for upon perceiving that Hughes was not alone she moved quickly if clumsily to the farthest reaches of the root cellar which her leg iron allows. Hughes attempted to coax her in a really remarkable approximation of what he says is her own speech, saying that I was not there to aggravate her with further questions as the other white men had done. She, however, would approach us no closer than just enough to ease the tension on her chains. Still, I can imagine the dangerously excitable state which Hughes confirms characterized her actions upon first being apprehended. According to Hughes, she was like a cat at that time, spitting, biting, scratching, apparently unconcerned about the harm her actions might bring to her child. The prosecutor was naturally relentless in his questioning and it is only since being removed to this farm that she has achieved a state of relative calm. Yet, to see in this one common negress the she-devil of Wilson's delirium is the grossest piece of nonsense. Hughes agrees with me, saying privately that he always believed that Wilson's loud harshness toward the blacks in his coffles hid a cowardly nature. Hughes, of course, has had more opportunity to judge of this than I, for Wilson has been bringing his coffles through Marengo County for well onto seven years. And this also confirms my own opinion of him. Even in that one brief visit I had with him in Selma, I detected the tone, the attitude of the braggart and bully.

I shall speak with Hughes about making other provisions for a meeting place. Even had I been of a mind to talk with the negress, the stench of the root cellar — composed almost equally I suspect of stale negro and whatever else has been stored there through the years — would have driven me away within the minute. And that would be a pity for there is no doubt that the negress was one of the leaders in the bloody proceeding. Her own testimony supports the findings of the Court. Now, she will be brought to re-create that event and all that led up to it for me. Ah, the work, *The Work* has at last begun.

June 13, 1829.

Each day I become more convinced of the necessity, the righteousness even of the work I have embarked upon. Think, I say to myself as I sit looking into the negress's face, think how it might have been had there been a work such as I envision after the Prosser uprising of 1800. Would the Vesey conspiracy and all the numerous uprisings which took place in between these two infamous events, would they have occurred? Would this wretched wench even now be huddled before me? No, I say. No, for the evil seeds which blossomed forth in her and her companions would never have been planted. I feel more urgency about the completion of *The Roots of Rebellion and the Means of Eradicating Them* (I have settled upon this as a compelling short title) than ever I did about writing *The Complete Guide for Competent Masters in Dealing with Slaves and Other Dependents.* I am honest enough to agree with those of my detractors who claim that *The Guide* is no more than a compendium of sound, commonsense practices gathered together in book form (they forget, however, that it is I who first hit upon the idea of compiling such a book and the credit of being first must always be mine). *The Guide* was, in some sense, a mere business venture. But *Roots* — even though the first word has yet to be written — looms already in my mind as a *magnum opus.*

Yet, being closeted with the negress within the small confines of the root cellar is an unsettling experience. Thus far, I have not been able to prevail upon Hughes to allow us the freedom of the yard for our meetings. Despite his bluff firmness in dealing with her, he is loath to allow the negress beyond the door of the root cellar. It is preposterous to suppose that anything untoward could happen. He vouches for the loyalty of his own darkies and has strictly forbidden them to have any intercourse whatsoever with her unless a white person is also present. The negress would, of course, be chained and perhaps under the open sky, I can free myself from the oppressive sense of her eyes casting a spell, not so much upon me (I know that should it ever come to a contest, God will prove stronger than the black devils she no doubt worships). No, not upon me is the spell cast, but upon the whole of the atmosphere from which I must draw breath. This last I know is fanciful; I laugh even as I write it, and it is not *the* reason for my long silence. She refused on two occasions to speak with me. I forebore carrying this tale to Hughes. He is a crude, vulgar, even brutal man who would doubtless feel that the best solution to the negress's stubbornness is a judicious application of the whip. In another situation I might be inclined to agree with him — the whip is most often the medicine to cure a recalcitrant slave. In this instance, however, I feel that the information I require must, if it is to be creditable, be freely given. I trust that I have not placed too much dependence upon her intelligence and sensitivity. Or, more likely, upon that innate stubbornness and intractableness for which I believe blacks from certain parts of the dark continent are well known. I think not, for upon the first occasion she appeared unmoved when I reminded her that although the child she carries may save her yet a while from a hanging, it was certainly not proof against a whipping. She cannot be said to roll her eyes (a most lamentable characteristic of her race), rather she *flicks* them across one — much in the same manner a horse uses his tail to flick a bothersome fly. It is a most offensive gesture. It was thus that she greeted this statement. I was so angered that I struck her in the face, soiling my hand and bloodying her nose, and called to Hughes to open the door. I was almost immediately sorry for my impetuous action. Hughes thinks of me as an expert negro tamer and although he has not, as he told me, read *The Guide*, he has heard from respectable sources that it has a "right good bit o' learnin and common sense" in it. I, therefore, do not want it ever to appear, for even a moment, that I have been or will ever be defeated by a negress. As I take pains to point out in *The Guide*, it is seldom necessary to strike a darky with one's hand and to do so, except in the most unusual circumstances, is to lower one's self almost to the same level of random violence which characterizes the action of the blacks among themselves. It is always a lowering, even repellent, reflection to know that one has forgotten the sense of one's own teachings. It was Willis, I believe, on the plantation of Mr. Charles Haskins near Valdosta in Lowndes County, Georgia, who carried a riding whip in order to correct just such subtle signs of insolence as the negress has tried my patience with. But the violence of my reaction has perhaps made any such response unnecessary in the future.

My latest attempt to have speech with her was this morning and I find it difficult to interpret her attitude. We heard upon approaching the cellar a humming or moaning. It is impossible to precisely define it as one or the other. I was alarmed, but Hughes merely laughed it off as some sort of "nigger business." He was perhaps right, for upon opening the door and climbing down the steps into the cellar proper, we found her with arms crossed in front of her chest, her hands grasping her shoulders. She was seated in the stream of light which comes through the one window — an odd instance in itself for always before she had crouched away from the light so that her eyes gleamed forth from the darkness like those of a beast surprised in its lair. She rocked to and fro and at first I thought the sounds which came from her some kind of dirge or lamentation. But when I ventured to suggest this to Hughes, he merely laughed, asking how else could a nigger in her condition keep happy save through singing and loud noise, adding that a loud nigger was a happy one; it is the silent ones who bear watching. I asked tartly if he made no distinction between moaning and singing. Why should I, he replied with a hearty laugh, the niggers don't. I am obliged to rely upon Hughes' judgment in this matter; as slaveholder and sheriff he has had far greater contact with various types of darkies than I should ever wish for myself. And this last piece of information tallies with what I heard again and again while doing the research for *The Guide.*

Hughes left at this point and I was alone with the wench. I admit to being at a loss as to how to begin, but just as I was about to order her to cease her noise, she lurched to her feet and her voice rose to a climactic pitch. She uttered the words, "I bes. I bes." Just those two words on a loud, yes, I would say, even exultant note. Her arms were now at her sides and she stood thus a moment in the light. Her face seemed to seek it and her voice was like nothing I had ever heard before. "I bes. I. And he in air on my tongue the sun on my face. The heat in my blood. I bes he; he me. He me. And it can't end in this place, not this time. Not this time. Not this. But if it do, if it do, it was and I bes. I bes."

I did not exist for her. And I knew then that to talk to her while she remained in such a state would be to talk to the air she now seems to claim to be. We will try what a little pressure can accomplish with her reluctant tongue. Perhaps a day spent on nothing but salt water will make her realize how lightly we have thus far held the reins.

I am somewhat surprised that she feels so little inclined toward boasting of her deeds, dark though they are. I do not make the mistake of putting her silence down to modesty or even fear but the above-mentioned stubbornness. She will find, however, that there are as many ways to wear stubbornness thin as there are to wear away patience.

June 17, 1829.

I have spent the last few days at the courthouse, going through the trial records of this appalling incident, hoping to get a better under-standing of what transpired and some insight into the motivation of the darkies. It is a measure of Judge Hoffer's confidence in me and the work upon which I am engaged that I was allowed access to the rec-ords. While I do not envision a narrative such as was made of the trial records of the Denmark Vesey case (which was later destroyed because of the inflammatory material it contained), I shudder to think of the uses to which the information contained in these records might be put should they fall into the wrong hands. The trials were conducted in closed sessions so that, while the records themselves contain little more than what Wilson and Hughes have already told me, none of this in-formation is for public consumption.

The bare outline is this: Wilson picked up a consignment of slaves in Charleston at the end of March. While in the area, he attended a private sale where he heard of a wench, just entered upon childbearing age, and already increasing, that was being offered for sale on the plantation of Mr. Terrell Vaungham. He inquired at the plantation and was told that the wench was being sold because she had assaulted Vaugnham. There is always a ready market for females of childbearing age with proven breeding capacity, so, despite the disquieting circum-stances, Wilson chose to inspect the wench. There were still signs of punishment, raw welts and burns across the wench's buttocks and the inside of her thighs. Being in places which would only be inspected by the most careful buyer, such marks were not likely to impair her value. Thus satisfied, Wilson paid three hundred eighty-five dollars specie for her: she would fetch at least twice that much in New Orleans. The wench gave every appearance of being completely cowed at the time of purchase and throughout the rest of the journey; thus no special guard was placed upon her. Also purchased at this time, through regular channels, were two bucks who were later whipped and branded as runaways because of their parts in the uprising. These purchases brought the number of slaves in the coffle to eighty: fifty males and thirty females ranging in age from about eleven to thirty (but then, no slave dealer will ever admit that any slave he wants to sell is older than thirty or younger than ten). Wilson will not take pickaninnies on these overland trips, feeling that they are more trouble than the price which they are like to fetch on the block warrants. Wilson and his partner, Darkmon, had with them six other men who acted as guards and drivers. It is generally agreed that this one-to-ten ratio is a proper one on a trip of this nature.

On the morning of March 30, 1829, they set out on the journey which would eventually end in New Orleans around the middle of June — had all gone well. There were no untoward events during the first portions of the journey, in fact, the coffle moved so smoothly that the regular security measures may have been somewhat relaxed (and Wilson's adamant denial of this does not convince me in the least. Men of his stripe are always more than willing to lay the blame for their own ineptness and laxity at someone else's door). As usual, Wilson continued to sell off and buy up slaves at each stop along the way. This practice, according to Wilson, serves to prevent trouble during the journey. The number of slaves on the coffle remains constant; there is, however, a continuous turnover of bodies. Thus, there is little chance for the blacks to become too intimate with one another. However, in checking the manifest (a copy of which was admitted as evidence) against the list of those apprehended, killed or convicted, I discovered a fact which had evidently escaped notice: a small group of twelve slaves had been with the coffle since Charleston. Of these, ten were directly involved in the uprising. It is also significant that two of the other blacks who were named as ringleaders had been with the coffle for some time. One must therefore conclude that a rapid and regular turnover of slaves does much to prevent the spread of discontent among them (perhaps this axiom can be modified and extended to include slaves on plantations and small farms).

Wilson had lately taken to chaining the blacks in groups of four and five to trees or other natural projections when no housing was available at night. He found that this method allowed them a more comfortable repose at night which in turn meant they were able to travel faster during the day and were also in better condition when they arrived at the market. He had saved considerable sums because the slaves no longer required expensive conditioning and grooming before being put up for sale. The darkies were strung together in the familiar single file when the coffle was ready to move. It is my firm belief that had Wilson used the tried and true method all along, he could have saved himself subsequent grief. A group of darkies had only to break away from the central chain which bound them to a projection in order to be free. This is precisely what happened.

In the early hours of April 29, the wench and the four bucks in her chain group managed to free themselves (whether with a file — which seems most likely — or because the locks were not properly secured — a terrifying oversight in a coffle of that size — was not revealed, even under the most intensive and painful methods of questioning. And the chains were never found). Two of these went to subdue the guards and drivers while the other three attacked Wilson and Darkmon, searching for the keys which would free the rest of the coffle. The negress attacked Darkmon and it was his death screams which awakened Wilson. He was immediately fighting for his own life, of course, and just as he managed to climb atop the darky and had raised his arm to strike him with the very rock with which he himself had been attacked, the negress fell upon him. She wielded a pick made from a stone sharpened to a stiletto point (the same one which she later used in attacking members of the posse). Evidently, her screams and "gleaming eyes" struck terror in Wilson's heart, for he is unable to recount what happened after this. Apparently, though, after Darkmon had been so foully murdered and while the negress went to the aid of the buck who had attacked Wilson, the other black used Darkmon's keys to free the others in the coffle. These quickly dispatched the drivers and guards who had not been subdued in the first onslaught. The darkies then took the horses and pack animals, some provisions and all the firearms and other weapons, and left Wilson and two of the drivers for dead. These lone survivors were found the next day on the trail to Linden, weak from loss of blood and babbling deliriously. A posse was quickly formed and set out in pursuit. They soon came upon the horses and other animals which the darkies had loosed, the better to cover their trail. The posse also found, throughout the course of their pursuit, a number of darkies who either could not keep up with the main body of renegades or who had repented of their impetuous action in following the malcontents and were eager to help in the capture. After three days of tracking the renegades back and forth in a northwesterly direction, the posse surprised them in a camp they had made some thirty-five miles north of Linden. After a fierce gun battle in which seven of the posse were wounded, two of whom did not recover from their wounds, the slaves were finally subdued in hand-to-hand combat at a cost to the posse of three dead and numerous minor injuries. A few renegades tried to slip away during the battle: they, too, were recaptured. However, three, seeing that the battle was lost, fled, and have thus far eluded capture. All told, there were some sixty-three blacks retaken, four having been killed in the initial skirmish with the drivers, eight, either outright or later as a result of their wounds, in the battle with the posse. The posse came up with the renegades on May 4; on the afternoon of the 6th, they arrived in Linden and the trials were held all day on the 8th. The slaves were tried in three groups: those who were thought to be ringleaders, those who were known to have been most directly involved in the attacks, either on the drivers or the posse (these groups often overlapped), and those who, perhaps, had been coerced into participation in these infamous proceedings. The sentences were carried out during the week of the 11th. The slaves were subjected to continual questioning from the time of their arrest until the time at which their sentences were carried out. I must commend the sheriff, the prosecutor and the judge on their ability to obtain so much information in such a short period of time.

Thirty-three blacks were tried (all adults above the age of fifteen): six were hanged and quartered as ringleaders, thirteen were hanged and quartered because of the ferocity with which they fought the posse (of these last two totals, six were females); three were whipped only; seven were branded only and three were whipped and branded (these last punishments infuriated Wilson when he learned of them. Branding makes the slave almost worthless, for no one in his right mind would buy a slave with such an extensive history of running away and re- belliousness as branding signifies. Wilson had preferred that they be hanged along with the others and thus save himself the cost of housing and feeding them). The negress still awaits her fate. The three bucks who eluded the posse were Big Nathan, a major plotter who had been chained with the negress the night of the uprising; Harker, who had been purchased in Atlanta; and Proud's Cully, who had been pur- chased in Jeffersonville just across the line in Georgia. According to the testimony of the slaves, it was this wench, the men in her chain group and five blacks from another group who were the sole plotters. The others had neither a part in the planning nor in the execution of these plans until all had been set free. This seems rather farfetched to me. Wilson, in his written statement to the Court, said that he changed the chain groupings at regular intervals. This would have made it easy for any plot to spread rapidly through the coffle. But as all maintained this posture, the Court accepted the statement of the blacks as true. In fact, one plotter, Elijah (charged by two of the others with being a "root-man," a dealer in black magic; but as there was no further sub- stantiation of this charge, he was not tried on this count), was even rather contemptuous of the idea of telling any of the other slaves about the rebellion plot. They were, he said, white men's niggers who would have betrayed the plans at the first opportunity and who would accept freedom only if it were shoved down their throats. Big Nathan, Mungo and Elijah, who were hanged and quartered, and Black David, who was killed in the battle with the posse, were to lead them all to freedom, but none could specify where this place of freedom was. Elijah said that God would reveal the direction of and route to the free place at the proper time, that the means of escape had likewise been delivered into their hands by God and he would not question the will of God. This was all the "information" which the Court could obtain from any of them — save that the negress, when asked why she, rather than one of the males, had been chosen for so dangerous a task as securing the keys, would say only that it was best that way. (Questioning of her was not as severe as with the others. Wilson has developed an almost fanatical resolve to see in chains the child she carries and the doctor feared that, should she lose the baby before this had been accom- plished, it might overset Wilson's reason. The Court took this medical opinion into account when deciding to delay the consummation of the wench's sentence.) It is my own belief that she was chosen because of her very unlikeliness. Who would think a female so far gone in the breeding process capable of such treacherous conduct?

That, in bare outline, is what happened; my chore now is to fill in that outline, to discover and analyze the motivating factors which culminated in this outrage against the public safety. I feel that I have been richly rewarded for these past few days of work. In retelling this outline, I am filled again with a sense of my mission. I look forward to dealing with the negress again on Monday.

June 29, 1829.

"Was I white, I might woulda fainted when Emmalina told me that Mas had done gon up-side Kaine head, nelly bout kilt him iff'n he wa'n't dead already. Fainted and not come to myself til it was ova, least ways all of it that could eva get ova. I guess when you faints you be out of the world, that how Kaine say it be. Say that how Mist's act up at the House when Mas or jes any lil thang don't be goin to suit her. Faint, else cry and have em all, Aunt Lefonia, Feddy and the rest, comin, runnin and fannin and carin on, askin what wrong, who did it. Kaine hear em from the garden and he say he be laughin fit to split his side and diggin, diggin and laughin to hear how one lil sickly white woman turn a house that big upside down. I neva rightly believe it could be that way. But wa'n't no way fo me to know fo sho — I work the fields and neva goes round the House neitha House niggas, cept only Aunt Lefonia. Kaine, when me and him first be close and see us want be closer, he try to get me up to the House, ask Aunt Lefonia if she see what she can do, talk to Mist's maybe. But Aunt Lefonia say I too light for Mist's and not light nough fo Mas. Mist's ascared Mas gon be likin the high colored gals same as he was fo they was married so she don't low nothin but dark uns up to the House else ones too old for Mas to be beddin. So I stays in the fields like I been. Kaine don't like it when Aunt Lefonia tell him that and he even ask Mist's please could I change, but Mist's see me and say no. Kaine mad but he finally jes laugh, say, what kin a nigga do? But I see Mist's that time close-up and I can't rightly believe all what Kaine say. Maybe he jes make it mo'n it bes so when he tell it I laugh. But I neva do know fo sho. Kaine mus know though. He been round the Houses, most a House nigga hisself, though a House nigga neva say a nigga what tend flovas any betta'n one what tend corn. He jes laugh when Childer try to come the big nigga ova him, tell him, say, Childer, jes cause you open do's for the white folks don't make you white. And Childer puff all up cause he not like it, you don't be treatin him some big and he was raised up with the old Mas, too. Humph. So he say to Kaine, say, steadda Kaine talkin back at the ones what betta'n him, Kaine betta be seein at findin him a mo likely gal'n me."

She paused, her head lifted, her eyes closed as though listening. "He chosed me." I could not read the expression on her face; the cellar was too dark. Something, however, seemed to have crept into her voice and I waited, hoping she would continue. "He chosed me. Mas ain't had nothing to do wid that. It Kaine what pick me out and say I be his woman. Mas say you lay down wid this'n or that un and that be the one you lay wid. He tell Carrie Mae she lay wid that studdin nigga and that who she got to be wid. And we all be knowin that it ain't fo nothin but to breed and time the chi'ren be up in age, they be sold off to notha 'tation, maybe deep south. And she jes a lil bitty thang then and how she gon be holdin a big nigga like that, carryin that big nigga child. And all what mamma say, what Aunt Lefonia and Mamma Hattie say don't make Mas no ne'mind. 'Luke known fo makin big babies on lil gals,' Mas say and laugh. Laugh so hard, he don't be hearin Mamma Hattie say how Luke studdin days be ova 'fo' he eva touch Carrie. Mas, he don't neva know it, but Luke, he know it. But he don't tell cause the roots stop his mouth from talkin to Mas same as they stop his seed from touchin Carrie. Mas jes wonder and wonder and finally he say Luke ain't good fo nothing no mo cept fo to drive otha niggas inna field and fo to beat the ones what try fo to be bad. Carrie bedded wid David then and Mas gots three mo niggas fo to be studs, so he ain't too much carin. And Carrie gots a baby comin. Baby comin . . . baby comin. . . . But Kaine chosed me. He chosed me and when Emmalina meet me that day, tell me Kaine don took a hoe at Mas and Mas don laid into him wid a shovel, bout bus' in his head, I jes run and when the hoe gits in my way, I let it fall, the dress git in my way and I holds that up. Kaine jes layin there on usses pallet, head seepin blood, one eye closed, one bout gone. Mamma Hattie sittin side him wipin at the blood. 'He be dead o' sold. Dead o' sold.' I guess that what she say then. She say it so many times afta that I guess she say it then, too. 'Dead o' sold.' Kaine jes groan when I call his name. I say all the names I know, eva heard bout, thought bout, Lawd, Legba, Shango, Jesus. Anybody, jes so's Kaine could speak. "Nigga,' Kaine say. Nigga and my name. He say em ova and ova and I hold his hand cause I know that can't be all he wanna say. Nigga and my name, my name and nigga. 'Nigga,' he say. 'Nigga can do.' And he don't say no mo."

And that has what to do with you and the other slaves rising up and killing the trader and the drivers, I asked sharply, for it seemed as though she would not continue.

She opened her eyes and looked at me. Wide and black they are. She had had them closed or only half open as she talked, her head moving now and then, from side to side, in and out of the light coming in through the tiny unshuttered window. She opened her eyes and her head was silhouetted in the light. I understood then what Wilson meant when he talked in his delirium about "devil eyes," a "devil's stare." Long, black and the whites are unstained by red or even the rheumy color which characterizes the eyes of so many darkies whether of pure or mixed blood, and she does not often blink them. "I kill that white man," she said, and in the same voice in which she talked about being allowed to work in the big house, in which she had talked about the young darky's dying. They were all the same to her. "I kill that white man cause the same reason Mas kill Kaine. Cause I can." And she turned her head to the dark and would not speak with me anymore.

I have read again this first day's conversation with the negress. It is all here — even that silly folderol about "roots" — as much in her own words as I could make out. It would seem that one must be acquainted with darkies from one's birth in order to fully understand what passes for speech amongst them. It is obvious that I must speak with her again, perhaps several times more, for she answers questions in a random manner, a loquacious, roundabout fashion — if, indeed, she can be brought to answer them at all. This, to one of my habits, is exasperating to the point of fury. I must constantly remind myself that she is but a darky and a female at that. Copious notes seem to be the order of the day and I will cull what information I can from them. And, despite the rambling nature of today's discourse, the fact that she did talk re-

mains something of a triumph for *The Guide.* Light punishment followed by swift relaxation of the punitive measure is a trick I learned of
in Maryland, where they have long since realized what the whippings
which the abolitionists deplore are not the only way to bring a rebel-
lious darky to heel.

June 22, 1829.

    She has talked again, perhaps the influence of the open air or per-
haps there was one thing in the long string of questions I asked which
touched her thought more than another. I have asked the same basic
questions at each meeting. Today, I grew more than a little impatient
with the response — or lack thereof — which I have thus far elicited,
and would have despaired of completing my project, if completion depends upon this one negress — which, thank God! it does not. But it is
not in my nature to admit defeat so readily and so, thinking to return
to the one thing about which she had previously talked, I asked, How
did it happen that this darky of whom you spoke attacked Mr. Vaungham? I had phrased this question in various ways and been met with
silence. I had even nudged her slightly with the tip of my boot to assure
myself that she had not fallen into a doze (they fall asleep, I am told,
much as a cow will in the midst of a satisfying chew, though I, myself,
have not observed this), but aside from that offensive flicking of the eye,
she would not respond. I contained my irritation and my impatience
and went on with my questioning. Was he crazed, drunk? Where did
he get the liquor? She was seated on the ground at my feet, her back
against the tree trunk. The chain which attached to her ankle was
wound once around the tree and fastened to a rung of the chair in
which I sat. The chair was placed to one side and a little behind so that
she would have to look up at me. She would not. Sometimes she closed
her eyes or looked out into space. At these times she would hum, an
absurd, monotonous little tune in a minor key, the melody of which
she repeated over and over. Each morning, we are awakened by the
singing of the darkies and they often startle one by breaking into song
at odd times during the day. Hughes, of course, finds this comforting.
But thus far I have heard nothing but moaning from this wench. How
did it happen that this darky attacked Mr. Vaungham? and I raised my
voice so as to be heard over her humming.

She stopped humming for a second and when she resumed, she put words to the melody:

> *"Lawd, gimme wings like Noah's dove*
> *Lawd, gimme wings like Noah's dove*
> *I'd fly cross these fields to the one I loves,*
> *Say, hello darlin; say, how you be.*

Mamma Hattie say that playin wid God, puttin yo self on the same level's His peoples is on. But Kaine jes laugh and say she ain't knowed no mo bout God and the Bible than what the white folk tell her and that can't be too much cause Mas say he don't be likin religion in his slaves. So Kaine jes go on singin his songs to me in the e'nin afta I gets out the fields. I be layin up on usses pallet and he be leanin ginst the wall. He play sweet-soft cause he say that what I needs, soft sweetin put me to sleep afta I done work so all day. He really feel bad bout that, me inna field and him in the garden. He even ask Boss Smith could I come work at the House o' he come work the field. I scared when he do that. Nobody ask Boss Smith fo nothing cause that make him note you and the onliest way Boss Smith know to note you is wid that whip. But Boss Smith jes laugh and tell him he a crazy nigga. But Kaine not crazy. He the sweetest nigga as eva walk this earth. He play that banger, he play it so sweet til Mist's even have him up to the House to play and she talk bout havin a gang o' niggas to play real music fo when they be parties and such like at the House. Ole Mist's used to would talk like that, so Aunt Lefonia say, cause that was how they done in Ole Mist's home. But it don't nothin comma it then, not now neitha. Side, Kaine say the music he know to play be real nough fo him. Say that that his banger. He make it hisn' so it play jes what he want play. And he play it. Not jes strum strum wid all his fingers, but so you hear each strang when he touch it and each strang gots a dif-f'ent thang to say. And they neva talks bout being sad, being lonesome cause Kaine say I hep him put all that behind him. Even when us be workin and he be up to the House and I be out inna field, it not bad, cause he be knowin, when the bell rang, I be comin fix that lil bit ration and we lay up on usses pallet. 'Niggas,' he tell me, 'niggas jes only belongs to white folks and that bes all. They don't be belongin to they mammas and daddys, they sista, they brotha.' Kaine mamma be sold when he lil bit and he not even know her face. And sometime he thank maybe his first Mas o' the driva o' maybe jes some white man passin through be his daddy. Then he say mus been some fine, big, black man muscled up like strong tree what got sold cause he go fo bad. And he be wishin he took looks afta his daddy, be big and strong like him, be *bad*, steadda the way he do look, nappy head and light eyes. Have a black fo a daddy well as a white man, he say, but he can't neva know, not fo sho, no way. He be sold hisself lotta time fo he come to Mas 'tation. So he don't know bout stayin wid Mamma Hattie til you be big nough to work the fields, o' bein woked up by mamma and eatin dry cornbread and 'lasses fo day in the mornin wid evabody and hearin Jeeter tease the slow pokes and havin mamma fetch you a slap so Boss Smith won't fetch his whip at you fo tarryin so. Onlest folks he eva belongs to is the white folks and that not really like belongin to a body. He say first time he hear anybody play a banger, he have to stop, have to listen cause it seem like it talkin right at him. And the man what play it, he a Af'ca black, not a reg'la nigga like what you see eva day. And this Af'ca man say that the music he play be from his home, and his home be his; it don't be belongs to no white folks. Nobody there belongs to white folks, jes onlest theyselves and each otha. He tell Kaine lotta thang what Kaine don't member cause he lil bit then and this the first time he be sold. That in Charleston and I know that close to where I'm is and I wonder how it be if Mas had buyed Kaine then, steadda when Kaine be grown. But, it happen how it happen and that time in Charleston Kaine not know all what the Af'ca man say, cept bout the home and bout the banger, how to make it, how to play it. And he know that cause he know if he have it, home be his and the banger be his. Cept he ain't got no home, so he jes onlest have the banger.

"He make that banger hisself. Make it outen good parchment and seasoned wood he get hisself and when Mas break it seem like he break Kaine. Might well as had cause it not right wid him afta tha. And I can't make it right wid him. I tell him he can make notha one. I pick up wood fo him from Jim Boys at the carp'ter shed, get horsehair from Emmalina Joe Big down to the stables. But Kaine jes look at it. 'Mas can make notha one,' he say, 'Nigga can't do shit. Mas can step on a nigga hand, nigga heart, nigga life, and what can a nigga do? Nigga can't do shit.

> *What can a nigga do when Mas house on fire?*
> *What can a nigga do when Mas house on fire?*
> *Bet NOT do mo'n yell, Fire, Fire!*
> *Let some'un else brang the wata*
> *Cause a nigga can't do shit!*

He sing that and laugh. And one day Emmalina meet me when I come in outten the field and tell me Mas don shoved in the side of Kaine head."

She looked up at the sun and blinked her eyes rapidly several times. I did not question her anymore.

This is still a far cry from just how five slaves managed to free themselves and loose the rest of the coffle, how, having achieved this, they managed to murder the drivers and one trader and dangerously injure another (and I begin to think, too, that she must have some inkling of where the three darkies that the posse couldn't find have gotten to), but I begin to perceive how I may get to this point. We shall see tomorrow. Enough for tonight. I sat late with Hughes over a very smooth Kentucky whiskey (I must admit to having misjudged Hughes. I had not thought from either the appointments of his house or the fare at his table that he was capable of such fine taste. Perhaps it is only from want of proper exercise that his discriminating faculties are not more in evidence. What I had thought dead may only be dormant. As for means — in the case of the whiskey, I would say that being sheriff must not be without its advantages). It is curious, though, how the negress, well, how she looks in the sun. For a moment today as I watched her I could almost imagine how Vaungham allowed her to get close enough to stick a knife between his ribs.

June 23, 1829.

She demanded a bath this morning, which Hughes foolishly allowed her, and in the creek. Being without a bathing dress, she must perforce bathe in her clothes and dry in them also. A chill was the natural outcome, whose severity we have yet to determine. And were that not bad enough, she cut her foot, a deep slash cross the instep and ball, while climbing up the bank. Hughes thinks it a reasonably clean cut but she bathed near the place where the livestock come to water so there is no way of knowing. He claims that he was so nonplussed, "flustered" as he phrases it, at such a novel request coming from a nigger and a wench ready to be brought to light, too, that he had granted the request before he had time to think properly of the possible outcome. Since she was shackled during the whole business he thought no harm could be done, as though darkies are not subject to the same chills and sweats which overtake the veriest pack animals. It seems that I am never to be spared the consequences of dealing with stupid people. Pray God the wench doesn't die before I get my book.

June 27, 1829.

A curious session we had of it today. I know not what, even now, to make of it. She spoke of her own accord today, spoke to me, rather than the hot windless air, as has been her custom. The air, even now, is oppressive, hot, still, strangely dry, and it was obvious, even as Hughes brought her up from the cellar, that the negress also felt it. Her movements, always slow, were even slower, her walk, not stumbling but heavy as though her feet were weighted. She eased her bulk onto the ground beneath the tree and leaned back against its trunk. Her dark wooly hair — which fits upon her head almost like a nubby cap — seemed to merge into the deeper shadows cast by the thick low hanging branches of the tree. I sat in my habitual place just behind her, stripped to my shirt sleeves and feeling that even this was not enough to lessen the sun's onslaught. The sharp, bright sunlight was too painful to gaze at from the depth of that shadow and I must look down at the pages of my notebook, blank save for the day's date, or at her. We were silent for some moments after she was seated, I thinking how limited my vision had become and she engaged in God knows what cogitations.

"That writin what you put on that paper?" I was somewhat startled by the question and did not immediately answer. "You be writin down what I say?" She was on her knees, turned to me now to see what was in the notebook. Instinctively, I held it away from her eyes and told her that although I had written nothing that day — we had said nothing so far — (I fear that this little pleasantry escaped her) I did indeed write down much of what she said. On a happy impulse, I flipped back through the pages and showed her the notes I had made on some of our previous sessions. "What that there . . . and there . . . and that, too?" I told her and even read a little to her, an innocuous line or two. She was entranced. "I relly say that?" And when I nodded she sat back on her haunches. "What you gon do wid it?" I told her cautiously that I would use it in a book I hoped to write. I was totally unsure of whether she would comprehend the meaning of that. "Cause why?" She was thoroughly aroused by this time and seemed, despite the chain which bound her, about to flee.

Girl, I said to her, for at that moment, I could not for the life of me remember her name, Girl, what I put in this book cannot hurt you now. You've already been tried and judged. She seemed somewhat calmed by this utterance, perhaps as much by the tone of my voice, which I purposely made gentle, as by the statement itself.

"Then for what you wanna do it?"

I told her that I wrote what I did in the hope of helping others to be happy in the life that has been sent them to live, a response with which I am rather pleased. Certainly, it succeeded in its purpose of setting her mind at ease about the possible repercussions to herself in talking freely with me, for she seemed much struck by the statement, looking intently into my face for a long moment before she again settled down into her habitual pose. I allowed her to reflect upon this for a moment. She was silent for so long that I began to suspect her of dozing and leaned forward the better to see her. Her eyes were open (she seemed not to have the same problem as I with the harsh sunlight), her hands cupped beneath the roundness of her stomach. Your baby seems to have dropped; according to the old wives' tale, you'll be brought to bed soon. It was merely an attempt at conversation, of course; I know no more about that sort of business than I know about animal husbandry or the cultivation of cotton. She, of course, did not treat my words as the conversational gambit they were; she jumped as though stung. I cursed my stupidity, knowing what this unthinking comment must have brought to her mind, even as I realized that this was the first time I had seen her hands anywhere near her stomach. After the initial start, she straightened her back and scooted nearer to the tree, but said nothing. I waited, somewhat anxiously, for the blank sullen look to return. It did not, however, and, emboldened, I ventured quietly, Girl, where did the others get the file? even as she said:

"Kaine not want this baby. He want and don't want it. Babies ain't easy fo niggas, but still, I knows this Kaine's and I wants it cause that. And . . . and, when he ask me to go to Aunt Lefonia . . . I, I nelly bout died. I know what Aunt Lefonia be doin, though she don't be doin it too much cause Mas know it gotta be some nigga chi'ren comin in this world. And was anybody but, but Kaine, I do it, too. First time, a anyway. But, but this Kaine and it be like killin parta him, parta me. So I talk wid him; beg him. I say, this us baby, usses. We make it. How you can say, kill it. It mine and it yo's. He jes look at me. 'Same way Lefonia sons be hers when Mas decide that bay geldin he want worth mo to him than they is to her. Dessa,' and I know he don't want hurt me when he call my name, but it so sweet til it do hurt. Dessa, jes soft like that. 'Dess, where yo brotha, Jeeter, at now?' I'm cryin already, can't cry no mo, not fo Jeeter. He be gon, sold, south, somewhere; we neva do know. And finally I say 'run' and he laugh. He laugh and say, 'Run, Dessa (Lawd. Ain't no body neva say my name so sweet. Even when he mad like that, Dessa. Dessa I always know the way he call my name). Dessa, run where?' 'No'th,' I whisper. I whisper cause I don't rightly thank I eva heard no nigga say that out loud like when anybody, even yo own self's shadow could hear you, less'n it right up on you. 'No'th? And how we gon get there?' 'You know, Kaine.' And he know. I know he know. He know if he wanna know. 'And what we gon do when we gets there?' I jes look at him. Cause he know. 'Dessa.' Say my name agin. 'You know what is no'th? Huh? What is no'th? Mo whites. Jes like here. You don't see Aunt Lefonia, I see her fo you.' But I don't go, not then. I waits and one night Kaine talk to me. I don't *know*, not then, bout all what he says, but I try to learn most o' it by heart so I can thank bout it and thank bout it til I does know. He tell me then how he been sold way from some massas, runned way from othas. He run, he say, tryin to find no'th and he lil then and not even know no'th a direction and mo places than he eva be able to count. He jes thank he be free o' whippins, free to belongs to somebody what belongs to him jes so long as he be no'th. Last time he runned way, he most get there and he thank, now he know which way free land is, what is a free town, next time he get there. But neva is no next time cause same time's patterrollers takes him back, they takes back a man what been no'th, lived there and what know what free no'th is. 'Now,' Kaine say, 'now this man free, bo'n free, but still, any white man what say he a slave be believed cause a nigga can't talk fo the laws, not ginst no white man, not even fo his own self. So this man gots to get a notha white man fo to say he is free and he couldn't find one quick nough so then the Georgia Man, that be what the no'th man call the patterrollers, they takes him back fo to be slave. That's right. But even fo the patterrollers catched him, white man hit, he not lowed to hit back. He carpt'na but if the white mens on the job say they don't want work wid him, he don't work and sucha thangs as that. He say it hard bein a free man o' color, he don't say nigga, say free man o' color, but it betta'n bein a slave and if he get the chance he gon runned way.' But, Kaine say, he ask hisself, 'That free? How that gon be free? It still be two lists, one say "White Man Can," otha say "Nigga Can't" and white man still be the onliest one what can write on em.' So he don't run no mo. 'Run fo what,' he say. 'Get caught be jes that much worser off. Maybe is a place widout no white, nigga can be free.' But he don't know where that is. He find it, he say we have us chi'ren then. That why he say go see Aunt Lefonia, but I don't go. I jes can't. I know Kaine be knowin mo'n me. I know that. He — He told me lotta thang I not eva thank bout fo I wid him. But I does know us. I does. Me'n him. I knows that. And I knows this usses baby. And I thank bout what he say and I thank bout what I knows and I know they all bes the same thang. How they gon be diff'ent? I tell Kaine find it, least *try* fo you say see Aunt Lefonia. I don't be cryin now and he don't be mad. Jes, jes touch my face and say me name, Lawd, say my name. Say my name and his body be so hard, so hard and stiff ginst mine and I feel how he want me. 'I try, Dessa. I try what I can do.' No matter though," she said looking up at me. "Mas kill him fo it get time fo us to go."

We were both quiet for some time. I searched around in my mind for some way to bring her train of thought back to the immediate concern.

"You thank," she asked looking up at me, "you thank what I say now gon hep peoples be happy in the life they sent? If that be true," she said as I opened my mouth to answer, "Why I not be happy when I live it? I don't wanna talk no mo." And she did not.

It is only now that I become aware of my failure to employ the strategy I have devised. Yet, she now suffers from no more than a small case of the sniffles and the gash, while painful, perhaps, causes her no more than a slight limp. Monday will thus do as well as today, for I feel that we have achieved a significant level in our relationship. Today was a turning point and I am most optimistic for the future.

June 28, 1829.

As has been my custom in the past, I held no formal session with the negress this Sunday. But, in order to further cultivate the tentative rapport achieved in yesterday's session, I read and interpreted for her selected Bible verses. We were in our habitual place under the oak tree and I must admit that the laziness of the hot Sunday afternoon threatened at times to overcome me (as Hughes had warned me it would). As a consequence, he was reluctant to give me the keys to the cellar. He felt my vigilance would be impaired by the heat. I replied that in as much as the negress would remain chained as usual, there was no danger involved in such a venture — unless, of course, he feared that his own darkies would rise up and free her. He was somewhat stung by my retort, but he did surrender the keys. I shall make it my business to obtain another key to the cellar and to the chains with which she is bound to the tree — these are the only ones which in her quieted state she now wears. It is not to my liking to be required to *request* permission each time I wish to talk with the woman.

My drowsiness was compounded, I finally realized, by the monotonous melody which she hummed. I have grown, it appears, so accustomed to them that they seem like a natural part of the setting like the clucking of the hens or the lowing of the cattle. Thinking to trap her into an admission of inattention, I asked her to repeat the lessons I had just imparted to her. She did so and I was very pleased to find her so responsive. However, the humming became so annoying that I was forced to ask her to cease. She looked up at me briefly and though I had not threatened her, I believe she was mindful of previous punishments and of the fact that it is only through my influence that she is able to escape from her dark hole for these brief periods.

"Oh, this ain't no good-timin song. It say bout the righteousness and heaven, same as what you say."

I asked her to sing it and I set it down here as I remember and understand it.

Gonna march away in the gold band in the army bye'n bye.
Gonna march away in the gold band in the army bye'n bye.
Sinner, what you gon do that day?
Sinner, what you gon do that day?
When the fire arollin behind you in the army bye'n bye?

It is, of course, only a quaint piece of doggerel which the darkies cunningly adapt from the scraps of scriptures they are taught. Nevertheless, the tune was quite charming when sung; the words seemed to put new life into an otherwise annoying melody and I was quite pleased that she had shared it with me. We were both quiet for several moments after she had done. The heat was, by this time, an enervating influence upon me. She, too, seemed to be spent by that brief spurt of animation. After a few more moments of silence, I closed the Bible, prayed briefly for the deliverance of her soul, then returned her to the cellar.

June 29, 1829.

I asked how to pronounce the name of the young darky with whom she had lived (I am puzzled in my own mind about how to refer to him. Certainly, they were not married and she never speaks of having gone through even the slave ceremony of jumping over the broom). Did Kaine — is that how you pronounce — how you *say* his name? I asked her.

"You say it the same way you . . . you . . . spell? Spell it!"

Did Kaine talk much about freedom? This is part of my strategy, to frame all the questions in such a way that Kaine can be referred to in some manner. Her attachment to this Kaine appears quite sincere and while it is probably rooted in the basest of physical attractions, I cannot summon up the same sense of contempt with which I first viewed this liaison. I must confess also that I feel some slight twinge — Not of guilt, rather of *compassion* in using her attachment to the young darky as a means of eliciting information from her. But the fact is that my stratagems — while not perhaps of the most noble *type* — are used in the service of a greater good and this consideration must sweep all else before it. And I fear that in concentrating upon obtaining this greater good, I had finished asking the first question before I realized that she had made a slight jest. Looking at her in some surprise, I told her that it was quite a good joke, both in what she had said and in my own rather slow and dull reaction to her pleasantry. She in turn smiled, revealing for the first time in my memory the even white teeth behind the long thick lips of her mouth. Kaine did speak, then, a great deal about freedom?

She sat back. "Don't no niggas be talkin too much bout freedom, cause they be knowing what good fo em."

I did not believe her, but I chose, for the time being at least, to allow her to think that I did. Then what was your idea in trying to escape from the coffle?

She picked up a twig and began to mark in the dirt and to hum — not the same tune as the previous days, but one equally monotonous. She looked up at me, finally, and widened her eyes. "Was you black, you wanna be sold deep south? I neva been deep south, but Boss Smith, he always threats lazy niggas wid that and they don't be too lazy no mo."

And the others, I asked, was this what was in their mind?

She shrugged her shoulders. "Onlest mind I be knowin is mines. Why fo you didn't ask them first?" I believe this was not insolence, rather it seems more simple curiosity, and I allowed it to pass, explaining that I had not heard of the incident until too late to speak with the others who had been charged as leaders. "You thank there be a place widout no whites?" I looked at her in some surprise and she continued to herself, in a deeper dialect than she had heretofore used, really almost a mumble, something about Emmalina's Joe Big (I have yet to determine if this is the name of Emmalina's son or her "husband." Because the father is seldom, if ever, of any consequence after conception, the children of these unions take their surnames from their owners and are distinguished from others of the same given names by prefacing their names with a possessive form of the mother's. This form of address, however, is also used in referring to spouses. The question of Joe Big's relationship to Emmalina, while of passing interest, is certainly extraneous to the present discussion, so I did not interrupt her ramblings) telling Kaine something and going, but where I could not make out. "They caught Bi— They caught the others what run?"

I asked quickly, perhaps too quickly, if she knew where they were and the blank sullen look immediately returned to her face. The humming started again. She moved as though uncomfortable and touched, almost as if frightened, the big mound which rises beneath her dress. When she spoke it was in the voice of the first day. "This all I gotta Kaine. Right here, in my belly. Mist's slap my face when I tell her that, say, don't lie, say, it must be Terrell, that how she call Mas, Terrell, say it mus be hissen, why else Mas want kill Kaine, best gard'er they eva has, what cost a pretty penny. She say, well, Terrell live, he live knowin his woman and his brat south in worser slavery than they eva thought of and Aunt Lefonia stop me fo I kills her, too."

It was almost like listening to the first day's recital and I knew when she turned her head from me that for this day, anyway, I had gotten all from her that I could. This, together with the oppressive heat (the air has now become laden with moisture — a relief from the furnace-like dryness of the last few days — and the whole atmosphere is pregnant with the storm which must break soon), made me close my notebook for the day. But I now know that the thick-lipped mouth, so savage in its sullen repose, can smile and even utter small jests, that lurking behind her all too often blank gaze is something more than the cunning stubbornness which, alone, I first perceived, even noted that her skin, which appeared an ashen black in the light of the root cellar, is the color of strong tea and that even in the shade it is tinged with gold (surely this is a sign of good health in her. The baby should fetch Wilson a handsome price to repay him in some measure for what he has had to suffer through her agency). So, this lapse does not unduly discourage me. I know that she does not understand the project — it would be a wretched piece of business if she did — but she begins to have less distrust of me. She was not overly free in her speech but I begin to believe that she inclines towards this more than in the past. I fancy that I am not overly optimistic in predicting that one, perhaps two more sessions and I will have learned all I need from her. I shall have to think of a provocative title for the section in which I deal with the general principles apparent in her participation in this bloody business. "The Female of the Species," something along those lines, perhaps.

Later

Hughes says there is talk of a "maroon" settlement, an encampment of runaway slaves, somewhere nearby. There have been signs of maraud-

ing about some of the farms and plantations farther out from town. In
the latest incident, several blacks (the wife of the farmer could not
give an accurate count) stole into a small farm about twenty miles east
of here and took provisions and the farm animals and murdered the
farmer when he tried to protect his property. Fortunately, the wife was
hidden during the raid and thus escaped injury. Hughes was inclined
to treat this as an isolated incident — claiming that the other cases had
happened so long ago that they had become greatly exaggerated in the
telling — and thus dismiss the maroon theory as merely a fearful fig-
ment in the imagination of the larger slaveholders. He put down the
missing provisions and the occasional loss of livestock to the thieving
of the planters' own darkies. I am aware, as I told him, that an un-
supervised darky will steal anything which is not nailed down, yet, in
light of Odessa's talk of a place without whites and her concern about
the three renegades who escaped capture by the posse — talk which I
repeated — I cannot dismiss the theory of an encampment of some sort
so easily. It is, of course, pure conjecture, but not, I believe, groundless
to say, as I did to Hughes, that perhaps these three had joined the ma-
roons — which would certainly be one place without whites. And, despite the babbling of the fanatic Elijah, it is obvious that the darkies
from the coffle had been making for *someplace* when they were apprehended. Hughes was much impressed with my theorizing and invited
me to join the posse which leaves at dawn tomorrow in search of the
renegades. I readily accepted, for, even knowing the imaginative flights
to which the darky's mind is prone, I put much faith in this information precisely because it was given inadvertently. What information
Hughes and the prosecutor were able to obtain from the others and
from Odessa herself regarding the uprising is as nothing compared to
this plum.

On the Trail
North and West of Linden

June 30, 1829.

We set out early this morning, picking up the trail of the renegades
at the farm where they were last seen. It led us in a northerly direction
for most of the day and then, just before we stopped for the night, it
turned to the west. Most of the posse feel this is a good sign, for had the

trail continued north we should have soon found ourselves in Indian territory and, with two enemies to contend with, the chances of being surprised in ambush would have greatly increased. The trackers expect to raise some fresher sign of them tomorrow, for they are laden with supplies and we are not (a fact to which my stomach can well attest. Dried beef and half-cooked, half-warmed beans are *not* my idea of appetizing fare). And, I am told, if the weather holds humid as it has been and does not rain, their scent will hold fresh for quite a while and the dogs will be able to follow wherever it leads.

I did see Odessa this morning before we departed. I heard singing and, at first, taking it to be the usual morning serenade of Hughes' darkies, I took no notice of it. My attention was caught, however, by the plaintive note of this song, a peculiar circumstance, for Hughes frowns upon the singing of any but the most lively airs. I listened and finally managed to catch the words:

> *Tell me, sista tell me, brother how long will it be?*
> *Tell me, brotha tell me, sista how long will it be*
> *That a poor sinner got to suffer, suffer here?*
> *Tell me, sista tell me, brotha when my soul be free?*
> *Tell me, oh please tell me, when I be free*
> *And the Lawd calla me home?*

I had no sooner figured out these words — and recognized Odessa's voice — when another voice, this one lower and more mellow, took up the melody, singing at a somewhat faster tempo while Odessa maintained her original pace.

> *Oh, it won't be long. Say, it won't be long*
> *Poor sinner got to suffer here.*
> *Soul's goin to heav'n, soul's gon ride that heav'nly train.*
> *Cause the Lawd have called us home.*

It gave the effect of close harmonic part singing and was rather interesting and pleasing to the ear, especially when other voices joined in, as they presently did.

I hoped that Odessa's singing betokened a reflective mood and I went round to the cellar window, thinking that I might induce her to talk. I called to her and she broke off her singing in mid-phrase. "Who dat?" She spoke barely above a whisper and I could catch no glimpse of her, hidden as she was in the dark recesses of the cellar. I stooped down by the window, the better to see her. "Who dat?" she called again. The appearance of her face at the window startled me, for I had heard no warning sound of her approach. Her eyes gleamed once briefly in her face and then she closed them or perhaps only turned her head. I could not tell which, for the early morning light was still uncertain. I told her that I would be leaving in a few minutes and I do not think I imagined her quickened interest. "You don't be comin back?" I then assured her that I would indeed return in a few days and we would resume our conversations at that time. Hoping in this way to elicit some further information from her, I told her that we were going in search of a nearby maroon settlement. She clutched the bars of the window and peered at me through them. "Maroon?" I explained this term to her, telling her that it is rumored that there is one in the vicinity. I thought I had perhaps imparted too much information, but what can such news avail her in that cellar? And she merely responded with a dumb stare. I am not even sure that she had understood what I said, for she asked, "You a *real* white man, fo true? You don't be talkin like one. Sometime I don't even be knowin what you be sayin. You don't be talkin like Mas and he a real uppity up white man, but not like trash neitha. Kaine says it bes white man what don't talk white man talk. You one like that, huh?" I had been angered, and, yes, I admit, a trifle offended by her question, and her emendations to the question only slightly mollified my emotions. I answered, somewhat haughtily, that I and others like me taught her master and his kind how to speak. My hauteur was, of course, lost on her, for she exclaimed happily that I was a "teacher man." It seemed unnecessarily heartless to destroy her felicitous mood by further probing so I held my peace, which proved to be a fortuitous choice. She continued, "Was a teacher man on the coffle. He teached hisself to read from the Bible, then he preach. But course, that only be to the niggas and he be all right til he want teach otha niggas fo to read the Good Word. That be what he call it, 'The Good Word,' and when his Mas find out what he be doin he be sold south same's if he be teachin a bad word or be a bad nigga or a prime field hand." I seized upon this, feeling that perhaps I had discovered the key to the insurrection, for no one of this description — except perhaps Elijah — had been implicated in the plot. Is he the one who

obtained the file, I asked, and she laughed. She laughed. "Onlest freedom he be knowin is what he say the 'righteous freedom,' that what
the Lawd be givin him or what the Mas be givin him and he was the
firstest one the patterrollers kills." She moved back into the darkness of
the cellar still laughing softly and when I called to her she would not
respond. Finally she moved back so that I could see the outline of her
form. "Whatcho want?" she called. "Whatcho want?" I could feel my
anger rising at the insolence of her tone, but just then Hughes called
that we were ready to start. I rose and brushed the dirt from the knees
of my trousers. I did not want to leave then, for I felt that some barrier
had risen between us which must be breached. I realize now, however,
that it was a fortuitous circumstance that Hughes called at just that
moment. Otherwise I might have been betrayed into some impetuous
action that might have permanently harmed this project. You will
learn what I require when I return, I flung at her, and went to join
Hughes. I could hear her voice raised, joining with the others in the
new song which the other darkies had commenced during my conversation with her:

> Good news, Lawd, Lawd, good news.
> My brotha got a seat and I so glad.
> I heard from heav'n today.
> Good news, Lawdy, Lawd, Lawd. Good news.
> I don't mind what Satan say
> Cause I heard, yes I heard, well I heard from heav'n today.

Pray God that nothing happens to upset the mood evinced by her singing. We have much to talk about, Odessa and I, when we resume our
conversations.

Somewhere West of Linden

July 3, 1829.

A wild-goose chase and a sorry time we have had of it. There is
doubt in my mind that such an encampment, as I first conceived of,
exists, at least in this vicinity, for we have searched a large area and
come up with nothing conclusive. Several times, we sighted what
might have been members of such a band, but the dogs could not tree
them and it was more than we ourselves could do to catch more than

what we *hope* were fleeting glimpses of black bodies. Whether they took, indeed, to the trees, as some in the posse maintain, or vanished into the air, I have no way of knowing. If they exist, they are as elusive as Indians, nay, as elusive as *smoke* and I feel it beyond the ability of so large a posse as ours to move warily enough to take them unawares. To compound matters, the storm which has been threatening for days finally broke this morning, putting an end to our search and drenching us in the process. We have stopped to rest the horses, for Hughes estimates that if we push hard, we should reach Linden by nightfall. A bed will be most welcome after having spent so many days upon the back of this wretched horse, and I look forward to resuming my conversations with Odessa. She has a subtle presence, almost an influence which I have only become aware of in its absence. Perhaps — but that is useless speculation and must wait upon the certainty of Wilson's return. Hughes has given the call to mount and so we are off.

July 4, 1829.
Early Morning.

I put the date in wearied surprise. We have been out most of the night scouring the countryside for signs of Odessa, but there were none that we found and the rain has by now washed away what we must have missed. It is as though the niggers who crept in and stole away with her were not human blood, human flesh, but sorcerers who whisked her away by magic to the accursed den they inhabit. Hughes maintained that the devil merely claimed his own and gave up the search around midnight. But reason tells me that the niggers were not supernatural, not spirits or "haints." They are flesh and bone and so must leave some trace of their coming and going. The smallest clue would have sufficed me, for I should have followed it to its ultimate end. Now the rain has come up and even that small chance is gone, vanished like Odessa.

And we did not even know that she was gone, had, in fact, sat down to eat the supper left warming at the back of the stove against the chance that we would return, to talk of the futile venture of the last few days, to conjecture on God knows what. Unsuspecting we were, until the darky that sleeps with Jemina came asking for her. Hughes went to inquire of his wife — who had not arisen upon our return, merely called down to us that she was unwell and that food had been left for us. I was immediately alarmed, prescience I now know, upon learning that the woman had not seen Jemina since the wench had taken supper to Odessa earlier in the evening. And Hughes' assurance that Jemina was a good girl, having been with the wife since childhood, did nothing to calm my fears. Such a slight indisposition as his wife evidently had was no reason to entrust the keeping of so valuable a prisoner to another negress who is no doubt only slightly less sly than Odessa herself. I protested thus to Hughes, too strongly I now see, for he replied heatedly that if I did not keep my tongue from his wife — I marvel, even now in my exhaustion, at the quaintness of his phrasing — my slight stature would not keep me from a beating. I am firm in my belief that these impetuous words of mine were a strong factor in his early abandonment of the search and I regret them accordingly. There are stronger words in my mind now, but I forbore, at that time, carrying the discussion farther. I knew, even then, without really knowing why, that time was of the essence. But he shall find on the morrow that even one of my *slight stature* has the means of prosecuting him for criminal neglect. To think of leaving Odessa in the care of another nigger!

The root cellar when we reached it was locked, but the relief I felt was short-lived. It was Jemina inside and the wench set up such a racket, then, when it could not possibly serve any useful purpose, that one would have thought the hounds of hell pursued her. Even had I not recognized that such a cacophony could never issue from Odessa's throat, Hughes' startled exclamation was enough to alert me. The wench was, of course, incoherent — when was a nigger in excitement ever anything else? — but we finally pieced together, between the wench's throwing her apron over her head and howling, "Oh, Mas, it terr'ble; they was terr'ble fierce," and pointing to her muddied gown to prove it, what must have happened. Three niggers (she said three the first time and the number has increased with each successive telling; perhaps there were only one or two, but I settle upon three as the most likely number, for they were obviously the niggers with whom Odessa was in league in the uprising on the coffle. I could scream to think that even as we were out chasing shadows, the cunning devils were even then lying in wait to spirit her away. And to think that she — *she* was so deep as to give never an indication that they were then lurking about. Both Jemina and that woman of Hughes swear that except for a natural melancholy — which in itself was not unusual — *I* have been the only one to succeed in coaxing her into animated spirits — there was nothing out of the ordinary in Odessa's demeanor these last days. And knowing now the cupidity of which she is capable, I must believe them). The three bucks overpowered the wench just as she opend the door to the cellar to hand down the evening meal to Odessa. At this point, Hughes ejaculated something to the effect that it was a good thing "my Betty" was not present, at which the negress began what must have been, had I not intervened, a long digression on the "Mist's" symptoms and how she might, at long last, be increasing. But I could *feel* those niggers getting farther away with Odessa and so could not bear the interruption. The niggers forced Jemina into the cellar, bound her, took up Odessa and escaped into the night. The wench swears she heard no names called, that except for one exclamation from Odessa, of surprise or dismay, she could not tell which, they fled in silence, swears also that she could not see well enough to describe either of the niggers, save to state that they were big and black and terrible as though that would help to distinguish them from any of the hundreds, *thousands* of niggers in this world who are equally as big and as black and as terrible. The wench could not even tell whether they went on horseback or afoot, nor explain how a woman almost nine months gone could move so quickly and so quietly as to give no clue to the direction they took, nor less explain how it came about that she herself did not cry out, for surely if she had someone must have heard. This last question was again the occasion for that banshee-like wail about how "terr'ble fierce" the niggers were.

Hughes numbers among his four slaves one he termed an expert tracker, skilled in the ways of the Indians in hunting and trapping, but we did not need his help in finding the place where they had lain in wait for someone to open the cellar door. The earlier rain had made their sign quite plain. We found, also, with heartening ease the place where they had tied their animals. It was muddied and much trampled so we could not tell what kind of animals they were — whether horses or mules — nor even how many. Hughes' jocular, and inappropriately so, prediction that we should find Odessa and her newborn brat — for what female as far gone as she could stand the strain of a quick flight without giving birth to something — lying beside the trail within a mile or so proved incorrect, for the tracks disappeared into the deep underbrush a short distance from the place where the animals had been tied. Both the nigger and the one bloodhound Hughes keeps were alike worthless in the quest. And then the rain came up, driven by a furious wind, lashing the needle-like drops into our faces; washing away all trace of Odessa. Hughes, in giving up the hunt, charged that I acted like one possessed. He could not say by what and I know that this was merely his own excuse for failing in his lawful duty. For myself, I have searched, hunted, called and am now exhausted. She is gone. Even the smallest clue — but there was nothing, no broken twig to point a direction, no scent which the hound could hold for more than a short distance. Gone. And I not even aware, not even suspecting, just — just gone.

SLAVERY

Damballah

by John Edgar Wideman

ORION LET THE DEAD, gray cloth slide down his legs and
stepped into the river. He picked his way over slippery stones till he
stood calf deep. Dropping to one knee he splashed his groin, then
scooped river to his chest, both hands scrubbing with quick, kneading
spirals. When he stood again, he stared at the distant gray clouds. A
hint of rain in the chill morning air, a faint, clean presence rising from
the far side of the hills. The promise of rain coming to him as all things
seemed to come these past few months, not through eyes or ears or
nose but entering his black skin as if each pore had learned to feel and
speak.

He watched the clear water race and ripple and pucker. Where the
sun cut through the pine trees and slanted into the water he could see
the bottom, see black stones, speckled stones, shining stones whose
light came from within. Above a stump at the far edge of the river,
clouds of insects hovered. The water was darker there, slower, appeared to stand in deep pools where tangles of root, bush and weed
hung over the bank. Orion thought of the eldest priest chalking a design on the floor of the sacred *obi*. Drawing the watery door no living
hands could push open, the crossroads where the spirits passed between worlds. His skin was becoming like that in-between place the
priest scratched in the dust. When he walked the cane rows and dirt
paths of the plantation he could feel the air of this strange land wearing
out his skin, rubbing it thinner and thinner until one day his skin

would not be thick enough to separate what was inside from everything outside. Some days his skin whispered he was dying. But he was
not afraid. The voices and faces of his fathers bursting through would
not drown him. They would sweep him away, carry him home again.

In his village across the sea were men who hunted and fished with
their voices. Men who could talk the fish up from their shadowy dwell-
ings and into the woven baskets slung over the fishermen's shoulders.
Orion knew the fish in this cold river had forgotten him, that they were
darting in and out of his legs. If the whites had not stolen him, he
would have learned the fishing magic. The proper words, the proper
tones to please the fish. But here in this blood-soaked land everything
was different. Though he felt their slick bodies and saw the sudden
dimples in the water where they were feeding, he understood that he
would never speak the language of these fish. No more than he would
ever speak again the words of the white people who had decided to
kill him.

The boy was there again hiding behind the trees. He could be the
one. This boy born so far from home. This boy who knew nothing but
what the whites told him. This boy could learn the story and tell it
again. Time was short but he could be the one.

"That Ryan, he a crazy nigger. One them wild African niggers act like
he fresh off the boat. Kind you stay away from less you lookin for
trouble." Aunt Lissy had stopped popping string beans and frowned
into the boy's face. The pause in the steady drumming of beans into the
iron pot, the way she scrunched up her face to look mean like one of
the Master's pit bulls told him she had finished speaking on the subject
and wished to hear no more about it from him. When the long green
pods began to shuttle through her fingers again, it sounded like she
was cracking her knuckles, and he expected something black to drop
into the huge pot.

"Fixin to rain good. Heard them frogs last night just a singing at the
clouds. Frog and all his brothers calling down the thunder. Don't rain
soon them fields dry up and blow away." The boy thought of the men
trudging each morning to the fields. Some were brown, some yellow,
some had red in their skins and some white as the Master Ryan black,
but Aunt Lissy blacker. Fat, shiny blue-black like a crow's wing.

"Sure nuff crazy." Old woman always talking. Talking and telling silly stories. The boy wanted to hear something besides an old woman's mouth. He had heard about frogs and bears and rabbits too many times. He was almost grown now, almost ready to leave in the mornings with the men. What would they talk about? Would Orion's voice be like the hollers the boy heard early in the mornings when the men still sleepy and the sky still dark and you couldn't really see nobody but knew they were there when them cries and hollers came rising through the mist.

Pine needles crackled with each step he took, and the boy knew old Ryan knew somebody spying on him. Old nigger guess who it was, too. But if Ryan knew, Ryan didn't care. Just waded out in that water like he the only man in the world. Like maybe wasn't no world. Just him and that quiet place in the middle of the river. Must be fishing out there, some funny old African kind of fishing. Nobody never saw him touch victuals Master set out and he had to be eating something, even if he was half crazy, so the nigger must be fishing for his breakfast. Standing there like a stick in the water till the fish forgot him and he could snatch one from the water with his beaky fingers.

A skinny-legged, black waterbird in the purring river. The boy stopped chewing his stick of cane, let the sweet juice blend with his spit, a warm syrup then whose taste he prolonged by not swallowing, but letting it coat his tongue and the insides of his mouth, waiting patiently like the figure in the water waited, as the sweet taste seeped away. All the cane juice had trickled down his throat before he saw Orion move. After the stillness, the illusion that the man was a tree rooted in the rocks at the riverbed, when motion came, it was too swift to follow. Not so much a matter of seeing Orion move as it was feeling the man's eyes inside him, hooking him before he could crouch lower in the weeds. Orion's eyes on him and through him boring a hole in his chest and thrusting into that space one word *Damballah*. Then the hooded eyes were gone.

On a spoon you see the shape of a face is an egg. Or two eggs because you can change the shape from long oval to moons pinched together at the middle seam or any shape egg if you tilt and push the spoon closer or farther away. Nothing to think about. You go with Mistress to the chest in the root cellar. She guides you with a candle and you make a pouch of soft cloth and carefully lay in each spoon and careful it don't jangle as up and out of the darkness following her rustling dresses and petticoats up the earthen steps each one topped by a plank which squirms as you mount it. You are following the taper she holds and the strange smell she trails and leaves in rooms. Then shut up in a room all day with nothing to think about. With rags and pieces of silver. Slowly you rub away the tarnished spots; it is like finding something which surprises you though you knew all the time it was there. Spoons lying on the strip of indigo: perfect, gleaming fish you have coaxed from the black water.

Damballah was the word. Said it to Aunt Lissy and she went upside his head, harder than she had ever slapped him. Felt like crumpling right there in the dust of the yard it hurt so bad but he bit his lip and didn't cry out, held his ground and said the word again and again silently to himself, pretending nothing but a bug on his burning cheek and twitched and sent it flying. Damballah. Be strong as he needed to be. Nothing touch him if he don't want. Before long they'd cut him from the herd of pickaninnies. No more chasing flies from the table, no more silver spoons to get shiny, no fat, old woman telling him what to do. He'd go to the fields each morning with the men. Holler like they did before the sun rose to burn off the mist. Work like they did from can to caint. From first crack of light to dusk when the puddles of shadow deepened and spread so you couldn't see your hands or feet or the sharp tools hacking at the cane.

He was already taller than the others, a stork among the chicks scurrying behind Aunt Lissy. Soon he'd rise with the conch horn and do a man's share so he had let the fire rage on half his face and thought of the nothing always there to think of. In the spoon, his face long and thin as a finger. He looked for the print of Lissy's black hand on his cheek, but the image would not stay still. Dancing like his face reflected in the river. Damballah. "Don't you ever, you hear me, ever let me hear that heathen talk no more. You hear me, boy? You talk Merican, boy." Lissy's voice like chicken cackle. And his head a barn packed with animal noise and animal smell. His own head but he had to sneak round in it. Too many others crowded in there with him. His head so crowded and noisy lots of time don't hear his own voice with all them braying and cackling.

Orion squatted the way the boy had seen the other old men collapse on their haunches and go still as a stump. Their bony knees poking up and their backsides resting on their ankles. Looked like they could sit that way all day, legs folded under them like wings. Orion drew a cross in the dust. Damballah. When Orion passed his hands over the cross the air seemed to shimmer like it does above a flame or like it does when the sun so hot you can see waves of heat rising off the fields. Orion talked to the emptiness he shaped with his long black fingers. His eyes were closed. Orion wasn't speaking but sounds came from inside him the boy had never heard before, strange words, clicks, whistles and grunts. A singsong moan that rose and fell and floated like the old man's busy hands above the cross. Damballah like a drum beat in the chant. Damballah a place the boy could enter, a familiar sound he began to anticipate, a sound outside of him which slowly forced its way inside, a sound measuring his heartbeat then one with the pumping surge of his blood.

The boy heard part of what Lissy saying to Primus in the cooking shed: "Ryan he yell that heathen word right in the middle of Jim talking bout Sweet Jesus the Son of God. Jump up like he snake bit and scream that word so everybody hushed, even the white folks what came to hear Jim preach. Simple Ryan standing there at the back of the chapel like a knot poked out on somebody's forehead. Lookin like a nigger caught wid his hand in the chicken coop. Screeching like some crazy hoot owl while Preacher Jim praying the word of the Lord. They gon kill that simple nigger one day."

Dear Sir:

    The nigger Orion which I purchased of you in good faith sight unseen on your promise that he was of sound constitution "a full grown and able-bodied house servant who can read, write, do sums and cipher" to recite the exact words of your letter dated April 17, 1852, has proved to be a burden, a deficit to the economy of my plantation rather than the asset I fully believed I was receiving when I agreed to pay the price you asked. Of the vaunted intelligence so rare in his kind, I have seen nothing. Not an English word has passed through his mouth since he arrived. Of his docility and tractability I have seen only the willingness with which he bares his leatherish back to receive the stripes constant misconduct earn him. He is a creature whose brutish habits would shame me were he quartered in my kennels. I find it odd that I should write at such length about any nigger, but seldom have I been so struck by the disparity between promise and performance. As I have accrued nothing but expense and inconvenience as a result of his presence, I think it only just that you return the full amount I paid for this flawed *piece of the Indies.*

You know me as an honest and fair man and my regard for those same qualities in you prompts me to write this letter. I am not a harsh master, I concern myself with the spiritual as well as the temporal needs of my slaves. My nigger Jim is renowned in this county as a preacher. Many say I am foolish, that the words of scripture are wasted on these savage blacks. I fear you have sent me a living argument to support the critics of my Christianizing project. Among other absences of truly human qualities I have observed in this Orion is the utter lack of a soul.

She said it time for Orion to die. Broke half the overseer's bones knocking him off his horse this morning and everybody thought Ryan done run away sure but Mistress come upon the crazy nigger at suppertime on the big house porch naked as the day he born and he just sat there staring into her eyes till Mistress screamed and run away. Aunt Lissy said Ryan ain't studying no women, ain't gone near to woman since he been here and she say his ain't the first black butt Mistress done seen all them nearly grown boys walkin round summer in the onliest shirt Master give em barely come down to they knees and niggers man nor woman don't get drawers the first. Mistress and Master both seen plenty. Wasn't what she saw scared her less she see the ghost leaving out Ryan's body.

The ghost wouldn't steam out the top of Orion's head. The boy remembered the sweaty men come in from the fields at dusk when the nights start to cool early, remembered them with the drinking gourds in they hands scooping up water from the wooden barrel he filled, how they throw they heads back and the water trickles from the sides of they mouth and down they chin and they let it roll on down they chests, and the smoky steam curling off they shoulders. Orion's spirit would not rise up like that but wiggle out his skin and swim off up the river.

The boy knew many kinds of ghosts and learned the ways you get round their tricks. Some spirits almost good company and he filled the nothing with jingles and whistles and took roundabout paths and sang to them when he walked up on a crossroads and yoo-hooed at doors. No way you fool the haunts if a spell conjured strong on you, no way to miss a beating if it your day to get beat, but the ghosts had every-thing in they hands, even the white folks in they hands. You know they there, you know they floating up in the air watching and counting and remembering them strokes Ole Master laying cross your back.

They dragged Orion across the yard. He didn't buck or kick, but it seemed as if the four men carrying him were struggling with a giant stone rather than a black bag of bones. His ashy nigger weight swung between the two pairs of white men like a lazy hammock but the faces of the men all red and twisted. They huffed and puffed and sweated through they clothes carrying Ryan's bones to the barn. The dry spell had layered the yard with a coat of dust. Little squalls of yellow spurted from under the men's boots. Trudging steps heavy as if each man car-ried seven Orions on his shoulders. Four grown men struggling with one string of black flesh. The boy had never seen so many white folks dealing with one nigger. Aunt Lissy had said it time to die and the boy wondered what Ryan's ghost would think dropping onto the dust sur-rounded by the scowling faces of the Master and his overseers.

One scream that night. Like a bull when they cut off his maleness. Couldn't tell who it was. A bull screaming once that night and torches burning in the barn and Master and the men coming out and no Ryan.

Mistress crying behind a locked door and Master messing with Patty down the quarters.

In the morning light the barn swelling and rising and teetering in the yellow dust, moving the way you could catch the ghost of some-thing in a spoon and play with it, bending it, twisting it. That goldish ash on everybody's bare shins. Nobody talking. No cries nor hollers from the fields. The boy watched till his eyes hurt, waiting for a moment when he could slip unseen into the shivering barn. On his hands and knees hiding under a wagon, then edging sideways through the loose boards and wedge of space where the weathered door hung crooked on its hinge.

The interior of the barn lay in shadows. Once beyond the sliver of light coming in at the cracked door the boy stood still till his eyes adjusted to the darkness. First he could pick out the stacks of hay, the rough partitions dividing the animals. The smells, the choking heat there like always, but rising above these familiar sensations the buzz of flies, unnaturally loud, as if the barn breathing and each breath shook the wooden walls. Then the boy's eyes followed the sound to an open space at the center of the far wall. A black shape there. Orion there, floating in his own blood. The boy ran at the blanket of flies. When he stomped, some of the flies buzzed up from the carcass. Others too drunk on the shimmering blood ignored him except to join the ones hovering above the body in a sudden droning peal of annoyance. He could keep the flies stirring but they always returned from the recesses of the high ceiling, the dark corners of the building, to gather in a cloud above the body. The boy looked for something to throw. Heard his breath, heavy and threatening like the sound of the flies. He sank to the dirt floor, sitting cross-legged where he had stood. He moved only once, ten slow paces away from Orion and back again, near enough to be sure, to see again how the head had been cleaved from the rest of the body, to see how the ax and tongs, branding iron and other tools were scattered around the corpse, to see how one man's hat and another's shirt, a letter that must have come from someone's pocket lay about in a helter-skelter way as if the men had suddenly bolted before they had finished with Orion.

Forgive him, Father. I tried to the end of my patience to restore his lost soul. I made a mighty effort to bring him to the Ark of Salvation but he had walked in darkness too long. He mocked Your Grace. He denied Your Word. Have mercy on him and forgive his heathen ways as you forgive the soulless beasts of the fields and birds of the air.

She say Master still down slave row. She say everybody fraid to go down and get him. Everybody fraid to open the barn door. Overseer half dead and the Mistress still crying in her locked room and that barn starting to stink already with crazy Ryan and nobody gon get him.

And the boy knew his legs were moving and he knew they would carry him where they needed to go and he knew the legs belonged to him but he could not feel them, he had been sitting too long thinking on nothing for too long and he felt the sweat running on his body but his mind off somewhere cool and quiet and hard and he knew the space between his body and mind could not be crossed by anything, knew you mize well try to stick the head back on Ryan as try to cross that space. So he took what he needed out of the barn, unfolding, getting his gangly crane's legs together under him and shouldered open the creaking double doors and walked through the flame in the center where he had to go.

Damballah said it be a long way a ghost be going and Jordan chilly and wide and a new ghost take his time getting his wings together. Long way to go so you can sit and listen till the ghost ready to go on home. The boy wiped his wet hands on his knees and drew the cross and said the word and settled down and listened to Orion tell the stories again. Orion talked and he listened and couldn't stop listening till he saw Orion's eyes rise up through the back of the severed skull and lips rise up through the skull and the wings of the ghost measure out the rhythm of one last word.

Late afternoon and the river slept dark at its edges like it did in the mornings. The boy threw the head as far as he could and he knew the fish would hear it and swim to it and welcome it. He knew they had been waiting. He knew the ripples would touch him when he entered.

SLAVERY

Louisiana: 1850

by Jewelle Gomez

At night sleep locks me into an echoless coffin
sometimes at noon I dream
there is nothing to fear . . .

— Audre Lorde

THE GIRL SLEPT RESTLESSLY, feeling the prickly straw as if it were teasing pinches from her mother. The stiff moldy odor transformed itself into her mother's starchy dough smell. The rustling of the Girl's body in the barn hay was sometimes like the sound of fatback frying in the cooking shed behind the plantation's main house. At other moments in her dream it was the crackling of the brush as her mother raked the bristles through the Girl's thicket of dark hair before beginning the intricate pattern of braided rows.

She had traveled by night for fifteen hours before daring to stop. Her body held out until a deserted farmhouse, where it surrendered to this demanding sleep hemmed by fear.

Then the sound of walking, a man moving stealthily through the dawn light toward her. In the dream it remained what it was: danger. A white man wearing the clothes of an overseer. In the dream the Girl clutched tightly at her mother's large black hand, praying the sound of the steps would stop, that she would wake up curled around her mother's body on the straw and cornhusk mattress next to the big, old stove, grown cold with the night. In sleep she clutched the hand of her mother, which turned into the warm, wooden handle of the knife she had stolen when she ran away the day before. It pulsed beside her heart, beneath the rough shirt that hung loosely from her thin, young frame. The knife, crushed into the cotton folds near her breast, was invisible to the red-faced man who stood laughing over her, pulling her by one leg from beneath the pile of hay.

The Girl did not scream but buried herself in the beating of her heart alongside the hidden knife. She refused to believe that the hours of indecision and, finally, the act of escape were over. The walking, hiding, running through the Mississippi and Louisiana woods had quickly settled into an almost enjoyable rhythm; she was not ready to give in to those whom her mother had sworn were not fully human.

The Girl tried to remember some of the stories that her mother, now dead, had pieced together from many different languages to describe the journey to this land. The legends sketched a picture of the Fulani past — a natural rhythm of life without bondage. It was a memory that receded more with each passing year.

"Come on. Get up, gal, time now, get up!" The urgent voice of her mother was a sharp buzz in her dream. She opened her eyes to the streaking sun which slipped in through the shuttered-window opening. She hopped up, rolled the pallet to the wall, then dipped her hands quickly in the warm water in the basin on the counter. Her mother poured a bit more bubbling water from the enormous kettle. The Girl watched the steam caught by the half-light of the predawn morning rise toward the low ceiling. She slowly started to wash the hard bits of moisture from her eyes as her mother turned back to the large, black stove.

"I'ma put these biscuits out, girl, and you watch this cereal. I got to go out back. I didn't beg them folks to let you in from the fields to work with me to watch you sleepin' all day. So get busy."

Her mother left through the door quickly, pulling her skirts up around her legs as she went. The Girl ran to the stove, took the ladle in her hand, and moved the thick gruel around in the iron pot. She grinned proudly at her mother when she walked back in: no sign of sticking in the pot. Her mother returned the smile as she swept the ladle up in her large hand and set the girl onto her next task — turning out the biscuits.

"If you lay the butter cross 'em while they hot, they like that. If they's not enough butter, lay on the lard, make 'em shine. They can't tell and they take it as generous."

"Mama, how it come they cain't tell butter from fat? Baby Minerva can smell butter 'fore it clears the top of the churn. She won't drink no pig fat. Why they cain't tell how butter taste?"

"They ain't been here long 'nough. They just barely human. Maybe not even. They suck up the world, don't taste it."

The Girl rubbed butter over the tray of hot bread, then dumped the thick, doughy biscuits into the basket used for morning service. She loved that smell and always thought of bread when she dreamed of better times. Whenever her mother wanted to offer comfort she promised the first biscuit with real butter. The Girl imagined the home across the water that her mother sometimes spoke of as having fresh bread baking for everyone, even for those who worked in the fields. She tried to remember what her mother had said about the world as it had lived before this time but could not. The lost empires were a dream to the Girl, like the one she was having now.

She looked up at the beast from this other land, as he dragged her by her leg from the concealing straw. His face lost the laugh that had split it and became creased with lust. He untied the length of rope holding his pants, and his smile returned as he became thick with anticipation of her submission to him, his head swelling with power at the thought of invading her. He dropped to his knees before the girl whose eyes were wide, seeing into both the past and the future. He bent forward on his knees, stiff for conquest, already counting the bounty fee and savoring the stories he would tell. He felt a warmth at the pit of his belly. The girl was young, probably a virgin he thought, and she didn't appear able to resist him. He smiled at her open, unseeing eyes, interpreting their unswerving gaze as neither resignation nor loathing but desire. The flash-fire in him became hotter.

His center was bright and blinding as he placed his arms — one on each side of the Girl's head — and lowered himself. She closed her eyes. He rubbed his body against her brown skin and imagined the closing of her eyes was a need for him and his power. He started to enter her, but before his hand finished pulling her open, while it still tingled with the softness of her insides, she entered him with her heart which was now a wood-handled knife.

He made a small sound as his last breath hurried to leave him. Then he dropped softly. Warmth spread from his center of power to his chest as the blood left his body. The Girl lay still beneath him until her breath became the only sign of life in the pile of hay. She felt the blood draining from him, comfortably warm against her now cool skin.

It was like the first time her mother had been able to give her a real bath. She'd heated water in the cauldron for what seemed like hours on a night that the family was away, then filled a wooden barrel whose staves had been packed with sealing wax. She lowered the Girl, small and narrow, into the luxuriant warmth of the tub and lathered her with soap as she sang an unnamed tune.

The intimacy of her mother's hands and the warmth of the water lulled the Girl into a trance of sensuality she never forgot. Now the blood washing slowly down her breastbone and soaking into the floor below was like that bath — a cleansing. She lay still, letting the life flow over her, then slid gently from beneath the red-faced man whose cheeks had paled. The Girl moved quietly, as if he had really been her lover and she was afraid to wake him.

Looking down at the blood soaking her shirt and trousers she felt no disgust. It was the blood signaling the death of a beast and her continued life. The Girl held the slippery wood of the knife in her hand as her body began to shake in the dream/memory. She sobbed, trying to understand what she should do next. How to hide the blood and still move on. She was young and had never killed anyone.

She trembled, unable to tell if this was really happening to her all over again or if she was dreaming it — again. She held one dirty hand up to her broad, brown face and cried heartily.

That was how Gilda found her, huddled in the root cellar of her small farmhouse on the road outside of New Orleans in 1850. The Girl clutched the knife to her breast and struggled to escape her dream.

"Wake up, gal!" Gilda shook the thin shoulder gently, as if afraid to pull loose one of the shuddering limbs. Her voice was whiskey rough, her rouged face seemed young as she raised the smoky lantern.

The Girl woke with her heart pounding, desperate to leave the dream behind but seized with white fear. The pale face above her was a woman's, but the Girl had learned that they, too, could be as dangerous as their men.

Gilda shook the Girl whose eyes were now open but unseeing. The night was long, and Gilda did not have time for a hysterical child. The brown of her eyes darkened in impatience.

"Come on, gal, what you doin' in my root cellar?" The Girl's silence deepened. Gilda looked at the stained, torn shirt, the too-big pants tied tightly at her waist, and the wood-handled knife in the Girl's grip. Gilda saw in her eyes the impulse to use it.

"You don't have to do that. I'm not going to hurt you. Come on." With that Gilda pulled the Girl to her feet, careful not to be too rough; she could see the Girl was weak with hunger and wound tight around her fear. Gilda had seen a runaway slave only once. Before she'd recognized the look and smell of terror, the runaway had been captured and hauled off. Alone with the Girl, and that look bouncing around the low-ceilinged cellar, Gilda almost felt she should duck. She stared deeply into the Girl's dark eyes and said silently, *You needn't be afraid. I'll take care of you. The night hides many things.*

The Girl loosened her grip on the knife under the persuasive touch of Gilda's thoughts. She had heard of people who could talk without speaking but never expected a white to be able to do it. This one was a puzzlement to her: the dark eyes and pale skin. Her face was painted in colors like a mask, but she wore men's breeches and a heavy jacket.

Gilda moved in her small-boned frame like a team of horses pulling a load on a sodden road: gentle and relentless. "I could use you, gal, come on!" was all Gilda said as she lifted the Girl and carried her out to the buggy. She wrapped a thick shawl around the Girl's shoulders and held tightly to her with one hand as she drew the horse back onto the dark road.

After almost an hour they pulled up to a large building on the edge of the city — not a plantation house, but with the look of a hotel. The Girl blinked in surprise at the light which glowed in every room as if there were a great party. Several buggies stood at the side of the house with liveried men in attendance. A small open shed at the left held a few single, saddled horses that munched hay. They inclined their heads toward Gilda's horse. The swiftness of its approach was urgent, and the smell the buggy left behind was a perfumed wake of fear. The horses all shifted slightly, then snorted, unconcerned. They were eating, rested and unburdened for the moment. Gilda held the Girl's arm firmly as she moved around to the back of the house past the satisfied, sentient horses. She entered a huge kitchen in which two women — one black, one white — prepared platters of sliced ham and turkey.

Gilda spoke quietly to the cook's assistant. "Macey, please bring a tray to my room. Warm wine, too. Hot water first though." Not breaking her stride, she tugged the Girl up the back stairs to the two rooms that were hers. They entered a thickly furnished sitting room with books lining the small bookshelf on the north wall. Paintings and a few line drawings hung on the south wall. In front of them sat a deep couch, surrounded by a richly colored hanging fabric.

This room did not have the urgency of those below it. Few of the patrons who visited the Woodard place — as it was still known although that family had not owned it in years — had ever been invited into the private domain of its mistress. This was where Gilda retreated at the end of the night, where she spent most of the day reading, alone except for a few of the girls or Bird. Woodard's was the most prosperous establishment in the area and enjoyed the patronage of some of the most esteemed men and women of the county. The gambling, musical divertissements, and the private rooms were all well attended. Gilda employed eight girls, none yet twenty, who lived in the house and worked hard hours being what others imagined women should be. After running Woodard's for fifteen years, Gilda loved her home and her girls. It had been a wonderfully comfortable and relatively tiny segment of the 300 years she'd lived. Her private rooms held the treasures of several lifetimes.

She raised the lid of a chest and pulled out a towel and nightshirt. The Girl's open stare brushed over her, nudging at the weight of the years on her shoulders. Under that puzzled gaze the years didn't seem so grotesque. Gilda listened a moment to the throaty laughter floating up from the rooms below, where the musical entertainment had begun without her, and could just barely hear Bird introducing the evening in her deep voice. Woodard's was the only house with an "Indian girl," as her loyal patrons bragged. Although Bird now only helped to manage the house, many came just to see her, dressed in the soft cotton, sparely adorned dress that most of the women at Woodard's wore. Thin strips of leather bearing beading or quill were sometimes braided into her hair or sewn onto her dress. Townsmen ranked her among their local curiosities.

Gilda was laying out clothes when Macey entered the room lugging two buckets of water — one warm and one hot. While stealing glances at the Girl, she poured the water into a tin tub that sat in a corner of the room next to an ornate folding screen.

Gilda said, "Take off those clothes and wash. Put those others on." She spoke slowly, deliberately, knowing she was breaking through one reality into another. The words she did not speak were more important: *Rest. Trust. Home.*

The Girl dropped her dusty, blood-encrusted clothes by the couch. Before climbing into the warm water, she looked up at Gilda, who gazed discreetly somewhere above her head. Gilda then picked up the clothes, ignoring the filth, and clasped them to her as she left the room. When the Girl emerged she dressed in the nightshirt and curled up on the settee, pulling a fringed shawl from its back down around her shoulders. She'd unbraided and washed the thickness of her hair and wrapped it tightly in the damp towel.

Curling her legs underneath her to keep off the night chill, she listened to the piano below and stared into the still shadows cast by the lamp. Soon Gilda entered, with Macey following sullenly behind holding a tray of food. Gilda pulled a large, overstuffed chair close to the settee while Macey put the tray on a small table. She lit another lamp near them, glancing backward over her shoulder at the strange, thin black girl with the African look to her. Macey made it her business to mind her own business, particularly when it came to Miss Gilda, but she knew the look in Gilda's eyes. It was something she saw too rarely: living in the present, or maybe just curiosity. Macey and the laundress, neither of whom lived in the house with the others, spoke many times of the anxious look weighing in Gilda's eyes. It was as if she saw something that existed only in her own head. But Macey, who dealt mostly with Bernice and some with Bird, left her imagination at home. Besides, she had no belief in voodoo magic and just barely held on to her Catholicism.

Of course there was talk around most dinner tables in the parish, especially after Bird had come to stay at the house. Macey was certain that if there was a faith Gilda held, it was not one she knew. The lively look that filled her employer's eyes now usually only appeared when she and Bird spent their evenings talking and writing together.

Some things were best not pondered, so Macey turned and hurried back down to her card game with Bernice, the cook. Gilda prepared a plate and poured from the decanter of red wine. The Girl looked furtively in her direction but was preoccupied with the cleanliness of the room and the spicy smell of the food. Her body relaxed while her mind still raced, filled with the unknowns: how far she was from the plantation, who this woman might be, how she could get away from her.

Gilda was barely able to draw her excitement back inside herself as she watched the Girl. It was the clear purpose in the Girl's dark eyes that first caught her. A child's single-mindedness shone through. Deeper still was an adult perseverance. Gilda remembered that look many years before in Bird's eyes when she had returned from her one visit to her people, the Lakota. There was an intensity, curiosity, and vulnerability blended together behind a tight mask of resolve.

More importantly, Gilda saw herself behind those eyes — a younger self she barely remembered, one who would never be comfortable with having decisions made for her. Or with following a path she'd not laid herself. Gilda also saw a need for family that matched her own. She closed her eyes, and in her mind the musky smell of her mother's garments rose. She almost reached out to the phantom of her past there in the lamplit room but caught her breath and shook her head slightly. Gilda knew then she wanted the Girl to stay.

Answers to her questions slipped in among her thoughts as the Girl ate. She was startled to discover the understanding of where she was and who this woman might be. She set her glass down abruptly and stared at Gilda's narrow face which glowed with excitement even in the shadows of the lamplight. Her dark brown hair was wound low at the back of her neck leaving her tiny features exposed. Even within the tight bodice of the blue beaded dress she now wore, Gilda moved in her own deliberate way. The brown cigar she lit seemed too delicate for her broad gestures.

The Girl thought for a moment: *This is a man! A little man!*

Gilda laughed out loud at the idea in the Girl's head and said, "No, I'm a woman." Then without speaking aloud she said, *I am a woman, you know that. And you know I am a woman as no other you have known, nor has your mother known, in life or death. I am a woman as you are, and more.*

The Girl opened her mouth to speak, but her throat was too raw, her nerves too tight. She bent her mouth in recognition and puzzlement. This was a woman, and her face was not unlike her mother's despite the colors painted on it.

Its unwavering gaze was hard-edged yet full of concern. But behind the dark brown of Gilda's eyes the Girl recognized forests, ancient roots and arrows, images she had never seen before. She blinked quickly and looked again through the lamplight. There she simply saw a small woman who did not eat, who sipped slowly from a glass of wine and watched with a piercing gaze through eyes that seemed both dark and light at the same time.

When the Girl finished eating and sat back again on the settee, Gilda spoke aloud. "You don't have to tell me anything. I'll tell you. You just listen and remember when anyone asks: You're new in the house. My sister sent you over here to me as a present. You've been living in Mississippi. Now you live here and work for me. Nothing else, do you understand?" The Girl remained silent but understood the words and the reasons behind them. She didn't question. She was tired, and the more she saw of this white world, the more afraid she became that she could no longer hide from the plantation owners and the bounty hunters.

"There is linen in that chest against the wall. The chaise longue is quite comfortable. Go to sleep. We will rise early, my girl." With that, Gilda's thin face radiated an abundant smile as youthful as the Girl's. She turned out one of the lamps and left the room quickly. The Girl unfolded a clean sheet and thick blanket and spread them out smoothly, marveling at their freshness and the comforting way they clung to the bowed and carved wood of the chaise's legs. She disturbed the placid surface almost regretfully and slipped in between the covers, trying to settle into sleep.

This woman, Gilda, could see into her mind. That was clear. The Girl was not frightened though, because it seemed she could see into Gilda's as well. That made them even.

The Girl thought a little about what she had seen when the woman opened herself to her, what had made her trust her: an expanse of road stretching narrowly into the horizon, curving gently away from her; the lulling noise of rushing wind and the rustling of leaves that sounded like the soft brush of the hem of a dress on carpet. She stared down the road with her eyes closed until she lost the dream in deep sleep.

Gilda stood outside the door, listening for a moment to the Girl's restless movement. She easily quieted the Girl's turmoil with the energy of her thoughts. The music and talking from below intruded on Gilda, but she resisted, searching out the glimmerings of her past instead. How unnerving to have stumbled upon them in that moment of recognition while watching the Girl eat her supper. The memory was vague, more like a fog than a tide after so many years in which Gilda had deliberately turned away from the past.

With her eyes closed she could slip backward to the place whose name she had long since forgotten, to when she was a girl. She saw a gathering of people with burnished skin. She was among them. The spiced scent of their bodies was an aura moving alongside them as they crossed an arid expanse of land. She couldn't see much beyond the curved backs and dust-covered sandals of those walking in front of her. She held the hand of a woman she knew was her mother, and somewhere ahead was her father. Where were they all now? Dead, of course. Less than ashes, and Gilda could not remember their faces. She couldn't remember when their eyes and mouths had slipped away from her. Where had the sound of their voices gone? All that seemed left was the memory of a scented passage that had dragged her along in its wake and the dark color of blood as it seeped into sand.

She grimaced at the sense of movement, the thing she most longed to be free of. Even there, in that mythical past she could no longer see clearly, she had moved nomadically from one home to another. Through first one war then another. Which sovereign? Whose nation? She had left those things behind sometime in the past three hundred years — perhaps even longer.

She opened her eyes and looked back toward the door to the room where the Girl slept, smiling as her own past dissolved. She no longer needed those diaphanous memories. She wanted to look only forward, to the future of the Girl and Bird, and to her own resting place where she would finally have stillness.

Again the music broke into her thoughts. For the first time in a long while she was eager to join the girls in the downstairs parlor for the evening, to watch Bird moving quickly among the rooms, and to listen to the languidly told stories the girls perfected to entertain the gentlemen and make the time pass for themselves. And when the night was edged by dawn she would gratefully lie down next to Bird, welcoming the weight of her limbs stretched across her body and the smell of her hair permeating her day of rest.

During her first few months at Woodard's the Girl barely spoke but did the chores she was directed to in the house. She began to accompany Bird or Gilda some months after, to shop for the house or buy presents for members of the household, which Gilda did quite frequently. The Girl carried the packages and straightened up Gilda's suite of rooms, carefully dusting the tiny vases and figurines, the shelves of books, and rearranging fresh flowers, which she picked from the garden once she became comfortable enough to venture outside alone.

Sometimes she would sit in the pantry while the girls were around the table in the kitchen eating, talking over previous evenings, laughing at stories, or discussing their problems.

"Don't tell me I'm ungrateful. I'm grown. I want what I want and I ain't nobody's mama!" Rachel shouted at Fanny, who always had an opinion.

"Not that we know of," was Fanny's vinegary retort. Rachel only stared at her coldly, so Fanny went on. "You always want something, Rachel, and you ain't coming to nothing with this dream stuff. Running off, leavin' everythin' just 'cause you had a dream to do something you don't know nothin' 'bout."

"It's my dream an' my life, ain't it, Miss Bird? You know 'bout dreams an' such."

Bird became the center of their attention as she tried to remember what would mean the most to these girls, who were really women, who had made their home with her and Gilda.

"Dreaming is not something to be ignored."

"But going to a place like that, next to the water — ready to fall in 'cording to her dream, mind you, not mine — is just foolish," Fanny insisted.

"It's a dream, not a fact. Maybe the dream just means change, change for the better. If Rachel has a dream, she reads it. Nobody else here can do that for her," Bird said.

"Anyway, I ain't packed nothin'. I'm just tellin' you my dream, is all. Damn you, Fanny, you a stone in my soup every time!"

The women laughed because Rachel always had a way with words when they got her excited.

Occasionally Gilda sat with them, as if they did not work for her, chiming in with stories and laughter just the same as Bernice, the dark, wary cook, or Rachel, the one full of ambition. There were also Rose, kind to a fault; Minta, the youngest; and the unlikely pair who were inseparable — Fanny, the opinionated, and Sarah, the appeaser. Mostly the Girl kept apart from them. She had never seen white women such as these before, and it was frightening not to know where she fit in. She had heard of bawdy houses from her mother who had heard from the men who sipped brandy in the library after dinner. But the picture had never added up to what she saw now.

These women embodied the innocence of children the Girl had known back on the plantation, yet they were also hard, speaking of the act of sex casually, sometimes with humor. And even more puzzling was their debate of topics the Girl had heard spoken of only by men. The women eagerly expressed their views on politics and economics: what slavery was doing to the South, who was dominating politics, and the local agitation against the Galatain Street "houses."

Located further from the center of activity, Gilda's house was run with brisk efficiency. She watched over the health of the women and protected them. But her presence was usually more presumed than actual. Most often she locked herself in her room until six in the evening. There she slept, read, and wrote in the voluminous journals she kept secured in a chest.

Bird managed the everyday affairs, supervising most of the marketing and arbitrating disputes with tradesmen or between the girls. She also directed the Girl in doing the sundry tasks assigned to her. And it was Bird who decided that she would teach the Girl to read. Every afternoon they sat down in Bird's shaded room with the Bible and a newspaper, going over letters and words relentlessly.

The Girl sat patiently as Bird told a story in her own words, then picked out each syllable on paper until they came together in the story she had just recited. At first the Girl did not see the sense of the lessons. No one she knew ever had need of reading, except the black preacher who came over on Saturday nights to deliver a sermon under the watchful gaze of the overseer. Even he was more likely to thwack the Bible with his rusty hand than read from it.

But soon the Girl began to enjoy the lessons. She liked knowing what Fanny was talking about when she exclaimed that Rachel was "as hard headed as Lot's wife," or recognizing the name of the Louisiana governor when she heard it cursed around the kitchen table. Another reason she enjoyed the lessons was that she liked the way Bird smelled. When they sat on the soft cushions of the couch in Bird's room, bending over the books and papers, the Girl was comforted by the pungent earthiness of the Lakota woman. She did not cover herself with the cosmetics and perfumes her housemates enjoyed. The soft scent of brown soap mixed with the leather of her headband and necklace created a familiar aura. It reminded the Girl of her mother and the strong smell of her sweat dropping onto the logs under the burning cauldrons. The Girl rarely allowed herself to miss her mother or her sisters, preferring to leave the past alone for a while, at least until she felt safe in this new world.

Sitting in the room with the Girl, Bird was no longer aloof. She was tender and patient, savoring memories of herself she found within the Girl. Bird gazed into the African eyes which struggled to see a white world through words on a page. Bird wondered what creatures, as invisible as she and the Girl were, did with their pasts.

Was she to slip it off of her shoulders and fold it into a chest to be locked away for some unknown future? And what to do with that future, the one that Gilda had given Bird with its vast expanse of road? Where would she look to read that future? What oracle could she lay on her lap to pick out the words that would frame it?

Bird taught the Girl first from the Bible and the newspaper. Neither of them could see themselves reflected there. Then she told the Girl stories of her own childhood, using them to teach her to write. She spoke each letter aloud, then the word, her own hand drawing the Girl's across the worn paper. And soon there'd be a sentence and a legend or memory of who she was. And the African girl then read it back to her. Bird enjoyed these lessons almost as much as her evenings spent alone with Gilda. And with the restlessness that agitated Gilda more each year, those times together had grown less frequent.

Gilda and Bird sometimes retreated to the farmhouse for a day or more, spending most of the time walking in the evening, riding, or reading together silently, rarely raising questions. Sometimes Gilda went to the farmhouse alone, leaving Bird anxious and irritable. This afternoon Bird prolonged the lesson with the Girl a bit. Uncertainty hung in the air around her, and she was reluctant to leave the security of the Girl's eagerness to learn. She asked her to read aloud again from the sheets of paper on which they'd just printed words. The halting sound of the Girl's voice opened a space inside of Bird. She stood quickly, walking to the curtained window.

"Go on if you understand the words, stop if you do not," Bird said with her back to the room.

She pulled the curtain aside and tied it with a sash, then fingered the small bits of pearlized quill stitched onto the leather band around her neck. Outside, the stableman was raking out hay for the horses of the evening visitors. Bird was pleased with the comfort she felt at the normal movements around the house and at the sound of the Girl's voice, which in the past year had lightened to seem more like a child's than when she'd first come. Bird turned when she heard a question.

"Tell me again of this *pox* please?" the Girl asked, pointing at the word on the paper.

"It came with the traders. They stole many things and breathed the disease into my people and sold it to us in their cloth. It makes the body feverish and causes spots over the body and many deaths."

"Why did you not die?" the Girl asked, carefully matching her words to the rhythm she had heard in Gilda's voice, just as she often imitated her walk when no one watched. She wondered if Bird's escape from the pox was connected to the rumors that she and Gilda were conjure women. She had seen many oddities since coming to the house, but none of them seemed near to conjuring to the Girl so she generally dismissed the talk.

Bird stared at her silently, startled for a moment to hear the familiar inflections from the Girl. "When the deaths came, some members of my clan moved away from the others. My mother and her brothers thought we could escape the air that was killing us. We came south to the warmth to burn away the disease from our spirits. I was sick for a time as we traveled, but we left it on the trail behind us." Bird ached as she spoke, remembering the brothers who'd become fearful of her when she'd fallen ill with the disease and then suspicious when she recovered.

In the end they were convinced she was a witch because she had survived. They chased her away from their small band into the night that had become her friend.

"Do you still have the spots?"

Bird laughed, and the small scar that lanced her eyebrow rose slightly. "Yes, there are some on my back. There is no more infection, simply the mark. Did you not have this disease before . . ." Bird's voice trailed off. She did not want to remind the Girl of past sadness.

"No disease with spots. Some fevers came, through the waters my mother said. Can I see your spots?"

Bird undid the tiny buttons at her wrists and down the front of her shirtwaist, shrugged her shoulders from the cotten dress, then turned her back toward the lamp. The Girl's eyes widened at the small raised circles that sprayed across the brown skin. She let her fingers brush the places where disease had come and placed a small finger gently atop one spot, fitting it into the indentation at its center.

"Your skin is smooth like a baby's," she said.

"Gilda has a lotion she used to rub into my back when I first came here. It makes the skin soft."

"Can I have some for my hands?"

Bird reached down and took the Girl's two hands in her own. Their fingertips were calloused in a way that Bird knew was not the result of the light cleaning and washing done at the house. She nodded and pressed the small hard hands to her face quickly, then let them go.

"Why white people feel they got to mark us?" the Girl asked, slipping back into her own vocal rhythm. Bird pushed her arms back into her sleeves as she thought for a moment.

"Maybe they're afraid they'll be forgotten." She gathered the papers from the table, then added, "They don't know that we easily forget them, who they might be. All we ever remember is their scars."

The Girl saw the deeply etched whip marks that had striped her mother's legs as she looked down at her own thin, hardened fingers. She remained silent as Bird put the papers into the wooden box holding all their lessons.

Bird wanted to tell just one more story, a happy one, but saw that the Girl, a meticulous worker, was becoming anxious. Her chores for the evening still lay ahead of her, and guests would be arriving in several hours. Or, Bird thought, anxiety might be her natural state.

The Girl left and Bird followed, locking her door behind her. Upstairs at Gilda's door she used the same key to enter. She opened the drapes slightly once inside its blackness, to let the twilight seep in, and then lay down beside the still figure. Even at its cool temperature Gilda's body had warmed the satin that lay over the soft earth. Bird didn't sleep. She watched the shadows, enjoying the familiar quiet of the room, thinking about the Girl and Gilda.

Bird enjoyed the days more since the Girl's arrival. She was grateful for her earnest curiosity and she saw Gilda responding similarly. Yet Bird was uneasy with the new way of things. Gilda was, indeed, more open and relaxed, but she was also less fully present, as if her mind were in a future none of them would know. When she tried to draw her back, Gilda only talked of the true death, how soon her time might come. Then they argued.

Even after their new routine had become old and their futures seemed secure, Bird was certain Gilda still held thoughts of true death but would speak of them to her only obliquely. When Bird asked her about the Girl and what might become of her should they decide to leave Woodard's, Gilda remained cryptic.

"She will always be with us, just as I'll always be with you," Gilda answered with a smile.

"How can that be so?" Bird asked, certain Gilda was making a joke.

"She is as strong as either of us and knows our ways."

"She's a child; she can't make the decision you'd ask of her!" Bird said with alarm when she realized it was no jest.

"We were all children at one time. And time passes. I expect she will be ready when I am."

"Ready?" Bird responded, still not able to grasp the idea of the Girl becoming one of them.

Gilda understood Bird's reluctance and lightened her voice. "Yes, ready to challenge you, my dear one. She'll be the best student you've ever had, perhaps even a scholar. We will then turn Woodard's into a college for girls!" Gilda laughed loudly, steering the conversation away from anything Bird might pursue.

In remembering that talk, Bird decided not to broach the questions now, even with herself. She simply wanted to feel Gilda near, listen to the sound of her heart as she awakened. They would go out to find their share of the blood later, perhaps together, when there was darkness.

After her second year at Woodard's the Girl began to look upon it as a home. She had grown three inches by the end of her third year and had the rounded calves and breasts of a woman. Each morning she scrubbed herself clean with cool water before coming down to the kitchen and to Bernice, who had become accustomed to her solemn, shining face. She watched the Girl closely until it seemed to her that she had gained enough weight. And the women of the house teased her gently and asked her about her lessons. Most of them were, in spite of their paint, simple farm girls and sometimes liked having a younger one to look after.

When the Girl was not doing chores or studying with Bird she stayed to herself, working in the garden. Minta sometimes joined her there, her thin, pale skin hidden under a large hat. She was only two years older than the Girl, although she had been at Woodard's for several years and carried herself as if she had always lived in a brothel.

On Minta's twentieth birthday Gilda took her into town to buy her a new dress. Not an unusual event, but the party Gilda and Bird planned was. Everyone at Woodard's dressed for dinner that evening. The kitchen was filled with teasing laughter which continued in the salon late that evening. A few of the clients who came brought Minta flowers or small trinkets, but Minta was most pleased by the simple cotton blouse the Girl had sewn especially for her.

Pride suffused Gilda's smile as she watched the girls, all of whom were women now. Even her young foundling had become Bird's assistant in the management of the house. They all had the manners of ladies, could read, write, and shoot. Rachel, to whom Minta had been closest, left for California just before Minta's birthday, hoping to start a fresh life and find a husband. The talk heard most often in the salon now was about abolition and the rising temperatures of the North and South. Even at Minta's party the passion of politics couldn't be resisted.

An older Creole man, a frequent visitor to the house, was pounding the piano ineptly but with enthusiasm as a circle of women cheered him on. The Girl served a tray of champagne and stood by the settee near the door in order to listen for Bernice calling her to the kitchen. She placed herself so she would be able to overhear the many conversations in the salon.

But it was Gilda's voice, raised slightly at the other side of the room, that came to her. "I'll say this just once tonight. The years of bartering in human flesh are near their end. And any civilized man will be grateful for it." She peered sternly at a pinched-faced man standing against the window. "You may discuss Lincoln's election in your own parlors, but I will listen to no talk of war in my house tonight."

Fanny tried to turn the conversation to horses, a subject she was most familiar with, but two men cut her off. "Horses! Nigras! It's the same damn thing, more trouble than they're worth. I say we just ship . . ."

The man at the piano stopped playing.

"As I've said gentlemen, the only name on the deed to this place is mine." After a beat of deep silence, the piano music started again and the Girl began to gather empty glasses. She backed out of the room with a full tray.

In the kitchen Bernice asked, "What that ruckus 'bout in there?"

"War talk."

"Umph, men got nothin' but war talk. Like it more'n they like hoppin' on top 'a these girls." She sucked the air through her teeth as she poured more wine into the glasses. She passed one to the Girl, and they both drank quickly.

Bernice looked more like her mother than anyone the Girl had met since running away, but she seemed like a sister too.

"What you think . . . if they get freedom?" Bernice asked as she slid her tongue around the rim of the champagne glass.

"We free already, Bernice. Won't mean so much over here, you think?"

"Gal, they's whole lot of us ain't free, just down the road!"

"Think they gonna come here?" the Girl asked, having a difficult time making the full picture of the world take shape in her head. The memory of the women and men, her sisters still at the plantation, made her feel slightly faint.

"Who know what they do. If they got no work, who know. With nobody to take care 'bout and nobody to pay them like Miss Gilda do us. Who know." Bernice poured more champagne into their glittering crystal.

A surge of fear welled up in the Girl. "We gotta keep this place safe, Bernice, no matter how the war goes. They'll be people needin' to come here I 'spect," the Girl said, remembering the smell of the dark earth of the root cellar where she'd taken refuge.

"Umph," Bernice said, letting her voice drop slightly, "we keep our eye out, maybe some folks need to take to root, if you knows what I mean. Me an' you can do that. I been figurin' on something like that. It's not the war, it's the freedom we got to keep our eye on."

"I remember how to do that," the Girl said, taking the last sip from her glass.

As the Girl hurried back into the salon Minta stopped her at the door, taking two glasses from the tray and setting one behind her on the mantel. She whispered in the Girl's ear conspiratorially, "You'd think these gents would give up arguin' with Miss Gilda. She's stubborner than a crow. I can't says I blame her."

"Why you say that? Don't you think there's gonna be war?"

"Sure, for certain sure. Just ain't no need talkin' it up. Be here soon enough. They always got to spoil somethin'. I'll be goddamned if one of 'em is gonna spoil my birthday!"

The Girl was full of questions but was afraid to ask them here. Sarah and Fanny came over to them, Fanny saying, "You gonna drink 'em all just cause it's your birthday?"

"If that's my desire," Minta said, draining her glass with a flourish.

She turned on her heel, picked up her other drink from the mantel, and strode to the far side of the room.

"She's a terrible slut. I can't understand why Miss Gilda keeps her here," Fanny said.

"Oh, she's all right," Sarah responded, tickling Fanny under her breast. "You jes' jealous 'cause she got a special handmade blouse for her birthday." Fanny refused to smile as she took a glass from the tray.

The Girl smiled shyly. "Aw, Miss Fanny ain't got nothin' to worry 'bout. She gets presents everyday." Fanny tried to look remote and superior, but a tiny smile turned up the corners of her mouth.

Sarah threw her arm around Fanny's waist and pulled her away saying, "Yes, and if she's lucky I'll get to wear her new brooch this Saturday." The two women, who seemed to the Girl not much more than girls themselves, made their way to the piano. Gilda and Bird stood apart at the far end of the room.

The Girl approached them with the last two glasses on her tray. "Miss Gilda?" she said in a low voice.

Gilda took a glass and gave it to Bird. Then she said, "You have that one, child."

Bird tapped the rim of the Girl's glass with her own before sipping. She turned to Gilda. "I think we're ready to move on to French."

"So soon!" Gilda was surprised and pleased.

"If we're learning one grammar, it might as well be two."

The Girl's head buzzed with excitement. She was still shocked that she could put letters and words together and make sense of them in English and that Bird had been able to teach her to understand the words of her nation. Sometimes when they were shopping in town she and Bird confused the shopkeepers along Rue Bourbon by switching back and forth between languages.

Their arrival was inevitably met by either bold, disdainful smirks or surreptitious glances. Everyone knew of the Indian from Woodard's place and now found the addition of the "dark one" a further curiosity they couldn't resist. Bird and the Girl were self-consciously erect as they meandered from one shop to the next, making their way easily among the creamy-colored quadroons who, with mighty effort, pretended they did not see them. It was some time before the Girl understood that these graceful, cold women shared her African blood. She had been so confused and upset by it that she cried as Bird tried to explain the social system of New Orleans, the levels of deceit and manners that afforded the fairer-skinned their privileges and banished the darker ones from society.

For many weeks the Girl could not bring herself to return to town to shop with Bird. First she feigned illness, then begged off because of duties with Bernice. She didn't understand her own fear of these people who tried to look through Bird as if she were glass and simply dismissed her as a slave. Only after an afternoon of making an effort to help Bernice in exchange for being excused from the shopping trip did the Girl find it possible to resume her routine. Bernice had asked her, directly, to explain herself. The Girl found the words for the shame she felt in front of those women, although she could not say why she thought this was so.

"I'll tell you what the problem is . . . you shamed all right," Bernice said in her now familiarly blunt manner, "but it's them you shamed of. Know how I knows? 'Cause long as you been here you ain't never looked shamed about nothin'. Even that first night when she dragged you in here like a sack. You was your mama's daughter and that was that. What you shamed about is them folks thinkin' they white and they ain't. Thinkin' being nasty to dark folks is gonna help make them white. That's a shame all right. Not yours . . . theirs, so just go on 'bout your business."

The Girl resumed her shopping with Bird from that afternoon on. Soon they started to speak the languages as often as they could and watched the shopkeepers' and customers' discomfort. Then they would leave the store choking back their giggles. Now to add French! She would be able to understand what she'd been certain were remarks being made about her and speak as well as they did, for Bird had said her facility with languages was excellent. The Girl was even happier than when she'd constructed her first sentence on paper. Gilda was pleased that she'd been correct; the girl was the one who would give Bird her connection to life. Bird had opened herself to her as she had with no one else at the house except Gilda.

"So Français it is, *ma chère.*"

Gilda's unwavering gaze both excited and discomfited the Girl. She sensed some question being answered in Gilda's mind.

"Can I take that Miss Bird?" the Girl said, lifting her tray. She was relieved to have a reason to leave the room for a moment. She needed to think about what had been raised this evening: war, French, as well as the look of satisfaction in Gilda's eyes. She had tried to read Gilda's thoughts as she had been able to do on occasions in the past but was not completely successful now. She perceived a sense of completion that was certainly focused on her, but the pictures that sometimes formed in her mind when she had questions did not appear this time. She left the glasses and tray in the kitchen and stepped into the small den that was used for coats, wanting to sit quietly for a moment. The bubbling wine and excitement had given her a slight headache, and she waited for it to recede so she could rejoin the others when Minta played the piano. She rose as a gentleman entered looking for his coat.

"May I help you, sir?" she inquired.

"You sure can, little gal," he said, smiling blandly. "I've been over here to New Orleans more than a couple of times now. And I got to say this is the best house west of Chicago."

His look appraised her although he was speaking of Woodard's. She continued to meet his almost-translucent eyes, as if she might hold his gaze and keep it from traveling over her body.

"Thank you, sir. I'll be sure and tell Miss Gilda you said so." The

Girl waited for the man to point toward his coat, but he stood silently with his eyes on her. The Girl had not known the auction block. She had never stood upon one and had never had any occasion to see the one used regularly in the center of the city. His look, however, made her know it intimately. The gaze from his hazel eyes seared her skin, but her face remained impassive as she spoke.

"Your coat, sir?"

"Not just yet. How old would you say you were, little gal?" The Girl's eyes were almost on a level with his.

"About seventeen. Miss Gilda gave me a birthday party last year. She said she figured I was about seventeen."

"How's it come you don't remember how old you are?" Even after the uneventful years that had passed since her arrival at the house, the Girl was still wary of white men asking questions. The talk of abolition and maybe a war meant little to her. Any of these men could capture her and take her back to the plantation.

"I was really sick for a while when I was little. My mistress, Miss Gilda's sister, died before she could tell Miss Gilda the exact information."

"Well, you don't look more'n fourteen to me."

She wondered why he told such a foolish lie. "Could be, sir, but I don't think so."

"Come over here and let me get a closer look at you."

The Girl took two steps nearer, not sure what to expect. He reached out and rubbed her breast. The Girl jumped back, startled. "Aw come on, little gal, let me just get a little somethin' here."

"No, sir!"

"Then we'll go up to your room. I'll pay the regular price."

"No, sir! I just do housekeeping for Miss Gilda. If you want I'll call one of the other girls in."

"I don't want one of the other gals. I'm looking to get to you right now. Come on upstairs."

The Girl recognized the look in his eye. It came back to her from a place far away. She had the dream only rarely now, but whenever she did she awoke crying in terror. Here, not sleeping, the nightmare stood before her, and instead of fear she felt an icy anger. Her hands clenched and unclenched fitfully, as she thought how she would distract his attention and run from the room. She did not want to cause a fuss and spoil Minta's birthday. She closed her eyes, and her mother's face was pictured clearly. Often it had been hard to remember what her mother looked like, but now here was the African face that had comforted her so often. The Girl was awash with tears.

The girls talked often of the gentlemen, usually with a tinge of indulgence as if they were children being kept busily playing while the women did important things. Never had they indicated any fear of the men who visited Woodard's. Whatever gossip she had heard about violence seemed to come from town, frequently about the haughty, fair-skinned ones and their white lovers. Mistreatment was something she knew Gilda would never tolerate, and the Girl realized just then that neither could she.

When she opened her eyes the moisture spilled out and she said, "Please sir, Miss Gilda will be looking for me in the kitchen. I got chores now."

"This won't take long," he said and took her wrist.

"Sir, I've explained —"

She stopped short as Gilda opened the door.

"May I help you, sir?" Gilda's voice was sweet, her anger concealed under the syrup of manners. He loosened his grip on the Girl and gave a deep bow in Gilda's direction.

"Just thought I'd have a little entertainment here."

"I'm sorry, sir. The Girl works only in the kitchen. I'm sure there are others you'd like to meet."

"Don't you think it's about time you broke this one in?"

"No, sir. I don't. If you'll leave the management of my girls to me, you just go about having a good time. Why don't we rejoin the party?" She turned toward the Girl. "Go to Bernice. I'm sure she could use your help. They're about to bring out the cake." The Girl squeezed past Bird who had appeared silently in the doorway.

"I bet you could do a lot of business with that nigra gal, Miss Gilda. You don't know what kind of opportunity you lettin' pass by."

"As I said, let me do the managing. You just enjoy yourself."

"I was kinda hopin' to enjoy myself with her," he said insistently.

"Well, that's not possible," Gilda said. The syrup froze around the sentence, and her back stiffened. Without turning she felt Bird enter the room and said, "Will you see that this gentleman gets a fresh glass of champagne? I have to go out for a while." Gilda left through the kitchen.

Bernice started to speak but stopped herself when she saw the jerky movement and aura of rage that swept along beside Gilda.

Gilda welcomed the coolness of the night air against her cheeks. They were flushed with anger. She was surprised by the rage she had felt when she sensed the Girl was in trouble.

In her lifetime, Gilda had killed reluctantly and infrequently. When she took the blood there was no need to take life. But she knew that there were those like her who gained power as much from the terror of their prey as from the life substance itself. She had learned many lessons in her time. The most important had been from Sorel and were summed up in a very few words: the source of power will tell in how long-lived that power is. He had pointed her and all of his children toward an enduring power that did not feed on death. Gilda was sustained by sharing the blood and by maintaining the vital connections to life. Her love for her family of friends had fed her for three hundred years. When Bird chose to join her in this life, Gilda was filled with both joy and dread. The weight of the years she had known subsided temporarily; at last there would be someone beside her to experience the passage of time. Bird's first years at Woodard's were remote now — Bird moving silently through their lives, subtly taking control of management, finding her place closer and closer to Gilda without having to speak of it.

Before she had even considered bringing Bird into her life she had wanted to feel her sleeping beside her. She had not been willing to risk their friendship, though, until she was certain. And Bird had opened to her, deliberately, to let her know her desires were the same as Gilda's. When they first lay together, Gilda sensed that Bird already knew what world it was Gilda would ask her to enter. She had teased Gilda later with sly smiles, about time and rushing through life, until Gilda had finally been certain Bird was asking to join her.

Despite the years of joy they had known together, tonight, walking along the dark road, Gilda felt she had lived much too long. Only now was it clear to her why. The talk of war, the anger and brutality that was revealed daily in the townspeople, was a bitter taste in her mouth. She had seen enough war and hatred in her lifetime. And although her abolitionist sentiments had never been hidden, she didn't know if she had the heart to withstand the rending effects of another war.

And as always, when Gilda reflected on these things she came back to Bird: Bird, who had chosen to be a part of this life, a choice she seemed to have made effortlessly. Gilda had never said the word *vampire*. She had only asked if Bird would join her as partner in the business and in life. In the years since she'd come to the house she always knew as much as was needed and challenged Gilda any time she tried to hide information from her. Bird listened inside of Gilda's words, hearing the years of isolation and discovery. There was in Gilda an unfathomable hunger — a dark, dry chasm that Bird thought she could help fill.

But now it was the touch of the sun and the ocean Gilda hungered for, and little else. She ached to rest, free from the intemperate demands of time. Often she'd tried to explain this burden to Bird, the need to let go. And Bird saw it only as an escape from *her* — rather than a final embrace of freedom.

Thoughts jostled inside her as she moved — so quickly she was invisible — through the night. She slowed a few miles west of the Louisiana state line, then turned back toward her township. When she came to a road leading to a familiar horse ranch within miles of her farmhouse, she slackened her pace and walked to the rear of the wood-frame building.

All of the windows were black as she slipped around to the small bunkhouse at the back where hands slept. She stood in the shadows listening. Once inside she approached the nearest man, the larger of the two she could see in the darkness. She began to probe his dreams, then sensed an uncleanness in his blood and recoiled. His sleeping face did not bear the mark of the disease that coursed through his body, but it was there. She was certain. Gilda was saddened as she moved to the smaller man who slept at the other end of the room.

He had fallen asleep in his clothes on top of the blankets and smelled of whiskey and horses. She slipped inside his thoughts as he dreamed of a chestnut-colored bay. Under his excitement lay anxiety, his fear of the challenge of this horse. Gilda held him in sleep while she sliced through the flesh of his neck, the line of her nail leaving a red trail. She extended his dream, making him king of the riders as she took her share of the blood. He smiled with triumph at his horsemanship, the warmth of the whiskey in him thundering through her. She caught her breath, and the other ranch hand tossed restlessly in his sleep. Although she no longer feared death she backed away, her instincts readying her hands to quiet the restless worker if he awoke. Her touch on the other sleeper sealed his wound cleanly. Soon his pulse was steady and he continued to explore the dreams she had left with him. As their breathing settled into a calm rhythm, Gilda ran from the bunkhouse flushed with the fullness of blood and whiskey.

The road back felt particularly dark to Gilda as she moved eastward. The clouds left little moonlight visible, but she was swift. Blood pounded in her head, and she imagined that was what she would feel once she finally lay down in the sea and gave up her life. Her heart beat with excitement, full of the need to match its rhythm with that of an ocean. There, Gilda would find her tears again and be free of the sounds of battles and the burden of days and nights piled upon each other endlessly. The dust from the road flew up around her as she made her way toward home. She remembered the dusty trek that was the one clear image of her childhood. They had been going toward water, perhaps the sea. The future had lain near that sea, somehow. It was survival for her mother, father, and the others who had moved relentlessly toward it. Now it was that again for Gilda — now and more. The sea would be the place to rest her spirit.

Once back in her room she changed her dusty jacket and breeches and sat quietly alone in the dark. As dawn appeared on the horizon behind the house, Gilda let down her dark hair and was peaceful in her earthen bed. She was relieved to finally see the end of the road.

In the soft light of a fall afternoon the Girl worked in the garden as she had done for so many years. By now she knew the small plot well, picking the legumes and uprooting the weeds without much thought, enjoying the sun and air. When she looked up at the house Bird waved to her, then pulled the curtain tight across the window of Gilda's room. The Girl's reverie was lazy and undirected. She started at Minta's shadow when it crept over her.

They both sat quietly for some time before the Girl asked Minta, "How long you been here at Woodard's?"

"I was younger than you was when you come," she answered proudly, "but I think I'm gonna move on soon, though. Been savin' my money and thinkin' about goin' west where Rachel is. Look around for a while."

"How long Bird . . . has Bird been here?" the Girl asked, picking her way through the rules of grammar.

"I don't know. Long as any of us can remember. She left once, that's what I heard Bernice say, but she come back quick. Them Indian folks she come from didn't want her back."

Both girls were quiet for a moment, each feeling younger than either had since going out into the world on her own. Minta spoke with hard resolve as if to cover her vulnerability. "When I leave, I'm gone. Gonna make me a fortune in California, get away from this war talk."

"You think Rachel let you stay with her?"

"Well, she sent me a letter with her address and everything. She went to that man Miss Gilda said would give her a hand if she need it. And he put her up in a place 'til she got her own and said he'd help her find a little shop." Minta could feel the Girl's unspoken doubt. She pushed ahead with assurance as much for herself as for the Girl. "She right there on the water and got lotsa business. And she say there not enough women for anybody." A smirk opened her mouth then, but she tried to continue in a businesslike way. "She want to move if she save the money. Get in a quiet district with the swells." Simply talking about Rachel and her new life seemed to make Minta breathless. "She said the women and men there wear the prettiest clothes she ever seen. She want to get a place nearer to the rich people and leave them sailors behind."

The Girl looked aghast, trying to picture Rachel alone in a western city, owning a shop, mixing with rich people who weren't trying to get in her bed. But the image was too distant to get it into focus.

"Say, you think you want to come too? I bet we could get us a little business goin' out there the way you can sew and all."

Leave Gilda and Bird? The thought was a shock to the Girl who had never considered such a possibility; it seemed ludicrous as she knelt under the warm sun feeling the softness of the earth's comfort beneath her. And even with the war coming and talk of emancipation and hardship, the Girl had little in mind she would run away to. "Naw, this is my home now, I guess."

"Well, you just be careful."

"What do you mean?"

"Watch yourself, is all." Minta said it softly and would speak no more. The Girl was puzzled and made anxious by the edge in Minta's voice as well as the silence that followed. Her look of frustration tugged at Minta. "There's lots of folk down this way believe in ha'nts and such like. Spirits. Creoles, like Miss Gilda, and Indians, they follow all that stuff." Minta spoke low, bending at the waist as if to make the words come out softer. "I like her fine, even though some folks don't. Just watch, is all." She skittered through the garden to the kitchen door.

The Girl finished her weeding, then went to the kitchen steps to rinse her hands at the pump and dust her clothes. Bernice watched from the back porch.

"What you say to Minta, she run upstairs?"

"I ain't certain. She's so nervous I can't get hold to what she sayin' half a while. I know she wants me to go out there with her to stay with Rachel."

"What else?"

"She afraid of something here. Sometimes I think maybe it's Miss Gilda. What you think?"

Bernice's face closed as if a door had been locked. "You ain't goin', is you?"

"I'm here for the war no matter what, if there's gonna be one."

"Listen gal, you been lucky so far. You got a life, so don't toss it in the air just to stay 'round here." Behind Bernice's voice the Girl could sense her conflict, her words both pushing the Girl away and needing her to stay.

"My life's here with you and Miss Gilda and Bird. What would I do in California — wear a hat and play lady?" she said, laughing loudly, nervously. She saw the same wary look on Bernice's face that had filtered through Minta's voice.

"What is it? Why you questioning me with that look?" the Girl asked with a tinge of anger in her voice.

"Nothin'. They just different. Not like regular people. Maybe that's good. Who gonna know 'til they know?"

"You sayin' they bad or somethin'?" The challenge wavered in the Girl's throat as her own questions about Gilda and Bird slipped into her mind.

"No." The solid response reminded the Girl of how long Bernice had been at Woodard's. "I'm just saying I don't know who they are. After all the time I been here I still don't know who Miss Gilda is. Inside I don't really know what she thinkin' like you do with most white folks. I don't know who her people is. White folks is dyin' to tell each other that. Not her. Now Bird, I got more an idea what she's up to. She watch over Miss Gilda like . . . like . . ." Bernice's voice trailed off as she struggled for words that spoke to this child who was now almost a woman.

"That ain't hurt you none, now has it?" The Girl's response was hard with loyalty to the women who'd drawn her into their family.

"Not me. I'm just waitin' for the river to rise." Bernice didn't really worry about who Gilda and Bird were. Her concern was what would become of this Girl on her own.

On a day soon after Gilda took the Girl and Bird with her to the farm-house, Minta stood by the empty horse stall nearest the road. Her face was placid, yet she was again bent at the waist as if still whispering. The Girl caught a glimpse of her when the buggy rounded the bend in the road, and she leaned over looking back. She was excited about this journey away from the house, but Minta's warnings itched her like the crinoline one of the girls had given her last Christmas.

The evening sky was rolling with clouds as they drove the buggy south to the farm, yet the Girl could feel Gilda's confidence that there would be no storm. They talked of many things but not the weather. Still, from simply looking into Gilda's eyes and touching Bird's hand she knew there was a storm somewhere. She felt a struggle brewing and longed to speak out, to warn them of how much everyone in town would need them when the war came. She knew that would not be the thing to say — Gilda liked to circle her point until she came to a place she thought would be right for speaking. It didn't come on the road to the farmhouse.

When the three arrived at the farmhouse, the Girl stored her small traveling box under the eaves in the tiny room she slept in whenever they visited here. She wondered if Minta knew Gilda spoke without speaking. That might be the reason she had cautioned her. But the Girl had no fear. Gilda, more often aloof than familiar, touched the Girl somehow. Words were only one of many ways of stepping inside of someone. The Girl smiled, recollecting her childish notion that Gilda was a man. Perhaps, she thought, living among the whites had given her a secret passage, but knowledge of Gilda came from a deeper place. It was a place kept hidden except from Bird.

The fields to the north and west of the farmhouse lay fallow, trimmed but unworked. It was land much like the rest in the Delta sphere, warm and moist, almost blue in its richness — blood soil, some said. The not-tall house over the shallow root cellar seemed odd with its distinct aura of life set in the emptiness of the field. Gilda stood at the window looking out to the evening dark as Bird moved around her placing clothes in chests. Gilda tried to pull the strands together, to make a pattern of her life that was recognizable, therefore reinforce-able. The farmhouse offered her peace but no answers. It was simply privacy away from the dissembling of the city and relief from the tides, which each noon and night pulled her energy, sucking her breath and leaving her lighter than air. The quietness of the house and its eager-ness to hold her safe were like a firm hand on her shoulder. Here Gilda could relax enough to think. She had hardly come through the door before she let go of the world of Woodard's. Still her thoughts always turned back toward the open sea and the burning sun.

The final tie was Bird. Bird, the gentle, stern one who rarely flinched yet held on to her as if she were drowning in life. Too few of their own kind had passed through Woodard's, and none hand stayed very long. On their one trip west to visit Sorel, neither could tolerate the dust and noise of his town for more than several weeks. And until the Girl's ar-rival, Gilda had met no one she sensed was the right one. To leave Bird alone in this world without others like herself would be more cruel than Gilda could ever be. The Girl must stay. She pushed back all doubts: Was the Girl too young? Would she grow to hate the life she'd be given? Would she abandon Bird? The answer was there in the child's eyes. The decision loosened the tight muscles of Gilda's back as if the deed were already done.

The Girl did not know why they had included her in the trip to the farmhouse this time. They rarely brought her along at midseason. The thought that they might want her to leave them made her more anx-ious than Minta's soft voice. Yet each day Bird and she sat down for their lessons, and in the evening when Gilda and Bird talked quietly together, they sought her out to join them. She would curl up in the corner, not speaking, only listening to the words that poured from them as they talked of the women back at the house, the politics in town, the war, and told adventurous stories. The Girl thought, at first, that they were made up but she soon heard in the passion of their voices the truth of the stories Gilda and Bird had lived.

Sometimes one of them would say, "Listen here, this is something you should know." But there was no need for that. The Girl, now tall and lean with adulthood, clung to their words. She enjoyed the contrasting rhythms of their voices and the worlds of mystery they revealed.

She sensed an urgency in Gilda — the stories had to be told, let free from her. And Bird, who also felt the urgency, did not become preoccupied with it but was happy that she and Gilda were spending time together again as it had been before. She unfolded her own history like soft deerskin. Bird gazed at the Girl, wrapped in a cotton shirt, her legs tucked under her on the floor, and felt that her presence gave them an unspoken completeness.

She spoke before she thought. "This is like many times before the fire in my village."

"Ah, and who's to play the part of your toothless elders, me or the Girl?" Gilda asked, smiling widely.

The Girl laughed softly as Bird replied, "Both."

Gilda rose from the dark velvet couch. Her face disappeared out of the low lamplight into the shadow. She stooped, lifted the Girl in her arms, and lay her on the couch. She sat down again and rested the Girl's head in her lap. She stroked the Girl's thick braids as Bird and she continued talking.

In the next silence she asked the Girl, "What do you remember of your mother and sisters?" The Girl did not think of them except at night, just before sleeping, their memory her nightly prayers. She'd never spoken of them to Gilda, only to Bird when they exchanged stories during their reading lessons. Now the litany of names served as memory: Minerva, small, full of energy and questions; Florine, two years older than the Girl, unable to ever meet anyone's eyes; and Martha, the oldest, broad-shouldered like their mother but more solemn. She described the feel of the pallet where she slept with her mother, rising early for breakfast duties — stirring porridge and setting out the rolls. She described the smell of bread, shiny with butter, and the snow-white raw cotton tinged with blood from her fingers.

Of the home their mother spoke about, the Girl was less certain. It was always a dream place — distant, unreal. Except the talk of dancing. The Girl could close her eyes and almost hear the rhythmic shuffling of feet, the bells and gourds. All kept beat inside her body, and the feel of heat from an open fire made the dream place real. Talking of it now, her body rocked slightly as if she had been rewoven into that old circle of dancers. She poured out the images and names, proud of her own ability to weave a story. Bird smiled at her pupil who claimed her past, reassuring her silently.

Each of the days at the farmhouse was much like the others. The Girl rose a bit later than when they were in the city, for there was little work to be done here. She dusted or read, walked in the field watching birds and rabbits. In the late afternoon she would hear Bird and Gilda stirring. They came out to speak to her from the shadows of the porch, but then they returned to their room, where the Girl heard the steady sound of their voices or the quiet scratching of pen on paper.

The special quality of their life did not escape the Girl; it seemed more pronounced at the farmhouse, away from the activity of Woodard's. She had found the large feed bags filled with dirt in the root cellar where she hid so long ago. She had felt the thin depth of soil beneath the carpets and weighted in their cloaks. Although they kept the dinner hour as a gathering time, they had never eaten in front of her. The Girl cooked her own meals, often eating alone, except when Bird prepared a corn pudding or a rabbit she had killed. Then they sat together as the Girl ate and Bird sipped tea. She had seen Gilda and Bird go out late in the night, both wearing breeches and woolen shirts. Sometimes they went together, other times separately. And both spoke to her without voices.

· The warning from Minta and the whispers of the secret religion, vodun, still did not frighten her. She had known deep fear and knew she could protect herself when she must. But there was no cause for fear of these two who slept so soundly in each other's arms and treated her with such tenderness.

On the afternoon of the eighth day at the farmhouse the Girl returned from a walk through the fields to get a drink of water from the back pump. She was surprised to hear, through the kitchen window, Gilda's voice drawn tight in argument with Bird. There was silence from the rest of the room, then a burst of laughter from Gilda.

"Do you see that we're fighting only because we love each other? I insist we stop right this minute. I won't have it on such a glorious evening."

The Girl could hear her moving around the small wooden table, pulling back a chair. Gilda did not sit in the chair, instead lowering herself onto Bird's lap. Bird's expression of surprise turned into a laugh, but the tension beneath it was not totally dispelled.

"I'm sick of this talk. You go on about this leaving as if there is somewhere in the world you could go without me."

Her next words were cut short by Gilda's hand on her mouth. And then Gilda's soft, thin lips pressed her back in the chair.

"Please, my love, let's go to our room so I can feel the weight of your body on mine. Let's compare the tones of our skin as we did when we were young."

Bird laughed just as she was expected to do. The little joking references to time and age were their private game. Even knowing there was more to the kisses and games right now, she longed to feel Gilda's skin pressed tightly to her own. She stood up, still clasping Gilda to her breasts, and walked up the stairs with her as if she were a child.

The Girl remained on the porch looking out into the field as the sun dropped quickly behind the trees. She loved the sound of Gilda and Bird laughing, but it seemed they did so only when they thought no others were listening. When it was fully dark she went into the kitchen to make supper for herself. She put on the kettle for tea, certain that Bird and Gilda would want some when they came down. She rooted through the clay jars until she had pulled together a collection of sweet-smelling herbs she thought worthy. She was eager to hear their laughter again.

That evening Bird took the buggy out and called to the Girl to help load the laundry bags inside. The Girl was silent as she lifted the bags up to the buckboard platform to Bird, who kept glancing up at the windows.

"Tell Minta I said hello." The Girl spoke tentatively when the quiet seemed too long. "Tell her not to leave without me." She figured that was a good enough joke since Minta had been deviling everybody with her dreamtalk of going west.

Bird stood straight, dropping the final bundle on the floor of the buckboard, and looked down at the Girl. "What does that mean?"

"I'm teasin'. She keep talkin' about movin' out there with Rachel like I goin' with her."

Bird turned silent, sat, and grasped the reins of the restless horse. The Girl felt more compelled to fill the air. "I'm not goin'."

"You could, you might want to. Eventually you'll want to start your own life, your own family somewhere." Bird's voice was even, but the Girl recognized a false quiet in it from the times she had heard her arguing with Gilda or talking to drunken clients.

"Any family startin' to do will be done right here." The Girl felt safe having finally said what she wanted out loud. She looked up at Bird's face shyly and was pleased to see the flash of Bird's teeth sparking her grin.

Bird climbed up to the seat and spoke casually, the voice of the woman who always kept the house. "I'll stay in town tonight and return tomorrow evening for tea. If there is any danger, you have only to call out to me."

Bird drew the horse out onto the road, leaving the Girl on the porch wondering what danger there might be. Her warning not to have concern was more frightening to her than Minta's cautionary words.

Upstairs, Gilda was silent in her room. She did not join the Girl after Bird was gone but came down later in the evening. She moved about the parlor, making a circle before resting on the arm of the sofa across from the Girl who sat in Bird's favored chair. The Girl's dark face was smooth, her brow wide and square under the braided rows that drew her thick, springy hair to the nape of her neck. Gilda wore pants and a shirt cinched tightly at her waist by soft leather studded with small white beads. She spoke to the Girl in silence. *Do you know how many years I have lived?*

"Many more years than anyone."

Gilda rose and stood over the girl. "I have Bird's love and yours, I think?" The end of the sentence curled upward in a question.

The Girl had not thought of love until the word was spoken. Yes, she loved them both. The remembered face of her mother was all she had loved until now. Tears slipped down her cheeks. Gilda's sadness washed over her, and she felt the loss of her mother, new and cutting.

"We can talk when I return." Gilda closed the door and was lost in the darkness.

The Girl walked through the house looking at their belongings as if it were the first time she had seen them — their dresses folded smoothly and the delicate linens, the chest that held small tailored breeches and flannel shirts that smelled of earth and lavender water.

She touched the leather spines of the books which she longed to read; some were in languages she did not recognize. Sitting on the edge of the bed that Gilda and Bird shared, she looked patiently at each item in the room, inhaling their scent. The brushes, combs, and jars sat neatly aligned on the dressing table. The coverlet, rugs, and draperies felt thick, luxurious, yet the room was plain. Without Gilda and Bird in the house the rooms seemed incomplete. The Girl walked slowly through each one as if it were new to her, crossing back and forth, searching for something to soothe the unease that crept up into her. Everything appeared just as it had during all the days she had been with Gilda and Bird, except that she felt someone had gone before her as she did now, examining objects, replacing them, pulling out memories, laying them aside.

When the house became cold, the Girl built a fire and curled up on the sofa under her cotton sheet. She fingered the small wooden frame with its rows of beads that Bird had been using to teach her accounting. The clicking of wood on wood was comforting. When Gilda returned she found the Girl asleep, clutching the abacus to her breast as she might a doll. The Girl woke up feeling Gilda's eyes on her and knew it was late by the chill of the air. The fire glowed faintly under fresh logs.

"We can talk now," Gilda said as if she'd never gone out. She sat beside the Girl and held her hand.

"There's a war coming. It's here already, truth be told . . ." She stopped. The effort of getting out those few words left her weary.

"Do you understand when I tell you I can live through no more?"

The Girl did not speak but thought of the night she decided to escape from the plantation.

Gilda continued. "I've been afraid of living too long, and now is the end of my time. The night I found you in the cellar seems only a minute ago. But you were such a child, so full of terror, your journey had been more than the miles of road. When I picked you up your body relaxed into mine, knowing part of your fight was done. I sensed in you a spirit and understanding of the world; that you were the voice lacking among us. Seeing this world with you has given me wonderful years of pleasure. Now my only fear is leaving Bird alone. It's you she needs here with her."

The Girl looked at Gilda's face, the skin drawn tightly across the tiny bones, her eyes glistening with flecks of orange. She wanted to comfort this woman who'd lifted her out of her nightmares.

"You must want to stay. You must need to live. Will you trust me?"

"I never thought to leave you or the house. My home is here as long as you'll have me," the Girl said in a clear voice.

"What I ask is not an easy thing. You may feel you have nothing to go back to, but sooner or later we all want to go back to something. Usually some inconsequential thing to which we've never given much thought before. But it will loom there in our past entreating us cruelly because there is no way to ever go back. In asking this of you, and in the future should you ask it of others, you must be certain that you — that others — are strong enough to withstand the complete loss of those intangibles that make the past so alluring.

The Girl said nothing, not really certain what Gilda meant. She felt a change in the room — the air was taut with energy.

"There are only inadequate words to speak for who we are. The language is crude, the history false. You must look to me and know who I am and if the life I offer is the life you choose. In choosing you must pledge yourself to pursue only life, never bitterness or cruelty."

The Girl peered deeply into the swirling brown and flickering orange of Gilda's eyes, feeling herself opening to ideas and sensations she had never fully admitted before. She drew back, startled at the weight of time she saw behind those eyes.

"Don't be frightened by the idea of death; it is part of life in all things. It will only become worrisome when you decide that its time has come. Power is the frightening thing, not death. And the blood, it is a shared thing. Something we must all learn to share or simply spill onto battlefields." Gilda stopped, feeling the weight of all she wanted to say, knowing it would be too much at once. She would leave the rest to Bird.

The Girl listened to the words. She tried to look again into the world behind Gilda's eyes and understand what was being asked of her. What she saw was open space, no barriers. She saw a dusty road and heard the silence of determination as she felt the tribe close around her as it had closed around Gilda, the child. She saw forests spanning a distance of green too remote for even Gilda to remember.

"My dream was to see the world, over time. The real dream is to make a world — to see the people, and still want to make a world."

"I haven't seen much, but what I've seen doesn't give me much appetite," the Girl said, remembering the chill she felt from Bernice's words about the war's aftermath.

"But what of the people?" Gilda's voice rose slightly. "Put aside the faces of those who've hunted you, who've hurt you. What of the people you've loved? Those you could love tomorrow?"

The Girl drew back from the fire in Gilda's voice. Her mother's hands reaching down to pull the cloth up to her chin as she lay on the mattress filled her vision. Her mother's darkened knuckles had loomed large and solid, something she had not articulated her love for. She remembered hearing Bird's voice for the first time below her in the house announcing the entertainment. The deep resonance sent a thrill through her body. Minta's soft warning was all but forgotten, but her tender concern which showed in the bend of her body filled the Girl with joy. The wary, protective way Bernice had watched her grow, their evenings alone in the kitchen talking about the ways of the world — these were things of value. She opened her eyes and looked into Gilda's. She found love there, too. And exhaustion beyond exploration. She could see no future in them although this was what Gilda wanted to promise her.

Reading the thoughts that Gilda tried to communicate, the Girl picked her way through. "You're offerin' me time that's not really time? Time that's gonna leave me by myself?"

"I've seen this world moving on many different paths. I've walked each road with curiosity, anxious to see what we would make of our world. In Europe and to the south of us here have been much the same. When I came here the world was much larger, and the trip I had to make into the new world was as fearful as the one you've made. I was a girl, too, much too young to even be afraid.

"Each time I thought taking a stand, fighting a war would bring the solution to the demons that haunted us. Each time I thought slavery or fanaticism could be banished from the earth with a law or a battle. Each time I've been wrong. I've run out of that youthful caring, and I know we must believe in possibilities in order to go on. I no longer believe. At least for myself."

"But the war is important. People have got to be free to live."

"Yes, and that will no doubt be accomplished. But for men to need war to make freedom . . . I have never understood. Now I am tired of trying to understand. There are those of our kind who kill every time they go out into the night. They say they need this exhilaration in order to live this life. They are simply murderers. They have no special need; they are rabid children. In our life, we who live by sharing the life blood of others have no need to kill. It is through our connection with life, not death, that we live."

Both women were silent. The Girl was uncertain what questions she might even ask. It was like learning a new language. When she looked again into Gilda's eyes she felt the pulsing of blood beneath the skin. She also sensed a rising excitement that was unfamiliar to her.

"There is a joy to the exchange we make. We draw life into ourselves, yet we give life as well. We give what's needed — energy, dreams, ideas. It's a fair exchange in a world full of cheaters. And when we feel it is right, when the need is great on both sides, we can re-create others like ourselves to share life with us. It is not a bad life," Gilda said.

The Girl heard the edge in Gilda's voice but was fascinated by the pulsing blood and the swirling colors in Gilda's eyes.

"I am on the road I've chosen, the one that is right for me. You must choose your path again just as you did when you ran from the plantation in Mississippi. Death or worse might have met you on that road, but you knew it was the one you had to take. Will you trust me?" Gilda closed her eyes and drew back a little, freeing the girl from her hypnotic gaze.

The Girl felt a chill, as if Gilda's lowered lids had shut off the sun, and for a moment she was afraid. The room was all shadows and unnatural silence as Gilda disappeared behind her closed eyes. Finally, confusion lifted from the Girl who was intent on listening to more than the words: the highs and lows, the pitch, the rhythm were all molded by a kind of faith the Girl hoped she would reach. It was larger than simply a long life. It was a grand adventure for which her flight into freedom had only begun to prepare her.

"Yes," the Girl whispered.

Gilda opened her eyes, and the Girl felt herself drawn into the flowing energy. Her arms and legs became weak. She heard a soft humming that sounded like her mother. She couldn't look away from Gilda's gaze, which held her motionless. Yet she felt free and would have laughed if she had had the strength to open her mouth. She sensed rather than felt Gilda pull her into her arms. She closed her eyes, her muscles softened under the touch of Gilda's hand on her arm. She curled her long body in Gilda's lap like a child safe in her mother's arms.

She felt a sharpness at her neck and heard the soothing song. Gilda kissed her on the forehead and neck where the pain had been, catching her in a powerful undertow. She clung to Gilda, sinking deeper into a dream, barely hearing Gilda as she said, "Now you must drink." She held the Girl's head to her breast and in a quick gesture opened the skin of her chest. She pressed the Girl's mouth to the red life that seeped from her.

Soon the flow was a tide that left Gilda weak. She pulled the suckling girl away and closed the wound. Gilda sat with the Girl curled in her lap until the fire died. As the sun crept into the dark room she carried the Girl upstairs to the bedroom, where they slept the day through. Gilda awoke at dusk, the Girl still tight in her arms. She slipped from the bed and went downstairs to put a tub of water to boil. When she returned to finish dressing, the Girl watched her silently.

"I'm not well," the Girl said, feeling the gorge rising in her throat.

"Yes, you'll be fine soon," Gilda said, taking her into her arms and carrying her downstairs and outside. The evening air made the Girl tremble in her thin shirt. Gilda held the Girl's head down over the dirt, then left her sitting alone on the back stairs. She returned with a wet cloth and wiped her mouth and face, then led her inside again. She helped her remove her clothes and lifted her into the large tub standing beside the kitchen table. Then she soaped, rinsed, and massaged the Girl into restfulness, drawing out the fear and pain with her strong, thin hands as she hummed the tune from the Girl's childhood. She dressed her in a fresh gown, one of her own bordered with eyelet lace, smelling of lavender, then put her back to bed.

"Bird will return soon. You mustn't be afraid. You will ask her to complete the circle. It is she who will make you our daughter. Will you remember that?"

"Yes," the Girl said weakly.

"You must also remember, later, when time weighs on you like

hard earthenware strapped to your back, it is for love that we do this."
Gilda's eyes were fiery and unfocused. The power of them lulled the
Girl into sleep, although she felt a pang of unease and hunger inside of
her. Gilda's lips again brushed her forehead. Then she slept without
dreaming.

She awoke abruptly to find Bird standing over her in darkness shad-
owed even further by a look of destructive anger, her eyes unblinking
and dry.

"When did she leave you?" Bird's voice was tight with control although her hands shook as they clutched several crumpled sheets of
paper.

Gilda had said don't be afraid and she wasn't, only anxious to understand what would happen now. "It seems long ago, before dark. She
wore her walking clothes and said you would complete the circle. I was
to be sure and tell you that."

Bird stalked from the room. Downstairs she stood on the porch,
turning east and west as if listening to thoughts on the wind. She ran
to the west, through the field, and disappeared for three hours. Her
clothes were full of brambles when she returned. She went to the cellar
and climbed part way through the door. She could see the new sacks
of fresh soil stacked beside the ones she and Gilda had prepared so long
ago. She stepped back outside and let the cellar door drop with a re-
sounding thud, then came into the house where the Girl lay weak,
unmoving except for her eyes, now dark brown flecked with pale
yellow.

Bird looked down at her as if she were a stranger, turned away, and
lit a lantern. Again she read the crumpled pages she'd dropped to the
floor, then paced, trying not to listen to the Girl's shallow breathing.
The darkest part of night passed. Bird stood on the porch again and
peered at the stars as if one might signal her.

When the sun began its rise Bird retreated to the shadows of the
house, moving anxiously from corner to corner, listening. She was uncertain what to expect, perhaps a ripping sound or scream of pain inside her head. She felt only the Girl weakening upstairs and a cloying
uneasiness. In her head she replayed recent conversations with Gilda.
Each one came closer and closer to the core.

Gilda had needed Bird to step away so she could end this long life
with the peace she sought. And each time Bird had resisted, afraid of

losing the love of a woman who was the center of her world. Upstairs was the Girl, now in her charge, the one who'd given that permission for which Gilda had yearned.

Full daylight came behind the closed drapes. Bird stood tense, her body a bronze rod, dull and aching, her full length of flesh and hair calling out for hours. The answer came like the sunlight it was. She felt Gilda lying naked in the water, marveling at its coolness and silence. Then she dove into the darkness of the tide. Without the power of her native soil woven into her breeches, she surrendered easily. The air was squeezed from her lungs and she eagerly embraced her rest. Bird felt a moment of the sun's warmth, her head filled with Gilda's scent. In her ear was the soft sigh of pleasure she recognized from many mornings of their past together, the low whisper of her name, then silence. She knew the knife-edged sun rays stripped the flesh from Gilda's bones. The heat seared through Bird, lightning on her skin and in her marrow. Then, like the gradual receding of menstrual pain, Bird's muscles slackened and her breathing slowed. The crackling was silenced. It was over. Gilda was in the air no more.

Bird went upstairs to the Girl whose face was ashen, her dark eyes now flecked with orange. A frost of perspiration covered her body, and tears ran down the sides of her face. She opened her mouth but no sounds came out. Bird sat against the pillows and pulled the Girl into her arms. She was relieved by the cool tears washing over her brown arm as if she were weeping herself. Bird pulled aside her woolen shirt and bared her breasts.

She made a small incision beneath the right one and pressed the Girl's mouth to it. The throbbing in her chest became synchronous with the Girl's breathing. Soon the strength returned to the Girl's body; she no longer looked so small.

Bird repeated the exchange, taking from her as Gilda had done and returning the blood to complete the process. She finally lay her head back on the pillows, holding the Girl in her arms, and rested. Their breathing and heartbeats sounded as one for an hour or more before their bodies again found their own rhythms. Even then, Bird remained silent.

"She's gone then?" Bird heard her ask. She only nodded and eased her arms from around the Girl's body.

"I'll build a fire," she said and rose quickly from the bed. Alone in the room Bird found the crumpled letter and returned it to the box Gilda had left on the dressing table. She heard the sound of a robe brushing the carpet below as the Girl moved about laying wood on the fire, then settling the kettle atop the stove in the kitchen. She called to Bird to come down. Her voice, now strong and vibrant, was a shock in the late afternoon quiet without Gilda.

They sat in the twilight in front of the low flames, not speaking for some time. Then Bird said, "She wanted you to be called Gilda."

"I know."

"Will you?"

"I don't know."

"It will be dark soon — we must go out. Are you afraid?"

"She said there's little to fear and you'll teach me, as always." They were quiet again.

"She loved you very much, Bird."

"Loved me so much that she traded her life for yours?" Bird almost shouted. In all else there'd been some reasoning, but she could find none in this. Here in the place of the woman to whom she'd given her life sat a child.

"I'm not a child, Bird. If I can hear her words and understand her need, why can't you? I didn't steal her life. She took her road to freedom — just like I did, just like you did. She made a fair exchange. For your sake."

"Fair exchange?" Bird was unnerved by the words she had heard so often in the past when she had been learning the manner of taking the blood and leaving something in return — how to partake of life and be certain not to take life. She chafed under the familiar words and inflection. "You for her?" Bird spit it out. "Hundreds of years of knowledge and wit in exchange for a girl who hasn't lived one lifetime yet."

"It's not just me, it's you. Her life, her freedom for our future. You are as much a part of the bargain as I am. She brought me to this place for your need as well as for mine. It's us seeing the future together that satisfies her needs."

Bird heard the past speaking to her, words she had chosen to ignore. Tonight she stood face to face with their meaning: Gilda's power over her own death was sacred, a decision all others were honor bound to respect. Bird had denied Gilda's right to her quietus and refused to even acknowledge that decision. It was a failure she could not wear easily.

Darkness seeped through the drawn curtains of the parlor. The glow of the almost-steady flame burned orange in the room, creating movement where there was none. The two women sat together as if they were still at their reading lessons. Finally Bird spoke.

"Gilda?"

"Yes."

"It's time now."

They dressed in the warm breeches and dark shirts. Bird took Gilda's hand and looked into the face of the woman who had been her pupil and saw the childlike roundness of her had melted away. Hunger filled her eyes.

"It is done much as it was done here. Your body will speak to you. Do not return to take from anyone too soon again: it can create the hunger in them. They will recover though, if it is not fed. And as you take from them you must reach inside. Feel what they are needing, not what you are hungering for. You leave them with something new and fresh, something wanted. Let their joy fill you. This is the only way to share and not to rob. It will also keep you on your guard so you don't drain life away."

"Yes, these are things she wanted me to know."

"I will teach you how to move about in indirect sunlight, as you've seen us do, and how to take your rest. Already your body sheds its mortal softness. You'll move faster than anyone, have the strength of many. It's that strength that you must learn to control. But we will talk more of these things later. It is better to begin before there is pain."

Gilda and Bird turned west. Their path through the flat field was invisible. Bird pushed aside all thoughts for the moment, remembering only her need to instruct, to insure that the girl gained enough knowledge for her survival. Gilda allowed the feeling of loss to drift through her as they sped into the darkness. Along with it came a sense of completion, too. There was certain knowledge of the world around her, excitement about the unknown that lay ahead, and comfort with her new life. She looked back over her shoulder, but they had moved so quickly that the farmhouse was all but invisible. Inside, the fire was banked low, waiting for their return.

A PERSONAL PAST

Remember Him a Outlaw

By Alexis DeVeaux

Remember him a outlaw. living in the bowery. didnt hardly work. he couldnt he roars. tobacco smiles. in baggy dove-colored khaki pants and big orange workboots. he is slew-foot. doing his wine walk. hips swaying west down 112 street. he tips his cap to the women. he grins at stoops. talking loud to other bums old friends. the sky or garbage. up the street at the corner of 5th & 112 he stops. to salute cars. to wait. to cross. his sober eye always leary. he crosses to our corner.

> *ma! ma! here come uncle willie! ma!*
> *hey uncle willie!*

mommie from somewhere inside the house runs to the window on instinct. she pops out. relief spreads over her yellow face. we run and climb at uncle willie. a mountain to jump on.

> *take me for a piggy-back uncle willie!*
> *take me first!*
> *look! i got on your hat uncle willie ooooooh what you got in your pocket*
> *is that candy??*

a long face melts in his shoulder cage. on his head hair beads. eyes like stars and rot-gut wine. medicine for his thick smooth lips. he sweats. his black skin wet tar. a reflection to look at and never see in. a cherub. an old womans son. uncle willie wasnt 43.

he is drunk. desperate to hold all of us. at the same time. he throws a few jabs to odell. ducks. fat vickie is teased. rosie runs to him. hugging me round the neck. twins we walk together. booboo and nell squint their eyes to look up. the sun has a new face.

   up to the stoop uncle willie is a father who visits. knows we love him boisterous. he stops to see mommie in the 2nd floor window. she shakes her head and grins. glad to see him. saying nothing saying

   willie nigger when you gon change?

uncle willie rears back in the heat. he sways. wipes sweat in a dingy rag from his neck. he throws back his head to talk

   hey mae! mae! where you get all those ugly children from?
   oh shut up. what you got in your pockets willie what you done stole?

the stoop is crowded with our friends. they stare and giggle. they are kidnapped. cannot play ball or rope. fascinated children at a circus. he is their uncle and pied piper. willie breaks up to laugh. he bends over. slaps his knees. we feel his pockets with silent permission. he winks at mommie

   now mae you know i dont steal. borrows well what you borrowed?

we already know. cherries and penny-candies flow from his pockets. it is a stream. it cannot stop.

   lord ha' mercy willie. they gon catch you one day on that market.
   look mae. this my family. my nieces an nefew.
   hope yall dont make no faggot outta him. they know uncle willie al-ways gon bring them something they know uncle willie dont steal. yall give some to your lil friends.

we are bombarded from the ringside. fingers poke my face hungry. odell wants more candy. he is searching. he discovers in a back pocket. spanish neighbors snicker and point. in the window mommie laughs

   willie! odell got your stuff!

odell is an imp running. his thin brown-body flies over the sidewalk. over cracks and cans. he cackles. escaping uncle willies chase

   come back here boy! dont you fall and break my jug!
   if you do ill break both your legs
   come here boy!

odell stops to be caught. his miniature face a pearl shining sweat. uncle willie blows a sigh of relief. he chuckles. glad to have the pint of purple-wine back safe.

aint he something? dont know where you found that one at mae. listen momma- im taking rose an lex on the avenue. buy the kids some ice cream.
we be right back. rest of yall stay here.

we walk on 5th avenue with uncle willie. he stops every 2 feet. dudes who ran with his brother in 45 and then. numbers runners. fathers. enemies. remember when niggers wore clothes made in italy and talked mafia. up and down lenox avenue. on 5th. numbers. getting over the war of. the good cocaine guineas brought up town the year before real dope came. jim-jam is dead. 8th avenue turned dope. tried to cheat georgie out some pay off money. found him in the elevator. no head. remember the lames busted. still in there. old playmates. couldnt get high no more off gin or jonnie walker red.

uncle willie pulls us from behind him. marshmallow fingers squeeze and held our shy hands. we sweat and are introduced celebrities.

richie in the joint man. yeah. got a pound jack.
blew a nigger in 2 114 street. he dont play jack.
my brother. these his kids. dont they look like him?
mean an black just like they daddy.
richie kids? didnt know that yeah look just like richie spit!
nawww man
sure they do
here honey. yall buy yourself something

coins roll out our hands to the sidewalk. silver dimes and quarters run curving in circles. fall on their faces in the gutter. uncle willie chases a nickel. under his boot its freedom is squashed.

we move from one stoop-crowd to another. down the line uncle willie waves. talks. here is black-father the watermelon man. and miss king. always dressed in black. summer or winter. old miss goldberg in the door of her laundromat. spit creeps from a corner of her mouth. she puffs a corn pipe. in front of her uncle willie stops. uncle willie feels her dead tits. leaves. he makes her hairy face turn pink for him. she dribbles as he walks away. she dreams on one day having him. right in the laundromat. on the ground me and rosie are hiding giggles.

uncle willie steps inside the ice cream place. on the big stools our sandaled feet dangle high off the floor. uncle willie reaches to kiss a big woman behind the counter.

> *nigger where you been? dont put your greasy lips on me. much as you smell.*
> *you know you like it. stop actin so funny.*
> *your nigger must be somewhere in here. listen flossy — let me have 6 cones. yeah 6. these richie kids. whats the damage on that? put it on my bill you aint got no bill here*
> *long as this your store momma — i got me a bill*

flossy looks at him. she smiles. her mouth pauses in a day like this before. when uncle willie walked thru the door. young and polished. he teases her. he waits for closing time. waits to claim the chocolate gold his night for love.

the sun melts our ice cream-on-credit. outside uncle willie hurries us to the block. we are 3 hurries. careful to hold the melting vanilla drips over our fingers. against our clothes. the 2 scoops disappear in to 1. we lick the sweet cream from our hands. as it runs we turn the corner. back.

> *ok mae   take care momma. im going over to see grammie. every-*
> *body got ice cream. uncle willie dont have nothing. dont get no kiss?*

odell is always first to him. i am always last. we walk back to the corner. watch as he fades across the street in colors and noises up the west side. uncle willie moves. hips like a swan. he stops to bum a cigarette. he shares his purple magic and continues. the beginning of our sunset.

and after that when he moved out the bowery grammie took him back. we moved to the bronx. always saw him on saturdays 114 street. in front of 216. uncle willie sweats. looking for a womans packages to carry up. to collect his jug-money. tip his cap. downstairs he waits. he spots me. grabs my hand. proud to own me. his sho-nuff blood. rushed upstairs to see grammie. she pleads with me not to stay long but to stay a virgin. she gives me my allowance. she kisses me behind the door. i say goodbye and go. downstairs uncle willie is waiting.

come on baby   ill walk you to the subway.
momma give you your money? dont say nothing.
shhh

we tip to 7th avenue. grammie rattles in the window. the veins of her small throat strain and pop. she yells

willie willie! dont you take that child money!
dont worry about nothing momma!
i aint gon take her money just walking to the train station. dont want
none a these low niggers putting they hands on her thats all!

at the liquor store where grammie cannot see i give uncle willie his 50 cent allowance. and wait briefly outside as he turns my quarters into purple-sweet juice. he is a magician. war counselor. he is my main man. coming out grinning. he clutches my shoulder. in his hand is love. we walk. for a quick taste he steps in a hallway. out of respect for me. it was easy to peep. him his head bent backwards. wine drops from his mouth. he jams his magic in a favorite pocket. uncle willie flows back into the light. every saturday our sacred routine. every year uncle willie and me.

   til the week or summer richie came home. back to the pit. go down make it rich. to snort more poison. to infest his begging matter. hustle his mother. anybody. make a flunkie of his brothers love. for him uncle willie runs the street. collects his old boys together. spreads news richies out. boasting with pride when richie got his eldorado. never let uncle willie sit in the front seat. gratefully taking the 5s and 10s richie shoved at him saying

nigger you need to buy yourself some new clothes
man raggidty as you is

pretty little black man. richie hill is a name. like 8th avenue. the powder he peddles. between niggers he shot and the .38 under his left arm pit. sharp fists that splattered a nigger jaw. richie is power over the dope-sick. a fox is a vulture. slick hair nigger back out the joint. blackberry face in skin the color of new coal around smooth lips like uncle willie.

   friday is a carnival afternoon 114 street. a vacuum sucks the souls of its people in the nauseous heat. buildings squat together an infinite line of faces. and bodies chatter hanging from the windows. to feel the breezes that never come. women shout from one side of the narrow street to the other. mating calls. and stray husbands in search of the number or gossip. wasting time. pasted on stoops hordes of people. little ones. ½ naked tar-babies run from the spray and coldness of a fire hydrant. they are laughing. people fill every empty space here fleeing from the shit poor.

   uncle willie prances up and down in front of 216. he grins and sweats. he is fresh and clean. his head is inflated. his eyes strut. in an unnatural fashion he is clean. in shoes of alligator green. italian knit sweater. silk green pants hang loose against his hips. not use to the rich feel of soft fiber. uncle willie is a dream in green. leather cap and green socks silk. the new pants have no back pocket to carry anything. uncle willie sees me. coconut eyes run to him.

hey uncle willie! hey man you looking too good!
when did you fall into this
yeah momma im moving up. now that richie out —
you working for him or something?
make me a cupla bills   you know.
nothing too tough. no more days niggers out here
gon run over me   who that lil monster
you was talking to on the corner.
who. duck?
baby i know you take care of yourself but if one of these chumps out
here mess around we straighten him out. know none a them wanna
run up on richie. he wanna see you.
momma showed us your picture in the paper black as you is. always
knew you be the one lex. told mae and momma. mae always fussing
cause you in a book. uncle willie was the first one to recognize you   so
they give you 8-grand for your college huh? where is it
cornell university. upstate next to the farms
what you gon take up momma
everything. psychology. i dont know
when you leaving?
tuesday night it all begins
uncle willie been waiting a long time to see this baby. im prouda you.
gon cut that picture out an put it right in my new wallet. show all the

niggers my niece going to one the best colleges.
richard around?
yeah got a place 111 street. him an his man red.
told me to bring you over there soon as you came.
hes prouda you momma.

uncle willies new shoes clop a hollow sound. thru the tribes the faces of poets and whores tangled together we move. up the block to 8th avenue the air is a vise no one can escape. bloated junkies in packs like wolves pace down and up. their nervous eyes glitter. at 6:00 the sun cooks the street. smells of chicken and watermelon mix with us. 8th avenue spreads gangrehea. it is us. rhythms are gospel from the dark cool bars. fingers pop. bop. in the heats beat. a toothless woman stops. in the middle of the street. her hips move like a snake charmed. she is voodoo. she is happy. while the cars and buses scream. they are in a hurry. they do not understand. she is free.

at the corner of 111 street we turn. up the long stairs of a ½ condemned building we stop on the 6th floor. knock and puff at the 2nd door. hear feet slowly answer the noise we make.

red! red! willie. open up. i got lexie.
richie here?

the doors eye opens and closes.

yeah   hes in the front. richie! wake up man!
you got company

down the empty-blue hallway hear glass knock against glass on the floor. a fan hums low. jazz whispers in the walls. it is hot like the street. smell wolves here. red walks behind us. he is skinny. his red bare chest a map of battle scars.

in the tiny front-room 2 chairs and a love seat are squeezed. a big coffee table you step over to get by is covered with coke bottles and cigarette ash.

hey richard. whats happn

in a coarse voice the black-berry face speaks.

hi   stuff. scuse me for not having my clothes on.
so hot in this room

he has been sleeping.
he is asleep.

> *come here baby. let me see you. watch yourself!*
> *willie! get a broom. sweep this mess out the way!*
> *you want her to think we pigs? hey red aint she grown up stuff? baby*
> *red is my right arm.*

uncle willie is a maid. he sweeps the floor. he wipes the coffee table. he
sweats in brown garbage bags. he is glad to help. i open a window. the
telephone rings in another tiny room richie answers

> *yeah i got it sucka. just have your man there*
> *when? right now?? no im waiting for sugar. sent him crosstown. wont*
> *be back til 7. cant send red man. need him here. what??*
> *just lay cool. youll get it in 20 minutes.*
> *ill send willie. yeah man   yeah.*

the telephone is quiet. richie stands in the doorway. he looks at uncle
willie. he lights a cigarette.

> *red! get that thing together. nigger over there cant wait. look at that*
> *lame! gave him 200 dollars. look what the nigger do. probably bought*
> *a case of pluck by now. willie. willie! pull yourself together man. need*
> *you for something*

red goes to the kitchen. his eyes are sealed in sweat-covers. he sleeps.
from the pink kitchen he returns. he shoves pork chops and frozen
hamburgers in a shopping bag.

> *here it is richie. maybe i should put it in 2 bags.*
> *yeah, willie got enough sense to carry it — just be his luck to break it.*
> *wake up man!*
> *yeah jack yeah. i hear you. what you want me to do go over to 108*
> *street central park west. where we stopped off yesterday? the orange*
> *stoop. 1st floor left in the back —*
> *the bald head chump   richie?*
> *uhhuh. suckas name is randolph. the one hand dude.*
> *owe him a grand. he get it when im ready.*
> *dont know who the lame think he dealing with.*
> *tell him to meet me in joe-blo about 9.*

> *shouldnt take you more than 15 minutes willie.*
> *take it straight there.*

red gives the fat shopping bag to uncle willie.

> *you kidding me   richie??*
> *bulls out there gon think i took off some supermarket.*
> *this randolph cat a butcher jack?*
> *salready dripping blood on me.*
> *take the thing an get back man!*
> *here baby. put this in your pocket. 50 dollars enough? make sure you*
> *come by an see me. take you downtown monday night. we hang out*
> *together. momma said you leaving tuesday. let me know if you need*
> *some dust. make sure she get to the subway willie. take care of yourself*
> *baby.*

hustled out the door   blood comes after business. outside uncle willie stoops to wipe pale-red juice from his shoes. down the street we are
conspicuous. on the sidewalk pork chops run away. the shopping bag
is too full. 50 dollars causes a fire in my skirt pocket. hear the siren
scream. red city-wagons surround me. pink faces in gas masks and
plastic coats drown me. laughing because i am a fire. smoke puffs. sail
away over roof tops. wonder where my 50 dollars is. i pat my pocket
for an answer.

> *uncle willie you dont have to walk me to the subway.*
> *go ahead. to 108 street. that bag might break.*
> *nawwwww momma. uncle willie can handle this.*
> *must be something for your father to give away all this meat. sure you*
> *can make it to the train?*
> *tell mae you saw richie. wheres your money keep your hands on it.*
> *chumps out here.*
> *aww aint no body thinking about getting me uncle willie. ill see you*
> *monday or tuesday*
> *before i go.*
> *alright momma get home safely*

down 8th avenue uncle willie goes away. he leans to one side walking.
careful to dodge blood drops from the bag. he is a green dream. he is
gone.

i am out. back from the subways and downtown. saturday is ½ spent. the paper money in my pocket just change left over from the boxes and bags i carry up stairs. climb 3 flights to #9. the door kicks open. a trumpet is assaulted. trumped by a strange smell. the air is cold. coming out. hollow sound. dont go in. see gray. see mommie quiet. her eyes at me quiver in their sockets. a whisper drips

lexie? close the door an come here
put those things there an sit down

sit. do not move. the couch wants to speak. what i do now. it wasnt me ma. how come vickie is crying? brought home some change just like you told me. whats wrong with rosie? dont ask. choke. think. ithaca. hallucinate new life. grow up. think. in the ivy league wonderland. a cow grows milk from a tree. tuesday bus ticket #94376. fly brown butterfly. farms are cartoon in storybooks. sunsets are black.

mommie your eyes have turned in
mommie where are your lips

uncle willie died

burst firecracker. burst. blop. blop. what? too much too many. blop. blop. what?? cows dont grow on trees. huh? speak slow. huh. leave uncle willie? dead. i am in ithaca. white lake in the pink sun. a sable moonface. you kidding me?? mommie i am going apart.

no   it isnt cold.
                        no more wine.
this is september.
                        it aint cold.

stand up. sit down. my belly is a fever humming. the world spins around.

play trumpet. say.
play. screech. screech. trumpet.
scream notes.

crack my head. mommie is a spiritual

allah, allah
damn!

allah
this is quicksand
stop
dont tell me
grammie called. not too long ago. say police found him early this morn-
ing. on some roof 108 street. ice box-cold. just his pants an wallet. laid
up there. dont know what he was doing. willie never bes over there.
didnt use that stuff.
willie was too afraid. somebody drew out his blood seem like   an shot
him full of poison.
gets in your blood
makes you fly
   black dot
   heart drops

thats ridiculous. i see uncle willie right now. saw him yesterday. talk.
shine. walk. in purple magic. long face i love you. head of hair beads.
eye of stars and rot-gut. medicine wine for his thick smooth lips

   lexie —

   mommie he sweats —

   no —

   mommie i see him

   they will lock you in a box
   will they give me to the worms?
   they will make you dust   in green

remember him   a outlaw.

Mother

by Andrea Lee

IN THE SUMMER my mother got up just after sunrise, so that when she called Matthew and me for breakfast, the house was filled with sounds and smells of her industrious mornings. Odors of frying scrapple or codfish cakes drifted up the back stairs, mingling sometimes with the sharp scent of mustard greens she was cooking for dinner that night. Up the laundry chute from the cellar floated whiffs of steamy air and the churning sound of the washing machine. From the dining room, where she liked to sit ironing and chatting on the telephone, came the fragrance of hot clean clothes and the sound of her voice: cheerful, resonant, reverberating a little weirdly through the high-ceilinged rooms, as if she were sitting happily at the bottom of a well.

My father left early in the morning to visit parishioners or to attend church board meetings. Once the door had closed behind him, the house entered what I thought of as its natural state — that of the place on earth that most purely reflected my mother. It was a big suburban house, handsomer than most, built of fieldstone in a common, vaguely Georgian design; it was set among really magnificent azaleas in a garden whose too-small size gave the house a faintly incongruous look, like a dowager in a short skirt. The house seemed little different from any other in my neighborhood, but to me, in my early-acquired role as a detective, a spy, a snooper into dark corners, there were about it undeniable hints of mystery. The many closets had crooked shapes that suggested secret passages; in the basement, the walls of the wine cellar — its racks filled by our teetotaling family with old galoshes and rusty roller skates — gave a suspicious hollow sound when rapped; and on the front doorbell, almost obliterated by the pressure of many fingers, was printed a small crescent moon.

The house stayed cool on breathless summer days when tar oozed in the streets outside, the heat excluded by thick walls and drawn shades, and the dim rooms animated by a spirit of order and abundance. When I came dawdling down to breakfast, long after Matthew had eaten and gone plunging off on his balloon-tired Schwinn, I usually found my mother busy in the kitchen, perhaps shelling peas, or stringing beans, or peeling a basket of peaches for preserves. She would fix me with her lively, sarcastic dark eyes and say, "Here comes Miss Sarah, the cow's tail. What, pray tell, were you doing all that time upstairs?"

"Getting dressed."

What I'd been doing, in fact — what I did every summer morning — was reading. Lounging voluptuously in my underpants on the cool bare expanse of my bed, while flies banged against the screen and greenish sunlight glowed through the shades, I would read with the kind of ferocious appetite that belongs only to garden shrews, bookish children, and other small creatures who need double their weight in nourishment daily. With impartial gluttony I plunged into fairy tales, adult novels, murder mysteries, poetry, and magazines while my mother moved about downstairs. The sense of her presence, of, even, a sort of tacit complicity, was always a background at these chaotic feasts of the imagination.

"You were reading," Mama would say calmly when I stood before her in the kitchen. "You must learn not to tell obvious lies. Did you make up your bed?"

"I forgot."

"Well, you're not going outside until you've done something to that room of yours. It looks like a hooraw's nest. Your place is set at the table, and the cantaloupe is over there — we've had such delicious cantaloupe this week! Scrape out the seeds and cut yourself a slice. No — wait a minute, come here. I want to show you how to cut up a chicken."

Each time she did this I would wail with disgust, but I had to watch. The chicken was a pimply yellow-white, with purplish shadows and a cavernous front opening; my mother would set her big knife to it, bar-ing her teeth in an ogress's grin that made fun of my squeamishness. "You saw along the backbone like this — watch carefully; it takes a strong arm — and then you *crack* the whole thing open!"

In her hands the cave would burst apart, exposing its secrets to the light of day, and with another few strokes of the knife would be transformed into ordinary meat, our uncooked dinner.

It was easy for me to think of my mother in connection with caves, with anything in the world, in fact, that was dimly lit and fantastic. Sometimes she would rivet Matthew and me with a tale from her childhood: how, at nine years old, walking home through the cobblestone streets of Philadelphia with a package of ice cream from the drugstore, she had slipped and fallen down a storm drain accidentally left uncovered by workmen. No one was around to help her; she dropped the ice cream she was carrying (something that made a deep impression on my brother and me) and managed to cling to the edge and hoist herself out of the hole. The image of the little girl — who was to become my mother — hanging in perilous darkness was one that haunted me; sometimes it showed up in my dreams.

Perhaps her near-fatal tumble underground was responsible for my mother's lasting attraction to the bizarre side of life. Beneath a sometimes prudish exterior, she quivered with excitement in the same way her children did over newspaper accounts of trunk murders, foreign earthquakes, Siamese twins, Mafia graves in the New Jersey pine barrens. When she commented on these subjects, she attempted a firm neutrality of tone but gave herself away in the heightened pitch of her voice and in a little breathy catch that broke the rhythm of each sentence she spoke. This was the voice she used to whisper shattering bits of gossip over the phone. "When Mr. Tillet died," I heard her say once, with that telltale intake of breath, "the funeral parlor did such a poor job that his daughter had to *wire her own father together!*"

My mother, Grace Renfrew Phillips, had been brought up with all the fussy little airs and graces of middle-class colored girls born around the time of World War I. There was about her an endearing air of a provincial maiden striving for sophistication, a sweet affectation of culture that reminded me, when I was older, of Emma Bovary. She and her cluster of pretty, light-skinned sisters grew up in a red-brick house with marble steps in South Philadelphia. They all played the piano, knew a bit of French and yards of Wordsworth, and expected to become social workers, elementary-school teachers, or simply good wives to suitable young men from their own background — sober young doctors, clergymen, and postal administrators, not too dark of complexion. Gracie Renfrew fit the pattern, but at the same time dismayed her family by attending Communist Party meetings, joining a theater group, and going off to a Quaker work camp.

When she married my father, the prescribed young minister, my mother had become, inevitably, a schoolteacher — a beautiful one. She was full-faced, full-bodied, with an indestructible olive skin and an extraordinary forehead — high, with two handsome hollows over the temples. She had a bright, perverse gaze, accentuated by a slight squint in her left eye, and a quite unusual physical strength. She swam miles every summer at the swim club, and at the small Quaker school, where I was a student and she taught sixth grade, it was common to see her jumping rope with the girls, her large bosom bobbing and a triumphant, rather disdainful smile on her face. Her pupils adored her, probably because her nature held a touch of the barbarism that all children admire: she would quell misbehavior, for instance, by threatening in a soft, convincing voice to pull off the erring student's ears and fry them for supper.

At home Mama was a housekeeper in the grand old style that disdains convenience, worships thrift, and condones extravagance only in the form of massive Sunday dinners, which, like acts of God, leave family members stunned and reeling. Her kitchen, a long, dark, inconvenient room joined to a crooked pantry, was entirely unlike the cheerful kitchens I saw on television, where mothers who looked like June Cleaver unwrapped food done up in cellophane. This kitchen had more the feeling of a workshop, a laboratory in which the imperfect riches of nature were investigated and finally transformed into something near sublimity. The sink and stove were cluttered with works in progress: hot plum jelly dripping into a bowl through cheesecloth; chocolate syrup bubbling in a saucepan; string beans and ham bones hissing in the pressure cooker; cooling rice puddings flavored with almond and vanilla; cooked apples waiting to be forced through a sieve to make applesauce; in a vat, a brownish, aromatic mix for root beer.

The instruments my mother used were a motley assemblage of blackened cast-iron pots, rusty-handled beaters, graters, strainers, and an array of mixing bowls that included the cheapest plastic variety as

well as tall, archaic-looking stoneware tubs inherited from my grandmother, who had herself been a legendary cook. Mama guarded these
ugly tools with jealous solicitude, suspicious of any new introductions,
and she moved in her kitchen with the modest agility of a master
craftsman.

Like any genuine passion, her love of food embraced every aspect of
the subject. She read cookbooks like novels, and made a businesslike
note in her appointment book of the date that Wanamaker's received
its yearly shipment of chocolate-covered strawberries. Matthew and I
learned from her a sort of culinary history of her side of the family: our
grandfather, for instance, always asked for calf brains scrambled with
his eggs on weekend mornings before he went out hunting. Grandma
Renfrew, a sharp-tongued beauty from North Carolina, loved to drink
clabbered milk, and was so insistent about the purity of food that once
when Aunt Lily had served her margarine instead of butter, she had
refused to eat at Lily's table again for a year. My mother's sole memory of her mother's mother, a Meherrin Indian called Molly, was of
the withered dark-faced woman scraping an apple in the corner of the
kitchen, and sucking the pulp between her toothless jaws.

Mama took most pleasure in the raw materials that became meals.
She enjoyed the symmetry, the unalterable rules, and also the freaks
and vagaries that nature brought to her kitchen. She showed me with
equal pleasure the handsome shape of a fish backbone; the little green
gallbladder in the middle of a chicken liver; and the double-yolked eggs,
the triple cherries, the peculiar worm in a cob of corn. As she enjoyed
most the follies, the bizarre twists of human nature and experience, so
also she had a particular fondness for the odd organs and connective
tissues that others disdained. "Gristle is delectable," she would exclaim
as Matthew and I groaned. "The best part of the cow!"

I was a rather lazy and dunderheaded apprentice to my mother. She
could be snappish and tyrannical, but I hung around the kitchen anyway, in quest of scrapings of batter, and because I liked to listen to her.
She loved words, not as my father the minister did, for their ceremonial
qualities, but with an off-handed playfulness that resulted in a combination of wit and nonsense. In her mischievous brain, the broad country imagery of her Virginia-bred mother mingled with the remains of a
lady-like education that had classical pretensions. When she was an-
noyed at Matthew and me, we were "pestilential Pestalozzis"; we were

also, from time to time, as deaf as adders, as dumb as oysters, as woolly as sheep's backs; we occasionally thrashed around like horses with the colic. At odd moments she addressed recitations to the family cat, whom she disliked; her favorite selections were versions of "O Captain! My Captain!" ("O Cat! my Cat! our fearful trip is done . . .") and Cicero's address to Catiline ("How long, Cat, will you abuse our patience? . . .").

On summer evenings, after the dinner dishes had been washed and as the remains of the iced tea stood growing tepid in the pitcher, my mother, dreamy and disheveled, finally would emerge from the kitchen. "Look at me," she'd murmur, wandering into the living room and patting her hair in the mirror over the piano. "I look like a Wild Man of Borneo."

She would change into a pair of oxfords and take a walk with me, or with a neighbor. At that time of day June bugs hurled themselves against the screens of the house, and my father, covered with mosquito repellent and smoking cigarette after cigarette, sat reading under the maple tree. In the diffuse light after sunset, the shadows around the perfectly ordinary houses up and down the street made the unambitious details of their designs — turrets, round Victorian towers, vague half-timbering — seem for once dramatic. All the backyards of the town seemed to have melted into one darkening common where packs of kids yelled faintly and fought their last battles before bedtime. Cars pulled out of driveways and headed for movie theaters or the shopping centers along the Pike, and the air smelled like honeysuckle and onion grass. When Mama and I walked together, we would wander up and down the long blocks until the streetlights came on.

One evening during the summer that I was six years old, we stopped to visit a neighboring family in which something sad and shocking had happened the previous winter. The father, a district judge named Roland Barber, had driven one gray afternoon to the marshland outside the airport and there had shot himself. Judge Barber, a short, grave, brown-skinned man with a curiously muted voice, had been a member of my father's congregation and had served with him on the board of the NAACP. His suicide, with hints of further-reaching scandal, sent a tremendous shock through the staid circles of my parents' friends, a shock that reached down even into the deep waters that normally insulated Matthew and me from adult life. For a few weeks after the suicide we held long grisly discussions on arcane, even acrobatic ways to do away with oneself.

The house in which Mrs. Barber continued to live with her teenage daughter was little different from our house, or any other in our neighborhood: a brick Colonial with myrtle and ivy planted around it instead of grass, and a long backyard that sloped down to a vegetable garden. I knew the Barbers' yard well, because there was an oak tree near the vegetable garden, with a swing in it that neighborhood kids were allowed to use. On the evening my mother and I came to visit, the daylight was fading, and the windows of the house were dark. It seemed that no one was home, but in the summers in our town, people often waited a long time in the evening before turning on lamps. It occurred to me as we walked up the driveway that the house itself seemed to be in mourning, with its melancholy row of blue spruces by the fence; I gave way, with a feeling that was almost like ecstasy, to a sudden shudder. Mama rubbed my goose-pimply arms. "We'll just stay a minute," she said.

My mother was carrying a recipe for peach cobbler. It was intended for Mrs. Barber, a bony woman who had fascinated me even before her husband's death, because she wore a very thick pair of elasticized stockings. However, after we'd knocked and waited for a while, the front door was finally opened by Phyllis, the Barbers' sixteen-year-old daughter. Mama, who had taught Phyllis, sometimes referred to her as "the fair and brainless"; I had seen her plenty of times at the swim club, pretty and somewhat fat-faced, drawing the stares of the men to her plump legs in Bermuda shorts. That night, though it was only about eight o'clock, she opened the door in a light summer bathrobe and peered out at us without turning on the porch lights.

"Hello, Mrs. Phillips. Hi, Sarah," she said in a low, hesitant voice. She came out onto the dark steps as she spoke, and let the screen door bang behind her. She explained that her mother wasn't there, and that she had been taking a shower when the bell rang; she radiated a fresh scent of soap and shampoo. When my mother asked her how she was feeling, she answered in the same hesitant tone, "All right."

I looked at her with a kind of awe. It was the first time I had seen her since I had heard the news about Judge Barber, and the first time I had ever stood right in front of anyone associated with an event that had caused such a convulsion in the adult world. In the light-colored robe, with her wet hair — which normally she wore flipped up at the ends and pulled back with a band, like other high-school girls in the neighborhood — combed back from her forehead, she had a mysterious, imposing look that I never would have suspected of her. I immediately ascribed it — as I was ascribing the ordinary shadow of the summer twilight around the doorway — to the extraordinary thing that had happened to her. Her face seemed indefinably swollen, whether with tears or temper, and she kept her top lip tightly clenched as she talked to my mother. She looked beautiful to me, like a dream or an illustration from a book, and as I stared at her, I felt intensely interested and agitated.

In a few minutes Phyllis went back inside. My mother and I, as we had done many times before, walked quietly up the Barbers' driveway and through the backyard to the swing in the oak tree. Mama stopped to pick a few tomatoes from the overloaded plants in the Barbers' vegetable garden, and I helped her, though my second tomato was a rotten one that squashed in my fingers.

It was completely dark by then. Lightning bugs flashed their cold green semaphores across the backyards of the neighborhood, and a near-tropical din of rasping, creaking, buzzing night insects had broken out in the trees around us. I walked over and sat down in the oak-tree swing, and Mama, pausing occasionally to slap at mosquitoes, gave me a few good pushes, so that I flew high out of the leaves, toward the night sky.

I couldn't see her, but I felt her hands against my back; that was enough. There are moments when the sympathy between mother and child becomes again almost what it was at the very first. At that instant I could discern in my mother, as clearly as if she had told me of it, the same almost romantic agitation that I felt. It was an excitement rooted in her fascination with grotesque anecdotes, but it went beyond that. While my mother pushed me in the swing, it seemed as if we were conducting, without words, a troubling yet oddly exhilarating dialogue about pain and loss.

In a few minutes I dragged my sneakered feet in a patch of dust to stop the swing. The light of a television had gone on inside the Barber house, and I imagined fat, pretty Phyllis Barber carefully rolling her hair on curlers, alone in front of the screen. I grabbed my mother's hand and said, "It's very sad, isn't it?"

"It certainly is," said Mama.

We took a shortcut home, and by the time we got there, it was time for me to scrub my grimy arms and legs and to go bed. Mama went immediately to the refrigerator and got out an uncooked roast of pork, which she stood contemplating as if it were the clue to something. She smelled of sage and dried mustard when she came upstairs to kiss Matthew and me goodnight.

A PERSONAL PAST

Long Distances

by Jewell Parker Rhodes

NATE COULDN'T REMEMBER the moment when it had happened, let alone why. Was it in the supermarket buying kidney beans or touring through Allegheny Park with its man-made pond when he knew just from looking at her, he would have to go to California? Knew from fixed stares, drooping mouth, her restlessness.

Knew he'd have to leave his humid and river-choked valley with its steel-mill-sooted hills to drive across Plains, Rockies and desert until sand gave way to heaving ocean. And for what? Her dreaming?

Three thousand miles. A man could get lost.

Della showed him a postcard picture book of California. Flat-topped roofs and pastel stucco. Palm trees bent by breezes. He'd be trapped by distance. Sunshine.

"We'll be pioneers," Della said.

He wondered if he'd miss shoveling snow, crushing ice while sprinkling salt? If he'd miss the ugliness of brick homes with rain slicking off slant roofs into mud-packed gutters? He'd never see the three rivers overflow.

Would he miss driving over cobblestones, getting his wheels caught by streetcar tracks the city was too cheap to dig up? Or parking on hills with the clutch in, the tires turned toward the curb?

He'd miss his mother.

For what? Della's dreaming? Or his fear she'd go with or without him? No matter.

Nate had traded in his muscle Chevy for a dreamboat Chrysler. A

300 with a red interior that wasn't as bright as the red metal outside and never would be. The skinny-ass man who sold him the car said it would get him around the world if that's where he wanted to go. He said he didn't. But Della had been sold with that line. And here he was driving on a stretch of highway about ready to cross into INDIANA WELCOME. A truck was coming out of Indiana, flicking its headlights to low. It started to rain. He turned on his windshield wipers, his high beams. Night driving was dangerous. But Della couldn't wait another day. Had to leave at midnight to make better time. Now she and the kids were sleeping.

He looked at the trip odometer: 270 miles. At least two more days and nights of driving. 800, 1,000 miles a day. No unnecessary stops. No motels. Della needed to get to Los Angeles fast, to make it big. Somehow. He'd drive until his mind warped and then maybe he'd forget his guilt. Forget his momma's unnatural quiet, forget her solemn shuffling about the house. Forget her leaning over a porch railing, watching them pack up as if she couldn't believe it. Forget her refusing to say or wave goodbye. Nate wished he had a drink. He'd promised to call his momma from Wheeling. But it'd seemed like too soon. He plain forgot to call at Dayton.

He looked in the side mirror and saw the Ford his father-in-law, Ben Williams, was driving. Ben was no comfort. For weeks, Ben told folks at the *Pier Point Bar*, "No way I'd allow my baby girl travel from Pittsburgh to L.A. alone."

"What you mean *alone*, Ben? Nate's going. He's her husband, ain't he?"

Then Ben Williams would puff his chest, suck his gut, and glare until the person nervously admitted, "Ain't right to let a woman travel alone. Not with two kids."

A dozen slicks and low-lifes had told Nate that Ben was drinking bourbon and calling him a faggot. But what was he supposed to do? Beat up on an old man? Have his wife holler? Nate gripped the steering wheel.

Since the first time he called on Della, the old man kept one-upping him. Nate remembered being seventeen, squirming on a plastic-covered sofa, his hands itching with sweat. Ben Williams, an ex-cop, had a bit of money. He had a bit of Irish too. He was a freckle-faced Negro and proud of it. Nate was just poor and black.

Ben Williams slipped in questions like artillery fire:

"Where you been, boy?"

"Home." He remembered how his plain, brown-faced momma could make a run-down house seem like the world. Make you never want to leave. He promised he'd never leave.

"Where you going, boy?"

"Uh, work, sir. I be wanting my own butcher shop." He liked the feel of a cleaver ripping away flesh from bone and the soft whishing sound of bloodied sawdust beneath his feet.

"What do you want with my girl?"

That one he couldn't answer.

Looking at Della with her head leaning up against the window and slightly cocked back, breathing through her nose in a slight snore — he still didn't know. Now she didn't look so pretty and when she was angry, she seemed less so. Maybe it was the old man that made him want her. Him with his attitude that his baby girl was so special and Nate was just another no-good hood from the streets.

Nate sighed, pressing the aching small of his back into the vinyl seat. He was twenty-eight. Still poor and black with a wife longing for the "opportunities" of California. She used to long for him.

At fifteen, Della was eager to do it anywhere. He remembered her hitching up her dress, begging him in the laundromat. Together they moaned; he had a kid. Responsibilities. Della was smart — she finished school. He dropped out to cut beef full-time. God, how his momma screamed. Wasn't a man supposed to support his family? What choice did he have?

Another pretty baby. Della was less eager to do it. She started spreading her legs again when she started talking California. When he'd admitted he was scared that if the family couldn't make it in Pittsburgh, they couldn't make it anywhere, she pressed him down upon her breasts, reminding him while he suckled that he'd promised California. He rubbed himself between her thighs until the world and regrets faded.

Momma never liked Della. "She attracts men like bugs to flypaper. Her uppity dad is a yellow fool. Her momma is just as bad." Then she would grin, smack her hips, before uttering her final condemnation. "Spoiled."

The smell and sound of stale heat passing through vents sickened Nate. He felt like rolling down the window, but the cool wind would cut right back to the children. His two daughters, Carrie and Jackie, almost smothered beneath blankets, were two squirrelly balls in the back. He wondered when his momma would see her grandkids again? No more dressing them in white and carrying them to church to sing, shout and Praise the Lord. Who would she rock and sing lullabies to? It was his fault they were leaving. Dammit, why couldn't he say "no" to Della? He should've called his momma from Dayton.

A yellow sign with a vertical ripple told him the road up ahead was curved. Nate took one hand away from the wheel. His right hand adjusting the turn of the wheel was all he really needed. He loved the feel of cars. Even this one. And as the green fluorescent speedometer showed his increase in speed, the better he felt. 70, 75, 80. Without looking in the mirror, he knew the old man would be straining his car to keep up with him. He could just about hear Ben Williams cursing. Ben needed to be with his daughter more than he needed to breathe. What do I need? Nate thought.

As the asphalt turnpike straightened itself out, Nate lowered the speed. He didn't understand his feelings, but it didn't much matter. If he understood everything, he'd still hurt. Understanding didn't ease pain.

He was eight when his momma told him matter-of-factly his dad and Sondra were gone. They were at the kitchen table eating collard greens and rice. Even at eight, he'd understood the attraction of the neighbor woman with her flowery dresses and jasmine perfume. Him and his dad both laughed and smiled at her jokes. He understood his momma was too fat, awkward, and glum around Miss Sondra. Nonetheless he'd kicked the wall and tried to hide his crying. That night he slept on his daddy's side of the bed. Curled in the crook of his mother's arms, touching her round face, he promised he'd never leave. She didn't ask him to say it. But he was eight and thought words had power. For many nights thereafter, before uncoiling his wiry body against hers, he'd whisper, "I'll be here." And when he married, it was simple enough to live in the same house, two floors up, across the hall. Della hadn't threatened to take the kids. He couldn't even use that excuse.

The car was pulling him farther away from his mother.

At the point where the skyline met the road in his vision, Nate was sure he could see her. Her breasts sagging, her eyes dim. Was there a difference between what the two of them were feeling? His mother, flat in bed, hearing the sound of no one breathing; him, maneuvering through rain, hearing the car and bodies exhaling the same heated air. Who would care for his mother? He wished he could turn on the radio. There were buttons to push rather than knobs to turn. Too much noise though. Besides, he'd probably only get country.

Nate wanted to piss and buy some coffee. A red neon sign blinked, Food, Gas, 5 miles, Terre Haute. He would call his mother and tell her he loved her. He would get change. A hundred quarters. Call her every stop from a pay phone. First, Terre Haute. Then, St. Louis. Topeka. Denver. Would she weep?

He wanted to hit something. Wanted to run the car off the road. A twist to the right, and into the embankment. Kill them all. Metal, concrete, blood. The car would pleat like an accordion. He wished he could see Ben Williams's face then. Yeah. What would Ben say seeing his daughter smashed up? Her toes meeting her elbows; her head twisted off. What would Ben do?

Nate missed the exit. A dairy truck hauling cows rumbled past. The rain was easing. He looked at his watch: 4:28 A.M. His momma was probably asleep now. He should wait till morning. After he crossed the Mississippi. Columbia, Missouri, then. He'd call her there. Veins popped up like worms along his hands. What if she refused to talk to him? He stumbled a bent Kool out of his right pocket. He lit the cigarette, dragged deep, and smoke filled his lungs like a caress. He exhaled. Smoke blanketed the dash. He stubbed the cigarette out.

"Della," he whispered plaintively. "Della."

Her eyes opened. Disoriented, she registered the night, the bold headlights whizzing by, Route 70 heading across the Wabash River and into Illinois.

She turned her head to the left and looked at Nate. "What is it?"

He grit his teeth and stared straight ahead at the road.

"Would you have gone without me?" His voice was barely a whisper. The heater's fan kicked in again.

"Yes," she said.

He felt like the time a line drive hit him in the gut. Wind went right out of him. Driving was easy. Automatic. He concentrated on feeling the murmurs of the engine.

The sky was clear. He switched off the wipers and rear window defrost. Della was sleeping.

Kansas City. Maybe he'd call his mother then. She'd be up. 10:00 A.M. Monday was laundry day. She'd be gathering clothes, stuffing them into her basket to carry them down the first flight of steps. She needn't worry anymore about shaking out sawdust, starching his collars, or lifting bloodstains from his shirts. He'd probably miss her if he called. When the phone would ring, she'd already be racketing her way down the basement steps. He'd call her that evening. After dinner. In Wichita.

Maybe Colorado Springs? Yeah. She'd have more time to adjust to him being gone. Another 1,000 miles, he'd be in Los Angeles. His family needed him. Nate pressed his foot hard on the gas. Los Angeles. He'd call his mother there and tell her he loved her nonetheless.

"Pop?" It was Jackie.

"Sssh. You'll wake your momma and sister up."

"Carrie keeps kicking me."

"In her sleep, she don't mean it."

Nate watched his daughter scowl in the mirror. She was resting her chin on top of the front seat, next to his shoulder — her fuzzy blue blanket covering her head like a nun's cloth.

"Can I help drive?"

"Come on, but be careful."

Jackie lifted her tennis shoe foot over and onto the front seat. Nate, with his right hand, grabbed her by her collar and pulled her down between him and Della. Jackie shifted herself onto his lap. He relaxed, feeling her small hands gripping his two hands on the wheel.

"Wow. I ain't never drove on the turnpike before."

"You just keep your eyes on the road so none of us don't get killed."

Jackie tightly clutched her father's hands. "Can I turn on the radio?"

"No."

"Aw, Pop."

Nate nudged her head with the side of his jaw.

Together, they watched the road. A clear, straight line to the horizon. Him looking over the arch of the wheel, Jackie right beneath it. It felt good to have company. He needed the distraction.

"Look, there's a dog, Pop. Running across the road."

Nate didn't see anything but he pumped the brakes anyway so Jackie could be satisfied they wouldn't hit the animal.

"And there. It's a raccoon. See it? Scootin' across the road."

"Nothing's there."

"It *is.*"

Nate pumped the brakes. He felt his heart lighten at his daughter's silliness. He slowed for deer, a wily old fox. Ben Williams must be thinking he's driving crazy. Nate didn't care. Jackie was the child most like himself. Carrie took after Della, feminine and sweet when she wanted something. Jackie was the one who should've been a boy.

Feeling her shoes bang his knees, her spine curling into his chest, and a stumpy braid tickling his chin, Nate felt more her father than any other time he could remember. They were alone in the car, driving to California. The sun was coming up.

"Angels are digging out the sun to wake up the world," said an awed Jackie. "Digging it right out of the earth."

"The sun doesn't come out of the earth."

"Does so," she said, fiercely whispering, staring at him through the mirror. "Right now, it's half in and half out."

"Who told you that?"

"Grandma."

Nate felt shaken. He remembered his momma telling him such things too. Telling him that stars were God's words in light. The moon, His mirror. Rainbows were the fluttering glow of angels' wings. The horizon was the blue gust of God's breath. All of a sudden his mother's presence was real.

"If Grandma said it, it must be true," Nate whispered.

Jackie tried burying her face in his shoulder. "I didn't want to leave," she said.

"I didn't want to go." Nate hugged his daughter closer, and hearing, feeling her soft shuddering sigh, he had a clear sense of what a damn fool he'd been.

"You think she'll forget me?" asked Jackie.

"Naw," he said. "Your grandma loves you."

"She wouldn't let me kiss her goodbye."

"She was just hurt."

Nate stared straight ahead at the gray roadway. He didn't want to look up and see Jackie's reflection in the overhead mirror. He didn't want to look up and see her looking at him. "There's a cat," he said, pumping the brakes, trying to stop his headlong drive. In his mind, he lost the image of a road map. He couldn't see a red-marked line named 70 winding its way to California. He saw him and his daughter marooned in a car, whispering secrets.

When the sun was halfway up in the sky, Jackie fell asleep. Her hands slipped off his hands and he could feel her fingers lightly touching the hair on his arms. "Jackie?" All the women in the car were sleeping.

In the side mirror, Nate looked yearningly at Ben Williams's car. He wished the old Ford would catch up with him. They could drive side by side past cornfields and wheat, at least until the Rockies.

Sunlight was baking him. He couldn't slip off his jacket without disturbing Jackie. He cursed under his breath. In the grease-slicked patches on the road, he saw shreds of rainbows. The sun loomed. He knew angels were moving it.

If Grandma said it, it must be true.

After Dreaming of President Johnson

by Howard Gordon

So MANY PEOPLE can easily recall that precise moment when they learned of President Kennedy's assassination. And, they can remember exactly how they reacted to the news. They have never forgotten who they were with, or what they had eaten, or even which clothes they happened to be wearing.

Until recently, I remembered none of such carefully recorded details. I was always a boy of disturbingly vague dreams, and perhaps on November 22, 1963, I restlessly fell asleep in order to forget everything I had learned.

What I did remember was that my life was much like the world of other children. School was important to us only because it presented an opportunity to mold sacred friendships. All adults were to be viewed as disciplinarians who occupied one stratum in a three-tiered system. Parents, teachers, and the police, of course, were the gatekeepers of each of these despised tiers. And fun — the sort of fun children had passion for — could not be discovered with an attitude of looking forward to becoming an adult; it had to be found in comic books, in block parties, and in imaginary adventures.

I was an only child in a lower-income family. The year of my tenth birthday, my father packed our meager belongings into his pickup and moved us to the city. The city was Rochester. We had moved there from

Benoit, a sleepy farming enclave of three hundred residents. Benoit was the kind of town where a father could send his child to the local store for a newspaper and know he'd return safely, know there was never a need to worry over city ruffians or the dangers of constant traffic. So quiet was Benoit that my father claimed he could hear moths pupating as he sat rocking on the front porch. Every summer evening, he sat there with my mother on their wicker sofa, and he would point out the endless stars among a web of constellations, all the while pretending to know their names, though never at all fooling my mother. But she went along with his dubious expertise, because both of us liked to hear him talk. His soft voice assured us he was in control, and he seemed to hum many of his words as if composing tunes we could cherish in another lifetime.

"MMM mmm you can hide out here," my father would tell us. Then he'd sigh wishfully.

And it made sense. Out there under the stars everything was so small and dark. Even our tiny farmhouse seemed hidden by the darkness. The three of us were like children playing in the tall grasses, listening and watching for something invisible or magic, yet hoping that, like us, whatever we found could just be left alone.

My father's aversion to the noise and crime of the big city created a perseverance for the harsh, western New York winters, which dropped savage snows into our valley and made the dirt roads as impenetrable as the meadows blanketed under knee-high drifts. During such storms, we risked the fifteen-mile trip into Rochester only once a month.

My mother and I bought groceries at the A&P while my father, hands on hips, patrolled the aisles for the hooligans who, he had often predicted, would swipe the food of hardworking folks right out of their grocery carts. I quickly learned to recognize these thugs, since my father had made a habit of pointing them out.

"Don't talk to him," he would warn me, as he ignored the friendly nod of a flat-nosed man. Or he might admonish me with, "Uh-um, stay away from them," directed at a horde of children in rumpled clothing who tugged at their mother's dress. They were curious but amiable children, asking me, "Who you be?" But I was aware of my father looming over us, his eyes red and cold, as though he were intoxicated by his own rage. As I became older, it was clear to me that my father hated these people because we were just like them. They, too, had very little money to spend, and only humble possessions. The only difference between us was the distance separating our homes.

What's more, my father hated these people in a way that made me fear him. I can't remember ever being afraid of anyone but my father. I now understand that he needed to keep us secure within our own isolation, yet horrified of stepping outside of it. If he could have had his way, we would have remained forever removed from their kind; but lack of income had made the need to relocate inevitable.

Once we had moved to Rochester, my father labored as an auto junkyard mechanic when he could find steady work; when he couldn't, he accepted seasonal employment on the custodial staff in one of the then still segregated cemeteries. My mother found a job as an occasional fruit-canner in an aged factory ten miles outside the city. It was she who had convinced my father we had to leave. He had held out for the quiet and simple life, but my mother was always more practical.

"Simple is what we'll be if we stay out here," she had argued.

He had thought about it for a moment, then answered her with one of his patented hums, a grumble of recognition that our lives were changing.

Much of that first year in Rochester somehow evaporated. Perhaps I simply became older and forgot, the way children tend to forget, the way they lose much of what happened early in their lives. But even now, I am always trying to remember. There are fragments. I do recollect that it was July when Sonny Liston knocked out Floyd Patterson and when the Mets, my father's favorite baseball team, finally ended their twenty-two game losing streak by beating the Los Angeles Dodgers. I remember *the* march, hundreds of thousands of people at the Lincoln Memorial.

We knew that we lived in hard times. Still, like every boy and girl my age, I was quickly schooled with the notion that each of us had an equal chance to live the American Dream. Ours was indeed a young country. The times were steeped in an ambience of limitless possibilities. The space race had yet to be won, and the new president was both a leader who promised us all a "Great Society" and a man whom every child could emulate.

Our family life became quite predictable; on Sundays we worshiped at the Church of God, and every Thursday evening I participated in the Brothers in Youth Fellowship, learning about equality under God and reinforcing that new direction in which the country seemed headed. Life at home was conducted under a simple philosophy: If you have a home, praise the Lord. If you lose your home, praise the Lord, and the next time you build one, make it His so that you will be blessed.

So we were blessed, my parents informed me. I learned to be thankful for the food on our dinner table, no matter how small the portions. Our survival in the face of poverty was an example of the divine intervention my parents often spoke about. Faithfully, we blessed each of our meals, and we chanted solemn prayers before slipping into bed. But, whenever I slept, I had a recurring dream, one that startled me awake.

Most dreams are so real that you begin to believe you are actually experiencing whatever you do in them. But this one dream was so far from real that I always knew I was asleep, or going mad, and that I had to hurry and awaken.

He was right there in front of me, telling me to come closer, and his face, rugged and lined, seemed to float so easily in a clearing of placards and effervescent smiles that I was unaware it was attached to a body. This was not just a man in front of me; it was the president of the United States — President Johnson. And he beckoned me, "Come here, little boy." I did. I let go of my father's hand and walked through the maze of bodies clad in flower-print dresses and dark three-piece suits. But this could not be real. I felt as if I were pressing my face against a television screen. I was finally standing right next to the man. He had been kissing babies. He seemed to shake everyone's hand. Such a big man. Huge hands. Balloons drifted over the crowd. Then he saw me again. My small hand was open. He looked right at me and smiled, but I hesitated. His stare seemed to say, "Well?" I felt ashamed and looked down at his rust-colored boots. Cowboy boots. Before I knew what was happening, the leader of the free world had turned around, shaken more hands, and was gone.

My father often reprimanded me for looking down and away from his gaze. I am awake now, and November 22, 1963, is clear again. A year that was gone is back. I didn't call it back. It just came on its own, as though it were a stain hidden somewhere but never really washed away. After dreaming of President Johnson, I no longer wanted to be like him — his ears were much too big, anyway.

In 1963, I am eleven, a shy and quiet child whose face can barely reach the middle of my father's chest, let alone his fierce eyes.

"A boy who can't return a stare will never be a man," he says.

I want very much to be a man. In the world in which I find myself growing up, nothing is greater or more significant. But I had hoped the metamorphosis into manhood would occur naturally and be as un-eventful as losing one's baby teeth or gaining height. Instead, it has become clear to me that the process of becoming a man is a loudly announced rite of passage to be witnessed by the entire world.

"Wilson," my father shouts, "mmm look at me when I'm talking to you, boy."

Even my name draws unwanted attention. I hate it, and long for something common, like Peter or John.

My newest friend's name is John. He and I met in gym class on the second day of the school year. We played on the same sixth-grade kick-ball team, and we wrestled for five minutes without either of us being able to pin the other. I told Johnny that Peter was really my first name, but that everyone dishonors me by calling me Wilson. Johnny has agreed to call me Pete.

I have a reason for admiring a name that is not my own. My best friend is Oliver Trinidad. He and I have been neighbors since my family moved into the city. Oliver shares everything with me, including his new comic books. But one particular comic he had shown me during the summer is called *The Amazing Spider-Man*, whose superhero is se-cretly Peter Parker, an unlikely teenage crime fighter who is as shy and unassuming as am I.

Oliver and I walk home together from school as we always do. We stand in front of my apartment building. With his foot, Oliver prods a bird that sits on the sidewalk. The bird just seems to ball itself up tightly in its feathers, as if doing so will protect it from Oliver's toe. A lover of animals and anything small, I protest.

"Leave it alone, man."

"Aw, I ain't gonna hurt it doin' this."

"I can't come over later and play," I tell Oliver. He wants me to go with him to the woods, to a place we call the Backhills. But I tell him that Johnny has invited me to his home, where he promises to show me his collection of Marvel comics. I am excited because he has every back issue of *Spider-Man* along with my own favorites: *Fantastic Four, Sub-Mariner, Dr. Doom, Thor, Captain America, Incredible Hulk, Iron-Man, Avengers* — all of the hottest and most sought-after comic adventurers. But Spider-Man has become my recent obsession. Until I met Johnny, I hadn't really paid any attention to the superhero, hadn't read a single issue about him even though the series had been out at least a year. I thought, How can a little insect be a superhero? But Johnny told me that spiders are not insects, and that Spider-Man is the best. Unlike other superheroes, his mask completely hides his face. No one can know who he really is.

"So you hangin' out with that white boy now, huh?" Oliver says.

"But you're my friend, too," I say.

"Naw I ain't," Oliver says. And he gives the bird such a hard kick that his shoe makes a *twaaack!* sound. "So there," he says, and he runs next door to his own house. He stares at me from his porch. I look away.

The bird has landed six feet away in the middle of the road. It lies on one side, unmoving. Its beak is open, and one of its wings has partially unfolded. I decide not to see whether it is dead. A strange feeling strikes me, like I've eaten too much junk food and need to throw up but can't. The vomit reaches my throat, then reverses itself, and my entire body shakes as if it's cold. My legs are no good to me. They refuse to walk even though I need to get away.

Johnny lives on Bertham Avenue, about three miles from my neighborhood. He gave me easy directions, though I feel disoriented long before I leave the Third Ward boundary. You learn to know the people and the neighborhood, because their personalities are unmistakably stamped into it. The artists use abandoned buildings and alley walls as canvasses for life-sized self-portraits and colorful graffiti. The romantics await rescue from their ghettoized existence by enduring nonstop ballads cranked from scratched 45s by the Marvelettes or the Impressions or Jackie Wilson; you know who the best dancers are because they automatically kick into the jerk or the popeye as soon as you pass by their porches, or every time a car turns the corner. There is no star-gazing or storytelling within the city confines. And all of the singers here — the confident ones, at least — congregate on street corners, harmonizing for all the world to hear, while those who lack the same bravado practice in bathrooms and alleys, hoping that the echo-chamber effect will disguise their group's off-key notes. On other corners stand members of the Fruit of Islam, soft-spoken young men with Caesar haircuts — men who dress in pin-striped gray and blue suits and plain but spotlessly polished shoes, and who are as recognizable by their radiant bow ties as they are for the sincere smiles that remain on their faces even if you do not purchase their bean pies or their *Muhammad Speaks* newspapers.

I know the hopes and talents and even the limitations of the people who occupy the neighborhood. I know their dreams and fears — know the gossip they pass among themselves.

And I know something else about these people, something they would never guess. I secretly hate them. They are loud. They shout their conversations at each other. They use imperfect English and have other conspicuous faults. Their coarse and knotty hair does not fall from their heads in wondrous dark bangs or curl into blond locks like the hair of Hollywood movie stars. Their noses have no length and are rarely pointed or hooked, they are crude and flat and nearly touch their jutted mouths, which do not have the perfectly thin lips that seem painted onto faces I admire. Nor are their clothes anything like those owned by people who appear on television or in my magazines. And these people do not own the stores my family shops in downtown or the banks from which my parents borrow money. They aren't the teachers in my school or the policemen who drive through our neighborhood, and they have as little chance of becoming bus drivers as they do of becoming secret service agents for President Kennedy.

Many of them are criminals. I read, and I am told this. They are the dark, sweating men who appear in WANTED posters, the evil men who must be apprehended for rape and murder and robbery of decent folks. I am beginning to understand my father's loathing. These are people who must be handcuffed and taken away — locked up with their own kind behind prison bars. I am told this in school, and I read about much of their crime in the newspapers.

These people make me hate myself, make me wish I had nothing in common with them. Maybe they are *bad guys*, the hooligans my father

warns me about. They may represent the reasons a world holds out
hope for real superheroes.

People stare at me as I make my way to Johnny's. It jump-starts my
imagination. Many of them stop as I approach, then watch me until I
pass. But I don't return their stares. Maybe they know I am somehow
different. Perhaps they suspect I harbor some great secret, or even
amazing powers that can never be understood. They stare at me as if I
am really wearing blue tights and red boots.

Johnny had told me that he wanted to be Spider-Man. I hadn't argued. He looks a bit like Peter Parker. Nearly a year older than me, he
is taller, lean, though not skinny, and he does wear glasses. Let him be
Spider-Man. I know we will soon become the best of friends. I don't
need Oliver Trinidad, or anyone like him. But Johnny and I will be like
brothers. Together we will fight crime and protect the innocent. We'll
swing over the rooftops, soar above obstacles, and somersault out of
danger.

Johnny's gate is unlocked, but I climb over it anyway. Nimbly, I leap
over the five steps onto the porch without losing my balance. The front
door is open. I peek through the screen at a man couched in front of a
television. His feet are propped up on a small table. The man has not
heard my soft footfalls. I start to knock, but something tells me that I
would disturb this man, that it would not be right to indicate my presence. The man has no shoulders, only a tremendously long neck that
starts at his oversized ears and takes on the shape of a tree trunk
stripped of its bark. His arms appear to grow right out of that neck. He
turns to me slowly, and his eyes frown. This time, my own stare does
not falter. His does. He turns back to the TV as he yells, "Betty."

A woman appears. She wipes her hands on an apron she is carrying
and stoops to see me more clearly. She has a poisoned sort of look, a
frosty half-smile of someone who has swallowed a bitter pill. And she,
too, stares at me for a moment. But she never touches the screen door.

"Well, what do you want?" the woman says.

"Is Johnny home?" I say.

She looks at me again and her half-smile disappears. She turns toward the direction from which she entered the room.

"Johnny," she shouts, "there's a nigger out here to see you."

The woman walks away, but I can't move. My legs feel stuck to the porch, and a rushing sound fills my ears, as if there's a train inside my head. I'm getting that queasy feeling again, the rising sickness that tickles my throat. Something is happening on the television that I can't quite make out. A black car in a procession. A woman on top of the car. And something about the president being shot. Somehow I manage to step away from the screen door. I hear Johnny, or someone, coming, but I jump off the porch and land on one knee. I don't know if I'm hurt; I just run.

And I run as if everything in front or behind me is an enemy, as if the big houses along the street have eyes instead of windows, and the lawns are traps beneath my sneakers. I run away from people and fire hydrants and from cars honking at me. I run until I reach my own street and see Oliver poking listlessly at the dead bird with a stick.

"Told you to leave that bird alone," I yell at him. I stare him down until he drops the stick.

We don't say anything for quite a while. But I'm glad to see him.

"Man, why you cryin'?" Oliver finally says.

"For nothin'," I say.

I wipe my eyes.

"You see the comics?"

"I don't need any stupid old comics," I tell him. He doesn't ask me about them again.

We stand on the corner watching cars flash by. Oliver offers me a candy cigarette. I forgot about the dead bird. It is no longer important. After a while, everything is back to normal again, and we're looking for something to do.

"Hey, wanna go to the Backhills?" Oliver says.

"Let's go," I say.

And we start running.

THE CHANGING TIMES

Neighbors

by Diane Oliver

THE BUS TURNING THE CORNER of Patterson and Talford Avenue was dull this time of evening. Of the four passengers standing in the rear, she did not recognize any of her friends. Most of the people tucked neatly in the double seats were women, maids and cooks on their way from work or secretaries who had worked late and were riding from the office building at the mill. The cotton mill was out from town, near the house where she worked. She noticed that a few men were riding too. They were obviously just working men, except for one gentleman dressed very neatly in a dark gray suit and carrying what she imagined was a push-button umbrella.

He looked to her as though he usually drove a car to work. She immediately decided that the car probably wouldn't start this morning so he had to catch the bus to and from work. She was standing in the rear of the bus, peering at the passengers, her arms barely reaching the overhead railing, trying not to wobble with every lurch. But every corner the bus turned pushed her head toward a window. And her hair was coming down too, wisps of black curls swung between her eyes. She looked at the people around her. Some of them were white, but most of them were her color. Looking at the passengers at least kept her from thinking of tomorrow. But really she would be glad when it came, then everything would be over.

She took a firmer grip on the green leather seat and wished she had on her glasses. The man with the umbrella was two people ahead of her on the other side of the bus, so she could see him between other people very clearly. She watched as he unfolded the evening news-paper, craning her neck to see what was on the front page. She stood, impatiently trying to read the headlines, when she realized he was star-ing up at her rather curiously. Biting her lips she turned her head and stared out of the window until the downtown section was in sight.

She would have to wait until she was home to see if they were in the newspaper again. Sometimes she felt that if another person snapped a picture of them she would burst out screaming. Last Mon-day reporters were already inside the pre-school clinic when she took Tommy for his last polio shot. She didn't understand how anyone could be so heartless to a child. The flashbulb went off right when the needle went in and all the picture showed was Tommy's open mouth.

The bus pulling up to the curb jerked to a stop, startling her and confusing her thoughts. Clutching in her hand the paper bag that con-tained her uniform, she pushed her way toward the door. By standing in the back of the bus, she was one of the first people to step to the ground. Outside the bus, the evening air felt humid and uncomfortable and her dress kept sticking to her. She looked up and remembered that the weatherman had forecast rain. Just their luck — why, she won-dered, would it have to rain on top of everything else?

As she walked along, the main street seemed unnaturally quiet but she decided her imagination was merely playing tricks. Besides, most of the stores had been closed since five o'clock.

She stopped to look at a reversible raincoat in Ivey's window, but although she had a full-time job now, she couldn't keep her mind on clothes. She was about to continue walking when she heard a horn blowing. Looking around, half-scared but also curious, she saw a man beckoning to her in a gray car. He was nobody she knew but since a nicely dressed woman was with him in the front seat, she walked to the car.

"You're Jim Mitchell's girl, aren't you?" he questioned. "You Ellie or the other one?"

She nodded yes, wondering who he was and how much he had been drinking.

"Now honey," he said leaning over the woman, "you don't know me but your father does and you tell him that if anything happens to that boy of his tomorrow we're ready to set things straight." He looked her straight in the eye and she promised to take home the message.

Just as the man was about to step on the gas, the woman reached out and touched her arm. "You hurry up home, honey, it's about dark out here."

Before she could find out their names, the Chevrolet had disappeared around a corner. Ellie wished someone would magically appear and tell her everything that had happened since August. Then maybe she could figure out what was real and what she had been imagining for the past couple of days.

She walked past the main shopping district up to Tanner's where Saraline was standing in the window peeling oranges. Everything in the shop was painted orange and green and Ellie couldn't help thinking that poor Saraline looked out of place. She stopped to wave to her friend who pointed the knife to her watch and then to her boyfriend standing in the rear of the shop. Ellie nodded that she understood. She knew Sara wanted her to tell her grandfather that she had to work late again. Neither one of them could figure out why he didn't like Charlie. Saraline had finished high school three years ahead of her and it was time for her to be getting married. Ellie watched as her friend stopped peeling the orange long enough to cross her fingers. She nodded again but she was afraid all the crossed fingers in the world wouldn't stop the trouble tomorrow.

She stopped at the traffic light and spoke to a shrivelled woman hunched against the side of a building. Scuffing the bottom of her sneakers on the curb she waited for the woman to open her mouth and grin as she usually did. The kids used to bait her to talk, and since she didn't have but one tooth in her whole head they called her Doughnut Puncher. But the woman was still, the way everything else had been all week.

From where Ellie stood, across the street from the Sears and Roebuck parking lot, she could see their house, all of the houses on the single street white people called Welfare Row. Those newspaper men always made her angry. All of their articles showed how rough the people were on their street. And the reporters never said her family wasn't on welfare, the papers always said the family lived on that street. She paused to look across the street at a group of kids pouncing on one rubber ball. There were always white kids around their neighborhood mixed up in the games, but playing with them was almost an unwritten rule. When everybody started going to school nobody played together any more.

She crossed at the corner ignoring the cars at the stop light and the closer she got to her street the more she realized that the newspaper was right. The houses were ugly, there were not even any trees, just patches of scraggly bushes and grasses. As she cut across the sticky asphalt pavement covered with cars she was conscious of the parking lot floodlights casting a strange glow on her street. She stared from habit at the house on the end of the block and except for the way the paint was peeling they all looked alike to her. Now at twilight the flaking gray paint had a luminous glow and as she walked down the dirt sidewalk she noticed Mr. Paul's pipe smoke added to the hazy atmosphere. Mr. Paul would be sitting in that same spot waiting until Saraline came home. Ellie slowed her pace to speak to the elderly man sitting on the porch.

"Evening, Mr. Paul," she said. Her voice sounded clear and out of place on the vacant street.

"Eh, who's that?" Mr. Paul leaned over the rail. "What you say, girl?"

"How are you?" she hollered louder. "Sara said she'd be late tonight, she has to work." She waited for the words to sink in.

His head had dropped and his eyes were facing his lap. She could see that he was disappointed. "Couldn't help it," he said finally. "Reckon they needed her again." Then as if he suddenly remembered he turned toward her.

"You people be ready down there? Still gonna let him go tomorrow?"

She looked at Mr. Paul between the missing rails on his porch, seeing how his rolled up trousers seemed to fit exactly in the vacant banister space.

"Last I heard this morning we're still letting him go," she said.

Mr. Paul had shifted his weight back to the chair. "Don't reckon they'll hurt him," he mumbled, scratching the side of his face. "Hope he don't mind being spit on though. Spitting ain't like cutting. They can spit on him and nobody'll ever know who did it," he said, ending his words with a quiet chuckle.

Ellie stood on the sidewalk grinding her heel in the dirt waiting for the old man to finish talking. She was glad somebody found something funny to laugh at. Finally he shut up.

"Goodbye, Mr. Paul," she waved. Her voice sounded loud to her own ears. But she knew the way her head ached intensified noises. She walked home faster, hoping they had some aspirin in the house and that those men would leave earlier tonight.

From the front of her house she could tell that the men were still there. The living room light shone behind the yellow shades, coming through brighter in the patched places. She thought about moving the geranium pot from the porch to catch the rain but changed her mind. She kicked a beer can under a car parked in the street and stopped to look at her reflection on the car door. The tiny flowers of her printed dress made her look as if she had a strange tropical disease. She spotted another can and kicked it out of the way of the car, thinking that one of these days some kid was going to fall and hurt himself. What she wanted to do she knew was kick the car out of the way. Both the station wagon and the Ford had been parked in front of her house all week, waiting. Everybody was just sitting around waiting.

Suddenly she laughed aloud. Reverend Davis' car was big and black and shiny just like, but no, the smile disappeared from her face, her mother didn't like for them to say things about other people's color. She looked around to see who else came, and saw Mr. Moore's old beat-up blue car. Somebody had torn away half of his NAACP sign. Sometimes she really felt sorry for the man. No matter how hard he glued on his stickers somebody always yanked them off again.

Ellie didn't recognize the third car but it had an Alabama license plate. She turned around and looked up and down the street, hating to go inside. There were no lights on their street, but in the distance she could see the bright lights of the parking lot. Slowly she did an about-face and climbed the steps.

She wondered when her mama was going to remember to get a yellow bulb for the porch. Although the lights hadn't been turned on, usually June bugs and mosquitoes swarmed all around the porch. By the time she was inside the house she always felt like they were crawling in her hair. She pulled on the screen and saw that Mama finally had made Hezekiah patch up the holes. The globs of white adhesive tape scattered over the screen door looked just like misshapen butterflies.

She listened to her father's voice and could tell by the tone that the men were discussing something important again. She rattled the door once more but nobody came.

"Will somebody please let me in?" Her voice carried through the screen to the knot of men sitting in the corner.

"The door's open," her father yelled. "Come on in."

"The door is not open," she said evenly. "You know we stopped leaving it open." She was feeling tired again and her voice had fallen an octave lower.

"Yeah, I forgot, I forgot," he mumbled walking to the door.

She watched her father almost stumble across a chair to let her in. He was shorter than the light bulb and the light seemed to beam down on him, emphasizing the wrinkles around his eyes. She could tell from the way he pushed open the screen that he hadn't had much sleep either. She'd overheard him telling Mama that the people down at the shop seemed to be piling on the work harder just because of this thing. And he couldn't do anything or say anything to his boss because they probably wanted to fire him.

"Where's Mama?" she whispered. He nodded toward the back.

"Good evening, everybody," she said looking at the three men who had not looked up since she entered the room. One of the men half stood, but his attention was geared back to something another man was saying. They were sitting on the sofa in their shirt sleeves and there was a pitcher of ice water on the window sill.

"Your mother probably needs some help," her father said. She looked past him trying to figure out who the white man was sitting on the end. His face looked familiar and she tried to remember where she had seen him before. The men were paying no attention to her. She bent to see what they were studying and saw a large sheet of white drawing paper. She could see blocks and lines and the man sitting in the middle was marking a trail with the eraser edge of the pencil.

The quiet stillness of the room was making her head ache more. She pushed her way through the red embroidered curtains that led to the kitchen.

"I'm home, Mama," she said, standing in front of the back door facing the big yellow sun Hezekiah and Tommy had painted on the wall above the iron stove. Immediately she felt a warmth permeating her skin. "Where is everybody?" she asked, sitting at the table where her mother was peeling potatoes.

"Mrs. McAllister is keeping Helen and Teenie," her mother said. "Your brother is staying over with Harry tonight." With each name she uttered, a slice of potato peeling tumbled to the newspaper on the table. "Tommy's in the bedroom reading that Uncle Wiggily book."

Ellie looked up at her mother but her eyes were straight ahead. She knew that Tommy only read the Uncle Wiggily book by himself when he was unhappy. She got up and walked to the kitchen cabinet.

"The other knives dirty?" she asked.

"No," her mother said, "look in the next drawer."

Ellie pulled open the drawer, flicking scraps of white paint with her fingernail. She reached for the knife and at the same time a pile of envelopes caught her eye.

"Any more come today?" she asked, pulling out the knife and slipping the envelopes under the dish towels.

"Yes, seven more came today," her mother accentuated each word carefully. "Your father has them with him in the other room."

"Same thing?" she asked picking up a potato and wishing she could think of some way to change the subject.

The white people had been threatening them for the past three weeks. Some of the letters were aimed at the family, but most of them were directed to Tommy himself. About once a week in the same handwriting somebody wrote that he'd better not eat lunch at school because they were going to poison him.

They had been getting those letters ever since the school board made Tommy's name public. She sliced the potato and dropped the pieces in the pan of cold water. Out of all those people he had been the only one the board had accepted for transfer to the elementary school. The other children, the members said, didn't live in the district. As she cut the eyes out of another potato she thought about the first letter they had received and how her father just set fire to it in the ashtray. But then Mr. Belk said they'd better save the rest, in case anything happened, they might need the evidence for court.

She peeped up again at her mother, "Who's that white man in there with Daddy?"

"One of Lawyer Belk's friends," she answered. "He's pastor of the church that's always on television Sunday morning. Mr. Belk seems to think that having him around will do some good." Ellie saw that her voice was shaking just like her hand as she reached for the last potato. Both of them could hear Tommy in the next room mumbling to himself. She was afraid to look at her mother.

Suddenly Ellie was aware that her mother's hands were trembling violently. "He's so little," she whispered and suddenly the knife slipped out of her hands and she was crying and breathing at the same time.

Ellie didn't know what to do but after a few seconds she cleared away the peelings and put the knives in the sink. "Why don't you lie down?" she suggested. "I'll clean up and get Tommy in bed." Without saying anything her mother rose and walked to her bedroom.

Ellie wiped off the table and draped the dishcloth over the sink. She stood back and looked at the rusting pipes powdered with a whitish film. One of these days they would have to paint the place. She tiptoed past her mother who looked as if she had fallen asleep from exhaustion.

"Tommy," she called softly, "come in and get ready for bed."

Tommy sitting in the middle of the floor did not answer. He was sitting the way she imagined he would be, crosslegged, pulling his ear lobe as he turned the ragged pages of *Uncle Wiggily at the Zoo*.

"What you doing, Tommy?" she said squatting on the floor beside him. He smiled and pointed at the picture of the ducks.

"School starts tomorrow," she said, turning a page with him. "Don't you think it's time to go to bed?"

"Oh Ellie, do I have to go now?" She looked down at the serious brown eyes and the closely cropped hair. For a minute she wondered if he questioned having to go to bed now or to school tomorrow.

"Well," she said, "aren't you about through with the book?" He shook his head. "Come on," she pulled him up, "you're a sleepy head." Still he shook his head.

"When Helen and Teenie coming home?"

"Tomorrow after you come home from school they'll be here."

She lifted him from the floor thinking how small he looked to be facing all those people tomorrow.

"Look," he said breaking away from her hand and pointing to a blue shirt and pair of cotton twill pants, "Mama got them for me to wear tomorrow."

While she ran water in the tub, she heard him crawl on top of the bed. He was quiet and she knew he was untying his sneakers.

"Put your shoes out," she called through the door, "and maybe Daddy will polish them."

"Is Daddy still in there with those men? Mama made me be quiet so I wouldn't bother them."

He padded into the bathroom with bare feet and crawled into the water. As she scrubbed him they played Ask Me A Question, their own version of Twenty Questions. She had just dried him and was about to have him step into his pajamas when he asked: "Are they gonna get me tomorrow?"

"Who's going to get you?" She looked into his eyes and began rubbing him furiously with the towel.

"I don't know," he answered. "Somebody I guess."

"Nobody's going to get you," she said, "who wants a little boy who gets bubblegum in his hair anyway — but us?" He grinned but as she hugged him she thought how much he looked like his father. They walked to the bed to say his prayers and while they were kneeling she heard the first drops of rain. By the time she covered him up and tucked the spread off the floor the rain had changed to a steady downpour.

When Tommy had gone to bed her mother got up again and began ironing clothes in the kitchen. Something, she said, to keep her thoughts busy. While her mother folded and sorted the clothes Ellie drew up a chair from the kitchen table. They sat in the kitchen for a while listening to the voices of the men in the next room. Her mother's quiet speech broke the stillness in the room.

"I'd rather," she said, making sweeping motions with the iron, "that you stayed home from work tomorrow and went with your father to take Tommy. I don't think I'll be up to those people."

Ellie nodded. "I don't mind," she said, tracing circles on the oilcloth-covered table.

"Your father's going," her mother continued. "Belk and Reverend Davis are too. I think that white man in there will probably go."

"They may not need me," Ellie answered.

"Tommy will," her mother said, folding the last dish towel and storing it in the cabinet.

"Mama, I think he's scared," the girl turned toward the woman. "He was so quiet while I was washing him."

"I know," she answered, sitting down heavily. "He's been that way all day." Her brown wavy hair glowed in the dim lighting of the kitchen. "I told him he wasn't going to school with Jakie and Bob any more but I said he was going to meet some other children just as nice."

Ellie saw that her mother was twisting her wedding band around and around on her finger.

"I've already told Mrs. Ingraham that I wouldn't be able to come out tomorrow." Ellie paused. "She didn't say very much. She didn't even say anything about his pictures in the newspaper. Mr. Ingraham said we were getting right crazy but even he didn't say anything else."

She stopped to look at the clock sitting near the sink. "It's almost time for the cruise cars to begin," she said. Her mother followed Ellie's eyes to the sink. The policemen circling their block every twenty minutes was supposed to make them feel safe, but hearing the cars come so regularly and that light flashing through the shade above her bed only made her nervous.

She stopped talking to push a wrinkle out of the shiny red cloth, dragging her finger along the table edges. "How long before those men going to leave?" she asked her mother. Just as she spoke she heard one of the men say something about getting some sleep. "I didn't mean to run them away," she said smiling. Her mother half-smiled too. They listened for the sound of motors and tires and waited for her father to shut the front door.

In a few seconds her father's head pushed through the curtain. "Want me to turn your bed now, Ellie?" She felt uncomfortable staring up at him, the whole family looked drained of all energy.

"That's all right," she answered. "I'll sleep in Helen and Teenie's bed tonight."

"How's Tommy?" he asked looking toward the bedroom. He came in and sat down at the table with them.

They were silent before he spoke. "I keep wondering if we should send him." He lit a match and watched the flame disappear into the ashtray, then he looked into his wife's eyes. "There's no telling what these fool white folks will do."

Her mother reached over and patted his hand. "We're doing what we have to do, I guess," she said. "Sometimes though I wish the others weren't so much older than him."

"But it seems so unfair," Ellie broke in, "sending him there all by himself like that. Everybody keeps asking me why the MacAdams didn't apply for their children."

"Eloise." Her father's voice sounded curt. "We aren't answering for the MacAdams, we're trying to do what's right for your brother. He's not old enough to have his own say so. You and the others could decide for yourselves, but we're the ones that have to do for him."

She didn't say anything but watched him pull a handful of envelopes out of his pocket and tuck them in the cabinet drawer. She knew that if anyone had told him in August that Tommy would be the only one going to Jefferson Davis they would not have let him go.

"Those the new ones?" she asked, "What they say?"

"Let's not talk about the letters," her father said. "Let's go to bed."

Outside they heard the rain become heavier. Since early evening she had become accustomed to the sound. Now it blended in with the rest of the noises that had accumulated in the back of her mind since the whole thing began.

As her mother folded the ironing board they heard the quiet wheels of the police car. Ellie noticed that the clock said twelve-ten and she wondered why they were early. Her mother pulled the iron cord from the switch and they stood silently waiting for the police car to turn around and pass the house again, as if the car's passing were a final blessing for the night.

Suddenly she was aware of a noise that sounded as if everything had broken loose in her head at once, a loudness that almost shook the foundation of the house. At the same time the lights went out and instinctively her father knocked them to the floor. They could hear the tinkling of glass near the front of the house and Tommy began screaming.

"Tommy, get down," her father yelled.

She hoped he would remember to roll under the bed the way they had practiced. She was aware of objects falling and breaking as she lay perfectly still. Her breath was coming in jerks and then there was a second noise, a smaller explosion but still drowning out Tommy's cries.

"Stay still," her father commanded. "I'm going to check on Tommy. They may throw another one."

She watched him crawl across the floor, pushing a broken flower vase and an iron skillet out of his way. All of the sounds, Tommy's crying, the breaking glass, everything was echoing in her ears. She felt as if they had been crouching on the floor for hours but when she heard the police car door slam, the luminous hands of the clock said only twelve-fifteen.

She heard other cars drive up and pairs of heavy feet trample on the porch. "You folks all right in there?"

She could visualize the hands pulling open the door, because she knew the voice. Sergeant Kearns had been responsible for patrolling the house during the past three weeks. She heard him click the light switch in the living room but the darkness remained intense.

Her father deposited Tommy in his wife's lap and went to what was left of the door. In the next fifteen minutes policemen were everywhere. While she rummaged around underneath the cabinet for a candle, her mother tried to hush up Tommy. His cheek was cut where he had scratched himself on the springs of his bed. Her mother motioned for her to dampen a cloth and put some petroleum jelly on it to keep him quiet. She tried to put him to bed again but he would not go, even when she promised to stay with him for the rest of the night. And so she sat in the kitchen rocking the little boy back and forth on her lap.

Ellie wandered around the kitchen but the light from the single candle put an eerie glow on the walls making her nervous. She began picking up pans, stepping over pieces of broken crockery and glass-ware. She did not want to go into the living room yet, but if she listened closely, snatches of the policemen's conversation came through the curtain.

She heard one man say that the bomb landed near the edge of the yard, that was why it had only gotten the front porch. She knew from their talk that the living room window was shattered completely. Suddenly Ellie sat down. The picture of the living room window kept flashing in her mind and a wave of feeling invaded her body making her shake as if she had lost all muscular control. She slept on the couch, right under that window.

She looked at her mother to see if she too had realized, but her mother was looking down at Tommy and trying to get him to close his eyes. Ellie stood up and crept toward the living room trying to prepare herself for what she would see. Even that minute of determination could not make her control the horror that she felt. There were jagged holes all along the front of the house and the sofa was covered with glass and paint. She started to pick up the picture that had toppled from the book shelf, then she just stepped over the broken frame.

Outside her father was talking and, curious to see who else was with him, she walked across the splinters to the yard. She could see pieces of the geranium pot and the red blossoms turned face down. There were no lights in the other houses on the street. Across from their house she could see forms standing in the door and shadows being pushed back and forth. "I guess the MacAdams are glad they just didn't get involved." No one heard her speak, and no one came over to see if they could help; she knew why and did not really blame them. They were afraid their house could be next.

Most of the policemen had gone now and only one car was left to flash the revolving red light in the rain. She heard the tall skinny man tell her father they would be parked outside for the rest of the night. As she watched the reflection of the police cars returning to the station, feeling sick on her stomach, she wondered now why they bothered.

Ellie went back inside the house and closed the curtain behind her. There was nothing anyone could do now, not even to the house. Everything was scattered all over the floor and poor Tommy still would not go to sleep. She wondered what would happen when the news spread through their section of town, and at once remembered the man in the gray Chevrolet. It would serve them right if her father's friends got one of them.

Ellie pulled up an overturned chair and sat down across from her mother who was crooning to Tommy. What Mr. Paul said was right, white people just couldn't be trusted. Her family had expected anything but even though they had practiced ducking, they didn't really expect anybody to try tearing down the house. But the funny thing was the house belonged to one of them. Maybe it was a good thing her family were just renters.

Exhausted, Ellie put her head down on the table. She didn't know what they were going to do about tomorrow, in the day time they didn't need electricity. She was too tired to think any more about Tommy, yet she could not go to sleep. So, she sat at the table trying to sit still, but every few minutes she would involuntarily twitch. She tried to steady her hands, all the time listening to her mother's sing-songy voice and waiting for her father to come back inside the house.

She didn't know how long she lay hunched against the kitchen table, but when she looked up, her wrists bore the imprints of her hair. She unfolded her arms gingerly, feeling the blood rush to her fingertips. Her father sat in the chair opposite her, staring at the vacant space between them. She heard her mother creep away from the table, taking Tommy to his room.

Ellie looked out the window. The darkness was turning to gray and the hurt feeling was disappearing. As she sat there she could begin to look at the kitchen matter-of-factly. Although the hands of the clock were just a little past five-thirty, she knew somebody was going to have to start clearing up and cook breakfast.

She stood and tipped across the kitchen to her parents' bedroom. "Mama," she whispered, standing near the door of Tommy's room. At the sound of her voice, Tommy made a funny throaty noise in his sleep. Her mother motioned for her to go out and be quiet. Ellie knew then that Tommy had just fallen asleep. She crept back to the kitchen and began picking up the dishes that could be salvaged, being careful not to go into the living room.

She walked around her father, leaving the broken glass underneath the kitchen table. "You want some coffee?" she asked.

He nodded silently, in a strange contrast she thought to the water faucet that turned with a loud gurgling noise. While she let the water run to get hot she measured out the instant coffee in one of the plastic cups. Next door she could hear people moving around in the Williams' kitchen, but they too seemed much quieter than usual.

"You reckon everybody knows by now?" she asked, stirring the coffee and putting the saucer in front of him.

"Everybody will know by the time the city paper comes out," he said. "Somebody was here last night from the *Observer*. Guess it'll make front page."

She leaned against the cabinet for support watching him trace endless circles in the brown liquid with the spoon. "Sergeant Kearns says they'll have almost the whole force out there tomorrow," he said.

"Today," she whispered.

Her father looked at the clock and then turned his head.

"When's your mother coming back in here?" he asked, finally picking up the cup and drinking the coffee.

"Tommy's just off to sleep," she answered. "I guess she'll be in here when he's asleep for good."

She looked out the window of the back door at the row of tall hedges that had separated their neighborhood from the white people for as long as she remembered. While she stood there she heard her mother walk into the room. To her ears the steps seemed much slower than usual. She heard her mother stop in front of her father's chair.

"Jim," she said, sounding very timid, "what we going to do?" Yet as Ellie turned toward her she noticed her mother's face was strangely calm as she looked down on her husband.

Ellie continued standing by the door listening to them talk. Nobody asked the question to which they all wanted an answer.

"I keep thinking," her father said finally, "that the policemen will be with him all day. They couldn't hurt him inside the school building without getting some of their own kind."

"But he'll be in there all by himself," her mother said softly. "A hundred policemen can't be a little boy's only friends."

She watched her father wrap his calloused hands, still splotched with machine oil, around the salt shaker on the table.

"I keep trying," he said to her, "to tell myself that somebody's got to be the first one and then I just think how quiet he's been all week."

Ellie listened to the quiet voices that seemed to be a room apart from her. In the back of her mind she could hear phrases of a hymn her grandmother used to sing, something about trouble, her being born for trouble.

"Jim, I cannot let my baby go." Her mother's words, although quiet, were carefully pronounced.

"Maybe," her father answered, "it's not in our hands. Reverend Davis and I were talking day before yesterday how God tested the Israelites, maybe he's just trying us."

"God expects you to take care of your own," his wife interrupted. Ellie sensed a trace of bitterness in her mother's voice.

"Tommy's not going to understand why he can't go to school," her father replied. "He's going to wonder why, and how are we going to tell him we're afraid of them?" Her father's hand clutched the coffee cup. "He's going to be fighting them the rest of his life. He's got to start sometime."

"But he's not on their level. Tommy's too little to go around hating people. One of the others, they're bigger, they understand about things."

Ellie still leaning against the door saw that the sun covered part of the sky behind the hedges and the light slipping through the kitchen window seemed to reflect the shiny red of the table cloth.

"He's our child," she heard her mother say. "Whatever we do, we're going to be the cause." Her father had pushed the cup away from him and sat with his hands covering part of his face. Outside Ellie could hear a horn blowing.

"God knows we tried but I guess there's just no use." Her father's voice forced her attention back to the two people sitting in front of her. "Maybe when things come back to normal we'll try again."

He covered his wife's chunky fingers with the palm of his hand and her mother seemed to be enveloped in silence. The three of them remained quiet, each involved in his own thoughts, but related, Ellie knew, to the same thing. She was the first to break the silence.

"Mama," she called after a long pause, "do you want me to start setting the table for breakfast?"

Her mother nodded.

Ellie turned the clock so she could see it from the sink while she washed the dishes that had been scattered over the floor.

"You going to wake up Tommy or you want me to?"

"No," her mother said, still holding her father's hand, "let him sleep. When you wash your face, you go up the street and call Hezekiah. Tell him to keep up with the children after school, I want to do something to this house before they come home."

She stopped talking and looked around the kitchen, finally turning to her husband. "He's probably kicked the spread off by now," she said. Ellie watched her father, who without saying anything walked toward the bedroom.

She watched her mother lift herself from the chair and automatically push in the stuffing underneath the cracked plastic cover. Her face looked set, as it always did when she was trying hard to keep her composure.

"He'll need something hot when he wakes up. Hand me the oatmeal," she commanded, reaching on top of the icebox for matches to light the kitchen stove.

The Witness

by Ann Petry

IT HAD BEEN SNOWING for twenty-four hours, and as soon as it stopped, the town plows began clearing the roads and sprinkling them with a mixture of sand and salt. By nightfall the main roads were what the roadmaster called clean as a whistle. But the little winding side roads and the store parking lots and the private walkways lay under a thick blanket of snow.

Because of the deep snow, Charles Woodruff parked his station wagon, brand-new, expensive, in the road in front of the Congregational church rather than risk getting stuck in the lot behind the church. He was early for the minister's class so he sat still, deliberately savoring the new-car smell of the station wagon. He found himself sniffing audibly and thought the sound rather a greedy one and so got out of the car and stood on the snow-covered walk, studying the church. A full moon lay low on the horizon. It gave a wonderful luminous quality to the snow, to the church, and to the branches of the great elms dark against the winter sky.

He ducked his head down because the wind was coming in gusts straight from the north, blowing the snow so it swirled around him, stinging his face. It was so cold that his toes felt as though they were freezing and he began to stamp his feet. Fortunately his coat insulated his body against the cold. He hadn't really planned to buy a new coat but during the Christmas vacation he had been in New York City and he had gone into one of those thickly carpeted, faintly perfumed, crystal-chandeliered stores that sell men's clothing and he had seen the coat hanging on a rack — a dark gray cashmere coat, lined with nutria and adorned by a collar of black Persian lamb. A tall, thin salesman who smelled of heather saw him looking at the coat and said: "Try it on, sir — it's toast-warm, cloud-light, guaranteed to make you feel like a prince — do try it on, here let me hold your coat, sir." The man's voice sounded as though he were purring and he kept brushing against Woodruff like a cat, and managed to sell him the coat, a narrow-brimmed felt hat, and a pair of fur-lined gloves.

If Addie had been alive and learned he had paid five hundred dollars for an overcoat, she would have argued with him fiercely, nostrils flaring, thin arched eyebrows lifted. Standing there alone in the snow, in front of the church, he permitted himself a small indulgence. He pretended Addie was standing beside him. He spoke to her, aloud: "You always said I had to dress more elegantly than my students so they would respect my clothes even if they didn't respect my learning. You said —"

He stopped abruptly, thinking he must look like a lunatic, standing in the snow, stamping his feet and talking to himself. If he kept it up long enough, someone would call the state police and a bulletin about him would go clattering out over the teletype: "Attention all cruisers, attention all cruisers, a black man, repeat, a black man is standing in front of the Congregational church in Wheeling, New York; description follows, description follows, thinnish, tallish black man, clipped moustache, expensive (extravagantly expensive, outrageously expensive, unjustifiably expensive) overcoat, felt hat like a Homburg, eyeglasses glittering in the moonlight, feet stamping in the moonlight, mouth muttering in the moonlight. Light of the moon we danced. Glimpses of the moon revisited . . ."

There was no one in sight, no cars passing. It was so still it would be easy to believe that the entire population of the town had died and lay buried under the snow and that he was the sole survivor, and that would be ironic because he did not really belong in this all-white community.

The thought of his alien presence here evoked an image of Addie — dark-skinned, intense, beautiful. He was sixty-five when she died. He had just retired as professor of English at Virginia College for Negroes. He had spent all of his working life there. He had planned to write a grammar to be used in first-year English classes, to perfect his herb

garden, catalogue his library, tidy up his files, and organize his clippings — a wealth of material in those clippings. But without Addie
these projects seemed inconsequential — like the busywork that grade
school teachers devise to keep children out of mischief. When he was
offered a job teaching in a high school in a small town in New York, he
accepted it quickly.

Everybody was integrating and so this little frozen Northern town
was integrating, too. Someone probably asked why there were no black
teachers in the school system and the school board and the Superinten-
dent of Schools said they were searching for "one" — and the search
yielded that brand-new black widower, Charles Woodruff (nigger in the
woodpile, he thought, and then, why that word, a word he despised
and never used so why did it pop up like that, does a full moon really
affect the human mind) and he was eager to escape from his old envi-
ronment and so for the past year he had taught English to academic
seniors in Wheeling High School.

No problems. No hoodlums. All of his students were being herded
toward college like so many cattle. He referred to them (mentally) as
the Willing Workers of America. He thought that what was being done
to them was a crime against nature. They were hard-working, courteous, pathetic. He introduced a new textbook, discarded a huge anthology that was filled with mutilated poetry, mutilated essays, mutilated
short stories. His students liked him and told him so. Other members of
the faculty said he was lucky but just wait until another year — the
freshmen and the sophomores were "a bunch of hoodlums" — "a
whole new ball game —"

Because of his success with his English classes, Dr. Shipley, the Congregational minister, had asked him if he would assist (Shipley used
words like "assist" instead of "help") him with a class of delinquent
boys — the class met on Sunday nights. Woodruff felt he should make
some kind of contribution to the life of this small town which had
treated him with genuine friendliness so he had said yes.

But when he first saw those seven boys assembled in the minister's
study, he knew that he could neither help nor assist the minister with
them — they were beyond his reach, beyond the minister's reach.
They sat silent, motionless, their shoulders hunched as though against
some chill they found in the air of that small book-lined room. Their
eyelids were like shutters drawn over their eyes. Their long hair cov-

ered their foreheads, obscuring their eyebrows, reaching to the collars of their jackets. Their legs, stretched out straight in front of them, were encased in pants that fit as tightly as the leotards of a ballet dancer.

He kept looking at them, studying them. Suddenly, as though at a signal, they all looked at him. This collective stare was so hostile that he felt himself stiffen and sweat broke out on his forehead. He assumed that the same thing had happened to Dr. Shipley because Shipley's eyeglasses kept fogging up, though the room was not overly warm.

Shipley had talked for an hour. He began to get hoarse. Though he paused now and then to ask a question and waited hopefully for a reply, there was none. The boys sat mute and motionless.

After they left, filing out, one behind the other, Woodruff had asked Shipley about them — who they were and why they attended this class in religion.

Shipley said, "They come here under duress. The Juvenile Court requires their attendance at this class."

"How old are they?"

"About sixteen. Very bright. Still in high school. They're all sophomores — that's why you don't know them. Rambler, the tall thin boy, the ringleader, has an IQ in the genius bracket. As a matter of fact, if they weren't so bright, they'd be in reform school. This class is part of an effort to — well — to turn them into God-fearing responsible young citizens."

"Are their families poor?"

"No, indeed. The parents of these boys are — well, they're the backbone of the great middle class in this town."

After the third meeting of the class where the same hostile silence prevailed, Woodruff said, "Dr. Shipley, do you think we are accomplishing anything?" He had said "we" though he was well aware that these new young outlaws spawned by the white middle class were, praise God, Shipley's problem — the white man's problem. This cripplingly tight shoe was usually on the black man's foot. He found it rather pleasant to have the position reversed.

Shipley ran his fingers through his hair. It was very short hair, stiff-looking, crew-cut.

"I don't know," he said frowning. "I really don't know. They don't even respond to a greeting or a direct question. It is a terribly frustrating business, an exhausting business. When the class is over, I feel as though I had spent the entire evening lying prone under the unrelieved weight of all their bodies."

Woodruff, standing outside the church, stamping his feet, jumped and then winced because he heard a sound like a gunshot. It was born on the wind so that it seemed close at hand. He stood still, listening. Then he started moving quickly toward the religious education building which housed the minister's study.

He recognized the sound — it was made by the car the boys drove. It had no muffler and the snorting, back-firing sounds made by the spent motor were like a series of gunshots. He wanted to be out of sight when the boys drove up in their rusted car. Their lithe young bodies were a shocking contrast to the abused and ancient vehicle in which they traveled. The age of the car, its dreadful condition, was like a snarled message aimed at the adult world: All we've got is the crumbs, the leftovers, whatever the fat cats don't want and can't use; the turnpikes and the throughways and the seventy-mile-an-hour speedways are filled with long, low, shiny cars built for speed, driven by bald-headed, big-bellied rat finks and we're left with the junk, the worn-out beat-up chassis, the thin tires, the brakes that don't hold, the transmission that's shot to hell. He had seen them push the car out of the parking lot behind the church. It wouldn't go in reverse.

Bent over, peering down, picking his way through the deep snow lest he stumble and fall, Woodruff tried to hurry and the explosive sound of that terrible engine kept getting closer and closer. He envisioned himself as a black beetle in a fur-collared coat silhouetted against the snow trying to scuttle out of danger. Danger: Why should he think he was in danger? Perhaps some sixth sense was trying to warn him and his beetle's antenna (did beetles have antennae, did they have five senses and some of them an additional sense, extrasensory —) picked it up — by the pricking of my thumbs, something wicked this way comes.

Once inside the building he drew a deep breath. He greeted Dr. Shipley, hung his hat and coat on the brass hat rack, and then sat down beside Shipley behind the old fumed oak desk. He braced himself for the entrance of the boys.

There was the sound of the front door opening followed by the click-clack sound of their heavy boots, in the hall. Suddenly they were all there in the minister's study. They brought cold air in with them. They sat down with their jackets on — great quilted dark jackets that had been designed for European ski slopes. At the first meeting of the class, Dr. Shipley had suggested they remove their jackets and they simply sat and stared at him until he fidgeted and looked away obviously embarrassed. He never again made a suggestion that was direct and personal.

Woodruff glanced at the boys and then directed his gaze away from them, thinking, if a bit of gilt braid and a touch of velvet were added to their clothing, they could pass for the seven dark bastard sons of some old and evil twelfth-century king. Of course they weren't all dark. Three of them were blond, two had brown hair, one had red hair, only one had black hair. All of them were white. But there was about them an aura of something so evil, so dark, so suggestive of the far reaches of the night, of the black horror of nightmares, that he shivered deep inside himself whenever he saw them. Though he thought of them as being black, this was not the blackness of human flesh, warm, soft to the touch, it was the blackness and the coldness of the hole from which D. H. Lawrence's snake emerged.

The hour was almost up when to Woodward's surprise, Rambler, the tall boy, the one who drove the ramshackle car, the one Shipley said was the leader of the group, began asking questions about cannibalism. His voice was husky, low in pitch, and he almost whispered when he spoke. Woodruff found himself leaning forward in an effort to hear what the boy was saying. Dr. Shipley leaned forward, too.

Rambler said, "Is it a crime to eat human flesh?"

Dr. Shipley said, surprised, "Yes. It's cannibalism. It is a sin and it is also a crime." He spoke slowly, gently, as though he were wooing a timid, wild animal that had ventured out of the woods and would turn tail and scamper back if he spoke in his normal voice.

"Well, if the cats who go for this human flesh bit don't think it's a sin and if they eat it because they haven't any other food, it isn't a sin for them, is it?" The boy spoke quickly, not pausing for breath, running his words together.

"There are many practices and acts that are acceptable to non-Christians which are sinful. Christians condemn such acts no matter what the circumstances."

Woodruff thought uncomfortably, why does Shipley have to sound so pompous, so righteous, so from-off-the-top-of-Olympus? The boys were all staring at him, bright-eyed, mouths slightly open, long hair obscuring their foreheads. Then Rambler said, in his husky whispering voice, "What about you, Doc?"

Dr. Shipley said, "Me?" and repeated it, his voice losing its coaxing tone, rising in pitch, increasing in volume. "Me?" What do you mean?"

"Well, man, you're eatin' human flesh, ain't you?"

Woodruff had no idea what the boy was talking about. But Dr. Shipley was looking down at his own hands with a curious self-conscious expression and Woodruff saw that Shipley's nails were bitten all the way down to the quick.

The boy said, "It's self-cannibalism, ain't it, Doc?"

Shipley put his hands on the desk, braced himself, preparatory to standing up. His thin, bony face had reddened. Before he could move, or speak, the boys stood up and began to file out of the room. Rambler leaned over and ran his hand through the minister's short-cut, bristly hair and said, "Don't sweat it, Doc."

Woodruff usually stayed a half-hour or more after the class ended. Dr. Shipley liked to talk and Woodruff listened to him patiently, though he thought Shipley had a second-rate mind and rambled when he talked. But Shipley sat with his head bowed, a pose not conducive to conversation and Woodruff left almost immediately after the boys, carrying in his mind's eye a picture of all those straight, narrow backs with the pants so tight they were like elastic bandages on their thighs, and the oversized bulky jackets and the long, frowsy hair. He thought they looked like paper dolls, cut all at once, exactly alike with a few swift slashes of scissors wielded by a skilled hand. Addie could do that — take paper and fold it and go snip, snip, snip with the scissors and she'd have a string of paper dolls, all fat, or all thin, or all bent, or all wearing top hats, or all bearded Santas or all Cheshire cats. She had taught arts and crafts in the teacher-training courses for elementary-school teachers at Virginia College and so was skilled in the use of crayon and scissors.

He walked toward his car, head down, picking his way through the snow and then he stopped, surprised. The boys were standing in the road. They had surrounded a girl. He didn't think she was a high school girl though she was young. She had long blond hair that spilled over the quilted black jacket she was wearing. At first he couldn't tell what the boys were doing but as he got closer to them, he saw that they were moving toward their ancient car and forcing the girl to move with them though she was resisting. They were talking to each other and to her, their voices companionable, half-playful.

"So we all got one in the oven."

"So it's all right if it's all of us."

The girl said, "No."

"Aw, come on, Nellie, hurry up."

"It's colder'n hell, Nellie. Move!"

They kept pushing her toward the car and she turned on them and said, "Quit it."

"Aw, get in."

One of them gave her a hard shove, sent her closer to the car and she screamed and Rambler clapped his hand over her mouth and she must have bitten his hand because he snatched it away and then she screamed again because he slapped her and then two of them picked her up and threw her on the front seat and one of them stayed there, holding her.

Woodruff thought, There are seven of them, young, strong, satanic. He ought to go home where it was quiet and safe, mind his own business — black man's business; leave this white man's problem for a white man, leave it alone, not his, don't interfere, go home to the bungalow he rented — ridiculous type of architecture in this cold climate, developed for India, a hot climate, and that open porch business —

He said, "What are you doing?" He spoke with the voice of authority, the male schoolteacher's voice and thought, Wait, slow down, cool it, you're a black man speaking with a white man's voice.

They turned and stared at him; as they turned, they all assumed what he called the stance of the new young outlaw: the shoulders hunched, the hands in the pockets. In the moonlight he thought they looked as though they belonged in a frieze around a building — the hunched-shoulder posture repeated again and again, made permanent in stone. Classic.

"What are you doing?" he said again, voice louder, deeper.

"We're standin' here."

"You can see us, can't you?"

"Why did you force that girl into your car?"

"You're dreamin'."

"I saw what happened. And that boy is holding her in there."

"You been readin' too much."

They kept moving in, closing in on him. Even on this cold, windy night he could smell them and he loathed the smell — cigarettes, clothes washed in detergents and not rinsed enough and dried in automatic driers. They all smelled like that these days, even those pathetic college-bound drudges, the Willing Workers of America, stank so that he was always airing out his classroom. He rarely ever encountered the fresh clean smell of clothes that had been washed in soap and water, rinsed in boiling water, dried in the sun — a smell that he associated with new-mown hay and flower gardens and — Addie.

There was a subtle change in the tone of the voice of the next speaker. It was more contemptuous and louder.

"What girl, ho-daddy, what girl?"

One of them suddenly reached out and knocked his hat off his head, another one snatched his glasses off and threw them in the road and there was the tinkling sound of glass shattering. It made him shudder. He was half-blind without his glasses, peering about, uncertain of the shape of objects — like the woman in the Thurber cartoon, oh, yes, of course, three balloons and an H or three cats and a dog — only it was one of those scrambled alphabet charts.

They unbuttoned his overcoat, went through the pockets of his pants, of his jacket. One of them took his wallet, another took his car keys, picked up his hat, and then was actually behind the wheel of his station wagon and was moving off in it.

He shouted, "My car. Damn you, you're stealing my car —" his brand-new station wagon; he kept it immaculate, swept it out every morning, washed the windows. He tried to break out of that confining circle of boys and they simply pushed him back toward their car.

"Don't sweat it, man. You goin' ride with us and this little chick-chick."

"You goin' be our pro-tec-shun, ho-daddy. You goin' be our protec-shun."

They took his coat off and put it around him backward without putting his arms in the sleeves and then buttoned it up. The expensive coat was just like a straitjacket — it pinioned his arms to his sides. He tried to work his way out of it by flexing his muscles, hoping that the buttons would pop off or a seam would give, and thought, enraged,

They must have stitched the goddamn coat to last for a thousand years and put the goddamn buttons on the same way. The fur collar pressed against his throat, choking him.

Woodruff was forced into the back seat, two boys on each side of him. They were sitting half on him and half on each other. The one holding his wallet examined its contents. He whistled. "Hey!" he said, "Ho-daddy's got one hundred and forty-four bucks. We got us a rich ho-daddy —"

Rambler held out his hand and the boy handed the money over without a protest, not even a sigh. Then Rambler got into the front seat behind the wheel. The girl was quiet only because the boy beside her had his hand around her throat and from the way he was holding his arm, Woodruff knew he was exerting a certain amount of pressure.

"Give the man a hat," Rambler said.

One of the boys felt around until he found a cap. They were so close to each other that each of his movements slightly disrupted their seating arrangement. When the boy shifted his weight, the rest of them were forced to shift theirs.

"Here you go," the boy said. He pulled a black wool cap down on Woodruff's head, over his eyes, over his nose.

He couldn't see anything. He couldn't breath through his nose. He had to breath through his mouth or suffocate. The freezing cold air actually hurt the inside of his mouth. The overcoat immobilized him and the steady pressure of the fur collar against his windpipe was beginning to interfere with his normal rate of breathing. He knew that his whole circulatory system would gradually begin to slow down. He frowned, thinking what a simple and easily executed method of rendering a person helpless — just an overcoat and a knit cap. Then he thought, alarmed, If they should leave me out in the woods like this, I would be dead by morning. What do they want of me anyway?

He cleared his throat preparatory to questioning them but Rambler started the car and he could not make himself heard above the sound of the engine. He thought the noise would shatter his eardrums and he wondered how these boys could bear it — the terrible cannon fire sound of the engine and the rattling of the doors and the windows. Then they were off and it was like riding in a jeep — only worse because the seat was broken and they were jounced up out of the seat and then back down into a hollowed-out place, all of them on top of each other. He tried to keep track of the turns the car made but he couldn't, there were too many of them. He assumed that whenever they stopped it was because of a traffic light or a stop sign.

It seemed to him they had ridden for miles and miles when the car began to jounce up and down more violently than ever and he decided they had turned onto a rough, rutted road. Suddenly they stopped. The car doors were opened and the boys pushed him out of the car. He couldn't keep his balance and he stumbled and fell flat on his face in the snow and they all laughed. They had to haul him to his feet for his movements were so constricted by the overcoat that he couldn't get up without help.

The cap had worked up a little so that he could breathe more freely and he could see anything that was in his immediate vicinity. Either they did not notice that the cap had been pushed out of place or they didn't care. As they guided him along he saw that they were in a cemetery that was filled with very old tombstones. They were approaching a small building and his station wagon was parked to one side. The boy who had driven it opened the door of the building and Woodruff saw that it was lighted inside by a big bulb that dangled from the ceiling. There were shovels and rakes inside and a grease-encrusted riding mower, bags of grass seed, and a bundle of material that looked like the artificial grass used around new graves.

Rambler said, "Put the witness here."

They stood him against the back wall, facing the wall.

"He's here and yet he ain't here."

"Ho-daddy's here — and yet — he ain't here."

"He's our witness."

And then Rambler's voice again, "If he moves, ice him with a shovel."

The girl screamed and then the sound was muffled, only a kind of far-off moaning and sound coming through something. They must have gagged her. All the sounds were muffled — it was like trying to see something in a fog or hear something when other sounds overlay the one thing you're listening for. What had they brought him here for? They would go away and leave him with the girl but the girl would know that he hadn't —

How would she know? They had probably blindfolded her, too. What where they doing? He could see shadows on the wall. Sometimes they moved, sometimes they were still, and then the shadows moved again and then there would be laughter. Silence after that and then thuds, thumps, silence again. Terrible sounds behind him. He started to turn around and someone poked him in the back, sharply, with the handle of a shovel or a rake. He began to sweat despite the terrible cold.

He tried to relax by breathing deeply and he began to feel as though he were going to faint. His hands and feet were numb. His head ached. He had strained so to hear what was going on behind him that he was afraid he had impaired his own hearing.

When Rambler said, "Come on, ho-daddy, it's your turn," he was beginning to lose all feeling in his arms and legs.

Someone unbuttoned his coat, plucked the cap off his head. He let his breath out in a long drawn-out sigh. He doubted that he could have survived much longer with that pressure on his throat. The boys looked at him curiously. They threw his coat on the hard-packed dirt floor and tossed the cap on top of it. He thought that the black knit cap they'd used, like a sailor's watch cap, was as effective a blindfold as could be found — providing, of course, the person couldn't use his hands to remove it.

The girl was lying on the floor, half-naked. They had put some burlap bags under her. She looked as though she were dead.

They pushed him toward her saying, "It's your turn."

He balked, refusing to move.

"You don't want none?"

They laughed. "Ho-daddy don't want none."

They pushed him closer to the girl and someone grabbed one of his hands and placed it on the girl's thigh, on her breasts, and then they laughed again. They handed him his coat, pulled the cap down on his head.

"Let's go, ho-daddy. Let's go."

Before he could put his coat back on they hustled him outdoors. One of them threw his empty wallet at him and another aimed his car keys straight at his head. The metal stung as it hit his cheek. Before he could catch them the keys disappeared in the snow. The boys went back inside the building and emerged carrying the girl, half-naked, head hanging down limply the way the head of a corpse would dangle.

"The girl —" Woodruff said.

"You're our witness, ho-daddy. You're our big fat witness."

They propped the girl up in the back seat of their car. "You're the only witness we got," they repeated it, laughing. "Take good care of yourself."

"She'll freeze to death like that," he protested.

"Not Nellie."

"She likes it."

"Come on, man, let's go, let's go, let's go," Rambler said impatiently.

Woodruff's arms and hands were so numb that he had trouble getting his coat on. He had to take his gloves off and poke around in the snow with his bare hands before he could retrieve his wallet and the car keys. The pain in his hands was as sharp and intense as if they had been burned.

Getting into his car he began to shake with fury. Once he got out of this wretched cemetery he would call the state police. Young animals. He had called them outlaws; they weren't outlaws, they were animals. In his haste he dropped the keys and had to feel around on the floor of the car for them.

When he finally got the car started he was shivering and shaking and his stomach was quivering so that he didn't dare try to drive. He turned on the heater and watched the tiny taillight on Rambler's car disappear — an old car and the taillight was like the end of a pencil glowing red in the dark. The loud explosive sound of the engine gradually receded. When he could no longer hear it, he flicked on the light in his car and looked at his watch. It was quarter past three. Wouldn't the parents of those godforsaken boys wonder where they were at that hour? Perhaps they didn't care — perhaps they were afraid of them — just as he was.

Though he wanted to get home as quickly as possible, so he could get warm, so he could think, he had to drive slowly, peering out at the narrow rutted road because he was half blind without his glasses. When he reached the cemetery gates he stopped, not knowing whether to turn right or left for he had no idea where he was. He took a chance and turned right and followed the macadam road, still going slowly, saw a church on a hill and recognized it as the Congregational church in Brooksville, the next town, and knew he was about five miles from home.

By the time he reached his own driveway, sweat was pouring from his body just like water coming out of a showerhead — even his eyelashes were wet; it ran down his ears, dripped off his nose, his lips, even the palms of his hands.

In the house he turned on the lights, in the living room, in the hall, in his bedroom. He went to his desk, opened a drawer and fished out an old pair of glasses. He had had them for years. They looked rather like Peter Cooper's glasses — he'd seen them once in the Cooper Union Museum in New York — small-lensed, with narrow, silvery-looking frames. They evoked an image of a careful scholarly man. When he had started wearing glasses, he had selected frames like Peter Cooper's. Addie had made him stop wearing them. She said they gave him the look of another era, made it easy for his students to caricature him — the tall, slender figure, slightly stooped, the steel-rimmed glasses. She said that his dark, gentle eyes looked as though they were trapped behind those little glasses.

Having put on the glasses, he went to the telephone and stood with one hand resting on it, sweating again, trembling again. He turned away, took off his overcoat and hung it on a hanger and placed it in the hall closet.

He began to pace up and down the living room — a pleasant spacious room, simply furnished. It had a southern exposure and there were big windows on that side of the room. The windows faced a meadow. The thought crossed his mind, lightly, like the silken delicate strand of a cobweb, that he would have to leave here and he brushed it away — not quite away, a trace remained.

He wasn't going to call the police. Chicken. That was the word his students used. Fink was another one. He was going to chicken out. He was going to fink out.

Why wasn't he going to call the police? Well, what would he tell them? That he'd been robbed? Well, that was true. That he'd been kidnapped? Well, that was true, too, but it seemed like a harsh way of putting it. He'd have to think about that one. That he'd been witness to a rape? He wasn't even certain that they had raped the girl. No? Who was he trying to kid? Himself? Himself.

So why wasn't he going to the police? He hadn't touched the girl. But those horrible little hoods, toads rather, why toads, toe of frog ingredient of witches' brew, poisonous substance in the skin — bufotenine, a hallucinogen found in the skin of the frog, of the toad. Those horrible toadlike hoods would say he had touched her. Well, he had.

Hadn't he? They had made sure of that. Would the police believe him? The school board? The PTA? "Where there's smoke there must be fire." "I'm not going to let my daughter stay in his class."

He started shivering again and made himself a cup of tea and sat down on the window seat in the living room to drink it and then got up and turned off the lights and looked out at the snow. The moonlight was so bright that he could see wisps of tall grass in the meadow — yellow against the snow. Immediately he thought of the long blond hair of that starvation-thin young girl. Bleached hair? Perhaps. It didn't lessen the outrage. She was dressed just like the boys — big quilted jacket, skin-tight pants, even her hair worn like theirs, obscuring the forehead, the sides of the face.

There was a sudden movement outside the window and he frowned and leaned forward, wondering what was moving about at this hour. He saw a pair of rabbits, leaping, running, literally playing games with each other. He had never before seen such free joyous movement, not even children at play exhibited it. There was always something unrelaxed about the eyes of children, about the way they held their mouths, wrinkled their foreheads — they looked as though they had been cornered and were impelled to defend themselves or that they were impelled to pursue some object that forever eluded them.

Watching this joyous heel-kicking play of the rabbits, he found himself thinking, I cannot continue to live in the same small town with that girl and those seven boys. The boys knew, before he did, that he wasn't going to report this — this incident — these crimes. They were bright enough to know that he would quickly realize how neatly they had boxed him in and thus would keep quiet. If he dared enter a complaint against them they would accuse him of raping the girl, would say they found him in the cemetery with her. Whose story would be believed? "Where there's smoke there's fire."

Right after that he started packing. He put his clothes into a foot locker. He stacked his books on the floor of the station wagon. He was surprised to find among the books a medical textbook that had belonged to John — Addie's brother.

He sat down and read all the material on angina pectoris. At eight o'clock he called the school and said he wasn't feeling well (which was true) and that he would not be in. Then he called the office of the local doctor and made an appointment for that afternoon.

When he talked to the doctor he described the violent pain in his chest that went from the shoulder down to his finger tips on the left side, causing a squeezing, crushing sensation that left him feeling faint, dizzy.

The doctor, a fat man in an old tweed jacket and a limp white shirt, said after he examined him, "Angina. You'll have to take three or four months off until we can get this thing under control."

"I will resign immediately."

"Oh, no. That isn't necessary. Besides I've been told you're the best English teacher we've ever had. It would be a great pity to lose you."

"No," Woodruff said, "it is better to resign." Come back here and look at that violated little girl? Come back here? Ever?

He scarcely listened to the detailed instructions he was to follow, did not even glance at the three prescriptions he was handed, for he was eager to be on his way. He composed a letter of resignation in his mind. When he went back to the bungalow he wrote it quickly and then put it on the front seat of the station wagon to be mailed en route.

Then he went back into the house and stayed there just long enough to call his landlord. He said he'd had a heart attack and was going back to Virginia to convalesce, that he had turned the thermostat down to sixty-five and he would return the house keys by mail. The landlord said, My goodness, you just paid a month in advance, I'll mail you a refund, what's your new address, so sorry, ideal tenant.

Woodruff hung up the receiver and said, "Peace be with you, brother —" There was already an echo in the room though it wasn't empty — all he'd removed were his books and his clothes.

He put on his elegant overcoat. When he got back to Virginia, he would give the coat away, his pleasure in it destroyed now for he would always remember the horrid feel of the collar tight across his throat, even the feel of the fabric under his finger tips would evoke an image of the cemetery, the tool shed, and the girl.

He drove down the road rather slowly. There were curves in the road and he couldn't go fast, besides he liked to look at this landscape. It was high rolling land. Snow lay over it — blue-white where there were shadows cast by the birch trees and the hemlocks, yellow-white and sparkling in the great meadow where he had watched the heel-kicking freedom of the rabbits at play.

At the entrance to the highway he brought the car to a halt. As he sat there waiting for an opportunity to get into the stream of traffic, he heard close at hand the loud explosive sound of an engine — a familiar sound. He was so alarmed that he momentarily experienced all the symptoms of a heart attack, the sudden terrible inability to breathe and the feeling that something was squeezing his chest, kneading it so that pain ran through him as though it were following the course of his circulatory system.

He knew from the sound that the car turning off the highway, entering the same road that he was now leaving, was Rambler's car. In the sunlight, silhouetted against the snow, it looked like a junkyard on wheels, fenders dented, sides dented, chassis rusted. All the boys were in the car. Rambler was driving. The thin blond girl was in the front seat — a terrible bruise under one eye. For a fraction of a second Woodruff looked straight into Rambler's eyes, just visible under the long, untidy hair. The expression was cold, impersonal, analytical.

After he got on the highway, he kept looking in the rearview mirror. There was no sign of pursuit. Evidently Rambler had not noticed that the car was loaded for flight — books and cartons on the seats, foot locker on the floor, all this was out of his range of vision. He wondered what they were doing. Wrecking the interior of the bungalow? No. They were probably waiting for him to return so they could blackmail him. Blackmail a black male.

On the turnpike he kept going faster and faster — eighty-five miles an hour, ninety, ninety-five, one hundred. He felt exhilarated by this tremendous speed. It was clearing his mind, heartening him, taking him out of himself.

He began to rationalize about what had happened. He decided that Rambler and his friends didn't give a damn that he, Woodruff, was a black man. They couldn't care less. They were very bright boys, bright enough to recognize him for what he was: a black man in his sixties, conditioned all his life by the knowledge that "White woman taboo for you" (as one of his African students used to say). The moment he attempted to intervene there in front of the church, they decided to take him with them. They knew he wasn't going to the police about any matter which involved sex and a white girl, especially where there was the certainty that all seven of them would accuse him of having relations with the girl. They had used his presence in that tool shed to give an extra exquisite fillip to their dreadful game.

He turned on the radio and waited impatiently for music, any kind of music, thinking it would distract him. He got one of those stations that play what he called thump-and-blare music. A husky-voiced woman was shouting a song — not singing, shouting:

> *I'm gonna turn on the big beat*
> *I'm gonna turn up the high heat*
> *For my ho-daddy, ho-daddy,*
> *For my ho-daddy, ho-daddy.*

He flipped the switch, cutting off the sound and he gradually diminished the speed of the car, slowing, slowing, slowing. "We got us a rich ho-daddy." That's what one of the boys had said there in front of the church when he plucked the money out of Woodruff's wallet. A rich ho-daddy? A black ho-daddy. A witness. Another poor scared black bastard who was a witness.

THE CHANGING TIMES

Steady Going Up

by Maya Angelou

THE MORNING'S RAIN had left the highway wet, but the big tires grabbed the pavement and almost in the same instant kissed it a noisy farewell. What with the licking, kissing sound and the moan of the heavy motor, Robert was coaxed to sleep. It was just that the space between his seat and the one in front of him wasn't enough to get comfortable in. He turned sideways and made a four-legged z of his body. That was even worse. There was no earthly reason for him to choose this seat except that from habit he had gone to the back of the bus. He opened his eyes and looked to see how full the front of the bus was. He knew they had made one stop. He hadn't been in a deep sleep, just dead-tired dozing, and hadn't bothered to look before. His glance skidded over the same Negro that had been sitting across the aisle when he got on in Memphis and on to the front. Everything looked about the same, except that the two white men's heads seemed closer to him than they had been earlier. Robert decided he was going to move up front, where at least he could stretch out his legs.

When he stood up the woman across the aisle said, "So you got your sleep out, huh?"

"Not yet, but I'm going to get me a better seat . . ."

She said, "Here, sit down with me for a little while. You a tall one, ain't you? How far you going?" She removed what he knew was a box lunch and put it on the floor under her seat, but she kept the Bible on her lap.

Robert said, "Well, just for a minute." He folded himself down beside her. "I'm going to Cincinnati. But I work nights, so I ain't been to bed and I mean I'm beat." He didn't want to sound like he wasn't anxious about sleeping or the old lady's company, but truth to tell, he wouldn't make no kind of company, the shape he was in. But he had to be polite.

He asked, "How far you going?"

She said, "To Cleveland." She patted the Bible with big mannish hands. "If life last and death pass and the good Lord says the same."

Robert thought, that's just like our people. She got the ticket and she's on the bus, but is scared to be hopeful in case something might happen. Like the bus run off the road or we get hit by a tornado. "Well, I guess we'll make it, seems like He's willing." Robert started edging toward the end of the seat. Five more minutes and he'd begin to nod, and the next thing he knew he'd be asleep and probably on this woman's shoulder.

"Son! Why don't you go back to your seat?"

He looked directly at her and saw her caring about him.

"While you was asleep, them two white men was talking about you. They turned around and looked at you and said something, then they moved to the last seat in the White section. They been drinking."

Robert said, "I don't know them, and, Miss, I ain't running from nobody. I mean, ain't nobody out looking for me. But . . ."

The woman said, "I didn't say you was running, I'm just telling you that they trash and when trash git trash inside them, what you think that add up to?"

There wasn't nothing Robert could say to that; he realized that the woman was trying to look after him. "Yes, ma'am. Thank you. I'll go on back to my seat."

She asked him how old he was, and when he told her "Twenty-two," she said, "You ain't nothing but a baby, and my own skin too. You know it's a pore chopper cain't hoe his own row."

That's the same way all the old ladies were in the Gordon section of Memphis. Looking out for the younger people. They had helped him to raise Baby Sister and himself too.

He eased himself up. "I'm so sleepy, you excuse me, I'll go on back now." Then he stretched himself out of the seat and without standing up straight drifted down into his own chair across the aisle. He glared up front. Now don't that beat all. White folks was really something. Over the rim of the seat in front, he tried to find some familiar trace in the heads and necks of the two white men. But they were completely strange to Robert. Then the one on the outside got up and leaned into the overhead rack. He pulled down a little blue plastic shaving kit, and in front of God and everybody pulled out a pint of bourbon. He pushed the kit back into the rack and, beginning to sit back down, caught a glimpse of Robert. He said something to his companion, and his head swiveled round and he looked at Robert too. Now Robert was sure after seeing the men's faces that he didn't know them from Adam's off ox. They probably got him mistaken for somebody they knew, or something like that. He turned to look out the window. Wasn't no use thinking anything else. No reason to think about any other reason. He had enough trouble going on right now, what with Baby Sister and all. The bus was really traveling now. They had moved out of the rain belt, yet only the telephone poles were clear in the rushing twilight, and the lights in a few lonely-looking farmhouses. This was the blue-grass state Robert had heard about, but he had never traveled across the Tennessee border before. Maybe on the way back, after he had picked up Baby Sister, they'd come in the daytime and get to see some of the tobacco fields and the blue grass. It might be something to get her to look forward to.

Baby Sister didn't have nobody but him. He scrunched down in his seat, his whole right side had gone to sleep. Of course he didn't have nobody but Baby Sister since their parents died — died within six months of each other. He was three years older than she when, at fifteen, he took over as head of the family. He got that job with Mr. Willie in the auto-mechanic shop. That was funny. He almost laughed to think that anybody could be as dumb as he had been. He didn't know a camshaft from a carburetor when he went there. But Dippermouth (it took him three months to be able to call that man Dippermouth — seemed so insulting) told him, "Aw, man, everybody got to start sometime." And little by little he picked up the understanding of how motors work. And now he was getting on to be a head mechanic. And he took care of Baby Sister. Like a father. Sent her to school and bought her clothes, and even passed on the boys she could take company with. The bus must of hit a pothole. It shook and Robert slid, putting his head against the cold window. Outside, the whole world was like the moon and stars had been switched off. It was dark inside too, but the blue lights on the dashboard, way up front, reminded him of the Bijou Theatre, where Baby Sister went every Saturday, come rain or shine. He didn't mind her going. It was a nice outing for her, long as she didn't use the balcony seats for a courting bench.

Baby Sister looked just like Mama except that she was littler and she was easier to talk to. There was the time she drank some sloe gin. Till he saw the bottle he thought it was spelled "slow gin" and that it worked slow. She had been to a reception party after a wedding and came home, after he had got off from work, high. That's the truth, she was almost wobbling and her big eyes were shining. Her clothes were neat okay, but something about the way she come up on the porch made her look as if something was hanging out. Like an underslip showing. He asked her had she been drinking and she said she had some mint drink that was like syrup but they put Seven-Up in it and it was good. He told her that that was sloe gin and that any boy that gave it to her must of wanted to take advantage of her and she better not see whoever it was again. She had said no and that it was Billy Sheppard and he was real nice and that she liked him and that after all Robert wasn't her daddy and that he wasn't more than three year and two months older than her. Then she went to bed, flouncing off.

Robert didn't sleep much that night; he lay awake wondering how he was going to be able to do what Daddy asked him to do: "Put Baby Sister under your wing and don't let nothing happen to her." If she got a stiff neck, he wasn't going to be able to do nothing with her.

Then the next morning, when he got up, he smelled biscuits. On a school day, it must have meant that she had got up at daybreak to make a fire in the woodstove so that the oven would get hot enough to bake beaten biscuits. Mixed with the aroma of baking bread was the home-cured ham. Robert went out the side door of the house Daddy left for the two of them and washed up in the spring morning by the well. When he came back into the kitchen, Baby Sister was singing, some old hymn . . . and humming; then she stopped.

"Don't look at me, Daddy, cause I got something to say." She was leaning over the worktable that he had made for Mama when he was ten. "Last night I acted like a fool. I know I sassed you, and all I can think is that the stuff I was drinking took my good sense and threw it out the window. I'm sorry and I'm grateful to you for everything. I mean, I'm glad to be your baby sister and I promise you that won't happen again. And if you don't want me to take company with Billy

Sheppard, okay, then I won't even let him come up on the porch again."

That's what made it so easy to do things for her. "Now, Buddy, if you forgive me, let's don't talk about it anymore, and when I turn around let's act just like this is any other day. Okay?"

He said softly, "Okay, Baby Sister." Then she bent down and took a pan of biscuits out of the oven and brought them to the table, smiling.

"Morning, Buddy. I thought maybe we'd have a surprise this morning. Even pulled down some tomato preserves."

Over breakfast, he asked her what she planned to do next Sunday after church. When she said she hadn't planned anything, he said with just a little joke in his voice, "Why don't you make some nice caramel cake and punch, and maybe we could ask Barbara Kendrick over here and that nice boy Billy Sheppard." She looked at him for just a moment to see if he was kidding and what kind of kidding he was doing; then they started to laugh, and laughed while she cleaned up the dishes, and even down the street until they had to separate they were still laughing.

What he had liked best about Baby Sister was that she needed him. So it took a lot for him to agree to let her go to Cincinnati to a nursing school. But she got around him by simply not whining and trying to get around him. She reminded him about the time Mama had been sick and how she had wished that she was a nurse, then she could have taken care of Mama herself. Then Daddy just dropped dead without any warning six months later. Doc Burton said he had always had a big heart, and even then Baby Sister said, she was going to be a nurse. Then she'd know how to prevent that sort of thing from happening to anybody else. Sure, it meant that Robert had to do his work at the shop and even take jobs after work to buy her clothes she'd need in a big town like Cincinnati, and then to pay her tuition and give her a little spending money on the side.

But even if she hadn't said, "I promise you, Buddy, I'll pay back every cent," and even if he didn't take her word for it, still he would have done it. Barbara Kendrick had helped him to come to that point of view. It was understood that they would be marrying in two years, and she told him she'd be proud to have a nurse in the family and to be able to tell her children that Aunt Baby Sister was a nurse. And now Baby Sister, who wanted so much to help other sick people, was sick herself. The head of the school had written him a letter saying that she would have to have absolute rest for at least six months and that she would have to have a special diet. Could be kidney trouble. Daddy always said it ran in the family. Robert didn't write to tell her he was coming, or to ask questions; he just got the letter last night when he came home from Barbara's house to change for work. So he caught the bus this morning. He'd find out everything when he got to Cincinnati.

He turned over away from the window and felt the bus slowing down. He turned back, and the brightness of a business winked at the bus. They came to a halt in front of a restaurant which flickered EATS, EATS, EATS. COVINGTON. The bus lights came on, and the bus driver was gazing down the aisle as people began to stir in the uncomfortable seats.

"Last stop before Cincinnati. We'll only be here ten minutes. If you don't have to get off, then wait. In another half hour we'll be in Cincinnati."

The two men in the forward seat got up. The tall one pulled the shaving kit down and took something from it and put it back; then he and the fat man walked down the aisle and out the door.

Robert wished he didn't have to go to the toilet, or at least wished the two men hadn't got off before him. He wasn't sure why they had been staring at him so hard. But anyway there were two things. They hadn't looked his way in a long time and then he wasn't sure he could wait another thirty minutes. And also, he was sure the toilets were marked COLORED and WHITE, so he didn't have to run into them at all. So he got up.

The old lady in the other seat was awake and still holding her Bible. "Son, you not getting off to get nothing to eat, is you? Cause I still got some fried chicken in this-here box."

"No'm. I got to get off for something else."

The woman frowned in the gloomy corner of her seat. "Cain't you wait thirty minutes?" Robert couldn't tell her what he was thinking, You gotta go, you gotta go, so he just said, "No, ma'am, but I won't be long." Then he was going down the aisle.

"If you want to, you can bring me a Dr Pepper," the old lady's whisper said in a hard loud sound from the back of the bus.

"Yes, ma'am, I will."

The air was cool and the ground felt good to his feet. Even if he was a good mechanic, Robert didn't think he'd ever have a car. Honestly, he didn't like riding anything but a horse. The sign MEN then COLORED, was painted in white on a door behind the café.

Inside, the yellow smell of old urine rammed itself up his nose. He thought they must not have cleaned in here since this place was built. And the grit on the floor itched beneath the soles of his shoes. Like scraping a fingernail on a windowpane. If only he could hold his breath and not touch nothing till he got out, he'd be all right. He felt the release of a deflated bladder all the way up his back. If a bean is a bean, as the old people say, then a pee is really a relief. He wasn't going to wash his hands in here, probably even the water out of the taps was dirty.

"See, Abe, I told you he'd be in here."

They did want him, but for what?

The tall one called Abe said, "Yeah, Slim, you was right again."

Robert raced his mind over his life like a drowning man. "You all looking for me?"

Slim, the fat one, said, "You damn right. You know you the only nigger on that bus?" Abe was leaning on the door, holding something, maybe a gun, under his shirt.

He said to Slim, " 'Cept for that old mammy."

Slim sucked his teeth and said, "I ain't counting her. All the niggers is running away from the South. How come, boy? How come you running to get up North? You gone slip in the sheets with some white lady?"

They were drunk and the smell of liquor even cut the lemon-sour smell of pee.

Abe drawled from the door, "What you gone take to them white women up North? Let's see what you gone put up in 'em."

Slim was leaning on the grimy face bowl, acting as if he was relaxing, but Robert saw the lines in his face get deeper and the great cord of muscle in his neck was tight even under the layers of fat.

"Why you all want to mess with me? I'm on my way to Cincinnati to get my baby sister . . . who's sick." Oh Lord, Baby Sister.

"Abe, maybe he'd loosen up if he had a little drink. That's how Harry used to be."

Robert couldn't stand the intention of meanness; these folks were planning to do something to him. He had to get out, and if he missed that bus . . .

Abe was reaching under his coat . . . "Yeah, that nigger didn't just run away with that cheating bitch; he used to drink up my liquor too."

When he pulled out the bottle, at first Robert's knees got weak and there was a taste in his mouth as if he'd had something too sweet. Then he thought again about the bus. He wasn't going to get left with these two crazy men.

The one called Abe unscrewed the top of the bottle of whiskey and started toward Robert. At the same time Slim began to stand up away from the sink. There just wasn't much time to think. Robert pushed his body forward to meet Abe. He reached for the bottle at the same time his knee found the soft place between the thin man's legs. The whiskey washed over his hands and he had the bottle. Abe was bending over, holding his privates, mumbling.

Then the fat man lunged. "You rotten nigger, I'm going to kill you . . ." Robert moved back . . . Fatty was moving faster than Robert thought he could; then the man had caught his shirt and was trying to knee him too. Robert brought the bottle down with all his might on Slim's head. They both grunted but the man still held his shirt. He hit him again, it was like a bad dream, he didn't feel like the bottle was even touching the man. But he felt the slick white-folks hair dampen and the bottle slip off, only to bring it down again, once more, then again. Finally, slowly letting go of Robert's shirt front, the man sunk down to the floor. That was when Robert saw the blood. Over his hands and on his shirt. Oh my God, these people would kill him now; he looked at the thin man, he wasn't out, but he had slid down the door and was sitting in the toilet filth. No time for Robert to wash even if he wanted to . . . At the door, hurrying now, he snatched the thin man's jacket and pulled at him just enough so he could open the door. Outside, it was dark, but the air was so clean and cool that it caught and nearly strangled Robert. Robert bumped into the bus driver before he knew it. He jumped.

The bus driver said, "You almost got left, boy. We're pulling out right now."

"Yes, sir. I'm sorry." He kept talking, it was too dark for the man to see the blood, but he must of smelt the liquor.

The driver said, "Hey wait, you ain't seen two white men that was on the bus, did you?"

"Naw, I ain't seen nobody." He was nearly at the bus, with the driver walking behind him. It looked sweet, like home after you have been walking for miles.

"Well, we going to leave them. I looked in the café and in the toilet."

Robert could feel a little kind of laugh cause the driver didn't think about there being more than one toilet. On the steps, he wondered if it would get the man to look in the Colored one and at the same time he knew it wouldn't. The lights were on in the bus and Robert tried to keep his arms in front of him, maybe shield the dark stains down the front of his shirt.

The old woman had moved into the seat in the aisle, and she was sitting up straight-like, as in church.

"Oooh, chile, I was getting scared for you . . ."

He knew she wanted to talk, but all he could think about was letting the bus get started and leaving those crazy men before they got a chance to call for help . . .

Robert sat down in his seat. "Yes'm. I'm sorry, I didn't have time to get you a Dr Pepper."

Then he felt the big motor turn and the lights darkened and that old big baby pulled away from the sidewalk and on its way to Cincinnati.

The Lesson

by Toni Cade Bambara

BACK IN THE DAYS when everyone was old and stupid or young and foolish and me and Sugar were the only ones just right, this lady moved on our block with nappy hair and proper speech and no makeup. And quite naturally we laughed at her, laughed the way we did at the junk man who went about his business like he was some big-time president and his sorry-ass horse his secretary. And we kinda hated her too, hated the way we did the winos who cluttered up our parks and pissed on our handball walls and stank up our hallways and stairs so you couldn't halfway play hide-and-seek without a goddamn gas mask. Miss Moore was her name. The only woman on the block with no first name. And she was black as hell, cept for her feet, which were fish-white and spooky. And she was always planning these boring-ass things for us to do, us being my cousin, mostly, who lived on the block cause we all moved North the same time and to the same apartment then spread out gradual to breathe. And our parents would yank our heads into some kinda shape and crisp up our clothes so we'd be presentable for travel with Miss Moore, who always looked like she was going to church, though she never did. Which is just one of the things the grown-ups talked about when they talked behind her back like a dog. But when she came calling with some sachet she'd sewed up or some gingerbread she'd made or some book, why then they'd all be too embarrassed to turn her down and we'd get handed over all spruced up. She'd been to college and said it was only right that she should take responsibility for the young ones' education, and she not even related by marriage or blood. So they'd go for it. Specially Aunt Gretchen. She was the main gofer in the family. You got some ole dumb shit foolishness you want somebody to go for, you send for Aunt Gretchen. She been screwed into the go-along for so long, it's a blood-deep natural thing with her. Which is how she got saddled with me and Sugar and Junior in the first place while our mothers were in a la-de-da apartment up the block having a good ole time.

So this one day Miss Moore rounds us all up at the mailbox and it's puredee hot and she's knockin herself out about arithmetic. And school suppose to let up in summer I heard, but she don't never let up. And the starch in my pinafore scratching the shit outta me and I'm really hating this nappy-head bitch and her goddamn college degree. I'd much rather go the pool or to the show where it's cool. So me and Sugar leaning on the mailbox being surly, which is a Miss Moore word. And Flyboy checking out what everybody brought for lunch. And Fat Butt already wasting his peanut-butter-and-jelly sandwich like the pig he is. And Junebug punchin on Q.T.'s arm for potato chips. And Rosie Giraffe shifting from one hip to the other waiting for somebody to step on her foot or ask her if she from Georgia so she can kick ass, preferably Mercedes'. And Miss Moore asking us do we know what money is, like we a bunch of retards. I mean real money, she say, like it's only poker chips or monopoly papers we lay on the grocer. So right away I'm tired of this and say so. And would much rather snatch Sugar and go to the Sunset and terrorize the West Indian kids and take their hair ribbons and their money too. And Miss Moore files that remark away for next week's lesson on brotherhood, I can tell. And finally I say we oughta get to the subway cause it's cooler and besides we might meet some cute boys. Sugar done swiped her mama's lipstick, so we ready.

So we heading down the street and she's boring us silly about what things cost and what our parents make and how much goes for rent and how money ain't divided up right in this country. And then she gets to the part about we all poor and live in the slums, which I don't feature. And I'm ready to speak on that, but she steps out in the street and hails two cabs just like that. Then she hustles half the crew in with her and hands me a five-dollar bill and tells me to calculate 10 percent tip for the driver. And we're off. Me and Sugar and Junebug and Flyboy hangin out the window and hollering to everybody, putting lipstick on each other cause Flyboy a faggot anyway, and making farts with our sweaty armpits. But I'm mostly trying to figure how to spend this money. But they all fascinated with the meter ticking and Junebug starts laying bets as to how much it'll read when Flyboy can't hold his breath no more. Then Sugar lays bets as to how much it'll be when we get there. So I'm stuck. Don't nobody want to go for my plan, which is to jump out at the next light and run off to the first bar-b-que we can find. Then the driver tells us to get the hell out cause we there already. And the meter reads eighty-five cents. And I'm stalling to figure out the tip and Sugar say give him a dime. And I decide he don't need it bad as I do, so later for him. But then he tries to take off with Junebug foot still in the door so we talk about his mama something ferocious. Then we check out that we on Fifth Avenue and everybody dressed up in stockings. One lady in a fur coat, hot as it is. White folks crazy.

"This is the place," Miss Moore say, presenting it to us in the voice she uses at the museum. "Let's look in the windows before we go in."

"Can we steal?" Sugar asks very serious like she's getting the ground rules squared away before she plays. "I beg your pardon," say Miss Moore, and we fall out. So she leads us around the windows of the toy store and me and Sugar screamin, "This is mine, that's mine, I gotta have that, that was made for me, I was born for that," till Big Butt drowns us out.

"Hey, I'm going to buy that there."

"That there? You don't even know what it is, stupid."

"I do so," he say punchin on Rosie Giraffe. "It's a microscope."

"Whatcha gonna do with a microscope, fool?"

"Look at things."

"Like what, Ronald?" ask Miss Moore. And Big Butt ain't got the first notion. So here go Miss Moore gabbing about the thousands of bacteria in a drop of water and the somethin or other in a speck of blood and the million and one living things in the air around us is invisible to the naked eye. And what she say that for? Junebug go to town on that "naked" and we rolling. Then Miss Moore ask what it cost. So we all jam into the window smudgin it up and the price tag say $300. So then she ask how long'd take for Big Butt and Junebug to save up their allowances. "Too long," I say. "Yeh," adds Sugar, "outgrown it by that time." And Miss Moore say no, you never outgrow learning instruments. "Why, even medical students and interns and," blah, blah, blah. And we ready to choke Big Butt for bringing it up in the first damn place.

"This here costs four hundred eighty dollars," say Rosie Giraffe. So we pile up all over her to see what she pointin out. My eyes tell me it's a chunk of glass cracked with something heavy, and different-color inks dripped into the splits, then the whole thing put into a oven or something. But for $480 it don't make sense.

"That's a paperweight made of semi-precious stones fused together under tremendous pressure," she explains slowly, with her hands doing the mining and all the factory work.

"So what's a paperweight?" asks Rosie Giraffe.

"To weigh paper with, dumbbell," say Flyboy, the wise man from the East.

"Not exactly," say Miss Moore, which is what she say when you warm or way off too. "It's to weigh paper down so it won't scatter and make your desk untidy." So right away me and Sugar curtsy to each other and then to Mercedes who is more the tidy type.

"We don't keep paper on top of the desk in my class," say Junebug, figuring Miss Moore crazy or lyin one.

"At home, then," she say. "Don't you have a calendar and a pencil case and a blotter and a letter-opener on your desk at home where you do your homework?" And she know damn well what our homes look like cause she nosys around in them every chance she gets.

"I don't even have a desk," say Junebug. "Do we?"

"No. And I don't get no homework neither," say Big Butt.

"And I don't even have a home," say Flyboy like he do at school to keep the white folks off his back and sorry for him. Send this poor kid to camp posters, is his specialty.

"I do," says Mercedes. "I have a box of stationery on my desk and a picture of my cat. My godmother bought the stationery and the desk. There's a big rose on each sheet and the envelopes smell like roses."

"Who wants to know about your smelly-ass stationery," say Rosie Giraffe fore I can get my two cents in.

"It's important to have a work area all your own so that . . ."

"Will you look at this sailboat, please," say Flyboy, cuttin her off and pointin to the thing like it was his. So once again we tumble all over each other to gaze at this magnificent thing in the toy store which is just big enough to maybe sail two kittens across the pond if you strap them to the posts tight. We all start reciting the price tag like we in assembly. "Handcrafted sailboat of fiberglass at one thousand one hundred ninety-five dollars."

"Unbelievable," I hear myself say and am really stunned. I read it again for myself just in case the group recitation put me in a trance. Same thing. For some reason this pisses me off. We look at Miss Moore and she lookin at us, waiting for I dunno what.

Who'd pay all that when you can buy a sailboat set for a quarter at Pop's, a tube of glue for a dime, and a ball of string for eight cents? "It must have a motor and a whole lot else besides," I say. "My sailboat cost me about fifty cents."

"But will it take water?" say Mercedes with her smart ass.

"Took mine to Alley Pond Park once," say Flyboy. "String broke. Lost it. Pity."

"Sailed mine in Central Park and it keeled over and sank. Had to ask my father for another dollar."

"And you got the strap," laugh Big Butt. "The jerk didn't even have a string on it. My old man wailed on his behind."

Little Q.T. was staring hard at the sailboat and you could see he wanted it bad. But he too little and somebody'd just take it from him. So what the hell. "This boat for kids, Miss Moore?"

"Parents silly to buy something like that just to get all broke up," say Rosie Giraffe.

"That much money it should last forever," I figure.

"My father'd buy it for me if I wanted it."

"Your father, my ass," say Rosie Giraffe getting a chance to finally push Mercedes.

"Must be rich people shop here," say Q.T.

"You are a very bright boy," say Flyboy. "What was your first clue?" And he rap him on the head with the back of his knuckles, since Q.T. the only one he could get away with. Though Q.T. liable to come up behind you years later and get his licks in when you half expect it.

"What I want to know is," I says to Miss Moore though I never talk to her, I wouldn't give the bitch that satisfaction, "is how much a real boat costs? I figure a thousand'd get you a yacht any day."

"Why don't you check that out," she says, "and report back to the group?" Which really pains my ass. If you gonna mess up a perfectly good swim day least you could do is have some answers. "Let's go in," she say like she got something up her sleeve. Only she don't lead the way. So me and Sugar turn the corner to where the entrance is, but when we get there I kinda hang back. Not that I'm scared, what's there to be afraid of, just a toy store. But I feel funny, shame. But what I got to be shamed about? Got as much right to go in as anybody. But somehow I can't seem to get hold of the door, so I step away for Sugar to lead. But she hangs back too. And I look at her and she looks at me and this is ridiculous. I mean, damn, I have never ever been shy about doing nothing or going nowhere. But then Mercedes steps up and then Rosie Giraffe and Big Butt crowd in behind and shove, and next thing we all stuffed into the doorway with only Mercedes squeezing past us, smoothing out her jumper and walking right down the aisle. Then the rest of us tumble in like a glued-together jigsaw done all wrong. And people lookin at us. And it's like the time me and Sugar crashed into the Catholic church on a dare. But once we got in there and everything so hushed and holy and the candles and the bowin and the handker-chiefs on all the drooping heads, I just couldn't go through with the plan. Which was for me to run up to the altar and do a tap dance while Sugar played the nose flute and messed around in the holy water. And Sugar kept givin me the elbow. Then later teased me so bad I tied her up in the shower and turned it on and locked her in. And she'd be there till this day if Aunt Gretchen hadn't finally figured I was lyin about the boarder takin a shower.

Same thing in the store. We all walkin on tiptoe and hardly touchin the games and puzzles and things. And I watched Miss Moore who is steady watchin us like she waitin for a sign. Like Mama Drewery watches the sky and sniffs the air and takes note of just how much slant is in the bird formation. Then me and Sugar bump smack into each other, so busy gazing at the toys, 'specially the sailboat. But we don't laugh and go into our fat-lady bump-stomach routine. We just stare at that price tag. Then Sugar run a finger over the whole boat. And I'm jealous and want to hit her. Maybe not her, but I sure want to punch somebody in the mouth.

"Watcha bring us here for, Miss Moore?"

"You sound angry, Sylvia. Are you mad about something?" Givin me one of them grins like she tellin a grown-up joke that never turns out to be funny. And she's lookin very closely at me like maybe she plannin to do my portrait from memory. I'm mad, but I won't give her that satisfaction. So I slouch around the store bein very bored and say, "Let's go."

Me and Sugar at the back of the train watchin the tracks whizzin by large then small then gettin gobbled up in the dark. I'm thinkin about this tricky toy I saw in the store. A clown that somersaults on a bar then does chin-ups just cause you yank lightly at his leg. Cost $35. I could see me askin my mother for a $35 birthday clown. "You wanna who that costs what?" she'd say, cocking her head to the side to get a better view of the hole in my head. Thirty-five dollars could buy new bunk beds for Junior and Gretchen's boy. Thirty-five dollars and the whole household could go visit Granddaddy Nelson in the country. Thirty-five dollars would pay for the rent and the piano bill too. Who are these people that spend that much for performing clowns and $1,000 for toy sailboats? What kinda work they do and how they live and how come we ain't in on it? Where we are is who we are, Miss Moore always pointin out. But it don't necessarily have to be that way, she always adds then waits for somebody to say that poor people have to wake up and demand their share of the pie and don't none of us know what kind of pie she talkin about in the first damn place. But she ain't so smart cause I still got her four dollars from the taxi and she sure ain't gettin it. Messin up my day with this shit. Sugar nudges me in my pocket and winks.

Miss Moore lines us up in front of the mailbox where we started from, seem like years ago, and I got a headache for thinkin so hard. And we lean all over each other so we can hold up under the draggy-ass lecture she always finishes us off with at the end before we thank her for borin us to tears. But she just looks at us like she readin tea leaves. Finally she say, "Well, what did you think of F.A.O. Schwartz?"

Rosie Giraffe mumbles, "White folks crazy."

"I'd like to go there again when I get my birthday money," says Mercedes, and we shove her out the pack so she has to lean on the mailbox by herself.

"I'd like a shower. Tiring day," say Flyboy.

Then Sugar surprises me by sayin, "You know, Miss Moore, I don't think all of us here put together eat in a year what that sailboat costs." And Miss Moore lights up like somebody goosed her. "And?" she say, urging Sugar on. Only I'm standin on her foot so she don't continue.

"Imagine for a minute what kind of society it is in which some people can spend on a toy what it would cost to feed a family of six or seven. What do you think?"

"I think," say Sugar pushing me off her feet like she never done before, cause I whip her ass in a minute, "that this is not much of a democracy if you ask me. Equal chance to pursue happiness means an equal crack at the dough, don't it?" Miss Moore is besides herself and I am disgusted with Sugar's treachery. So I stand on her foot one more time to see if she'll shove me. She shuts up, and Miss Moore looks at me, sorrowfully I'm thinkin. And somethin weird is goin on, I can feel it in my chest.

"Anybody else learn anything today?" lookin dead at me. I walk away and Sugar has to run to catch up and don't even seem to notice when I shrug her arm off my shoulder.

"Well, we got four dollars anyway," she says.

"Uh hunh."

"We could go to Hascombs and get half a chocolate layer and then go to the Sunset and still have plenty money for potato chips and ice-cream sodas."

"Uh hunh."

"Race you to Hascombs," she say.

We start down the block and she gets ahead which is O.K. by me cause I'm goin to the West End and then over to the Drive to think this day through. She can run if she want to and even run faster. But ain't nobody gonna beat me at nuthin.

THE CHANGING TIMES

Kiswana Browne

by Gloria Naylor

FROM THE WINDOW of her sixth-floor studio apartment, Kiswana could see over the wall at the end of the street to the busy avenue that lay just north of Brewster Place. The late afternoon shoppers looked like brightly clad marionettes as they moved between the congested traffic, clutching their packages against their bodies to guard them from sudden bursts of the cold autumn wind. A portly mailman had abandoned his cart and was bumping into indignant window-shoppers as he puffed behind the cap that the wind had snatched from his head. Kiswana leaned over to see if he was going to be successful, but the edge of the building cut him off from her view.

A pigeon swept across her window, and she marveled at its liquid movements in the air waves. She placed her dreams on the back of the bird and fantasized that it would glide forever in transparent silver circles until it ascended to the center of the universe and was swallowed up. But the wind died down, and she watched with a sigh as the bird beat its wings in awkward, frantic movements to land on the corroded top of a fire escape on the opposite building. This brought her back to earth.

Humph, it's probably sitting over there crapping on those folks' fire escape, she thought. Now, that's a safety hazard. . . . And her mind was busy again, creating flames and smoke and frustrated tenants whose escape was being hindered because they were slipping and sliding in pigeon shit. She watched their cussing, haphazard descent on the fire escapes until they had all reached the bottom. They were milling around, oblivious to their burning apartments, angrily planning to march on the mayor's office about the pigeons. She materialized placards and banners for them, and they had just reached the corner, boldly sidestepping fire hoses and broken glass, when they all vanished.

A tall copper-skinned woman had met this phantom parade at the corner, and they had dissolved in front of her long, confident strides. She plowed through the remains of their faded mists, unconscious of the lingering wisps of their presence on her leather bag and black fur-trimmed coat. It took a few seconds for this transfer from one realm to another to reach Kiswana, but then suddenly she recognized the woman.

"Oh, God, it's Mama!" She looked down guiltily at the forgotten newspaper in her lap and hurriedly circled random job advertisements.

By this time Mrs. Browne had reached the front of Kiswana's building and was checking the house number against a piece of paper in her hand. Before she went into the building she stood at the bottom of the stoop and carefully inspected the condition of the street and the adjoining property. Kiswana watched this meticulous inventory with growing annoyance but she involuntarily followed her mother's slowly rotating head, forcing herself to see her new neighborhood through the older woman's eyes. The brightness of the unclouded sky seemed to join forces with her mother as it highlighted every broken stoop railing and missing brick. The afternoon sun glittered and cascaded across even the tiniest fragments of broken bottle, and at that very moment the wind chose to rise up again, sending unswept grime flying into the air, as a stray tin can left by careless garbage collectors went rolling noisily down the center of the street.

Kiswana noticed with relief that at least Ben wasn't sitting in his usual place on the old garbage can pushed against the far wall. He was just a harmless old wino, but Kiswana knew her mother only needed one wino or one teenager with a reefer within a twenty-block radius to decide that her daughter was living in a building seething with dope factories and hang-outs for derelicts. If she had seen Ben, nothing would have made her believe that practically every apartment contained a family, a Bible, and a dream that one day enough could be scraped from those meager Friday night paychecks to make Brewster Place a distant memory.

As she watched her mother's head disappear into the building,

Kiswana gave silent thanks that the elevator was broken. That would give her at least five minutes' grace to straighten up the apartment. She rushed to the sofa bed and hastily closed it without smoothing the rumpled sheets and blanket or removing her nightgown. She felt that somehow the tangled bedcovers would give away the fact that she had not slept alone last night. She silently apologized to Abshu's memory as she heartlessly crushed his spirit between the steel springs of the couch. Lord, that man was sweet. Her toes curled involuntarily at the passing thought of his full lips moving slowly over her instep. Abshu was a foot man, and he always started his lovemaking from the bottom up. For that reason Kiswana changed the color of the polish on her toenails every week. During the course of their relationship she had gone from shades of red to brown and was now into the purples. I'm gonna have to start mixing them soon, she thought aloud as she turned from the couch and raced into the bathroom to remove any traces of Abshu from there. She took up his shaving cream and razor and threw them into the bottom drawer of her dresser beside her diaphragm. Mama wouldn't dare pry into my drawers right in front of me, she thought as she slammed the drawer shut. Well, at least not the *bottom* drawer. She may come up with some sham excuse for opening the top drawer, but never the bottom one.

When she heard the first two short raps on the door, her eyes took a final flight over the small apartment, desperately seeking out any slight misdemeanor that might have to be defended. Well, there was nothing she could do about the crack in the wall over that table. She had been after the landlord to fix it for two months now. And there had been no time to sweep the rug, and everyone knew that off-gray always looked dirtier than it really was. And it was just too damn bad about the kitchen. How was she expected to be out job-hunting every day and still have time to keep a kitchen that looked like her mother's, who didn't even work and still had someone come in twice a month for general cleaning. And besides . . .

Her imaginary argument was abruptly interrupted by a second series of knocks, accompanied by a penetrating, "Melanie, Melanie, are you there?"

Kiswana strode toward the door. She's starting before she even gets in here. She knows that's not my name anymore.

She swung the door open to face her slightly flushed mother. "Oh, hi, Mama. You know, I thought I heard a knock, but I figured it was for the people next door, since no one hardly ever calls me Melanie." Score one for me, she thought.

"Well, it's awfully strange you can forget a name you answered to for twenty-three years," Mrs. Browne said, as she moved past Kiswana into the apartment. "My, that was a long climb. How long has your elevator been out? Honey, how do you manage with your laundry and groceries up all those steps? But I guess you're young, and it wouldn't bother you as much as it does me." This long string of questions told Kiswana that her mother had no intentions of beginning her visit with another argument about her new African name.

"You know I would have called before I came, but you don't have a phone yet. I didn't want you to feel that I was snooping. As a matter of fact, I didn't expect to find you home at all. I thought you'd be out looking for a job." Mrs. Browne had mentally covered the entire apartment while she was talking and taking off her coat.

"Well, I got up late this morning. I thought I'd buy the afternoon paper and start early tomorrow."

"That sounds like a good idea." Her mother moved toward the window and picked up the discarded paper and glanced over the hurriedly circled ads. "Since when do you have experience as a fork-lift operator?"

Kiswana caught her breath and silently cursed herself for her stupidity. "Oh, my hand slipped — I meant to circle file clerk." She quickly took the paper before her mother could see that she had also marked cutlery salesman and chauffeur.

"You're sure you weren't sitting here moping and daydreaming again?" Amber specks of laughter flashed in the corners of Mrs. Browne's eyes.

Kiswana threw her shoulders back and unsuccessfully tried to disguise her embarrassment with indignation.

"Oh, God, Mama! I haven't done that in years — it's for kids. When are you going to realize that I'm a woman now?" She sought desperately for some womanly thing to do and settled for throwing herself on the couch and crossing her legs in what she hoped looked like a nonchalant arc.

"Please, have a seat," she said, attempting the same tones and gestures she'd seen Bette Davis use on the late movies.

Mrs. Browne, lowering her eyes to hide her amusement, accepted the invitation and sat at the window, also crossing her legs. Kiswana saw immediately how it should have been done. Her celluloid pose clashed loudly against her mother's quiet dignity, and she quickly uncrossed her legs. Mrs. Browne turned her head toward the window and pretended not to notice.

"At least you have a halfway decent view from here. I was wondering what lay beyond that dreadful wall — it's the boulevard. Honey, did you know that you can see the trees in Linden Hills from here?"

Kiswana knew that very well, because there were many lonely days that she would sit in her gray apartment and stare at those trees and think of home, but she would rather have choked than admit that to her mother.

"Oh, really, I never noticed. So how is Daddy and things at home?"

"Just fine. We're thinking of redoing one of the extra bedrooms since you children have moved out, but Wilson insists that he can manage all that work alone. I told him that he doesn't really have the proper time or energy for all that. As it is, when he gets home from the office, he's so tired he can hardly move. But you know you can't tell your father anything. Whenever he starts complaining about how stubborn you are, I tell him the child came by it honestly. Oh, and your brother was by yesterday," she added, as if it had just occurred to her.

So that's it, thought Kiswana. That's why she's here.

Kiswana's brother, Wilson, had been to visit her two days ago, and she had borrowed twenty dollars from him to get her winter coat out of layaway. That son-of-a-bitch probably ran straight to Mama — and after he swore he wouldn't say anything. I should have known, he was always a snotty-nosed sneak, she thought.

"Was he?" she said aloud. "He came by to see me, too, earlier this week. And I borrowed some money from him because my unemployment checks hadn't cleared in the bank, but now they have and everything's just fine." There, I'll beat you to that one.

"Oh, I didn't know that," Mrs. Browne lied. "He never mentioned you. He had just heard that Beverly was expecting again, and he rushed over to tell us."

Damn. Kiswana could have strangled herself.

"So she's knocked up again, huh?" she said irritably.

Her mother started. "Why do you always have to be so crude?"

"Personally, I don't see how she can sleep with Willie. He's such a dishrag."

Kiswana still resented the stance her brother had taken in college. When everyone at school was discovering their blackness and protesting on campus, Wilson never took part; he had even refused to wear an Afro. This had outraged Kiswana because, unlike her, he was dark-skinned and had the type of hair that was thick and kinky enough for a good "Fro." Kiswana had still insisted on cutting her own hair, but it was so thin and fine-textured, it refused to thicken even after she washed it. So she had to brush it up and spray it with lacquer to keep it from lying flat. She never forgave Wilson for telling her that she didn't look African, she looked like an electrocuted chicken.

"Now that's some way to talk. I don't know why you have an attitude against your brother. He never gave me a restless night's sleep, and now he's settled with a family and a good job."

"He's an assistant to an assistant junior partner in a law firm. What's the big deal about that?"

"The job has a future, Melanie. And at least he finished school and went on for his law degree."

"In other words, not like me, huh?"

"Don't put words into my mouth, young lady. I'm perfectly capable of saying what I mean."

Amen, thought Kiswana.

"And I don't know why you've been trying to start up with me from the moment I walked in. I didn't come here to fight with you. This is your first place away from home, and I just wanted to see how you were living and if you're doing all right. And I must say, you've fixed this apartment up very nicely."

"Really, Mama?" She found herself softening in the light of her mother's approval.

"Well, considering what you had to work with." This time she scanned the apartment openly.

"Look, I know it's not Linden Hills, but a lot can be done with it. As soon as they come and paint, I'm going to hang my Ashanti print over the couch. And I thought a big Boston fern would go well in that corner, what do you think?"

"That would be fine, baby. You always had a good eye for balance."

Kiswana was beginning to relax. There was little she did that attracted her mother's approval. It was like a rare bird, and she had to tread carefully around it lest it fly away.

"Are you going to leave that statue out like that?"

"Why, what's wrong with it? Would it look better somewhere else?"

There was a small wooden reproduction of a Yoruba goddess with large protruding breasts on the coffee table.

"Well," Mrs. Browne was beginning to blush, "it's just that it's a bit suggestive, don't you think? Since you live alone now, and I know you'll be having male friends stop by, you wouldn't want to be giving them any ideas. I mean, uh, you know, there's no point in putting yourself in any unpleasant situations because they may get the wrong impressions and uh, you know, I mean, well . . ." Mrs. Browne stammered on miserably.

Kiswana loved it when her mother tried to talk about sex. It was the only time she was at a loss for words.

"Don't worry, Mama." Kiswana smiled. "That wouldn't bother the type of men I date. Now maybe if it had big feet . . ." And she got hysterical, thinking of Abshu.

Her mother looked at her sharply. "What sort of gibberish is that about feet? I'm being serious, Melanie."

"I'm sorry, Mama." She sobered up. "I'll put it away in the closet," she said, knowing that she wouldn't.

"Good," Mrs. Browne said, knowing that she wouldn't either. "I guess you think I'm too picky, but we worry about you over here. And you refuse to put in a phone so we can call and see about you."

"I haven't refused, Mama. They want seventy-five dollars for a deposit, and I can't swing that right now."

"Melanie, I can give you the money."

"I don't want you to be giving me money — I've told you that before. Please, let me make it by myself."

"Well, let me lend it to you, then."

"No!"

"Oh, so you can borrow money from your brother, but not from me."

Kiswana turned her head from the hurt in her mother's eyes. "Mama, when I borrow from Willie, he makes me pay him back. You never let me pay you back," she said into her hands.

"I don't care. I still think it's downright selfish of you to be sitting over here with no phone, and sometimes we don't hear from you in two weeks — anything could happen — especially living among these people."

Kiswana snapped her head up. "What do you mean, *these people.* They're my people and yours, too, Mama — we're all black. But maybe you've forgotten that over in Linden Hills."

"That's not what I'm talking about, and you know it. These streets — this building — it's so shabby and rundown. Honey, you don't have to live like this."

"Well, this is how poor people live."

"Melanie, you're not poor."

"No, Mama, *you're* not poor. And what you have and I have are two totally different things. I don't have a husband in real estate with a five-figure income and a home in Linden Hills — *you* do. What I have is a weekly unemployment check and an overdrawn checking account at United Federal. So this studio on Brewster is all I can afford."

"Well, you could afford a lot better," Mrs. Browne snapped, "if you hadn't dropped out of college and had to resort to these dead-end clerical jobs."

"Uh-huh, I knew you'd get around to that before long." Kiswana could feel the rings of anger begin to tighten around her lower backbone, and they sent her forward onto the couch. "You'll never understand, will you? Those bourgie schools were counterrevolutionary. My place was in the streets with my people, fighting for equality and a better community."

"Counterrevolutionary!" Mrs. Browne was raising her voice. "Where's your revolution now, Melanie? Where are all those black revolutionaries who were shouting and demonstrating and kicking up a lot of dust with you on that campus? Huh? They're sitting in wood-paneled offices with their degrees in mahogany frames, and they won't even drive their cars past this street because the city doesn't fix the potholes in this part of town."

"Mama," she said, shaking her head slowly in disbelief, "how can you — a black woman — sit there and tell me that what we fought for during the Movement wasn't important just because some people sold out?"

"Melanie, I'm not saying it wasn't important. It was damned important to stand up and say that you were proud of what you were and to get the vote and other social opportunities for every person in this country who had it due. But you kids thought you were going to turn the world upside down, and it just wasn't so. When all the smoke had cleared, you found yourself with a fistful of new federal laws and a country still full of obstacles for black people to fight their way over — just because they're black. There was no revolution, Melanie, and there will be no revolution."

"So what am I supposed to do, huh? Just throw up my hands and not care about what happens to my people? I'm not supposed to keep fighting to make things better?"

"Of course, you can. But you're going to have to fight within the system, because it and these so-called 'bourgie' schools are going to be here for a long time. And that means that you get smart like a lot of your old friends and get an important job where you can have some influence. You don't have to sell out, as you say, and work for some corporation, but you could become an assemblywoman or a civil liberties lawyer or open a freedom school in this very neighborhood. That way you could really help the community. But what help are you going to be to these people on Brewster while you're living hand-to-mouth on file-clerk jobs waiting for a revolution? You're wasting your talents, child."

"Well, I don't think they're being wasted. At least I'm here in day-to-day contact with the problems of my people. What good would I be after four or five years of a lot of white brainwashing in some phony, prestige institution, huh? I'd be like you and Daddy and those other educated blacks sitting over there in Linden Hills with a terminal case of middle-class amnesia."

"You don't have to live in a slum to be concerned about social conditions, Melanie. Your father and I have been charter members of the NAACP for the last twenty-five years."

"Oh, God!" Kiswana threw her head back in exaggerated disgust. "That's being concerned? That middle-of-the-road, Uncle Tom dumping ground for black Republicans!"

"You can sneer all you want, young lady, but that organization has been working for black people since the turn of the century, and it's still working for them. Where are all those radical groups of yours that were going to put a Cadillac in every garage and Dick Gregory in the White House? I'll tell you where."

I knew you would, Kiswana thought angrily.

"They burned themselves out because they wanted too much too fast. Their goals weren't grounded in reality. And that's always been your problem."

"What do you mean, my problem? I know exactly what I'm about."

"No, you don't. You constantly live in a fantasy world — always going to extremes — turning butterflies into eagles, and life isn't about that. It's accepting what is and working from that. Lord, I remember how worried you had me, putting all that lacquered hair spray on your head. I thought you were going to get lung cancer — trying to be what you're not."

Kiswana jumped up from the couch. "Oh, God, I can't take this anymore. Trying to be something I'm not — trying to be something I'm not, Mama! Trying to be proud of my heritage and the fact that I was of African descent. If that's being what I'm not, then I say fine. But I'd rather be dead than be like you — a white man's nigger who's ashamed of being black!"

Kiswana saw streaks of gold and ebony light follow her mother's flying body out of the chair. She was swung around by the shoulders and made to face the deadly stillness in the angry woman's eyes. She was too stunned to cry out from the pain of the long fingernails that dug into her shoulders, and she was brought so close to her mother's face that she saw her reflection, distorted and wavering, in the tears that stood in the older woman's eyes. And she listened in that stillness to a story she had heard from a child.

"My grandmother," Mrs. Browne began slowly in a whisper, "was a full-blooded Iroquois, and my grandfather a free black from a long line of journeymen who had lived in Connecticut since the establishment of the colonies. And my father was a Bajan who came to this country as a cabin boy on a merchant mariner."

"I know all that," Kiswana said, trying to keep her lips from trembling.

"Then know this." And the nails dug deeper into her flesh. "I am alive because of the blood of proud people who never scraped or begged or apologized for what they were. They lived asking only one thing of this world — to be allowed to be. And I learned through the blood of these people that black isn't beautiful and it isn't ugly — black is! It's not kinky hair and it's not straight hair — it just is.

"It broke my heart when you changed your name. I gave you my grandmother's name, a woman who bore nine children and educated them all, who held off six white men with a shotgun when they tried to drag one of her sons to jail for 'not knowing his place.' Yet you needed to reach into an African dictionary to find a name to make you proud.

"When I brought my babies home from the hospital, my ebony son and my golden daughter, I swore before whatever gods would listen — those of my mother's people or those of my father's people — that I would use everything I had and could ever get to see that my children were prepared to meet this world on its own terms, so that no one could sell them short and make them ashamed of what they were or how they looked — whatever they were or however they looked. And Melanie, that's not being white or red or black — that's being a mother."

Kiswana followed her reflection in the two single tears that moved down her mother's cheeks until it blended with them into the woman's copper skin. There was nothing and then so much that she wanted to say, but her throat kept closing up every time she tried to speak. She kept her head down and her eyes closed, and thought, O, God, just let me die. How can I face her now?

Mrs. Browne lifted Kiswana's chin gently. "And the one lesson I wanted you to learn is not to be afraid to face anyone, not even a crafty old lady like me who can outtalk you." And she smiled and winked.

"Oh, Mama, I . . ." and she hugged the woman tightly.

"Yeah, baby." Mrs. Browne patted her back. "I know."

She kissed Kiswana on the forehead and cleared her throat. "Well, now, I better be moving on. It's getting late, there's dinner to be made, and I have to get off my feet — these new shoes are killing me."

Kiswana looked down at the beige leather pumps. "Those are really classy. They're English, aren't they?"

"Yes, but, Lord, do they cut me right across the instep." She removed the shoe and sat on the couch to massage her foot.

Bright red nail polish glared at Kiswana through the stockings. "Since when do you polish your toenails?" she gasped. "You never did that before."

"Well . . ." Mrs. Browne shrugged her shoulders, "your father sort of talked me into it, and, uh, you know, he likes it and all, so I thought, uh, you know, why not, so . . ." And she gave Kiswana an embarrassed smile.

I'll be damned, the young woman thought, feeling her whole face tingle. Daddy's into feet! And she looked at the blushing woman on her couch and suddenly realized that her mother had trod through the same universe that she herself was now traveling. Kiswana was breaking no new trails and would eventually end up just two feet away on that couch. She stared at the woman she had been and was to become.

"But I'll never be a Republican," she caught herself saying aloud.

"What are you mumbling about, Melanie?" Mrs. Browne slipped on her shoe and got up from the couch.

She went to get her mother's coat. "Nothing, Mama. It's really nice of you to come by. You should do it more often."

"Well, since it's not Sunday, I guess you're allowed at least one lie."
They both laughed.

After Kiswana had closed the door and turned around, she spotted an envelope sticking between the cushions of her couch. She went over and opened it up; there was seventy-five dollars in it.

"Oh, Mama, darn it!" She rushed to the window and started to call to the woman, who had just emerged from the building, but she suddenly changed her mind and sat down in the chair with a long sigh that caught in the upward draft of the autumn wind and disappeared over the top of the building.

PART II

AFFIRMING . . .

THE FAMILY

Second-Hand Man

by Rita Dove

VIRGINIA COULDN'T STAND IT when someone tried to shorten her name — like *Ginny*, for example. But James Evans didn't. He set his twelve-string guitar down real slow.

"Miss Virginia," he said, "you're a fine piece of woman."

Seemed he'd been asking around. Knew everything about her. Knew she was bold and proud and didn't cotton to no silly niggers. Vir-gin-ee-a he said, nice and slow. Almost Russian, the way he said it. Right then and there she knew this man was for her.

He courted her just inside a year, came by nearly every day. First she wouldn't see him for more than half an hour at a time. She'd send him away; he knew better than to try to force her. Another fellow did that once — kept coming by when she said she had other things to do. She told him he do it once more, she'd be waiting at the door with a pot of scalding water to teach him some manners. Did, too. Fool didn't believe her — she had the pot waiting on the stove and when he came up those stairs, she was standing in the door. He took one look at her face and turned and ran. He was lucky those steps were so steep. She only got a little piece of his pant leg.

No, James knew his stuff. He'd come on time and stay till she told him he needed to go.

She'd met him out at Summit Beach one day. In the Twenties, that was the place to go on hot summer days! Clean yellow sand all around the lake, and an amusement park that ran from morning to midnight.

She went there with a couple of girl friends. They were younger than her and a little silly. But they were sweet. Virginia was nineteen then. "High time," everyone used to say to her, but she'd just lift her head and go on about her business. She weren't going to marry just any old Negro. He had to be perfect.

There was a man who was chasing her around about that time, too. Tall dark Negro — Sterling Williams was his name. Pretty as a panther. Married, he was. Least that's what everyone said. Left a wife in Washington, D.C. A little crazy, the wife — poor Sterling was trying to get a divorce.

Well, Sterling was at Summit Beach that day, too. He followed Virginia around, trying to buy her root beer. Everybody loved root beer that summer. Root beer and vanilla ice cream — the Boston Cooler. But she wouldn't pay him no mind. People said she was crazy — Sterling was the best catch in Akron, they said.

"Not for me," Virginia said. "I don't want no second-hand man."

But Sterling wouldn't give up. He kept buying root beers and having to drink them himself.

Then she saw James. He'd just come up from Tennessee, working his way up on the riverboats. Folks said his best friend had been lynched down there and he turned his back on the town and said he was never coming back. Well, when she saw this cute little man in a straw hat and a twelve-string guitar under his arm, she got a little flustered. Her girlfriends whispered around to find out who he was, but she acted like she didn't even see him.

He was the hit of Summit Beach. Played that twelve-string guitar like a devil. They'd take off their shoes and sit on the beach toward evening. All the girls loved James. "Oh, Jimmy," they'd squeal, "play us a *loooove* song!" He'd laugh and pick out a tune:

> *I'll give you a dollar if you'll come out tonight*
> *If you'll come out tonight,*
> *If you'll come out tonight.*
> *I'll give you a dollar if you'll come out tonight*
> *And dance by the light of the moon.*

Then the girls would giggle. "Jimmy," they screamed, "you outta be 'shamed of yourself!" He'd sing the second verse then:

I danced with a girl with a hole in her stockin',
And her heel kep' a-rockin',
And her heel kep' a-rockin';
I danced with a girl with a hole in her stockin',
And we danced by the light of the moon.

Then they'd all priss and preen their feathers and wonder which would be best — to be in fancy clothes and go on being courted by these dull factory fellows, or to have a hole in their stockings and dance with James.

Virginia never danced. She sat a bit off to one side and watched them make fools of themselves.

Then one night near season's end, they were all sitting down by the water, and everyone had on sweaters and was in a foul mood because the cold weather was coming and there wouldn't be no more parties. Someone said something about hating having the good times end, and James struck up a nice and easy tune, looking across the fire straight at Virginia:

As I was lumb'ring down de street,
Down de street, down de street,
A han'some gal I chanced to meet,
Oh, she was fair to view!

I'd like to make dat gal my wife,
Gal my wife, gal my wife.
I'd be happy all my life
If I had her by me.

She knew he was the man. She'd known it a long while, but she was just biding her time. He called on her the next day. She said she was busy canning peaches. He came back the day after. They sat on the porch and watched the people go by. He didn't talk much, except to say her name like that:

"Vir-gin-ee-a," he said, "you're a mighty fine woman."

She sent him home a little after that. He showed up again a week later. She was angry at him and told him she didn't have time for playing around. But he'd brought his twelve-string guitar, and he said he'd been practicing all week just to play a couple of songs for her. She let him in then and made him sit on the stool while she sat on the porch swing. He sang the first song. It was a floor thumper.

> *There is a gal in our town,*
> *She wears a yallow striped gown,*
> *And when she walks the streets aroun',*
> *The hollow of her foot makes a hole in the ground.*

> *Ol' folks, young folks, cl'ar the kitchen,*
> *Ol' folks, young folks, cl'ar the kitchen,*
> *Ol' Virginny never tire.*

She got a little mad then, but she knew he was baiting her. Seeing how much she would take. She knew he wasn't singing about her, and she'd already heard how he said her name. It was time to let the dog in out of the rain, even if he shook his wet all over the floor. So she leaned back and put her hands on her hips, real slow.

"I just *know* you ain't singing about me."

"Virginia," he replied, with a grin would've put Rudolph Valentino to shame, "I'd *never* sing about you that way."

He pulled a yellow scarf out of his trouser pocket. Like melted butter it was, with fringes.

"I saw it yesterday and thought how nice it would look against your skin," he said.

That was the first present she ever accepted from a man. Then he sang his other song:

> *I'm coming, I'm coming!*
> *Virginia, I'm coming to stay.*
> *Don't hold it agin' me*
> *For running away.*

> *And if I can win ya,*
> *I'll never more roam,*
> *I'm coming Virginia,*
> *My dixie land home.*

She was gone for him. Not like those girls on the beach: she had enough sense left to crack a joke or two. "You saying I look like the state of Virginia?" she asked, and he laughed. But she was gone.

She didn't let him know it, though, not for a long while. Even when he asked her to marry him, eight months later, he was trembling and thought she just might refuse out of some woman's whim. No, he courted her proper. Every day for a little while. They'd sit on the porch until it got too cold and then they'd sit in the parlor with two or three bright lamps on. Her mother and father were glad Virginia'd found a beau, but they weren't taking any chances. Everything had to be proper.

He got down, all trembly, on one knee and asked her to be his wife. She said yes. There's a point when all this dignity and stuff get in the way of Destiny. He kept on trembling; he didn't believe her.

"What?" he said.

"I said yes," Virginia answered. She was starting to get angry. Then he saw that she meant it, and he went into the other room to ask her father for her hand in marriage.

But people are too curious for their own good, and there's some things they never need to know, but they're going to find them out one way or the other. James had come all the way up from Tennessee and that should have been far enough, but he couldn't hide that snake any more. It just crawled out from under the rock when it was good and ready.

The snake was Jeremiah Morgan. Some fellows from Akron had gone off for work on the riverboats, and some of these fellows had heard about James. That twelve-string guitar and straw hat of his had made him pretty popular. So, story got to town that James had a baby somewhere. And joined up to this baby — but long dead and buried — was a wife.

Virginia had been married six months when she found out from sweet-talking, side-stepping Jeremiah Morgan who never liked her no-how after she'd laid his soul to rest one night when he'd taken her home from a dance. (She always carried a brick in her purse — no man could get the best of her!)

Jeremiah must have been the happiest man in Akron the day he found out. He found it out later than most people — things like that have a way of circulating first among those who know how to keep it from spreading to the wrong folks — then when the gossip's gotten to everyone else, it's handed over to the one who knows what to do with it.

"Ask that husband of your'n what else he left in Tennessee besides his best friend," was all Jeremiah said at first.

No no-good Negro like Jeremiah Morgan could make Virginia beg for information. She wouldn't bite.

"I ain't got no need for asking my husband nothing," she said, and walked away. She was going to choir practice.

He stood where he was, yelled after her like any old common person. "Mrs. Evans always talking about being Number 1! It looks like she's Number 2 after all."

Her ears burned from the shame of it. She went on to choir practice and sang her prettiest; and straight when she was back home she asked:

"What's all this number two business?"

James broke down and told her the whole story — how he'd been married before, when he was seventeen, and his wife dying in child-birth and the child not quite right because of being blue when it was born. And how when his friend was strung up he saw no reason for staying. And how when he met Virginia, he found out pretty quick what she'd done to Sterling Williams and that she'd never have no second-hand man, and he had to have her, so he never said a word about his past.

She took off her coat and hung it in the front closet. She unpinned her hat and set it in its box on the shelf. She reached in the back of the closet and brought out his hunting rifle and the box of bullets. She didn't see no way out but to shoot him.

"Put that down!" he shouted. "I love you!"

"You were right not to tell me," she said, "because I sure as sin wouldn't have married you. I don't want you now."

"Virginia!" he said. He was real scared. "How can you shoot me down like this?"

No, she couldn't shoot him when he stood there looking at her with those sweet brown eyes, telling her how much he loved her.

"You have to sleep sometime," she said, and sat down to wait.

He didn't sleep for three nights. He knew she meant business. She sat up in their best chair with the rifle across her lap, but he wouldn't sleep. He sat at the table and told her over and over that he loved her and he hadn't known what else to do at the time.

"When I get through killing you," she told him, "I'm going to write to Tennessee and have them send that baby up here. It won't do, farming a child out to any relative with an extra plate."

She held on to that rifle. Not that he would have taken it from her — not that that would've saved him. No, the only thing would've saved him was running away. But he wouldn't run either.

Sitting there, Virginia had lots of time to think. He was afraid of what she might do, but he wouldn't leave her, either. Some of what he was saying began to sink in. He had lied, but that was the only way to get her — she could see the reasoning behind that. And except for that, he was perfect. It was hardly like having a wife before at all. And the baby — anyone could see the marriage wasn't meant to be anyway.

On the third day about midnight, she laid down the rifle.

"You will join the choir and settle down instead of plucking on that guitar anytime anyone drop a hat," she said. "And we will write to your aunt in Tennessee and have that child sent up here." Then she put the rifle back in the closet.

The child never made it up to Ohio — it had died a month before Jeremiah ever opened his mouth. That hit James hard. He thought it was his fault and all, but Virginia made him see the child was sick and was probably better off with its Maker than it would be living out half a life.

James made a good tenor in the choir. The next spring, Virginia had her first baby and they decided to name her Belle. That's French for beautiful. And she was, too.

THE FAMILY

Crusader Rabbit

by Jess Mowry

Y OU COULD BE MY DAD.

Jeremy stood, waist-deep in the dumpster, his arms slimed to the elbows from burrowing, and dropped three beer cans to the buckled asphalt.

Raglan lined them up, pop-tops down, and crushed them to crinkled discs under his tattered Nike, then added them to the half-full gunnysack. Finally he straightened, and studied the boy in the dumpster. It wasn't the first time. "Yeah. I guess I could be."

Jeremy made no move to climb out, even though the stink seemed to surround him like a bronze-green cloud, wavering upward like the heat-ghosts off the other dumpster lids along the narrow alley. The boy wore only ragged jeans, the big Airwalks on his sockless feet buried somewhere below. His wiry, dusk-colored body glistened with sweat.

Not for the first time Raglan thought that Jeremy was a beautiful kid; thirteen, small muscles standing out under tight skin, big hands and feet like puppy paws, and hair like an ebony dandelion puff. A ring glistened gold and fierce in his left ear, and a faded red bandanna, sodden with sweat, hung loosely around his neck. His eyes were bright obsidian but closed now, the bruise-like marks beneath them were fading, and his teeth flashed strong and white as he panted.

Raglan could have been a larger copy of the boy; twice his age but looking it only in size, and without the earring. There was an old knife slash on his chest; a deep one with a high ridge of scar.

The Oakland morning fog had burned off hours before, leaving the alley to bake in tar-and-rot smell, yet Raglan neither panted nor sweated. There were three more dumpsters to check, and the recycle place across town would be closing soon, but Raglan asked, "Want a smoke?"

Jeremy watched through lowered lashes as Raglan's eyes changed, not so much softening as going light-years away somewhere. Jeremy hesitated, his long fingers clenching and unclenching on the dumpster's rusty rim. "Yeah. . . . No . . . I think it's time."

Jeremy's movements were stiff and awkward as he tried to climb out. Garbage sucked wetly at his feet. Raglan took the boy, slippery as a seal, under the arms and lifted him over the edge. Together, they walked back to the truck.

It was a '55 GMC one-ton, as rusted and battered as the dumpsters. There were splintery plywood sideboards on the bed. The cab was crammed with things, as self-contained as a Land Rover on safari. Even after almost two months it still surprised Jeremy sometimes what Raglan could pull from beneath the seat or out of the piled mess on the floor . . . toilet paper, comic books, or a .45 automatic.

Raglan emptied the gunnysack into an almost full garbage can in the back of the truck, then leaned against the sideboard and started to roll a cigarette from Bugler tobacco while Jeremy opened the driver's door and slipped a scarred old Big Bird Band-Aids box from under the floormat. The boy's hands shook slightly. He tried not to hurry as he spread out his things on the seat: a little rock bottle, but with grayish-brown powder in the bottom instead of crack crystals; a puff of cotton, stub of a candle, needle, and flame-tarnished spoon. On the cab floor by the shift lever was a gallon plastic jug from Pay-Less Drugs that at one time had held "fresh spring water from clear mountain streams." Raglan filled it from gas station hoses, and the water always tasted like rubber. Jeremy got it out, too.

Raglan finished rolling his cigarette, fired it with a Bic, handed the lighter to Jeremy, then started making another as he smoked. His eyes were still far away.

Jeremy looked up while he worked. "Yo. I know your other name. I seen it on your driver license. Why you call yourself Raglan?"

Smoke drifted from Raglan's nostrils. He came close to smiling. "My dad always called me that. Sposed to be from an old-time cartoon. On TV. When he was only a little kid. *Crusader Rabbit.* I never seen it.

The rabbit's homeboy was a tiger. Raglan T. Tiger. Maybe they was somethin like the Ninja Turtles . . . had adventures an stuff like that. It was a long time ago."

"Oh." Jeremy sat on the door sill. He wrapped a strip of innertube around his arm. It was hard to get it right, one-handed. He looked up again. "Um . . . ?"

"Yeah." Raglan knelt and pulled the strip tighter. His eyes were distant once more, neither watching nor looking away as he put the needle in. "You got good veins. Your muscles make 'em stand out."

Jeremy's eyes shifted from the needle, lowering, and his chest hardened a little. "I do got some muscles, huh?"

"Yeah. You ain't a bad-lookin kid. Little more exercise . . ."

Jeremy chewed his lip. "I used to miss 'em. . . . My veins, I mean. A long time ago. An, sometimes I poked right through."

"Yeah. I done that too. A long time ago."

The boy's slender body tensed for a moment, then relaxed with a sigh, his face almost peaceful and his eyes closed. But a few seconds later they opened again and searched out Raglan's. "It only makes me normal now."

Raglan nodded. "Yeah. On two a day that's all, folks." He handed Jeremy the other cigarette and fired the lighter.

The boy pulled in smoke, holding it a long time, then puffing out perfect rings and watching them float in the hot, lifeless air. "Next week it only gonna be one." He held Raglan's eyes. "It gonna hurt some more, huh?"

"Yeah."

"Um, when you stop wantin it?"

Raglan stood, snagging the water jug and taking a few swallows. Traffic rumbled past the alley mouth. Exhaust fumes drifted in from the street. Flies buzzed in clouds over the dumpsters, and a rat scuttled past in no particular hurry. "When you decide there's somethin else you want more."

Jeremy began putting his things away. The little bottle was empty. It would take most of today's cans to score another for tomorrow. "Yo. You gots to be my dad, Raglan. Why else you give a shit?"

"You figure it out, you let me know."

Raglan could have added that when he'd first found Jeremy laying behind a dumpster, the boy hadn't even been breathing. A minute more and it would have been *that's all, folks.* Why? Who in hell knew. Never ask questions if you don't want the answers.

Raglan dropped his cigarette on the pavement, slipped the sack off the sideboard, and started toward the other dumpsters. There really wasn't much reason to check them: this was the worst part of West Oaktown, and what poor people threw away was pitiful . . . everything already scraped bony and bare, rusted or rotted or beaten beyond redemption, and nothing left of any value at all. Jeremy followed, his moves flowing smooth like a kid's once again.

A few paces in front of the boy, Raglan flipped back a lid so it clanged against the sooty brick wall. Flies scattered in swarms. For a second or two he just stood and looked at what lay on top of the trash. He'd seen this before, too many times, just as he'd seen the other Jeremys. But somehow this was even harder to get used to. His hand clamped on Jeremy's shoulder, holding the boy back. But Jeremy saw the baby anyhow.

" . . . Oh . . ." Jeremy pressed suddenly close to Raglan, and Raglan's arm went around him.

"I . . . heard 'bout them," whispered Jeremy, as if scared he might wake something sleeping. "But . . . I never seen one for real."

Raglan's gaze was distant once more, seeing but not seeing the little honey-brown body, the tiny and perfect fingers and toes.

Jeremy swallowed. Then his lean chest expanded to pull in air. "What should we do?"

Raglan's eyes had turned hard. He was thinking of smirking white cops and their stupid questions . . . or smirking black cops, what in hell was the difference? He could make a quick call from a pay phone: there was one at the recycle place. Time was running short. The recycle center closed soon. The truck's tank was still almost full, but there was food to buy after Jeremy's need, and the cans were the only money. Still, he asked, "What you want to do?"

The boy looked back at the baby. Automatically he waved flies away. "What do they . . . do with 'em?" He turned to Raglan. "Is there some little coffin . . . An flowers?"

Raglan took his hand off the boy. "They burn 'em."

"*No!*"

"The ones they find. Other times they just get hauled to the dump, an the bulldozers bury 'em. You been to the dump with me."

Almost, the boy clamped his hands to his ears, but then his fists clenched. "NO! Shut the fuck up, goddamn you!"

The boy's chest heaved, muscles standing out stark. Raglan stayed quiet a moment. Finally he gripped Jeremy's shoulder once more. Why? Who in hell knew. "Okay."

Raglan walked to the truck while Jeremy watched from the dumpster, still waving away flies. Raglan stopped around back. There was a ragged canvas tarp folded behind the cab. On rainy nights he spread it over the sideboards to make a shelter. A piece of that would do. Who in hell cared? Salty sweat burned Raglan's eyes, and he blinked in the sunlight stabbing down between the buildings. The canvas was oily, and stank. Going around to the cab, he pulled one of his T-shirts from behind the seat.

The old GMC was a city truck . . . an inner city truck . . . that measured its moves in blocks, not miles. It burned oil, the radiator leaked, and its tires were worn almost bald. There were two bullet holes in the right front fender. But it managed to maintain a grudging 55, rattling first across the Bay Bridge into San Francisco, and then over the Golden Gate, headed north. Tourists were taking pictures, but not of the truck. It had a radio/tape-deck, but Jeremy didn't turn on KMEL or play the old Kriss-Kross cassette he'd found in a dumpster and patiently rewound with a pencil. He just stayed silent, rolling cigarettes for Raglan and himself, and looking sometimes through the grimy back window at the little bundle in the bed. Even when they turned off 101 near Novato onto a narrow two-lane leading west, Jeremy only stared through the windshield, his own eyes a lot like Raglan's now, even though an open countryside of gentle green hills spread out around them.

It was early evening with the sunlight slanting gold when Raglan slowed the truck and scanned the roadside ahead. The air was fresh and clean, scented with things that lived and grew, and tasting of the ocean somewhere close at hand. There was a dirt road that Raglan almost missed, hardly much more than twin tracks with a strip of yellow dandelions between. It led away toward more low hills, through fields of tall grass and wild mustard flowers. Raglan turned the truck off the pavement, and they rolled slowly to the hills in third gear.

Jeremy began to watch the flowered fields passing by, then looked at
Raglan.

"Yo. You been here before?"

"A long time ago."

"I never knew there was places like this . . . pretty, an 'out no other
people an cars. Not for real."

The road entered a cleft between hills, and a little stream ran down
to meet it, sparkling over smooth rocks. For a while the road followed
the splashing water, then turned and began to wind upward. The truck
took the grade, growling in second. The road seemed to fade as it
climbed, then finally just ended at the top of a hill. Raglan switched off
the engine. A hundred feet ahead a cliff dropped sheer to the sea. Big
waves boomed and echoed on rocks somewhere below. Silver stream-
ers of spray drifted up.

Jeremy seemed to forget why they'd come. He jumped from the
truck and ran to the cliff, stopping as close to the edge as he could, as
any boy might. Then he just stood, gazing out over the water.

Raglan leaned on the fender and watched.

Jeremy spread his arms wide for a moment, his head thrown back.
Raglan watched until the boy seemed to discover that if he took off his
shoes the grass would feel good underfoot. Then Raglan went to the
rear of the truck. There was an old square-nosed cement shovel and an
Army trenching tool.

Jeremy joined him, his half-naked body gleaming with sea-spray. He
was solemn, though his eyes had a sparkle. Raglan said nothing, just
taking the shovel in one hand and the little bundle in the crook of his
arm. Jeremy followed with the trenching tool.

The ground rose again nearby to a point that looked out on the
ocean. Raglan and Jeremy climbed to the top. Raglan cut the sweet-
smelling sod into blocks with his shovel, and Jeremy set them aside.
Earth-scent filled the air. Then they both dug. The sun was almost gone
when they finished. Though the evening was growing cooler, Jeremy
was sheened with sweat once more. But he picked some of the wild
mustard and dandelion flowers and laid them on the little mound.

Far out on the water the sun grew huge and ruddy as it sank.
Raglan built a fire near the truck, and Jeremy unrolled their blankets.
He was surprised again when Raglan conjured two dusty cans of
Campbell's soup and a pint of Jack Daniel's from somewhere in the

cab. A little later, when it was dark and the ocean boomed softly below, and the food was warm inside them, they sat side-by-side near the fire, smoking and sipping the whiskey.

"Is this campin out?" asked Jeremy.

Raglan looked around. "I guess it is."

Jeremy passed the bottle back to Raglan, then glanced at the truck: it seemed small by itself on a hilltop. "Um, we don't got enough gas to get back, huh?"

Raglan gazed into the flames. "Maybe there's someplace around here that buys cans. We'll check it out in the mornin."

Jeremy stared into the fire for a time. "It gonna hurt a lot, huh?"

"Yeah. But, I be here with you."

"I still glad we come, Raglan."

Jeremy moved close to Raglan, shivering. "So, you never seen that Crusader Rabbit? Don't know what he looked like?"

"I think he carried a sword . . . an fought dragons."

Jeremy smiled. "My dad would say somethin like that."

THE FAMILY

Silences

by Helen Elaine Lee

FROM THE BEGINNING, they were consigned to narrowed space. To cubicles with proportions that seemed just right to those safely distanced by the refuge of their personal judgments. For others, these were the spaces where she and Zella had lived, squeezed and folded in by the theories that explained her fall.

Some said curiosity was her undoing. Others said the hunter had found its prey. Some said she had met with shrunken choice. And just about everyone said it was a terrible shame.

She stood at the casket, slightly bent, leaning on solid arms. Her ceremonial wig hugged her forehead where the elastic gripped too tight, and the toe of one foot rested, poised to pivot, on the polished floor. She stared, struggling with an impulse to peel back the expression of arranged peace, searching for the woman she had known. She looked for the dark eyes that could flash caustic or tender. For the warm flush of vibrant copper skin. She looked for Zella in the face before her.

The mouth once carved and full was pinched shut. Hair that was worn loose had been set into waves and dips of unsettling symmetry. All of her features looked insistent, exaggerated by the funereal make-up that, seeking desperately to recapture life, only makes more real the passing on. As she stood staring, groping for the past, she opened and closed her hands over the worn rungs of her crutches, gathering close the fragments of their forty-seven years.

The summer of 1924, the summer they had met, she had always

privately called her "swan song." She had swung her corset-cinched body along the streets of St. Louis with long steady strides, smiling but never meeting the eyes of those who paused from whatever they were doing to partake of her radiance. The world would come to prefer the starved look, and her grand-niece would exclaim in horror at the rounded bodies in the crumbling snapshots taken in long thigh-length bathing bloomers. But in those days, she had the ideal form, "ample and forgiving," in Zella's words. She carried herself with a sense that something wonderful might happen to her. And just freed from the weakness incarnate she had married out of carnal guilt, her step was invigorated by a newfound liberation. The final act of extrication had been to tell her father, who was puzzled by the union from the first, that she was coming home.

Since her mother's death when she was barely twelve, her father had been confused to find himself alone and raising girls. They focused on the practical demands of each day, never speaking of the void her death had left, never remembering her out loud. Her father had offered a titular guidance, had offered what he knew, from the Pullman cars that were his mobile home. She could still see him standing on the platform, his brow a map of furrowed ground. He had fumbled, with the help of his dead wife's sister, Rose, to raise them right. And when she announced her intention to return home, he stood there mutely, nodding and frowning, sticking to his policy of never asking those questions whose answers he might not want to hear.

That summer had been hers, and in her memory it inhabited a soft violet space. As with all treasured time, the lens had gradually softened, rendering indistinct the sharp edges of growth, polishing smooth the glory of her freed beauty. From the vantage point of her manicurist's table at the Marquis Barber Shop, she had surveyed the range of the possible, and for the first time in her life, she felt she owned the choice. From the spin of options, she made assessments. And she did some choosing.

She chose the dark barber who, passing by throughout the day, tormented and drew her with the economy of his attention. She chose the white patron who brought fine linens and embossed leather as barter for the pulse of life she gave. For the exotic spark that he might capture, like a firefly, within his palm. And then, to everyone's astonishment, she chose Zella, in whom she had sensed something unplaceable from the first.

Maybe it was the disregard in the set of her jaw. Or the untamed richness of her laugh. She remembered sharing the knowledge that she had thought secret with her sister, Mattie. The late-night revelation that she had met a girl who was "different."

It wasn't long before she heard Zella spoken of in curtained words, in phrases of whispered violence. BulldaggerBulldaggerBulldagger. Sealed by a switchblade fold of hands and an abruptly turned back. But her fear was heightened only for an instant, and the warnings washed right over her. She had reached through the ugly words, past the fear in other eyes, scattering an arc of their beaded unshed tears. Reaching anyway. Reaching because of. Reaching for the knowing.

There was polite speculation at first about the nature of the friendship, but others found solace in her enjoyment of the company of men. As she and Zella grew closer, some distanced themselves from the taint of the "unnatural," and, more and more, she and Zella found themselves speaking in conspiratorial tones. Heads shook slowly in condemnation, and leaned closer for details. Couldsheisshedoesshe? Photos of stilted poses that would yellow over the years in dusty attic boxes betrayed a subtle intimacy that would have rendered inquiry unnecessary.

How many distant arcs had spiralled off that early meeting, fused from passion and nearly disarming understanding? Arcs like arms that would flail and smooth and push, and draw them in again and again across the years.

It was Zella who had helped her stem the fevered blood of that stagnant day, that night of rent flesh. Zella had pleaded hopelessly against the clumsy unclean slashing out of unwanted life, begging it for her own, and had stopped in alarm, midway through the barren landscape of dry ragged brush and fallen leaves, to arrange the discarded towels and newspapers. Zella had gone for help. And that was only the beginning. Over time, she had cradled her in those places that they inhabited alone.

It was Zella whose legs had been there when her own stiffened from the infection that sped through her body when help came, but didn't matter. She had spent months suspended in traction. And more months

standing in naked humiliation before rooms of white doctors who
shook their heads at such ravaged beauty, while "studying" the workings of her steel pinned joints.

About her illness no one spoke. What could be said of such a thing,
the causes of which were guarded and tinged with shame? Because it
was easier to skirt the discomfort of tragedy and send a card, visits
were infrequent and shortlived. During her one-year stay at a Boston
hospital, Zella moved there in order to be near. She had helped her
through that time, coming daily with flowers, pears and chocolates . . .
the little things with which the confined order time.

It was Zella who had built her a house without stairs. She remembered approaching it for the first time, after leaving another hospital
where she had spent two years. She had seen it from a block away,
from a little circle rubbed from the frosted car window. They had been
the first colored on the block, and she would never forget the look of
choked rage on her neighbor's flaming face as she opened her door and
stood watching them struggle to move in. The hostile stares persisted
until the area began to change, and they could finally release the
breaths they had held for decades. One more reason to keep to themselves. One more silent space.

They would spend forty-two years together in that house, washed
in the prism of afternoon light that spilled in from the window of tiny
stained glass panes. They had watched so many things pass from their
living room chairs. Joe Louis and "Amos 'n Andy" in the magic word-
picture times before TV. Assassinations that had left them speechless.
Stonewall and the slow gains of Sixties marches. And Bob Gibson's
Cardinals. And "Porgy and Bess" on the hi-fi relegated later to the
basement. And all the little changes wrought by mornings and dusks.
There had been many an outburst in that room, where discussions
were never tame. She would hold forth, gesticulating with impassioned
handphrases, while Zella waited quietly for the chance to slice in with
sharp concise rebuttals. How many times had she hoisted herself up,
snatched her crutches, and disappeared before Zella could come up
with a response?

She thought, too, of the kitchen sink, where she had stood so often,
continuing with the daily tasks that move life forward. She was sure
that if she added up the time she had spent there it would amount to
years, passed in that familiar pose. Crutches abandoned, she stood with

arms firmly placed. As she washed and chopped, she looked out through her collection of African violets, sifting time. Assessing and reassessing the past. Imagining things to come. Zella would enter and stop short, struck by the strength of her pose, mumbling, "I don't know who's disabled and who's not."

They had taken cooking seriously, and unlike the women of today, she had never really worried about getting fat. "You can't get too much of a good thing," Zella used to say. Both had their specialties, and they were always feeling some craving coming on. Zella made homemade soup with everything leftover thrown in, and seafood was an undying passion. But no matter what season or hour, it was always time for barbecue. They had sat devouring a slab one evening thirty years ago and pledged, hands raised to the heavens, that they would never stop eating ribs. Zella used to get a notion to barbecue in the middle of January sometimes, and she would find her out there in her beaver coat and boots.

They had always believed in eating and drinking, and had hosted slews of parties in the early years. Zella mixing and passing round the designated cocktail. They had spent three weeks on Margaritas once, stuck on a double-edged Tequila rush. There had been chitterling parties on the back porch. And bridge games that extended into night, stretched by the requisite bout for biggest talker of shit. Twin titles, "Bridge" and "Shit," that Zella often won.

Gathering regularly with other sharers of clandestine love, they had celebrated the move from muted tones to full voice. Waves of unencumbered expression swept a house filled with their expanding numbers. There had been such carrying on. She would never forget the time Calvin Styles had joined into the discussion of the Kinsey Report to say that such theories were originated by the great Roman philosopher, Julius Octavius Flavius. He had everyone going, taken in by the casual nature of the lie, until Zella went for the encyclopedia. The stories that man told, you never knew what was fiction and what was fact. He wove them together deftly, scorning the effort at distinction.

There were poetry readings and charades. The contest for "Homecoming Queen" that the girls judged. And that unforgettable Sunday morning after a party that had left the floor littered with sleeping bodies, when Lanie Johnson had awakened them with a lampshade on her head to serve bacon and eggs.

Zella had been comfortable in putting aside the style prescribed for women. Designated handsome, even as a girl, she had always featured tailored clothes. Back in the Forties, she wore pleated trousers and button-down shirts when not at work. She remembered the first pair of trousers they had bought. Marching into the Men's Department at Famous, she had scandalized the place. And then, moving directly into Lingerie, she had satisfied her passion for lace and silk. Zella had been thought so daring. So bold. And so many other things with which she didn't concern herself.

Zella had considered herself so tough. She walked alone at night, convinced that attitude was a foolproof repellant. And to her colleagues, she was a teacher, nothing more. No one would ever ask about the missing pictures of husband and kids. No one would visit her at home. She had mastered the protective device of distance early on, so that it was clear that things private were forever closed topics.

None of them knew how gentle she really was. But for her and their animals, who loved without judgment or condition, she would rearrange the stars. She had treated their cats like her own babies, feeding them only fresh liver from the deli down the street. "They live better than we do," she used to say, feigning outrage at their indolence, scolding them for not getting jobs.

What a legend Zella had been at Central High. Thousands of students had come through her classroom in forty years of teaching. She had touched so many lives. In the later years they had assigned her the "problem" students, knowing she could whip them into shape. For it was common knowledge that Ms. Bridgeforth took no shit. Soon thereafter, she tired of her role as enforcer, and figured forty years was long enough to spend at most things.

Former students of all ages stopped her on the street and called. One had phoned last month, an outstanding student who had become a teacher herself. The brilliant ones flourished under her tutelage . . . and none forgot her. People were still telling the story of the sleeping student who awoke to find a sign reading "Rest in Peace" hanging from her neck.

While Zella was at school, she turned to profit her gift for shaping fabric into clothes, tucking and pleating silks for white ladies who could afford such customized things. She felt at peace only when creating, and was mostly glad to have the time to herself. But sometimes her loneliness was something tangible, her companion. The quiet time was punctuated only by the humming of the machine and her outbursts at mistakes. She was swept up with profanity for a time, calling out curses with increasing fervor. She had been surprised at the particular pleasure she had found in the word "shit."

Seeking always, always, to quiet restless hands, she had mastered the entire array of needlecrafts. Her fingers took off like hummingbirds, as if to make up for what her legs could not do. She had quilted, clothed, sweatered, and afghaned her entire family, so that Mattie's child had never known a store-bought dress until the age of 21. Sewing was something her mother had given her, and she could still see her quilting in dim evening light. She had meant to pull her weight with Zella, honing her one marketable skill, the joining of needle and thread. As soon as she moved in, she ordered a brand new Singer and set in to making slipcovers. She never wanted Zella to look back and wonder if she had been saddled with an invalid.

She had forfeited her chance to go to college by marrying right out of high school and beginning a quick slide into financial ruin. Although there had never been a lot of extra money around when she was growing up, her father and Aunt Rose had been smart with what they had. Suddenly, there wasn't enough money for rent and Billy had come home with a silver flask or a new pair of snakeskin shoes. She had known that, although his family owned the first colored drug store in St. Louis, he was spoiled and weak.

But she had had to turn his fumbling and persistent conquest into something. And besides, everyone thought that marriage might grow him up. She had tried to will their union into rightness for three years, but he moved from job to job by day, and prowled at night, propelled only by the drive to enjoy life and look good in the process. It seemed like money slipped through his fingers. Suddenly it was gone, and he had nothing to show for it. Until the day he died, people would say of Billy Sampson that he could "fuck some money up."

Despite the world of her aborted plans, she had set out to expand herself through books. Her mother had read to them ritually, and had told them stories as she finished the sewing that she took in. She remembered jumping on her bed as a little girl to recite her favorite poem with great drama, "to strive to seek to find and not to yield!" Her mother was so surprised that she forgot to scold. The books that Zella couldn't manage to bring arrived by the bookmobile that visited "shut-ins" once a week. She liked to mix up the classics and the latest offerings, and kept a record of what she read, charting her journeys into other worlds. Many a time she and Zella sat up far into the night discussing their favorites. Sharing stanzas from Robert Hayden and Keats. Arguing whether *Finnegans Wake* was worth the try.

They had fought, venting anger in curses uttered with sweeping arms. Wounding with immediate regret. But then, they were devout about everything they did. Her jealous passion had erupted more than once at intruders, real or imagined. There was a dent in the dining room wall to memorialize one explosion. The cut glass pitcher had sailed through the air in slow motion, of its own volition, it seemed, just missing Zella's head. She had reached out to snatch it back, and then stared, shocked at what her hands had done.

Afterwards, there was only silence as they turned aside from the brush with loss. After walking around it for an entire day, she had quietly gone for the broom and dust pan and had swept the broken glass. They had been speechless for days, and then one afternoon Zella had returned from school with a bouquet of soaring birds of paradise . . . there must have been two dozen . . . and left it on the bed.

They had moved past the pain, but she had tucked it away with the other disillusionments, cordoned off with her indignation. She kept it in a place not too far back. Accessible. Where she could reach it to probe the soreness, or pull it out for view. She knew, now, how little it had mattered, and regretted that she had nurtured it so long.

Some of the best times she could remember were the Scrabble bouts at the folding card table they kept in the vestibule. Both determined and fiercely competitive. Both holding out for the seven-letter word. They had had to institute a timer to keep decisions from stretching into night. In summer they had taken the board to the shaded porch with cool drinks to ease the suffocating heat. To watch for the landing of wings and the drifting down of forsythia clouds.

And there were the summer visits to see Mattie's family in Detroit. They set off at dawn with waxed-paper lined tins of fried chicken and devilled eggs that were gone by the time they hit Louisville, entertaining themselves with word games and twenty questions as they drove. They came, like the seasons, for long spells at a time. One day in early June they would pull up to Mattie's two-family to find someone on the stoop relaying cries of "They're here" to those out back. Bedrooms were switched, furniture rearranged and projects begun. Summer curtains took shape in the dining room workshop where she sequestered herself on cooler days. Pound cakes, preserves, and watermelon pickles appeared, as she swung around the kitchen with the deftness of impassioned determination.

Since Mattie had sat hugging her knees and wide-eyed at the news of Zella's otherness, she had asked no questions. She had listened silently over the years to the things carefully selected for sharing. She figured that what her "sisser" chose must be okay, and when she heard the word "lesbian," she never thought of her. In decades of long-distance holiday calls and letters, Mattie had never failed to include Zella. She had loved her, like a sister, but had kept her distance from the hazy spaces where strange love lived.

She and Zella guarded Mattie's ignorance carefully, displaying just enough affection. Stilling touch. She had wondered often if sudden rage lurked below the surface calm. But in the rare moment when intimacy bled through, when their fingers brushed or she caught something in their eyes for which she had no comfortable name, Mattie turned and busied herself with straightening up.

With Mattie's child, the nature of her love for Zella was never broached. In their zealous protection of her niece's innocence, in their attempt to keep this child from the dangers of things sexual, they had sealed her off from understanding. The not telling grew, until it was larger than the reason why. And soon it was herself, and not her niece, that she protected. She didn't know what the exposure would mean for their love. Would it keep? Would it keep? Would she hesitate before she hugged? Would she pull away behind her eyes in confusion? In anger at her prolonged ignorance? In horror at the shame that implicitly accompanies such silence? Because she could not risk this magic, she was an accomplice in the hiding. Here she had chosen not to speak. She had chosen not to be known.

Disapprovals were never voiced at family reunions on the Cape Cod shore. No openly expressed disdain, even from those with connections more tenuous than blood. Just a veering from all dangerous ground, and the cool whispers that faded on their approach. That one unbelievable time, at the Wilson cottage, when Mattie had burst into a discussion on sleeping arrangements with, "You all need a room away from everyone else, the way you carry on," those nearby had turned away politely with raised eyebrows to gossip behind closed doors.

At times she had longed for open scorn. For the honesty of direct confrontation. And she had tried to use her mechanism for physical suffering on the psychic pain. To apply the coping game that she was already playing now with death. In an hour it will still throb. In a day it will wane. In a month it will scar. In a year it will fade. But she found that unarticulated condemnation made wounds that burned freezer sharp. Wounds that would never make scars. Wounds that would never heal.

She and Zella had grown old together. She remembered when they had first found gray pubic hair. They had laughed, saying it was time to get rid of those tired old things. And she had been shy about her scars at first, covering her nakedness even when alone. But Zella had embraced it all, seeing beauty even in her mangled joints. There had been wrinkles, sagging breasts, and sometimes a passing glance in the mirror that made you stop and look for the girl you had been. In forty years of Sunday afternoon massaging and lathering Zella's hair, she had watched it move through shades of gray into solid white.

And then the stroke came, suddenly, after all the years of encroaching decay, with so little concern for easing them into death. It had raged violently, knocking her from her chair, so that before she realized what was happening, Zella was lying at her side. Zella had lingered a few weeks, recognizing no one, in a place where antiseptic dispositions and artificial cheer were the only weapons against certain death. She had managed to struggle there to see her only once. With all of her illnesses, she had outlived Zella. They had never imagined it like this.

She stood there at the casket, back suddenly in the present. Although only a few moments had elapsed, their years together had passed before her in their richness. She glanced across the room of heavy drapery and slim armless chairs, completing her formal goodbye. And then she moved on, past the section where Zella's family sat, to stand with the close friends.

The parlor filled with eyes that evaded hers, unsure of the response to match the occasion. As she looked around and arranged her crutches to leave, she felt trapped within the walls erected by their fears. She realized that none of them would rock her from grief into acceptance. None of them knew the shape of her love. For forty-seven years, she had lived in a world of reduced proportions, exiled by their theories to untravelled silent space.

THE FAMILY

Proper Library

by Carolyn Ferrell

BOYS, MEN, GIRLS, CHILDREN, MOTHERS, BABIES. You got to feed them. You always got to keep them fed. Winter summer. They always have to feel satisfied. Winter summer. But then you stop and ask: Where is the food going to come from? Because it's never-ending, never-stopping. Where? Because your life is spent on feeding them and you never stop thinking about where the food is going to come from.

Formula, pancakes, syrup, milk, roast turkey with cornbread stuffing, Popsicles, love, candy, tongue kisses, hugs, kisses behind backs, hands on faces, warmth, tenderness, Boston cream pie, fucking in the butt. You got to feed them, and it's always going to be you. Winter summer.

My ma says to me, Let's practice the words this afternoon when you get home, baby. I nod to her. I don't have to use any words with her to let her know I will do what she wants. When family people come over and they see me and Ma in the kitchen like that with the words, they say she has the same face as the maid in the movies. She does have big brown hands like careful shovels, and she loves to touch and pat and warm you up with them. And when she walks, she shuffles. But if anyone is like the maid in the movies, it is Aunt Estine. She likes to give mouth, 'specially when I got the kids on my hands. She's sassy. She's got what people call a bad attitude. She makes sure you hear her heels clicking all the time, 'specially when you are lying in bed before dawn and thinking things in order, how you got to keep moving, all day long.

Click, click. Ain't nobody up yet? Click. Lazy-ass Negroes, you better not be 'specting me to cook y'all breakfast when you do get up! Click, click. I'm hungry. Click. I don't care what time it is, I'm hungry y'all and I'm tired and depressed and I need someone to talk to. Well, the hell with all y'all. That's my last word. Click, click, click.

My ma pats her hands on my schoolbag, which is red like a girl's, but that's all right. She pats it like it was my head. The books I have in it are: Biology, Woodworking for You, Math 1, The History of Civilization.

I'm supposed to be in Math 4, but the people keep holding me back. I know it's no real fault of mind. I been teaching the kids Math 4 from a book I took out the Lending Mobile in the schoolyard. The kids can do most of Math 4. They like the way I teach it to them, with real live explanations, not the kind where you are supposed to have everything already in your head and it's just waiting to come out. And the kids don't ask to see if I get every one right. They trust me. They trust my smart. They just like the feel of the numbers and seeing them on a piece of paper: division of decimals, division of fractions. It's these numbers that keep them moving and that will keep them moving when I am gone. At school I just keep failing the City Wide Tests every May and the people don't ask any questions: they just hold me back. Cousin Cee Cee said, If you wasn't so stupid you would realize the fact of them holding you back till you is normal.

The kids are almost as sad as Ma when I get ready to go to school in the morning. They cry and whine and carry on and ask me if they can sit on my lap just one more time before I go, but Ma is determined. She checks the outside of my books to make sure nothing is spilled over them or that none of the kids have torn out any pages. Things got to be in place. There got to be order if you gonna keep on moving, and Ma knows that deep down. This morning I promise to braid Lasheema's hair right quick before I go, and as I'm braiding, she's steady smiling her four-year-old grin at Shawn, who is a boy and therefore has short hair, almost a clean shave, and who can't be braided and who weeps with every strand I grease, spread, and plait.

Ma warns me, Don't let them boys bother you now, Lorrie. Don't let 'em.

I tell her, Ma, I have not let you down in a long time. I know what I got to do for you.

She smiles but I know it is a fake smile, and she says, Lorrie, you are my only son, the only real man I got. I don't want them boys to get you from me.

I tell her because it's the only thing I can tell her, You cooking up something special tonight?

Ma smiles and goes back to fixing pancake mix from her chair in the kitchen. The kids are on their way to forgetting about me 'cause they love pancakes more than anything and that is the only way I'll get out of here today. Sheniqua already has the bottle of Sugar Shack Syrup and Tonya is holding her plate above her nappy lint head.

Tommy, Lula Jean's Navy husband, meets me at the front door as I open it. Normally he cheers me up by testing me on Math 4 and telling me what a hidden genius I am, a still river running deep, he called it one time. He likes to tell me jokes and read stories from the Bible out loud. And he normally kisses my sister Lula Jean right where I and everybody else can see them, like in the kitchen or in the bedroom on the bed, surrounded by at least nine kids and me, all flaming brown heads and eyes. He always says: This is what love should be. And he searches into Lula Jean's face for whole minutes.

I'm leaving for Jane Addams High School and I meet Tommy and he has a lady tucked under his arm and it ain't Lula Jean. Her hair is wet and smells like mouthwash and I hate him in a flash. I never hate anybody, but now I hate him. I know that when I close the door behind me a wave of mouths will knock Tommy and this new lady down but it won't drown them. My sister Anita walks into the room and notices and carries them off into the bathroom, quick and silent. But before that she kisses me on my cheek and pats her hand, a small one of Ma's, on my chest. She whispers, You are my best man, remember that. She slips a letter knife in my jacket pocket. She says, If that boy puts his thing on you, cut it off. I love you, baby. She pushes me out the door.

Layla Jackson who lives in the downtown Projects and who might have AIDS comes running up to me as I walk out our building's door to the bus stop. She is out of breath. I look at her and could imagine a boy watching her chest heave up and down like that and suddenly get romantic feelings, it being so big and all, split like two kickballs bouncing. I turn my eyes to hers, which are crying. Layla Jackson's eyes are red. She has her baby Tee Tee in her arms but it's cold out here and she doesn't have a blanket on him or nothing. I say to her, Layla, honey, you gonna freeze that baby to death.

And I take my jacket off and put it over him, the tiny bundle.

Layla Jackson says, Thanks Lorrie man I got a favor to ask you please don't tell me no please man.

Layla always makes her words into a worry sandwich.

She says, Man, I need me a new baby-sitter 'cause I been took Tee Tee over to my mother's but now she don't want him with the others and now I can't do nothing till I get me a sitter.

I tell her, Layla, I'm going back to school now. I can't watch Tee Tee in the morning but if you leave him with me in the cafeteria after fifth period I'll take him on home with me.

She says, That means I got to take this brat to Introduction to Humanities with me. Shit, man. He's gonna cry and I won't pass the test on Spanish Discoverers. Shit, man.

Then Layla Jackson thinks a minute and says, Okay, Lorrie, I'll give Tee to you at lunch in the cafeteria, bet. And I'll be 'round your place 'round six for him or maybe seven, thanks, man.

Then she bends down and kisses Tee Tee on his forehead and he glows with what I know is drinking up an oasis when you are in the desert for so long. And she turns and walks to the downtown subway, waving at me. At the corner she comes running back because she still has my jacket and Tee Tee is waving the letter knife around like a flag. She says that her cousin Rakeem was looking for me and to let me know he would waiting for me 'round his way. *Yes.* I say to her, See you, Layla, honey.

Before I used to not go to Jane Addams when I was supposed to. I got in the habit of looking for Rakeem, Layla's cousin, underneath the Bruckner Expressway, where the Spanish women sometimes go to buy oranges and watermelons and apples cheap. He was what you would call a magnet, only I didn't know that then. I didn't understand the different flavors of the pie. I saw him one day and I had a feeling like I wanted him to sit on my lap and cradle me. That's when I had to leave school. Rakeem, he didn't stop me. His voice was just as loud as the trucks heading towards Manhattan on the Bruckner above us: This is where your real world begins, man. The women didn't watch us. We stared each other in the eyes. Rakeem taught me how to be afraid of school and of people watching us. He said, Don't go back, and I didn't. A part of me was saying that his ear was more delicious than Math 4. I didn't go to Jane Addams for six months.

On the BX 17 bus I see Tammy Ferguson and her twins and Joe Smalls and that white girl Laura. She is the only white girl in these Bronx projects that I know of. I feel sorry for her. She has blue eyes and red hair and one time when the B-Crew-Girls were going to beat her butt in front of the building, she broke down crying and told them that her real parents were black from the South. She told them she was really a Negro and they all laughed and that story worked the opposite than we all thought. Laura became their friend, like the B-Crew-Girls' mascot. And now she's still their friend. People may laugh when she ain't around but she's got her back covered. She's loyal and is trying to wear her thin flippy hair in cornrows, which in the old days woulda made the B-Crew, both boys and girls, simply fall out. When Laura's around, the B-Crew-Girls love to laugh. She looks in my direction when I get on the bus and says, Faggot.

She says it loud enough for all the grown-up passengers to hear. They don't look at me, they keep their eyes on whatever their eyes are on, but I know their ears are on me. Tammy Ferguson always swears she would never help a white girl, but now she can't pass up this opportunity, so she says, You tight-ass homo, go suck some faggot dick. Tammy's kids are taking turns making handprints on the bus window.

I keep moving. It's the way I learned: keep moving. I go and sit next to Joe Smalls in the back of the bus and he shows me the Math 3 homework he got his baby's mother Tareen to do for him. He claims she is smarter now than when she was in school at Jane Addams in the spring. He laughs.

The bus keeps moving. I keep moving even though I am sitting still. I feel all of the ears on us, on me and Joe and the story of Tareen staying up till 4 A.M. on the multiplication of fractions and then remembering that she had promised Joe some ass earlier but seeing that he was sound asleep snoring anyway, she worked on ahead and got to the percent problems by the time the alarm went off. Ha ha. Joe laughs, I got my girl in deep check. Ha ha.

All ears are on us, but mainly on me. Tammy Ferguson is busy slapping the twins to keep quiet and sit still, but I can feel Laura's eyes like they are a silent machine gun. Faggot faggot suck dick faggot. Now repeat that one hundred times in one minute and that's how I am feeling.

Keep moving. The bus keeps rolling and you also have to keep moving. Like water like air like outer space. I always pick something for my mind. Like today I am remembering the kids and how they will be waiting for me after fifth period and I remember the feel of Lasheema's soft dark hair.

Soft like the dark hair that covers me, not an afro, but silky hair, covering me all over. Because I am so cold. Because I am so alone. A mat of thick delicious hair that blankets me in warmth. And therefore safety. And peace. And solitude. And ecstasy. Lasheema and me are ecstatic when we look at ourselves in the mirror. She's only four and I am fourteen. We hold each other smiling.

Keep moving. Then I am already around the corner from school while the bus pulls away with Laura still on it because she has fallen asleep in her seat and nobody has bothered to touch her.

On the corner of Prospect Ave. and East 167th Street where the bus lets me out, I see Rakeem waiting for me. I am not supposed to really know he's there for me and he is not supposed to show it. He is opening a Pixie Stick candy and then he fixes his droopy pants so that they are hanging off the edge of his butt. I can see Christian Dior undies. When I come nearer he throws the Pixie Stick on the ground next to the other garbage and gives me his hand just like any B-Crew-Boy would do when he saw his other crew member. Only we are not B-Crew members, we get run over by the B-Crew.

He says, Yo, man, did you find Layla?

I nod and listen to what he is really saying.

Rakeem says, Do you know that I got into Math 3? Did you hear that shit? Ain't that some good shit?

He smiles and hits me on the back and he lets his hand stay there.

I say, See what I told you before, Rakeem? You really got it in you to move on. You doing all right, man.

He grunts and looks at his sneakers. Last year the B-Crew-Boys tried to steal them from him but Rakeem screamed at them that he had AIDS from his cousin and they ran away rubbing their hands on the sides of the buildings on the Grand Concourse.

Rakeem says, Man, I don't have nothing in me except my brain that tells me: Nigger, first thing get your ass up in school. Make them know you can do it.

I say, Rakeem, you are smart, man! I wish I had your smart. I would be going places if I did.

He says, And then, Lorrie, I got to get people to like me and to stop seeing me. I just want them to think they like me. So I got to hide *me* for a while. Then you watch, Lorrie, man: *much* people will be on my side!

I say to him, Rakeem, you got Layla and baby Tee Tee and all the teachers on your side. And you got smart. You have it made.

He answers me after he fixes his droopy pants again so that they are hanging off exactly the middle of his ass: Man, they are whack! You know what I would like to do right now, Lorrie? You know what I would like? Shit, I ain't seen you since out went back to school and since I went back. Hell, you know what I would like? But it ain't happening 'cause you think Ima look at my cousin Layla and her bastard and love them and that will be enough. But it will never be enough.

I think about sitting on his lap. I did it before but then I let months go by because it was under the Bruckner Expressway and I believed it could only last a few minutes. It was not like the kind of love when I had the kids because I believed they would last forever.

He walks backwards away and when he gets to the corner, he starts running. No one else is on the street. He shouts, Rocky's Pizza! Ima be behind there, man. We got school fooled. This is the master plan. Ima be there, Lorrie! *Be there.*

I want to tell Rakeem that I have missed him and that I will not be there but he is gone. The kids are enough. The words are important. They are all enough.

The front of Jane Addams is gray-green with windows with gates over all of them. I am on the outside.

The bell rings first period and I am smiling at Mr. D'Angelo and feeling like this won't be a complete waste of a day. The sun has hit the windows of Jane Addams and there is even heat around our books. Mr. D'Angelo notices me but looks away. Brandy Bailey, who doesn't miss a thing, announces so that only us three will hear: Sometimes when a man's been married long he needs to experience a new kind of loving, ain't that what you think, Lorrie?

For that she gets thrown out of the classroom and an extra day of in-school suspension. All ears are now on me and Mr. D'Angelo. I am beyond feeling but I know he isn't. And that makes me happy in a way, like today ain't going to be a complete waste of a day.

He wipes his forehead with an imported handkerchief. He starts out saying, Class, what do we remember about the piston, the stem, and the insects? He gets into his questions and his perspiration stops and in two minutes he is free of me.

And I'm thinking: Why couldn't anything ever happen, why does every day start out one way hopeful but then point to the fact that ain't nothing ever going to happen? The people here at school call me ugly, for one. I know I got bug eyes and I know I am not someone who lovely things ever happen to, but I ask you: Doesn't the heart count? Love is a pie and I am lucky enough to have almost every flavor in mine. Mr. D'Angelo turns away from my desk and announces a surprise quiz and everybody groans and it is a sea of general unhappiness but no one is more than me, knowing that nothing will ever happen the way I'd like it to, not this flavor of the pie. And I am thinking: Mr. D'Angelo, do you know that I would give anything to be like you, what with all your smarts and words and you know how to make the people here laugh and they love you. And I would give anything if you would ask me to sit on your lap and ask me to bite into your ear so that it tingles like the bell that rips me in and out of your class. I would give anything. Love is a pie. Didn't you know that? Mr. D'Angelo, I am in silent love in a loud body.

So don't turn away. *Sweat.*

Mrs. Cabrini pulls me aside and whispers, My dear Lorrie, when are you ever going to pass this City Wide? You certainly have the brains. And I know that your intelligence will take you far, will open new worlds for you. Put your mind to your dreams, my dear boy, and you will achieve them. You are your own universe, you are your own shooting star.

People 'round my way know me as Lorrie and the name stays. Cousin Cee Cee says the name fits and she smacks her gum in my face whenever she mentions that. She also adds that if anyone ever wants to kick my ass, she'll just stand around and watch because a male with my name and who likes it just deserves to be watched when whipped.

Ma named me for someone else. My real name is Lawrence Lincoln Jefferson Adams. It's the name on my school records. It's the name Ma says I got to put on my application to college when the time comes. She knows I been failing these City Wide Tests and that's why she wants to practice words with me every day. She laughs when I get them wrong but she's afraid I won't learn them on my own, so she asks me to practice them with her and I do. Not every day, but a whole lot: look them up and pronounce them. Last Tuesday: Independence. Chagrin. Symbolism. Nomenclature. Filament. On Wednesday: only Apocrypha. Ma says they have to be proper words with proper meanings from a dictionary. You got to say them right. This is important if you want to reach your destiny, Ma says.

Like for instance the word *Library*. All my life I been saying that "Liberry." And even though I knew it was a place to read and do your studying, I still couldn't call it right. Do you see what I mean? I'm about doing things, you see, *finally* doing things right.

Cousin Cee Cee always says, What you learning all that shit for? Don't you know it takes more than looking up words to get into a college, even a damn community college? Practicing words like that! Is you a complete asshole?

And her two kids, Byron and Elizabeth, come into the kitchen and ask me to teach them the words too, but Cee Cee says it will hurt their eyes to be doing all that reading and besides they are only eight and nine. When she is not around I give them words with up to ten letters, then they go back to TV with the other kids.

When we have a good word sitting, me and Ma, she smooths my face with her hands and calls me Lawrence, My Fine Boy. She says, You are on your way to good things. You just got to do things the proper way.

We kiss each other. Her hands are like the maid in the movies. I know I am taken care of.

Zenzile Jones passes me a note in History of Civilization. It's the part where Ptolemy lets everyone know the world is round. Before I open it, I look at her four desks away and I remember the night when I went out for baby diapers and cereal and found her crying in front of a fire hydrant. I let her cry on my shoulder. I told her that her father was a sick man for sucking on her like that.

The note says, Please give me a chance.

Estine Smith, my mother's sister who wants me and the kids to call her by both names, can't get out of her past. Sometimes I try on her clothes when I'm with the kids and we're playing dress-up. My favorite dress is her blue organza without the back. I seen Estine Smith wear this during the daytime and I fell in love with it. I also admired her for wearing a dress with the back out in the day, but it was only a ten-second admiration. Because then she opens her mouth and she is forever in her past. Her favorite time to make us all go back to is when they lynched her husband, David Saul Smith, from a tree in 1986 and called the TV station to come and get a look. She can't let us go one day without reminding us in words. I never want to be like her, ever. Everybody cries when they are in her words because they feel sorry for her, and Estine Smith is not someone but a walking hainted house.

Third period. I start dreaming about the kids while the others are standing in line to use the power saw. I love to dream about the kids. They are the only others who think I am beautiful besides Ma and Anita. They are my favorite flavor of the pie, even if I got others in my mind.

Most of the time there are eight but when my other aunt, Samantha, comes over I got three more. Samantha cries in the kitchen and shows Ma her blue marks and it seems like her crying will go on forever. Me, I want to take the kids' minds away. We go into Ma's room where there is the TV and we sing songs like "Old Gray Mare" and "Bingo Was His Name O" or new ones like "Why You Treat Me So Bad?" and "I Try to Let Go." Or else I teach them Math 4. Or else I turn on the TV so they can watch Bugs or He-Man and so I can get their ironing done.

Me, I love me some kids. I need me some kids.

Joe Smalls talks to me in what I know is a friendly way. The others in Woodworking for You don't know that. They are like the rest of the people who see me and hear the action and latch on.

Joe Smalls says, Lorrie, man, that bitch Tareen got half the percentage problems wrong. Shit. Be glad you don't have to deal with no dumb-ass Tareen bitch. She nearly got my ass a F in Math 3.

I get a sad look on my face, understanding, but it's a fake look because I'm feeling the rest of the ears on us, latching, readying. I pause to Heaven. I am thinking I wish Ma had taught me how to pray. But she doesn't believe in God.

Junior Sims says, Why you talking that shit, Joe, man? Lorrie don't ever worry about bitches!

Perry Samson says, No, Lorrie never ever thinks about pussy as a matter of fact. Never ever.

Franklin says, Hey, Lorrie, man, tell me what you think about, then? What can be better than figuring out how you going to get that hole, man? Tell me what?

Mr. Samuels, the teacher, turns off the power saw just when it gets to Barney Moore's turn. He has heard the laughter from underneath the saw's screeching. Everybody gets quiet. His face is like a piece of lumber. Mr. Samuels is never soft. He doesn't fail me even though I don't do any cutting or measuring or shellacking. He wants me the hell out of there.

And after the saw is turned off, Mr. Samuels, for the first time in the world, starts laughing. The absolute first time. And everybody joins in because they are afraid of this and I laugh too because I'm hoping all the ears will go off me.

Mr. Samuels is laughing Haw Haw like he's from the country. Haw Haw. Haw Haw. His face is red. Everyone cools down and is just smiling now.

Then he says, Class, don't mess with the only *girl* we got in here!

Now it's laughter again.

Daniel Fibbs says, Yeah, Mr. Samuels is *on!*

Franklin laughs, No fags allowed, you better take your sissy ass out of here less you want me to cut it into four pieces.

Joe Smalls is quiet and looking out the window.

Junior Sims laughs, Come back when you start fucking bitches!

Keep moving, keep moving.

I pick up my red bag and wade towards the door. My instinct is the only thing that's working, and it is leading me back to Biology. But first out the room. Inside me there is really nothing except for Ma's voice:

Don't let them boys. But inside there is nothing else. My bones and my brain and my heart would just crumble if it wasn't for that swirling wind of nothing in me that keeps me moving and moving.

Perry laughs, I didn't know Mr. Samuels was from the South.

With his eyelashes, Rakeem swept the edges of my face. He let me know they were beautiful to him. His face went in a circle around mine and dipped in my eyes and dipped in my mouth. He traveled me to a quiet place where his hands were the oars and I drifted off to sleep. The thin bars of the shopping cart where I was sitting in made grooves in my back, but it was like they were rows of tender fingers inviting me to stay. The roar of the trucks was a lullaby.

Layla Jackson comes running up to me but it's only fourth period because she wants to try and talk some sense into Tyrone. She hands me little Tee Tee. Tyrone makes like he wants to come over and touch the baby but instead he flattens his back against the wall to listen to Layla. I watch as she oozes him. In a minute, they are tongue-kissing. Because they are the only two people who will kiss each other. Everyone says that they gave themselves AIDS and now have to kiss each other because there ain't no one else. People walk past them and don't even notice that he has his hand up her shirt, squeezing the kickball.

Tee Tee likes to be in my arms. I like for him to be there.

The ladies were always buying all kinds of fruits and vegetables for their families underneath the Bruckner Expressway. They all talked Spanish and made the sign of the cross and asked God for forgiveness and gossiped.

Rakeem hickeyed my neck. We were underneath the concrete bridge supports and I had my hands on the handle of a broken shopping cart, where I was sitting. Don't go back, Rakeem was telling me, don't go back. And he whispered in my ear. And I thought of all the words I had been practicing, and how I was planning to pass that City Wide. Don't go back, he sang, and he sat me on his lap and he moved me around there. They don't need *you*, he said, and *you* don't need *them.*

But I do, I told him.

This feeling can last forever, he said.

No, it can't, I said, but I wound up leaving school for six months anyway. That shopping cart was my school.

I am thinking: It will never be more. I hold Tee Tee carefully because he is asleep on my shoulder and I go to catch the BX 17 back to my building.

Estine Smith stays in her past and that is where things are like nails. I want to tell her to always wear her blue organza without the back. If you can escape, why don't you all the time? You could dance and fling your arms and maybe even feel love from some direction. You would not perish. *You* could be free.

When I am around and she puts us in her past in her words, she tells me that if I hada twitched my ass down there like I do here, they woulda hung me up just by my black balls.

The last day Rakeem and I were together, I told him I wanted to go back, to school, to everyone. The words, I tried to explain about the words to Rakeem. I could welcome him into my world if he wanted me to. Hey, wasn't there enough room for him and me and the words?

Hell no, he shouted, and all the Spanish women turned around and stared at us. He shouted, You are an ugly-ass bastard who will always be hated big time and I don't care what you do; this is where your world begins and this is where your world will end. Fuck you. You are a pussy, man. Get the hell out of my face.

Ma is waiting for me at the front door, wringing her hands. She says it's good that I am home because there is trouble with Tommy again and I need to watch him and the kids while she goes out to bring Lula Jean home from the movies, which is where she goes when she plans on leaving Tommy. They got four kids here and if Lula Jean leaves, I might have to drop out of school again because she doesn't want to be tied to anything that has Tommy's stamp on it.

I set Tee Tee down next to Tommy on the sofa bed where I usually sleep. Tommy wakes up and says, Hey, man, who you bringing to visit me?

I go into the kitchen to fix him some tea and get the kids' lunch ready. Sheniqua is playing the doctor and trying to fix up Shawn, who always has to have an operation when she is the doctor. They come into the kitchen to hug my legs and then they go back in the living room.

Tommy sips his tea and says, Who was that chick this morning, Lorrie, man?

I say I don't know. I begin to fold his clothes.

Tommy says, Man, you don't know these bitches out here nowadays. You want to show them love, a good time, and a real deep part of yourself and all they do is not appreciate it and try to make your life miserable.

He says, Well, at least I got Lula. Now that's some woman.

And he is asleep. Sheniqua and her brother Willis come in and ask me if I will teach them Math 4 tonight. Aunt Estine rolls into the bedroom and asks me why do I feel the need to take care of this bum, and then she hits her head on the doorframe. She is clicking her heels. She asks, Why do we women feel we always need to teach them? They ain't going to learn the right way. They ain't going to learn shit. That's why we always so alone. Click, click.

The words I will learn before Ma comes home are: Soliloquy, Disenfranchise, Catechism. I know she will be proud. This morning before I left she told me she would make me a turkey dinner with all the trimmings if I learned four new words tonight. I take out my dictionary but then the kids come in and want me to give them a bath and baby Tee Tee has a fever and is throwing up all over the place. I look at the words and suddenly I know I will know them without studying.

And I realize this in the bathroom and then again a few minutes later when Layla Jackson comes in cursing because she got a 60 on the Humanities quiz. She holds Tee but she doesn't touch him. She thinks Tyrone may be going to some group where he is meeting other sick girls and she doesn't want to be alone. She curses and cries, curses and cries. She asks me why things have to be so fucked. Her braids are coming undone and I tell her that I will tighten them up for her. That makes Layla Jackson stop crying. She says, And to top it off, Rakeem is a shit. He promised me he wouldn't say nothing but now that he's back in school he is broadcasting my shit all over the place. And that makes nobody like me. And that makes nobody want to touch me.

I put my arm around Layla. Soon her crying stops and she is thinking about something else.

But me, I know these new words and the old words without looking at them, without the dictionary, without Ma's hands on my head. Lasheema and Tata come in and want their hair to be like Layla's and they bring in the Vaseline and sit around my feet like shoes. Tommy wakes up still in sleep and shouts, Lula, get your ass on in here. Then he falls back to sleep.

Because I know I will always be able to say the words on my own. I can do the words on my own and that is what matters. I have this flavor of the pie and I will always have it. Here in this kitchen I was always safe, learning the words till my eyes hurt. The words are in my heart.

Ma comes in and shoves Lula Jean into a kitchen chair. She says, Kids, make room for your cousin, go in the other room and tell Tommy to get his lame ass out here. Layla, you can get your ass out of here and don't bring it back no more with this child sick out his mind, do your 'ho'ing somewhere out on the street where you belong. Tommy, since when I need to tell you how to treat your wife? You are a stupid heel. Learn how to be a man.

Everybody leaves and Ma changes.

She says, I ain't forgot that special dinner for you, baby. I'm glad you're safe and sound here with me. Let's practice later.

I tell her, Okay, Ma, but I got to go meet Rakeem first.

She looks at me in shock and then out the corner of my eye I can tell she wants me to say no, I'll stay, I won't go to him. Because she knows.

But I'm getting my coat on and Ma has got what will be tears on her face because she can't say no and she can't ask any questions. Keep moving.

And I am thinking of Rocky's Pizza and how I will be when I get there and how I will be when I get home. Because I am coming back home. And I am going to school tomorrow. I know the words, and I can tell them to Rakeem and I can share what I know. Now he may be ready. I want him to say to me in his mind: Please give me a chance. And I know that behind Rocky's Pizza is the only place where I don't have to keep moving. Where there is not just air in me that keeps me from crumbling, but blood and meat and strong bones and feelings. I will be me for a few minutes behind Rocky's Pizza and I don't care if it's quiet just a few minutes. I pat my hair down in the mirror next to the kitchen door. I take Anita's letter knife out my jacket pocket and leave it on the table next to where Tommy is standing telling his wife that she never knew what love was till she met him and why does she have to be like that, talking about leaving him and shit? You keep going that way and you won't ever know how to keep a man, bitch.

THE FAITH

The Diary of an African Nun

by Alice Walker

OUR MISSION SCHOOL is at the foot of lovely Uganda mountains and is a resting place for travelers. Classrooms in daylight, a hotel when the sun sets.

The question is in the eyes of all who come here: Why are you — so young, so beautiful (perhaps) — a nun? The Americans cannot understand my humility. I bring them clean sheets and towels and return their too much money and candid smiles. The Germans are very different. They do not offer money but praise. The sight of a black nun strikes their sentimentality; and, as I am unalterably rooted in native ground, they consider me a work of primitive art, housed in a magical color; the incarnation of civilization, anti-heathenism, and the fruit of a triumphing idea. They are coolly passionate and smile at me lecherously with speculative crystal eyes of bright historical blue. The French find me *charmant* and would like to paint a picture. The Italians, used as they are to the habit, concern themselves with the giant cockroaches in the latrines and give me hardly a glance, except in reproach for them.

I am, perhaps, as I should be. *Gloria Deum. Gloria in excelsis Deo.*

I am a wife of Christ, a wife of the Catholic church. The wife of a celibate martyr and saint. I was born in this township, a village "civilized" by American missionaries. All my life I have lived here within walking distance of the Ruwenzori mountains — mountains which show themselves only once a year under the blazing heat of spring.

2

When I was younger, in a bright blue school uniform and bare feet, I came every day to the mission school. "Good morning," I chanted to the people I met. But especially to the nuns and priests who taught at my school. I did not then know that they could not have children. They seemed so productive and full of intense, regal life. I wanted to be like them, and now I am. Shrouded in whiteness like the mountains I see from my window.

At twenty I earned the right to wear this dress, never to be without it, always to bathe myself in cold water even in winter, and to wear my mission-cropped hair well covered, my nails clean and neatly clipped. The boys I knew as a child are kind to me now and gentle, and I see them married and kiss their children, each one of them so much what our Lord wanted — did he not say, "Suffer little children to come unto me"? — but we have not yet been so lucky, and we never shall.

3

At night I sit in my room until seven, then I go, obediently, to bed. Through the window I can hear the drums, smell the roasting goat's meat, feel the rhythm of the festive chants. And I sing my own chants in response to theirs: "*Pater noster, qui es in caelis, sanctificetur nomen tuum, adveniat regnum tuum, fiat voluntas tua, sicut in caelo et in terra. . . .*" My chant is less old than theirs. They do not know this — they do not even care.

Do *I* care? Must I still ask myself whether it was my husband, who came down bodiless from the sky, son of a proud father and flesh upon the earth, who first took me and claimed the innocence of my body? Or was it the drumbeats, messengers of the sacred dance of life and deathlessness on earth? Must I still long to be within the black circle around the red, glowing fire, to feel the breath of love hot against my cheeks, the smell of love strong about my waiting thighs! Must I still tremble at the thought of the passions stifled beneath this voluminous rustling snow!

How long must I sit by my window before I lure you down from the sky? Pale lover who never knew the dance and could not do it!

*I bear your colors, I am in your livery, I belong to you. Will you not come
down and take me! Or are you even less passionate than your father who
took but could not show his face?*

4

Silence, as the dance continues — now they will be breaking out the
wine, cutting the goat's meat in sinewy strips. Teeth will clutch it,
wring it. Cruel, greedy, greasy lips will curl over it in an ecstasy which
has never ceased wherever there were goats and men. The wine will
be hot from the fire; it will cut through the obscene clutter on those lips
and turn them from their goat's meat to that other.

At midnight a young girl will come to the circle, hidden in black she
will not speak to anyone. She has said good morning to them all, many
mornings, and has decided to be like them. She will begin the dance —
every eye following the blue flashes of her oiled, slippery body, every
heart pounding to the flat clacks of her dusty feet. She will dance to her
lover with arms stretched upward to the sky, but her eyes are leveled
at her lover, one of the crowd. He will dance with her, the tempo will
increase. All the crowd can see the weakening of her knees, can feel in
their own loins the loosening of her rolling thighs. Her lover makes her
wait until she is in a frenzy, tearing off her clothes and scratching at
the narrow cloth he wears. The eyes of the crowd are forgotten. The
final taking is unbearable as they rock through the oldest dance.
The red flames roar and the purple bodies crumple and are still. And
the dancing begins again and the whole night is a repetition of the
dance of life and the urgent fire of creation. Dawn breaks finally to the
acclaiming cries of babies.

5

"Our father, which art in heaven, hallowed be thy name, thy kingdom
come, thy will be done on earth —" And in heaven, would the ecstasy
be quite as fierce and sweet?

"Sweet? Sister," they will say. "Have we not yet made a convert of
you? Will you yet be a cannibal and eat up the life that is Christ because it eases your palate?"

What must I answer my husband? To say the truth would mean

oblivion, to be forgotten for another thousand years. Still, perhaps I shall answer this to him who took me:

"Dearly Beloved, let me tell you about the mountains and the spring. The mountains that we see around us are black, it is the snow that gives them their icy whiteness. In the spring, the hot black soil melts the crust of snow on the mountains, and the water as it runs down the sheets of fiery rock burns and cleanses the naked bodies that come to wash in it. It is when the snows melt that the people plant their crops; the soil of the mountains is rich, and its produce plentiful and good.

"What have I or my mountains to do with a childless marriage, or with eyes that can see only the snow; or with you or friends of yours who do not believe that you are really dead — pious faithful who do not yet realize that barrenness is death?

"Or perhaps I might say, 'Leave me alone; I will do your work'; or, what is more likely, I will say nothing of my melancholia at your lack of faith in the spring. . . . For what is my faith in the spring and the eternal melting of snows (you will ask) but your belief in the Resurrection? Could I convince one so wise that my belief bears more fruit?"

How to teach a barren world to dance? It is a contradiction that divides the world.

My mouth must be silent, then, though my heart jumps to the booming of the drums, as to the last strong pulse of life in a dying world.

For the drums will soon, one day, be silent. I will help muffle them forever. To assure life for my people in this world I must be among the lying ones and teach them how to die. I will turn their dances into prayers to an empty sky, and their lovers into dead men, and their babies into unsung chants that choke their throats each spring.

6

In this way will the wife of a loveless, barren, hopeless Western marriage broadcast the joys of an enlightened religion to an imitative people.

In a House of Wooden Monkeys

by Shay Youngblood

SUMMER RAIN sounded heavy on the new tin roof. Loud whispers ran up and down the rough wooden pews. Father MacIntyre was getting impatient. He knew Moses would not come and he could not perform the ceremony if Moses was not there.

"Yate where is Moses? We have waited long enough." The Father said.

"He soon come Father. He know we waiting for he." The young woman answered, lowering her eyes to the fat brown baby she held close to her heart. She didn't seem to notice the impatience in the air, but her throat was as tight as a witch's drum and her spine tingled with the tension. On this most important day she and Moses had fought over the ritual to baptize the baby in Holy Water to protect it. Moses had raised his hand to slap her, a thing he had never done, and left before he did. She was in misery, but could not show it before all those who had come to witness.

The child in Yate's arms was restless and cried. Yate carefully opened her worn, white cotton blouse and offered her breast, full with milk, to the child. She guided her tender nipple into her baby's mouth, it sucked noisily. Her clear brown eyes watched, her full dark lips smiled at her baby, the most happiness she had ever had in her young life, because she got to keep this one. She had lost two babies already.

Hill folk said Widow took her babies. The first one Widow drowned in a dream sack, told folk she dreamed Yate's baby would be born dead, and it was. The second time, Widow strangled her baby with the mother's string. Everyone knew Widow had done it. Widow was a toothless young woman who had come to Greenlove Mountain as a girl to live with her grandmother, a rootwoman, in a wood shack by the road. Her grandmother died shortly after she came and as she was strange and thought to be blessed of evil, no one would take her in. So she lived high up on the mountain. She got the name Widow by the birthmark shaped like a black widow spider she carried on her forehead and by her dark attitude and visions of death.

The third time Yate discovered that there was a child growing inside of her, she began to go to Greenlove Mountain church on sundays. The whiteman had come from England to teach her people about his god, who he said was the All Mighty and All Powerful one. He certainly was a rich god. He allowed the priest to dress in fancy velvet robes and white satin hats, to perform grand rituals with white candles set in heavy brass and drink French red wine, he called blood, from an inlaid golden chalice.

Yate burned offerings at the breaking of each day and went to the church services every sunday morning to pray to the whiteman's god, hoping his prayer and juju would be stronger than Widow's magic, this time. She prayed with a desperate passion to Jesus and she prayed to the Virgin Mary, whom she pitied, to save her baby. Baby Gillian was born in her Mama Etta's house, arriving lungs filled with fear and clenched fists beating the air that smelled so of blood. Yate cried, praised the Lord and her personal juju. She kissed the Holy Medal she wore around her neck. Moses, he laughed at her, shaking his dreadlocks from side to side at his woman's foolishness.

"It is Jah taking care of thee woman, you betta forget dis jesus nonsense." He said, lighting a bowl of herb, smoke and scent of it rising in the air between them. More had come between them because of her promise to the whiteman's god.

Moses was pleased at the birth of a living child. For two years they had only stolen hours. Mama Etta had kept a sharp eye on her daughter, sending her to town school hoping to keep the young lovers apart. With the birth of Baby Gillian even Mama Etta could not hold Yate, they could live together as man and wife. Mama Etta poured rum into the earth and slit the throat of a baby goat.

For as long as Yate could remember there were babies in Mama Etta's house. Soft, fat, warm, brown babies that cried when pinched, and
laughed when teased in tender spots. Mama Etta was a rich woman,
because she would always have someone to care for her. She had fifteen children to her credit. Her sons would provide for her and carry
the family name to another generation and her daughters when educated would marry well and visit her often with many grandchildren
to warm her lap. To Yate these things were important, to have someone
to love you always, a man could leave you. To deliver a living, growing
thing from her body was a miracle she wanted to bear. She knew that
Mama Etta could not keep her from her man, even though he was a
Rastaman, if she were to bear his child. She loved Moses enough, she
could feel it in her heart and blood and limbs whenever he watched
her undress at the river or touched her body with a reverence and
ritual she marveled at when they made love on mossy patches of damp
earth beneath the coolness of the waterfall.

Yate promised Jesus she would go up the hill to the whiteman's
church everyday if her baby was allowed to be among the living, and
so she did. When Baby Gillian was born alive and kicking, Yate invited
all her friends and family, many of whom had never been to church, to
come see her baby be blessed with Holy Water. Some came only for the
spectacle, as they were suspicious of a man with only one god.

Saint Julien came because she was Yate's best girlfriend. They were
friends and lovers long before she met Moses. Saint Julien's husband
was at sea for many months of the year, it was only natural that she
longed for hands and lips of passion on her breasts and on the soft spot
between her thighs and warm arms to hold her through the endless
nights her husband was away. So many men of the village loved the
sea. She also could not have a baby by Yate to anger her husband. She
often wished that many things were not as they were, but when the
men returned from the sea, the women turned from each other in that
intimate way, back to their men. It had always been the way, from her
grandmother's time and before.

The faithful of the congregation were waiting, hands pressed in respect for the ritual. This was to be the first christening in the church.
Four families were present with new babies to be sprinkled with the
priest's Holy Water. Father MacIntyre blew his nose into a white lace

handkerchief and cleared his throat, as he did when he was about to speak on some important subject in his sunday morning talks to them.

"I can wait no longer. Let us begin." The Father said.

"But my Gillian, will you bless her?" Yate whispered, tears reaching for the edge of her eyes.

The Father turned away from her tears and to those who had come for the ceremony. He was so cold his words chilled like ice.

"A man who would allow his child to be punished for his sins is not a man. If a woman is loose and without moral responsibility, she is the devil's sin and so is her child. In good conscience I cannot perform the rites for Yate's bastard child."

Angry looks flew above the injustice of his words. Up to this point there had been silence, but Mama Etta spilled herself into the room and stepped like a queen up to the altar, to her daughter's side.

"She is a daughter of the gods and loved not less. She ain't belonging to no Rastaman, to no devil, no other woman, just me. I give her life and breath from between these thighs, something you can never do, because it is you who are evil and cannot bear a miracle. You are a no feeling wooden monkey and so are the people of this house." She spit in the dust before him.

Taking her daughter's arm, they made their way down the aisle and through the doors of the church. Father MacIntyre stood stiffly before the podium and watched helplessly as the pews emptied behind Mama Etta, Yate and Baby Gillian. The silent procession of those who had lost faith wound down the dirt path to the village.

Widow stood grinning in the doorway after most all had gone but the Father. She said a few words that made no sense to human ears, shook some feathers, then squat to pee on the threshold. The remaining of the congregation watched in surprise as the Father seized his throat and choked himself to the ground, where he wallowed like a dog. Widow watched him some then turned to follow the others.

THE FAITH

Young Reverend Zelma Lee Moses

by Joyce Carol Thomas

A HOOT OWL feasted round eyes on the clapboard building dipped in April shadow at the edge of a line of magnolia and redbud trees.

The owl peered through the budding branches until he focused on the kitchen, in which a mother, brown and fluffy as buttermilk biscuits, stood by the muslin-draped window, opening glass jars of yams, okra, tomatoes, spinach, and cabbage and stirred the muted colors in a big, black cast-iron pot. Then she raised the fire until she set the harvest green and red colors of the vegetables bubbling before fitting the heavy lid in place and lowering the flame.

She watched the blaze, listening to the slow fire make the food sing in low lullaby.

When it was time, she ladled the stew onto warmed platters, sliced warm-smelling red-pepper cornbread into generous wedges, and poured golden tea into three fat clay mugs.

"Dinner!" her voice sang.

"Coming, Mama," said tall Zelma, who was leaning over stoking the fire in the wood fireplace. Her shadow echoed an angular face, backlit by the light from the flames.

When she turned around, her striking features showed misty black eyes in a face which by itself was a chiseled beauty mark. Indeed, she gave the phrase "colored woman" its original meaning. She was colored, with skin the sugar brown of maple syrup.

At the kitchen table she sat between her aging parents. Her father, his earthen face an older, darker, lined version of Zelma's, his hair thick as white cotton and just as soft and yielding to Zelma's touch, started the blessing.

"We thank thee for this bountiful meal. . . ."

"May it strengthen us in our comings and goings," Zelma continued.

"Lord, do look down and watch over us for the work that lies ahead," chanted the father and daughter together.

"And bless the hands of the cook who prepared this meal."

"Amen," said the mother.

They ate as the quiet light outside their window began to fall in whispers. Zelma told time by how long the fire in the fireplace at their backs danced. She counted the dusky minutes in how long it took to clear the table, to clean and place the dishes in their appointed places in the cabinet, to scrub the black cast-iron pot until it gleamed black as night.

Then it was the hushing hour, the clock of the trees and the sky and the flying crickets said, "Come, let us go into the house of the Lord." And they started out, hands holding hands, down the red clay dusty road together.

Before long they were joined by Mother Augusta, a pillar of the community and cornerstone of the church.

The eighty-year-old Mother Augusta, who like a seer was frequently visited by psychic dreams, enjoyed a reputation as the wrinkleless wonder because her face was so plump no lines could live there, causing folks to say, "She either a witch or she been touched by God." Today Mother Augusta kept up a goodly pace with her wooden cane. Augusta and her late husband had broken the record for the longest continuous years of service as board members to the church. She was a live oak living on down through the years and keeping up the tradition now that her husband was gone on.

Today as the family walked along, Mother Augusta smiled at Zelma, thinking it was just about wedding time for the young woman. The older Mother Augusta's head flooded with memories of Zelma and how she had always been special, but one memory stood out from the rest. One April memory many years back.

The Bible Band of preschoolers had come marching into the church that Easter looking so pretty, and all the children serious, strict-postured, the girls with black braids laced with ribbons like rainbows. A few with hot-iron curls.

Each of the ten children had stepped forward and given a biblical recitation, a spring poem, a short song. The church house nodded, a collection of heads in a show of approval as one child with pink ribbons sat down.

Another reciter in a little Easter-egg-yellow child's hat stood up and delivered an age-old poem. Finishing, she gave a sigh of relief, curtsied, and took her seat.

Then Zelma, pressed and curled, stepped forward, her maple hands twisting shyly at the sleeves of her lavender-blue and dotty-green organdy dress. In white cotton stockings and ebony patent leather shoes so shiny and carefully walked in no mud scuffed the mirror bright surface, her feet just wouldn't stay still. Zelma couldn't get settled; she nervously listed from one foot to the other.

She started her speech in an expressionless, singsong tone. No color anywhere near it. It was a typical Bible Band young people's performance that the whole church endured, as yet another duty, as yet another means of showering encouragement upon the young.

Zelma recited:

> *"It's raining, it's raining;*
> *The flowers are delighted;*
> *The thirsty garden greens will grow,*
> *The bubbling brooks will quickly flow;*
> *It's raining, it's raining, a lovely rainy day."*

Now instead of curtsying and sitting herself down, Zelma stared suddenly at the crucifix above the sanctuary door.

She stared so hard until every head followed her gaze that had settled on the melancholy light beaming on the crucifix.

Then in a different voice she started to speak.

"And Jesus got up on the cross and He couldn't get down."

Mother Augusta had moved forward in her seat as if to say, "Hear tell!"

And Zelma went on like that, giving her own interpretation of the crucifixion, passion making her voice vibrate.

An usher moved forward to stop her, but Mother Augusta waved the usher back.

"Well?" said Mother Augusta.

"If He could have got down, He would've," Zelma supposed.

Zelma talked about stubbing her toe, about how much it hurt, and she reported the accident she had of once stepping on a rusty nail.

"If one nail could hurt so bad, how painful the Christ nails piercing Him in His side must have been," Zelma decided.

"And so I think He didn't get down, because you see," she added in a whisper, "something was holding Him there.

"It was something special."

"Yes?" called Mother Augusta just as a deacon moved to herd the child to her pew. Bishop Moses waved the deacon back.

"I know He wanted to get down. Why else would He have said, 'My Lord, my Lord, why hast Thou forsaken me?'"

"Amen," said the first usher.

"But you see," said Zelma, "something was holding my Lord there, something was nailing Him to that old rugged cross, and it wasn't just metal nails."

Now the entire church had gotten into the spirit with young Zelma.

"Wasn't just metal nails," sang the church in response.

"It was nails of compassion."

"Nails of compassion," repeated the church.

"He was nailed with nails of sorrow," Zelma preached.

"Nails of sorrow," the church rang out.

"Nailed for our iniquity," Zelma called.

"Nailed," the church responded.

"He was nailed, he was bruised for our transgression."

Then Zelma let go. "The nail, the nail that wouldn't let Him down, the nail that would give Him no peace, the nail that held Him there was the nail of love."

"Love," shouted the church.

"Jesus," Zelma said, in a lower muted voice, "Jesus got up on the cross and He couldn't get down, and because He couldn't get down, and because He couldn't get down, He saved a world in the name of a nail called Love!"

It was all told in rhythms.

As the church went ecstatic with delight, somebody handed Zelma her guitar.

Another child hit the tambourine.

And the music started talking to itself.

"She been called to preach," announced Mother Augusta.

Bishop Moses, scratching his getting-on-in-years head, was as thunderstruck as the other members of the congregation. He flitted from one to the other as they stood outside in the church yard to gossip and to appraise the service.

One of the elder deacons opened his mouth to object, starting to say something backward, something about the Bible saying fellowship meant fellows not women, but the eldest sister on the usher board proclaimed, "God stopped by here this morning!"

Who could argue with that?

This evening as Augusta walked along with Zelma's family skirting the honeysuckle-wrapped trees of the Sweet Earth woods, they eagerly approached that same church, now many years later. Two mockingbirds singing and chasing each other in the tulip trees just by the tamed path leading into the church house reminded Mother Augusta that it was almost Easter again.

Spring was lifting her voice through the throats of the brown thrashers and the wood thrushes and the wild calls coming from the woods.

And in the light colors of bird feathers, beauty spread her charm all over the land.

Inside the church a wine-red rug stitched with Cherokee roses led the way down the center aisle around a pot-bellied stove and continued up three steps. Behind the lectern sat three elevated chairs for Bishop Benjamin Moses, Zelma Lee Moses, and any dignitary who might come to visit. Then behind the three chairs perched seats for the choir members who filled them when the singers performed formally and on Sundays.

The church had been there so long that the original white paint on the pew armrests had been worn and polished by generations of the members' hands until in spots the pure unadulterated rosewood peeked through.

The Bishop opened the weeknight service by saying a prayer. All over the building the members stood, knelt, sat, waiting for the rapture.

Soon Testimony Service was over and the congregational singing had been going on for some time before they felt that special wonder when the meeting caught fire. First they felt nothing and then they all felt the spirit at one time.

The soul-thrilling meters, the changing rhythms, the syncopated tambourine beats trembled inside every heart until they were all of one accord.

Stripes of music gathered and fell across the people's minds like lights.

Melodies lifted them up to a higher place and never let them down.

The notes rang out from the same source: the female, powerhouse voice of Zelma Lee Moses. She bounced high on the balls of her feet as she picked the guitar's steely strings, moving them like silk ribbons. The congregation felt the notes tickling from midway in their spines and on down to the last nerve in their toes.

Zelma gave a sweet holler, then lowered her voice to sing so persuasively that the people's shoulders couldn't stay still, just had to move into the electrifying rhythm and get happy.

Zelma gospel-skipped so quick in her deep-blue robe whirling with every step she took, somebody had to unwrap the guitar from around her neck. She was a jubilee all by herself.

And the people sang out her name, her first two names, so musically that they couldn't call one without calling the other: *Zelma Lee.*

Perfect Peace Baptist Church of Sweet Earth, Oklahoma, sat smack-dab in the middle of a meadow near the piney woods. This zigzag board wooden building with the pot-bellied stove in its center served as Zelma Lee Moses's second home.

Here she sang so compellingly that shiny-feathered crows from high in the treetops winged lower, above the red clay earth, roosted on black tupelo tree branches, peeked in the church window and bobbed their heads, flapped their glossy feathers, cawing in time to the quickened-to-perfection, steady beat.

Reverend Zelma Lee Moses closed her eyes and reached for the impossible note made possible by practice and a gift from God. Row after row of worshippers commenced to moaning watching her soul, limited only by her earthly body, full and brimming over, hop off the pulpit. She sang, "Lord, just a little mercy's all I need."

And she didn't need a microphone.

"Look a yonder, just a skipping with the gift and the rhythm of God." Mother Augusta over in the Amen Corner clapped her hands in syncopated time. At home, Sister Moses, Zelma's blood mother, was the woman of the house, but in the sanctuary Mother Augusta, the mother of the church, was in charge.

Zelma began and ended every sermon with the number "Lord, Just a Little Mercy's All I need."

The sound tambourined and the Sweet Earth sisters swooned and swooned, the ushers waved their prettiest embroidered handkerchiefs under the noses of the overcome, but they couldn't revive the fainting women as long as young Reverend Zelma Lee Moses dipped into her soul and crooned,

> *"Lord, just a little mercy's all I need.*
> *If I have sinned in any way,*
> *Down on my knees I'll stay and pray,*
> *Lord, just a little mercy's all I need."*

How her silver voice swooped over the words, coloring them a mystery color that did not exist except in the mind which received it, forgot it, then gave it back.

Daniel, a newcomer who'd only been in town for one year, wanted Zelma to pay him some attention; how she had stayed unattached puzzled him. He knew the statuesque Reverend Zelma Lee Moses easily attracted men. On this third visit to church Daniel saw how men flocked like butterflies to Zelma's color-rich flower garden, to the sunbows in her throat every time she opened her mouth to preach or sing. Out flew the apricot hues of hollyhock. The gold of the goldenrod, the blue pearl of Jacob's ladder. Daniel got a little jealous watching Zelma study the fellows, her camera eyes pausing on one young man's skin that rivaled the brown feather colors of a red-tailed hawk. Her admiring gaze directed briefly at the young man made Daniel itch around the collar. He turned neon red inside watching her watching him.

But it was on Daniel that Zelma's camera stopped scanning and focused. She saw his skin flirting with light, his inky hair accepting the brilliance like a thirsty canvas accepts a crown of black beads dabbed by a painter's shimmering brush.

His eyes shone with such a joy-lit intensity of sparkling double black flecked with the silver crescents of the moon that looking into them made her want to die or live forever.

Now Zelma, already so touched with talent that limousined producers from New York came down and waved rock and roll contracts in front of her, wanted to ask Daniel his opinion of the intricate offers.

"What do you think about this here music contract," she asked him one night after service.

"Rock and roll? I don't know. Seems to me you ought to keep singing gospel. But take your time," he advised after studying the papers.

"Time," she said thoughtfully, and when she looked in Daniel's eyes, she knew he was just thinking about what was best for her.

"Think I'll write gospel right next to rock and roll," she said.

"Makes sense to me," said Daniel.

"What you studying to be?" she asked.

"How do you know I'm studying anything?" he teased.

"You're getting lots of books in the mail."

"Oh that! I'm studying to be an electrician or a bishop like your daddy," he said, handing the music recording agreement back to her.

"So that's why you're always carting the Bible and those big mail-order books around!"

"That's the truth," he acknowledged with a grin.

"An electrical bishop."

"An electrician-bishop," said Daniel.

"Uh-hm," said Zelma Lee in her most musical-speaking voice.

When she took her time about signing the contracts, the producers resorted to recording her mellifluous gospel voice to see if they could find someone else to match it who wouldn't study too long over the words in their contracts. But they never could.

Nobody else had that red clay memory in her throat, fat gold floating in the colored notes.

So they returned to try again and again until the young singer, after understanding as best she could all the small print and inserting the part about gospel, took pen in hand and signed the document.

That night her voice rivered out melodies so clear that when the music company visitors from the outside world heard the rhythms rinsed in some heavenly rain, they either thought of art or something dangerous they could not name.

Since the producers were coming with music on their minds, they only thought of songs and never perceived the threat.

The producers seemed so out of place in that place that welcomed everybody, common and uncommon, that they sometimes giggled suddenly without warning and thought that instead of stained glass they saw singing crows dressed in polka dot hats looking in the windows.

When they packed up their recording gear and stood on the outside of the church by the side of the road where the wild irises opened their blue mouths, Mother Augusta, leaning on her cane, bent an ear to the limousine and commented, "Say, good sirs, that motor's running so soft on this long machine you can hear the flowers whisper. Umph, umph, umph!"

"What?"

The music merchants leaned back in their accordion cars and waved the chauffeur forward. They eased on down the road shaking their heads, couldn't figure out what she was talking about.

One said to the other, "Whispering flowers? Another one of those old Oklahoma fogeyisms."

"No doubt," agreed his partner, hugging the hard-earned contract to his breast.

Reverend Zelma Lee Moses only sang so the people could rejoice.

"A whole lot of people will rejoice when you sign this contract," the producer had said.

"Will?" said Zelma.

"Of course I'll be one of them." The record company man smiled as he extended the pen.

And more people did rejoice about a year after she'd signed the contract.

The echo of colors flew across the airwaves. The song "A Little More Mercy" made women listening to the radio as they pressed clothes still their irons in the middle of rough, dried collars, watching the steam weave through the melody.

Daniel, in his pine thick backyard chopping wood, his head awash in the sound, wondered at the miracle of vinyl, catching a voice like that and giving it back so faithfully. He reached inside the open kitchen window and turned up the homemade radio he had assembled with his own hands. The sound flowed out to him even more distinctly. He raised the ax, chopping more rhythmically, clef signs scoring the wood.

More and more people rejoiced.

Both Zelma's mothers, Augusta and her natural mother, ended up with limousines, if they wanted them, turning the dials to their favorite gospel stations, which always played their favorite artist to the additional accompaniment of limousine tires dancing down the road.

Zelma only sang so the people could rejoice.

And therein lay the danger. Preachers who had that kind of gift had to be around folks who loved them, for the devil stayed busy trying to stick the old pitchfork in. Zelma kept herself too wrapped up with her gift to notice the devil's works; those around her had to be aware, wary, and protective.

She preached one Sunday till her voice rang hoarse with power and her guitar hit a note so high it rang heaven's doorbell. And all up and down the rows, women stood up, their tambourines trembling like rhinestones.

Palm Sunday, the Sunday when visiting congregations from as far away as New Orleans, Louisiana, arrived with their clothes speckled with the Texas dust they passed through to get to Sweet Earth, Oklahoma, and the new gospel recording star; the visiting Louisiana choir, hot from their journey, crowded the choir stands to overflowing and mopped sweat from their curious brows.

Palm Sunday in Sweet Earth at Perfect Peace Baptist Church, the deacons with trembling hands, babies sucking blisters on their thumbs, folks so lame they had to wheel themselves in in wheelchairs, eyeglassed teachers, and farmers with weed cuts persisting around their scrubbed nails, all stepped out, in shined shoes, pressed suits, spring dresses, and assorted hats, coming to hear the female preacher perform on Palm Sunday, and she didn't disappoint them; she preached until her robe stuck to her sculptured body, wringing wet. She preached until dear Daniel, in an evergreen shirt of cotton and linen, Daniel so handsome she could squeeze the proud muscles straining against his shirt sleeves, until Daniel who had been tarrying for a year on the altar, dropped his tambourine and fell out in the sanctuary overcome by the holy spirit.

A cloud of "Hallelujah's" flew up like joy birds from the congregation when Daniel got religion. Still the Sweet Earth saints in front of Zelma with their mouths stretched open on the last syllable of Halle-lujah, had not *shouted,* had not danced in the spirit.

Only one mover shook loose in the whole flock of them. And that was dimpled Daniel, an earth angel dressed in light and leaf green and smelling of musky sweet spring herbs, stepping all up and down and inside the gospel beat, a human drum.

It was just about time for Zelma to wind up the sermon and finish with the song "Lord, Just a Little Mercy's All I Need."

And she felt as if she hadn't done her job at all if she couldn't get ten sisters and several deacons moved from their sanctified seats.

The visiting choir voices behind her had sunk and their volume di-minished. She was used to more call and response and certainly much more shouting.

"Why's this church so cold?" she asked.

Stopped in the middle of her sermon and asked it.

What she could not see behind her were the visiting choir members being carried off the stage one by one. The entire soprano section of the New Orleans New Baptist Youth Choir had danced until they fainted, until only one or two straggly alto voices were left.

The Sweet Earth congregation gazed so amazed at the rapture and the different shouting styles of the Louisiana choir that they settled back and, instead of joining in the commotion, sat transfixed on their chairs like they were in a downtown theater watching a big city show on tour.

Nobody told Zelma she had preached so hard that she had set a record for the number of folks falling out in one sermon.

She wasn't aware of the record she'd just broken because she couldn't see the Louisiana choir behind her, she only saw dear Daniel in a golden trance, speaking in tongues, Daniel who made her feel like an angel every time she beheld his face.

When she pronounced Daniel "saved" and accepted him into the church, she made a silent promise, looking into Daniel's deep dark gaze, finding her passion in the curve of his molasses colored lips.

Before the week-long revival was over Daniel would be proud of her.

And then it came to her, not from God but from the soft place in the center of her soul-filled passion.

She would do what nobody else had done.

Come Sunday, the crowning day of the revival, young Reverend Zelma Lee Moses would fly.

"On Easter Sunday," she announced, talking to the Church but looking Daniel in the eyes, "on the last day of the revival, on the day Christ came forth from the tomb, Church, it's been given me to fly."

Their opened mouths opened even wider.

The New Orleans New Baptist Youth Choir, scheduled to be in concert in Louisiana on Eastern Sunday, took a vote and sent back word that their Oklahoma stay would be extended and that the Sunday School Choir would have to sing two extra numbers instead to make up for their absence.

Since the Reverend Zelma Lee Moses's voice had moved over them like a mighty wind, knocking them from their perches in the choir stand and rendering them senseless from the mighty impact of her spirit, they could not leave, even if they wanted to.

"Young Reverend Zelma Lee Moses's gonna fly come Sunday evening," the ecstatic choir director chanted over the Oklahoma-to-Louisiana telephone wires.

That very night, beneath her flower garden patched quilt, Mother Augusta dreamed. First she saw Zelma Lee inside the church, making the announcement about flying, then she saw a red-dressed she-devil down in her hell home listening to Zelma's promise to fly on Sunday. Slack-jawed, the devil looked up at the church and the people being moved like feathers and got jealous.

"Flying on Sunday? Zelma Lee's gonna fly!" The next day these two phrases lit up the telephone wires in Sweet Earth.

The funny thing about all of this, of course, was that passion was playing hide-and-seek.

Daniel wanted Zelma as much as Zelma wanted him, but she did not know this.

"I want this Zelma," Daniel whispered to himself in the still hours of the night when the lightning bugs flew like earth stars outside his window. It was then he spoke, forgetting his Sweet Earth enunciation, in the lyrical thick accent of the swamp place from which he came.

As experienced with women as Daniel was he had never seen anybody like Zelma, and so he studied her carefully; he slowly wondered how to approach her. He didn't want to make even one false move.

Just seeing her was sometimes enough to take his breath away. Zelma had already stolen his heart when he saw her sitting in the pulpit between the visiting evangelist and Bishop Moses that first Sunday he visited Perfect Peace.

Because the visiting evangelist preached, Zelma was not required to speak or sing. It was her presence alone that had attracted him. He didn't even know she could talk, let alone sing. Even quiet she was a sight.

Hearing her sing on his second Sunday visit brought him to his knees. Folks thought he had fallen down to pray.

Eventually he did kneel to pray all the subsequent Sundays, but his belly still quivered like Jell-O even now remembering what the woman did to his mind.

And Zelma had never had so much as one boyfriend before. Since she was a preacher's daughter, she was expected, when it came to passion, to wait 'til her appointed time. Music had been her passion; music had been enough.

Then came Daniel. When she looked at Daniel, her heart opened on a door to a God she had not known was even there.

Daniel she wanted to impress even though he was already smitten.

Anything she did beyond being who she already was was needless, was superfluous, but young Zelma didn't know this.

As Mother Augusta might have said, "Humph. The devil found work."

The first thing Zelma did wrong was she built a short platform out of the wrong wood and didn't ask the deacons of the church to help her out.

"Didn't ask nobody nothing," complained Deacon Jones, he was so mad his trembling bottom lip hung down almost to his knees. "Got to drive a nail in at the right angle or it won't hold!"

Second thing Zelma did wrong was she went downtown to some unsanctified, whiskey-drinking folks and had them sew some wings onto her robe; looking like vultures roosting, they sewed crooked, leaving tobacco smoke lingering in the cloth.

"You don't tell sinning people nothing sacred," Mother Augusta clucked in a chastening voice to whoever's ears were free to listen.

"Sinning people! They nature is such that they misunderstand the mysteries.

"If they see trumpets on your head, they refer to them as horns.

"Now and then you run across an exception, but half the time they don't know *what* they looking at," said Mother Augusta.

And too, the seasoned women in the church primped their mouths and got offended, because for as long as they could remember they had personally sewn the sacred robe with the smoke blue thread that had been blessed and sanctified in a secret ritual that nobody discussed, lest a raven run away with their tongue.

"Who knows what them drunk people put in them wings?"

Mother Augusta, the human *Jet* and *Ebony* combined, kept a running oral column going among the older people all the revival days approaching Easter Sunday.

In the meantime Mother Augusta wanted to have words with the young preacher, but the members of the New Orleans New Baptist Youth Choir kept Zelma so occupied the female preacher didn't even have time for her own Sweet Earth congregation.

Even her own father, the retired Bishop Benjamin Moses, couldn't get a word in edgewise. Between counseling the New Orleans young folk, Zelma studied the Bible in the day and slept in the church house at night after falling out exhausted from continuous prayer. In the wee hours of the morning she slipped home, where her mother had prepared steaming hot bathwater and laid out fresh clothes. She refused her mother's platters of peppergrass greens, stewed turkey wings and Sunday rice, including her favorite dewberry biscuits. She was fasting and only took water.

But the community fed the Louisiana visitors. The gray-haired, white-capped mothers of the church, mothers of the copper kettles and porcelain pans, kept their kitchens bustling with younger Sweet Earth women. They instructed these sisters of the skillet in the fine art of baking savory chicken-and-dressing and flaky-crusted peach cobblers.

"Put a little more sage in that cornbread.

"Make that dumpling plumper than that," Mother Augusta ordered, throwing out to the birds a pan of dough that didn't pass her inspection.

She personally turned over each peach, seeing with her farsighted eyes what stronger, younger eyes often missed.

The young Louisiana people stood around, underfoot, mesmerized by Zelma, but Mother Augusta saw what they couldn't see and what Zelma's mother's eyes wouldn't see.

She prayed, Mother Augusta did.

Zelma prayed, but her love for Daniel had her all puffed up and half-drunk with passion.

Come Easter Sunday she would fly, then after church she would offer Daniel her hand, and if he held it much longer than friendly, they would be companions.

Every night she preached and promised to fly on Sunday.

Every night the crowd got thicker.

By Sunday night the standing-room-only audience pushed and elbowed each other in competition with the cawing crows for a low, window-level place on the tupelo branches above the clay by the window.

Oh, the crowd and the crows!

The church house sagged, packed to the rafters. And Mother Augusta ordered the carpenter to check the floor planks because they might not be able to take the whipping she knew Zelma was going to give them once she got started stomping the floor and making the Bible holler.

"Tighten that board over yonder," she ordered.

Another sound that added to the clamor was the hum of more buses arriving from New Orleans. Some members back home in the Louisiana church were so intrigued by the choir's decision to remain in Sweet Earth that they boarded yet another bus and struck out for northeast Oklahoma to see what the excitement was all about, driving on through the sleepless night so they could reach Perfect Peace in time for Sunday service and the promised night of miracles.

The New Orleans contingency was so glad to have made it in time, they entered the church swaying down the aisle, fingers circling circles in the air, uncrossed feet whipping up the holy dance.

As the evening lengthened, something softened in the air. Maybe it was the effect of the full moon.

The Reverend Zelma Lee Moses preached about wings that Sunday night.

The soft shadows cast by the full moon looked like veils hanging over the sanctuary.

She took her text from Psalms.

"Read, Brother Daniel!"

Daniel opened his Bible and quoted, "Keep me as the apple of thy eye, hide me under the shadow of thy wings.

"And He shall cover thee with his feathers, and under his wings shalt thou trust: his truth shall be thy shield and buckler."

"Read!"

Daniel found the next Psalm and continued, "Be merciful unto me, O God, be merciful unto me: for my soul trusteth in thee: yea, in the shadow of thy wings will I make my refuge. . . ."

"Read!"

". . . Who layeth the beams of his chambers in the waters; who maketh the clouds his chariot: who walketh upon the wings of the wind."

Now the great flying moment the Sweet Earth people had been anticipating for a whole week arrived. The spectacle that the New Orleans visitors awaited was here at last.

As she approached the platform, the young Zelma Lee Moses began to sing the closing number, "Lord, just a little mercy's all I need."

One sister let out a long, low holler. Transfigured, a ghost took over her throat, and it was like a special spirit had flown in through the open church window; like the miracle of the cross, Christ ascending into heaven would be repeated in another way.

It was too crowded for the people to cut loose. They swayed backward, swooned; and the crush of their numbers held each member up.

Now Zelma Lee Moses approached the foot of the launching platform, the platform built without consulting the deacons.

She mounted it and spread the arms of her robe, revealing the drunk-people-made wings.

And the congregation hushed.

Neither crowd nor crows flapped.

Young Zelma Lee Moses leaped!

But instead of being taken up by a mighty wind into the rafters above the gaping crowd, she plopped, sprawled, spread out on the oak floor at the feet of the frowning deacons, under the scrutinizing gaze of Mother Augusta, dragging her wings in the sawdust.

"The hem's crooked. And the thread's red wrong." Mother Augusta pointed, almost choking.

"Caw!" sang a crow.

Zelma scrambled back up, sure that the Lord had not forsaken her.

Maybe all she needed was a little speed to prime her wings: Recalling the way kites had to be hoisted, remembering her long adolescent legs running down the weed fields fast and far enough before the kite yielded to the wind and took off, she opened her hands and spread her wings.

And with her long arms out as far as she could fling them, she ran, up and down the aisles, her arms moving up and down, her hands making circles. Up and down the aisles.

Up. Down.

Fast, faster.

Up. Down.

Fast. Faster.

She ran past her future sweetheart-to-be and Daniel saw that she could not fly.

And she could not fly.

Finally her mother said, "Daughter?"

And the people got mad.

"Limp-winged!" somebody said in an un-Christian voice.

They chased her on out of the church house. Out across the weed field like a carnival of people chasing a getting-away kite. They ran her under the full moon, under the crows shadowing and cawing above them and on into the woods. She disappeared right through a grove of white oak and yellow pines. The last thing Daniel saw was Zelma's left foot, looking like a wing, as she slipped farther into the piney woods.

The people stopped right at the lush wildness, which was a curtain of green forest pulled like a secret against the place where unknown lakes and streams flowed and where wild foxes and all sorts of untamed creatures roamed.

Daniel was the only one who could have followed her there into the wildness, for he knew wild places like the back of his hand. But the look Zelma had shot him had said No.

And then he remembered that the piney woods was a natural bird refuge. There also doves flew in the thicket, marsh hens strutted proud, and quail called across the muddy and winding Sweet Earth River. He saw Zelma trembling there among the white and golden lilies and the singing crowd. And Daniel knew this red earth of willow trees, dogwoods, and redbuds could hypnotize a person like Zelma who had wings in her feet, until it would be difficult for her to leave its allure.

As the church people ended their chase, he also stopped. It seemed as if she had been gone for weeks already. But instead of following her, he did the best thing: He turned back with the others.

Mother Augusta now raised her trembling hand and directed the choir to sing Zelma's favorite number, "Lord, Just a Little Mercy's All I Need," which they began singing softly, and she conducted the song so that it slowed down to a soothing pace. Finally the Louisiana choir dispersed, gathered their belongings, got on board and continued their sweet, wafting music on the midnight bus as they started out for home and Louisiana.

"She'll be back," Mother Augusta promised Daniel, who was sitting by the altar, head sadly bowed, looking long-faced, sifting the sawdust through his fingers, sawdust Zelma Lee Moses made rise by pounding the oak into powder while doing one of her gospel-skipping holy dances.

"She'll be back," Mother Augusta repeated in a knowing voice, then added as she took apart the launching platform, "This church is full of God's grace and mercy. Zelma's seen to that." She was remembering Zelma's invisible flight of the soul every time she looked at Daniel.

"When?" asked Daniel in that deep baritone voice.

"In three days," Mother Augusta answered, mumbling something about God making humans just a little bit lower than the angels.

"Being a little spryer than a timeworn woman, she didn't know she couldn't fly," sighed Mother Augusta. "Yet we hear her flying every Sunday morning on the radio."

"Well then why did the people come if they knew she couldn't fly?" asked Daniel, forgetting the miracle of the sawdust in his hand and the clef notes in the wood he chopped that radio afternoon when Zelma's first record came over the airwaves.

"Listen," said Mother Augusta.

"I'm listening."

"They came for the same reason they got mad," answered Mother Augusta. "They didn't want to miss it just in case she could." The elderly woman paused, then added, "When she realizes she already can fly, she'll be back. Take a lesson from the crow. Why should a bird brag about flying — that jet bird just spreads two easy wings. When Zelma knows that lesson, and she will know it, she'll return, she'll sure enough return."

The next day the women gathered in the morning pews and Mother Augusta offered up a prayer of early thanks.

The deacons joined in, serving the women broom-wheat tea, gathering the cloth to help the sisters in the sanctuary sew a new gown fit for a child of God.

Somebody started lining a hymn.

It started out as a low moan.

Then it grew until it was full to bursting.

It exploded and the right word dropped from a mouth, scooted along the floor, lifted its head, flapped in place, flew up and became a note hanging from the light bulb in the rafters of the church.

A moan. A lyric.

And it went on like that, from moan to lyric.

Until the song was fully realized.

Three long days passed with the people sitting, waiting, sewing, singing.

Mother Augusta was lining a hymn and she was lining a hem.

And on the third day, and on the third day they heard the crows gathering around the church.

But they did not open their beaks.

The hymn stopped, circled the light bulb above their heads.

The sound of silence.

The sound of waiting.

Then the next sound they heard was the door of the church opening softly.

"Who is it?" Daniel asked.

"Sh!" Mother Augusta whispered.

Nobody turned around except the waiting silence.

The silence stood up and opened its welcome arms.

Zelma.

Zelma Lee.

Zelma Lee Moses.

On the third day Zelma Lee Moses, looking a little down at the heel, stepped through Perfect Peace, paused and put on her long sanctified robe of invisible wings, picked up her guitar, mounted the steps to the pulpit, opened her mouth, and began to sing a crescendo passage in a higher voice with light wings glittering in the fire-singed notes, "Lord, just a little mercy's all I need."

And she looked at Daniel with a look that some folks claimed she got from talking to the devil for three days. But this was not true.

The look was all mixed up with angels, mockingbird flights, burnished butterflies, and tree-skimming kites.

After the service Daniel took her hand and held it longer than friendly.

When Zelma glanced up at the crucifix it seemed to her that Jesus, through a divine transformation, was winking through His pain. Or maybe it was just the effect of the morning sun kindling His expression, beaming only on those muscles of the mouth that brightened the corners of His lips.

As they left the church they walked under the crucifix over the doorway.

As if he too saw the same expression on the Christ, Daniel squeezed Zelma Lee's hand tighter. And she could feel electricity pulse back and forth from his fingers to hers.

And they flew away to a place where wings grew from their ribs.

And they were standing still flying.

THE SELF

Tell Me How Long the Train's Been Gone

by James Baldwin

MY BROTHER, CALEB, was seventeen when I was ten. We were very good friends. In fact, he was my best friend and, for a very long time, my only friend.

I do not mean to say that he was always nice to me. I got on his nerves a lot, and he resented having to take me around with him and be responsible for me when there were so many other things he wanted to be doing. Therefore, his hand was often up against the side of my head, and my tears caused him to be punished many times. But I knew, somehow, anyway, that when he was being punished for my tears, he was not being punished for anything he had done to me; he was being punished because that was the way we lived; and his punishment, oddly, helped unite us. More oddly still, even as his great hand caused my head to stammer and dropped a flame-colored curtain before my eyes, I understood that he was not striking *me*. His hand leaped out because he could not help it, and I received the blow because I was there. And it happened, sometimes, before I could even catch my breath to howl, that the hand that had struck me grabbed me and held me, and it was difficult indeed to know which of us was weeping. He was striking, striking out, striking out; the hand asked me to forgive him. I felt his bewilderment through the membrane of my own. I also felt that he was trying to teach me something. And I had, God knows, no other teachers.

For our father — how shall I describe our father? — was a ruined Barbados peasant, exiled in a Harlem which he loathed, where he never saw the sun or sky he remembered, where life took place neither indoors nor without, and where there was no joy. By which I mean no joy that he remembered. Had he been able to bring with him any of the joy he had felt on that far-off island, then the air of the sea and the impulse to dancing would sometimes have transfigured our dreadful rooms. Our lives might have been very different.

But no, he brought with him from Barbados only black rum and blacker pride and magic incantations, which neither healed nor saved.

He did not understand the people among whom he found himself; they had no coherence, no stature and no pride. He came from a race which had been flourishing at the very dawn of the world — a race greater and nobler than Rome or Judea, mightier than Egypt — he came from a race of kings, kings who had never been taken in battle, kings who had never been slaves. He spoke to us of tribes and empires, battles, victories and monarchs of whom we had never heard — they were not mentioned in our textbooks — and invested us with glories in which we felt more awkward than in the secondhand shoes we wore. In the stifling room of his pretensions and expectations, we stumbled wretchedly about, stubbing our toes, as it were, on rubies, scraping our shins on golden caskets, bringing down, with a childish cry, the splendid purple tapestry on which, in pounding gold and scarlet, our destinies and our inheritance were figured. It could scarcely have been otherwise, since a child's major attention has to be concentrated on how to fit into a world which, with every passing hour, reveals itself as merciless.

If our father was of royal blood and we were royal children, our father was certainly the only person in the world who knew it. The landlord did not know it; our father never mentioned royal blood to *him*. When we were late with our rent, which was often, the landlord threatened, in terms no commoner had ever used before a king, to put us in the streets. He complained that our shiftlessness, which he did not hesitate to consider an attribute of the race, had forced him, an old man with a weak heart, to climb all these stairs to plead with us to give him the money we owed him. And this was the last time; he wanted to make sure we understood that this was the last time.

Our father was younger than the landlord, leaner, stronger and bigger. With one blow, he could have brought the landlord to his knees. And we knew how much he hated the man. For days on end, in the wintertime, we huddled around the gas stove in the kitchen, because the landlord gave us no heat. When windows were broken, the landlord took his time about fixing them; the wind made the cardboard we stuffed in the windows rattle all night long; and when snow came, the weight of the snow forced the cardboard inward and onto the floor. Whenever the apartment received a fresh coat of paint, we bought the paint and did the painting ourselves; we killed the rats. A great chunk of the kitchen ceiling fell one winter, narrowly missing our mother.

We all hated the landlord with a perfectly exquisite hatred, and we would have been happy to see our proud father kill him. We would have been glad to help. But our father did nothing of the sort. He stood before the landlord, looking unutterably weary. He made excuses. He apologized. He swore that it would never happen again. (We knew that it *would* happen again.) He begged for time. The landlord would finally go down the stairs, letting us and all the neighbors know how goodhearted he was, and our father would walk into the kitchen and pour himself a glass of rum.

But we knew that our father would never have allowed any black man to speak to him as the landlord did, as policemen did, as storekeepers and welfare workers and pawnbrokers did. No, not for a moment. He would have thrown him out of the house. He would certainly have made a black man know that he was not the descendant of slaves! He had made them know it so often that he had almost no friends among them, and if we had followed his impossible lead, we would have had no friends, either. It was scarcely worthwhile being the descendant of kings if the kings were black and no one had ever heard of them.

And it was because of our father, perhaps, that Caleb and I clung to each other, in spite of the great difference in our ages; or, in another way, it may have been precisely the difference in our ages that made the clinging possible. I don't know. It is really not the kind of thing anyone can ever know. I think it may be easier to love the really helpless younger brother, because he cannot enter into competition with one on one's own ground, or on any ground at all, and can never question one's role or jeopardize one's authority. In my own case, certainly, it did not occur to me to compete with Caleb, and I could not have questioned his role or his authority, because I needed both. He was my touchstone, my model and my only guide.

Anyway, our father, dreaming bitterly of Barbados, despised and mocked by his neighbors and all but ignored by his sons, held down his unspeakable factory job, spread his black gospel in bars on the weekends, and drank his rum. I do not know if he loved our mother. I think he did.

They had had five children — only Caleb and I, the first and the last, were left. We were both dark, like our father; but two of the three dead girls had been fair, like our mother.

She came from New Orleans. Her hair was not like ours. It was black, but softer and finer. The color of her skin reminded me of the color of bananas. Her skin was as bright as that, and contained that kind of promise, and she had tiny freckles around her nose and a small black mole just above her upper lip. It was the mole, I don't know why, which made her beautiful. Without it, her face might have been merely sweet, merely pretty. But the mole was funny. It had the effect of making one realize that our mother liked funny things, liked to laugh. The mole made one look at her eyes — large, extraordinary dark eyes, eyes which seemed always to be amused by something, eyes which looked straight out, seeming to see everything, seeming to be afraid of nothing. She was a soft, round, plump woman. She liked nice clothes and dangling jewelry, which she mostly didn't have, and she liked to cook for large numbers of people, and she loved our father.

She knew him — knew him through and through. I am not being coy or colloquial but bluntly and sadly matter-of-fact when I say that I will now never know what she saw in him. What she saw was certainly not for many eyes; what she saw got him through his working week and his Sunday rest; what she saw saved him. She saw that he was a man. For her, perhaps, he was a great man. I think, though, that, for our mother, any man was great who aspired to become a man; this meant that our father was very rare and precious. I used to wonder how she took it, how she bore it — his rages, his tears, his cowardice.

On Saturday nights, he was almost always evil, drunk and maudlin. He came home from work in the early afternoon and gave our mother some money. It was never enough, of course, but he always kept enough to go out and get drunk. She never protested, at least not as far as I know. Then she would go out shopping. I would usually go with her, for Caleb would almost always be out somewhere, and our mother didn't like the idea of leaving me alone in the house. And this was probably, after all, the best possible arrangement. People who disliked our father were sure (for that very reason) to like our mother; and people who felt that Caleb was growing to be too much like his father could feel that I, after all, might turn out like my mother. Besides, it is not, as a general rule, easy to hate a small child. One runs the risk of looking ridiculous, especially if the child is with his mother.

And especially if that mother is Mrs. Proudhammer. Mrs. Proudhammer knew very well what people thought of Mr. Proudhammer. She knew, too, exactly how much she owed in each store she entered, how much she was going to be able to pay, and what she had to buy. She entered with a smile, ready.

"Evening. Let me have some of them red beans there."

"Evening. You know, you folks been running up quite a little bill here."

"I'm going to give you something on it right now. I need some cornmeal and flour and some rice."

"You know, I got my bills to meet, too, Mrs. Proudhammer."

"Didn't I just tell you I was going to pay? I want some cornflakes too, and some milk." Such merchandise as she could reach, she had already placed on the counter.

"When do you think you're going to be able to pay this bill? All of it, I mean."

"You know I'm going to pay it just as soon as I can. How much does it all come to? Give me that end you got there of that chocolate cake." The chocolate cake was for Caleb and me. "Well, now you put this against the bill." Imperiously, as though it were the most natural thing in the world, she put two or three dollars on the counter.

"You lucky I'm softhearted, Mrs. Proudhammer."

"Things sure don't cost this much downtown — you think I don't know it? Here." And she paid him for what she had bought. "Thank you. You been mighty kind."

And we left the store. I often felt that in order to help her, I should have filled my pockets with merchandise while she was talking. But I never did, not only because the store was often crowded or because I was afraid of being caught by the storekeeper, but because I was afraid of humiliating her. When I began to steal, not very much later, I stole in stores that were not in our neighborhood, where we were not known.

When we had to do "heavy" shopping, we went marketing under the bridge at Park Avenue — Caleb, our mother and I; and sometimes, but rarely, our father came with us. The most usual reason for heavy shopping was that some relatives of our mother's, or old friends of both our mother's and our father's, were coming to visit. We were certainly not going to let them go away hungry — not even if it meant, as it often did, spending more than we had. In spite of what I have been suggesting about our father's temperament, and no matter how difficult he may sometimes have been with us, he was much too proud to offend any guest of his; on the contrary, his impulse was to make them feel that his home was theirs; and besides, he was lonely, lonely for his past, lonely for those faces which had borne witness to that past. Therefore, he would sometimes pretend that our mother did not know how to shop, and our father would come with us, under the bridge, in order to teach her.

There he would be, then, uncharacteristically, in shirt-sleeves, which made him look rather boyish; and as our mother showed no desire to take shopping lessons from him, he turned his attention to Caleb and me. He would pick up a fish, opening the gills and holding it close to his nose. "You see that? That fish looks fresh, don't it? Well, that fish ain't as fresh as I am, and I *been* out of the water. They done doctored that fish. Come on." And we would walk away, a little embarrassed but, on the whole, rather pleased that our father was so smart.

Meantime, our mother was getting the marketing done. She was very happy on days like this, because our father was happy. He was happy, odd as his expression of it may sound, to be out with his wife and his two sons. If we had been on the island that had been witness to his birth, instead of the unspeakable island of Manhattan, he felt that it would not have been so hard for us all to trust and love each other. He sensed, and I think he was right, that on that other, never to be recovered island, his sons would have looked on him very differently, and he would have looked very differently on his sons. Life would have been hard there, too; we would have fought there, too, and more or less blindly suffered and more or less blindly died. But we would not have been (or so it was to seem to all of us forever) so wickedly menaced by the mere fact of our relationship, would not have been so frightened of entering into the central, most beautiful and valuable facts of our lives. We would have been laughing and cursing and tussling in the water, instead of stammering under the bridge; we would have known less about vanished African kingdoms and more about each other. Or, not at all impossibly, more about both.

If it was summer, we bought a watermelon, which either Caleb or our father carried home, fighting with each other for this privilege. They looked very like each other on those days — both big, both black, both laughing.

Caleb always looked absolutely helpless when he laughed. He laughed with all his body, perhaps touching his shoulder against yours, or putting his head on your chest for a moment, and then careening off you, halfway across the room or down the block. I will always hear his laughter. He was always happy on such days, too. If our father needed his son, Caleb certainly needed his father. Such days, however, were rare — one of the reasons, probably, that I remember them now.

Eventually, we all climbed the stairs into that hovel which, at such moments, was our castle. One very nearly felt the drawbridge rising behind us as our father locked the door.

The bathtub could not yet be filled with cold water and the melon placed in the tub, because this was Saturday, and, come evening, we all had to bathe. The melon was covered with a blanket and placed on the fire escape. Then we unloaded what we had bought, rather impressed by our opulence, though our father was always, by this time, appalled by the money we had spent. I was always sadly aware that there would be nothing left of all this once tomorrow had come and gone and that most of it, after all, was not for us, but for others.

Our mother was calculating the pennies she would need all week — carfare for our father and for Caleb, who went to a high school out of our neighborhood; money for the life insurance; money for milk for me at school; money for light and gas; money put away, if possible, toward the rent. She knew just about what our father had left in *his* pockets and was counting on him to give me the money I would shortly be demanding to go to the movies. Caleb had a part-time job after school and already had his movie money. Anyway, unless he was in a very good mood or needed me for something, he would not be anxious to go to the movies with me.

Our mother never insisted that Caleb tell her where he was going, nor did she question him as to how he spent the money he made. She was afraid of hearing him lie, and she did not want to risk forcing him to lie. She was operating on the assumption that he was sensible and had been raised to be honorable and that he, now more than ever, needed his privacy.

But she was very firm with him, nevertheless. "I do not want to see you rolling in here at three in the morning, Caleb. I want you here in time to eat, and you know you got to take your bath."

"Yes, indeed, ma'am. Why can't I take my bath in the morning?"

"Don't you start being funny. You know you ain't going to get up in time to take no bath in the morning."

"Don't nobody want you messing around in that bathroom all morning long, man," said our father. "You just git back in the house like your ma's telling you."

"Besides," I said, "you never wash out the tub."

Caleb looked at me in mock surprise and from a great height, allowing his chin and his lids simultaneously to drop and swiveling his head away from me.

"I see," he said, "that everyone in this family is ganging up on me. All right, Leo. I was planning to take you to the show with me, but now I've changed my mind."

"I'm sorry," I said quickly. "I take it back."

"You take *what* back?"

"What I said — about you not washing out the tub."

"Ain't no need to take it back," our father said stubbornly. "It's true. A man don't take back nothing that's true."

"So *you* say," Caleb said, with a hint of a sneer. But before anyone could possibly react to this, he picked me up, scowling into my face, which he held just above his own. "You take it back?"

"Leo ain't going to take it back," our father said.

Now I was in trouble. Caleb watched me, a small grin on his face. "You take it back?"

"Stop teasing that child, and put him down," our mother said. "The trouble ain't that Caleb don't wash out the tub — he just don't wash it out very clean."

"I never knew him to wash it out," our father said, "unless I was standing behind him."

"Well, ain't neither one of you much good around the house," our mother said.

Caleb laughed and set me down. "You didn't take it back," he said.

I said nothing.

"I guess I'm just going to have to go on without you."

Still, I said nothing.

"You going to have that child to crying in a minute," our mother said. "If you going to take him go on and take him. Don't do him like that."

Caleb laughed again. "I'm going to take him. The way he got them eyes all ready to water, I'd better take him somewhere." We walked toward the door. "But you got to make up *your* mind," he said to me, "to say what *you* think is right."

I grabbed Caleb's hand, the signal for the descent of the drawbridge. Our mother watched us cheerfully as we walked out; our father watched us balefully. Yet there was a certain humor in his face, too, and a kind of pride.

"Dig you later," Caleb said, and the door closed behind us.

The hall was dark, smelling of cooking, of stale wine, of rotting garbage. We dropped down the stairs, Caleb going two at a time, pausing at each landing, briefly, to glance back up at me. I dropped down behind him as fast as I could. When I reached the street level, Caleb was already on the stoop, joking with some of his friends, who were standing in the doorway — who seemed always to be in the doorway.

I didn't like Caleb's friends, because I was afraid of them. I knew the only reason they didn't try to make life hell for me, the way they made life hell for a lot of the other kids, was because they were afraid of Caleb. I went through the door, passing between my brother and his friends, down to the sidewalk, feeling, as they looked briefly at me and then continued joking with Caleb, what they felt — that here was Caleb's round-eyed, frail and useless sissy of a little brother. They pitied Caleb for having to take me out. On the other hand, they also wanted to go to the show, but didn't have the money. Therefore, in silence, I could crow over them even as they despised me. But this was always a terribly risky, touch-and-go business, for Caleb might, at any moment, change his mind and drive me away.

I always stood, those Saturday afternoons, in fear and trembling, holding on to the small shield of my bravado, while waiting for Caleb to come down the steps of the stoop, away from his friends, to me. I braced myself, always, for the moment when he would turn to me, saying, "Okay, kid. You run along. I'll see you later."

This meant that I would have to go to the movies by myself and hang around in front of the box office, waiting for some grown-up to take me in. I could not go back upstairs, for this would be informing my mother and father that Caleb had gone off somewhere after promising to take me to the movies.

Neither could I simply hang around, playing with the kids on the block. For one thing, my demeanor, as I came out of the house, very clearly indicated that I had better things to do than play with *them;* for another, they were not terribly anxious to play with *me;* and, finally, my remaining on the block would have had exactly the same effect as my going upstairs. To remain on the block after Caleb's dismissal was to put myself at the mercy of the block and to put Caleb at the mercy of our parents.

So I prepared myself, those Saturdays, to respond with a cool "Okay. See you later," and then to turn indifferently away, and walk. This was surely the most terrible moment. The moment I turned away, I was committed, I was trapped, and I then had miles to walk, so it seemed to me, before I would be out of sight, before the block ended and I could turn onto the avenue. I wanted to run out of that block, but I never did. I never looked back. I forced myself to walk very slowly, looking neither right nor left, striving to seem at once distracted and offhand; concentrating on the cracks in the sidewalk and stumbling over them; trying to whistle, feeling every muscle in my body, feeling that all the block was watching me, and feeling, which was odd, that I deserved it.

And then I reached the avenue, and turned, still not looking back, and was released from those eyes at least; but now I faced other eyes, eyes coming toward me. These eyes were the eyes of children stronger than me, who would steal my movie money; these eyes were the eyes of white cops, whom I feared, whom I hated with a literally murderous hatred; these eyes were the eyes of old folks, who might wonder what I was doing on this avenue by myself.

And then I got to the show. Sometimes someone would take me in right away, and sometimes I would have to stand there and wait, watching the faces coming to the box office. And this was not easy, since I didn't, after all, want everyone in the neighborhood to know I was loitering outside the movie house waiting for someone to take me in. If it came to our father's attention, he would kill both Caleb and me.

Eventually, I would see a face which looked susceptible. I would rush up to him — it was usually a man, for men were less likely to be disapproving — and whisper, "Take me in," and give him my dime. Sometimes the man simply took the dime and disappeared inside; sometimes he gave my dime back to me and took me in anyway. Sometimes I ended up wandering around the streets — but I couldn't wander into a strange neighborhood, because I would be beaten up if I did — until I figured the show was out. It was dangerous to get home too early, and, of course, it was practically lethal to arrive too late. If all went well, I could cover for Caleb, saying that I had left him with some boys on the stoop. Then, if *he* came in too late, it could not be considered my fault.

But if wandering around this way was not without its dangers, neither was it without its discoveries and delights. I discovered subways. I discovered, that is, that I could ride on subways by myself and, furthermore, that I could usually ride for nothing. Sometimes, when I ducked under the turnstile, I was caught, and sometimes great black ladies seized on me as a pretext for long, very loud, ineffably moral lectures about wayward children breaking their parents' hearts. Sometimes, doing everything in my power not to attract their attention, I endeavored to look as though I were in the charge of a respectable-looking man or woman, entering the subway in their shadow and sitting very still beside them. It was best to try to sit *between* two such people, for each would automatically assume that I was with the other. There I would sit, then, in a precarious anonymity, watching the people, listening to the roar, watching the lights of stations flash by. It seemed to me that nothing was faster than a subway train, and I loved the speed, because the speed was dangerous.

For a time, during these expeditions, I simply sat and watched the people. Lots of people would be dressed up, for this was Saturday night. The women's hair would be all curled and straightened, and the lipstick on their full lips looked purple and make-believe against the dark skins of their faces. They wore very fancy capes or coats, in wonderful colors, and long dresses, and sometimes they had jewels in their hair, and sometimes they wore flowers on their dresses. They were almost as beautiful as movie stars. And so the men with them seemed to think.

The hair of the men was slick and wavy, brushed up into pompadours; or they wore very sharp hats, brim flicked down dangerously over one eye, with perhaps one flower in the lapel of their many-colored suits. They laughed and talked with their girls, but quietly, for there were white people in the car. The white people would scarcely ever be dressed up and did not speak to each other at all — only read their papers and stared at the advertisements. But they fascinated me more than the colored people did, because I knew nothing at all about them and could not imagine what they were like.

Underground, I received my first apprehension of New York neighborhoods and, underground, first felt what may be called a civic terror. I very soon realized that after the train had passed a certain point, going uptown or downtown, all the colored people disappeared. The first time I realized this, I panicked and got lost. I rushed off the train, terrified of what these white people might do to me, with no colored person around to protect me — even to scold me, even to beat me; at least, their touch was familiar, and I knew that they did not, after all, intend to kill me — and got on another train only because I saw a black man on it. But almost everyone else was white.

The train did not stop at any of the stops I remembered. I became more and more frightened, frightened of getting off the train and frightened of staying on it, frightened of saying anything to the man and frightened that he would get off the train before I could say anything to him. He was my salvation, and he stood there in the unapproachable and frightening form that salvation so often takes. At each stop, I watched him with despair.

To make matters worse, I suddenly realized that I had to pee. Once I realized it, this need became a torment; the horror of wetting my pants in front of all these people made the torment greater. Finally, I tugged at the man's sleeve. He looked down at me with a gruff, amused concern; then, reacting, no doubt to the desperation in my face, he bent closer.

I asked him if there was a bathroom on the train.

He laughed. "No," he said, "but there's a bathroom in the station." He looked at me again. "Where're you going?"

I told him that I was going home.

"And where's home?"

I told him.

This time he did not laugh. "Do you know where you are?" he said.

I shook my head. At that moment, the train came into a station, and after several hours, it rolled to a stop. The doors opened, and the man led me to the bathroom. I ran in, and hurried, because I was afraid he would disappear. But I was glad he had not come in with me.

When I came out, he stood waiting for me. "Now," he said, "you in Brooklyn. You ever hear of Brooklyn? What you doing out here by yourself?"

"I got lost," I said.

"I *know* you got lost. What I want to know is how *come* you got lost? Where's your mamma? Where's your daddy?"

I almost said that I didn't have any, because I liked his face and his voice and was half hoping to hear him say that *he* didn't have any little boy and would just as soon take a chance on me. But I told him my mama and daddy were at home.

"And do they know where *you* are?"

I said, "No." There was a pause.

"Well, I know they going to make your tail hot when they see you." He took my hand. "Come on."

And he led me along the platform and then down some steps and along a narrow passage and then up some steps onto the opposite platform. I was very impressed by this maneuver; in order to accomplish the same purpose, I had always left the subway station and gone up into the street. Now that the emergency was over, I was in no great hurry to leave my savior. I asked him if he had a little boy.

"Yes," he said, "and if *you* was my little boy, I'd paddle your behind so you couldn't sit down for a week."

I asked him how old was his little boy, what was his name and if his little boy was at home."

"He *better* be at home!" He looked at me and laughed. "His name is Jonathan. He ain't but five years old." His gaze refocused, sharpened. "How old are you?"

I told him that I was ten, going on eleven.

"You a pretty bad little fellow," he said then.

I tried to look repentant, but I would not have dreamed of deny-ing it.

"Now, look here," he said, "this here's the uptown side. Can you read, or don't you never go to school?" I assured him that I could read. "Now, to get where you going, you got to change trains." He told me where. "Here, I'll write it down for you." He found some paper in his pockets but no pencil. We heard the train coming. He looked about him in helpless annoyance, looked at his watch, looked at me. "It's all right. I'll tell the conductor."

But the conductor, standing between two cars, had rather a mean pink face.

My savior looked at him dubiously. "He *might* be all right. But we better not take no chances." He pushed me ahead of him into the train. "You know you right lucky that I got a little boy? If I didn't, I swear I'd just let you go on and *be* lost. You don't know the kind of trouble you going to get me in at home. My wife ain't *never* going to believe *this* story."

I told him to give me his name and address and I would write a letter to his wife and to his little boy, too.

This caused him to laugh harder than ever. "You only say that because you know I ain't got no pencil. You are one *hell* of a shrewd little boy."

I told him that then maybe we should get off the train and that I would go back home with him.

This made him grave. "What does your father do?"

This question made me uneasy. I stared at him for a long time before I answered. "He works in a —" I could not pronounce the word — "he has a job."

He nodded. "I see. Is he home now?"

I really did not know, and I said I did not know.

"And what does your mother do?"

"She stays home."

Again he nodded. "You got any brothers or sisters?"

I told him no.

"I see. What's your name?"

"Leo."

"Leo what?"

"Leo Proudhammer."

He saw something in my face. "What do you want to be when you grow up, Leo?"

"I want to be —" and I had never said this before — "I want to be a — a movie actor. I want to be a — actor."

"You pretty skinny for that," he said.

"That's all right," I told him. "Caleb's going to teach me to swim. That's how you get big."

"Who's Caleb?"

I opened my mouth, I started to speak. I checked myself as the train roared into a station. He glanced out the window, but did not move. "He swims," I said.

"Oh," he said after a very long pause, during which the doors slammed and the train began to move. "Is he a good swimmer?"

I said that Caleb was the best swimmer in the world.

"Okay," my savior said, "okay," and put his hand on my head again and smiled at me.

I asked him what his name was.

"Charles," he said, "Charles Williams. But you better call me *Uncle* Charles, you little devil, because you have certainly ruined my Saturday night." The train came into a station. "Here's where we change," he said.

We got out of the train and crossed the platform and waited.

"Now," he said, "this train stops exactly where you going. Tell me where you going."

I stared at him.

"I want you," he said, "to tell me exactly where you *going.* I can't be fooling with you all night."

I told him.

"You sure that's right?"

I told him I was sure.

"I got a very good memory," he said. "Give me your address. Just say it, I'll remember it."

So I said it, staring into his face as the train came roaring in.

"If you don't go straight home," he said, "I'm going to come see your daddy, and when we find you, you'll be mighty sorry." He pushed me into the train and put one shoulder against the door. "Go on, now," he said, loud enough for all the car to hear. "Your mama'll meet you at the station where I told you to get off." He repeated my subway stop, pushed the angry door with his shoulder, and then said gently, "Sit down, Leo." He remained in the door until I sat down. "So long, Leo," he said then, and stepped backward out. The doors closed. He grinned at me and waved, and the train began to move.

I waved back. Then he was gone, the station was gone, and I was on my way back home.

I never saw that man again, but I made up stories about him, I dreamed about him, I even wrote a letter to him and his wife and his little boy, but I never mailed it.

I never told Caleb anything about my solitary expeditions. I don't know why. I think that he might have liked to know about them. I suppose, finally, at bottom, I said nothing because my expeditions belonged to me.

Another time, it was raining, and it was still too early for me to go home. I felt very, very low that day. It was one of the times that my tongue and my body refused to obey me, and I had not been able to work up the courage to ask anyone to take me in to the show. The ticket taker was watching me, or so I thought, with a hostile suspicion. Actually, it's very unlikely he was thinking at all, and certainly not of me. But I walked away from the show, because I could no longer bear his eyes, or anybody's eyes.

I walked the long block east of the movie house. The street was empty, black and glittering. The water soaked through my coat at the shoulders, and water dripped down my neck from my cap. I began to be afraid. I could not stay out in the rain, because then my father and mother would know I had been wandering the streets. I would get a beating, and, though Caleb was too old to get a beating, he and my father would have a terrible fight, and Caleb would blame it all on me and would not speak to me for days.

I began to hate Caleb. I wondered where he was. I started in the direction of our house, only because I did not know what else to do. Perhaps Caleb would be waiting for me on the stoop.

The avenue, too, was very long and silent. Somehow, it seemed old, like a picture in a book. It stretched straight before me, endless, and the streetlights did not so much illuminate it as prove how dark it was. The rain was falling harder. Cars sloshed by, sending up sheets of water. From the bars, I heard music, faintly, and many voices. Straight

ahead of me a woman walked, very fast, head down, carrying a shopping bag. I reached my corner and crossed the wide avenue. There was
no one on my stoop.

Now I was not even certain what time it was; but I knew it wasn't time
yet for the show to be over. I walked into my hallway and wrung out
my cap. I was sorry that I had not made someone take me in to the
show, because now I did not know what to do. I *could* go upstairs and
say that we had not liked the movie and had left early and that Caleb
was with some boys on the stoop. But this would sound strange, and
Caleb, who would not know what story I had told, would, therefore, be
greatly handicapped when he came home.

I could not stay in my hallway, because my father might not be at
home and might come in. I could not go into the hallway of another
building, because if any of the kids who lived in the building found me,
they would have the right to beat me up. I could not go back out into
the rain. I stood next to the big, cold radiator, and I began to cry. But
crying wasn't going to do me any good, either, especially as there was
no one to hear me.

So I stepped out on my stoop again and stood there for a long time,
wondering what to do. Then I thought of a condemned house, around
the corner from us. We played there sometimes, though it was very
dangerous and we were not supposed to. What possessed me to go
there now, I don't know, except that I could not think of another dry
place in the whole world. I started running east, down our block. I
turned two corners and came to the house, with its black window sockets. The house was completely dark. I had forgotten how afraid I was
of the dark, but the rain was drenching me. I ran down the cellar steps
and clambered into the house through one of the broken windows. I
squatted there in a still, dry dread, not daring to look into the house
but staring outward. I was holding my breath. I heard an endless scurrying in the darkness, a perpetual busyness, and I thought of rats, of
their teeth and ferocity and fearful size, and I began to cry again.

I don't know how long I squatted there this way or what was in
my mind. I listened to the rain and the rats. Then I was aware of another sound — I had been hearing it for a while without realizing it.
This was a moaning sound, a sighing sound, a sound of strangling,
which mingled with the sound of the rain and with a muttering, curs-

ing human voice. The sounds came from the door that led to the backyard.

I wanted to stand, but I crouched lower; wanted to run, but could not move. Sometimes the sounds seemed to come closer, and I knew that this meant my death; sometimes they diminished or ceased altogether, and then I knew that my assailant was looking for me. I looked toward the backyard door, and I seemed to see, silhouetted against the driving rain, a figure, half bent, moaning, leaning against the wall, in indescribable torment; then there seemed to be two figures, sighing and grappling, moving so quickly that it was impossible to tell which was which, two creatures, each in a dreadful, absolute, silent single-mindedness attempting to strangle the other!

I watched, crouching low. A very powerful and curious excitement mingled itself with my terror and made the terror greater. I could not move. I did not dare move. The figures were quieter now. It seemed to me that one of them was a woman, and she seemed to be crying, pleading for her life. But her sobbing was answered only by a growling sound. The muttered, joyous curses began again; the murderous ferocity began again, more bitterly than ever. The sobbing began to rise in pitch, like a song.

Then everything was still, all movement ceased. Then I heard only the rain and the scurrying of the rats. It was over; one of them, or both of them, lay stretched out, dead or dying in this filthy place. It happened in Harlem every Saturday night. I could not catch my breath to scream. Then I heard a laugh, a low, happy, wicked laugh, and the figure turned in my direction and seemed to start toward me.

Then I screamed and stood up straight, bumping my head on the window frame and losing my cap, and scrambled up the cellar steps. I ran head down, like a bull, away from that house and out of that block. I ran up the steps of my stoop and bumped into Caleb.

"Where the hell have you been? Hey! What's the matter with you?"

I had jumped up on him, almost knocking him down, trembling and sobbing.

"You're *soaked.* Leo, what's the matter? Where's your cap?"

But I could not say anything. I held him around the neck with all my might, and I could not stop shaking.

"Come on, Leo," Caleb said, in a different tone, "tell me what's the matter." He pried my arms loose and held me away from him, so that he could look into my face. "Oh, little Leo. Little Leo. What's the matter, baby?" He looked as though he were about to cry himself, and this made me cry harder than ever. He took out his handkerchief and wiped my face and made me blow my nose. My sobs began to lessen, but I could not stop trembling. He thought that I was trembling from cold, and he rubbed his hands roughly up and down my back and rubbed my hands between his. "What's the matter?"

I did not know how to tell him.

"Somebody try to beat you up?"

I shook my head. "No."

"What movie did you see?"

"I didn't go. I couldn't find nobody to take me in."

"And you just been wandering around in the rain all night?"

"Yes."

He sat down on the hallway steps. "Oh, Leo." Then, "You mad at me?"

I said, "No. I was scared."

He nodded. "I reckon you were, man." He wiped my face again. "You ready to go upstairs? It's getting late."

"Okay."

"How'd you lose your cap?"

"I went in a hallway to wring it out — and — I put it on the radiator, and I heard some people coming — and — I ran away, and I forgot it."

"We'll say you forgot it in the movies."

"Okay."

We started up the stairs.

"Leo," he said, "I'm sorry about tonight. I'm really sorry. I won't let it happen again. You believe me?"

"Sure. I believe you." I smiled up at him.

He squatted down. "Give us a kiss."

I kissed him.

"Okay. Climb up. I'll give you a ride. Hold on, now."

He carried me piggyback up the stairs.

Thereafter, we evolved a system, which did not, in fact, work too badly. When things went wrong and he could not be found, I was to leave a message for him at a certain store on the avenue. This store had a bad reputation — more than candy and hot dogs and soda pop

were sold there; Caleb himself had told me this and told me not to hang
out there. But he said he would see to it that they treated me all right.

I went in the store one Saturday night, and one of the boys who was
always there, a boy about Caleb's age, looked up and smiled and said,
"You looking for your brother? Come on, I'll take you to him."

This was not the agreed-on formula. I was to be *taken* to Caleb only
in cases of real emergency, which wasn't the case this time. I was there
because the show was over a little earlier than usual, and since it was
only about a quarter past eleven, I figured I had about half an hour to
wait for Caleb.

When the boy made his invitation, I assumed it was because of some
prearrangement with the owner of the store, a very dour, silent black
man, who looked at me from behind his counter and said nothing.

I said, "Okay," and the boy, whose name was Arthur, said, "Come
on, Sonny. I'm going to take you to a party." He took my hand and led
me across the avenue and into a long, dark block.

We walked the length of the block in silence, crossed another avenue and went into a big house in the middle of the block. We were in a
big vestibule, with four locked apartment doors staring away from each
other. It was not really clean, but it was fairly clean. We climbed three
flights of stairs. Arthur knocked on the door, a very funny knock, not
loud. After a moment, I heard a scraping sound, then the sound of a
chain rattling and a bolt being pulled back. The door opened.

A lady, very black and rather fat, wearing a blue dress, held the door
for us. She said, "Come on in. Now, what you doing here with this
child?"

"Had to do it. It's all right. It's Caleb's brother."

We started down a long, dark hall, with closed rooms on either side
of it, toward the living room. One of the rooms was the kitchen. A smell
of barbecue made me realize that I was hungry. The living room was
really two living rooms. The far one looked out on the street. There
were six or seven people in the room, women and men. They looked
exactly like the men and women who frightened me when I saw them
standing on the corners, laughing and joking in front of the bars. But
they did not seem frightening here. A record player was going, not very
loud. They had drinks in their hands, and there were half-empty plates
of food around the room. Caleb was sitting on the sofa, with his arm
around a girl in a yellow dress.

"Here's your little brother," said the fat black lady in blue.

Arthur said to Caleb, "It was just better for him not to have to wait there tonight."

Caleb smiled at me. I was tremendously relieved that he was not angry. I was delighted by this party, even though it made me shy. "Come on over here," Caleb said. I went to the sofa. "This is my kid brother. His name is Leo. Leo, this is Dolores. Say hello to Dolores."

Dolores smiled at me — I thought she was very pretty — and said, "I'm very happy to meet you, Leo. How've you been?"

"Just fine," I said.

"Don't you want to know how *she's* been?" Caleb grinned.

"No," said the fat black lady, and laughed. "I'm sure he don't want to know that. I bet he's hungry. You been stuffing yourself all night, Caleb. Let me give him a little bit of my barbecue and a glass of ginger ale." She already was beginning to propel me out of the room.

I looked at Caleb. Caleb said, "Just remember we ain't got all night. Leo, this is Miss Mildred. She cooked everything, and she's a might good friend of mine. What do you say to Miss Mildred, Leo?"

"Dig Caleb being the big brother," Arthur murmured, and laughed.

"Thank you, Miss Mildred," I said.

"Come on in the kitchen," she said, "and let me try to put some flesh on them bones." She walked me into the kitchen. "Now, you sit right over there," she said. "Won't take me but a minute to warm this up." She sat me at the kitchen table and gave me a napkin and poured the ginger ale. "What grade you in at school, Leo?" I told her. "You must be a right smart boy, then," she said, with a pleased smile. "Do you like school, Leo?"

I told her what I liked best was Spanish and history and English composition.

This caused her to look more pleased than ever. "What do you want to be when you grow up?"

Somehow, I could not tell her what I had told the man, my friend, on the train. I said I wasn't sure, that maybe I would be a schoolteacher.

"That's just what I wanted to be," she said proudly, "and I studied right hard for it, too, and I believe I would have made it, but then I had to go and get myself mixed up with some no-count nigger. I didn't have no sense. I didn't have no better sense but to marry him. Can you beat that?" And she laughed and set my plate in front of me. "Go on, now, eat. Foolish me. Now, your brother," she said suddenly, "he's a right fine boy. He wants to make something of himself. He's got ambition. That's what I like — *ambition.* Don't you let him be foolish. Like me. You like my barbecue?"

"Yes, ma'am," I said. "It's good."

"Let me give you some more ginger ale," she said, and poured it.

I was beginning to be full. But I didn't want to go, although I knew that, now, it was really beginning to be late. While Miss Mildred talked and moved about the kitchen, I listened to the voices coming from the other room, the voices and the music. They were playing a kind of purple, lazy dance music, a music that was already in my bones, along with the wilder music from which the purple music sprang. The voices were not like the music, though they corroborated it. I listened to a girl's voice, gravelly and low, indignant and full of laughter. The room was full of laughter. It exploded, at intervals, and rolled through the living room and hammered at the walls of the kitchen.

Every once in a while, I heard Caleb, booming like a trumpet, drowning out the music. I wondered how often Caleb came here and how he had met these people, who were so different, at least as it seemed to me, from any of the people who ever came to our house.

Then Caleb's hand was on my neck. Dolores stood in the doorway, smiling. "You stuffed yourself enough, little brother?" Caleb said. "Because we got to get out of here now."

We walked slowly down the hall, Miss Mildred, Dolores and Caleb and me. We reached the door, which had a metal pole built into it in such a way as to prevent its being opened from the outside, and a heavy piece of chain around the top of the three locks.

Miss Mildred began, patiently, to open the door. "Leo," she said, "don't you be no stranger. You make your brother bring you back to see me, you hear?" She got the pole out of the way and then undid the chain. To Caleb, she said, "Bring him by some afternoon. I ain't got nothing to do. I'll be glad to look after him." The last lock yielded, and Miss Mildred opened the door. We were facing the bright hall lights: no, the building was not very clean. "Good night, Leo," Miss Mildred said, and then she said good night to Dolores and Caleb. She closed the door.

I heard the scraping sound again, and we walked down the stairs.

"She's nice," I said.

Caleb said, yawning, "Yeah, she's a very nice lady." Then he said, "Now, I don't want you telling anybody at home about this, you hear?" I swore I wouldn't tell. "It's our secret," Caleb said.

It was colder in the streets than it had been before.

Caleb took Dolores' arm. "Let's get you to your subway," he said.

We started walking up the wide, dark avenue. We reached the brightly lit kiosk, which came up out of the sidewalk like some unbelievably malevolent awning or the suction apparatus of a monstrous vacuum cleaner.

"Bye-bye," Caleb said, and kissed Dolores on the nose. "I got to run. See you Monday after school."

"Bye-bye," Dolores said. She bent down and kissed me quickly on the cheek. "Bye-bye, Leo. Be good." She hurried down the steps.

Caleb and I began walking very fast, down the avenue, toward our block. The subway station was near the movie house, and the movie house was dark. We knew we were late; we did not think we were *that* late.

"It was a *very* long show, wasn't it?" Caleb said.

"Yes," I said.

"What did we see? Better tell me about *both* pictures. Just in case."

I told him as well as I could as we hurried down the avenue. Caleb had great powers of concentration and could figure out enough from what I said to know what to say if the necessity arose.

But our troubles, that night, came from a very different source than our parents. I had just reached the point in my breathless narration where the good girl is murdered by the Indians and the hero vows revenge. We were hurrying down the long block that led east to our house when we heard a car braking and were blinded by bright lights and were pushed up against a wall.

"Turn around," a voice said. "And keep your hands in the air."

It may seem funny, but I felt as though Caleb and I had conjured up a movie — that if I had not been describing a movie to him, we would not have suddenly found ourselves in the middle of one. Or was it the end? I had never been so frightened in my life.

We did as we were told. I felt the grainy brick beneath my fingers. A hand patted me all over my body, every touch humiliating. Beside me, I heard Caleb catch his breath.

"Turn around," the voice said.

The great lights of the police car had gone out; I could see the car at the curb, the doors open. I did not dare look at Caleb, for I felt that this would, somehow, be used against us. I stared at the two policemen, young, white, tight-lipped and self-important.

They turned a flashlight first on Caleb, then on me. "Where you boys going?"

"Home," Caleb said. I could hear his breathing. "We live in the next block." And he gave the address.

"Where've you been?"

Now I heard the effort Caleb was making not to surrender either to rage or panic. "We just took my girl to the subway station. We were at the movies." And then, forced out of him, weary, dry and bitter, "This here's my brother. I got to get him home. He ain't but ten years old."

"What movie did you see?"

And Caleb told them. I marveled at his memory. But I also knew that the show had let out about an hour or so before. I feared that the policemen might also know this. But they didn't.

"You got any identification?"

"My brother doesn't. I do."

"Let's see it."

Caleb took out his wallet and handed it over.

They looked at his wallet, looked at us, handed it back. "Get on home," one of them said. They got into their car and drove off.

"Thanks," Caleb said. "Thanks, all you scum-bag Christians." His accent was now as irredeemably of the islands as was the accent of our father. I had never heard this sound in his voice before. And then, suddenly, he looked down at me and laughed and hugged me. "Come on, let's get home. Little Leo. Were you scared?"

"Yes," I said. "Were you?"

"Damn right, I was scared. But — damn! — they must have seen that you weren't but ten years old."

"You didn't *act* scared," I said.

We were in our own block, approaching our stoop. "Well. We certainly have a good excuse for being late," he said. He grinned. Then he said, "Leo, I'll tell you something. I'm glad this happened. It had to happen one day, and I'm glad it happened while I was with you — of course, I'm glad you were with *me*, too, because if it hadn't been for you, they'd have pulled me."

"What for?"

"Because I'm black," Caleb said. "That's what for."

I said nothing. I said nothing, because what he said was true, and I knew it. It seemed, now, that I had always known it, though I had never been able to say it. But I did not understand it. I was filled with an awful wonder; it hurt my chest and paralyzed my tongue. *Because you're black.* I tried to think, but I couldn't. I only saw the policemen, those murderous eyes again, those hands. Were they people?

"Caleb," I asked, "are white people people?"

"What are you talking about, Leo?"

"I mean, are white people — *people?* People like us?"

He looked down at me. His face was very strange and sad. It was a face I had never seen before. We were in the house now, and we climbed a few more stairs, very slowly. Then, "All I can tell you, Leo, is — well, *they* don't think they are."

I thought of the landlord. Then I thought of my schoolteacher, a lady named Mrs. Nelson. I liked her very much. I thought she was very pretty. She had long yellow hair, like someone I had seen in the movies, and a nice laugh, and we all liked her, all the kids I knew. The kids who were not in her class wished they were. I liked to write compositions for her, because she seemed really interested. But she was white. Would she hate me all my life because I was black? It didn't seem possible. She didn't hate me now; I was pretty sure of that. And yet, what Caleb had said was true.

"Caleb," I asked, "are all white people the same?"

"I never met a good one."

I asked, "Not even when you were little? In school?"

Caleb said, "Maybe. I don't remember." He smiled at me. "I never met a good one, Leo. But that's not saying that *you* won't. Don't look so frightened."

We were in front of our door. Caleb raised his hand to knock.

I held his hand. "Caleb," I whispered, "what about Mama?"

"What do you mean, what about Mama?"

"Well, Mama." I stared at him; he watched me very gravely. "Mama — Mama's almost white."

"But that don't make her white. You got to be *all* white to be white." He laughed. "Poor Leo. Don't feel bad. I know you don't understand it now. I'll try to explain it to you, little by little." He paused. "But our mama is a colored woman. You can tell she's a colored woman because she's married to a colored *man,* and she's got two colored *children.* Now, you know ain't no white lady going to do a thing like that." He watched me, smiling. "You understand that?" I nodded. "Well, you going to keep me here all night with your questions, or can we go on in now?"

He knocked, and our mother opened the door. "About time," she said drily. She had her hair piled in a knot on the top of her head. I liked her hair that way. "You must have sat through that movie four or five times. You're going to ruin your eyes, and that'll just be too bad for you, because you know, we ain't got no money to be buying you no glasses. Leo, you go on inside and get ready to take your bath."

"Let him come over here a minute," our father said. He was sitting in the one easy chair, near the window. He was drunk, but not as drunk as I had seen him, and this was a good-mood drunk. In this mood, he talked about the islands, his mother and father and kinfolk and friends, the feast days, the singing, the dancing and the sea.

I approached him, and he pulled me to him, smiling, and held me between his thighs. "How's my big man?" he asked, smiling and rubbing his hand, gently, over my hair. "Did you have a good time tonight?"

Caleb sat on a straight chair near him, leaning forward. "Let Leo tell you why we so late. Tell them what happened Leo."

"We were coming down the block," I began — and I watched my father's face. Suddenly, I did not want to tell him. Something in Caleb's tone had alerted him, and he watched me with a stern and frightened apprehension. My mother came and stood beside him, one hand on his shoulder. I looked at Caleb. "Maybe you could tell it better," I said.

"Go on, start. I'll fill in."

"We were coming down the block," I said, "coming from the movies." I looked at Caleb.

"It's not the way we usually come," Caleb said.

My father and I stared at each other. There was, suddenly, between us, an overwhelming sorrow. It had come from nowhere. "We got stopped by the cops," I said. Then I could not continue. I looked helplessly at Caleb, and Caleb told the story.

As Caleb spoke, I watched my father's face. I don't know how to describe what I saw. I felt his arm tighten, tighten; his lips became bitter, and his eyes grew dull. It was as though — after indescribable, nearly mortal effort, after grim years of fasting and prayer, after the loss of all he had, and after having been promised by the Almighty that he had paid the price and no more would be demanded of his soul, which was harbored now — it was as though in the midst of his joyful feasting and dancing, crowned and robed, a messenger arrived to tell him that a great error had been made, and that it was all to be done again. Before his eyes, then, the banquet and the banquet wines and the banquet guests departed, the robe and crown were lifted, and he was alone, frozen out of his dream, with all that before him which he had thought was behind him.

My father looked as stunned and still and as close to madness as that, and his encircling arm began to hurt me, but I did not complain. I put my hand on his face, and he turned to me; he smiled — he was very beautiful then! — and he put his great hand on top of mine. He turned to Caleb. "That's all that happened? You didn't say nothing?"

"What could I say? It might have been different if I'd been by myself. But I had Leo with me, and I was afraid of what they might do to Leo."

"No, you did right, man. I got no fault to find. You didn't take their badge number?"

Caleb snickered. "What for? You know a friendly judge? We got money for a lawyer? Somebody they going to *listen* to? They get us in that precinct house and make us confess to all kinds of things and sometimes even kill us, and don't nobody give a damn. Don't nobody care what happens to a black man. If they didn't need us for work, they'd have killed us all off a long time ago. They did it to the Indians."

"That's the truth," our mother said. "I wish I could say different, but it's the truth." She stroked our father's shoulder. "We just thank the Lord it wasn't no worse. We just got to say: Well, the boys got home safe tonight."

I asked, "Daddy, how come they do us like they do?"

My father looked at us for a long time. Finally, he said, "Leo, if I could tell you that, maybe I'd be able to make them stop. But don't let them make you afraid. You hear?"

I said, "Yes, sir." But I knew that I was already afraid.

"Let's not talk about it no more," our mother said. "If you two is hungry, I got some pork chops back there."

Caleb grinned at me. "Little Leo might be hungry. He stuffs himself like a pig. But I ain't hungry. Hey, old man —" he nudged my father's shoulder; nothing would be refused us tonight — "why don't we have a taste of your rum? All right?"

Our mother laughed. "I'll go get it," she said. She started out of the room.

"Reckon we can give Leo a little bit, too?" our father asked. He pulled me onto his lap.

"In a big glass of water," our mother said, laughing. She took one last look at us before she went into the kitchen. "My," she said, "I sure am surrounded by some pretty men! My, my, my!"

THE SELF

By the Way of Morning Fire

by Michael Weaver

BRUNSWICK COUNTY, VIRGINIA, 1968

IN THE WINTER, the large, black, wood-burning stove downstairs in the kitchen, a pot-bellied stove, and the fireplace in the front bedroom were the only sources of heat, the only places to go and take the stiff chill out of their toes. Before going to school in the mornings, they would take time to go into the yard and chop the short logs of dry wood into smaller, slender pieces to feed the dimming fire in the stove. Holding the logs with one hand while placing the axe in the top side, the children took turns banging the wood against the huge trunk which served as a table until the log split neatly down the middle. On those cold winter mornings the only sound was that of the wood banging against the makeshift table, and their grandfather working the phlegm out of his throat with long, hacking coughs. Once they were making their way through the woods to school, they could look back at their house and see the smoke spiralling upwards from the chimney by the kitchen stove.

Moses Lee was in charge of his younger brother and sister. When they reached the one-lane highway that snaked though the county, Moses Lee was the one to take their hands in his whether they could hear cars approaching the hidden curves or not. He was responsible for them. In the warm days of late spring when the shrubbery growth made it difficult to see the black snakes that habitually made their way through the pine forests, Moses Lee was the one who carried the long stick and steered the babies away from the serpents. Moses Lee answered questions, parceled out the syrup and honey biscuits, found shelter in unexpected rain, and suffered the wrath of his mother for failing to obey. Of all his duties, the questions were the most difficult, and his sister Elvira the most inquisitive.

"Moses Lee, why our Daddy got to be still using mules when everybody else's papa got tractors? He gonna kill hisself."

"Daddy just like workin hard, Vira. You know that."

"That ain't no excuse, Moses Lee. You just tryin to ignore me. I ain't no fool."

"You ain't old enough to be nothin, Vira, fool or otherwise. You know what Mama told you about usin that word."

"I'm just talkin bout myself. Ain't no wrong or right in that."

"I ought to tell Mama."

"I sure hope we don get stuck wit you fore we get grown. You one contrary colored boy!"

"By the time y'all get grown, I'll be grown and gone, thank the Lord."

Although he never openly admitted it, Moses Lee too felt his father was an embarrassment, an accident which defied logical explanation. Summers, when everyone else had long departed the field and returned to the house for the afternoon break, they could look out into the long rows of tobacco and see Lincoln Thomas winding his way around the end of the row, turning the mule slowly and positioning the sled to make another trip down the row, catching the leaves his younger son, Jesse, threw in playfully. Moses Lee too wondered why he kept mules in a time when men looked forward confidently to traveling to other stars. Sometimes, he felt a deepening urge to leave his limited world and step forward in time to the real world that had long since marched on. He's sit on the porch and pour water on his naked feet to wash away the stain of the clay, and mourn his security.

Summer afforded the luxury of wishing, but winter forced a painful pragmatism. If the wood was not prepared properly and in an ample supply before they left for school, it severely hampered their mother's work of cooking and cleaning. If the hog slop wasn't thickened and taken down to be thrown in the troughs, the chore became another in a long list of overly physical tasks for Lincoln, who was already addicted to exhaustion. If they didn't go to school, they might be denied the chance to know, to understand, to perceive.

The forest was Moses Lee's confidant. He took long, solitary walks to sort and straighten out the questions that grew to burrs inside him — sticking prickly, indecipherable prods against the routine of working, schooling and thanking God for the opportunities that had come to his life. Walking along, kicking the twigs and fallen pine needles, the wondering would bunch inside his stomach as he cursed the air whistling coldly about his ears. He kicked trees, sent small stones hurtling into the air with makeshift bats, and stoned squirrels shooting past; all the while pondering alternatives to becoming an adult in the same forest, trapped by the questions that brought him there now. The world of television and power steering, of foreign languages and vastly different people, of distinctly different and beautiful ways of living — all the possibilities were becoming rapidly more inviting and inaccessible, more troubling.

Then he would turn to see the spiralling smoke from his mother's stove where she prepared the Sunday dinner. She hummed a tune and occasionally sang one, moved back and forth between the steaming pots on the stove and the dining room table where she placed the dishes and Bible. As she worked, Lincoln Thomas sat in the living room with his father filling rolling paper with Prince Albert tobacco. Moses Lee saw them in his aborted dreams in the forest, and turned homeward to the hot food.

At the end of a narrow path through the woods bordering the corn field, there was a small store with a single gas pump in the middle of a dirt lot. The store was owned by the Ingrams, a white family that also owned a feed store nearby and controlled most of the public offices in the county. Moses Lee and his father would occasionally walk to the store together. Lincoln Thomas made these walks opportunities to educate his son about the perils of becoming a man.

One day in the spring of the last year Moses Lee spent with his family, he and his father walked to the store to buy a new box of Prince Albert tobacco and two Coca-Colas. Old Man Ingram was sitting out front on the cement ledge facing the gasoline pump.

"Good evening, Lincoln."

"How you, Mr. Ingram sir?"

"Weren't for the gout and this crazy government, I'd be all right. Y'all go on in, Lonnie'll take care of you."

Lonnie Ingram was the dullest of the six boys of Old Man Ingram. The other five were well established in their own lines of work, either some profession or government office in the county. Moses Lee had heard that one of them had a statewide office. But Lonnie was hateful as a snake and extremely moody. He would often lash out against whoever happened along when he was low. Sometimes it was his father, but more often the victim was a poor soul who could ill afford to retaliate. After Lonnie had placed the Prince Albert on the counter, Lincoln Thomas asked him about the two Coca-Colas.

Leaning over the counter on his fists, Lonnie slowly reminded him, "Lincoln, you know damn well that's a white man's drink."

Lincoln was taken aback. He had been concentrating on the lecture he was preparing to deliver to Moses Lee about the importance of the company a young man keeps, how there were many different kinds of women, and about the important power money wielded in most circles. He had been busy sorting all the thoughts that swirled inside him when Lonnie wiped the slate absolutely clean. It had been a good five years since Old Man Ingram had stopped insisting that blacks buy orange or grape — anything but Coca-Cola. He looked immediately at the door and saw the shadow of the old monarch brushing a freckled hand past his face.

"What you lookin out there for, boy? I asked you a question, damnit!"

"You didn't ask nothin, Lonnie. You just told me."

That said, Lincoln turned to leave when he heard the old man say, "Now go on, Lincoln. You know how the boy is. Just go on over to the soda chest and get you and your boy two grape sodas. We's all out of orange."

Lincoln motioned Moses Lee to the chest. Inside there were three dozen orange sodas freshly packed in ice. Moses fished for two grape sodas and opened them with the bottle opener fastened on the corner of the chest just above the Coke logo written in white, cursive lettering. Without saying a word, Lincoln paid Lonnie and left.

On the way home there was nothing either of them could find to say. For Moses Lee every word was conjured, then caught in a feverish bubbling that started in the corner of his eyes and filtered down to his stomach where it curled and struck out at his heart with a long, poisonous tongue. Halfway down the dirt path, Lincoln picked up the pace and left Moses behind. He looked up to see his father's overalls flapping against the dirt and raising small clouds of dust around his feet.

May was the time for Moses Lee to get used to the sun again, time to write letters to his cousin in Washington and ask him to bring a fresh batch of books, time to watch the ground for the first bursting of new crops in the fields and the multicolored flowers in his mother's garden. It was time to forget that an ordered world could be woefully upset by such small things as Cokes and privilege.

That time past, another came, and in June, Moses Lee's uncle, William Thomas, came to visit. As he knelt with his family around the dining room table to say their Sunday prayer, Moses Lee heard the occasional grinding bump of a rear chassis against the high, grassy sections of the path that led to their house. He was almost sure. Then he peeked through clasped hands to see a shiny automobile approaching the house.

Excitement overruled propriety.

"Daddy, here come Uncle William wit a new car."

His father pinched him behind the ear to remind him that his grandfather was still saying grace. The eldest of the Thomases had not broken his stride a bit. He was thanking God for everything.

"For the strength Dear God against all kinds of trials. The crops planted safely in the field, the glory of a bright mornin. Lord for the patience we thank you. As we are about to partake of this meal Jesus . . ."

Lincoln held his son's ear tightly, and Moses knew from experience that he dare not scream or cry out. When Uncle William walked into the house, he knew instinctively what was taking place and held his family at the doorway with bowed heads until Grandfather finished.

After they had finished dinner, Lincoln and his brother walked out to the yard to examine the new car, a 1968 Buick Electra. They walked around the car several times before popping the hood to examine the car's heart — the engine.

Moses Lee sat on the back porch and talked with his cousin Bobby, a tall, lean muscular boy of 18 years, just two months older than Moses. He was wearing a pair of expensive-looking trousers and a cotton shirt with a large collar and blue cuff links at the end of long, starched sleeves.

Moses Lee questioned him about the long-sleeved shirt. "Mighty hot for that shirt, ain't it, Bobby?"

"No. Well, it's cool up North. Don't you know nothin, boy? The further north you go, the cooler it gets. Damn, boy, you just about eighteen and nearly retarded."

"No such thing, goddamnit. Why didn't you answer my letter?"

"What letter?"

"I wrote you two or three weeks ago about some more books."

"That mail got a long way to go too, you know. Washington is a long way off. You ought to read some more mature shit anyway."

"Why you cuss so much, Bobby? Mama is right there in the house, and you out here trying to be mannish. Our papas will cut us too short to shit wit them straps they carry. Even though we is eighteen."

In the past Moses Lee had enjoyed Bobby's visits, but now his cousin bored and angered him. As Bobby explained how he was making headway with a senator's niece, Moses Lee stared meekly at the ground in front of him, making designs in the dirt with a small twig. It was one lie after another — a college scholarship, wealthy friends, liquor-drinking sprees and more. Moses Lee took a deep breath, swelling his chest till it seemed it would burst, and then walked away leaving Bobby to boast to the chickens and the huge, gray cats snoozing in the afternoon shade.

Bobby shouted after him, "You dummy, big country dummy!"

Moses Lee turned immediately and replied, "This country dummy'll lay a whippin on your black ass you'll never get over."

"Well then, do it, dummy."

"Bring your black city ass down here and get it."

Moses Lee was standing near the wood pile, and as Bobby approached, he grabbed the big axe that stood lodged in the tree stump. With his cousin chasing him down toward the pine forest, Bobby screamed for his father.

"Help! Daddy! Moses Lee done lost his mind!"

When they reached the edge of the woods, Moses Lee took a wild swing at his cousin and missed. The axe hit a tree instead and stuck there so tightly that Moses Lee lost sight of his prey as he fought to remove it. Still struggling with the axe, Moses Lee felt a sudden, sharp, cutting sensation across his back. It was his father applying discipline. His Uncle William shot past him into the woods after Bobby with his belt swinging wildly beside him.

Moses Lee hollered to Bobby, "Motherfucker!" and his father slapped him alongside his cheek so hard his mouth began to bleed — an outburst of his father's anger he had never known.

The remainder of the visit was torment for the two cousins. For two weeks Uncle William's family remained at the farm, helping Lincoln in the fields during the day and riding down the dirt path in the Electra to seek out other kin in the evening. Moses disowned the whole crew, scornfully referring to them as the DC bunch. Almost daily, Vira would approach him as he sulked on the back porch or under the apple tree on the side of the house.

"Moses Lee, if you hadn't been so hot on being a man, you wouldn't a got your hind whopped so bad in front of everybody. You such a fool even though you my brother. Moses Lee, you listenin to me, fool?"

But Moses Lee had stopped talking. Now all he did was sit and consider the meaning of Coca-Colas, climate control and power windows, the lofty arrogance of white skin and distance — the space between here and the North, the space between what ran through his heart and the jumbled mush that came from his mouth when he had tried to speak of his feelings. He had hidden his true emotions about so many things for so long that he had difficulty understanding such awesome and fearful things as the hate and lust he felt when he wanted to kill his cousin — to good feelings that surged through him without legitimate provocation. Moses Lee wanted to be free of restraint, to leave.

In August Lincoln Thomas began preparations for the tobacco harvest. He assembled his makeshift sleds that were used to haul the large, waxy leaves back to the barn where they were hung to dry. From the family of a neighbor, he hired two teen-aged boys to help him with the work. It was the first time he'd had to resort to outside labor. In the past Moses Lee had been able to do the work of three boys like them, but now he just sat around the edges of the house, chasing the shade and staring quietly out into space. Lincoln and his wife consulted a midwife who examined Moses Lee and declared him insane.

But she was wrong. A vibrant host of images flashed across the forefront of Moses Lee's mind — images that he now gave all the attention he had denied them for years. Behind the blank stare was a soul that smiled vengefully and plotted its escape.

It came that same August. His family trusted him as they would have a small child. Once he was fed and clothed for the day, they left him to his own devices as they went about the work of maintaining the farm. He just walked away quietly in the heat of one routine work-day, unseen. He didn't bother to take anything but the twenty dollars he'd saved working for Old Man Ingram. After making his way to the highway which connected the county with the North Carolina state line, he turned southward, and hailed a pickup that approached him after he had gone nearly two miles. There was a small light-skinned black man sitting behind the wheel.

He asked Moses Lee slowly, "Where you goin, boy?"

Moses Lee hadn't talked in two months and it was a strange sensation to form his mouth for something other than eating or blowing leaves across the water in the huge tubs his mother kept filled in the back of their house. But he answered, "South. I'm goin south."

"You in the South, boy."

"I know, but I'm goin deeper — where it's a little richer. Closer to the fire."

THE SELF

China

by Charles Johnson

If one man conquer in battle a thousand men, and if another conquers himself, he is the greatest of conquerors.

— The Dhammapada

EVELYN'S PROBLEMS with her husband, Rudolph, began one evening in early March — a dreary winter evening in Seattle — when he complained after a heavy meal of pig's feet and mashed potatoes of shortness of breath, an allergy to something she put in his food perhaps, or brought on by the first signs of wild flowers around them. She suggested they get out of the house for the evening, go to a movie. He was fifty-four, a postman for thirty-three years now, with high blood pressure, emphysema, flat feet, and, as Evelyn told her friend Shelberdine Lewis, the lingering fear that he had cancer. Getting old, he was also getting hard to live with. He told her never to salt his dinners, to keep their Lincoln Continental at a crawl, and never run her fingers along his inner thigh when they sat in Reverend William Merrill's church, because anything, even sex, or laughing too loud — Rudolph was serious — might bring on heart failure.

So she chose for their Saturday night outing a peaceful movie, a mildly funny comedy a *Seattle Times* reviewer said was fit only for titters and nasal snorts, a low-key satire that made Rudolph's eyelids droop as he shoveled down unbuttered popcorn in the darkened, half-empty theater. Sticky fluids cemented Evelyn's feet to the floor. A man in the last row laughed at all the wrong places. She kept the popcorn on her lap, though she hated the unsalted stuff and wouldn't touch it, sighing as Rudolph pawed across her to shove his fingers inside the cup.

She followed the film as best she could, but occasionally her eyes frosted over, flashed white. She went blind like this now and then. The fibers of her eyes were failing; her retinas were tearing like soft tissue. At these times the world was a canvas with whiteout spilling from the far left corner toward the center; it was the sudden shock of an empty frame in a series of slides. Someday, she knew, the snow on her eyes would stay. Winter eternally: her eyes split like her walking stick. She groped along the fractured surface, waiting for her sight to thaw, listening to the film she couldn't see. Her only comfort was knowing that, despite her infirmity, her Rudolph was in even worse health.

He slid back and forth from sleep during the film (she elbowed him occasionally, or pinched his leg), then came full awake, sitting up suddenly when the movie ended and a "Coming Attractions" trailer began. It was some sort of gladiator movie, Evelyn thought, blinking, and it was pretty trashy stuff at that. The plot's revenge theme was a poor excuse for Chinese actors or Japanese (she couldn't tell those people apart) to flail the air with their hands and feet, take on fifty costumed extras at once, and leap twenty feet through the air in perfect defiance of gravity. Rudolph's mouth hung open.

"Can people really do that?" He did not take his eyes off the screen, but talked at her from the right side of his mouth. "Leap that high?"

"It's a *movie*," sighed Evelyn. "A *bad* movie."

He nodded, then asked again, "But can they?"

"Oh, Rudolph, for God's sake!" She stood up to leave, her seat slapping back loudly. "They're on *trampolines!* You can see them in the corner — there! — if you open your eyes!"

He did see them, once Evelyn twisted his head to the lower left corner of the screen, and it seemed to her that her husband looked disappointed — looked, in fact, the way he did the afternoon Dr. Guylee told Rudolph he'd developed an extrasystolic reaction, a faint, moaning sound from his heart whenever it relaxed. He said no more and, after the trailer finished, stood — there was chewing gum stuck to his trouser seat — dragged on his heavy coat with her help and followed Evelyn up the long, carpeted aisle, through the exit of the Coronet Theater, and to their car. He said nothing as she chattered on the way home, reminding him that he could not stay up all night puttering in his base-ment shop because the next evening they were to attend the church's revival meeting.

Rudolph, however, did not attend the revival. He complained after lunch of a light, dancing pain in his chest, which he had conveniently whenever Mount Zion Baptist Church held revivals, and she went alone, sitting with her friend Shelberdine, a beautician. She was forty-one; Evelyn, fifty-two. That evening Evelyn wore spotless white gloves, tan therapeutic stockings for the swelling in her ankles, and a white dress that brought out nicely the brown color of her skin, the most beautiful cedar brown, Rudolph said when they were courting thirty-five years ago in South Carolina. But then Evelyn had worn a matching checkered skirt and coat to meeting. With her jet black hair pinned behind her neck by a simple wooden comb, she looked as if she might have been Andrew Wyeth's starkly beautiful model for *Day of the Fair.* Rudolph, she remembered, wore black business suits, black ties, black wing tips, but he also wore white gloves because he was a senior usher — this was how she first noticed him. He was one of four young men dressed like deacons (or blackbirds), their left hands tucked into the hollow of their backs, their right carrying silver plates for the offer-ing as they marched in almost military fashion down each aisle: Chris-tian soldiers, she'd thought, the cream of black manhood, and to get his attention she placed not her white envelope or coins in Rudolph's plate but instead a note that said: "You have a beautiful smile." It was, for all her innocence, a daring thing to do, according to Evelyn's mother — flirting with a randy young man like Rudolph Lee Jackson, but he did have nice, tigerish teeth. A killer smile, people called it, like all the boys in the Jackson family: a killer smile and good hair that needed no more than one stroke of his palm to bring out Quo Vadis rows pomaded sweetly with the scent of Murray's.

And, of course, Rudolph was no dummy. Not a total dummy, at least. He pretended nothing extraordinary had happened as the con-gregation left the little whitewashed church. He stood, the youngest son, between his father and mother, and let old Deacon Adcock re-mark, "Oh, how strong he's looking now," which was a lie. Rudolph was the weakest of the Jackson boys, the pale, bookish, spiritual child born when his parents were well past forty. His brothers played foot-ball, they went into the navy; Rudolph lived in Scripture, was labeled

4-F, and hoped to attend Moody Bible Institute in Chicago, if he could ever find the money. Evelyn could tell Rudolph knew exactly where she was in the crowd, that he could feel her as she and her sister, Debbie, waited for their father to bring his DeSoto — the family prize — closer to the front steps. When the crowd thinned, he shambled over in his slow, ministerial walk, introduced himself, and unfolded her note.

"You write this?" he asked. "It's not right to play with the Lord's money, you know."

"I like to play," she said.

"You do, huh?" He never looked directly at people. Women, she guessed, terrified him. Or, to be exact, the powerful emotions they caused in him terrified Rudolph. He was a pud puller, if she ever saw one. He kept his eyes on a spot left of her face. "You're Joe Montgomery's daughter, aren't you?"

"Maybe," teased Evelyn.

He trousered the note and stood marking the ground with his toe. "And just what you expect to get, Miss Playful, by fooling with people during collection time?"

She waited, let him look away, and, when the back-and-forth swing of his gaze crossed her again, said in her most melic soft-breathing voice: "*You.*"

Up front, portly Reverend Merrill concluded his sermon. Evelyn tipped her head slightly, smiling into memory; her hand reached left to pat Rudolph's leg gently; then she remembered it was Shelberdine beside her, and lifted her hand to the seat in front of her. She said a prayer for Rudolph's health, but mainly it was for herself, a hedge against her fear that their childless years had slipped by like wind, that she might return home one day and find him — as she had found her father — on the floor, bellied up, one arm twisted behind him where he fell, alone, his fingers locked against his chest. Rudolph had begun to run down, Evelyn decided, the minute he was turned down by Moody Bible Institute. They moved to Seattle in 1956 — his brother Eli was stationed nearby and said Boeing was hiring black men. But they didn't hire Rudolph. He had kidney trouble on and off before he landed the job at the Post Office. Whenever he bent forward, he felt dizzy. Liver, heart, and lungs — they'd worn down gradually as his belly grew, but none of this was as bad as what he called "the Problem." His pecker shrank to no bigger than a pencil eraser each time he saw her undress. Or when Evelyn, as was her habit when talking, touched his arm. Was she the cause of this? Well, she knew she wasn't much to look at anymore. She'd seen the bottom of a few too many candy wrappers. Evelyn was nothing to make a man pant and jump her bones, pulling her fully clothed onto the davenport, as Rudolph had done years before, but wasn't sex something else you surrendered with age? It never seemed all that good to her anyway. And besides, he'd wanted oral sex, which Evelyn — if she knew nothing else — thought was a nasty, unsanitary thing to do with your mouth. She glanced up from under her spring hat past the pulpit, past the choir of black and brown faces to the agonized beauty of a bearded white carpenter impaled on a rood, and in this timeless image she felt comforted that suffering was inescapable, the loss of vitality inevitable, even a good thing maybe, and that she had to steel herself — yes — for someday opening her bedroom door and finding her Rudolph face down in his breakfast oatmeal. He would die before her, she knew that in her bones.

And so, after service, Sanka, and a slice of meat pie with Shelberdine downstairs in the brightly lit church basement, Evelyn returned home to tell her husband how lovely the Griffin girls had sung that day, that their neighbor Rod Kenner had been saved, and to listen, if necessary, to Rudolph's fear that the lump on his shoulder was an early-warning sign of something evil. As it turned out, Evelyn found that except for their cat, Mr. Miller, the little A-frame house was empty. She looked in his bedroom. No Rudolph. The unnaturally still house made Evelyn uneasy, and she took the excruciatingly painful twenty stairs into the basement to peer into a workroom littered with power tools, planks of wood, and the blueprints her husband used to make bookshelves and cabinets. No Rudolph. Frightened, Evelyn called the eight hospitals in Seattle, but no one had a Rudolph Lee Jackson on his books. After her last call the starburst clock in the living room read twelve-thirty. Putting down the wall phone, she felt a familiar pain in her abdomen. Another attack of Hershey squirts, probably from the meat pie. She hurried into the bathroom, lifted her skirt, and lowered her underwear around her ankles, but kept the door wide open, something impossible to do if Rudolph was home. Actually, it felt good not to have him underfoot, a little like he was dead already. But the last thing Evelyn wanted was that or, as she lay down against her lumpy backrest, to fall asleep, though she did, nodding off and dreaming until something shifted down her weight on the side of her bed away from the wall.

"Evelyn," said Rudolph, "look at this." She blinked back sleep and squinted at the cover of a magazine called *Inside Kung-Fu*, which Rudolph waved under her nose. On the cover a man stood bowlegged, one hand cocked under his armpit, the other corkscrewing straight at Evelyn's nose.

"Rudolph!" She batted the magazine aside, then swung her eyes toward the cluttered nightstand, focusing on the electric clock beside her water glass from McDonald's, Preparation H suppositories, and Harlequin romances. "It's morning!" Now she was mad. At least, working at it. "Where have you been?"

Her husband inhaled, a wheezing, whistlelike breath. He rolled the magazine into a cylinder and, as he spoke, struck his left palm with it. "That movie we saw advertised? You remember — it was called *The Five Fingers of Death*. I just saw that and one called *Deep Thrust*."

"Wonderful." Evelyn screwed up her lips. "I'm calling hospitals and you're at a Hong Kong double feature."

"Listen," said Rudolph. "You don't understand." He seemed at that moment as if he did not understand either. "It was a Seattle movie premiere. The Northwest is crawling with fighters. It has something to do with all the Asians out here. Before they showed the movie, four students from a kwoon in Chinatown went onstage —"

"A what?" asked Evelyn.

"A kwoon — it's a place to study fighting, a meditation hall." He looked at her but was really watching, Evelyn realized, something exciting she had missed. "They did a demonstration to drum up their membership. They broke boards and bricks, Evelyn. They went through what's called kata and kumite and . . ." He stopped again to breathe. "I've never seen anything so beautiful. The reason I'm late is because I wanted to talk with them after the movie."

Evelyn, suspicious, took a Valium and waited.

"I signed up for lessons," he said.

She gave a glacial look at Rudolph, then at his magazine, and said in the voice she used five years ago when he wanted to take a vacation to Upper Volta or, before that, invest in a British car she knew they couldn't afford:

"You're fifty-*four* years old, Rudolph."

"I know that."

"You're no Muhammad Ali."

"I know that," he said.

"You're no Bruce Lee. Do you want to be Bruce Lee? Do you know where he is now, Rudolph? He's dead — dead here in a Seattle cemetery and buried up on Capital Hill."

His shoulders slumped a little. Silently, Rudolph began undressing, his beefy backside turned toward her, slipping his pajama bottoms on before taking off his shirt so his scrawny lower body would not be fully exposed. He picked up his magazine, said, "I'm sorry if I worried you," and huffed upstairs to his bedroom. Evelyn clicked off the mushroom-shaped lamp on her nightstand. She lay on her side, listening to his slow footsteps strike the stairs, then heard his mattress creak above her — his bedroom was directly above hers — but she did not hear him click off his own light. From time to time she heard his shifting weight squeak the mattress springs. He was reading that foolish magazine, she guessed; then she grew tired and gave this impossible man up to God. With a copy of *The Thorn Birds* open on her lap, Evelyn fell heavily to sleep again.

At breakfast the next morning any mention of the lessons gave Rudolph lockjaw. He kissed her forehead, as always, before going to work, and simply said he might be home late. Climbing the stairs to his bedroom was painful for Evelyn, but she hauled herself up, pausing at each step to huff, then sat on his bed and looked over his copy of *Inside Kung-Fu.* There were articles on empty-hand combat, soft-focus photos of ferocious-looking men in funny suits, parables about legendary Zen masters, an interview with someone named Bernie Bernheim, who began to study karate at age fifty-seven and became a black belt at age sixty-one, and page after page of advertisements for exotic Asian weapons: nunchaku, shuriken, sai swords, tonfa, bo staffs, training bags of all sorts, a wooden dummy shaped like a man and called a Mook Jong, and weights. Rudolph had circled them all. He had torn the order form from the last page of the magazine. The total cost of the things he'd circled — Evelyn added them furiously, rounding off the figures — was $800.

Two minutes later she was on the telephone to Shelberdine.

"Let him tire of it," said her friend. "Didn't you tell me Rudolph had Lower Lombard Strain?"

Evelyn's nose clogged with tears.

"Why is he doing this? Is it me, do you think?"

"It's the Problem," said Shelberdine. "He wants his manhood back. Before he died, Arthur did the same. Someone at the plant told him he could get it back if he did twenty-yard sprints. He went into convulsions while running around the lake."

Evelyn felt something turn in her chest. "You don't think he'll hurt himself, do you?"

"Of course not."

"Do you think he'll hurt *me?*"

Her friend reassured Evelyn that Mid-Life Crisis brought out these shenanigans in men. Evelyn replied that she thought Mid-Life Crisis started around age forty, to which Shelberdine said, "Honey, I don't mean no harm, but Rudolph always was a little on the slow side," and Evelyn agreed. She would wait until he worked this thing out of his system, until Nature defeated him and he surrendered, as any right-thinking person would, to the breakdown of the body, the brutal fact of decay, which could only be blunted, it seemed to her, by decaying *with* someone, the comfort every Negro couple felt when, aging, they knew enough to let things wind down.

Her patience was rewarded in the beginning. Rudolph crawled home from his first lesson, hunched over, hardly able to stand, afraid he had permanently ruptured something. He collapsed face down on the living room sofa, his feet on the floor. She helped him change into his pajamas and fingered Ben-Gay into his back muscles. Evelyn had never seen her husband so close to tears.

"I can't *do* push-ups," he moaned. "Or sit-ups. I'm so stiff — I don't know my body." He lifted his head, looking up pitifully, his eyes pleading. "Call Dr. Guylee. Make an appointment for Thursday, okay?"

"Yes, dear." Evelyn hid her smile with one hand. "You shouldn't push yourself so hard."

At that, he sat up, bare-chested, his stomach bubbling over his pajama bottoms. "That's what it means. *Gung-fu* means 'hard work' in Chinese. Evelyn" — he lowered his voice — "I don't think I've ever really done hard work in my life. Not like this, something that asks me to give *every*thing, body and soul, spirit and flesh. I've always felt . . ." He looked down, his dark hands dangling between his thighs. "I've never been able to give *every*thing to *any*thing. The world never let me. It won't let me put all of myself into play. Do you know what I'm saying? Every job I've ever had, everything I've ever done, it only demanded part of me. It was like there was so much *more* of me that went unused after the job was over. I get that feeling in church sometimes." He lay back down, talking now into the sofa cushion. "Sometimes I get that feeling with you."

Her hand stopped on his shoulder. She wasn't sure she'd heard him right, his voice was so muffled. "That I've never used all of you?"

Rudolph nodded, rubbing his right knuckle where, at the kwoon, he'd lost a stretch of skin on a speedbag. "There's still part of me left over. You never tried to touch all of me, to take everything. Maybe you can't. Maybe no one can. But sometimes I get the feeling that the unused part — the unlived life — *spoils*, that you get cancer because it sits like fruit on the ground and rots." Rudolph shook his head; he'd said too much and knew it, perhaps had not even put it the way he felt inside. Stiffly, he got to his feet. "Don't ask me to stop training." His eyebrows spread inward. "If I stop, I'll die."

Evelyn twisted the cap back onto the Ben-Gay. She held out her hand, which Rudolph took. Veins on the back of his hand burgeoned abnormally like dough. Once when she was shopping at the Public Market she'd seen monstrous plastic gloves shaped like hands in a magic store window. His hand looked like that. It belonged on Lon Chaney. Her voice shook a little, panicky, "I'll call Dr. Guylee in the morning."

Evelyn knew — or thought she knew — his trouble. He'd never come to terms with the disagreeableness of things. Rudolph had always been too serious for some people, even in South Carolina. It was the thing, strange to say, that drew her to him, this crimped-browed tendency in Rudolph to listen with every atom of his life when their minister in Hodges, quoting Marcus Aurelius to give his sermon flash, said, "Live with the gods," or later in Seattle, the habit of working himself up over Reverend Merrill's reading from Ecclesiastes 9:10: "Whatsoever thy hand findeth to do, do it with all thy might." Now, he didn't *really* mean that, Evelyn knew. Nothing in the world could be taken that seriously; that's *why* this was the world. And, as all Mount Zion knew, Reverend Merrill had a weakness for high-yellow choirgirls and gin, and was forever complaining that his salary was too small for his family. People made compromises, nodded at spiritual commonplaces — the high seriousness of biblical verses that demanded nearly superhuman duty and self-denial — and laughed off their lapses into sloth, envy, and the other deadly sins. It was what made living so enjoyably *human:* this built-in inability of man to square his performance with perfection. People were naturally soft on themselves. But not her Rudolph.

Of course, he seldom complained. It was not in his nature to complain when, looking for "gods," he found only ruin and wreckage. What did he expect? Evelyn wondered. Man was evil — she'd told him that a thousand times — or, if not evil, hopelessly flawed. Everything failed; it was some sort of law. But at least there was laughter, and lovers clinging to one another against the cliff; there were novels — wonderful tales of how things should be — and perfection promised in the afterworld. He'd sit and listen, her Rudolph, when she put things this way, nodding because he knew that in his persistent hunger for perfection in the here and now he was, at best, in the minority. He kept his dissatisfaction to himself, but occasionally Evelyn would glimpse in his eyes that look, that distant, pained expression that asked: *Is this all?* She saw it after her first miscarriage, then her second; saw it when he stopped searching the want ads and settled on the Post Office as the fulfillment of his potential in the marketplace. It was always there, that look, after he turned forty, and no new, lavishly praised novel from the Book-of-the-Month Club, no feature-length movie, prayer meeting, or meal she fixed for him wiped it from Rudolph's eyes. He was, at least, this sort of man before he saw that martial-arts B movie. It was a dark vision, Evelyn decided, a dangerous vision, and in it she whiffed something that might destroy her. What that was, she couldn't say, but she knew her Rudolph better than he knew himself. He would see the error — the waste of time — in his new hobby, and she was sure he would mend his ways.

In the weeks, then months that followed Evelyn waited, watching her husband for a flag of surrender. There was no such sign. He became worse than before. He cooked his own meals, called her heavy soul food dishes "too acidic," lived on raw vegetables, seaweed, nuts, and fruit to make his body "more alkaline," and fasted on Sundays. He ordered books on something called Shaolin fighting and meditation from a store in California, and when his equipment arrived UPS from Dolan's Sports in New Jersey, he ordered more — in consternation,

Evelyn read the list — leg stretchers, makiwara boards, air shields, hand grips, bokken, focus mitts, a full-length mirror (for heaven's sake) so he could correct his form, and protective equipment. For proper use of his headgear and gloves, however, he said he needed a sparring partner — an opponent — he said, to help him instinctively understand "combat strategy," how to "flow" and "close the Gap" between himself and an adversary, how to create by his movements a negative space in which the other would be neutralized.

"Well," crabbed Evelyn, "if you need a punching bag, don't look at *me.*"

He sat across the kitchen table from her, doing dynamic-tension exercises as she read a new magazine called *Self.* "Did I ever tell you what a black belt means?" he asked.

"You told me."

"Sifu Chan doesn't use belts for ranking. They were introduced seventy years ago because Westerners were impatient, you know, needed signposts and all that."

"You told me," said Evelyn.

"Originally, all you got was a white belt. It symbolized innocence. Virginity." His face was immensely serious, like a preacher's. "As you worked, it got darker, dirtier, and turned brown. Then black. You were a master then. With even more work, the belt became frayed, the threads came loose, you see, and the belt showed white again."

"Rudolph, I've heard this before!" Evelyn picked up her magazine and took it into her bedroom. From there, with her legs drawn up under the blankets, she shouted: "I *won't* be your punching bag!"

So he brought friends from his kwoon, friends she wanted nothing to do with. There was something unsettling about them. Some were street fighters. Young. They wore tank-top shirts and motorcycle jackets. After drinking racks of Rainier beer on the front porch, they tossed their crumpled empties next door into Rod Kenner's yard. Together, two of Rudolph's new friends — Truck and Tuco — weighed a quarter of a ton. Evelyn kept a rolling pin under her pillow when they came, but she knew they could eat that along with her. But some of his new friends were students at the University of Washington. Truck, a Vietnamese only two years in America, planned to apply to the Police Academy once his training ended; and Tuco, who was Puerto Rican, had been fighting since he could make a fist; but a delicate young man named Andrea, a blue sash, was an actor in the drama department at the university. His kwoon training, he said, was less for self-defense than helping him understand his movements onstage — how, for example, to convincingly explode across a room in anger. Her husband liked them, Evelyn realized in horror. And they liked him. They were separated by money, background, and religion, but something she could not identify made them seem, those nights on the porch after his class, like a single body. They called Rudolph "Older Brother" or, less politely, "Pop."

His sifu, a short, smooth-figured boy named Douglas Chan, who Evelyn figured couldn't be over eighteen, sat like the Dalai Lama in their tiny kitchen as if he owned it, sipping her tea, which Rudolph laced with Korean ginseng. Her husband lit Chan's cigarettes as if he were President Carter come to visit the common man. He recommended that Rudolph study T'ai Chi, "soft" fighting systems, ki, and something called Tao. He told him to study, as well, Newton's three laws of physics and apply them to his own body during kumite. What she remembered most about Chan were his wrist braces, ornamental weapons that had three straps and, along the black leather, highly polished studs like those worn by Steve Reeves in a movie she'd seen about Hercules. In a voice she thought girlish, he spoke of eye gouges and groin-tearing techniques, exercises called the Delayed Touch of Death and Dim Mak, with the casualness she and Shelberdine talked about bargains at Thriftway. And then they suited up, the boyish Sifu, who looked like Maharaj-ji's rougher brother, and her clumsy husband; they went out back, pushed aside the aluminum lawn furniture, and pommeled each other for half an hour. More precisely, her Rudolph was on the receiving end of hook kicks, spinning back fists faster than thought, and foot sweeps that left his body purpled for weeks. A sensible man would have known enough to drive to Swedish Hospital pronto. Rudolph, never known as a profound thinker, pushed on after Sifu Chan left, practicing his flying kicks by leaping to ground level from a four-foot hole he'd dug by their cyclone fence.

Evelyn, nibbling a Van de Kamp's pastry from Safeway — she was always nibbling, these days — watched from the kitchen window until twilight, then brought out the Ben-Gay, a cold beer, and rubbing alcohol on a tray. She figured he needed it. Instead, Rudolph, stretching under the far-reaching cedar in the backyard, politely refused, pushed the tray aside, and rubbed himself with Dit-Da-Jow, "iron-hitting wine," which smelled like the open door of an opium factory on a hot summer day. Yet this ancient potion not only instantly healed his wounds (said Rudolph) but prevented arthritis as well. She was tempted to see if it healed brain damage by pouring it into Rudolph's ears, but apparently he was doing something right. Dr. Guylee's examination had been glowing; he said Rudolph's muscle tone, whatever that was, was better. His cardiovascular system was healthier. His erections were outstanding — or upstanding — though lately he seemed to have no interest in sex. Evelyn, even she, saw in the crepuscular light changes in Rudolph's upper body as he stretched: Muscles like globes of light rippled along his shoulders; larval currents moved on his belly. The language of his new, developing body eluded her. He was not always like this. After a cold shower and sleep his muscles shrank back a little. It was only after his workouts, his weight lifting, that his body expanded like baking bread, filling out in a way that obliterated the soft Rudolph-body she knew. This new flesh had the contours of the silhouetted figures on medical charts: the body as it must be in the mind of God. Glistening with perspiration, his muscles took on the properties of the free weights he pumped relentlessly. They were profoundly tragic, too, because their beauty was earthbound. It would vanish with the world. You are ugly, his new muscles said to Evelyn; old and ugly. His self-punishment made her feel sick. She was afraid of his hard, cold weights. She hated them. Yet she wanted them, too. They had a certain monastic beauty. She thought: *He's doing this to hurt me.* She wondered: What was it like to be powerful? Was clever cynicism — even comedy — the by-product of bulging bellies, weak nerves, bad posture? Her only defense against the dumbbells that stood between them — she meant both his weights and his friends — was, as always, her acid southern tongue:

"They're all fairies, right?"

Rudolph looked dreamily her way. These post-workout periods made him feel, he said, as if there were no interval between himself and what he saw. His face was vacant, his eyes — like smoke. In this afterglow (he said) he saw without judging. Without judgment, there were no distinctions. Without distinctions, there was no desire. Without desire . . .

He smiled sideways at her. "Who?"

"The people in your kwoon." Evelyn crossed her arms. "I read somewhere that most body builders are homosexual."

He refused to answer her.

"If they're not gay, then maybe I should take lessons. It's been good for you, right?" Her voice grew sharp. "I mean, isn't that what you're saying? That you and your friends are better'n everybody else?"

Rudolph's head dropped; he drew a long breath. Lately, his responses to her took the form of quietly clearing his lungs.

"You should do what you *have* to, Evelyn. You don't have to do what anybody else does." He stood up, touched his toes, then brought his forehead straight down against his unbent knees, which was physically impossible, Evelyn would have said — and faintly obscene.

It was a nightmare to watch him each evening after dinner. He walked around the house in his Everlast leg weights, tried push-ups on his finger-tips and wrists, and, as she sat trying to watch "The Jeffersons," stood in a ready stance before the flickering screen, throwing punches each time the scene, or shot, changed to improve his timing. It took the fun out of watching TV, him doing that — she preferred him falling asleep in his chair beside her, as he used to. But what truly frightened Evelyn was his "doing nothing." Sitting in meditation, planted cross-legged in a full lotus on their front porch, with Mr. Miller blissfully curled on his lap, a Bodhisattva in the middle of houseplants she set out for the sun. Looking at him, you'd have thought he was dead. The whole thing smelled like self-hypnosis. He breathed too slowly, in Evelyn's view — only three breaths per minute, he claimed. He wore his gi, splotchy with dried blood and sweat, his calloused hands on his knees, the forefingers on each tipped against his thumbs, his eyes screwed shut.

During his eighth month at the kwoon, she stood watching him as he sat, wondering over the vivid changes in his body, the grim firmness where before there was jolly fat, the disquieting steadiness of his posture, where before Rudolph could not sit still in church for five minutes without fidgeting. Now he sat in zazen for forty-five minutes a day, fifteen when he awoke, fifteen (he said) at work in the mailroom during his lunch break, fifteen before going to bed. He called this withdrawal (how she hated his fancy language) similar to the necessary silences in music, "a stillness that prepared him for busyness and sound." He'd never breathed before, he told her. Not once. Not clear to the floor of himself. Never breathed and emptied himself as he did now, picturing himself sitting on the bottom of Lake Washington: himself, Rudolph Lee Jackson, at the center of the universe; for if the universe was infinite, any point where he stood would be at its center — it would shift and move with him. (That saying, Evelyn knew, was minted in Douglas Chan's mind. No Negro preacher worth the name would speak that way.) He told her that in zazen, at the bottom of the lake, he worked to discipline his mind and maintain one point of concentration; each thought, each feeling that overcame him he saw as a fragile bubble, which he could inspect passionlessly from all sides; then he let it float gently to the surface, and soon — as he slipped deeper into the vortices of himself, into the Void — even the image of himself on the lake floor vanished.

Evelyn stifled a scream.

Was she one of Rudolph's bubbles, something to detach himself from? On the porch, Evelyn watched him narrowly, sitting in a rain-whitened chair, her chin on her left fist. She snapped the fingers on her right hand under his nose. Nothing. She knocked her knuckles lightly on his forehead. Nothing. (Faker, she thought.) For another five minutes he sat and breathed, sat and breathed, then opened his eyes slowly as if he'd slept as long as Rip Van Winkle. "It's dark," he said, stunned. When he began, it was twilight. Evelyn realized something new: He was not living time as she was, not even that anymore. Things, she saw, were slower for him; to him she must seem like a woman stuck in fast-forward. She asked:

"What do you see when you go in there?"

Rudolph rubbed his eyes. "Nothing."

"Then *why* do you do it? The world's out here!"

He seemed unable to say, as if the question were senseless. His eyes angled up, like a child's, toward her face. "Nothing is peaceful sometimes. The emptiness is full. I'm not afraid of it now."

"You empty yourself?" she asked. "Of me, too?"

"Yes."

Evelyn's hand shot up to cover her face. She let fly with a whimper. Rudolph rose instantly — he sent Mr. Miller flying — then fell back hard on his buttocks; the lotus cut off blood to his lower body — which provided more to his brain, he claimed — and it always took him a few seconds before he could stand again. He reached up, pulled her hand down, and stroked it.

"What've I done?"

"That's it," sobbed Evelyn. "I don't know what you're doing." She lifted the end of her bathrobe, blew her nose, then looked at him through streaming, unseeing eyes. "And you don't either. I wish you'd never seen that movie. I'm sick of all your weights and workouts — sick of them, do you hear? Rudolph, I want you back the way you were: *sick.*" No sooner than she said this Evelyn was sorry. But she'd done no harm. Rudolph, she saw, didn't want anything; everything, Evelyn included, delighted him, but as far as Rudolph was concerned, it was all shadows in a phantom history. He was humbler now, more patient, but he'd lost touch with everything she knew was normal in people: weakness, fear, guilt, self-doubt, the very things that gave the world thickness and made people do things. She *did* want him to desire her. No, she didn't. Not if it meant oral sex. Evelyn didn't know, really, what she wanted anymore. She felt, suddenly, as if she might dissolve before his eyes. "Rudolph, if you're 'empty,' like you say, you don't know who — or what — is talking to you. If you said you were praying, I'd understand. It would be God talking to you. But this way . . ." She pounded her fist four, five times on her thigh. "It could be *evil* spirits, you know! There *are* evil spirits, Rudolph. It could be the Devil."

Rudolph thought for a second. His chest lowered after another long breath. "Evelyn, this is going to sound funny, but I don't believe in the Devil."

Evelyn swallowed. It had come to that.

"Or God — unless we are gods."

She could tell he was at pains to pick his words carefully, afraid he might offend. Since joining the kwoon and studying ways to kill, he seemed particularly careful to avoid her own most effective weapon: the wry, cutting remark, the put-down, the direct, ego-deflating slash. Oh, he was becoming a real saint. At times, it made her want to hit him.

"Whatever is just *is,*" he said. "That's all I know. Instead of worrying about whether it's good or bad, God or the Devil, I just want to be quiet, work on myself, and interfere with things as little as possible. Evelyn," he asked suddenly, "how can there be *two* things?" His brow wrinkled; he chewed his lip. "You think what I'm saying is evil, don't you?"

"I think it's strange! Rudolph, you didn't grow up in China," she said. "They can't breathe in China! I saw that today on the news. They burn soft coal, which gets into the air and turns into acid rain. They wear face masks over there, like the ones we bought when Mount St. Helens blew up. They all ride bicycles, for Christ's sake! They want what we have." Evelyn heard Rod Kenner step onto his screened porch, perhaps to listen from his rocker. She dropped her voice a little. "You grew up in Hodges, South Carolina, same as me, in a right and proper colored church. If you'd *been* to China, maybe I'd understand."

"I can only be what I've been?" This he asked softly, but his voice trembled. "Only what I was in Hodges?"

"You can't be Chinese."

"I don't want to be Chinese!" The thought made Rudolph smile and shake his head. Because she did not understand, and because he was tired of talking, Rudolph stepped back a few feet from her, stretching again, always stretching. "I only want to be what I *can* be, which isn't the greatest fighter in the world, only the fighter *I* can be. Lord knows, I'll probably get creamed in the tournament this Saturday." He added, before she could reply, "Doug asked me if I'd like to compete this weekend in full-contact matches with some people from the kwoon. I have to." He opened the screen door. "I will."

"You'll be killed — you know that, Rudolph." She dug her fingernails into her bathrobe, and dug this into him: "You know, you never were very strong. Six months ago you couldn't open a pickle jar for me."

He did not seem to hear her. "I bought a ticket for you." He held the screen door open, waiting for her to come inside. "I'll fight better if you're there."

She spent the better part of that week at Shelberdine's mornings and Reverend Merrill's church evenings, rinsing her mouth with prayer, sitting most often alone in the front row so she would not have to hear Rudolph talking to himself from the musty basement as he pounded out bench presses, skipped rope for thirty minutes in the backyard, or shadowboxed in preparation for a fight made inevitable by his new muscles. She had married a fool, that was clear, and if he expected her to sit on a bench at the Kingdome while some equally stupid brute spilled the rest of his brains — probably not enough left now to fill a teaspoon — then he was wrong. How could he see the world as "perfect"? — That was his claim. There was poverty, unemployment, twenty-one children dying every minute, every day, every year from hunger and malnutrition, over twenty murdered in Atlanta; there were sixty thousand nuclear weapons in the world, which was dreadful, what with Seattle so close to Boeing; there were far-right Republicans in the White House: *good* reasons, Evelyn thought, to be "negative and life-denying," as Rudolph would put it. It was almost sin to see harmony in an earthly hell, and in a fit of spleen she prayed God would dislocate his shoulder, do some minor damage to humble him, bring him home, and remind him that the body was vanity, a violation of every verse in the Bible. But Evelyn could not sustain her thoughts as long as he could. Not for more than a few seconds. Her mind never settled, never rested, and finally on Saturday morning, when she awoke on Shelberdine's sofa, it would not stay away from the image of her Rudolph dead before hundreds of indifferent spectators, paramedics pounding on his chest, bursting his rib cage in an effort to keep him alive.

From Shelberdine's house she called a taxi and, in the steady rain that northwesterners love, arrived at the Kingdome by noon. It's over already, Evelyn thought, walking the circular stairs to her seat, clamping shut her wet umbrella. She heard cheers, booing, an Asian voice with an accent over a microphone. The tournament began at ten, which was enough time for her white belt husband to be in the emergency ward at Harborview Hospital by now, but she had to see. At first, as she stepped down to her seat through the crowd, she could only hear — her mind grappled for the word, then remembered — kiais, or "spirit shouts," from the great floor of the stadium, many shouts, for contests were progressing in three rings simultaneously. It felt like a circus. It smelled like a locker room. Here two children stood toe to toe until one landed a front kick that sent the other child flying fifteen feet. There two lean-muscled female black belts were interlocked in a delicate ballet, like dance or a chess game, of continual motion. They had a kind of sense, these women — she noticed it immediately — a feel for space and their place in it. (Evelyn hated them immediately.) And in the farthest circle she saw, or rather felt, Rudolph, the oldest thing on the deck, who, sparring in the adult division, was squared off with another white belt, not a boy who might hurt him — the other man was middle-aged, graying, maybe only a few years younger than Rudolph — but they were sparring just the same.

Yet it was not truly him that Evelyn, sitting down, saw. Acoustics in the Kingdome whirlpooled the noise of the crowd, a rivering of voices that affected her, suddenly, like the pitch and roll of voices during service. It affected the way she watched Rudolph. She wondered: Who are these people? She caught her breath when, miscalculating his distance from his opponent, her husband stepped sideways into a roundhouse kick with lots of snap — she heard the cloth of his opponent's gi crack like a gunshot when he threw the technique. She leaned forward, gripping the huge purse on her lap when Rudolph recovered and retreated from the killing to the neutral zone, and then, in a wide stance, rethought strategy. This was not the man she'd slept with for twenty years. Not her hypochondriac Rudolph who had to rest and run cold water on his wrists after walking from the front stairs to the fence to pick up the *Seattle Times.* She did not know him, perhaps had never known him, and now she never would, for the man on the floor, the man splashed with sweat, rising on the ball of his rear foot for a flying kick — was he so foolish he still thought he could fly? — would outlive her; he'd stand healthy and strong and think of her in a bubble, one hand on her headstone, and it was all right, she thought, weeping uncontrollably, it was all right that Rudolph would return home after visiting her wet grave, clean out her bedroom, the pillboxes and paperback books, and throw open her windows to let her sour, rotting smell escape, then move a younger woman's things onto the floor space darkened by her color television, her porcelain chamber pot, her antique sewing machine. And then Evelyn was on her feet, unsure why, but the crowd had stood suddenly to clap, and Evelyn clapped, too, though for an instant she pounded her gloved hands together instinctively until her vision cleared, the momentary flash of retinal blindness giving way to a frame of her husband, the postman, twenty feet off the ground in a perfect flying kick that floored his opponent and made a Japanese judge who looked like Oddjob shout "ippon" — one point — and the fighting in the farthest ring, in herself, perhaps in all the world, was over.

PART III

REVEALING THE SELF DIVIDED . . .

WE WHO HAVE

Blackness

by Jamaica Kincaid

HOW SOFT is the blackness as it falls. It falls in silence and yet it is deafening, for no other sound except the blackness falling can be heard. The blackness falls like soot from a lamp with an untrimmed wick. The blackness is visible and yet it is invisible, for I see that I cannot see it. The blackness fills up a small room, a large field, an island, my own being. The blackness cannot bring me joy but often I am made glad in it. The blackness cannot be separated from me but often I can stand outside it. The blackness is not the air, though I breathe it. The blackness is not the earth, though I walk on it. The blackness is not water or food, though I drink and eat it. The blackness is not my blood, though it flows through my veins. The blackness enters my many-tiered spaces and soon the significant word and event recede and eventually vanish: in this way I am annihilated and my form becomes formless and I am absorbed into a vastness of free-flowing matter. In the blackness, then, I have been erased. I can no longer say my own name. I can no longer point to myself and say "I." In the blackness my voice is silent. First, then, I have been my individual self, carefully banishing randomness from my existence, then I am swallowed up in the blackness so that I am one with it . . .

There are the small flashes of joy that are present in my daily life: the upturned face to the open sky, the red ball tumbling from small hand to small hand, as small voices muffle laughter; the sliver of orange on the horizon, a remnant of the sun setting. There is the wide stillness, trembling and waiting to be violently shattered by impatient demands.

("May I now have my bread without the crust?"

"But I long ago stopped liking my bread without the crust!")

All manner of feelings are locked up within my human breast and all manner of events summon them out. How frightened I became once on looking down to see an oddly shaped, ash-colored object that I did not recognize at once to be a small part of my own foot. And how powerful I then found that moment, so that I was not at one with myself and I felt myself separate, like a brittle substance dashed and shattered, each separate part without knowledge of the other separate parts. I then clung fast to a common and familiar object (my lamp, as it stood unlit on the clean surface of my mantelpiece), until I felt myself steadied, no longer alone at sea in a small rowboat, the waves cruel and unruly. What is my nature, then? For in isolation I am all purpose and industry and determination and prudence, as if I were the single survivor of a species whose evolutionary history can be traced to the most ancient of ancients; in isolation I ruthlessly plow the deep silences, seeking my opportunities like a miner seeking veins of treasure. In what shallow glimmering space shall I find what glimmering glory? The stark, stony mountainous surface is turned to green, rolling meadow, and a spring of clear water, its origins a mystery, its purpose and beauty constant, draws all manner of troubled existence seeking solace. And again and again, the heart — buried deeply as ever in the human breast, its four chambers exposed to love and joy and pain and the small shafts that fall with desperation in between.

I sat at a narrow table, my head, heavy with sleep, resting on my hands. I dreamed of bands of men who walked aimlessly, their guns and cannons slackened at their sides, the chambers emptied of bullets and shells. They had fought in a field from time to time and from time to time they grew tired of it. They walked up the path that led to my house and as they walked they passed between the sun and the earth; as they passed between the sun and the earth they blotted out the daylight and night fell immediately and permanently. No longer could I see the blooming trefoils, their overpowering perfume a constant giddy delight to me; no longer could I see the domesticated animals feeding in the pasture; no longer could I see the beasts, hunter and prey, leading a guarded existence; no longer could I see the smith moving cautiously in a swirl of hot sparks or bent over anvil and bellows. The bands of men marched through my house in silence. On their way, their breath scorched some flowers I had placed on a dresser, with their bare hands they destroyed the marble columns that strengthened the foundations of my house. They left my house, in silence again, and they walked across a field, opposite to the way they had come, still passing between the sun and the earth. I stood at a window and watched their backs until they were just a small spot on the horizon.

I see my child arise slowly from her bed. I see her cross the room and stand in front of the mirror. She looks closely at her straight, unmarred body. Her skin is without color, and when passing through a small beam of light, she is made transparent. Her eyes are ruby, revolving orbs, and they burn like coals caught suddenly in a gust of wind. This is my child! When her jaws were too weak, I first chewed her food, then fed it to her in small mouthfuls. This is my child! I must carry a cool liquid in my flattened breasts to quench her parched throat. This is my child sitting in the shade, her head thrown back in rapture, prolonging some moment of joy I have created for her.

My child is pitiless to the hunchback boy; her mouth twists open in a cruel smile, her teeth becoming pointed and sparkling, the roof of her mouth bony and ridged, her young hands suddenly withered and gnarled as she reaches out to caress his hump. Squirming away from her forceful, heated gaze, he seeks shelter in a grove of trees, but her arms, which she can command to grow to incredible lengths, seek him out and tug at the long silk-like hairs that lie flattened on his back. She calls his name softly and the sound of her voice shatters his eardrum. Deaf, he can no longer heed warnings of danger and his sense of direction is destroyed. Still, my child has built for him a dwelling hut on the edge of a steep cliff so that she may watch him day after day flatten himself against a fate of which he knows and yet cannot truly know until the moment it consumes him.

My child haunts the dwelling places of the useless-winged cormorants, so enamored is she of great beauty and ancestral history. She traces each thing from its meager happenstance beginnings in cool and slimy marsh, to its great glory and dominance of air or land or sea, or to its odd remains entombed in mysterious alluviums. She loves the thing untouched by lore, she loves the thing that is not cultivated, and yet she loves the thing built up, bit carefully placed upon bit, its very beauty eclipsing the deed it is meant to commemorate. She sits idly on a shore, staring hard at the sea beneath the sea and at the sea beneath even that. She hears the sounds within the sounds, common as that is to open spaces. She feels the specter, first cold, then briefly warm, then cold again as it passes from atmosphere to atmosphere. Having observed the many differing physical existences feed on each other, she is beyond despair or the spiritual vacuum.

Oh, look at my child as she stands boldly now, one foot in the dark, the other in the light. Moving from pool to pool, she absorbs each special sensation for and of itself. My child rushes from death to death, so familiar a state is it to her. Though I have summoned her into a fleeting existence, one that is perilous and subject to the violence of chance, she embraces time as it passes in numbing sameness, bearing in its wake a multitude of great sadnesses.

I hear the silent voice; it stands opposite the blackness and yet it does not oppose the blackness, for conflict is not a part of its nature. I shrug off my mantle of hatred. In love I move toward the silent voice. I shrug off my mantle of despair. In love, again, I move ever toward the silent voice. I stand inside the silent voice. The silent voice enfolds me. The silent voice enfolds me so completely that even in memory the blackness is erased. I live in silence. The silence is without boundaries. The pastures are unfenced, the lions roam the continents, the continents are not separated. Across the flat lands cuts the river, its flow undammed. The mountains no longer rupture. Within the silent voice, no mysterious depths separate me; no vision is so distant that longing is stirred up in me. I hear the silent voice — how softly now it falls, and all of existence is caught up in it. Living in the silent voice, I am no longer "I." Living in the silent voice, I am at last at peace. Living in the silent voice, I am at last erased.

WE WHO HAVE

Lost in the City

by Edward P. Jones

WHEN THE TELEPHONE RANG about three o'clock that morning, she sat bolt upright in her bed, as if a giant hand had reached through the ceiling and snatched her up. The man sleeping beside her did not stir until the seventh ring, and then only to ask "What? What?" of nothing in particular before returning to sleep. She first sat on the side of the bed and began to hope: a wrong number, or Gail, drunk, in from an evening of bar-hopping, calling to talk about a man. She then sat in the dark on the floor in front of the nightstand. If it was true what her mother had once told her, then nothing rang the telephone like death in the middle of the night.

On the fifteenth ring, she picked up the telephone and said nothing.

"Ms. Walsh? Ms. Lydia Walsh?" a woman said.

"Yes."

"We are very sorry to call at such a time, but your mother died twenty minutes ago." The woman was waiting. "Ms. Walsh?"

"Yes. I'll be there soon as I can," Lydia said.

"Very well. We, the entire staff here at George Washington, are very sorry. Your mother was an exemplary patient," the woman said. "We will expect you very soon."

"Listen," Lydia said. "Don't . . . don't put that sheet over her face until I get there, okay? I don't want to walk in and see that sheet over her."

"Very well," the woman said. "We will expect you soon. And again, we at George Washington are very sorry."

Lydia hung up the telephone. She continued sitting on the floor and watched the clock that could tell her the time in the dark. The minute numbers on the clock moved ahead one, two, and then three more minutes. Twenty minutes ago, what had she been dreaming? Try to remember, she told herself, for all of it must go in the diary: On the night of June 29th, I was dreaming such-and-such and such-and-such when my mother passed away. Try to remember where you were.

She tapped the base of the brass lamp once and the bulb's lowest setting came on. The man in the bed was naked, as was she. There was a foreign smell about herself and she realized that it was his cologne, a popular and very expensive concoction that many of the men she knew wore because someone in their world had decided that the smell conveyed power and success. She thought she had been dreaming of Antibes and the naked Texan on the beach when her mother died, but the more she thought the more it seemed that Antibes had actually been on her mind when she came the first time hours ago.

What is his name? she asked herself of the sleeping man. From a nightstand drawer she took one of the three appointment books she kept in the town house. On the June 29 page there were the initials JL scrawled across all the hours after eight in the evening. She remembered they had met at Trader Vic's for dinner after she had come from the hospital, and then they had come to her place. But what had she called him all those hours? She flipped back through the pages: "Gyn-nw dia" on the 22nd morning; "B Kaufman — Sen Fin" lunch on the 20th; "Taylor — Amer. Con Life Bst" at two on the 19th afternoon. Finally, on the evening of the 15th, she found "Dinner and ?????? with Jack Lawrence, Amer. Bankers. . . ."

"He's pretty light-skinned, ain't he?" her mother had said of the first boy she had ever slept with, though all her mother knew at that time was that the boy had taken her to a movie and Mile Long for a steak sandwich. "Does he come from a sickly family?" her mother had asked. She told her diary about the evening the boy busted her cherry: "The movie was *Who's Afraid of Virginia Woolf?* He told me that I was the most beautiful girl at Dunbar, but when he walked me back home after the 'dirty deed' was done, he acted like he didn't know me anymore."

She shook Jack Lawrence from Amer. Bankers, who was not light-skinned but the color of dark honey. He grabbed her hand and squeezed it so hard she thought she heard her bones cracking — in his sleep he had perceived some threat to himself. She screamed and he woke up, his hand still holding hers and his head turning about to find out where in the world he was. He released her and she rubbed her hand. "What the hell's wrong with you?" she said.

"Sorry . . . sorry," he said. "I must have been dreaming." The way he said "dreaming" prompted more details about him. Something he called fate had plucked him from the streets of Harlem and sent him to Horace Mann prep, then sent him to Dartmouth, then sent him to Harvard Law. At their first dinner, he had said of the place where she had gone, "I would have gone to Yale Law, but there was something I didn't like about the white guy that interviewed me." "You okay?" he said now. He was still lying down.

"I'll be all right. I have to go," Lydia said. "My mother has died and I have to go to her."

"Oh, Cynthia, I'm very sorry."

My name is Cynthia and I come from Washington, she chanted in her head. What was that from? Jumping rope or playing hopscotch? He does not even know my name on the very night my mother has died, she thought, wanting him out of her bed and out of her house. "You can get some sleep," she said. "Make sure the door is locked when you leave."

He yawned. "Yeah, I'm beat," he said. The way he said "beat" brought more details about him. He turned over and pulled the sheet up to his shoulders. Even now, she thought that they were nice shoulders.

"I can't believe I'm walkin the same paths that my Lord walked," her mother had said that second day in Israel, standing at the Church of Gethsemane. Lydia had presented the trip to her mother on her sixty-fifth birthday, and had even paid the way for Georgia Evans, her mother's best friend. Lydia had not wanted to go, but her mother had insisted. "Oh, Lydia," her mother had said, "what would the Holy Land mean to me without you bein there with me?"

Georgia, lazy, far less religious that her mother, had complained about all the hills. "How did Jesus get any preachin done goin up and down these hills?" she said the second day. Georgia would drink all the water she carried, then want more from Lydia and her mother. "I never done so much walkin in all my life. Never drunk so much water either." On the third day, after the Via Dolorosa, Georgia was unable to go on and spent the next days moping about the hotel. "I never thought all I'd get to see of the Holy Land was a big old hotel. Must be a sin in that somewhere."

My mother lies moldering . . .

She tapped the base of the lamp three times and the bulb went through the rest of the settings, then the room went dark. In the living room, she knew she needed some coke. One line, she said to herself, one line and no more. This fur and no further. With the gold razor blade, she spread out the cocaine on the black marble tray, then inhaled a line of two inches or so through the crystal straw Gail Saunders had brought back from Bonn. "I hereby make this oath, this pledge, this whatever," Gail said the night of her return. "I'll sleep with no more white men. They make you feel like you should be grateful."

In the shower, Lydia held her face as close as she could to the nozzle. After she had finished, she soaped herself again. "Best get his smell off me," she said to the water. "Or else when I walk in there, they'll know I've been fucking. The nurses and doctors will look at me and they'll say, 'Why, Ms. Walsh, your mother lies moldering and you've been fucking.'"

"Forgive me, Father, for I have been fucking," she said to the mirror as she toweled off. The exhaust fan made a low humming sound, barely audible even in the quiet of the night. But though the repair people had been there four times, it was still too loud for her. "No sound," she had said to the second repairman. "Absolutely no sound whatsoever. Can you manage that?" She did not want to go back to her bedroom, to her closet, so she dressed in the clothes she had returned home in the evening before. They, the clothes, were scattered about the living room, where Amer. Bankers had taken her the first time and where Antibes had entered her head. That first Sunday in Antibes, she had done as the natives did and gone naked on the beach, and a stranger, the naked Texan reading Ayn Rand, had said in the most exquisite French that her breasts were perfect. *Je m'appelle Lydia et j'habite à Washington.*

She called a Capitol cab, because that was the company her mother had always used. "Trust Capitol to get you there and back in one piece," her mother had said. "Don't trust D.C. National or Empire." Lydia opened the front door and listened to the night sounds. She felt the coke was wearing off. Way off to the left, through the thick leaves of June, she thought she saw the sun inching up, but she knew how deceptive the light in Washington could be. Once, as a girl, she had traveled with her mother's church through most of the night to an edge-of-the-world mountain town in Virginia, where the church members had held Easter sunrise services as the sun came up over the mountains. "We proclaim," the preacher had said, "that Jesus has risen." "We proclaim it so," the congregation had said, huddled in blankets and covered with dew. "We proclaim it so."

She did another line of cocaine. Her town house was in an enclosed area in Southwest protected by a guard in his tiny house at the entrance. Generally, the guard would call to tell her that a cab was coming to her door, but she felt she might want to go out to the entrance and meet the cab. But then, as the coke flowed through her, she relaxed and thought it best for him to come and get her. "Ten-dollar tip," she said to the marble tray and raised her eyebrows up and down several times. Before closing the crystal canister that contained the drug, she put some in a plastic packet with the small gold spoon she kept in the canister. "Who knows what evil lurks in a hospital," she said, laughing.

On that sixth morning in Israel, Georgia had gone back to her bed after breakfast and seemed unable to move, but she had insisted that Lydia and her mother go on without her. When mother and daughter returned from floating on the Dead Sea, they found Georgia in a lounge chair at the swimming pool, descending into drunkenness, not quite certain who they were or where she was. When Lydia's mother told her that she was in the Holy Land, the land of Jesus, Georgia said, "Yes. Yes. I been to that place." Then, after Lydia's mother slapped her, Georgia asked her friend for forgiveness.

Back in the room the two older women shared, Lydia had tried to reassure a sobbing Georgia. Her mother refused to say anything more to Georgia. "It's all right," Lydia said to Georgia as she put her to bed. The old woman kept saying that she was going to die in the Holy Land and Lydia kept telling her that she wouldn't. They left her and had dinner in the hotel dining room, but her mother only picked at her food.

Georgia was contrite throughout the last six days, and though it was clear to Lydia that the woman's legs and feet could not manage it, Georgia, uncomplaining, went out each day for the rest of the tour.

Each place along the way, in Jericho, in Bethany, in Nazareth, she stayed close to Lydia's mother, but Cornelia paid her no mind, and it showed on Georgia's face.

On the living-room wall in Lydia's town house, among the photographs of places she had visited around the world, between the pictures of her standing before the Kremlin on a winter day and of her in a cavernous room in a Danish castle the guide said was haunted, there was the picture of Lydia and Cornelia and Georgia standing where the tourist bureau said Joseph's carpentry shop had been, Georgia in her hideous wig standing on one side and her mother in the middle. It was the tenth day of the trip.

She did two more lines of cocaine. "Just a shorty shorty this time, girl," she said as she spread out the drug. All of this and more I offer to you if you would but bow down and worship me. . . .

She did not know how long the cab driver had been standing in the doorway when he said, "Lady, you call for a cab?" He was an old man who had probably done nothing but work all his life. Father, may I? . . . What would that old man have said to see her perfect breasts adorning the beach at Antibes? Have you seen the Egyptian pyramids? the naked Texan asked, fingering the pages of Ayn Rand.

"Yes," she said to the old man, sounding as if there had been a death in the family. "It's for me. My mother has died." Immediately, he took off his hat and made the sign of the cross. She stood and put her things, including the packet of cocaine, into the Fendi bag.

"My heart goes out to you, lady," the cab driver said. "It really does. I know what it's like to lose a mother. And a father too." Through the screen door, he looked about the room as if there might be others to whom he should express condolences.

At the door, she could see that he was not just an old man, but an extremely old man. Her father, had he lived, would have been such a man. She closed the door and locked it. The sounds of birds were louder, and she knew the sun was not far off. The old man helped her down the three brick stairs and held the cab door for her. She had wanted to buy a second town house in the area as another investment and have her mother and Georgia live there, but her mother told her that she did not know if she could live among so many white people. "I'm not used to their ways and such like you are, Lydia," and Lydia had been offended.

The old man drove out of the compound and turned right on G Street. He was looking at her in the rearview mirror. She smelled dead fish from the wharf. At 7th the man turned right again. "I knew folks who lived in Southwest before they threw the colored out and made it for the wealthy," her mother had said when Lydia told her she had bought a town house there.

"Ma'am, maybe you should tell me where you goin?" the cab driver said.

"Just get me lost in the city," she said.

"What, ma'am?"

"Just keep on driving and get us lost in the city. I'll pay you. I have the money."

"No, ma'am, it ain't a matter of money. I just thought. . . . You know, your mother. . . . And besides, ma'am, I'm a Capitol cab driver and I ain't allowed to get lost."

"Try," she said. "Try ever so hard." She took two twenty-dollar bills from her bag, leaned forward and placed them on the seat beside him. "And the more lost you get us, the more you get paid. Or is it, the more loster, or the most lost? There are, you know, Mr. Cab Driver, so many grammatical rules that the grammar people say we must not break."

"Yes, ma'am, I know. I've heard it said."

He did not know what else to do, so he continued driving. He passed the federal buildings along 7th, then the mall and its museums. In one of the museums white men had allowed her father to make a living pushing a broom, and now she was paid in one year more than her parents had earned in both their lifetimes. Soon, she would pass a point in her life where she would have earned more than all her ancestors put together, all of them, all the way back to Eve.

At New York Avenue, he turned right, then left on 5th Street. He thought that maybe she had been born elsewhere, that she did not know Washington, would not know the streets beyond what the white people called the federal enclave. But in fact, the farther north he went, the more she knew about where they were going. My name is Lydia. . . . Say it loud. . . .

"You gettin us lost?"

"Yes, ma'am, I'm tryin."

"All right. Try very hard." She placed another twenty beside the other two.

They passed where the K Street market once had been. Two pounds of chicken wings for twenty cents. Had she remembered to finally write down her mother's recipe for that wondrous beef stew somewhere in one of the appointment books? They continued on up 5th Street. Her father had died at 1122 5th Street in a back room on the top floor where they had lived when she was four. It occurred to Lydia that in the world there was now no one from whom she could get that full medical history she had always planned to get. Who now could tell her if there was a history of breast cancer among the women in her family?

"I'm sorry for all this," her father had said on his death bed to her mother. "I'm very sorry for all this, Cornelia." They had not known that she was standing in the doorway watching them.

"For what?" her mother said to her father. "What's there to be sorry about? You do know that I love you. You do know that, don't you? If you go away with nothin else, go away with that."

At 5th and Ridge streets, she asked the cab driver, "Hi you doin up there, buddy? You doin okay?"

"Yes, ma'am, just fine, thank you."

While living at 457 Ridge Street, in the downstairs apartment, they had come to know Georgia, who lived in the upstairs apartment. Georgia would never have children of her own and, except for Lydia, was uncomfortable around other people's children. Until Lydia was fourteen, she gave her a doll every Christmas. "Now see, if you pull the string Chatty Cathy will talk to you, honey. Tell Chatty Cathy your name, honey." "My name is Lydia Walsh and I live in Washington."

The sun was even higher when he turned right at O Street. In one of the houses on that street her mother lived until Lydia's last year of law school. She had once brought down from New Haven a professor of linguistics who thought the sun rose and set on her. He had had a kind heart, the professor had, but his love for her had shown through all too clearly, and that was his downfall. For thirty days during the month of her birthday he had sent her the reddest roses she had seen up to then: one on the first day, two on the second day, three on the third, and so on. "How much do professors of linguistics make?" she asked a friend on the twentieth day, looking down at his name on the card that came with the roses. "Does he come from a sickly family?" her mother had asked while the man was in the bathroom.

She wanted more coke and she began to cry. "And first prize, for her particularly beautiful enunciation, goes to . . ." John Brown lies mold-erin where my mother lies molderin. . . . The cab driver thought that her crying meant that maybe it had finally hit her that her mother had died and that soon his passenger would be coming to herself.

At New Jersey Avenue, the cab driver turned left, then right at Rhode Island down past Frazier's Funeral Home. At a large apartment building on Rhode Island where the Safeway now stood, they had lived on the same floor as a woman who was terrified that her husband would leave her. "So all the time bein scared of him leavin," her mother told Lydia years later when she thought her daughter was old enough to understand, "she just became his slave. He was a night foreman at a bakery way out in Northeast. I guess some thought he was a hand-some man, but I never cared for him. Had what they call that good hair. Night and day she worried that he'd leave her. She begged me and all the other women not to take him from her. She wouldn't be-lieve that I whatn't studyin bout him. She worried herself sick and they came and took her away to St. Lizabeths one day. In those days, they gave you twenty-five dollars if you turned in a crazy person. Twenty-five dollars and a pat on the back. Somebody turned her in, but it whatn't me."

WE WHO HAVE

Run, Mourner, Run

by Randall Kenan

... for there is no place that does not see you. You must change your life.

— Rilke

DEAN WILLIAMS SITS in the tire. The tire hangs from a high and fat sycamore branch. He swings back and forth, back and forth, so that the air tickles his ears. His legs, now lanky and mannish, drag the ground. Not like the day his father first hung the tire and hoisted a five-year-old Dean up by the waist and pushed him and pushed him, higher and higher — "Daddy, don't push so hard!" — until Dean, a little scared, could see beyond the old truck and out over the field, his heart pounding, his eyes wide; and his daddy walked off that day and left Dean swinging and went back to the red truck and continued to tinker under the hood, fixing ... Dean never knew what.

Eighteen years later Dean sits in the tire. Swinging. Watching the last fingers of the late-October sun scratch at the horizon. Waiting. Looking at an early migration of geese heading south. Swinging. Waiting for his mama to call him to supper — canned peas, rice, Salisbury steak, maybe. His daddy always use to say Ernestine wont no good cook, but ah, she's got.

Dean Williams stares off at the wood in the distance, over the soybean fields to the pines' green-bright, the oaks and the sycamores and the maples all burnt and brittle-colored. Looking at the sky, he remembers a rhyme:

> *A red sky at night is a shepherd's delight*
> *A red sky in the morning is a shepherd's warning.*

Once upon a time — what now seems decades ago rather than ten or fifteen years — Dean had real dreams. In first grade he wanted to be a doctor; in second, a lawyer, in third, an Indian chief. He read the fairy stories and nursery rhymes, those slick shiny oversized books, over and over, and Mother Goose became a Bible of sorts. If Pigs could fly and foxes could talk and dragons were for real, then surely he could be anything he wanted to be. Not many years after that he dropped out and learned to dream more mundane dreams. Yet those nuggets from grade school stayed with him.

Dean Williams sits in the tire his daddy made for him. Thinking: For what?

See, there's somebody I want you to . . . to . . . Well, I want you to get him for me. So to speak.

Percy Terrell had picked him up that day, back in March. Percy Terrell, driving his big Dodge truck, his Deere cap perched on his head, his gray hair peeking out, his eyes full of mischief and lies and greed and hate and.

Son, I think I got a job for you.

Sitting in the cab of that truck, groceries in his lap (his Ford Torino had been in need of a carburetor that day), he wondered what Percy was up to.

Now of course this is something strictly between me and you.

On that cemetery-calm day in March, staring into the soybean field and his mama's house, the truck stopped on the dirt road between the highway, he wondered whether Percy wanted to make a sexual proposition. It wouldn't have been the first time a gray-haired granddaddy had stopped his truck and invited Dean in. Dean had something of a reputation. Maybe Percy had found out that Dean had been sleeping with burly Joe Johnson, the trucker. Maybe somebody had seen him coming out of a bar in Raleigh or in Wilmington or in.

. . . if you dare tell a soul, it'll be your word against mine, boy. And well . . . you'd just be fucking yourself up then.

How could he have known what he'd be getting himself into? If some fortune-teller had sat him down and explained it to him, detail by detail; if he'd had some warning from a crow or a woodchuck; if he'd had a bad dream the night before that would.

Land.

Land?

They own a parcel of land I want. Over by Chitaqua Pond. In fact they own the land under Chitaqua Pond. It got them surrounded a hundred acres on one side, two hundred acres on one side, one fifty on the other.

How much land is it?

It ain't how much that matters, son. They're blocking me. See? I want — I need that land. Niggers shouldn't own something as pretty as Chitaqua Pond. Got a house on it they call their homeplace. Don't nobody live in it. Say they ain't got no price. We'll see.

When he was only a tow-headed twenty-four-year-old with a taste for hunting deer and redheads, Percy Terrell had inherited from his daddy, Malcolm Terrell, about three thousand acres and a general store to which damn-near everyone in Tims Creek was indebted. Yet somehow fun-loving Percy became Percy the determined; hell-raising Percy became Percy the cunning, Percy the sly, Percy the conniving, and had manipulated and multiplied his inheritance into a thousand acres more land, two textile mills, a chicken plant, part ownership in a Kentucky Fried Chicken franchise in Crosstown, and God only knew what else. The day he picked Dean up he had been in the middle of negotiating with a big corporation for his third textile mill. Before that day Percy had never said so much as "piss" to Dean. In Percy's eyes Dean was nothing more than poor white trash: a sweet-faced, dark-haired faggot with a broken-down Ford Torino, living with his chain-smoking mama in a damn-near condemned house they didn't even own. So it was like an audience with the king for Dean to be picked up by ole Percy on the side of the road, for him to stop the car, to turn to Dean and say: I want you to get to know him. Real good. You get my meaning?

Sir?

You know what I mean. He likes white boys. He'll just drool all over you. Who knows. He probably already does.

That day in March Dean hardly knew who Raymond Brown was. Only that he was the one colored undertaker in town. How could he have known he was something of a prince, something of a child, something of a little brown boy in a man's gray worsted-wool suit, with skin underneath smooth like silk? So he sat there thinking: This one of them dreams like on TV? Surely, he wasn't actually sitting in a truck with the richest white man in Tims Creek being asked to betray the richest black man in Tims Creek. . . . Shoot! Sure as hell must be a dream.

Sex with a black man. His first one — his only one till Ray — had been Marshall Hinton in the ninth grade just before Dean dropped out of high school. It had been nothing much: nasty, sweaty, heartbeat-quick — but Dean still remembered the touch of that boy's skin, petal-soft and hard at the same time — and the sensation lingered on his fingertips. With that on his mind, part of the same evil dream, with the shadow of Percy Terrell sitting there next to him in his shadow-truck, Dean had asked: Let's say I decide to go along with this. Let's just say. What do I get out of it?

What do I get?

Had he actually said that? He could easily have said at that point: No a thank you, Mr. Imaginary Percy Terrell. I know this is a test from the Lord and I ain't fool enough to go through with it. I ain't stupid enough. I ain't drunk enough. I ain't.

What do I get?

You know that factory I'm trying to buy from International Spinning Corporation? You work at that plant, don't you?

Yeah.

Well, how would you like a promotion to foreman? And a six-thousand-dollar raise?

More a dream or less a dream? Dean couldn't tell. But the idea — six thousand dollars — how much is that a month? — a promotion. How long does it take most people to get to foreman? John Hyde? Fred Lanier? Rick Batts? Ten, fifteen, seventeen years. And they're still on line. Foremen come in as foremen. That simple. People like Dean never get to be foremen . . . and six thousand dollars.

I don't understand, Mr. Terrell, how — ?

You just get him in bed. That's all. I'll worry about the rest.

But how do I — ?

Ever heard of a bar called The Jack Rabbit in Raleigh?

Yeah. A colored bar.

He goes there every second Saturday of every month, I'm told.

Dean stared at the dashboard. He admired the electronic displays and the tape deck with a Willie Nelson tape sticking out — What kind of guarantee I get?

Percy chuckled. A flat, good-old-boy chuckle, with a snort and a wheeze. For the first time Dean was a little scared. Son, you do my bidding you don't need no guarantee. This — he stuck out his hand — this is your guarantee.

Dean had walked into the kitchen that day and looked down at his mama, who sat at the kitchen table reading the *National Enquirer*, a cigarette hanging out of her mouth, ashes on her tangerine knit blouse, ashes on the table. Water boiling on the stove. The faucet they could never fix, dripping. Dripping. The linoleum floor needing mopping — it all seemed like a dream. Terrell.

Just get him in bed.

What Percy Terrell want with you? — She watched him closely as he put the grocery bags on the counter.

Nothing.

She harrumphed as she got up to take the cans out of the brown paper bag and finish supper. He stopped and took a good look at her; he noticed how thin his mama was getting. How her hair and her skin seemed washed out, all a pale, whitish-yellow color. Is that when he decided to do it? When he took in how the worry about money, worry about her doctor bills, the worry about her job — when she had a job — worry about her health, worry about Dean, had fretted away at her? Piece by piece, gnawing at her, so manless, so perpetually sad.

He remembered how she had been when his daddy was alive. Her hair black. Her eyes child-like and playful. Her body full and supple and eager to please a man. She did her nails a bright red then. Went to the beauty parlor. Now she bit her nails, and her head was a mess of split ends.

Dean sits in a tire. A tire hung off the great limb of a sycamore tree. Swinging. Watching smoke rising off in the distance a ways. Someone burning a field maybe. But it's the wrong time of year. People are still harvesting corn.

No, it wasn't for his mama that he did it. He hated the line. Hated the noise and the dust and the smell. But he hated the monotony and the din even more, those millions of damn millions of fucking strands of thread churning and turning and going on and on and on. What did he have to lose? What else did he have to trade on but his looks? A man once told him: Boy, you got eyes that could give a bull a hard-on. Why not use them?

> *Oh, Mother, I shall be married to*
> *Mr. Punchinello*
> *Mr. Punch*
> *Mr. Joe*
> *Mr. Nell*
> *Mr. Lo*
> *To Mr. Punch. Mr. Joe.*
> *To Mr. Punchinello.*

That very next day in March at McTarr's Grocery Store he saw him. Dean's mama had asked him to stop on the way back home and pick up a jar of mayonnaise. Phil Jones gave him a lift from the plant, and as he got out and was walking into the store Raymond Brown drove up in his big beige Cadillac.

He'd seen Ray Brown all his life, known who he was by sight and such, but he had never really paid him any mind. Over six foot and in a dark-navy suit. A fire-red tie. A mustache like a pencil line. Skin the color of something whipped, blended, and rich. A deep color. Ray walked with a minister's majesty. Upright. Solemn. His head held up. Almost looking down on folk.

Scuse me, Mr. Brown.

Had he ever really looked into a black man's eyes before then? Dean stood there, fully intending to find some way to seduce this man, and yet the old mixture of things he sensed coming out of him — a rock solidness, an animal tenderness, a cool wariness — made Dean step back.

Yeah? What can I do for you? — Ray spoke in a slow, round baritone. Very proper. (Does he like me?) He kept his too-small-for-a-black-man's nose in the air. (Does he know I'm interested?) Raised an eyebrow. (He just thinks I'm white trash.) — Can I help you, young man? — Ray started to step away.

W . . . what year is your car?

My? Oh, an '88.

Fleetwood?

No, Eldorado.

Drive good?

Exceedingly.

Huh?

Very.

Dean tried to think of something more to say without being too obvious to the folk going into the store. (What if Percy was tricking me? What if Ray Brown don't go in for men? What if — ?)

That it?

Ah . . . yeah, I —

Well, please excuse me. I'm in something of a hurry. Ray nodded and started to walk off.

Mr. Ray —

When Raymond Brown turned around, the puzzled look on his face softened its sternness: Dean saw a boy wanting to play. Ray smiled faintly, as if taking Dean in for the first time. His eyes drifted. — Well, what is it?

Nothing. See you later. — Dean smiled and looked down a bit, feigning shyness.

A grin of recognition passed over Ray's face. His eyes narrowed. At once he was all business again; he turned without a word or a gesture and walked into the store.

> *Lavender blue and rosemary green,*
> *When I am king you shall be queen;*
> *Call up my maids at four o'clock,*
> *Some to the wheel and some to the rock;*
> *Some to make hay and some to shear corn,*
> *And you and I will keep the bed warm.*

Dean Williams gazes down now at the trough in the earth in which his feet have been sliding. For eighteen years. Sliding. The red clay hard and baked after years of sun and rain and little-boy feet. Exposed. His blue canvas hightops beaten and dirty and frayed but comfortable. His mother says time and again he should get rid of them. A crow *caw-caw-ca-caws* as it glides over his head, as he swings in the old tire. As he thinks. As he wonders what Raymond Brown is doing. Thinking. At this moment.

Some things you just let happen, Ray had said that night. Dean never quite understood what he meant by that. Ray gestured grandly with his hands as he went on and on. He was a little pompous — is that the word? A little stuck-up. A little big on himself and his education. With his poetry and his books and his reading and his plays. But he had such large hands. Well-manicured. So clean. And a gold ring with a shiny black stone he called onyx. He said his great-granddaddy took it off the hand of his slavemaster after killing him. Dean had thought an undertaker's hands would be cold as ice; Ray's hands were always warm.

A few days after McTarr's, Dean finally made his play at The Jack Rabbit. A rusty, run-down, dank, dark, sleazy, sticky-floored sort of place, with a smudged, wall-length mirror behind the bar, a small dance floor crowded with men and boys, mostly black, jerking or gyrating to this guitar riff, to that satiny saxophone, to this syrupy siren's voice, gritty, nasty, hips, heads, eyes, grinding. Dean found Ray right off, standing at the edge of the bar, slurping a scotch and soda, jabbering to some straggly-looking, candy-assed blond boy with frog-big blue eyes, who looked on as if Ray were speaking in Japanese or in some number-filled computer language.

Scuse me, Mr. Ray.

Ray Brown's eyes narrowed again the way they had in front of McTarr's. This time Dean did not have to wonder if Ray was interested. The straggly-looking boy drifted away.

You're that Williams boy, aren't you?

Yeah.

Buy you a drink?

Some smoky voice began to sing, some bitter crooning, some heart-tugging melody, some lonely piano. They were playing the game now, old and familiar to Dean, like checkers, like Old Maid; they were dancing cheek to cheek, hip to thigh. Dean knew he could win. Would win.

Ray talked. Ray talked about things dean had no notion or knowledge of. Ray talked of school (Morehouse — the best years of my life. I should have become an academic. I did a year in Comp Lit at BU. Then my father died and my Aunt Helen insisted I go to mortuary school); Ray talked of his family (You know, my mother actually forbade me to marry Gloria. Said she was too poor, backward, and good-for-nothing. Wanted me to marry a Hampton or a Spellman girl); Ray talked of the funeral business (It was actually founded by my great-grandfather, Frederick Brown. What a man. Built it out of nothing. What a man.

Loved to hunt. He did); Ray talked of undertaking (I despise form-
aldehyde; I loathe dead people; I abhor funerals); Ray talked on the
President and the Governor and the General Assembly (Crooks! Liars!
Godless men!); Ray talked. In soft tones. In icy tones. In preacher-like
tones. This moment loud and thundering, his baritone making heads
turn; the next moment quiet, head tilted, a little boy in need of a shoulder to lean on. Dean had never heard, except maybe on the radio and
on TV, someone who knew so damn much, who carried himself just
so, who.

But my wife — Ray would somehow smile and look despairing at
the same time — I love her, you know. She could have figured it out
by now. She's not a dumb woman, really.

Why hasn't she?

Blinded. Blinded by the Holy Ghost. She's full of the Holy Ghost,
see. — Ray went off on a mocking rendition of a sermon, pounding his
fists on the bar for emphasis (cause we're all food for worms, we know
not the way to salvation, we must seek — yes, seek — Him). He broke
off. — Of course there's the money too.

The money?

Yeah, my money.

Oh.

Ray became silent. He stared at Dean. The bartender stood at the
opposite end of the bar wiping glasses with a towel; the smoky air had
cleared somewhat but still appeared blue-gray, alight with neon; one
lone couple ground their bodies into each other on the dance floor to a
smoldering Tina Turner number.

How about you?

What about me?

Whom do you love?

Dean laughed. — Who loves me is the real question. Don't nobody
give a shit about me. My mama, maybe.

Ray put his large hand over Dean's: Ray's full and strong, Dean's
dry and brittle and rough and small. — Well, I wouldn't put it exactly
like that. He kissed Dean's hand as though it were a small and frightened bird.

As simple as breaking bones. Had he thought of Percy and how he
was to betray this mesmerizing man? Did he believe he could? Would?

I want to show you something.

Yeah, I'll bet. — Dean smirked.

No, really. A place. Tonight. Come on.

They drove back to Tims Creek, down narrow back roads, through winding paths, alongside fields, into woods, into a meadow Dean had never seen before, near Chitaqua Pond. They arrived at the homeplace around midnight.

Is this where you take your boys?

Where did you think? To the mortuary?

So the house actually exists, Dean thought. This is for real. Part of him genuinely wanted to warn Ray, to protect him. But as Ray gave him a brief tour of the house where he had grown up (Can you believe this place is nearly ninety years old?): the kitchen with the deep enamel sink and the wood stove, the pantry with the neat rows of God-only-knows-how-old preserves and cans and boxes, the living room with the gaping fireplace where Christmas stockings had hung, the surprisingly functional bathroom; as they entered the bedroom where measles had been tended and babies created; as Ray rambled on absently about his Aunt Helen and Uncle Max (Aunt Helen is my great-granddaddy's youngest sister. She insists nothing change about this house. Nothing. If we sold it, it'd kill her); as he undressed Dean (No, please, allow me); as Dean, naked, stood with his back to Ray, those tender fingers exploring the joints and the hinges of his body; as a wet, warm tongue outlined, every so lightly, the shape of his gooseflesh-cold body, Ray mumbling trance-like (All flesh is grass, my love, sweet, sweet grass) between bites, between pinches; as they slid into the plump feather bed that *scree-ee-creeked* as they lay there, underneath a quilt made by Ray's great-grandmother, multicolored, heavy; as they joined at the mouth; as Dean trembled and tingled and clutched — all the while in his ears he heard a noise: faint at first, then loud, louder, then deafening: and he was not sure if the quickening *thu-thump-thump, thu-thump-thump* of his heartbeat came from Ray's bites on his nipples or from fear. Dean felt certain he heard the voices of old black men and old black women screaming for his death, his blood, for him to be strung up on a Judas tree, to die and breathe no more.

> *Far from home across the sea*
> *To foreign parts I go;*
> *When I am gone, O think of me*

And I'll remember you.
Remember me when far away,
Whether asleep or awake.
Remember me on your wedding day
And send me a piece of your cake.

Dean! — His mother calls to him from the door to the house where she stands. — Dean! Did you get me some Bisquick?

Noum, he yells back, not stopping his back-and-forth, the rope on the limb creaking like the door to a coffin opening and closing.

How could you forget? I asked you this morning.

I just did.

You 'just did.' Shit. Well, we ain't got no bread neither so you'll just eat with no bread. Boy, where is your mind these days?

Dean says nothing. He just rocks. Remembering. Noting the sky richening and deepening in color. Remembering. Seeing what he thinks might be a deer, way, way out. Remembering.

Remembering how it went on for a month, the meetings at the homeplace. Remembering how good being with Ray felt as spring crept closer and closer. Remembering the daffodils and the crocuses and the blessed jonquils and eating chocolate ice cream from the carton in bed afterward and mockingly calling each other honey and listening to the radio and singing, and Ray quoting some damn poet ('There we are two, content, happy in beauty together, speaking little, / perhaps not a word,' as Mr. Whitman would say), and would nibble at his neck and breathe deeply and let out a little sigh and say: I've got to get home. Gloria — yeah, yeah, I know. I know — remembering how he would tell himself: I ain't jealous of no black woman and of no black man. I don't care how much money he got. Remembering how he would drive home and climb into his cold and empty bed with the bad mattress and reach up and pull the metal chain on the light bulb that swung in the middle of the room. Remembering how he would huddle underneath the stiff sheets, thinking of Ray's voice, the feel of his skin, the smell of his aftershave, imagining Ray pulling into the driveway of his ranch-style brick house, dashing through rooms filled with nice things, wall-to-wall-carpeted floors, into the shower, complaining of the dealers and their boring conversations (I'm really sorry, honey, John Simon insisted we go to this barbecue joint in Goldsboro after the meeting and told me all this tedious foolishness about his mother-in-law and) — how he would probably kiss her while drying himself with a thick white towel as she sat reading a Bible commentary, and she would smile and say, Oh, I understand, Ray, and he would ooze his large mahogany body into a king-sized bed with her under soft damask sheets, fresh and clean and warm, and say, Night, honey, and melt away into dreams, perhaps not even of Dean. — Hell, I don't give a shit, Dean would think, staring into his bare, night-filled room. So what if he doesn't. So what if he does. Don't make no never mind to me, do it? I'm in it for the money. Right?

Yet Dean had no earthly idea what Percy had in mind for Ray and, after a few weeks, thought it might have already happened or maybe never would.

But one morning, one Sunday morning in April, when Gloria and the girls had gone to Philadelphia for a weekend to see a sick sister and Ray had decided to spend the night with Dean at the homeplace, the first and only time Dean was to see morning there (through the window that sunrise he could see a mist about the meadow and the pond), while they lolled, intertwined in dreams and limbs, he heard the barking of dogs. Almost imperceptible at first. They came closer. Louder. He heard men's voices. As he turned to jog Ray awake he heard someone kick in the front door. The sound of heavy feet trampling. Hooting. Jeering.

Where is they? Where they at? I know they're here.

The order and the rhyme of what happened next ricocheted in a cacophony in Dean's head even now: Ray blinks awake: Percy: his three sons: the sound *snap-click-whurr, snap-click-whurrr, snap-click-whurrr:* dogs yapping: tugging at their leashes: Well, well, well, look-a-here, boys, salt-n-pepper: a dog growls: the boys grin and grimace: Dean jumping up, naked, to run: Get back in that bed, boy: No I —: I said, get back in that bed: *snap-click-whurrr, snap-click-whurrr:* a Polaroid camera, the prints sliding out like playing cards from a deck: the sound of dogs panting: claws on wooden floors: the boys mumbling under their breath: fucking queers, fucking faggots: damn, out of film.

Like a voice out of the chaos Ray spoke, steely, calm, almost amused. — You know, you *are* trespassing, Terrell.

Land as good as mine now, son. I done caught you in what them college boys call *flagrante delecto*, ain't that what you'd call it, Ray? You one of them college boys. In the goddamn flesh. You got to damn-near give me this here piece of property now, boy.

How do you figure that, Percy?

You a smart boy, Ray. I expect you can figure it.

Ray reached toward the nightstand. (A gun?)

A Terrell boy slammed a big stick down on the table in warning. A dog snapped.

Ray shrugged sarcastically. — A cigarette, maybe?

Bewildered, the boy glanced to his father, who warily nodded okay. Ray pulled out a pack of Lucky Strikes — though Dean had never known him to smoke — and deftly thumped out a single one, popped it into his mouth, reached for his matches, lit it, inhaled deeply, and blew smoke into the dog's face. The hound whined.

You got to be kidding, Terrell. You come in here with your boys and your dogs and pull this bullshit TV-movie camera stunt and expect me to whimper like some snot-nosed pickaninny, 'Yassuh, Mr. Terrell, suh, I'll give you anything, suh. Take my house. Take my land. Take my wife. I sho is scared of you, suh.' Come off it. — He drew on his cigarette.

Percy's face turned a strawberry color. He stood motionless. Dean expected him to go beserk. Slowly he began to nod his head up and down, and to smile. He put his hands on his hips and took two steps back. — Now boys, I want you to look-a-here. I respect this man. I do. I really do. How many men do you know, black or white, could bluff, cool as a cucumber, caught butt-naked in bed with a damn whore? A white boy whore at that. Wheee-hooo, boy! you almost had me fooled. Shonuff did. — Percy curled his lip like one of his dogs. — But you fucked up, boy. May as well admit it.

Ray narrowed his eyes and puffed.

You a big man in this county, Ray. You know it and I know it. Think about it. Think about your ole Aunt Helen. Think about what that ole Reverend Barden'll say. A deacon and a trustee of his church. Can't have that. Think of your business. Who'll want you to handle their loved ones, Ray? Think of your *wife. Your girls.* I got me some eyewitnesses here, boy. Let somebody get one whiff of this . . . He turned with self-congratulatory delight to his boys. They all guffawed in unison, a sawing, inhuman sound.

Think on it, Ray. Think on it hard. Like I said, you're a smart boy.

I'll enjoy finally doing some business with you. And it won't be on a cool slab, I guarantee.

Percy walked, head down, feet clomping, over to Dean. He reached over and mussed Dean's hair as though he were some obedient animal. — You did a fine job, son. A mighty fine job. I'll take real good care of you. Just like I promised.

Dean had never seen Ray's face in such a configuration of anger, loathing, coldness, disdain, recognition, as though he suddenly realized he had been in bed with a cottonmouth moccasin or a stinking dog. It made the very air in the room change color. He stubbed out his cigarette and stared out the window. — Get out of my house, Terrell. — He said it quietly but firmly.

Oh, come on, Ray. Don't be sore. How else did you think you could get your hands on such a *fine* piece of white ass? I'm your pimp, boy. I'll send the bill directly.

Get out.

Percy patted Dean's head again. — I'll settle up with you later. Come on, boys. We's done here. — He tipped his hat to Ray, turned, and was gone, out the door, the boys and the dogs and the smell of mud and canine breath and yelping and stomping trailing out behind him like the cloak of some wicked king of darkness. Dean sat numb and naked, curled up in a tight ball like a cat. As if someone had snatched the covers from him and said: Wake up. Stop dreaming.

You get the hell out too. — Ray sat up, swinging his feet to the floor. He reached for another cigarette.

Dean began to shiver; more than anything else he could imagine at that moment, he wanted Ray to hold him, more than six thousand dollars, more than a new car. He felt like crying. He reached out and saw his pale hand against the broad bronze back and sensed the enormity of what he had done, that his hand could never again touch that back, never glide over its ridges and bends and curves, never linger over that mole, pause at this patch of hair, that scar. He looked about the room for some sign of change; but it remained the same: the oil lamp: the warped mirror: the walnut bureau: the cracked windowsill. But it would soon be gone. Percy would see to that.

Ray, I'm s—

I don't want to hear you. Okay? I don't want to see you. I don't want to know you. Or that you even existed. Ever. Get out. Now.

As Dean stood and pulled his clothes on, he wanted desperately to hate Ray, to dredge up every nigger, junglebunny, cocksucking, motherfucking, sambo insult he could muster; he wanted to relearn hate, fiery, blunt, brutal; he wanted to unlearn what he had learned in the very bed on which he was turning his back, to erase it from his memory, to blot it out, scratch over it. Forget. Walking out the door he paused, listening for the voices of those dark ancestors who had accosted him upon his first entering. They were still. Perhaps appeased.

> *Little Miss Tuckett*
> *Sat on a bucket,*
> *Eating some peaches and cream.*
> *There came a grasshopper*
> *And tried hard to stop her,*
> *But she said, "Go away, or I'll scream."*

Dean looks over at his Ford Torino and worries that it may never run again. It has been in need of so many things, a distributor cap, spark plugs. The wiring about shot. Radiator leaks. He just doesn't have the money. Will he ever? He stands up with the tire around him and walks back, back, back, and jumps up in the air, the limb popping but holding. He swings high. He pushes a little with his legs on the way back. He goes higher. Higher.

Who said money is the root of all evil? Or was it the love of money? Love.

Six thousand dollars. This is my guarantee.

Dean waited six months. Twenty-four weeks. April. May. June. July. August. September. He watched the spring mature into summer and summer begin to ripen into autumn. He waited as his mother went into the hospital twice. First for an ovarian cyst. Next for a hysterectomy. He waited as the bills the insurance company would not take care of piled high. He waited as his mother was laid off again. He waited as the news blared across the York Country *Cryer* and the Crosstown papers and the Raleigh papers: TERRELL FAMILY BUYS TEXTILE MILL, INTERNATIONAL SPINNING SOLD TO TERRELL INTERESTS, INTERNATIONAL SPINNING TO BECOME YORK EAST MILL. He waited through work, through the noise and the dust, through the gossip about daughters who ran off with young boys wanting to be country music stars, grandmothers going to the old folks' home, adulterous husbands and unwed mothers. He waited through some one-night stands with nameless truckers in nameless truckstops and bored workers at boring shopping malls. He waited. He waited through the times he ran into Ray, who ignored him. He waited through the times he had only a nickel and a dime in his pocket and had to borrow for a third time from his cousin Jimmy or his uncle Fred, and his mama would have to search and search in the cabinets for something to scare up supper with. He waited. He waited through the news of Terrell making a deal with the Brown family for a tiny piece of property over by Chitaqua Pond, and of Raymond Frederick Brown's great-aunt Helen making a big stink, and taking to her bed ill. They said she was close to dead. But Dean waited. And waited. One hundred sixty and eight days. Waiting.

I'm going to Terrell, he finally decided on the last day of September. A late-summer thundercloud lasted all that day. Terrell still worked out of the general store his father had built, in an office at the back of the huge, warehouse-like structure. His boys ran the store. What if he says he ain't gone do nothing? What do I do then? Dean stood outside the store peering inside, wind and rain pelting his face.

Terrell kept the store old-fashioned: a potbellied stove that blazed red-hot in winter: a glass counter filled with bright candies: a clanging granddaddy National Cash Register. The cabinets and the benches and the dirt all old and dark. Deer heads looked down from the walls. Spiderwebs formed an eerie tent under the ceiling. As Dean entered, he looked back to the antique office door with TERRELL painted on the glass; it seemed a mile from the front door.

What you want? The oldest Terrell boy held a broom.

Come to see your daddy.

What for?

Business.

What kind of business?

Between him and me.

The youngest Terrell walked up to Dean. — Like hell.

Dean saw Percy through the glass, preparing to leave. He jumped between the boys and ran.

Hey, where the hell you going?

Dean's feet pumped against the pine floor. He could hear six feet in pursuit. Terrell tapped on his hat as Dean slid into the wall like a runner into home plate, out of breath. — Mr. Terrell, Mr. Terrell, I got to talk to you. I got —

What you want, son?

Panting, Dean began to speak, the multitude of days piling up in the back of his throat crowding to get out all at once. — You promised. My mama been in the hospital twice since March. My car's broke down. I just need to know when. When I —

When what, son?

All he had wished to tell Percy seemed to dry up in his head like spit on a hot July sidewalk. His mouth hung open. No words fell out. — You . . . you guaranteed . . .

'Guaranteed'? Boy, what *are* you talking about? — Terrell turned the key in the office door.

Ray Brown. Ray. You know. You promised. You . . .

Son — Terrell picked up his briefcase and turned to go — I don't know what in the Sam Hill you talking about.

Dean grabbed Percy's sleeve. The boys tensed. — Please, Mr. Terrell. Please. I did everything you asked. I . . .

Percy stared at Dean's hand on his sleeve for an uncomfortably long period. He reached down with his free hand and knocked Dean's away as though it were a dead fly. — Don't you ever lay a hand on me again, faggot.

He began to walk away, calling behind him: Don't be too long closing up, boys. You know how your mama gets when you're late.

Dean stood in the shadows watching Percy walk away. — I'll tell, goddamnit. I'll tell. — Dean growled, not recognizing his own voice.

Percy stopped stock-still. With his back to them all, he raised his chin a slight bit. — Tell? Who, pray tell, will you tell? — He pivoted around, a look of disgust smearing his face. — And who the *fuck* would believe you?

Dean felt his breathing come more labored, heavy. He could not keep his mouth closed, though he could force out no words. He felt saliva drooling down his chin.

Look at you — Percy's head jerked back — Look-at-you! A pathetic white-trash faggot whore. Who would think any accusation you brought against me, specially one as far-fetched as what you got in mind to tell, would have ary one bit of truth to it. Shit. — Percy said under his breath. He walked to the door. — Show him the way out, boys. And don't be late now, you hear? — The wind *wa-banged* the door shut.

They beat him. They taunted him with limp wrists and effeminate whimpers and lisps. They kicked him. Finally they threw him out into the rain and mud. Through it all he said not a mumbling word. He did not weep. He sat in a puddle. In the rain. One eye closed. His bruises stinging. The taste of blood in his mouth. He sat in some strange limbo, some odd place of ghosts and shadows, knowing he must rise, knowing he had been badly beaten, knowing that the boys had stopped on their way out and, snickering, dropped a twenty-dollar bill in front of him (We decided we felt sorry for you. Here's a little something for you. Price of a blowjob), knowing he could use the money, knowing he would be late for supper, knowing he could never really explain, never really tell anyone what had happened, knowing he would surely die one day, hoping it would be now. He could not move.

After a while, though he had no idea how long a while, something stopped the rain from falling on him. An old man's voice spoke to him: You all right, son? You lose something?

Is that you, Lord? he thought. Have you come to take me? With all the energy he could gather he lifted his head and looked through his one good eye.

An umbrella. An old gray-haired, trampy-looking man Dean did not know. Not the Lord. Dean opened his mouth and the cut in his lip spurted fresh blood into his mouth. He moaned. No I'll be all right yes yes yes I will be all right yes.

Yes, sir. I did lose something. Something right fine.

> *Moses supposes his toeses are roses,*
> *But Moses supposes erroneously;*
> *For nobody's toeses are posies of roses*
> *As Moses supposes his toeses to be.*

Dean! — His mother calls to him. — Dean! Supper's ready. Better come on.

Dark has gobbled up the world. He can see the light from a house here and there. People are sitting down to suppers of peas and chicken. A bat's *ratta-tatta-tatta* wings dip by. He continues to swing. He continues to wait. He continues to wonder.

Wondering about how two weeks after going to Terrell's office —
two weeks after, the wounds and bruises had mostly healed — two
weeks after knowing he would not get a raise or a promotion, two
weeks of wondering if he should tell someone something, how he was
walking down the road toward home with two bags of groceries. How
the bag split and how rice, beans, canned tuna, garbage bags, white
bread, and all came tumbling to the ground (though the milk carton
didn't burst, he was happy to see), and how as he knelt down to pick
everything up a beige Cadillac drove up, and how he heard the electric
whur of the power windows going down, and how he heard a soft female voice say — Can I help you out?

He had never actually met Gloria Brown. She sat behind the wheel,
her honey skin lightly powdered and smooth, her lips covered in some
muted red like pink but not pink, her eyes intelligent and brown. In the
backseat perched her two daughters, Ray's two daughters, their hair
as shiny black as their patent-leather shoes. Their dresses white and
green and neat.

It's all right, ma'am. I'm just down the road a piece.

But it's on my way. And you do seem to be having a little trouble.
Hop on in. No trouble.

Dean collected the food and got into the front seat. I've never been
in this car, he thought, feeling somehow entitled while knowing he had
no right.

An a capella gospel song in six-part harmony rang out from the
stereo. Awful fine car, Dean wanted to say. But didn't.

We're heading to a revival meeting over at the Holiness Church. —
She held the wheel gingerly, as if intimidated by the big purring
machine. Her fingernails flashed an earthy orange color. Dean could
smell her sweet and subtle perfume.

What church do you belong to?

Me? I don't, ma'am.

That's a shame. Well, you know Jesus loves you anyway. Are you
saved?

Saved? From what?

Why, from Hell and Damnation, of course.

I guess not.

Well, keep your heart open. He'll speak to you. "For all have sinned
and fallen short of the will of God."

Dean felt slightly offended but could think of nothing to say. He groped for words. Finally he said: Some things you just let happen.

Gloria turned to him the way one would turn upon hearing the voice of someone long dead; at first puzzled, then intrigued. — My husband always says that. Now ain't that funny.

Dean forced a chuckle. — Yes, ma'am. I reckon it is.

Gloria dropped him off at his house, her voice lilting after him with concern (Can you get to the house all right? Want the girls to help you?). He thanked her, no, he could manage. The Cadillac drove off into the early evening. This a road of ghosts, he thought. Spooks just don't like for a soul to know peace. Keep on coming to haunt.

> *If all the world was apple pie*
> *And all the sea was ink,*
> *And all the trees were bread and cheese,*
> *What would we have to drink?*

Dean! Boy, you better bring your butt on in here, now. Food's getting cold.

He doesn't feel hungry. He doesn't feel like sitting at the table with his mama. He doesn't feel like listening to her talk and complain or to the TV or to the radio. He doesn't feel like telling her that he was notified today that as of next Friday he will be laid off "indefinitely." He feels like sitting in the tire. Like swinging. Like waiting.

Waiting for the world to come to an end. Waiting for this cruel dream world to pass away. Waiting for the leopard to lie down with the kid and the goats with the sheep. Waiting for everything to be made all right — cause I know it will be all right, it has to be all right — and he will sit like Little Jack Horner in a corner with his Christmas pie and put in a thumb and pull out a plum and say: What a good, what a good, Oh what a good boy am I.

WE WHO HAVE NOT

Blues for Little Prez

by Sam Greenlee

THE garbage collectors found Little Prez in the alley near Six-trey, OD'd away, layin' there cool and stiff, the tools of his burglar trade beside him and the shit for his fix there, too. He'd run across some of that almost pure smack only the rich white folks can get nowadays stuck behind a real Picasso drawing in a Sandburg Village townhouse on the North Side. Didn' pull no capers usually on the North Side 'cause rippin' off white folks was a one-way ticket to the slam, but he turned on all the afternoon before with some junkies he knew lived in Old Town, turnin' on, noddin' an' diggin' teevee an' the nex' mornin' everybody was gone an' no smack aroun' when he woke up an' he needed a fix quick so he walked over to the Village an' dug a backdoor with a lock jus' beggin' to be picked. So he slid in through the sci-fi electronic computerized plasticized kitchen that could do everything except fuck an' cook food you could taste, past the bit color console TV sittin' squat an' fat like some bloated Buddha gon' wrong diggin' him with its big charcoal-gray cyclops eye, an' on past the little brother Sony TV in the bedroom 'cause any Pig seein' a nigger walkin' down North State Street with a idiot box was gon' jack you up for sure. Dug a cassette recorder good enough for a fix, but the real score after he emptied all the dresser drawers on the floor lookin' for a stash o' cash was a fancy wristwatch good enough for the first fix of the day an' he could stick it in his pocket, an' then he dug the picture wasn' hangin' right in the way junkies have of focusin' in on jus' one thing an' foun' the package taped behind it and stuck it in his pocket when he heard a noise before he could check it out. He slid on back out the kitchen door of the white man's pad like his momma been doin' for more years than Little Prez been livin'. On out into the eye-blinkin' hard hot sun cuttin' through his shades like razor blades an' lettin' him know once more that daylight and junkies ain' no match. On down into the dank damp tube of the subway feelin' more like home where no daylight an' no eyeball burnin' sun could come. Bought two Hershey bars in the vending machine on the platform, his junkie juices flowing in his mouth askin' for some sugar, an' he tried to cool his junkie nerves jumpin' up and down his spine like grasshoppers up a long stalk of ragweed in a Woodlawn vacant lot where he used to play an' catch grasshoppers and make 'em spit tobacco an' tell ladybirds to fly away home 'cause they pad was on fire an' he didn' ever step on ants 'cause that would make it rain an' when it rained he'd have to stay in his funky crib in the middle of the rats and roaches an' the sound of the soap opera down the hall dealin' with silly-ass so-called hangups of jive-ass white folks whose ghost-white voices walked into the room an' took over. Tol' his grasshopper nerves to cool it an' his monkey to take a vacation 'cause he was gon' turn on soon as he hustled that fancy-ass watch layin' in his pocket nex' to his long unused dick cause smack been for a longtime his only ol' lady. Was sniffin' an' scratchin' but bein' cool with it 'cause they might be a undercover pig sittin' in the subway car waitin' to jack up some junkie 'cause he didn' have nothin' else to do an' it was easier than messin' with some beret-wearin' gang-banger who didn't give a shit an' might kick some pig's ass or worse an', shit, he sure wished the pigs would get off his back but he been cool since the last time he got out of the slam in Joliet an' he was stoolin' for the pigs now and so they let him alone an' even laid a lid on him now an' then when he said somethin' they wanted to hear, but right now he was out of his 'hood an' some motherfuckin' rookie lookin' for a promotion an' didn' know Little Prez might bust him or even rip him off 'cause the quickest way for a honky pig cop to get a promotion in Chicago was to off a nigger. So he wished the damn train would get him the hell on back to the South Side where he belonged an' he could get him a fix an' all his hangups take a vacation along with his monkey, an' all the time he had the best smack he ever had in his pocket but he forgot about it like everything else when he needed a fix, jus' thinkin' how much he needed to turn on an' how good he be feelin' after he

shoot up an' all the down things be movin' in his head while he noddin'. The El came on up out of the tube an' the sunlight hit him across
his eyes right through his shades as hard as a pig from the Southwes'
Side hatin' niggers an' hungup an' evil 'cause one of his neighbors sold
his crib to a nigger jus' three blocks away, an' even though the pig
pumped a full magazine of buckshot in through the nigger's picture
window they jus' boarded it over an' now they was "for sale" signs all
over the block an' nex' thing you know they be takin' over his neighborhood an' he moved twice already gettin' away from niggers. Little
Prez knew how to read all that shit in a honky pig's face, an' how much
shit the pig gon' make him take an' how much smilin' sometimes didn'
do no good 'cause a lot of them pigs got they kicks stompin' niggers.

Little Prez got off at Fifty-fifth, glad he was back in his own 'hood,
an' he hustled the watch to a barber for 35 bills, bought his shit, hurried to his crib an' knew he could make a thing out of his make 'cause
his monkey not buggin' him too much. Let himself into his funky-
junky pad with jus' a mattress on the floor an' a table an' a refrigerator
(didn' usually have nothin' in it, the only thing in the crib worth anything the stereo an' color teevee). He dug sittin' an' noddin' diggin'
TV with the sound off an' his earphones on, diggin' the sounds an'
watchin' TV without havin' to listen to them screechy honky voices
sounding like somebody scratchin' his fingernails across a blackboard
when he high. He had a small white enamel sterilizer he ripped off from
an abortionist one time an' that was a good score 'cause he foun' two
shoeboxes full of cash an' he didn' have to steal nothin' for months after
that caper. Little Prez dug he was a different kind of junkie shootin' up
with sterile needles and the only tracks in his arms was when he
turned on someplace else with some junkie friends or when he was too
strung-out to wait for the red light to go on on the sterilizer. But he
was scared of dirty needles; his momma always tol' him 'bout germs an'
shit, an' he knew a lota junkies got wasted from hepatitis an' shit from
turnin' on with dirty needles. He turned on the TV without no sound
to that soap opera always had somebody Black on it talkin' to white
folks all the time, an' Little Prez used to make up what they talkin'
about between nods diggin' the sounds on his headphones. Then he
took his time puttin' on a stack o' sounds: Prez, Stitt, Jug, Trane an' a
old Wardell outa print nowadays an' he tol' everybody it was one of his
"collector's items." He had some of the new sounds an' dug 'em, but

when he was turned on he mainly listened to the sounds was the sounds in the streets when he first got out there in 'em. He put the records on the box then started gettin' his make together diggin' Prez during his first administration winnin' the election for all-time in front of that bad-ass Basie band. He put the needle in the sterilizer. "Rock-a-Bye Basie," diggin' Earl Warren doin' a few Johnny Hodges type bars, then Prez fatter-toned than usual the band riffin' so bad behind him, an' then Sweets blowin' like he invented the Harmon mute. Little Prez hummin' along with 'em everyone of 'em and the band too, an' not missin' a note, gettin' the make ready, careful like he was gettin' his horn together in some funky backstage like Prez gettin' ready to blow. The red light went on an' tol' him the needle was ready, an' he got the rest of the make together while Prez was doin' trippin'-type things on "Taxi War Dance." Took out the needle and the tablespoon with the handle bent over double, made up over an alcohol lamp, Prez wailin' now, bootin' the band an' they talkin' to each other, Prez an' the brass section, an' Prez, four bars each an' them cats could say more in four bars than some of these young dudes in four sides. Herschell Evans blowin' now, deeper-toned than Prez, earthy sound like he had to keep his feet planted on the ground 'cause Prez always wantin' to fly, big fat sound no reed squeak, sound soundin' like it an' Herschel the same thing with the rhythm section rock-steady an' swingin' behind him. Whole band riffin' now an' Little Prez puttin' the rubber hose roun' his pipestem arm, flexin' his fist an' lookin' for a collapsed vein to show, gettin' uptight now 'cause it so close an', shit, where was the mother-fucker, the needle ready an' Prez sayin' things an' the earphones right there, shit, where was it, wantin' to put it in his arm an' beggin' for pussy he knew he wasn' go get, never as bad as waitin' for that vein to show an' give him a target for the clean dickhead of his needle, an' one showed an' he hit it an' slow slow makin' it last shot up an' pulled the needle out, still proud an' hard even when empty an' his own dick never been like that even when he was a stud an' hustlin' a stable of four of the finest whores on the South Side. He put the dick/needle in the sterilizer, put on the earphones an' waited for the flash, better than any orgasm he ever had an' didn' miss anymore 'cause he had all the sex he needed every day in Miss Skag an' it hit him an' he moaned an' Prez blowin' "D. B. Blues" an' Little Prez layin' there an' noddin' an' diggin' Lester, his man, President of all the tenor men.

II

We called him Little Prez 'cause he dug Lester so much. Could scat all Prez's solos note for note in the right key standin' there near the basketball backboard in McCosh playground, his hands shoulder high, holdin' an imaginary tenor like Prez downstage at the Regal Theater blowin' with that bootin' Basie band behind him. Jo Jones kickin' on drums. Freddie Green rockin' steady an' Walter Page walkin' strong, the brass bright an' bitin' punctuatin' the saxophone riffs, an' Prez would start out with his tenor hangin' low an' like it gettin' good to him comin' up slow 'til it shoulder-high an' him steppin' in place in time like it so good he can't stan' still an' the band kickin' twelve-bar ass behind him, an' we could see an' hear all that on a sunny day when bored with basketball, an' Little Prez doin' his thing. Was a little nigger, Little Prez, with a head too big for his scrawny body, lookin' skinny even under all those clothes his momma made him wear to keep him from catchin' cold but didn' work too well he was always sniffin', even in the summertime. Little Prez couldn' do nothin' but rap, was the Rap Master of the 'hood. Couldn' fight like Tampy, play basketball like Raby, football like Fuzz, run like C. B., hit a softball like Junior. Couldn' sing, dance, drink, fuck, steal, play games, hunt rats. Wasn' dumb or smart in school, didn' have a fine momma with a sharp boyfrien' with a big Cadillac or Lincoln. Couldn' do shit but rap, lie an' signify. Could play the dozens for days, talk about your momma bad enough to make you cry, run off 42 verses without repeatin' hisself. Sing-say the "Signifyin' Monkey" like nobody else. Couldn' do nothin' else 'cep rap an' he could rap like the real Prez blew, an' when Little Prez got big everybody knew he was gonna blow tenor too an' he would walk down to the pawnshop near Cottage Grove an' dig the horns in the barred window, mostly old beatup Martins and Selmers, but sometimes one or two lookin' bran' new, lef' by some strungout junky musician. Cheated on his lunch money, delivered the *Tribune* in the mornin's, sold the *Defender* an' the *Courier* on Fridays, hauled groceries from Kroger's in his wagon, an' finally he had the bread an' got his Selmer, walked out with it in the case on down Sixty-third in a crab-like shuffle jus' like Prez, an' everybody said if Little Prez could blow like he talked he'd be a bitch. He dug every tenor goin', dug Jug offin' everybody every Saturday afternoon at Al Benson's Battle of the Bands at the Pershing. Dug E. Parker Mc-Dougal an' Johnny Griffin still blowin' with the DuSable High School band before Hamp came through. Dug Dexter an' heard the cats in the playgroun' tryin' to put down Prez to the tune o' "Dexter's Deck"; "My name's Dexter, outblow Lester anyday . . ." and he laughed. Dug Jug an' Stitt, Wardell, Lockjaw an' Gator Tail, Quinichette, the vice pres, Ike Quebec, Ben Webster. Dug 'em at the Parkway, Savoy, Pershing, White City an' the Regal. In the Propeller Lounge, Blue Note, Bee Hive an' the Sutherland. Saw 'em come and disappear, saw 'em early an' saw 'em late, saw 'em try to imitate the President, an' Little Prez tried to deal with somethin' we didn' know: that Little Prez couldn' blow. All them sounds and notes and things runnin' roun' in his head and he couldn' bring 'em out through his horn. Wore a black porkpie like Prez, sometimes tossed his head in that faggot put-on like Prez, drank good Gordon's gin, wore eight-sided dark green tea glasses, big bold-look ties, pin-stripe double-breasted box-back suits like Prez. Lived, ate, slept Prez but couldn' blow like Prez. Practiced six, eight, 10 hours a day, treated his horn better than his momma, shaved his reeds, soaked his reeds, changed his mouthpiece, oiled his keys, polished the brass, an' Prez blew his nose better than Little Prez blew his horn. Couldn' deal with it, wouldn' deal with it, didn' want to deal with it 'cause he knew it was a lie 'cause his momma tol' him, his preacher tol' him, teacher tol' him, everybody tol' him hard work and sacrifice would suffice. Didn' know, couldn' know the only people really believed in the Protestant Ethic was Black folks, didn' know even though he'd grown up in a Black Baptist church what a Protestant Ethic was, jus' believed if you wanted somethin' bad enough and worked long enough and hard enough you had to get it, couldn' quit it, had to get it. If you worked hard enough you had to get it and didn', couldn' dig that the people worked hardest had the least. . . . An' all the time Little Prez blowin' an' not knowin' he doin' the right thing for the wrong reasons. Blowin' with visions of Cadillacs dancin' in his head, long an' lavender an' full o' chicks with hydramatic hips, a closet full of clothes an' enough shoes to change everyday for a month an' not wear the same pair twice. Didn' know, wouldn' know, couldn' know music ain' got nothin' to do with them kinda things. Didn' even stop to think Prez didn' have them kinda things, sittin' in a cheap hotel on Broadway lookin' at Birdland through gin-glazed eyes, diggin' all his imitators and emulators draggin' down all the bread for blowin' the shit he'd discarded 20 years before, an' all of 'em white boys.

So Little Prez blew ugly 'cause his head was ugly and he never knew the reason why. Tried everything twice and then once more 'til one day he discovered Smack. Started out sniffin' and found everything turned soft and warm, the hard edges roundin' off an' the sounds, smells and taste becomin' somethin' else, an' when he blew he sounded jus' like Prez — to hisself. Started out sniffin', then skin-poppin', an' had to put away his horn to go out in the streets to support his habit. Started snatchin' pocketbooks 'til a welfare mother with her check jus' cashed and five hungry kids to feed kicked his ass an' almos' held him 'til the pigs got there. Ran some whores on Sixty-third and Cottage 'till the shit turned him too greedy and impotent and one day he had to make a choice between a fix an' a payoff and the pigs he tried to stall busted him and he spent his first time in the slam and dug he could get all the shit he needed long as he had some bread, and between his momma and hustlin' his ass inside to guards and/or cons he was cool and wasn' even in a hurry to get out, but by the time he got out he'd had a full course in Breaking and Entering, an' now he was a full-time junkie and part-time thief. But the dream never deferred 'cause nex' week he was gon' renew his union card, get a band together, cut a record and blow everybody's mind. Spent time twice in the slam an' went to Lexington three times, not to kick his habit but reduce it when it got too expensive to support. An' you could see him on a corner on Six-trey noddin' his junkie nod and blowin' tenor sounds inside his head loud enough to drown out the racket of the El on its way between Cottage Grove and King Drive, which usta be South Park in his before-junkie days.

III

Little Prez sat up straight out of his nod like he was havin' a bad dream he couldn't remember. The box was still playin' the last record over and over. It was almos' dark outside, the sun comin' pale an' weak down the airshaft and crawlin' into his funky room on weak wino knees. He got up quick an' turned on the lights; big, bright, naked bulb 'cause he was afraid of the dark. A drag for a rip-off junkie, afraid of the dark 'cause the dark is when he had to work, slippin' down alleys in the dark into dark houses an' workin' with not much light, checkin' out whatever would bring the most bread with the least work: portable TV sets, watches an' jewelry and men's suits, if they wasn' too big or too small, but money the bes' 'cause you didn' get ripped off five-to-one by a fence or worse than that if you had to hustle somethin' quick on the streets. Move through the dark pad hopin' you was right they was no dog in it an' no silent burglar alarm, but even so knew no pigs would be in no hurry to answer an alarm from a nigger's home. Check out the bedroom first an' dump all the stuff from the drawers on the floor an' mos' times they was cash in there somewhere 'cause even credit-card niggers didn' really trust banks and usually had a stash somewhere in the pad. It was a drag havin' to work in the dark with the shadows long an' always lookin' like they movin' an' furniture sit-tin' there lookin' like people, so he always had to turn on before he went inside to keep from climbin' the walls. He got his shit together, his burglar tools in a attaché case — he thought that was cool puttin' rip-off tools in a attaché case of good pigskin he'd ripped off from a pad in Pill Hill but he usually worked Woodlawn where he grew up 'cause the pigs didn' give a damn and the folks lived there couldn' afford to buy and train them big man-eatin' dogs them saditty niggers had roun' the house an' he laughed like hell everytime he read 'bout one of them big motherfuckers turnin' on his owner. He was waitin' for the sterilizer to turn on the red light an' reached in his pocket and pulled out the envelope he forgot he had and opened it up and they was ten packets looked like Horse an' he opened one, wet his finger, dipped it in and tasted an' it was smack, tasted like good shit an' he almos' sat down and cried. Thought 'bout stayin' home an' turnin' on but he'd cased the job for a month an' he decided to do it and took one lid of the new stuff to turn on with before he went inside the pad he had staked out.

IV

He stood listening, in the dark alley not far from Six-trey. Good place for a rip-off an' he'd pulled four capers there in a year, only one dog, old and half-blind down at the other end o' the block and barked at everything including the El, so nobody paid him any mind. Had lived a whole history in Woodlawn alleys: ripped-off his first sweet potato from a store on Six-trey and cooked it over a fire in the alley; shot his first basketball and missed; smoked his first cigarette, his first joint, felt his first tit, drank his first wine, had his first fight, an' lost, had his first fuck leanin' against a garage, sniffed his first Horse and pulled his first B & E caper in alleys near Six-trey. Couldn' keep away, an' his momma still lived on Eberhart an' kep' a $20 bill in a sugar bowl so he wouldn' rip off her TV when he was uptight for a fix. Little Prez moved deeper into the shadows, made-up an' hit himself. Took loose the rubber tubing an' waited for the flash an' the white folks' almos' pure Horse galloped through his thin junkie veins an' smacked his ass for the las' time, the Horse too pure, too white for the Black junkie's heart, an' they foun' him the nex' day, OD'd away. No more Prez for Little Prez, his horn in its case in the closet. No more dreams of standing in the spot-light in eight-sided dark green tea glasses, his horn held high nex' to his right shoulder. No more rip-offs, an' no more monkeys to feed an' somewhere on the South Side a little Black kid saved his pennies to buy a horn so he could blow just like Trane. . . .

WE WHO HAVE NOT

Ma'Dear

by Terry McMillan

(for Estelle Ragsdale)

LAST YEAR the cost of living crunched me and I got tired of begging from Peter to pay Paul, so I took in three roomers. Two of 'em is live-in nurses and only come around here on weekends. Even then they don't talk to me much, except when they hand me their money orders. One is from Trinidad and the other is from Jamaica. Every winter they quit their jobs, fill up two and three barrels with I don't know what, ship 'em home, and follow behind on an airplane. They come back in the spring and start all over. Then there's the little college girl, Juanita, who claims she's going for architecture. Seem like to me that was always men's work, but I don't say nothing. She grown.

I'm seventy-two. Been a widow for the past thirty-two years. Weren't like I asked for all this solitude, just that couldn't nobody else take Jessie's place is all. He knew it. And I knew it. He fell and hit his head real bad on the tracks going to fetch us some fresh picked corn and okra for me to make us some succotash, and never come to. I couldn't picture myself with no other man, even though I looked after a few years of being alone in this big old house, walking from room to room with nobody to talk to, cook or clean for, and not much company either.

I missed him for the longest time and thought I could find a man just like him, sincerely like him, but I couldn't. Went out for a spell with Esther Davis's ex-husband, Whimpy, but he was crazy. Drank too much bootleg and then started memorizing on World War I and how hard he fought and didn't get no respect and not a ounce of recognition for his heroic deeds. The only war Whimpy been in is with me for not keeping him around. He bragged something fearless about how he coulda been the heavyweight champion of the world. Didn't weigh but 160 pounds and shorter than me.

Chester Rutledge almost worked 'ceptin' he was boring, never had nothing on his mind worth talking about; claimed he didn't think about nothing besides me. Said his mind was always clear and visible. He just moved around like a zombie and worked hard at the cement foundry. Insisted on giving me his paychecks, which I kindly took for a while, but when I didn't want to be bothered no more, I stopped taking his money. He got on my nerves too bad, so I had to tell him I'd rather have a man with no money and a busy mind, least I'd know he's active somewheres. His feelings was hurt bad and he cussed me out, but we still friends to this very day. He in the home, you know, and I visits him regular. Takes him magazines and cuts out his horoscope and the comic strips from the newspaper and lets him read 'em in correct order.

Big Bill Ronsonville tried to convince me that I shoulda married him instead of Jessie, but he couldn't make me a believer of it. All he wanted to do was put his big rusty hands all on me without asking and smile at me with that big gold tooth sparkling and glittering in my face and tell me how lavish I was, lavish being a new word he just learnt. He kept wanting to take me for night rides way out in the country, out there by Smith Creek where ain't nothin but deep black ditches, giant mosquitoes, loud crickets, lightning bugs, and loose pigs, and turn off his motor. His breath stank like whiskey though he claimed and swore on the Bible he didn't drink no liquor. Aside from that his hands were way too heavy and hard, hurt me, sometimes left red marks on me like I been sucked on. I told him finally that I was too light for him, that I needed a smaller, more gentle man, and he said he knew exactly what I meant.

If you want to know the truth, after him I didn't think much about men the way I used too. Lost track of the ones who upped and died or the ones who couldn't do nothing if they was alive nohow. So, since nobody else seemed to be able to wear Jessie's shoes, I just stuck to myself all these years.

*   *   *

My life ain't so bad now 'cause I'm used to being alone and takes good care of myself. Occasionally I still has a good time. I goes to the park and sits for hours in good weather, watch folks move and listen in on confidential conversations. I add up numbers on license plates to keep my mind alert unless they pass too fast. This gives me a clear idea of how many folks is visiting from out of town. I can about guess the color of every state now, too. Once or twice a month I go to the matinee on Wednesdays, providing ain't no long line of senior citizens 'cause they can be so slow; miss half the picture show waiting for them to count their change and get their popcorn.

Sometimes, when I'm sitting in the park, I feed the pigeons old cornbread crumbs, and I wonders what it'll be like not looking at the snow falling from the sky, not seeing the leaves form on the trees, not hearing no car engines, no sirens, no babies crying, not brushing my hair at night, drinking my Lipton tea, and not being able to go to bed early.

But right now, to tell you the truth, it don't bother me all *that* much. What is bothering me is my case worker. She supposed to pay me a visit tomorrow because my nosy neighbor, Clarabelle, saw two big trucks outside, one come right after the other, and she wondered what I was getting so new and so big that I needed trucks. My mama used to tell me that sometimes you can't see for looking. Clarabelle's had it out to do me in ever since last spring when I had the siding put on the house. I used the last of Jessie's insurance money 'cause the roof had been leaking so bad and the wood rotted and the paint chipped so much that it looked like a wicked old witch lived here. The house looked brand-new, and she couldn't stand to see an old woman's house looking better than hers. She know I been had roomers, and now all of a sudden my case worker claim she just want to visit to see how I'm doing, when really what she want to know is what I'm up to. Clarabelle work in her office.

The truth is my boiler broke and they was here to put in a new one. We liked to froze to death in here for two days. Yeah, I had a little chump change in the bank, but when they told me it was gonna cost $2,000 to get some heat, I cried. I had $862 in the bank; $300 of it I had just spent on this couch I got on sale; it was in the other truck. After twenty years the springs finally broke, and I figured it was time to buy a new one 'cause I ain't one for living in poverty, even at my age. I figured $200 was for my church's cross-country bus trip this summer.

Jessie's sister, Willamae, took out a loan for me to get the boiler, and I don't know how long it's gonna take me to pay her back. She only charge me fifteen or twenty dollars a month, depending. I probably be dead by the time it get down to zero.

My bank wouldn't give me the loan for the boiler, but then they keep sending me letters almost every week trying to get me to refinance my house. They must think I'm senile or something. On they best stationery, they write me. They say I'm up in age and wouldn't I like to take that trip I've been putting off because of no extra money. What trip? They tell me if I refinance my house for more than what I owe, which is about $3,000, that I could have enough money left over to go anywhere. Why would I want to refinance my house at fourteen and a half percent when I'm paying four and a half now? I ain't that stupid. They say dream about clear blue water, palm trees, and orange suns. Last night I dreamt I was doing a backstroke between big blue waves and tipped my straw hat down over my forehead and fell asleep under an umbrella. They made me think about it. And they asked me what would I do if I was to die today? They're what got me to thinking about all this dying mess in the first place. It never would've layed in my mind so heavy if they hadn't kept reminding me of it. Who would pay off your house? Wouldn't I feel bad leaving this kind of a burden on my family? What family they talking about? I don't even know where my people is no more.

I ain't gonna lie. It ain't easy being old. But I ain't complaining neither, 'cause I learned how to stretch my social security check. My roomers pay the house note and I pay the taxes. Oil is sky-high. Medicaid pays my doctor bills. I got a letter what told me to apply for food stamps. That case worker come here and checked to see if I had a real kitchen. When she saw I had a stove and sink and refrigerator, she didn't like the idea that my house was almost paid for, and just knew I was lying about having roomers. "Are you certain that you reside here alone?" she asked me. "I'm certain," I said. She searched every inch of my cabinets to make sure I didn't have two of the same kinds of food, which would've been a dead giveaway. I hid it all in the basement inside the washing machine and dryer. Luckily, both of the nurses was in the islands at the time, and Juanita was visiting some boy what live in D.C.

After she come here and caused me so much eruptions, I had to make trip after trip down to that office. They had me filling out all kinds of forms and still held up my stamps. I got tired of answering the same questions over and over and finally told 'em to keep their old food stamps. I ain't got to beg nobody to eat. I know how to keep myself comfortable and clean and well fed. I manage to buy my staples and toiletries and once in a while a few extras, like potato chips, ice cream, and maybe a pork chop.

My mama taught me when I was young that, no matter how poor you are, always eat nourishing food and your body will last. Learn to conserve, she said. So I keeps all my empty margarine containers and stores white rice, peas and carrots (my favorites), or my turnips from the garden in there. I can manage a garden when my arthritis ain't acting up. And water is the key. I drinks plenty of it like the doctor told me, and I cheats, eats Oreo cookies and saltines. They fills me right up, too. And when I feels like it, rolls, homemade biscuits, eats them with Alga syrup if I can find it at the store, and that sticks with me most of the day.

Long time ago, used to be I'd worry like crazy about gaining weight and my face breaking out from too many sweets, and about cellulite forming all over my hips and thighs. Of course, I was trying to catch Jessie then, though I didn't know it at the time. I was really just being cute, flirting, trying to see if I could get attention. Just so happens I lucked up and got all of his. Caught him like he was a spider and I was the web.

Lord, I'd be trying to look all sassy and prim. Have my hair all did, it be curled tight in rows that I wouldn't comb out for hours till they cooled off after Connie Curtis did it for a dollar and a Budweiser. Would take that dollar out my special savings, which I kept hid under the record player in the front room. My hair used to be fine, too: long and thick and black, past my shoulders, and the mens used to say, "Girl, you sure got a head of hair on them shoulders there, don't it make your neck sweat?" But I didn't never bother answering, just blushed and smiled and kept on walking, trying hard not to switch, cause mama told me my behind was too big for my age and to watch out or I'd be luring grown mens toward me. Humph! I loved it, though, made me feel pretty, special, like I had attraction.

Ain't quite the same no more, though. I looks in the mirror at myself and I sees wrinkles, lots of them, and my skin look like it all be trying to run down toward my toes but then it changed its mind and just stayed there, sagging and lagging, laying limp against my thick bones. Shoot, mens used to say how sexy I was with these high cheeks, tell me I looked swollen, like I was pregnant, but it was just me, being all healthy and everything. My teeth was even bright white and straight in a row then. They ain't so bad now, 'cause ain't none of 'em mine. But I only been to the dentist twice in my whole life and that was 'cause on Easter Sunday I was in so much pain he didn't have time to take no X-ray and yanked it right out 'cause my mama told him to do anything he had to to shut me up. Second time was the last time, and that was 'cause the whole top row and the fat ones way in the back on the bottom ached me so bad the dentist yanked 'em all out so I wouldn't have to be bothered no more.

Don't get me wrong, I don't miss being young. I did everything I wanted to do and then some. I loved hard. But you take Jessie's niece, Thelma. She pitiful. Only twenty-six, don't think she made it past the tenth grade, got three children by different men, no husband and on welfare. Let her tell it, ain't nothing out here but dogs. I know some of these men out here ain't worth a pot to piss in, but all of 'em ain't dogs. There's gotta be some young Jessies floating somewhere in this world. My mama always told me you gotta have something to give if you want to get something in return. Thelma got long fingernails.

Me, myself, I didn't have no kids. Not 'cause I didn't want none or couldn't have none, just that Jessie wasn't full and couldn't give me the juices I needed to make no babies. I accepted it 'cause I really wanted him all to myself, even if he couldn't give me no new bloodlines. He was satisfying enough for me, quite satisfying if you don't mind me repeating myself.

I don't understand Thelma, like a lot of these young peoples. I be watching 'em on the streets and on TV. I be hearing things they be doing to themselves when I'm under the dryer at the beauty shop. (I go to the beauty shop once a month 'cause it make me feel like thangs ain't over yet. She give me a henna so the silver have a gold tint to it.) I can't afford it, but there ain't too many luxuries I can. I let her put makeup on me, too, if it's a Saturday and I feel like doing some window shopping. I still know how to flirt and sometimes I get stares, too. It feel good to be looked at and admired at my age. I try hard to keep myself up. Every weekday morning at five-thirty I do exercises with the TV set, when it don't hurt to stretch.

But like I was saying, Thelma and these young people don't look healthy, and they spirits is always so low. I watch 'em on the streets, on the train, when I'm going to the doctor. I looks in their eyes and they be red or brown where they supposed to be milky white and got bags deeper and heavier than mine, and I been through some thangs. I hear they be using these drugs of variety, and I can't understand why they need to use all these thangs to get from day to day. From what I do hear, it's supposed to give 'em much pleasure and make their minds disappear or make 'em not feel the thangs they supposed to be feeling anyway.

Heck, when I was young, we drank sarsaparilla and couldn't even buy no wine or any kind of liquor in no store. These youngsters ain't but eighteen and twenty and buys anything with a bite to it. I've seen 'em sit in front of the store and drank a whole bottle in one sitting. Girls, too.

We didn't have no dreams of carrying on like that, and specially on no corner. We was young ladies and young men with respect for ourselfs. And we didn't smoke none of them funny cigarettes all twisted up with no filters that smell like burning dirt. I ask myself, I say Ma'Dear, what's wrong with these kids? They can read and write and do arithmetic, finish high school, go to college and get letters behind their names, but every day I hear the neighbors complain that one of they youngsters done dropped out.

Lord, what I wouldn'ta done to finish high school and been able to write a full sentence or even went to college. I reckon I'da been a room decorator. I know they calls it by that fancy name now, interior designer, but it boil down to the same thang. I guess it's 'cause I loves so to make my surroundings pleasant, even right pretty, so I feels like a invited guest in my own house. And I always did have a flair for color. Folks used to say, "Hazel, for somebody as poor as a church mouse, you got better taste in thangs than them Rockefellers!" Used to sew up a storm, too. Covered my mama's raggedy duffold and chairs. Made her a bedspread with matching pillowcases. Didn't mix more than two different patterns either. Make you dizzy.

Wouldn't that be just fine, being an interior designer? Learning the proper names of thangs and recognizing labels in catalogs, giving peoples my business cards and wearing a two-piece with white gloves. "Yes, I decorated the Hartleys' and Cunninghams' home. It was such a pleasant experience. And they're such lovely people, simply lovely," I'da said. Coulda told those rich folks just what they needed in their bedrooms, front rooms, and specially in the kitchen. So many of 'em still don't know what to do in there.

But like I was saying before I got all off the track, some of these young people don't appreciate what they got. And they don't know thangs like we used to. We knew about eating fresh vegetables from the garden, growing and picking 'em ourselves. What going to church was, being honest and faithful. Trusting each other. Leaving our front door open. We knew what it was like to starve and get cheated yearly when our crops didn't add up the way we figured. We suffered together, not separately. These youngsters don't know about suffering for any stretch of time. I hear 'em on the train complaining 'cause they can't afford no Club Med, no new record playing albums, cowboy boots, or those Brooke Shields–Calvin Klein blue jeans I see on TV. They be complaining about nonsense. Do they ever read books since they been taught is what I want to know? Do they be learning things and trying to figure out what to do with it?

And these young girls with all this thick makeup caked on their faces, wearing these high heels they can't hardly walk in. Trying to be cute. I used to wear high heels, mind you, with silk stockings, but at least I could walk in 'em. Jessie had a car then. Would pick me up, and I'd walk real careful down the front steps like I just won the Miss America pageant, one step at a time, and slide into his shiny black Ford. All the neighbors peeked through the curtains 'cause I was sure enough riding in a real automobile with my legitimate boyfriend.

If Jessie was here now I'd have somebody to talk to. Somebody to touch my skin. He'd probably take his fingers and run 'em through my hair like he used to; kiss me on my nose and tickle me where it made me laugh. I just loved it when he kissed me. My mind be so light, and I felt tickled and precious. Have to sit down sometime just to get hold of myself.

If he was here, I probably woulda beat him in three games of checkers by now and he'd be trying to get even. But since today is Thursday, I'd be standing in that window over there waiting for him to get home from work, and when I got tired or the sun be in my eyes, I'd hear the taps on his wing tips coming up the front porch. Sometime, even now, I watch for him, but I know he ain't coming back. Not that he wouldn't if he could, mind you, 'cause he always told me I made him feel lightning lighting up his heart.

Don't get me wrong, I got friends, though a heap of 'em is dead or got tubes coming out of their noses or going all through their bodies every which-a-way. Some in the old folks' home. I thank the Lord I ain't stuck in one of them places. I ain't never gonna get that old. They might as well just bury me standing up if I do. I don't want to be no nuisance to nobody, and I can't stand being around a lot of sick people for too long.

I visits Gunther and Chester when I can, and Vivian who I grew up with, but no soon as I walk through them long hallways, I get depressed. They lay there all limp and helpless, staring at the ceiling like they're really looking at something, or sitting stiff in their rocking chairs, pitiful, watching TV and don't be knowing what they watching half the time. They laugh when ain't nothing funny. They wait for it to get dark so they know it's time to go to sleep. They relatives don't hardly come visit 'em, just folks like me. Whimpy don't understand a word I say, and it makes me grateful I ain't lost no more than I have.

Sometime we sits on the sun porch rocking like fools; don't say one word to each other for hours. But last time Gunther told me about his grandson what got accepted to Stanford University, and another one at a university in Michigan. I asked him where was Stanford and he said he didn't know. "What difference do it make?" he asked. "It's one of those uppity schools for rich smart white people," he said. "The important thang is that my black grandson won a scholarship there, which mean he don't have to pay a dime to go." I told him I know what a scholarship is. I ain't stupid. Gunther said he was gonna be there for at least four years or so, and by that time he would be a professional. "Professional what?" I asked. "Who cares, Ma'Dear, he gonna be a professional at whatever it is he learnt." Vivian started mumbling when she heard us talking, 'cause she still like to be the center of attention. When she was nineteen she was Miss Springfield Gardens. Now she can't stand the thought that she old and wrinkled. She started yakking about all the places she'd been to, even described the landscape like she was looking at a photograph. She ain't been but twenty-two miles north of here in her entire life, and that's right there in that home.

Like I said, and this is the last time I'm gonna mention it. I don't mind being old, it's just that sometime I don't need all this solitude. You can't do everything by yourself and expect to have as much fun if somebody was there doing it with you. That's why when I'm feeling jittery or melancholy for long stretches, I read the Bible, and it soothes me. I water my morning glories and amaryllis. I baby-sit for Thelma every now and then, 'cause she don't trust me with the kids for too long. She mainly call on holidays and my birthday. And she the only one who don't forget my birthday: August 19th. She tell me I'm a Leo, that I got fire in my blood. She may be right, 'cause once in a while I gets a churning desire to be smothered in Jessie's arms again.

Anyway, it's getting late, but I ain't tired. I feel pretty good. That old case worker think she gonna get the truth out of me. She don't scare me. It ain't none of her business that I got money coming in here besides my social security check. How they 'spect a human being to live off $369 a month in this day and age is what I wanna know. Every time I walk out my front door it cost me at least two dollars. I bet she making thousands and got credit cards galore. Probably got a summer house on the Island and goes to Florida every January. If she found out how much I was getting from my roomers, the government would make me pay back a dollar for every two I made. I best to get my tail on upstairs and clear everything off their bureaus. I can hide all the nurse's stuff in the attic; they won't be back till next month. Juanita been living out of trunks since she got here, so if the woman ask what's in 'em, I'll tell her, old sheets and pillowcases and memories.

On second thought, I think I'm gonna take me a bubble bath first, and dust my chest with talcum powder, then I'll make myself a hot cup of Lipton's and paint my fingernails clear 'cause my hands feel pretty steady. I can get up at five and do all that other mess; case worker is always late anyway. After she leave, if it ain't snowing too bad, I'll go to the museum and look at the new paintings in the left wing. By the time she get here, I'ma make out like I'm a lonely old widow stuck in a big old house just sitting here waiting to die.

WE WHO HAVE NOT

Transaction

by Kelvin Christopher James

SITTING IN POSITION being invisible had become so comfortable, Omari was nodding off. Drowsiness seeped into his will like a fog, gently misting away the vibrant insistence of his purpose. His hovering dreamtime seesawed the plans for the scam, straddling them across the borders of reality: What he had to do was also what he might've done, or what might've been done, or even what he was going to do. Time frame shifted drunkenly, as insensitive to circumstance as his backside was numb to the damp coolness of the new-mown grass.

A smooth transition — and the giddy had resolved into reassurance. And all was well. He was doing it. He was being the lookout man. First one in. Last out. His job to divine trouble at the outset, and frustrate it after that. Until the play was done. Most of all, he was the man with the Might, the .38 arm of firepower. As usual, Jangles had assigned him alone that violence option.

He had entered the small East Side park half an hour ago, so ready and alert he almost twitched through the gate, concentration like a daze around him. His eyes, jackhammer rapid, darted about, wanting to check everywhere at once. The strain was controlling it all down to common sense. So that he could be the look-see man, and not conspicuous.

What his sweating anticipation had met was an innocent summer's day, ten o'clock peaceful with a morning-airing crowd. Nannies minding lazy babies lolling off in strollers. Some senior ladies brooding close-headed with their histories and who-knows in duos and trios. A bent-over old man carefully testing the pathway as if his third leg of a walking stick had a seeing eye. A few other walkers and sitters. All were too well kept or well off or well aged to be the Undercover Man.

Omari had muttered, "Beautiful." And became aware that his palms were wet, his jaw adroop. He got himself together, then set off to double-check the fortune of their good preparations.

His saunter through the park's morning calm only reassured him it was as harmless to their plans as it was pleasant. So Omari headed for his assigned post to signal and await the rest of the crew.

The second bench on the path from the entrance gate was the spot, snuggled right next to a dense, small-leafed bush sculpted into a man-high teacup. The giant cup handle touched one of the bench's arms, and the dark green bowl gave shade and color to the intimacy of the seat. Even though it was there in the open, next to the public path, it had the privacy of a nest, except for some watching body being bold and rude.

Jangles had named this as its best advantage, that plain-sight openness with politeness shades. Folks couldn't stare at coziness, he'd said, so this love seat was the perfect lookout for his lieutenant and advance man. It had been great strategy in the meeting. There was one problem now, though. During Omari's brief double-checking circuit, a woman had come in and sat there.

She was dressed straight out of a rich store window, shirt to shoes in shades of wealthy brown. The pocketbook, too, was a mahogany suede with a fat gold clasp. The outfit advertised spending bank.

This piece of dead time was clearly expensive to her. Each tick ground her down, taking valuable toll on her patience. Wasting many nerves, making her glance at her watch and, every other minute, at the entrance gate. Whenever someone strayed into her sights, he'd get a blast from her rat-a-tat vigil for her no-show target. And with every disappointment, she was building up more heat. Fine-adjusting her temper by recrossing model legs to models' poses. Unclasping the gold hold to finger tissues from the suede and press the tension out of her makeup.

With all her action, though, it was plain that something more powerful had her in control. Otherwise she would break, flail her arms and scream to the sky with rage red to blue. If she weren't dressed chic and proper, she would.

While appraising her — and not wanting to risk winding her up further — Omari had chosen an alternative spot some twenty feet over-shoulder to her. From there, feet out long, reclining on rump and elbows, he had eyes both on his job and on the benched busy-Mizzy.

Thus it was that twenty minutes later, with nothing much changed, relaxation began its creep-up assault, and the lazybones feeling started undermining his alertness. At the first, he took to easing his eyes only a little. Then he had discovered that even with the vision resting, he was still able to maintain his sense of the importance of the watch. The nods had fully conquered when he found himself time-sliding back to the meeting the night before.

Jangles had laid out this solid plan of a scam, guaranteeing some easy pawnshop cash. It was five minutes' action, no cops, no pain, and no chase. As usual with Jangles, the promise had turned to a neat adventure by the time he ran down the situation. His magic was sweet planning, and how he told it.

Jangles had scoped this park for weeks, learning its patterns. It was small, with a private-privileged look from its well-kept lawns and trimmed hedges and fresh-turned beds of varicolored tulips and ornamented bushes. It fitted in with its neighborhood: an East Side pocket of rich society living off the icing on the cake. The park had but one gate open for entrance and exit (the other secured by a two-inch-thick steel chain, as if it could break away). That convenient one-door resemblance to a shopping bag was Jangles's final persuasion that the park was easy pickings for the crew. And it should be worth the while. For its mainstay crowd was an older, better sort. Mostly heirloom conservators with family trees of gold, and jewels around their necks and wrists and fingers.

Yes! There was a cop. His beat took him by about midday. But he had taken up with a pretty nanny, who came with her kid like clockwork to help him with his workload. To synchronize and so on, they always shifted to the park's farthest end, him with his hat in his hand, her glowing like a happy baby.

After this was related, Tari had thrown out the idea of riffraffing some pussy if it showed up. That set Jangles wild. Like forever didn't matter, he began raining on speeches. Sermons on Selfishness, on Reason, on Stupidity. Then barbecuing the Ta' on a Brotherhood and Discipline grill, using Bitterness and Sarcasm for sauce. What would the cops and robbered say? How would the media put it? Even an off-color suggestion would be made into a sexual assault. One impetuous fondle would change their Well-Coordinated Caper into a Raping Rampage. From Proficient Tacticians, they'd become Heinous Hoodlums, or a Perverse Gang. Jangles might've ranted on, but for Tari screaming, "Time out!" to plead out with forced jokes, play tears, and genuine regret about his mouth mess.

Jangles quit then, after a final stutter or two of muttered remainders. The rest of the meeting had proceeded smoothly, everyone attentive and serious and mainly avoiding Jangles's word whip. His eloquence was a gift — his talent instead of science, basketball, or whatever — and it made him the major man. But it could make him a torture, too. . . .

As if a disco's door had busted open, loud beat music exploded, blowing Omari's idle-minding away. His heart abruptly pounded awakeness through him, and wrenching his neck about, with a shamed glance he raked the entrance where Jangles would be waiting; then he relaxed to find his man absent to his lieutenant's laxness. That anxiety cleared, he turned full-scowl vexation toward the noisy offender.

It was Dolfo and his jamma-blasta, posted near the gate between the fence and a tulip patch. Last night he had been insisting and whining and begging with Jangles about bringing the box. The police band on the radio could be used for checking on the law, he'd argued. When he noticed Jangles's interest in this point, he'd needled on with it until Jangles had said okay.

Omari'd been against it all along. To his mind, Dolfo would mess up and, as always, have his excuse afterward. And just as he'd expected, here was the Murf now, louding soul sounds into this elite setup. Dolfo seemed absolutely into the music. Finger-popping the rhythm, rocking his shoulders, boogying his ass where it leaned against the iron spears linking as fence.

Fiercing up his stare, Omari sat up and concentrated disgust thoughts at the asshole. No difference. Dolfo remained deeply into the current top o' the charts.

As far as Omari could judge, the music hadn't affected the folks too much. They didn't show serious alarm. Here and there was a glance at Dolfo, but no one was getting restless. The noise was just a commonplace annoyance to tolerate and ignore. Like an upset stomach, it would pass soon. When Omari noticed one of the nannies putting a little hip-hop in her strolling gait, he admitted that the tune wasn't so bad. The number moved (still carrying Dolfo) into its honey-crooning chorus.

This recalled to Omari the time somebody'd told Dolfo how he had a black hole in his head; any sense from his brain went into another dimension. Dolfo had laughed harder than everyone else. Longer, too. All that evening, again and again, he'd erupted in giggle fits and guffaws. As if it wasn't him the joke was on. As if the joke was that sweet. As if he had tasted it at all. But that was Dolfo, a guy Mr. Spock would've found "fascinating."

Now, as Omari set to heave himself up for a reminding (but casual) saunter over by the balloon-brained, Dolfo suddenly caught himself and reduced the radio's volume. So soft, Omari couldn't hear it, and his mind faltered on the ending part of the tune to which it had been humming a backup.

Dolfo was now casting sly glances around. Probably feeling that he hadn't been noticed, and looking furtive as a mouse in the cheese cupboard. Omari shifted his eyes away from the bother. All at once, his irritation changed to an odd cheerfulness. It was kinda funny, but even the Zero-head had come through in his weird way. It seemed that matters could only get better now.

Right then the woman halfway stood up to briefly arrange skirt creases at her bottom. Then, readied for whatever, she sat again, looking straight ahead. His instant check of the gate told Omari why. A man had entered and was approaching in a rush. And once more Omari was seized by tension, while his heartbeat started its own jam session in his chest.

But the man had eyes only for the woman in brown. He hurried straight to her like a late schoolboy with his upset mama whip-waiting. Omari thought, Punk! and his muscles and mind went mellow again, his heart quieting to relief.

The Punk might've been a model, too. Or maybe they dressed from the same store windows. He looked to be a diet-watcher who probably worked out yet still remained a slight-weight. One to whom even karate couldn't pass on aggression. A vulgar belch would blow him right away.

As he neared his date, he commenced an elaborate arm-stretching, wrist-bending, and elbow-jerking action, which ended in a studied glance at his watch. Although practiced and smooth, still it was a punkish move, not hiding the wimp behind it. He had to have known he was late. And worse, he had done his glance act, and it missed his audience. For the woman never gave him eye. She had remained looking frustrated at her morning, as if the piece of day were behaving unmanageably.

Standing his distance like a Boy Scout, the Punk hailed her, and maybe got the permission to sit. Or perhaps it was manners understanding. She still wasn't looking at him.

Now Omari saw that time-checking wasn't his only gimmick. The Punk was elaborate at sitting down, too. He had to pinch-hold the front pleats of his pants' legs just so, and throw a glance behind to guide his ass to sit. Then he did a softness test before committing the sensitive backside. He ended by crossing the gentleman's legs.

All this, and not yet a play from the woman.

With all their motions and gestures, Omari couldn't but notice the Punk's hands. He would've never recognized him by them. They looked real, foreign to the magazine-ad man they serviced. The right one showed a fresh-healed scar. They had fat veins, and long, strong, knobby fingers. Big enough to palm a basketball, they looked man's hands.

Omari realized that the woman had been fussing at the Punk while still gazing away. He heard some as the off-and-on breezes allowed her voice to reach him. A bit about him demeaning reality. Something else about winter and discontent. It was speechy complaining, sounding prepared, poor-felt, and distant. Omari relaxed out of their hassle. They couldn't be trouble, not with that quarreling like no-longer lovers. They weren't the undercover police trap he was wary about, only coupled rabbits setting up as prey.

He was thinking in terms of another Jangles idea: his Natural Survival Theory. When he'd dropped out of college, Jangles had kept up his self-education, reading majorly in biology. This he used as basis for interpreting the Life's systems.

By his Survival Theory, Out Here was a great human-species natural park. It had available for every want by everybody. No one ever had to go hungry. The catch was that each one was the food for another.

Whether dog eat dog, or wolf eat rabbit, or worm eat wolf, one guy had to depend on that one other for food.

Jangles saw that as a problem, this depending on one special food. As he said it, "If your burger joint closed down, y're starving!" According to him, the rats had found a solution: eat anything, live anywhere, adjust with instinct, and stay hungry. Using that plan, they owned everywhere man lived. And they never made a weapon.

Hear Jangles expound about rats, and they became most admirable. Their strength, intelligence, family ties, patience, and success against human oppression all gave them underdog glamour and heroic stature. From vermin they were changed to sophisticated social survivors. And this is how he wanted the crew to see themselves: as a gang of rats with hands, the ultimate candidates for the One Life Handicap Derby.

Something had made the Punk exert his voice. Maybe it was a squeezed ball, for he calmed down again after a fidget. But he was still talking back to her. With the breezes on hold, Omari could hear quite plainly, the Punk speaking each word FM perfect, from its beginning through to its end, extra-working his lips and tongue as if the language had bubble gum in it.

"I'm aware of my responsibilities in this. I am. Really I am. But there are other considerations." He managed two notes into "are." "The market is very dull. We aren't selling a thing. The work isn't moving. The agency promised to get rid of the 'Moonlight' piece, but I regard it as . . . It's a favorite, if not the best . . . I'm reluctant . . ."

She cut in, "Still the sentimental you, huh, always and forever? You'd sell this, but you like it too much. That one's too good for the money. Your pieces're like your children. You make them from stone, or mud, and sweat. And you love them so." Here she stopped and turned to give him the full-faced eye. "May I remind you that you have a flesh-and-blood creation that, this year, needs eight thousand for tuition, three thousand for clothes, and more for food and doctors. . . ."

She paused for breath, and the Punk made to slip in some speech, but she hammered him down with, "And I cannot ask my agent to get rid of her. You understand that? Whether she's my favorite piece or not!"

The Punk eased his tie's knot with the active fingers and swallowed some explanations. He tried another tack, changing his tone from explain to complain. "Well, what am I to do? You know my extent, my resources. Father refuses to come across. What am I supposed to do? You don't expect me to steal, do you?"

Eye-to-eye with him, the woman surveyed his seated stature. Up, then down, her formed eyebrows assessed him. Then, weighted with scorn, her voice fell from proper to common louding as she wiped him out.

"You don't have the balls!"

Omari didn't get to see the Punk's response. The distraction was Jangles strolling into his field of vision. His major man was smiling and relaxed, signaling all was well, and the action would be getting on.

Putting his concentration together, Omari examined the pair on his bench and decided what items he'd be having. The pocketbook, of course. He'd clean it out. And the Punk should have a wallet. Counting the visibles, there were also two watches, bracelet(s?), earrings, and at least one neck chain. Not too bad. He could evaluate maybe four, five hundred in dollars. Plus, luck might have the Punk carrying a stash despite his crying poor pockets.

Omari looked around at the other guys. They had all cut out their posing and seemed ready for business. Emark and Tari had grounded their Frisbee. Dolfo was in his position near the fence. Jangles was heading back to the gate after his quick overlook of the situation. When he got to where he could monitor the street, it would begin.

Briefly, Omari wondered how the fine folks in the park couldn't see it coming. It seemed as obvious as rain clouds in a clear blue sky.

Jangles reached the gate and pulled its iron wings shut with a bang. Ten guys who watched it happen moved into action as one. Omari quicked over to his bench and stood close over the couple. The woman, still working the Punk, didn't notice him.

Omari wasn't loud, but his voice was hard: "Shut up!"

She looked up at his command with bigging eyes, mouth agape. The hanging jaws sagged her cheeks, giving her a fish mouth.

"Gimme what y'got!" Omari told her.

In response she slumped down on the bench, propping her head up against the backrest.

The Punk took it much better. It was the startled look, then immediate understanding. He folded his arms and didn't try a word.

"Okay, okay. It's a takeoff," Omari continued quickly. "You don't panic, and y'don't bleed. So nothing fancy, okay? Mi' man there at the fence could blow y'fuckin' heads off anytime. Y'got it? So relax, okay?"

The woman's eyes wanted to look behind him at the fence, but they couldn't break the magnet of Omari's face. She had closed her mouth. Now a tic of a smile kept tugging it on one side only. Omari hoped she'd stay in shock and checked the Punk. He had closed his eyes and was shaking his head as if he didn't believe it was really happening to him.

She made a fart when Omari reached down and grabbed her mahogany suede pocketbook. Chuckling, he demanded her watch and earrings. Meantime he searched the pocketbook with half his eyes and five fingers. It had a checkbook, a small fold of bills, a change purse, some credit cards, and other pure feminine stuff. A second pass of his fingers found nothing but a pen. He kept the bills and chucked the suede back on the bench.

She was taking her time with the watch, slowly peeling it off as if it were wrist skin, wasting time and hoping.

"Give it here! Bitch!" Omari growled, and snatched at it.

That was enough grease, and the watch slid off immediately. Without urging, the earrings followed, offered from shaking, long-nailed fingers. Her neck chain, Omari saw, was a thin, delicate rope with a tiny pendant. As his pawnshop man bought gold by weight, he passed on it. So with the woman finished, he turned to the Punk.

"Awright, let's have it. And don't fuck up now."

The Punk took off his watch quickly. Next came a heavy gold ID band Omari hadn't even seen. Then the Punk hesitated.

"Your pockets, sucker!" Omari urged. He added a meaningful look at the Punk's jacket pockets. But turned insides out, they didn't yield the wallet Omari sought. He was growing impatient.

"I want your wallet, fuckhead!" he said.

The Punk stammered, "I . . . I, er, don't carry a, er, wallet, sir!"

Omari almost grinned. The Punk had called him "sir" as if he meant it. Mentally cursing the Luck of No Wallet, Omari was about to demand the Punk's finger ring when the woman's voice cut in.

"For God's sake, give him the damned wallet and stop trying to be a hero."

Omari shot a look at her. Her hand was reaching for her throat but wasn't quite there. It crouched nearer to her shoulder like a little animal caught undecided whether to stand or run. Her eyes slid away from his like a traitor's, and he felt a strong disgust at her. She shouldn't have blown the Punk's try. It wasn't her place to. A man had to try. But he reined in his vexation at her and turned his rage on the Punk.

"So, what's it goin' to be, huh, asshole? You want to see y'blood? Gimme it! Now!"

Omari pounced smelling-close to the Punk, staring right into the clean-shaven face, ready to break it with his fist as the anger roused by the woman's betrayal recharged from the man's attempted resistance. The combined underhandedness offended him so. He tensed himself to punch — just as the Punk gave in.

Lifting his foot to his lap, he reached inside his sock and pulled out a wallet. Loaded up to strike, breathing hard, Omari barely held in the energy. He kept the blow poised and said, "Just gimme the cash, man."

With deliberate speed, the Punk emptied his wallet and handed over the cash.

As Omari took the money, from the corner his eye he glimpsed the woman's crouching hand still fluttering near her throat. It suddenly occurred to him that the gesture held a suspicious stealthiness. He studied her face, her eyes scurrying about wildly, like cockroaches trapped in a light cage.

"What y'got there?" he asked softly, gesturing toward her hand.

Her answer was to make a fist over what she concealed.

The stupid defiance of the little fist slacked the bonds of his control. The silly, back-squeezing bitch. His time was almost up, and here she was playing her greedy ways with him. Furious, he stooped and hissed in her face, "Gimme. Here, here. Give it up!"

She was so out-of line. And he, near out-of-bounds of Jangles's rule, he wanted to punch the shit out of her. His fist was up, the blood charging through him.

The woman broke and sobbed, "Oh my God . . ." and she removed her hand.

It was a brooch. A golden, pinky-sized butterfly with spread wings and eyes of bulging ruby red; it was a big, beautiful, classy treasure on her chest. Now Omari realized why she had betrayed the Punk's wallet. It was to buy some opportunity to hide her fancy brooch,

As he discovered her fault, Omari beheld a crumpling of her made-up face. Cracks between where was paint and where was pallor had made a gap into her, like it was an earthquake. And he could see her greedy core. Not greedy from need, but from just wanting more. Automatic greedy, like a worm eating shit. Which was why he felt he could squash her face.

"You greedy bitch!" he snarled, and snatched at the jewel. But it was well pinned to the beige cashmere collar, so the grab only yanked her shoulder sideways, making her scream out fright and cower down.

"Don't," the Punk chimed in, "please don't. It's not her fault. . . ."

Surprised, Omari looked at him. He had raised his big, veiny hands, palms up and open, certainly not to attack. More forcing of a pause, like a guy wanting fairness, not fights. He continued talking into Omari's hesitation.

"It's my family's. An heirloom. I gave it to her as a wedding present. It's really for my daughter . . . a tradition. It's our way, sir."

He was explaining it strong-voiced, as if this was a western and he was the hero. He was being reasonable, until he got to the "sir." Only then it became appeal. The whole speech so surprised Omari that he met the fellow's eyes. And in that odd consternation — exchanging shocked, reseeing stares — they formed a wordless bargain.

Omari straightened up. "Okay, mi'man. Y'got it."

Right then he heard the scam being called. "Time! Time's cut!" He stepped back onto the pavement.

"Don't move till the gate bangs, okay?" he warned them. "You're still lined up. So don't spoil it now."

Just before turning away, he jumped close and faked a violent cuff at the woman. She made a retching, asthma-attack sound and threw her arms up over her hairdo. The guy didn't even flinch at the empty gesture, just sat there testing an ambiguous half smile.

As Omari split with the gang, his parting image was of the man comforting the woman, holding her head on his chest, stroking it slowly. Omari imagined him years hence telling the daughter how he'd saved the family heirloom. He hoped the guy would tell it like a hero.

A Loaf of Bread

by James Alan McPherson

IT WAS ONE of those obscene situations, pedestrian to most people, but invested with meaning for a few poor folk whose lives are usually spent outside the imaginations of their fellow citizens. A grocer named Harold Green was caught red-handed selling to one group of people the very same goods he sold at lower prices at similar outlets in better neighborhoods. He had been doing this for many years, and at first he could not understand the outrage heaped upon him. He acted only from habit, he insisted, and had nothing personal against the people whom he served. They were his neighbors. Many of them he had carried on the cuff during hard times. Yet, through some mysterious access to a television station, the poor folk were now empowered to make grand denunciations of the grocer. Green's children now saw their father's business being picketed on the Monday evening news.

No one could question the fact that the grocer had been overcharging the people. On the news even the reporter grimaced distastefully while reading the statistics. His expression said, "It is my job to report the news, but sometimes even I must dissassociate myself from it to protect my honor." This, at least, was the impression the grocer's children seemed to bring away from the television. Their father's name had not been mentioned, but there was a close-up of his store with angry black people, and a few outraged whites, marching in groups of three in front of it. There was also a close-up of his name. After seeing this, they were in no mood to watch cartoons. At the dinner table, disturbed by his children's silence, Harold Green felt compelled to say, "I am not a dishonest man." Then he felt ashamed. The children, a boy and his older sister, immediately left the table, leaving Green alone with his wife. "Ruth, I am not dishonest," he repeated to her.

Ruth Green did not say anything. She knew, and her husband did not, that the outraged people had also picketed the school attended by their children. They had threatened to return each day until Green lowered his prices. When they called her at home to report this, she had promised she would talk with him. Since she could not tell him this, she waited for an opening. She looked at her husband across the table.

"I did not make the world," Green began, recognizing at once the seriousness in her stare. "My father came to this country with nothing but his shirt. He was exploited for as long as he couldn't help himself. He did not protest or picket. He put himself in a position to play by the rules he had learned." He waited for his wife to answer, and when she did not, he tried again. "I did not make this world," he repeated. "I only make my way in it. Such people as these, they do not know enough to not be exploited. If not me, there would be a Greek, a Chinaman, maybe an Arab or a smart one of their own kind. Believe me, I deal with them. There is something in their style that lacks the patience to run a concern such as mine. If I closed down, take my word on it, someone else would do what has to be done."

But Ruth Green was not thinking of his leaving. Her mind was on other matters. Her children had cried when they came home early from school. She had no special feeling for the people who picketed, but she did not like to see her children cry. She had kissed them generously, then sworn them to silence. "One day this week," she told her husband, "you will give free, for eight hours, anything your customers come in to buy. There will be no publicity, except what they spread by word of mouth. No matter what they say to you, no matter what they take, you will remain silent." She stared deeply into him for what she knew was there. "If you refuse, you have seen the last of your children and myself."

Her husband grunted. Then he leaned toward her. "I will not knuckle under," he said. "I will *not* give!"

"We shall see," his wife told him.

The black pickets, for the most part, had at first been frightened by the audacity of their undertaking. They were peasants whose minds had long before become resigned to their fate as victims. None of them, before now, had thought to challenge this. But now, when they watched themselves on television, they hardly recognized the faces they saw beneath the hoisted banners and placards. Instead of reflecting the meekness they all felt, the faces looked angry. The close-ups looked especially intimidating. Several of the first pickets, maids who worked in the suburbs, reported that their employers, seeing the activity on the afternoon news, had begun treating them with new respect. One woman, midway through the weather report, called around the neighborhood to disclose that her employer had that very day given her a new china plate for her meals. The paper plates, on which all previous meals had been served, had been thrown into the wastebasket. One recipient of this call, a middle-aged woman known for her bashfulness and humility, rejoined that her husband, a sheet-metal worker, had only a few hours before been called "Mister" by his supervisor, a white man with a passionate hatred of color. She added the tale of a neighbor down the street, a widow-woman named Murphy, who had at first been reluctant to join the picket; this woman now was insisting it should be made a daily event. Such talk as this circulated among the people who had been instrumental in raising the issue. As news of their victory leaked into the ears of others who had not participated, they received all through the night calls from strangers requesting verification, offering advice, and vowing support. Such strangers listened, and then volunteered stories about indignities inflicted on them by city officials, policemen, other grocers. In this way, over a period of hours, the community became even more incensed and restless than it had been at the time of the initial picket.

Soon, the man who had set events in motion found himself a hero. His name was Nelson Reed, and all his adult life he had been employed as an assembly-line worker. He was a steady husband, the father of three children, and a deacon in the Baptist church. All his life he had trusted in God and gotten along. But now something in him capitulated to the reality that came suddenly into focus. "I was wrong," he told people who called him. "The onliest thing that matters in this world is *money*. And when was the last time you seen a picture of Jesus on a dollar bill?" This line, which he repeated over and over, caused a few callers to laugh nervously, but not without some affirmation that this was indeed the way things were. Many said they had known it all along. Others argued that although it was certainly true, it was one thing to live without money and quite another to live without faith. But still most callers laughed and said, "You right. You *know* I know you right. Ain't it the truth, though?" Only a few people, among them Nelson Reed's wife, said nothing and looked very sad.

Why they looked sad, however, they would not communicate. And anyone observing their troubled faces would have to trust his own intuition. It is known that Reed's wife, Betty, measured all events against the fullness of her own experience. She was skeptical of everything. Brought to the church after a number of years of living openly with a jazz musician, she had embraced religion when she married Nelson Reed. But though she no longer believed completely in the world, she nonetheless had not fully embraced God. There was something in the nature of Christ's swift rise that had always bothered her, and something in the blood and vengeance of the Old Testament that was mellowing and refreshing. But she had never communicated these thoughts to anyone, especially her husband. Instead, she smiled vacantly while others professed leaps of faith, remained silent when friends spoke fiercely of their convictions. The presence of this vacuum in her contributed to her personal mystery; people said she was beautiful, although she was not outwardly so. Perhaps it was because she wished to protect this inner beauty that she did not smile now, and looked extremely sad, listening to her husband on the telephone.

Nelson Reed had no reason to be sad. He seemed to grow more energized and talkative as the days passed. He was invited by an alderman, on the Tuesday after the initial picket, to tell his story on a local television talk show. He sweated heavily under the hot white lights and attempted to be philosophical. "I notice," the host said to him, "that you are not angry at this exploitative treatment. What, Mr. Reed, is the source of your calm?" The assembly-line worker looked unabashedly into the camera and said, "I have always believed in *Justice* with a capital *J*. I was raised up from a baby believin' that God ain't gonna let nobody go *too* far. See, in *my* mind God is in charge of *all* the capital letters in the alphabet of this world. It say in the Scripture He is Alpha and Omega, the first and the last. He is just about the *onliest* capitalizer they is." Both Reed and the alderman laughed. "Now, when *men* start to capitalize, they gets *greedy*. They put a little *j* in *joy* and a littler one in *justice*. They raise up a big *G* in *Greed* and a big *E* in *Evil*. Well, soon as they commence to put a little *g* in *god,* you can expect some kind of reaction. The Savior will just raise up the *H* in *Hell* and go on from there. And that's just what I'm doin', giving these sharpies *HELL* with a big *H."* The talk show host laughed along with Nelson Reed and the alderman. After the taping they drank coffee in the back room of the studio and talked about the sad shape of the world.

Three days before he was to comply with his wife's request, Green, the grocer, saw this talk show on television while at home. The words of Nelson Reed sent a chill through him. Though Reed had attempted to be philosophical, Green did not perceive the statement in this light. Instead, he saw a vindictive-looking black man seated between an ambitious alderman and a smug talk-show host. He saw them chatting comfortably about the nature of evil. The cameraman had shot mostly close-ups, and Green could see the set in Nelson Reed's jaw. The color of Reed's face was maddening. When his children came into the den, the grocer was in a sweat. Before he could think, he had shouted at them and struck the button turning off the set. The two children rushed from the room screaming. Ruth Green ran in from the kitchen. She knew why he was upset because she had received a call about the show; but she said nothing and pretended ignorance. Her children's school had been picketed that day, as it had the day before. But both children were still forbidden to speak of this to their father.

"Where do they get so much power?" Green said to his wife. "Two days ago, nobody would have cared. Now, everywhere, even in my home, I am condemned as a rascal. And what do I own? An airline? A multinational? Half of South America? *No!* I own three stores, one of which happens to be in a certain neighborhood inhabited by people who cost me money to run it." He sighed and sat upright on the sofa, his chubby legs spread wide. "A cab driver has a meter that clicks as he goes along. I pay extra for insurance, iron bars, pilfering by customers and employees. Nothing clicks. But when I add a little overhead to my prices, suddenly everything clicks. But for someone else. When was there last such a world?" He pressed the palms of both hands to his temples, suggesting a bombardment of brain-stinging sounds.

This gesture evoked no response from Ruth Green. She remained standing by the door, looking steadily at him. She said, "To protect yourself, I would not stock any more fresh cuts of meat in the store until after the giveaway on Saturday. Also, I would not tell it to the employees until after the first customer of the day has begun to check out. But I would urge you to hire several security guards to close the door promptly at seven-thirty, as is usual." She wanted to say much more than this, but did not. Instead she watched him. He was looking at the blank gray television screen, his palms still pressed against his ears. "In case you need to hear again," she continued in a weighty tone of voice, "I said two days ago, and I say again now, that if you fail to do this you will not see your children again for many years."

He twisted his head and looked up at her. "What is the color of these people?" he asked.

"Black," his wife said.

"And what is the name of my children?"

"Green."

The grocer smiled. "There is your answer," he told his wife. "Green is the only color I am interested in."

His wife did not smile. "Insufficient," she said.

"The world is mad!" he moaned. "But it is a point of sanity with me to not bend. I will not bend." He crossed his legs and pressed one hand firmly atop his knee. "*I will not bend,*" he said.

"We will see," his wife said.

Nelson Reed, after the television interview, became the acknowledged leader of the disgruntled neighbors. At first a number of them met in the kitchen at his house; then, as space was lacking for curious newcomers, a mass meeting was held on Thursday in an abandoned theater. His wife and three children sat in the front row. Behind them sat the widow Murphy, Lloyd Dukes, Tyrone Brown, Les Jones — those who had joined him on the first picket line. Behind these sat people who bought occasionally at the store, people who lived on the fringes of the neighborhood, people from other neighborhoods come to investigate the problem, and the merely curious. The middle rows were occupied by a few people from the suburbs, those who had seen the talk show and whose outrage at the grocer proved much more powerful than their fear of black people. In the rear of the theater crowded aging, old-style leftists, somber students, cynical young black men with angry grudges to explain with inarticulate gestures. Leaning against the walls, huddled near the doors at the rear, tape-recorder-bearing social scientists looked as detached and serene as bookies at the track. Here and there, in this diverse crowd, a politician stationed himself, pumping hands vigorously and pressing his palms gently against the shoulders of elderly people. Other visitors passed out leaflets, buttons, glossy color prints of men who promoted causes, the familiar and obscure. There was a hubbub of voices, a blend of the strident and the playful, the outraged and the reverent, lending an undercurrent of ominous energy to the assembly.

Nelson Reed spoke from a platform on the stage, standing before a yellowed, shredded screen that had once reflected the images of matinee idols. "I don't mind sayin' that I have always been a sucker," he told the crowd. "All my life I have been a sucker for the words of Jesus. Being a natural-born fool, I just ain't never had the *sense* to learn no better. Even right today, while the whole world is sayin' wrong is right and up is down, I'm so dumb I'm *still* steady believin' what is wrote in the Good Book . . ."

From the audience, especially the front rows, came a chorus singing, "Preach!"

"I have no doubt," he continued in a low baritone, "that it's true what is writ in the Good Book: 'The last shall be first and the first shall be last.' I don't know about y'all, but I have *always* been the last. I never wanted to be the first, but sometimes it look like the world get so bad that them that's holdin' onto the tree of life is the onliest ones left when God commence to blowin' dead leafs off the branches."

"Now you preaching," someone called.

In the rear of the theater a white student shouted an awkward "Amen."

Nelson Reed began walking across the stage to occupy the major part of his nervous energy. But to those in the audience, who now hung on his every word, it looked as though he strutted. "All my life," he said, "I have claimed to be a man without earnin' the right to call myself that. You know, the *average* man ain't really a man. The average man is a *boot-licker.* In fact, the *average* man would *run away* if he found hisself standing alone facin' down a adversary. I have done that *too many a time* in my life! But *not no more.* Better to be *once* was than *never* was a man. I will tell you tonight, there is somethin' *wrong* in being average. *I intend to stand up!* Now, if your average man that ain't really a man stand up, two things gonna happen: *One,* he g'on bust through all the weights that been place on his head, and, *two*, he g'on feel a lot of pain. But that same hurt is what make things fall in place. That, and gettin' your hands on one of these slick four-flushers tight enough so's you can squeeze him and say, '*No more!*' You do that, you g'on hurt some, but *you won't be average no more . . .*"

"No *more!*" a few people in the front rows repeated.

"I say *no more!*" Nelson Reed shouted.

"*No more! No more! No more!*" The chant rustled through the crowd like the rhythm of an autumn wind against a shedding tree.

Then people laughed and chattered in celebration.

As for the grocer, from the evening of the television interview he had begun to make plans. Unknown to his wife, he cloistered himself several times with his brother-in-law, an insurance salesman, and plotted a course. He had no intention of tossing steaks to the crowd. "And why should I, Tommy?" he asked his wife's brother, a lean, bald-headed man named Thomas. "I don't cheat anyone. I have never cheated anyone. The businesses I run are always on the up-and-up. So why should I pay?"

"Quite so," the brother-in-law said, chewing an unlit cigarillo. "The world has gone crazy. Next they will say that people in my business are responsible for prolonging life. I have found that people who refuse to believe in death refuse also to believe in the harshness of life. I sell well by saying that death is a long happiness. I show people the realities of life and compare this to a funeral with dignity, *and* the promise of a bundle for every loved one salted away. When they look around hard at life, they usually buy."

"So?" asked Green. Thomas was a college graduate with a penchant for philosophy.

"So," Thomas answered. "You must fight to show these people the reality of both your situation and theirs. How would it be if you visited one of their meetings and chalked out, on a blackboard, the dollars and cents of your operation? Explain your overhead, your security fees, all the additional expenses. If you treat them with respect, they might understand."

Green frowned. "That I would never do," he said. "It would be admission of a certain guilt."

The brother-in-law smiled, but only with one corner of his mouth. "Then you have something to feel guilty about?" he asked.

The grocer frowned at him. "*Nothing!*" he said with great emphasis.

"So?" Thomas said.

This first meeting between the grocer and his brother-in-law took place on Thursday, in a crowded barroom.

At the second meeting, in a luncheonette, it was agreed that the grocer should speak privately with the leader of the group, Nelson Reed. The meeting at which this was agreed took place on Friday afternoon. After accepting this advice from Thomas, the grocer resigned himself to explain to Reed, in as finite detail as possible, the economic structure of his operation. He vowed to suppress no information. He would explain everything: inventories, markups, sale items, inflation, balance sheets, specialty items, overhead, and that mysterious item called profit. This last item, promising to be the most difficult to explain, Green and his brother-in-law debated over for several hours. They agreed first of all that a man should not work for free, then they agreed that it was unethical to ruthlessly exploit. From these parameters, they staked out an area between fifteen and forty percent, and agreed that someplace between these two borders lay an amount of return that could be called fair. This was easy, but then Thomas introduced the factor of circumstance. He questioned whether the fact that one serviced a risky area justified the earning of profits, closer to the forty-percent edge of the scale. Green was unsure. Thomas smiled. "Here is a case that will point out an analogy," he said, licking a cigarillo. "I read in the papers that a family wants to sell an electric stove. I call the home and the man says fifty dollars. I ask to come out and inspect the merchandise. When I arrive I see they are poor, have already bought a new stove that is connected, and are selling the old one for fifty dollars because they want it out of the place. The electric stove is in good condition, worth much more than fifty. But because I see what I see I offer forty-five."

Green, for some reason, wrote down this figure on the back of the sales slip for the coffee they were drinking.

The brother-in-law smiled. He chewed his cigarillo. "The man agrees to take forty-five dollars, saying he has had no other calls. I look at the stove again and see a spot of rust. I say I will give him forty dollars. He agrees to this, on condition that I myself haul it away. I say I will haul it away if he comes down to thirty. You, of course, see where I am going."

The grocer nodded. "The circumstances of his situation, his need to get rid of the stove quickly, placed him in a position where he has little room to bargain?"

"Yes," Thomas answered. "So? Is it ethical, Harry?"

Harold Green frowned. He had never liked his brother-in-law, and now he thought the insurance agent was being crafty. "But," he answered, "this man does not *have* to sell! It is his choice whether to wait for other calls. It is not the fault of the buyer that the seller is in a hurry. It is the right of the buyer to get what he wants at the lowest price possible. That is the rule. That has *always* been the rule. And the reverse of it applies to the seller as well."

"Yes," Thomas said, sipping coffee from the Styrofoam cup. "But suppose that in addition to his hurry to sell, the owner was also of a weak soul. There are, after all, many such people." He smiled. "Suppose he placed no value on the money?"

"Then," Green answered, "your example is academic. Here we are not talking about real life. One man lives by the code, one man does not. Who is there free enough to make a judgment?" He laughed. "Now you see," he told his brother-in-law. "Much more than a few dollars are at stake. If this one buyer is to be condemned, then so are most people in the history of the world. An examination of history provides the only answer to your question. This code will be here tomorrow, long after the ones who do not honor it are not."

They argued fiercely late into the afternoon, the brother-in-law leaning heavily on his readings. When they parted, a little before 5:00 P.M., nothing had been resolved.

Neither was much resolved during the meeting between Green and Nelson Reed. Reached at home by the grocer in the early evening, the leader of the group spoke coldly at first, but consented finally to meet his adversary at a nearby drugstore for coffee and a talk. They met at the lunch counter, shook hands awkwardly, and sat for a few minutes discussing the weather. Then the grocer pulled two gray ledgers from his briefcase. "You have for years come into my place," he told the man. "In my memory I have always treated you well. Now our relationship has come to this." He slid the books along the counter until they touched Nelson Reed's arm.

Reed opened the top book and flipped the thick green pages with his thumb. He did not examine the figures. "All I know," he said, "is over at your place a can of soup cost me fifty-five cents, and two miles away at your other store for white folks you chargin' thirty-nine cents." He said this with the calm authority of an outraged soul. A quality of condescension tinged with pity crept into his gaze.

The grocer drummed his fingers on the countertop. He twisted his head and looked away, toward shelves containing cosmetics, laxatives, toothpaste. His eyes lingered on a poster of a woman's apple red lips and milk white teeth. The rest of the face was missing.

"Ain't no use to hide," Nelson Reed said, as to a child. "*I* know you wrong, *you* know you wrong, and before I finish, *everybody in this city* g'on know you wrong. God don't *like* ugly." He closed his eyes and gripped the cup of coffee. Then he swung his head suddenly and faced the grocer again. "Man, why you want to *do* people that way?" he asked. "We human, same as you."

"Before *God!*" Green exclaimed, looking squarely into the face of Nelson Reed. "Before God!" he said again. "*I am not an evil man!*" These last words sounded more like a moan as he tightened the muscles in his throat to lower the sound of his voice. He tossed his left shoulder as if adjusting the sleeve of his coat, or as if throwing off some unwanted weight. Then he peered along the countertop. No one was watching. At the end of the counter the waitress was scrubbing the coffee urn. "Look at these figures, please," he said to Reed.

The man did not drop his gaze. His eyes remained fixed on the grocer's face.

"All right," Green said. "Don't look. I'll tell you what is in these books, believe me if you want. I work twelve hours a day, one day off per week, running my business in three stores. I am not a wealthy person. In one place, in the area you call white, I get by barely by smiling lustily at old ladies, stocking gourmet stuff on the chance I will build a reputation as a quality store. The two clerks there cheat me; there is nothing I can do. In this business you must be friendly with everybody. The second place is on the other side of town, in a neighborhood as poor as this one. I get out there seldom. The profits are not worth the gas. I use the loss there as a write-off against some other properties," he paused. "Do you understand write-off?" he asked Nelson Reed.

"Naw," the man said.

Harold Green laughed. "What does it matter?" he said in a tone of voice intended for himself alone. "In this area I will admit I make a profit, but it is not so much as you think. But I do not make a profit here because the people are black. I make a profit because a profit is here to be made. I invest more here in window bars, theft losses, insurance, spoilage; I deserve to make more here than at the other places." He looked, almost imploringly, at the man seated next to him. "You don't accept this as the right of a man in business?"

Reed grunted. "Did the bear shit in the woods?" he said.

Again Green laughed. He gulped his coffee awkwardly, as if eager to go. Yet his motions slowed once he had set his coffee cup down on the blue plastic saucer. "Place yourself in *my* situation," he said, his voice high and tentative. "If *you* were running my store in this neighborhood, what would be *your* position? Say on a profit scale of fifteen to forty percent, at what point in between would you draw the line?"

Nelson Reed thought. He sipped his coffee and seemed to chew the liquid. "Fifteen to forty?" he repeated.

"Yes."

"I'm a churchgoin' man," he said. "Closer to fifteen than to forty."

"How close?"

Nelson Reed thought. "In church you tithe ten percent."

"In restaurants you tip fifteen," the grocer said quickly.

"All right," Reed said. "Over fifteen."

"How much over?"

Nelson Reed thought.

"Twenty, thirty, thirty-five?" Green chanted, leaning closer to Reed. Still the man thought.

"Forty? Maybe even forty-five or fifty?" the grocer breathed in Reed's ear. "In the supermarkets, you know, they have more subtle ways of accomplishing such feats."

Reed slapped his coffee cup with the back of his right hand. The brown liquid swirled across the countertop, wetting the books. "*Damn this!*" he shouted.

Startled, Green rose from his stool.

Nelson Reed was trembling. "I ain't *you*," he said in a deep baritone. "I ain't the *supermarket* neither. All I is is a poor man that works *too* hard to see his pay slip through his fingers like rainwater. All I know is you done *cheat* me, you done *cheat* everybody in the neighborhood, and we organized now to get some of it *back!*" Then he stood and faced the grocer. "My daddy sharecropped down in Mississippi and bought in the company store. He owed them twenty-three years when he died. I paid off five of them years and then run away to up here. Now, I'm a deacon in the Baptist church. I raised my kids the way my daddy raise me and don't bother nobody. Now come to find out, after all my runnin', they done lift that *same company store* up out of Mississippi and slip it down on us here! Well, my daddy was a *fighter*, and if he hadn't owed all them years he would of raise him some hell. Me, I'm steady my daddy's child, plus I got seniority in my union. I'm a free man. Buddy, don't you know *I'm gonna raise me some hell!*"

Harold Green reached for a paper napkin to sop the coffee soaking into his books.

Nelson Reed threw a dollar on top of the books and walked away.

"I *will not* do it!" Harold Green said to his wife that same evening. They were in the bathroom of their home. Bending over the face bowl, she was washing her hair with a towel draped around her neck. The grocer stood by the door, looking in at her. "I will not bankrupt myself tomorrow," he said.

"I've been thinking about it, too," Ruth Green said, shaking her wet hair. "You'll do it, Harry."

"Why should I?" he asked. "You won't leave. You know it was a bluff. I've waited this long for you to calm down. Tomorrow is Saturday. This week has been a hard one. Tonight let's be realistic."

"Of course you'll do it," Ruth Green said. She said it the way she would say "Have some toast." She said, "You'll do it because you want to see your children grow up."

"And for what other reason?" he asked.

She pulled the towel tighter around her neck. "Because you are at heart a moral man."

He grinned painfully. "If I am, why should I have to prove it to *them?*"

"Not them," Ruth Green said, freezing her movements and looking in the mirror. "Certainly not them. By no means them. They have absolutely nothing to do with this."

"Who, then?" he asked moving from the door into the room. "Who else should I prove something to?"

His wife was crying. But her entire face was wet. The tears moved secretly down her face.

"Who else?" Harold Green asked.

It was almost 11:00 P.M. and the children were in bed. They had also cried when they came home from school. Ruth Green said, "For yourself, Harry. For the love that live inside your heart."

All night the grocer thought about this.

Nelson Reed also slept little that Friday night. When he returned home from the drugstore, he reported to his wife as much of the conversation as he could remember. At first he had joked about the exchange between himself and the grocer, but as more details returned to his conscious mind he grew solemn and then bitter. "He ask me to put myself in *his* place," Reed told his wife. "Can you imagine that kind of gumption? I never cheated nobody in my life. All my life I have lived on Bible principles. I am a deacon in the church. I have worked all my life for other folks and I don't even own the house I live in." He paced up and down the kitchen, his big arms flapping loosely at his sides. Betty Reed sat at the table, watching. "This here's a low-down, ass-kicking world," he said. "I swear to God it is! All my life I have lived on principle and I ain't got a dime in the bank. Betty," he turned suddenly toward her, "don't you think I'm a fool?"

"Mr. Reed," she said. "Let's go on to bed."

But he would not go to bed. Instead, he took the fifth of bourbon from the cabinet under the sink and poured himself a shot. His wife refused to join him. Reed drained the glass of whiskey, and then another, while he resumed pacing the kitchen floor. He slapped his hands against his sides. "*I* think I'm a fool," he said. "Ain't got a dime in the bank, ain't got a pot to *pee* in or a wall to pitch it over, and that there *cheat* ask me to put myself inside *his* shoes. Hell, I can't even *afford* the kind of shoes he wears." He stopped pacing and looked at his wife.

"Mr. Reed," she whispered, "tomorrow ain't a work day. Let's go to bed."

Nelson Reed laughed, the bitterness in his voice rattling his wife. "The *hell* I will!" he said.

He strode to the yellow telephone on the wall beside the sink and began to dial. The first call was to Lloyd Dukes, a neighbor two blocks away and a lieutenant in the organization. Dukes was not at home. The second call was to McElroy's Bar on the corner of 65th and Carroll, where Stanley Harper, another of the lieutenants, worked as a bartender. It was Harper who spread the word, among those men at the bar, that the organization would picket the grocer's store the following morning. And all through the night, in the bedroom of their house, Betty Reed was awakened by telephone calls coming from Lester Jones, Nat Lucas, Mrs. Tyrone Brown, the widow-woman named Murphy, all coordinating the time when they would march in a group against the store owned by Harold Green. Betty Reed's heart beat loudly beneath the covers as she listened to the bitterness and rage in her husband's voice. On several occasions, hearing him declare himself a fool, she pressed the pillow against her eyes and cried.

The grocer opened later than usual this Saturday morning, but still it was early enough to make him one of the first walkers in the neighborhood. He parked his car one block from the store and strolled to work. There were no birds singing. The sky in this area was not blue. It was smog-smutted and gray, seeming on the verge of a light rain. The street, as always, was littered with cans, papers, bits of broken glass. As always the garbage cans overflowed. The morning breeze plastered a sheet of newspaper playfully around the sides of a rusted garbage can. For some reason, using his right foot, he loosened the paper and stood watching it slide into the street and down the block. The movement made him feel good. He whistled while unlocking the bars shielding the windows and door of his store. When he had unlocked the main door he stepped in quickly and threw a switch to the right of the jamb, before the shrill sound of the alarm could shatter his mood. Then he switched on the lights. Everything was as it had been the night before. He had already telephoned his two employees and given them the day off. He busied himself doing the usual things — hauling milk and vegetables from the cooler, putting cash in the till — not thinking about the silence of his wife, or the look in her eyes, only an hour before when he left home. He had determined, at some point while driving through the city, that today it would be business as usual. But he expected very few customers.

The first customer of the day was Mrs. Nelson Reed. She came in around 9:30 A.M. and wandered about the store. He watched her from the checkout counter. She seemed uncertain of what she wanted to buy. She kept glancing at him down the center aisle. His suspicions aroused, he said finally, "Yes, may I help you, Mrs. Reed?" His words caused her to jerk, as if some devious thought had been perceived going through her mind. She reached over quickly and lifted a loaf of whole wheat bread from the rack and walked with it to the counter. She looked at him and smiled. The smile was a broad, shy one, that rare kind of smile one sees on virgin girls when they first confess love to themselves. Betty Reed was a woman of about forty-five. For some reason he could not comprehend, this gesture touched him. When she pulled a dollar from her purse and laid it on the counter, an impulse, from no place he could locate with his mind, seized control of his tongue. "Free," he told Betty Reed. She paused, then pushed the dollar toward him with a firm and determined thrust of her arm. "Free," he heard himself saying strongly, his right palm spread and meeting her thrust with absolute force. She clutched the loaf of bread and walked out of his store.

The next customer, a little girl, arriving well after 10:30 A.M., selected a candy bar from the rack beside the counter. "Free," Green said cheerfully. The little girl left the candy on the counter and ran out of the store.

At 11:15 A.M. a wino came in looking desperate enough to sell his soul. The grocer watched him only for an instant. Then he went to the wine counter and selected a half-gallon of medium-grade red wine. He shoved the jug into the belly of the wino, the man's sour breath bathing his face. "Free," the grocer said. "But you must not drink it in here."

He felt good about the entire world, watching the wino through the window gulping the wine and looking guiltily around.

At 11:25 A.M. the pickets arrived.

Two dozen people, men and women, young and old, crowded the pavement in front of his store. Their signs, placards, and voices denounced him as a parasite. The grocer laughed inside himself. He felt lighthearted and wild, like a man drugged. He rushed to the meat counter and pulled a long roll of brown wrapping paper from the rack, tearing it neatly with a quick shift of his body resembling a dance step practiced fervently in his youth. He laid the paper on the chopping block and with the black-inked, felt-tipped marker scrawled, in giant letters, the word FREE. This he took to the window and pasted in place with many strands of Scotch tape. He was laughing wildly. "Free!" he shouted from behind the brown paper. "Free! Free! Free! Free! Free! Free!" He rushed to the door, pushed his head out, and screamed to the confused crowd, "*Free!*" Then he ran back to the counter and stood behind it, like a soldier at attention.

They came in slowly.

Nelson Reed entered first, working his right foot across the dirty tile as if tracking a squiggling worm. The others followed: Lloyd Dukes dragging a placard, Mr. and Mrs. Tyrone Brown, Stanley Harper walking with his fists clenched, Lester Jones with three of his children, Nat Lucas looking sheepish and detached, a clutch of winos, several bashful nuns, ironic-smiling teenagers and a few students. Bringing up the rear was a bearded social scientist holding a tape recorder to his chest. "Free!" the grocer screamed. He threw up his arms in a gesture that embraced, or dismissed, the entire store, "*All free!*" he shouted. He was grinning with the grace of a madman.

The winos began grabbing first. They stripped the shelf of wine in a matter of seconds. Then they fled, dropping bottles on the tile in their wake. The others, stepping quickly through this liquid, soon congealed it into a sticky, blood-like consistency. The young men went for the cigarettes and luncheon meats and beer. One of them had the prescience to grab a sack from the counter, while the others loaded their arms swiftly, hugging cartons and packages of cold cuts like long-lost friends. The students joined them, less for greed than for the thrill of the experience. The two nuns backed toward the door. As for the older people, men and women, they stood at first as if stuck to the wine-smeared floor. Then Stanley Harper, the bartender, shouted, "The man said *free*, y'all heard him." He paused. "Didn't you say *free* now?" he called to the grocer.

"I said free," Harold Green answered, his temples pounding.

A cheer went up. The older people began grabbing, as if the secret lusts of a lifetime had suddenly seized command of their arms and eyes. They grabbed toilet tissue, cold cuts, pickles, sardines, boxes of raisins, boxes of starch, cans of soup, tins of tuna fish and salmon, bottles of spices, cans of boned chicken, slippery cans of olive oil. Here a man, Lester Jones, burdened himself with several heads of lettuce, while his wife, in another aisle, shouted for him to drop those small items and concentrate on the gourmet section. She herself took imported sardines, wheat crackers, bottles of candied pickles, herring, anchovies, imported olives, French wafers, an ancient, half-rusted can of pâté, stocked, by mistake, from the inventory of another store. Others packed their arms with detergents, hams, chocolate-coated cereal, whole chickens with hanging asses, wedges of bologna and salami like squashed footballs, chunks of cheeses, yellow and white, shriveled onions, and green peppers. Mrs. Tyrone Brown hung a curve of pepperoni around her neck and seemed to take on instant dignity, much like a person of noble birth in possession now of a long sought-after gem. Another woman, the widow Murphy, stuffed tomatoes into her bosom, holding a half-chewed lemon in her mouth. The more enterprising fought desperately over the three rusted shopping carts, and the victors wheeled these along the narrow aisles, sweeping into them bulk items — beer in six-packs, sacks of sugar, flour, glass bottles of syrup, toilet cleanser, sugar cookies, prune, apple and tomato juices — while others endeavored to snatch the carts from them. There were several fistfights and much cursing. The grocer, standing behind the counter, hummed and rang his cash register like a madman.

Nelson Reed, the first into the store, followed the nuns out, empty-handed.

In less than half an hour the others had stripped the store and vanished in many directions up and down the block. But still more people came, those late in hearing the news. And when they saw the shelves were bare, they cursed soberly and chased those few stragglers still bearing away goods. Soon only the grocer and the social scientist remained, the latter stationed at the door with his tape recorder sucking in leftover sounds. Then he too slipped away up the block.

By 12:10 P.M. the grocer was leaning against the counter, trying to make his mind slow down. Not a man given to drink during work hours, he nonetheless took a swallow from a bottle of wine, a dusty bottle from beneath the wine shelf, somehow overlooked by the winos. Somewhat recovered, he was preparing to remember what he should do next when he glanced toward a figure at the door. Nelson Reed was standing there, watching him.

"All gone," Harold Green said. "My friend, Mr. Reed, there is no more." Still the man stood in the doorway, peering into the store.

The grocer waved his arms about the empty room. Not a display case had a single item standing. "All gone," he said again, as if addressing a stupid child. "There is nothing left to get. You, my friend, have come back too late for a second load. I am cleaned out."

Nelson Reed stepped into the store and strode toward the counter. He moved through wine-stained flour, lettuce leaves, red, green, and blue labels, bits and pieces of broken glass. He walked toward the counter.

"All day," the grocer laughed, not quite hysterically now, "all day long I have not made a single cent of profit. The entire day was a loss. This store, like the others, is *bleeding* me." He waved his arms about the room in a magnificent gesture of uncaring loss. "Now do you understand?" he said. "Now will you put yourself in my shoes? I have nothing here. Come, now, Mr. Reed, would it not be so bad a thing to walk in my shoes?"

"Mr. Green," Nelson Reed said coldly. "My wife bought a loaf of bread in here this mornin'. She forgot to pay you. I, myself, have come here to pay you your money."

"Oh," the grocer said.

"I think it was brown bread. Don't that cost more than white?"

The two men looked away from each other, but not at anything in the store.

"In my store, yes," Harold Green said. He rang the register with the most casual movement of his finger. The register read fifty-five cents.

Nelson Reed held out a dollar.

"And two cents tax," the grocer said.

The man held out the dollar.

"After all," Harold Green said. "We are all, after all, Mr. Reed, in debt to the government."

He rang the register again. It read fifty-seven cents.

Nelson Reed held out a dollar.

Backwacking, a Plea to the Senator

by Ralph Ellison

Braxas, Alabama
April 4th, 1953

To the Right Honorable
Senator Sunraider
Washington, D.C.

Dear Senator Sunraider:

This evening I take my pen in hand to write you our deep appreciation for all the good things you have been doing for this pore beat down country of ours. That Cadillac speech you gave us was straight forward and to the point and much needed saying. So I thank you and my wife Marthy wants to thank you. In fact we both thank you for looking out for folks like us who firmly believe that all this WELFARE the Guv. is shoveling out to the lazy nogooders and freeloaders is something that stinks in the nostril of Heaven worse than a batch of rotten catfish that some unGodly thief has stole and scattered all over Courthouse Square at high noon on the 4th day of July. We are with you Senator because you are a good man. You have done great things for the God-fearing folks of this country and we respect you for it. And as you are one of the very *few* men in Guv. who we can depend on when the going gets real TOUGH I now take the liberty of calling something to your kind attention that is taking place down here in these parts.

I refer to this new type of sinful activity that has cropped up amongst the niggers. It is known as "BACKWACKING," which I am prepared to say under oath is probably one of the most UNGODLY and also UNATURAL activity that anybody has ever yet invented! Senator, it is no less than RADICAL! And so naturally the nigger has been going at it so HARD that he is fast getting out of hand and out of control. Here is what he is doing. HE and his woman have taken to getting undressed and standing back to back and heel to heel, shoulderblade to shoulderblade, and tale to tale with his against her's and her's against his, and then after they have horsed around and manuvered like cats in heat and worked as tight together as a tick to a cow's tit, HE ups and starts in to HAVING AFTER HER BACKWARDS!

Now I know, Senator, that this sounds like he is taking a very roundabout and also mullet-headed path to Robin Hood's barn, but I have it on the most reliable authority that this is exactly how he is going about it. Yessir! The facts have been well established even though I have to admit that on account of he is not only defying common decency but also NATURE, I cannot explain in full detail just *how* the nigger is proceeding in this tradition busting business. Because naturally he thinks that he has him a good thing going and is trying to keep the WHITE MAN in the DARK. Even so, I want you to know that ever since it was brought to my attention I been putting a great deal of effort into trying to untangle what he is doing. I have figgered HARD and I have figgered LONG but to date nothing I have come up with seems to fit WHAT he is doing with HOW he is going about it. Neither, I am sad to report, has anybody else. So it appears that once again and after all the trouble we have seen we are being VICTIMIZED by yet another so-called "nigger mystery." It is a crying sin and a dirty shame but once again the nigger has tossed the responsible citizenry of these parts a terrible tough nut to crack. Once again it appears that like the time he came back from Cuba at the end of the Spanish American War and then again when he came back from Paris France after World War I, he is HELLBENT on taking advantage of our good nature. But be that as it may, I hasten to assure you that we down here are not taking it laying down. We are going after him not only with might and main but with foresight and hindsight. And as for me personal, I am doing my level best to bring him to heel and can be counted on to KEEP ON doing it! Senator, you have my word on that. I have known niggers all my life and am well acquainted with smart ones as well as dumb ones, but while heretofore this has been an advantage in many a tight place in my dealings with him, in this particular situation I am forced to admit that I have yet to come across any as backwards-acting as my most reliable information makes these here out to be. Evidently these are of a different breed, because considering that I am a GODFEARING white man in my 80th year if *I* have not heard of this "BACKWACKING" until now it has got to be something NEW! So in my considered opinion it is something that some black rascal has brought in here from somewheres else, probably from up NORTH.

But Senator, wherever this "BACKWACKING" comes from it calls for some ruthless INVESTIGATING and drastic CONTROL! Because not only is the nigger conducting himself in this UNGODLY jiggsawing fashion I have described to you, but there is OVERPOWERING evidence that he is doing it too much for his own or anybody elses good, and I say so for the following reasons. I am informed that when he and his woman reach the climax of this radical new way of sinning they get blasted by one of the *darndest* feelings that has ever been known to hit the likes of Man! My friend says it is like watching somebody being struck down by greased lightening, and he says that when it hits the nigger it is like seeing somebody being knocked down and dragged by an L & N freight train that has been doing a high-ball on a down-hill grade with its brakeshoes busted and with no red light ahead! Yes, sir! It is a mind graveler and a viscious back breaker. He says that watching it work on the black rascal is like seeing somebody get blasted to as close to dying as any normal human being can possibly come and still not die. Like he says this "BACKWACKING" is a real humdinging ripsnorter and a danger to life, limb and social order — only you wouldn't think so if you could see how some who are practicing it are around here strutting and grinning.

Yes, sir, Senator, they are out trying to make some slick nigger propaganda to the point that they had all at once jumped way ahead of the WHITE man! But of course and as we both well know, they are badly mistaken in this regard. Because if the truth be known, all they are doing is setting back their own RACE. There is no doubt about it, because it is a "well established fact" and as I have always held No race can pull itself up by their bootstraps and bring home the bacon that dedicates itself to indulging in such UNATURAL activity as the one these here are messing with. But yet and still and as niggers will, they are going at it like old fashioned common sense has gone plum out of style! Senator, the situation he is creating is no less than critical! And it is right here that we come face to face with the most confounding detail of this "BACKWACKING."

Now you would expect that all this powerful feeling he generates would knock the nigger out, and as I have stated it truly staggers him. It knocks the rascal as limber as a bacon rine that has been boiled in a mess of collards and turns his bones to rubber. Yes, sir! But then an absolutely CONFUSING thing takes place. Like I say, when this feeling strikes the nigger it blasts him so hard that it seems that it has knocked all such nasty notions out of his ignorant head. He goes out like a lantern in a wind storm and you would swear that he was already at the gates of hell, which is shorely where he is headed, yessir! But then it jacks him up, and the next thing you know he comes up with a quick second wind! That is the unGodly truth, Senator, and I'll swear to it. Instead of keeling over and breathing his last or at least taking him a nap, the nigger just lets out a big ole hoop-and-a-holler and leaps back to his position and commences to practicing this "BACKWACKING" again! So when you think about that and all the raw naked POWER he lets loose it is my firm opinion that this "BACKWACKING" must do no less than throw him into some new kind of TRANCE. Something about this new way of sinning he is practicing simply takes the rascal OVER. Otherwise I ask you how is it that as soon as he uses up his second-wind — which takes him a full five minutes longer by a good stop-watch — according to my friend he right away "BACKWACKS" his way into a third and then into a fourth and *fifth* wind? So it stands to reason that nothing less than a TRANCE can explain it, therefore I must stand on that. It simply has to be what happens, especially since he has been known to keep on going in this fashion until he is vibrating like a sheet-tin roof in a wind storm and his petered-out woman is wore plumb down to a slam-banging *frazzel!*

Senator, after observing this disgraceful business on several occasions, my friend holds that it is a crying pity and a down-right shame that it don't just knock the nigger out of commission the first shot out of the box, and I wholeheartedly agree. Because if this "BACKWACKING" was to kill off a few of the ornery ones who is practicing it this thing would be brought to a quick and abrupt conclusion. After that the rest of the niggers would sober up to the firmly grounded truth of the proposition which states that "No Race can prosper or long endure" that devotes itself to going against NATURE like these down here have been doing. Therefore they would go back and devote themselves to conducting their business in the old fashion way they was taught by the WHITE man back there in slavery.

Now mind you Senator, I say that that is the proposition the nigger OUGHT to be living by, but this being a new day and age, and one in which he has lost all sense of direction, he is NOT. Instead he is coming up daily with all KINDS of new minds and new notions, most of them nasty, radical and UNGODLY. So with the nigger continuing on his "BACKWACKING" rampage it is most unfortunate that some of the most responsible citizens in these parts are dying off while some of the rest have given up the struggle and grown discouraged. Some are even thinking about migrating to Australia! And only the other day a friend of mine was even talking about moving to South Africa, just to get away from some of the outrages taking place down here. He's ready to cut bait and run! "Let the nigger take over, and get out while the getting is good," he says "That's what I'm thinking, Just let him have it, lock, stock, barrel and gatepost, because that's exactly what he's out to do. One way or another, either by hook, or by crook or sinning, he means to seize control. So I'm going somewhere a WHITE man still has a chance to live in peace." That is what he says and he's from one of the finest old families in these parts. Yessir, that's just how pessimistic some folks have come to feel. But fortunately folks like my friend are in the minority and I hasten to assure you Senator that all is not lost, no sir! Not by a long shot. Because while a few have let themselves become discouraged and intimidated by this recent rash of nigger outrages a determined VANGUARD remains on the firing line and is putting up a firm resistance. And for this I say "Praise the LORD!" as there is a growing concern that if the nigger ain't soon checked and returned to his proper balance — and I mean by any means NECESSARY — or if he don't just naturally run out of gas on his own accord, he will keep on plunging down this unatural path he is on until he is out on the street grabbing and "BACKWACKING" each and every female woman he can lay his corrupted eyes on. Such is the terrible prospect we face in a nutshell.

So it is my considered opinion that we are confronted by a crisis the likes of which we haven't had to face since back in 1918 when the nigger come home trying to talk and act like French men. Therefore I have tried to the best of my ability to give you a clear and accurate picture of our situation. What we actually have down here is not only a serious threat to our orderly society but we are in the middle of something that can best be described as a "clear and present danger"! I insist on that, Senator, and it is a danger that threatens *everybody*, including the nigger, who seems bent on no less than downright self-annihilation! And what makes our predicament so untenable is the fact that the nigger is so sly and *devious*. He knows we're watching him so he's coming up with all kinds of "diversionary tactics." But while we have yet to discover what he is sneaking around eating and drinking in order to do what he is doing and while he is keeping his hand well hid, down here in Alabama his offenses to common decency is causing a terrible stir. Senator, our backs are against the wall and our nerves are on edge and our patience is running thin. And it is doing it so *fast* that I tell you confidential that all this "backwacking" he is doing has got our STORM WARNINGS up. By which I mean to say that this latest of many aggravating "nigger mysteries," grievous offenses, and attacks on moral integrity and clean living has got folks so flustered and upset that they are beginning to cry out loud for some RELIEF! So Senator it is in their name as well as my own that I am calling upon you to hurry down here with a committee of your best people and INVESTIGATE! We are calling upon you because from your Cadillac speech the other day we are firmly convinced that you are the ONE for the role. You have the "intestinal fortitude" to do what needs to be done and you have the authority to SEE that it is done. So please heed our plea. Because even if what the nigger is up to wasn't against NATURE, which it simply has to be, there is no question but that he is going both against the BIBLE and against our most hallowed tradition and therefore what he is doing calls for the firm and unyielding hand of the LAW!

Senator, the above constitutes our unhappy bill of particulars, and as I appreciate that you are a busy man I beg pardon for taking up so much of your precious time. But please understand that our situation is DESPERATE and we call upon your aid because you are one of the few that truly stands for LAW AND ORDER and really looks out for the welfare of the good WHITE people, who as I have tried to make crystal clear, are once again being sorely tried and tested. So in closing both me and

Marthy thank you in advance for your kind consideration and look
forward to the time when we will once again be safe and at peace with
our fine and honorable tradition and our straightforward way of doing
things. We wish you a long life and the best of everything, and we hope
and pray that you will soon find time to lay the firm hand of the law
on this "BACKWACKING" and bring it to a teeth-rattling HALT! Just look
into the nigger is all we ask, and GOD BLESS.

Respectfully Yrs.

Norm A. Mauler

A CONCERN CITIZEN

THEM AND US

The Woman Who Would Eat Flowers

by Colleen McElroy

CORA KAY waited until the old woman moved the broom a whisper away from her big toe before she yelled, "Don't be sweeping my feet! That broom mess my feet up from where I was going."

Kei-Shee mumbled something that probably sounded like "Shade-down," or "Chinatown," to most folks in the Flats, but Cora Kay's ear had been trained to understand a few Chinese phrases, and she knew when she'd heard one of those curses Kei-Shee muttered whenever she had the chance. That chance didn't happen very often, because it wasn't very often that Wu Yeung Lee allowed his mother to come out of the kitchen. In this respect, he was a good son, and she, obedient as any old-world Chinese woman, never entered the front part of Wu Fong's Eatery without her son's permission. In fact, through three generations of Chinese owners, none of the black folks in the Flats had seen any of the Chinese women waiting tables in Wu Fong's. Retired railroad men told stories about how their fathers had not seen old man Wu Fong's wife in the front of the restaurant when Wu Fong himself ran the place. Only men had waited tables until 1946, when Wu Fong's grandson, Wu Yeung Lee, hired Cora Ivory. Cora Kay had made the front of the Eatery her domain, and as she sat there, watching Yeung Lee's mother sweep the floor with a heavy straw broom, Cora Kay Ivory exercised her reign over this kingdom.

"You can just swallow that spit," she told the old woman. "You think I don't know what *shyä-dan* means? I ain't no lazy chicken, or whatever it is you be saying under your breath. And I ain't gone sit here and let you sweep me into my grave with that broom neither."

The old woman looked up and grinned, her one ragged tooth hanging like a loose nail from the top of her mouth.

"You know what I'm talking bout, don't you?" Cora Kay shouted.

Kei-Shee began swinging the broom back and forth as if she were getting ready to dance by swaying to the music. She moved closer to Cora Kay, swaying and grinning, the broom hissing against the wooden floor like the swish of a ball gown. Even though Kei-Shee had no ball gowns to remember, she remembered the brothel in San Francisco where she'd been trapped until, at eighteen, Yeung Lee's father had found her. And if she thought about the music of Chinatown streets, its nightlife similar to the stingy row of cafes and jook joints on either side of Wu Fong's Eatery, she could not stop her memories. But Cora Kay's knowledge of street life was too recent, so she did not move. There was nothing in Kei-Shee's muttered oaths that would have made Cora Kay budge. Moving would not enter her mind until the wall clock reached 4:00 P.M., which was when she was officially bound to begin waiting tables. Even then, nothing moved Cora Kay if she didn't want to move — a trait she kept intact until she encountered a skinny little hobo named Clarence Henry, but that was yet to be. At the time, Cora Kay was about the business of polishing her nails, and the notion of pulling her body from its slumped position was no more a part of this ritual than sweeping floors was a part of waiting tables.

Cora Kay watched Kei-Shee and cast a few oaths of her own. "You can grin all you want to, old lady, but if you come near me with that broom, I'm gone make you a picture up on that wall, you hear me?"

Kei-Shee made the sound of a broom singing to itself — "Säu, säu" — her eyes glittering as she moved closer to Cora Kay's feet. "Don't be sweeping my feet," Cora Kay warned her again.

The old woman did a little hop-step and turned within inches of Cora Kay. The broom went back and forth, back and forth, and on its third swing, the one that most certainly would have made contact with its target, Cora Kay picked up a soy bowl of salt and flung it across the room — not at the old lady, but not away from her either.

The kitchen doors slammed open. Yeung Lee stood there, his machete knife already slick with a coating of duck grease. He glared first at his mother posed stock-still in the center of the floor, the broom frozen midway in its downswing, then at Cora Kay, languishing in the third booth from the door. Neither woman acknowledged him until Yeung Lee yelled, "Mü-chin! Hwēi-chyu!"

The old woman nodded to her son and began shuffling toward the kitchen, dragging the broom behind her. When she reached the door, she turned and said, "Dzäi-djän."

Cora Kay stuck out her tongue. "So long yourself, you old bat."

Then she turned her frown on Yeung Lee. Although his lip curled once, he said nothing. But in the space of that look, the two of them wrestled with what little understanding they had growing between them. After a few moments, Yeung Lee marched back to the kitchen, cursing as he entered — his queue unleashed from its usual nest under his hat and quivering against his back. Cora Kay returned to the task of lacquering her nails. Seconds later, Yeung Lee's daughter, Tea Rose, resumed the sweeping her grandmother had abandoned. In the doorway, Kei-Shee waited to see what went on between her granddaughter and Cora Kay. She could have saved herself the trouble. Both girls set their expressions to appear as if they were alone in the room.

Tea Rose melted into the broom, its sweeping consuming all of her attention. She was a plump girl, about as old as Cora Kay, with a round face sharpened by the pinched set of her mouth and downcast eyes. Cora Kay was surprised at how the girl seemed to straddle two worlds. The way Tea Rose walked, like her speech, belonged to Kei-Shee, not the Flats, yet when she was out of Kei-Shee's sight, Tea Rose could be as much a part of the Strip as Cora Kay. Still Cora Kay was always amazed at how the girl scuttled away from the center of things. The day Cora Kay had moved into the spare room in the crook of the upstairs hallway, Tea Rose had stood just outside the door. At first, Cora Kay did not realize the girl was there. Then she'd seen a shadow, a movement like a falling leaf, or a cockroach hovering on the other side of the doorjamb. Cora Kay hated roaches, so she'd waited to squash the bug, the shoe in her hand raised at just the right level to make contact before the thing sensed danger. Nothing else moved, and as Cora Kay was about to relax, Tea Rose spoke. "You come live here?" Tea Rose had asked. "Your mama come live here?"

"I ain't saying nothing till you out from behind that door," Cora Kay had told her. But the girl had sidled down the hall.

The next chance she'd had to talk to Tea Rose was while the girl cleaned the hallway. Without breaking her rhythm of wiping down the walls with a damp rag, Tea Rose had asked her, "What name you have for papers?" Cora Kay had told her. The rag had slapped the wall once, twice, before Tea Rose had tried repeating the name. "Don't like that," she'd said finally. "That name only one you speak?" Cora Kay had shrugged. The rag had slapped-slapped, louder this time.

"My mama calls me Cinnamon," Cora Kay had said. "It's cause of my coloring. But she the onliest one I allow to call me that."

Tea Rose had begun to rinse the rag. "Sēn-nà-mēn," she'd said, moving to a new section of the wall. "Don't like that," she'd said, and once more, slammed the rag into action. "I call you Hoisin. Chinese spice. Hoisin same brown-red, like you. I say Hoisin." The rag had echoed the name as Tea Rose worked her way down the hall.

"Chile's always cleaning," Cora Kay told herself. *"Moving like one of them church folk who seen the spirit and can't speak up right."*

Not speaking up was hardly one of Cora Kay's faults. Even the act of blow-drying her newly applied nail polish was a form of speech, each puff a challenge to whatever thoughts anyone might harbor about assigning her to sweep the floor. Cora Kay blew two puffs of air on each nail, then extended her hands to gaze upon the perfection of her rust-brown fingers, their coral-red tips the same shade of polish Tea Rose would secretly spread on her toenails later that night. Cora Kay repeated the blow-drying process until each fingernail received some ten puffs of air, but as Yeung Lee had found out by the end of the first week of her employment, she'd still spend the next several hours of work avoiding any direct contact between fingertips and dishes of food. Some nights, her fear of ruining her nails drove her into making Tea Rose place the orders on a tray, then forcing the customers to pluck their own food from tray to table.

Now, as Tea Rose swept, Kei-Shee lurked in the doorway and clicked her tongue in disapproval of both girls. The old woman hunkered there until the minute hand made its usual little jump-click sixty seconds before the hour, then she turned back to the kitchen. Just as the clock pinged its first count of four, Cora Kay pulled herself away from the booth. Strolling toward the front door, she dropped the bottle of nail polish into Tea Rose's cupped hand. Tea Rose closed her fingers over the gift, flicked her pile of dust under the nearest booth, and scuttled into the kitchen without looking once at Cora Kay, who had already reached for the CLOSED/OPEN sign stuck in a corner of the front window. On the fourth chime of the hour, she flipped the sign, announcing Wu Fong's was ready for business. Then Cora Kay Ivory turned her back on all who entered.

Turning her back was how Cora Kay had learned to deal with the narrow little world of the Flats, and in the execution of that act, she fit right into the pattern of Wu Fong's Eatery. Wu Yeung Lee and his family had become masters at being both a party to, yet outside of the crumbling district of tar-paper shacks, tenements, and factories, interrupted by a sprinkling of bars, jook joints, and cheap stores that spread across the flatlands into a neighborhood of sorts — all of it belted together by the skinny street known as the Strip. Yeung Lee, like his grandfather, Wu Fong, held a thriving business for black folks who the law said couldn't eat in the same place as white folks. Everyone knew they'd all get the same service at Wu Fong's, regardless of their color. But while everyone knew the street side of Wu Fong's Eatery, few people knew the folks inside the restaurant.

Like most of those who lived in that part of town, Yeung Lee and his family had earned their living from the railroad at one time or another. In the 1800s, when the railroad was being built, Yeung Lee's grandfather, one of the few Mandarin Chinese to come West, had been a cook for the Chinese workers the railroad company had refused to feed, as it had done so willingly for their white co-workers. Later, when the company bosses ordered Wu Fong to cook for the bucket brigade of black men hauling stones from Cobbler's Creek, he'd fed them as well. And when the railroad finally had finished laying the east-west track cross-country, the occasion for that famous picture of the hookup of tracks at the California-Nevada border, publicity did not include the Chinese or black workers who'd labored for the companies. Company policy had split those men into racial groups as clearly as the tracks had split the land. Cora Kay didn't know it, but her grandfather, who had worked in the train yards most of his sixty-one years of life, had been one of the men fed by Wu Fong. And his son, Cora Kay's father, had died following an accident in the yards. After that, Cora Kay and her mother had lived in one of the shanties at the edge of the tracks, where hoboes had been setting up camp since the Great Depression.

In those days, black men headed north the way geese traveled the migratory patterns into Canada, but unlike the geese, those men had no intention of returning to the breeding grounds south of the Mason-Dixon. Some left home in the rickety wooden Jim Crow part of the train, the only part colored people were allowed to ride. Others traveled as best they could, grabbing a passing train like the wind grabbed the sound clacking in its wheels. And for the women in the shanties, those men often represented their tickets out of town. When Cora Kay was sixteen, her mother had given her a choice.

"Cinnamon, ain't nothing here for us," she'd said. "Ain't no needa staying here listening to them trains come and go when we could be the ones doing the going. I got a man wants us to come along to Chi-town. Come with me, Cinnamon. Come with me, baby girl."

But Cora Kay had chosen Wu Fong's — "a steady job where I ain't grabbing holt of no freight car and cooking beans on no tin plate."

"Ain't nothing for you here," her mother had repeated.

"I don't know what's here and what ain't," Cora Kay had told her, "but I don't aim to leave fore I find out."

"Well, you ain't gone find out working for that Chinaman. These white folks ain't gone do nothing but give that Chinaman a hard way to go and a short time to get there. They don't even let them men bring they wives over here. That's how come there ain't nothing but that old woman and that chile working in that Chinaman's restaurant."

After she moved into the room at the top of the stairs, Cora Kay discovered the loss of her mother gave her something in common with Tea Rose, whose mother had been forced to stay behind when Yeung Lee returned to the States following his obligatory trip to China to find a bride. Under immigration laws that made it nearly impossible for a Chinese worker to bring his wife into the country, Yeung Lee had returned with his child, but if the truth be known, he had listed six-year-old Tea Rose as male, and given her the name Hēu-hwēi, or Sorrow. Like Cora Kay, Tea Rose had grown up in the sorrow of the Strip, with its gambling men and hoboes, railroad families and Christians. When she was younger, Tea Rose had fled to the Eatery's roof to escape school and the taunts of children singing, "Chink, Chink. Chinaman, eat dead rats. Chew them up like ginger snaps." From the roof, Tea Rose could watch the orange clay hillside for the first sign of smoke from inbound trains that, her father once told her, might be the one bringing her mother from China. Until her father hired Cora Kay, that view of the train yards had sustained Tea Rose.

"What you looking at that mud hole for?" Cora Kay had asked. "My mother come sometime this track," Tea Rose had answered.

"Don't hold your breath," Cora Kay told her, but when Tea Rose's father sent the two of them to gather day lilies, chrysanthemums, and sweet flower grasses growing in the meadow near the Hodiman Road shantytown, both girls would stare into windows of trains that were slowing down to make the approach to the station. Those outings made Cora Kay pull on the memories of her mother's cooking, and she would include coltsfoot and fireweed in the bundles of herbs she and Tea Rose gathered. Although Cora Kay had brought a large box of ground cinnamon in an effort to teach Yeung Lee and his family how to say her nickname, that box remained untouched on the pantry shelf. But Yeung Lee used the selection of wild herbs she'd picked in the meadow to spice his soups and stews, and in doing so, added another reason to the list of those he'd concocted to rationalize hiring Cora Kay.

Still, some folks on the Strip claimed they never understood the whys-and-wherefores of how Cora Kay came to work at Wu Fong's Eatery, even though everyone knew that, in 1946, Cora Kay had been the first black woman in town employed to work right out front in a business that was not owned by someone who was black.

"She young, but she sho know how to take care of herself," Dee Streeter said. "I spect that come from being raised in shantytown."

Dee was sitting in a booth with LuRaye Turner and Patsy Granger. At least once a week, on those nights when they couldn't bring themselves to go home and cook in a second kitchen after a day full of kitchens out in the Belmont District, the women stopped by Wu Fong's for take-out. They were usually sitting in one of the front booths next to church ladies like Sister Vernida Garrison, the Ladies' Aid president, or Hattie Lou Pritchard, the doctor's wife, both of whom regularly brought Yeung Lee some of their Christian literature to heal the heathen ways they were sure infected the place, along with cockroaches and rats. Aside from spearheading a drive to get the city to tear down the shanties, these family women were among the first customers in the Eatery, and quite often they took it upon themselves to try "talking some sense into Cora Kay."

"Chile, that Chinaman's got you waiting tables every night. Go to school so you can get a good job," Sister Garrison would tell her.

Cora Kay would flick Sister Garrison's order of pork fried rice off the edge of her hip so quickly, rice skittered away from the plate and danced toward the end of the table before bouncing into the woman's ample lap. Cora Kay had no patience with these women. It was their children who'd run her home from school. "Your mama's like the railroad track," they'd laughed. "She been laid from one end of town to the other." They had teased her about what went on in the shanties the same way they'd picked on Tea Rose about being Chinese. So when Cora Kay reached the service window, she'd let Tea Rose know the church ladies had descended by writing the Chinese symbols for "religion-up-come" in the patina of grease covering the counter. In one way or another, those women paid for their cruel offspring.

"Lord, it's a sin and a shame that chile's mama up and left her by herself," Doc Pritchard's wife mumbled, her back teeth grinding sour against the extra dash of Szechwan vinegar Cora Kay had sprinkled on her order of Heavenly Greens. "That chile ain't got but one nerve and no manners," the doctor's wife added.

"And that Chinaman don't pay her enuf for room and board," Dee sniffed. "She got to live upstairs in that back room of his."

"But he do give her a place to stay," Patsy Granger muttered. "Out in Belmont, that white woman didn't even want to give me a room to myself. Said I had to share it with the wet nurse." Then Patsy took another sip of tea and complained about how it was so strong, "it burns clear through your throat like red-eye likker."

"May be a job, but Cora Kay do smell like food all the time," Sister Garrison said. "Garlic and onion. Trashy smells."

"Beats some other smells," the women grunted, all of them inching toward the first twinges of heartburn they'd suffer from that hefty dollop of Mongolian fire oil Tea Rose put in their pepper rice soup.

"That Chinaman don't seem to mind them smells," LuRaye noted, a hint of the devil in her eyes as she burped sweet-and-sour chicken.

The other women said, "Um-hum," and "I hear that," and stared at Cora Kay sauntering between tables, her age almost hidden behind a shabby dress that was permanently stained with the grease of fowl, pork, and fish. Then they turned their attention to the service window, where they could see Kei-Shee and Tea Rose, and behind them, Yeung

Lee chopping onions, chicken, and strips of pork on the butcher's block, his nostrils flaring with anticipation of the cut — the thunk of his machete knife and the gleam in his eyes as sure and definite as anger. That view prompted all sorts of comments about just what might be going on in those rooms at the top of the stairs. Though the women were unwilling to admit it, more than one of them had examined that six foot tall Chinaman with more than food on her mind. They all had noticed how Yeung Lee's eyebrows grew together over the bridge of his nose, like frayed bird wings — "wild like the night owls up in the woods," some said — and how his hair, with its waist-long queue, was black as light trapped in the deepest part of a well. Cora Kay could have told them how Yeung Lee's eyes changed from liquid darkness to smoke, and how his voice was ribbed with silk when he looked up from the storage shed behind the restaurant and called to her while she stood in her bedroom window, the moonlight fashioning her rough cotton shift into a shapely garment. Cora Kay could have told them this if she were of a mind to speak to them. As it was, she simply watched them load their dinner plates with questions.

"You see them eyes?" they whispered. "Them eyes cut right through you," they told each other when they felt him stare at their hips as they slid out of a booth. But more than one woman had tried to provoke a smile that raised the dimples on either side of Yeung Lee's Fu Manchu mustache and goatee, then fantasized herself trapped in a Charlie Chan spy scene, Yeung Lee bargaining for her body with sacks of jade or opium just as some beautiful black man, like James Edwards or Canada Lee, rushed through the door to save her. Their dreams were always cut short by Cora Kay's presentation of the bill.

"Don't give you no time to finish eating," they sniffed. "Always there asking for money, like we trying to get by without paying."

"Honey, that girl just too sloppy. Don't know what no man would see in her."

But if the women were curious, the men were outright baffled. It was a known fact that Wu Yeung Lee's daughter, Tea Rose, was old enough to wait those tables herself. And if Yeung Lee was trying to be so careful about hiding his daughter from their eyes, why hire Cora Kay to tempt them? Others said the reason was as plain as Cora Kay's wide hips and Yeung Lee's roving eye.

"Is you blind?" men like Butler Sykes would cackle. "Take yourself a look at Cora Ivory, then ask why that Chinaman wants her round him."

And his railroad buddies, Maroon-Willie Evans, Lip Wooten, Whitaker Yarrow, and the other men who ran the road, would nod their heads. Like them, Butler Sykes came home for a layover ready to see his woman, and ready for a scam. But like most of the married men, Butler didn't let go of the road just because the train had pulled into the station. Unless his wife caught him, he spent the first hours of his layover with the unmarried men, combing the Strip, and later, coaxing his friends into a little game in the room in back of his wife's funeral home. The problem was the funeral home game usually involved high stakes, and although gambling and women were almost second nature to railroad men, most of them didn't want to lose their entire paychecks on one game. Running the road meant having to sit on their feelings and memories of home until the train pulled in, and they wanted a little something in their pockets once they left that train behind them.

Necessity had taught the men to be careful about separating home and the railroad. When they dressed for work — checking shoes for rundown heels, double-checking facial hair, or checking for the least hint of manly scents that had to be removed before the head conductor finished his white-glove inspection — they'd had to shed all memories of home. To carry that memory past the threshold of the trains was dangerous. One racist remark too many, and home could grab a man's throat and rip it open — "Just come tumbling out fore you can snatch it back," Whitaker Yarrow would say. So while they had to scramble aboard the train, once they were released from duty, they were ready to run a game. Still, nobody played on an empty stomach, and they knew that, next to the chitterlings and collard greens folks loved to buy at Rosie's Bar-B-Q, there wasn't a better place to eat on the down side of town than at the restaurant owned by Wu Fong's grandson.

Maroon-Willie, chowing down at Wu Fong's, would praise Yeung Lee's cooking as he remembered serving under a vicious captain in the Merchant Marines, and how, mid-voyage, he had abandoned ship to escape the captain's wrath, thereby earning the name Maroon. "You sho get your money's worth at the Chinaman's," he'd tell the others. "Ain't like in the Merchant's when you be eating green chicken gizzards, or throwing up food done spoilt past rotten. They oughta have that Chinaman cooking on them boats. Make the Boss Cap'n eat that other slop himself. That's how come I'm running the road. Means I ain't never too far from eating good."

"Food's good, but that woman's got an attitude," Butler said.

"Still it be betta than some offa places," Lip Wooten told him. Lip had been running the road so long — some said before A. Philip Randolph started the Brotherhood of Sleeping Car Porters — that he'd grown gray-haired and bent-back. The other members of the Union protected him because he'd lost his strength, and the use of half of his mouth when he was hit in the face with a blackjack during a railroad strike before the war. They took up the slack when he doubled under the leadweight of a suitcase, or caught flak from white conductors who mimicked his thick-lipped speech.

"We'all ain't jus a membah of the Brothahhood," Lip added. "The Brothahhood be like fam-bily, but we'all still gots ta beg fuh food on that train. So longs ah git mah food heah-ah, don mattuh how Cora Ivory be actin'. See, ah members time when we'all pullup to Sa-town an they say: 'Don serv niggahs back heah-ah.'"

"Yeah, they say that in Chicago," Maroon-Willie nodded. "They say: 'Don't serve niggers here.'"

Whitaker laughed and said, "Well, Maroon, you and Lip shoulda told 'em: That's OK . . . we don't eat 'em neither.'"

Everyone howled at that inside joke, but the laughter died quickly when Whitaker added, "I still don't see why ain't no Chinawomen waiting tables." And until someone like Maroon-Willie said, "Pass me some more of them garlic ribs," they'd all look at the hip-riding tightness of Cora Kay's soiled dress as she leaned over to pick up a tray of dishes from a table. And they dreamed of train stops where fancy women catered to them.

While churchgoers and family folk were among the first round of customers at the Eatery, the railroad men and the rest of the night trade took over the place after dark, when flickering neon lit up the Strip from the Flame Bar's dancing lights at one end, down to the Glass Bar's Seagram's sign blinking at the opposite end. From that time till an hour or so past midnight, Wu Fong's Eatery belonged to the night crowd. And every night, those folks found Yeung Lee at his chopping block, the machete's blade hissing toward its target with unerring accuracy. Every night, while Cora Kay sidled from table to table, her skin most often as oily as the plates she piled on the counter over the sink,

Tea Rose sat in the back room, filling orders and folding dough for fortune cookies, while her grandmother listened to radio tales of the Shadow, the Green Hornet, and the Fat Man. Between episodes, Kei-Shee washed dishes, stirred fresh noodles into the ever-present pot of broth, and checked the bin of rice. At times she muttered some oath to rid the room of spirits, or to warn Yeung Lee of trouble. And even before Clarence Henry showed up, there was plenty of trouble on the Strip that could touch Wu Fong's.

Not that any owner of Wu Fong's had been unfamiliar with trouble. So many shady types had frequented Wu Fong's that the police simply cruised through the restaurant from time to time. It was not uncommon for a family of church folks to watch several tables of gambling men scramble for the side exit, or rush for the pantry in back of the kitchen, where the dim outline of a door was barely visible under a grease-stained bamboo curtain. For the generations of Wu Fong owners, this activity became a sort of stock-in-trade. The old man, Wu Fong himself, had likened it to the days of the Tong gangs back in China. He had neither encouraged nor obstructed this New World version of gangsters. He'd just learned their games, and in some ways, played them better than they had. That was one reason the restaurant had survived. Soon after opening his business, Wu Fong had hung up a scroll painting of a Chinese farm with a grass-writing motto:

> In a land where no rice grows, the man with full baskets
> is the cold wind biting the beggar's coat.

During his gambling days, Wu Fong's baskets were full, and for the white men, gambling with the same odds against the wind, that presented a problem. Gambling was a thin vein that ran through all the railroad men and gold miners, and the year he opened, Wu Fong had tried his hand at a bit of back-room gambling behind the restaurant's kitchen. His luck with cards had doubled his income. "Hit good pü-kē-pái," he'd said. "Dä-djïr-pái." But new money does not go unnoticed, especially in places like the Flats. Wu Fong's luck had almost cost him his life. One day the cops had raided a game and not only had destroyed the back room, but most of the restaurant as well. From that point on, Wu Fong confined his card playing to close friends, and when he did not have outside players, he'd used his family. And so it was that Yeung Lee inherited his grandfather's card luck, a skill he'd passed to Tea

Rose. And it was Tea Rose who perfected Cora Kay's beginner's luck, and later, Clarence Henry's fool's luck.

"Hoisin play low, win lump money," Tea Rose would tell Cora Kay.

They'd practice on Sunday afternoons, when the restaurant closed at ten to accommodate the sensibilities of their Christian neighbors. At first, Tea Rose would come to Cora Kay's room. Later, when Yeung Lee became more comfortable around Cora Kay, he joined their games. He'd move the cards in a fast shuffle that spread them in an even pattern across the table, like the Chinese fan he'd brought from the old country, the one he'd given to Cora Kay a month after she'd come to work for him. He'd move the cards with the same speed as he moved that machete knife. Between games, he'd offer a trick, closing his eyes and saying, "You think one card. I tell you number written that card." No matter what Cora Kay did, Yeung Lee picked the right cared every time.

"We oughta sit in on a real game," Cora Kay told him.

"No, no. I not allowed go play some pü-kē-pái card here."

"We could make some big money," Cora Kay reminded him.

For a moment, his eyes blinked with interest, but he had made his father two promises: He would not gamble, and he would not cut his queue. "Make lump money downstairs," he said, and folded the deck.

"Make lump money downstairs," Tea Rose echoed.

That stubbornness persisted until Tea Rose saw Clarence Henry. In fact, it was Tea Rose who spotted Clarence when he first came in the restaurant. She and her grandmother had a better chance of observing the comings and goings of both the restaurant and the street than Cora Kay did. Kei-Shee, occupying the woman's stool, sat high enough behind the kitchen service window to be in direct line with the front door and the street beyond. If the old woman signaled the approach of the police with, "Um cha hwēi-lai!", Cora Kay would quickly hide the cash box under the bin of fortune cookies, while Tea Rose helped her father open the door for the gamblers to scoot through. All of that was just a simple courtesy. Usually the law was after bigger fish, big-time gamblers like the district boss, John Gionio, who ate at Wu Fong's on a regular basis. The cops really didn't bother to harass the Chinaman, who, after all, was legally forbidden to give testimony in court by reason of a dusty 1800s edict.

"I no Emancipated! Dzēu-chyu!" Yeung Lee would shout when the cops burst through the door. And when the flurry died down, he'd feed them dishes of noodles and rice, and after a decent interval of delay, bow them back to their patrol cars.

But despite the traffic of Gionio and other up-and-coming hoodlums, the regular trade pretty much remained the same, and the service at Wu Fong's was dependable. Yeung Lee's generous bowls of sticky rice, the thin noodles in their broth of chicken feet and ginger, the pungent oxtail stew, or roast duck garnished with turnip roots, broccoli, and the leaves of sweet mustard and dandelion kept folks coming back. But just as Yeung Lee's knife cut-cut on the chopping block, those living above Wu Fong's, including Cora Kay, remained cut off from the world — East or West. And until Clarence Henry showed up, folks took it for granted that Tea Rose would be confined to the back room while Cora Kay waited tables out front.

"What's that Chinaman saying?" the railroad men would ask when Cora Kay served their food while Tea Rose peeked out at them from the kitchen. "He saying it be alright to have colored women working they butts off whilst he hides his own women in that back room?"

Wu Yeung Lee offered no answers, and neither did Cora Ivory. And in a way, Cora Kay made matters worse by ignoring the men.

"Ah spect Cora inna puttin out fuh the Chinee-man," Lip muttered.

"You just mad cause she ain't putting out for you," Maroon said.

"Ah don need it. Mah woman waitin fuh me at home heah-ah."

"Now Lip, where else that ugly woman gone be?" Whitaker asked.

"Don't be funning at Lip. All of y'all mad cause Cora Kay don't pay none of you no attention," Butler reminded the men.

They nodded. Certainly, all of them had tried to put a hit on Cora Kay at one time or another. Nothing seemed to impress her, and though the men boasted of seeing better looking women, all of them agreed that with her single braid of kinky rust-colored hair, thick ankles, and skin dusted a silk brown tinged with the light of an October's sunset, Cora Kay wasn't exactly an ugly woman. Her long legs and wide hips earned her the nickname, "High Pockets," and the men followed the sway of her ass while she waited tables. But none got close enough to do more than watch. The fact was that like any woman who kept herself a mystery, the men couldn't stay away from Cora Kay. So until Clarence Henry tumbled out of that freight car and got himself a room at the Proctor Hotel, where the unmarried railroad men stayed on their layovers, all they could do was keep a close watch on Cora Kay. They should have watched Tea Rose. Clarence Henry did.

The fate that brought Clarence Henry into Wu Fong's Eatery was as straight as the railroad tracks that brought him into town. Everyone knew railroad men were partial to the Chinaman's because of old man Wu Fong had fed their fathers, but they also knew Wu Fong's was one place where it didn't matter if a man was running the road on a job, or running to get away from where he'd been. Clarence Henry was running when he hit town. Butler Sykes spotted Clarence when he and Maroon-Willie were taking a break at the end of a trip. They were standing in the doorway of the train when it slowed down to make the bend where the tracks spread away from the main line on the town side of the hobo camp. Seeing Clarence made Butler elbow Maroon-Willie, and Maroon-Willie inched away from the door to pass the word along so other Brotherhood members could watch out for Clarence once the train was in the yards. That was when Butler swears he saw Cora Kay Ivory romping in a field of wildflowers with somebody wearing a small brocade hat — "a tassel on top like the Chinaman's," Maroon-Willie later offered. Cora Kay and Yeung Lee would have laughed to know the rumors about them were as thick as the egg-drop soup Yeung Lee served at the restaurant every Saturday night, but not everyone trusted what the men claimed they could see from a moving train.

"No, it were sho Cora Kay, and she were a sight," Butler said when the other men questioned him. "Had on one of them long dresses, like the women be wearing when they go to the dances. Cept it was broad daylight, and them weeds and flowers so tall, she couldn't hardly move. And somebody else was with her — though I couldn't rightly tell who."

"Well, I sho caught me a glimpse of something in the field cross from the processing plant. And that Chinaman's car was parked up by a tree over near Hodiman Road," Maroon-Willie added.

"You mean that DeSoto?" Whitaker asked. Butler nodded, but Whitaker shook his head. "Naw, naw . . . can't be."

"Ah heah-ah them Chinee-mans shooes it off like a pistol," Lip said. "Heard that myself," Maroon added. And all the men looked at Yeung Lee with a new bit of understanding glued to their eyes.

Still, Maroon-Willie and Butler had to admit they never had a clear view of whatever was going on in the field, because that was the same moment Butler saw Clarence Henry, limbs thin as a praying mantis', push himself out of a boxcar, and climb the ladder to the roof. Clarence had left that car intent on scrambling across the flatlands toward the town's black section, but when Butler spotted him, slipping two steps ahead of the yard bulls, he'd set Clarence on a straight line into the Black Belt, set him up the way he'd set up other black men who'd fallen off trains looking for work. Of all the railroad men, Butler had more pull than most, not only because his wife, Aleeda Grace, owned the colored funeral home, but also because he was the spokesman for the local Brotherhood Union. Butler's layover hadn't ended before he'd found Clarence a job working from 5:00 A.M. to midnight at the boxer's gym. There, Clarence cleaned up the resin and sweat of would-be prizefighters, white boys who had hopes of knocking the spit out of some black kid who wanted to be a champ like Jack Johnson and Joe Louis. But Clarence wasn't interested in fighting.

"It just be a job," he told Butler and the others when they came back to town that next weekend, and picked him up at the Proctor. "That job do for now, but I got me some plans."

They watched him straighten his square knot, then pull a loose thread into the inside seam of his shirt. It didn't take much for them to figure out where Clarence had bought his duds. On the train, the men hid behind their uniforms the same way Clarence his behind his mop and stacks of towels at the gym, but when there was a need to get dressed up, almost all of the men who lived in the Flats had bought swank clothes from Hoffmeyer's Pawnshop at one time or another. Those clothes helped them lose the leather-tight grins they'd learned to click into place when they boarded the trains, or shined shoes downtown by the courthouse, or chauffered cars in the Belmont District — or like Clarence, stacked towels at the gym. For Clarence, Florsheim shoes had replaced the beat-up work boots he'd been wearing when the men had found him in the train yards, but his one-button, rolled-lapel suit, with peg-legged trousers and jacket nipped at the waist, was, as Butler said, a dollar short and twenty years too late.

"Clarence, my man, peers to me you all dressed up and no one to fuck," Whitaker told him. The other men laughed and pulled themselves taller inside the black tailored pants the railroad bought for them.

But Clarence merely grinned at himself in the peeling mirror of the hotel's chifforobe and said, "Ain't nothing but a little bit for now." Then he smoothed each eyebrow into a velvet arch. "Just you wait and see what this brings me. My hands itching for some cards."

"Well, Slick, you just be sure that itching don't bring you a one-way ride out of town," Butler said.

Clarence kept smiling. "I come in on that train, so I can go out the same way." Then with a hairbrush in each hand, he plastered strands of hair against his skull, his hands moving so rapidly, the brushes crackled against kinky hair as if they were copying the sound of train wheels. The whistle of a southbound train had made Clarence Henry shudder until he was old enough to figure out his worry was just an urging to leave on one of the trains that passed the sharecropper farm his father worked, or closer still to the Louisiana-Arkansas state line, where Clarence finally had jumped a northbound freight after its whistle had roused the urge to move once too often.

"Listen to the man," Maroon-Willie snickered. "He don't know he can leave this town riding in a pine box steada the boxcar."

"And don't think that train gone be waiting for your black butt neither," Butler warned.

"That train wouldn't get nowhere if it wasn't for a colored man named Elijah McCoy," Clarence said.

Lip slapped his knee and hooted. "Thazz right. He the one be invent-ah fuh them steam fits. Call 'em The-Real-Mc-Coy, they do. Then come long them other cullard boys. Them call Winn and Woods, an they make 'em bettah even fore Mc-Coy."

"How you know so much?" Whitaker asked. He was really asking Clarence Henry, but for once, Lip Wooten had answers and he wasn't about to be outdone.

"Ah be readin aftah y'all be talkin," Lip said. "Sa'more cullard boys invent-ah fuh the rail too. Burr an Jackson, an Purvis an . . ."

Clarence interrupted him. "Man, I ain't got no time to be standing here whilst you list all them cats. Less you got somebody inventing fast cards, there's a game out there with my name on it. And in case anybody ask, you can tell 'em my name is Lucky. As the song goes, *I guess*

I'm just a lucky so-and-so." With that, he strutted out of the room and left them to close the door behind him.

As they headed for Wu Fong's, Whitaker told Butler, "You gone help one poor boy too many one of these days."

"Aw, he ain't doing nothing but blowing off steam," Butler said.

"I don't know," Whitaker muttered. "I seen boys acting half that bad jump up in your face asking for death."

With as much traveling as Whitaker had done on the railroad, he had reason to be suspicious of drifters like Clarence Henry. But who was to say why Kei-Shee never trusted Clarence? Perhaps she remembered San Francisco and the gold miners. Perhaps she remembered the gamblers who frequented the brothel where she had worked off the price of her ticket from China until Yeung Lee's father had brought her to town as his bride. Perhaps. At any rate, she was the one who overheard Tea Rose mutter, "Shēn-yan-sē-dē." So Kei-Shee turned to see just what patch of black skin had caught her granddaughter's eye, and made her lose all of her senses by speaking without permission.

Kei-Shee, who had been both teacher and mother to Tea Rose, was worried about her granddaughter's future. Not long before Clarence Henry arrived, Kei-Shee had tried talking to Yeung Lee. Len Poo Yen, the laundryman's son, had been killed two years before in the invasion of Normandy, and only the month before, Kei-Shee had urged Yeung Lee to put more money aside for a trip to China, or at least to the West Coast where young Chinese bachelors dreamed of finding a bride who already lived in the land of the Gold Mountain. Kei-Shee sensed the problems of finding a suitable husband for Tea Rose any place near the Strip, and the minute she saw Clarence Henry, she muttered. "Hēi-fon Kwei!" with such a vengeance, Cora Kay almost dropped the stack of dirty dishes she was putting on the counter.

For once, Cora Kay gave all of her attention to the restaurant. When she turned around, she saw several of the men from the cattle yards, high on their weekly pay and eating as much as they could before they had the rest boxed up as take-home for the family. She knew Kei-Shee would not have used them to mutter an oath about "foreign-black-devils." The old woman called working men, "Häu-kàn rēn," — good-look-men. Cora Kay saw them sitting near Sister Garrison and Doc Pritchard's wife, who were downing their usual Saturday night helping of shrimp fried rice. She was sick of throwing Christian pamphlets in the trash after they left, but it would be too much to hope the old woman was referring to them as "foreign devils." Other than one or two kids picking up take-out for their mamas, she only saw Maroon-Willie, Whitaker, and the usual crew of railroad men fitting themselves in a booth. True, they were loud and would try to cheat her every chance they got, but Butler Sykes' wife let the Chinese use her funeral home if one of them died, and none of the other men would have made the old woman spit out the words, "black devil." Then Cora Kay saw Clarence Henry — "six shades blacker than night," her mother would have said. When she turned back to Tea Rose, she knew by the look in the girl's eyes that she'd spotted Kei-Shee's "Hēi-fon Kwei."

At first nothing set Clarence apart from the others except his old-style pin-striped suit, its slightly musty odors marking its pawnshop origins. But mothballs could not compete with half a night's work already weaving the smell of onions and soy sauce into her clothes and hair, so Cora Kay had to look for some other sign. Clarence was a bit thin for her taste, his face a little too broad and his eyes somewhat shifty, but when he smiled, the chip in his front tooth made him look young and old at the same time. It also made Cora Kay remember a time when she was a little girl, before WWII, and a man who used to visit her mother. He had given her candies, and promised her a trip to the circus when he came back that next spring. But the war had started, and he'd never returned. Still, she recalled his laughter and how he'd told her he'd broken his tooth riding in a rodeo in some town out in Oklahoma where all the folks were black.

"Don't be telling that child all that devilment," her mother had said. "Whoever heard of such a thing? A town with no white folks in it and all the black ones riding horses like in them cowboy movies."

But the man had insisted there was such a town, and he'd gone off to find it, taking with him the devilment in his smile.

Cora Kay leaned across the service counter to signal Tea Rose, and once again, Key-Shee muttered, "Hēi-fon Kwei!"

"Shut up, snaggle-tooth. I ain't studying bout you," Cora Kay told her. But she kept her voice low in case Yeung Lee looked up from his chores of splitting celery root or cracking a duck's back with one stroke of his knife. "Why you always got to be flapping your lips?" Cora Kay hissed at the old woman. "Why you always got to be taking a look-see at what I do? Look-see, djäu. Humph! You think I'm seeing something? Think I'm looking at something to talk about?"

Then, satisfied that she'd given Tea Rose as many clues as she dared, Cora Kay started to worm her way between tables and booths, ignoring customers who signaled her as she aimed for Clarence Henry. Kei-Shee grumbled as she watched Cora Kay's progress, and had it not been for the old woman's mutterings, Yeung Lee would not have looked up from his chopping block. When he saw his daughter was also staring at something in the front of the restaurant, Yeung Lee went to the service window. And that was how, in the early spring of 1946, trouble came between Clarence Henry and Wu Yeung Lee. To his credit, that trouble was not all Clarence's fault, despite what anyone in the Flats might say. With Tea Rose's help, he unknowingly took a roundabout way of raising the Chinaman's hackles.

Clarence had made the right call when he claimed to be a lucky so-and-so. By the time Yeung Lee came to the service window, Clarence had started talking to Cora Kay, who was standing in the aisle. He'd had to turn around to talk to her, and in turning, saw Tea Rose staring at him, her round face perfect in its moon-shaped wonder. Of course, he also saw Yeung Lee — it was hard to miss the big Chinaman — but Clarence Henry believed in his luck, so he'd continued to stare at Tea Rose. It didn't take Yeung Lee long to discover the target of his daughter's admiring glances was the same beaming black face that held Cora Kay's attention. It was doubtful whether Yeung Lee tried dividing his anger equally between Cora Kay and Tea Rose, or whether he was aware of how tightly he gripped the knife's handle, or that he'd begun to shift his weight so his next step would lead him out of the kitchen. But none of it mattered, because at that moment, Clarence's luck held true. Just as Yeung Lee reached the kitchen door, machete in hand, the police burst through the front door on one of their routine raids of joints along the Strip.

The regular customers had practice at timing their scramble, but without knowing where the rear exit was, Clarence tried running toward the front door. Immediately he was turned back by the onslaught of cops. At one point, Maroon-Willie tried to reach him, but Clarence vaulted across tables to the other side of the restaurant. There the church ladies beat him back with their purses, and the cops would have tagged him if Tea Rose hadn't snatched him into the kitchen. Yeung Lee already had the pantry door open, but Tea Rose took Clarence through the alley to the storage shed, where she locked him in as tightly as her father had locked in the burlap-covered bales of rice and tea freight trains brought him from the West Coast.

And while her father cleared the air — shouting: "Here not allowed Tong! Here not allowed suckee yä-pyän! Not allowed card men! Herebelong only honest man!" — Tea Rose let the confusion help folks forget she'd neatly placed Clarence Henry in the storage shed. The whole business might have gone unnoticed if Yeung Lee hadn't been suspicious already. But he was, and long after the cops had left, he watched the two girls. So it was much later, after the Eatery had closed and Yeung Lee and his mother were snoring in unison, that Tea Rose was able to release Clarence from the storage shed.

"Where you going?" Cora Kay whispered. Tea Rose was at the end of the hall when she stopped her. "Make water," Tea Rose said, as if Cora Kay suddenly couldn't remember they were forced to use chamber pots at night like almost all of the folks in the Flats.

"What brand of truth you giving me?" Cora Kay asked. Tea Rose's eyes were like a night breeze flowing past her, a splinter of light caught in the cinders of coal piled at the edge of shantytown. "What you up to, girl?"

Tea Rose said, "I make someone belong-safe when cops come chyu-djēu."

For once, Cora Kay was impatient with the spider web of Chinese woven into English. "Where is he?" she hissed. "Where is he?"

Tea Rose bowed her head and moved away in what Cora Kay called her cockroach steps. Still, Cora had to walk fast to keep up with the girl, and Tea Rose, in her usual determination, never looked around to see how far away Cora Kay was.

When Tea Rose opened the shed, Clarence was a deeper shadow huddled in a corner and sleeping as if darkness were a solution to his problems. Tea Rose waited until Cora Kay closed the door before she lit the lantern, then they both watched Clarence rub sleep from his eyes. For a moment, the three of them inspected each other. Tea Rose drank in images of Clarence as if he were a vision she'd seen those nights when she'd escaped to the roof where, if she looked at it long enough, the sky's darkness seemed as thick as flesh. And Cora Kay stretched out toward something her mother told her about how a man smells when he awakens — the softness in back of his neck, the pillow of his shoulder. She fought to see Clarence for what he was — his razor-boned frame too loose and slippery to stay in one place. What Clarence saw was Cora Kay's skin under its red-brown covering — not just the patch of cinnamon the railroad men had dreamed when she served their food off her hip in the same way some women carried babies, or what made Yeung Lee remember a tapestry where dragon fire licked the edges of the ocean. But no vision pleased Clarence more than Tea Rose. Her hair, purple-black, softened and darkened a face so pale, he'd seen her clearly even before she'd held up the lantern. Whatever Clarence saw in her face made him shudder as much as a train's mournful whistle had. And those eyes, their lashes brushing down just before he could discover the secret they held. Already he was touching her — the sweet skin behind her knees, the small of her back, the inside of her thighs where the rush of smells would fill his head and leave him drowning.

"You gone get us killed," Cora Kay said to both of them. "Yeung Lee gone come out here and chop us all to little pieces the way he chops up them ducks. Y'all must be crazy. I'm outta here." She moved toward the door, but Tea Rose stayed where she was. "You hear me, girl?" Cora Kay asked her. "Your daddy don't play. Specially with the likes of that," she added, nodding toward Clarence Henry.

But Tea Rose was well past reason. "What name you call?" she asked Clarence. "What place you live? What place belong your wife?"

As Cora Kay left the shed, she rightly assumed she had trouble on her hands.

It wasn't long before Tea Rose and Clarence were meeting in secret on a regular basis. In fact, the two of them were at ease with the mess they were creating. As long as Tea Rose knew when Clarence was going to meet her, she easily assumed her expressionless pose behind the service window. Cora Kay, on the other hand, had to act as if Clarence were a piece of woodwork when he came into Wu Fong's with the railroad men.

"Well, Slick, she sho got your number fast," Whitaker told Clarence when Cora Kay barely stayed long enough to finish taking their order.

"Um-hum," Maroon-Willie added. "Come on strong the first time she seen you, now turning you cold as a tombstone."

"Hey, y'all know this cat's the best thing she seen since Wonder Bread," Butler laughed.

"Yeah, the butt enda bread," Lip said.

The others laughed, but Clarence said nothing. Like Cora Kay, he was relieved that the jokes reached Yeung Lee. After a while, the Chinaman stopped staring at him each time he came into the restaurant, so Clarence figured he was home free. But he didn't have to make excuses for the noises Yeung Lee heard drifting into the upstairs windows long after closing hours, when being with Cora Kay made his eyes glint black as the stones at the bottom of the creek. When Yeung Lee heard laughter, Cora Kay would hold him closer and say, "It's them foxes. They useta come right up to the door when I lived in shantytown." And when the shed door creaked against a rock Tea Rose hadn't kicked out of its path, Cora Kay would say, "It's them trains. Must be breaking in a new yard crew. Some ain't good for nothing."

After a while, Cora Kay began to look more strained than Tea Rose. Yeung Lee told her, "I no send you for flower-pick. You tired out work maybe."

"We need some place not for work," Tea Rose said. And after she'd gained her father's permission to return to the meadow, she told Clarence almost the same thing.

"We need some place invite me, huh?"

Cora Kay moved away from them. It wasn't that she wanted to leave them alone, but she simply did not want to hear Clarence's answer. More than once, they'd said too much around her. And once, when they'd been in the meadow, she'd seen them sink into the tall grass. She'd wandered away to look at the shadows of Indian Hills, visible on the horizon some thirty miles south of town and tinted pink by the sun, like the clumps of pale agates she used to find at the edge of Cobbler's Creek. The creek was like a bright silver guardrail guiding the way toward the valley. She'd searched the valley for a while, then turned back to where she'd last seen Clarence and Tea Rose. At first, the meadow had seemed empty. Then she'd spotted a slight depression in the grass. And with her hand shielding her eyes, she could see the two of them pillowed by wood violets and chicory bending under the weight of their bodies. A sparrow rustled the branches of a sycamore, and the flash of light was trapped in the movement of Tea Rose's arm curling toward Clarence Henry. If the wind blew just right, the grass spread back to its raw side and Cora Kay could clearly see them both: the smooth slant of Clarence Henry's back, humped marble-black like the rocks the railroad had used to shore up the trestle, and Tea Rose's legs, bent in that crooked way women assumed when they opened their bodies for birth or love. And the two of them moving, pulsing like snakes, or the very grass itself, flower petals falling in the wake of a breeze.

It wasn't as if the sight surprised Cora Kay — she'd witnessed more than that in shantytown — but the wonder of watching Tea Rose open herself to Clarence kept Cora Kay fixed on the scene. Later, she wished she'd had the sense to turn away, because it was at that point that, somehow, Cora Kay began to feel responsible for the conspiracy that hummed between those two. And it didn't take long for her part in the act to come due.

"Hoisin, you make card men say yes for lump money game?" Tea Rose asked her. "Henry C. good card man," she said, reversing his name, Chinese fashion.

"Humph. Good for nothing," Cora Kay snorted.

"No. Make lump money. Big game when Fù-chin fall-sleeping."

"Your daddy don't sleep that sound, and the onliest thing Clarence gone buy you is a space in the graveyard," Cora Kay told her.

But in the end, she found herself setting up the game. "*I'm running a fool,*" she told herself, but she'd seen Clarence Henry double-shuffle cards, his long fingers tapered like ribbons, so graceful, they seemed to flow into the act until cards and hands moved as one. Clarence had told them more than one story of how some redneck card player had been tempted to break those fingers just to erase their image from his memory. Cora Kay had to admit Clarence could move cards almost as well as Yeung Lee, but she still had her doubts about setting him up with the big-time gambling men.

"Takes more than the nerve of a brass monkey to shine in that game," Cora Kay told Clarence.

"Do I look like I'm short on nerve?" Clarence asked. "Besides, what I don't know, my woman know."

Cora Kay's eyes went from Clarence to Tea Rose. Tea Rose grinned. "Man, I think you musta hit your head when you fell off that train," Cora Kay said. "You think they gone let some Chinawoman come to a game with you?"

"Um-hum. And be glad for the gamble," Clarence laughed. Moving from the South to the North had been his biggest gamble, so a city game seemed like a piece of cake. His instinct always told him when to push for a bet and when to fold. Now it told him to bet. "You just tell 'em Tea Rose is ready. Can't be my doing, else they back off. You just pass the word at Wu Fong's."

"Hoisin, I have shïng-yün, much luck. We make lump money," Tea Rose said. "Invite you come big house."

"Not me," Cora Kay said. "I ain't going nowhere. Not to that game or some house you think you gone get. I'll do this and no more."

So the next time Cora Kay served the table of railroad men, she let Tea Rose's little firecracker drop. Clarence Henry's luck seemed to be spreading itself around, because not only were the railroaders there, but John Gionio and a few big-time gamblers were in the next booth. Cora Kay said it loud enough for both groups to listen. For a second, all conversation came to a halt.

"Maybe y'all didn't hear me right," she said. "Maybe I oughta be serving you them fortune cookies early."

Gionio bathed her in one of his dog's-head grins. "If there's some other gentlemen interested, then you can bring us a couple dozen thousand-year-old eggs. They gonna need that much luck."

Cora Kay looked at the booth full of railroad men. Clarence didn't signal until Butler and Whitaker nodded. Maroon shrugged, but Lip looked confused, so Cora Kay figured he wasn't coming. No matter. She already had enough players. "Thousand-year-old eggs," she said, as if she were writing down a regular order. "I guess we can get 'em to you a little after midnight."

"But you make sure that Chinawoman washes the grease off the money fore she hands it over," Gionio said, then patted Cora Kay's hip as if he were stroking a horse's flank.

Cora Kay smacked him with her pencil, and the sound of the wood whacking across Gionio's knuckles was almost as sharp as the crack of Yeung Lee's machete on his chopping block.

Gionio laughed and leaned away from the booth to catch Butler's eye. "I'll take that broad for my table," he said.

"You take what you get," Clarence snapped.

Butler hunched Clarence. "Don't pay no attention to him, Mr. Gionio. He just selling buffalo chips."

Later, Butler had a few choice words for Clarence. They had left the restaurant and were walking toward the funeral parlor where Clarence and the others would help Butler set up the gaming table.

"Man, why you want to front-off somebody?" Butler asked Clarence. "Ain't you got no better sense than to rile that white man? Watch your mouth. You asking for trouble."

"Trouble be my name, asking be my game," Clarence said.

"Well, Sporting Life, you best be asking for the right cards tonight," Whitaker told him. Maroon said, "Um-hum," wagging his head.

But Clarence just threw back his head and laughed, showing a row of sharp, even teeth. Whitaker sighed. Like most black folks born in Dixie, he remembered how death could as easily knock at his door in the form of a posse as it could creep up behind someone caught in the wrong place by accident of forgetfulness. All night, Whitaker was afraid he'd be caught in Clarence's accident of forgetfulness, so he kept his eyes peeled for trouble.

Trouble didn't come until late in the game. By all rights, Clarence and Tea Rose should have bought themselves out of the play at least an hour before Gionio started chomping on his losing streak. Perhaps it was knowing the pile of winnings in front of them meant they'd passed the point of no return, or perhaps it was the thick air that left them groggy and overconfident. Certainly the back room of the funeral parlor carried that smell peculiar to any house of the dead. As night crept toward dawn, the scent grew heavier — even with the blue smoke of tobacco and whiskey fumes, even with the card players' body odors in a neighborhood where the usual odors rising from cattle pens could reduce folks to lizards scurrying for a place among the rocks, and spitting words at each other when they couldn't find their real targets. Gionio was losing, and he needed a target.

"Leda got some fresh blood in here?" Gionio asked Butler.

"I don't be asking my wife who she burying," Butler said.

Gionio looked at the cards in his hand. "Whatever she's burying turned rancid fore it died." He looked around for a response.

Everyone intently studied their cards. Whitaker worried the end of a cigar, and Butler rubbed the stubble of his beard, while the dealer, Hugh Spalding, Gionio's cut-buddy who controlled the city's water rights, sliced his forehead into a frown that was deep enough to fold skin over skin. Only Clarence seemed at ease — Clarence and Tea Rose who was sitting right behind him. Tea Rose was wearing flowers in her hair, and each time she leaned forward to gaze at Clarence's hand, the petals quivered. Tea Rose's usual grease-stained smock had been replaced by a shantung dress, slit up both sides and so tight, it seemed to dance across her hips of its own accord, music or not. Gionio tried to imagine her naked and spread under him. When she leaned forward, and coached Clarence to ask for three cards, Gionio heard her whispered signal of "Yäu-sän-gē," as "Y'all singing." Tea Rose felt him staring and looked up. Gionio could only see half of her eyes under their slanted lids. He didn't like anything hidden, especially something Chinese.

"Maybe we ought tell Leda to get another coffin ready," he said. "Something's turning rotten sure as I'm sitting here."

Nobody responded. Hugh dealt against each player's discard. Butler called and raised the ante. Everyone threw in money, except Maroon and Whitaker, who folded. The play should have gone smoothly, Clarence hadn't been listening to Gionio's lament. Although Whitaker said, "Take it easy, man," Clarence raised the bet again before he called in the hand. Butler shook his head, Hugh folded, and Maroon-Willie looked around the room as if he were searching for a pool of water to throw himself into. That left Gionio and Clarence in a face-off. Like the motto on Wu Fong's grass-writing scroll, Gionio's look was colder than a wind biting a beggar's coat.

He said, "Lay them cards out careful, boy."

"Any way you want 'em," Clarence said. "Read 'em and weep."

Gionio pushed back from the table. "I don't weep for no niggers. And don't think you gone get rich off me, boy. I'll be here when they done buried your black ass six feet under in a pauper's grave."

It's anyone's guess as to whether John Gionio ever looked at Clarence Henry's winning hand. It would be a shame to think that big-dog spread of aces high, nine low mixed suit went unnoticed, but none of the players had time to attend to cards right at that moment, because Gionio came up from the chair with his gun drawn. The table spilled onto Hugh's lap, and Maroon raced Whitaker to the floor. It was probably Butler's alarmed cry of "John!" that stopped Gionio, who wasn't averse to killing, but had long since hired others to do his dirty work. So he looked at his gun. For Clarence, that hesitancy was another bit of luck. He and Tea Rose wasted no time leaving the room. One scoop, and the money was in his hat. Two steps, and Tea Rose snatched him through the door. Three steps, and before Butler could finish saying, "Ga'damn black mothah . . ." they were in the alley.

As Clarence well knew, running was an art only survivors lived long enough to brag about. Between his knowledge of the streets, and Tea Rose's history of clearing the restaurant during a raid, they were half-way to Wu Fong's before Gionio could call his boys. But both of them knew how small they'd carved that lead. They needed help. Tea Rose sprinkled Cora Kay's window with pebbles four times before Cora Kay lifted the sash. When she saw Tea Rose's panicky look, and the hatful of money Clarence was showing her, Cora grabbed her clothes and sneaked past Yeung Lee. By the time she reached the back door, by the time they told her Gionio was following them, she knew they would get nowhere on foot. And Yeung Lee's DeSoto was so conveniently parked by the storage shed.

Clarence's years of running had not put him in a place where he could have learned to drive, but once behind the wheel of the car, he had no recourse but to pretend he knew how. It had seemed so easy when he'd watched other men doing it. He fiddled with the gears, and keeping both feet on the brake and clutch, waited for something to happen. Cora Kay stared at him as if he'd ordered some odd combination of food, like sweet-and-sour ribs sprinkled with fried shrimp. She tried to be patient. "Put it in gear, Clarence. Move your feet, man."

By some accident, Clarence popped the clutch and stomped the accelerator. The DeSoto lurched forward, stopped, lurched, stopped.

"Hit that stick again," Cora Kay said.

He snatched it back and the gears screamed so loudly, Tea Rose slid to the floor, certain her father would wake up right at that moment and find them. She needn't have worried. Yeung Lee didn't wake up until Clarence had ground the gears for the third time, and Yeung Lee didn't reach the window until the car had rolled into the Mission Road intersection. They might have heard him shouting if Clarence hadn't been shoving the gears again. Cora Kay leaned over to see what his feet were doing. Her head was so close to his crotch, Clarence almost un-raveled. He slammed his foot against the accelerator once more, then, in an effort to hide his rapidly growing erection, lifted his leg from the clutch, and the car shot across the intersection as if it had been blown from one of the cannons circus stuntmen used to propel a body into the air. That move slammed Cora Kay into the dash, and nearly took off the top of her head. She moaned and sat up. The bundle of sage Yeung Lee had hung from the rearview mirror quivered.

Cora Kay managed to say, "Jesus, you bout killed me."

And Tea Rose shouted, "Hwēi-lai! Hwēi-chyu!" Those were the first words she'd spoken since they'd climbed into the DeSoto.

"What she saying?" Clarence asked.

"She saying: 'Go back,'" Cora Kay told him.

"I got to get turned around," Clarence said. But the car hit the first set of train tracks, and galloped from track to track before it died midway to the inbound line. Clarence yelled, "Shit!", but he had definitely passed the danger of his erection. Now he was sweating. He tried the motor again. The DeSoto protested. Tea Rose bounced up and down as if her backseat action would start the engine. Cora Kay wanted to wallop the girl.

"Why the hell am I here?" Cora Kay said to no one in particular.

She could smell the whiffs of sweet-sour cow manure, and the moldy yeast of grain elevators and old warehouses. On the other side of the tracks, she saw the beginning of the narrow streets that lead to shantytown where the road curved downhill toward the back side of the train yards. This wasn't her idea of coming home again, but then, none of it had ever been her idea. She turned to say something to this effect to Clarence when lights reflected in the back window caught her eye. Cora Kay blinked. There were all sorts of visions she might have imagined seeing, but none of them involved Yeung Lee waving his machete, and running down the road in front of several oncoming cars, motors churning on a low growl.

Clarence moaned. Tea Rose yelled, "Fù-chin! Fù-chin!" as if none of them could have recognized her father.

"Shit! And Gionio behind him! That does it!" Cora Kay shouted. "That's it! You see what y'all done done? First the car, then them damn gamblers chasing you. Now you got Yeung Lee ready to kill us. What else could . . ." she began. And as if it had been waiting for that question, an inbound train's whistle screamed twice.

Clarence yelled, "Shit fucka-roony!" and leaped out of the seat. Where his feet had clumsily sought brake pedal and clutch, they easily found ground level and headed up the tracks without missing a step.

Cora Kay screamed and pulled at the door latch. For want of a quick escape route. Tea Rose merely screamed, a long protracted sound like nails scratching glass, a sound that bypassed all of her language problems. Once more, a train answered, this one on the outbound track. Now, all of them abandoned the car. Cora Kay panted and looked both ways. Town was out of the question, and going up the tracks would merely put her in the station. Clarence had already doubled back, and was diving into the car to retrieve his hatful of money. "Leave the damn money!" Cora Kay shouted. But he stuffed some in his pockets, then threw the hat at Cora Kay. Without looking at how much it contained, she plopped it on her head. Clarence took off again, this time up the outbound train tracks.

Cora Kay turned to Tea Rose. "Com'on!" she yelled, trying to grab the girl to get her moving. "This way!" Cora Kay shouted. And she heard Yeung Lee shout something too. He was closer, close enough for her to see his queue streaming, like the tail of a stallion in full flight from the headlights of the cars behind him. And his machete blade picked up the glare of the car lights. He yelled again. This time, Cora Kay clearly heard him shout, "Djì-nyü!" She vaguely wondered just who he was calling a whore, but the approaching train whistles told her it didn't matter. The cars behind Yeung Lee added their horns to the noise. Cora Kay snatched at Tea Rose again. "Move it!" she yelled, and started running. Out of the corner of her eye, she saw Clarence had turned back one more time. Tea Rose was already running toward him when Cora Kay hurled herself into the row of jimson weed, skunk cabbage, and foxglove growing at the edge of the tracks.

Cora Kay cut diagonally across the tracks and slipped into the underbrush separating the railroad yards from shantytown. The ground was wet and she slid down the embankment, past someone's outhouse. Behind her, the shouts of men grew louder, and the trains were rumbling nearer. When she entered a rut between the shanties, she heard gunshots, then a long crunch as first one train, then the other, chewed Yeung Lee's DeSoto. Cora Kay's headlong plunge took her right into the arms of Sister Vernida Garrison and her little band of Ladies' Aid volunteers finishing their nightly shantytown mission. Sister Garrison didn't know whether it was man or woman falling into her arms — the hat askew on a hard, lumpy head, the face covered with stinking mud, and the dusty prickles of poisonous plants clinging to the arms that enfolded her.

"Lord help me! I been kissed by the evil eye," she screamed.

Folks say Vernida Garrison was never quite the same after Cora Kay Ivory plowed into her that night. Certainly Yeung Lee was never the same. Only the food was dependable — and Yeung Lee's anger as his machete sliced the air, and he muttered about the black-foreign-devil who wrecked his car and took his love away from him. Folks who ate at the Chinaman's waited to see if Tea Rose and that badass Clarence Henry ever returned to the Flats. Like Yeung Lee, they were disappointed. No one saw Tea Rose after that night, but folks on the Strip frequented Cinnamon's Bar, and if they were real nice she'd speak a few words of Chinese while she poured their drinks.

THEM AND US

— And Love Them?

by Thomas Glave

ONLY NOW I HATE THEM.

Well, no, I shouldn't say that, I really shouldn't and anyway you have to be careful saying things like that and especially who you say them to because it's the kind of thing they're always looking out for to hold against you, the kind of something or other they think they can use. And they always use it, without ever understanding the feeling. They always use it, without ever taking responsibility for their part in it. They're always waiting to jump on you for something, catch you in something — that's the way you've got to deal with them, that's what makes it so hard every time. And after a while you learn that you can't hate all of them anyway or all of anybody. Not for long. Sooner or later it passes into something else you recognize, and I guess deep down *hate* anyway isn't the right word. I consider myself an educated woman and I know that. I'm logical, I live in the world, I read the papers; I observe, I think, I respond. And react. I'm still pretty good-looking for my age, people tell me — you couldn't tell I'm getting close to forty-whatever, it doesn't matter how much, it's no big deal anyway and if it is you know it shouldn't be. A woman's life begins at forty, some people say, and I think they're right. Someone I used to know who's really honest, one of them but still really honest, told me once that I could still even pass for a teenager and I believed him because I know it's true — how you keep yourself, it's all in the mind. My mind's really sharp, that's what keeps me going. Like when I sit next to them on the train in the morning on the way to work and think about them. That's when I try to feel them, feel what they might be thinking or feeling. But most of the time it feels like you can never tell what they're thinking or feeling. One of them used to work with me at the office — a sweet, very charming girl from Guyana or one of those islands. She spoke so nicely on the phone, people said; she was so polite when she took messages and spelled out their names correctly. It was like she always had a smile in her voice. But she left two months ago — she was finally pregnant, she said, after trying so hard for so many years, and wanted to have the baby in Guyana or wherever it was. I found out later her husband was involved in some kind of trade union thing down there on one of the islands. I wish them a lot of happiness together. I certainly will miss her. She was so polite, so kind; what I call a real human being.

But that's what I mean — that way they have of holding back. I still can't understand it; it hurts me deep down and makes me really furious, to tell the absolute truth. And then after some more time of it I just get sick of it all, the same goddamned situation over and over again, and it's like I'm always thinking what should I say? What should I do? What went wrong *this* time? But you can't let *them* know that because all they ever are is angry, very angry, and it's like they think they've got an exclusive corner on it so they can bully the rest of the world into shutting up or being afraid. And as soon as you even try to open your mouth to explain that maybe, God forbid just maybe *you* might have some feelings too they give you that disgusting sickening awful look that's no look at all and then go into that sulky silence they're so good at. I'm pretty intuitive, I can tell moods. It's like they don't want you to know they're angry, oh no, but then, oh, believe it, they *do* want you to know. They force it on you. You've seen it: those ugly expressions. The ugliest expressions in the world. Their lips get thin then and they stare at you with that hating look. But then (if I said this to one of them, you could be sure they'd take it the wrong way) at least when they react that way you know, most of the time, that things won't get out of hand. It won't be like when they get *really* angry and go out into the street and do all the wild things they do, setting fires and turning over police cars and killing innocent people just in the name of anger. They're not human then. I've seen them, everyone's seen them — like what they did in L.A. in '92. The thing is — they could never understand this — I *agreed* with them. I didn't think they were wrong to be upset. I told two of them, friends of mine (Tracy and Angela, two girls who work with me in the legal division; they don't always seem to be looking for an argument like some of the others) — I told them, you're right, you've got every right to be angry, that was a ridiculous miscarriage of justice, I couldn't agree with you more (I told them this, oh yes, the truth, I told them), I can't believe that even with a videotape of them beating him and everything else that they still allowed those men to go free. Awful, I said; just not right, I said. And I meant it. It was all true. But then — here's where it gets so hard — I wanted to tell them that maybe they *should* have looked at it all a little more closely before they got so upset, because those men *were* police officers and they were only trying, really, finally, to do their job, can't you see? — it can't be easy going through what they have to go through every day of their lives, imagine being a policeman's wife, would *you* want to have to experience that trauma every day of your life? Well, yes, all right, you could say they went a little too far. I've never seen police violence like that before in my life. It upset me for an entire week, I almost had nightmares like everyone else, I've got feelings too; but maybe — did they ever stop to think? Did they ever try to have some compassion for the other people in the situation? — that guy, the criminal, might really have been dangerous, who can ever know these things when they're happening? — because even after they hit him a few times he kept on trying to rise up from the ground toward them. Maybe *they* were afraid, after all. Wouldn't you have been? Wouldn't anybody have been? Because you can't ever tell what someone's thinking. And they showed some compassion, finally, the officers, because they didn't shoot him the way they're trained to do. It's like you just can't tell who'll try to kill you in the world these days, everything is so dangerous now with all these drug dealers and crackheads and all out in the streets, everywhere, and all these rapists and serial killers too. But no, you can't tell *them* that. I couldn't tell them that. They would just get all upset again and tell me I'm being what they call you when they can't call you anything else — it makes them feel good when they call you that because then they can sit back and hate you and blame you all over again for everything that's wrong in the world like you made it that way. It's always you, never them. It's so hard, so sickening, because I really like Tracy and Angela, they're nice girls, so well-spoken; we even go out to lunch sometimes together and manage to talk about all kinds of things like books and music and even modern art — it shows you how much people can have going on up-stairs when they want to. I really value their friendship so I never tell them these things, and that's one of the things that makes this all so hard and horrible because — if you don't already know — imagine how hard it is to be friends with someone when you can't even tell them the truth because they're so sensitive about what they think is right that they can't deal with reality or what anyone else thinks. They're very emotional. All of them are, there's nothing wrong with it, it's just a cultural thing, and it's like you know they've probably been hurt in one way or another by things that have happened to them — little, stupid things. But after a while even that begins to sound too much like another excuse. Haven't we all been hurt by something? But some of us still manage to *think.*

Besides — and this I know I can say, it would make them smile — why do the people always burn their own neighborhoods? Why do they hurt themselves? It's always like that. If I was in their shoes, and I am in a way kind of because I'm a woman, I would march right on up there to the good neighborhoods, all those places in Beverly Hills and what not, and break a few windows and turn over some cars *there.* That'd show those rich bastards who's got the power! I did say that, and I meant it; and Tracy and Angela laughed, but they also looked at each other really quickly and strangely afterwards with that look, that look they're so fucking famous for, I've seen it before, you've seen it before, I know it like I know the back of my hand, but what they mean by it I couldn't tell you, I still can't tell you. And sometimes it's really like I just don't care anymore, I just get so sick of it. Another thing they keep to themselves, not really angry but not what I'd call friendly ei-ther. Had I said the wrong thing? And we laughed and laughed, yes, we laughed, on and on and loud, for sure, yes, but that's more of what I mean, do you see? — just that no matter how hard you try you can't please them. You can't win. You can't get through to someone on a really human level, never, not even when you have true painful com-passion for them; compassion so deep it hurts, what we've all felt at one time or another. Never. And you hate them for that, you can't help it, because they won't ever let you in.

I know I'm a very compassionate person. I can feel sorry for any-body. The world is so full of suffering. When I see those homeless people on the street talking to themselves, muttering to themselves, all bent over like cripples, I just want to cry — really, I want to cry. And some-times I do. Because you know people shouldn't have to live like that. You can't even call that living. It's wrong and it's unfair. I try to give them money when I can, to improve their lives in some little way so they'll be able to thank God again, feel alive again and know that somebody, even a stranger, cares for them; would like to help them; wants them to do well in the middle of all this crazy sickness. Some-times they say thank you and sometimes they don't. I know I can't change their lives — only Christ can do that, or the government — but a quarter or a dime will make their day a little nicer. You have to have compassion for people, no matter what color they are. It doesn't matter. I was brought up to believe that color doesn't matter, just like how much money someone has doesn't matter, or what kind of house they live in, or whether or not they're educated so they can get a good job; even if they're living on welfare with a whole bunch of kids be-cause they don't want to work, you shouldn't judge them — that woman you're judging might have been raped or maybe her husband beats her like lots of them do, or he's in jail. You don't know, so you shouldn't say anything. Only the person matters, my family always stressed to me. And the truth everybody knows is that we'd all get along better if it mattered less to them. They're the ones who al-ways bring it up. And then they'll look at you and say you hate them when they're really the ones who hate. That's when you know you should just try to rise above it and leave hatred in their laps because they're really the ones who want it. Always.

It's like that old man in the subway. Sometimes even now I think about him and even as I feel compassion for him I still get furious. He was a cruel old man, just cruel, that's all, and he didn't have to be. He was very old, filthy dirty and very black, sitting on the subway steps in everybody's way as we were coming out one morning on our way to work. That day I remember — it was such a pretty morning, the sun was out, and people in the rush didn't seem as pushy and nasty as usual. I didn't have any change left because just that minute I'd bought a ten pack of tokens to last me the week. Why did he have to pick me? — maybe because I looked at him? Or because of my clothes? (People are always envious, even homeless people, although you could tell he was a good type, sort of, not one of those people pretending to be blind or the kind who would try and rob you like some of them.) I just felt so sorry for him there, sitting there looking so old and dirty as everyone stepped around him and over him, and when I gave him a kind of sympathetic look he started screaming — *screaming* — that I wasn't going to give him any money because I was white, wasn't I, and why didn't I just go (he said something too unbelievable to repeat) because he didn't need my money anyway, you white bitch, he said, and kept on cursing, *you white bitch, you white bitch,* over and over. Over and over. He actually called me that. And I couldn't say anything. I couldn't feel anything except the hate and the real rage that came up. Because it was humiliating. Because I didn't deserve that. No one can tell me I deserved that. Not even the worst kind of person would deserve treatment like that. And for no reason, that's what makes it worse. Just because I happened to be the one he picked on, because he was a sick crazy old bastard who didn't have anyplace to live and needed to blame somebody for it. And I swear, and I'm not apologizing either, in that minute I wished something really horrible would happen to him — I didn't care what, just something to show him he should watch what he said to people, people who'd even wanted to help him and didn't have to but wanted to because that's what you should do for people who are suffering so much, they're so unhappy. I don't care if I shouldn't feel that way, I don't *care* what anyone says, I'd just like to know how one human being could say something like that to another. Especially when I felt so sorry for him sitting there so alone, so black and dirty. But then you learn that some people don't deserve anyone's compassion. You learn that they'll just take it and use it against you. Because I didn't cause his pain. I didn't put him on those subway steps. And you could look around and say that there are more of them that way than anybody else, but that's one thing they can't blame us for. I can't be held accountable for what society does to people and I shouldn't have to suffer for it. I wasn't around a hundred years ago and I've never stolen anything from one of them, never. But you see it in their eyes: how they try to put it all on you. And when I think of that I just want to scream, or break something, or kill any son of a bitch who even looks like him. Because . . . just ask yourself — how can they keep on blaming everybody for things that happened a hundred years ago, two hundred years ago? I've never even been in

Georgia or any of those places. And after that he could have sat there and starved to rotten death for all I cared. I know I'm a good person. I have a life I can call my own. And a *job*.

It's like what happened last week, I swear to God, the same thing almost, for nothing at all. One of them in the office got all mean over something really stupid. I'm talking about hair. Can you get that? Hair. I was like, let's get real already. It wasn't like I was asking her about God or her boyfriend or whatever. And then it's like, you try to talk, they won't even let you get out five words before they get all hysterical and upset. It's getting like you can't even ask how's it going or what'd you do this weekend, and, God in Heaven, don't dare to take it further. Let me tell you right now — I wouldn't *care* if anyone asked me about my hair. It's brown, I comb it out in the morning and tease it and put on some hair spray and sometimes a barrette if I have the time. That's all. But this one in the office, this girl who's always wearing all those African clothes and things, she had some fancy hairstyle one day, all curls and twists, and I thought it looked great, kind of foreign, almost, like what one of those models or someone would wear, and I asked her, all I did was ask her how she got it like that and how she washed it because it was great I thought how they could do all those things with their hair that nobody else can, make it long or short one day or stiff and what not. And the way she looked at me — like she wanted to kill me. Cut me out before the sight of God. Hate is what you call it. Hate. Over something stupid like hair. So she went around the rest of the day saying "Miss Blue Eyes wanted to know how I did my hair" to the rest of them, laughing, and they laughed too. I don't have blue eyes and I didn't like her tone — that nasty mean sound in her voice. It's what always happens, isn't it? — you can't be a real human being, except maybe with a very few — the nicer ones. And now I won't ask any-thing, never again. Ask and they'll laugh at you. Ask and they'll hu-miliate you. And then you know they'll say things — I've heard them, you've heard them — like how you don't ever want to "learn" about them and all kinds of things. What's there to learn that's so special it has to be a big deal all the time? People are people, and with all that it's just another example of how they always want to make themselves different like they're the only ones who have problems and all the rest of us are just living the high life. Am I living the high life? Do I have to pay taxes? Do I have to ride the subway every day and smell the vomit and the piss stink with everybody else, or what? And then it's like I want to say (but you can't tell them this, so it ends up burning you to death inside) that if I'd wanted to take care of children I would have had some by now, thank you. *Stupid* children. This same girl had the nerve to tell me once that if I wanted to learn anything I should go to the library. It was like she'd smacked me right in the face. Go to the library for *what?* I'd wanted to say. When I could just ask her, a real, living, breathing human being, and learn from her? That might have meant something to me. We might even have become friends if she hadn't been such a mean-spirited bitch. To tell you the truth, I don't even see why she always wears all those African clothes, either — she's not African. That's another thing now, another fad they can get angry about, every day something different, like how we're supposed to *say african-american* not *black*. People are never happy to be just who they are, I'm learning. They dig their own graves that way, holding on to all those labels, and then try to pull you down into the sickness with them.

She doesn't even know what kind of person I am. How I try, as God is my witness, how I try. Like that time I was walking down Lexington Avenue, alone, late at night, on a Sunday after some friends and I had gone to the movies up around Seventy-something Street and they all took cabs home because of the hour, but they knew me, I couldn't be bothered to spend that kind of money, you never know when you might need it and anyway I love to walk late at night sometimes and just feel the city quiet and sleeping around me, quiet and peaceful, so quiet. Yes, well, I know I could be raped sometime, I know what's happening in the world, but no one's ever done that and when they try it God forbid I'll be ready because I never go anywhere without my Mace and the pocketknife a friend gave me one Christmas. I could easily kill someone who'd try to rape me. I'd have no choice. What's a woman supposed to do, live locked up in a castle? You might as well be dead. Anyway, I'm walking down the avenue and it's dark, a really nice night, quiet, cool, the entire city sleeping behind windows, making love, maybe, or watching TV, maybe, or just out walking like me, thinking whatever. And after a little while I can tell there's someone walking behind me, kind of following not too fast but fast enough so I can tell he's there. I kind of look back, you know, just so that I can sort of see his outline, and I can see out of the corner of my eye this dark

guy, really tall, walking back there, keeping pace with me. Did I get
scared? Did I think about running? So maybe when I thought about it
later I did in a small way, you know, I thought plenty of women get
raped in this city, you have to be really alert for creeps if you're thinking at all. But this guy — just because he was a big one didn't mean I
had to be scared, really, maybe he was just out enjoying the night like
I was . . . people have all kinds of ways of enjoying life. And I'm telling
myself You're not going to scream, stupid, just let him walk behind
you, he's probably never even raped anybody, he's probably a really
good person with a job and everything, just because you see a lot of
them hanging out in front of those neighborhood stores doesn't mean
anything now, right now, just relax. But then all of a sudden he starts
walking faster, then faster and faster, and it's like I do start to get a little
just a little scared, not much but I'm also telling myself Stupid you
know people just like him in the office, Tracy and Angela sort of and
all the other girls too and the guys who work in the mailroom and the
messengers and that bitch who got so pissed off about her hair, remember that remember that you know all of them. But then it's like — I
don't know, all at once I'm thinking about how angry they can get
when all you do is ask them a simple question, oh God a simple question, that's all, and how angry they get at people who're just trying to
do their jobs like the cops, you see it on the news all the time, they're
ready to kill people who never did anything to them, just like that guy
who shot up or no he *massacred* all those people on the railroad that
time just because they were — just because they were there, just because they were — because they were *white,* he said, it's like Jesus God
how could anybody be filled with so much hate for anyone, it's like he
hated the whole country, how, why, for *what?* — ask yourself that,
then ask yourself why can't people forget about things and get on
with their lives, because for God's sake the people on the train weren't
doing anything to him and he even admitted it, remember, he said it
was because he was so angry and full of hate, he hated everybody,
even Chinese people who never do anything to anybody, they're so
quiet always and really decent and clean, they don't bother anybody,
everybody loves them. I cried and cried for days after and that time I
did have bad dreams, because think about it, those people could have
been anyone, they could have been you or me, and it's like you know
everybody shouldn't have called him an animal but that's something

only an animal would do, isn't it, only an animal, what else can you say? — that's it, that's how it always happens, they're ready to kill people just for looking, just for smiling, you can't smile, no, you can't look no, never, they'll kill you or start a fire or: — angry all the time for nothing at all really how can anyone live like that, that's why they die young, they live to be angry, killing people and even each other sometimes and then: — wondering I'm wondering really fast is this guy angry too for some reason because Jesus fucking Christ God I didn't cause any of it his pain or whatever they're complaining about now, living in the past still *they won't let go of it:* —

(should I scream or should I   )

(they won't get beyond it they won't

should I scream or   )

and so suddenly so fast I start to walk faster Jesus God walk faster almost running I should run but not almost running and trying to find the Mace my knife a cop I haven't got a gun why didn't I but I am not scared the Mace the Mace but it slips out of my hands or maybe I don't know I forgot to bring it this time I am not scared:

because lots of lots of women do get raped in this city   all over the world:

everywhere   Jesus God you better run you better fly or is there somebody a cop or: —

Because this anger in them that gets out of control it gets out of control and if he raped me but I can't imagine being raped but if he rapes me Jesus God Christ I'll die I won't

— survive I won't because it can happen to anyone and it's like this panic I'm not scared I'm not trying to run but running not running and is he there

running oh God   is he there

— and then I see him running out into the street and hailing a cab so I guess he must have money or something, only the cab doesn't stop for him and the next one doesn't either and the next doesn't either and you can see he gets this kind of frustrated look, sort of angry, always angry, and now I'm sort of calming down and thinking *I wasn't really scared I wasn't* — and what's happening is they're not stopping for him and you can't blame them but not because of how he looks or anything but they probably just want to go home and eat, they've worked hard for hours and it's late, really late, and they deserve a break too. I know because some of them wouldn't want to take me out of the city either. At this time of the night they only want to go to SoHo or Tribeca or

maybe the Upper West Side or the Village. They hate going anyplace else because they want to go home and eat. It's also really hard to get one these days because now lots of them are from so many foreign places like Pakistan or Africa and you know how people are in those countries, if they see a woman out late alone they'll take you for a whore because it's like they show on the news, in those countries you know a woman can't just be herself, she's either somebody's property or she's a whore, that's how it is. And now slowing down but still watching him, looking back, I feel this incredible warm feeling, it's like happiness or contentment, that he turned out to be a good person after all, I almost want to cry for some reason, and I look back at him and kind of wave and say (I don't know why my heart's jumping around like this, it's so stupid how darkness and dark streets can make you feel so jittery, nothing's ever happened to me after all, what would ever happen?), I say Having a hard time there, huh? — and I smile, really smile, because it's like this really human moment when there's nobody else around and it's just us two out in the dark in the middle of the quiet quiet city when nothing matters, none of it, we're past it, we're just two people. A truly human moment, and I feel like, God, what an incredible world this is in spite of all the pain and the suffering, and you can see some homeless people carrying their beer bottles and bags and everything down the street, looking the way they always do, dirty and run-down, but at least they're alive, thank God, they'll live to beg another day and you know somewhere deep down there's some kind of mercy in that at least. And now he's still out there and he looks back at me for a second before he turns his face back to the lights of the oncoming cars (his face, it's so beautiful, really, like one of those bears with the gentle eyes of a child), but then — I swear to God — looking out at me he gets this look on his face like he hates me. *Hates* me. And just that fast like before, so many times before I'm thinking I hate you too, you son of a bitch, somebody tries to reach out to you and be friendly, who the hell are *you?* I hope you never get a cab now, you bastard, and then I'm thinking something really awful and I'm sorry, I *know* I shouldn't think that, God forgive me, but it's just like before, like always . . . they drive you to it. You can't share anything, not the night, not the darkness, not any kind of human moment. And now it's like I feel a little sick, a little hot, the moment's over and it feels like somebody died, there's something dead here, ruined, and I'm sorry I went to the movies at all, something always has to spoil it, and I'm not walking alone anymore tonight I tell myself, no, I'm sick of walking and running out here and anyway you can't tell what kind of animals are out here at this time of night, you can't even walk alone without somebody coming up behind you. I put out a hand and hail a cab and one comes, thank God, everything'll be OK now, and yes, I'll pay the goddamn fare all the way home because I'm on my way back now anyway, after all, on my way home to a quiet quiet place. Get me home fast, I'm thinking as I get in. Fast. . . . It's safer that way.

And — just once — one time —
   I don't know why. I don't. I just —
   I dated one. . . .
   One time. Just once. A long time ago. Not now. When I was a little more . . . I know, I shouldn't talk about it. I should just let it rest and be quiet. Just forget about it already. It's all over now and it'd be better not to go over all that again but even now I have to, something inside me's saying I should, I have to. Get it out of my system. For the last time. Let it out. I have to.
   It's like I wonder sometimes how it happened at all. How it ever happened, I mean. It's not like I don't try to be really careful. Even back then when I didn't. . . . You know you can't ever tell about people. Like if some guy comes up to me and tells me I'm gorgeous that doesn't mean I'm going to go out with him. Even though I know I'm lucky, like I said I'm in great shape and everything, you know guys use that line with women all the time when they're looking for a good time, that's how they are. And maybe I shouldn't say *they're* especially like that but it's like I said too you have to be really careful with them always. I know that even more now, because it's like nothing every changes; you can't change things. And I guess that time I just *looked*. Everybody looks once in a while, right? And maybe you shouldn't. You know you really shouldn't, but it's like you can't always help it, they're out there more now, not just in their own neighborhoods, and then too sometimes you know some of them try a little harder, sometimes, like Tracy and Angela, they really try. That doesn't mean you're going to — but we did, that one time we did, and it's like now I still can't. . . . That's what scares me the most sometimes. Just that we — that all that stuff happened. I know — I know it was one of those times when it's

sort of like you just let go. You slip a little looking for something and you just let go. You don't know what it is maybe and maybe you don't even care. It's like all you know, you *feel* it, my God, like you want to really let go like you never did before. Not ever. And when you do that's when everything happens, when you end up alone wondering like oh my God how could you. . . . That's it. It's like you jump, really scary and far, and you fall. And maybe part of it was even my fault. Or even all of it. But it was like we never talked about any of it because I knew he was really embarrassed by what happened that time, and even though I think I'm a modern woman and everything, I mean even though I believe in equal rights and divorce and the right to do what I want to do with my own body and all that, still I know one of the worst things you can ever let a man feel is embarrassment because of something he did between you that he shouldn't have done, because you know how guys are with their egos and their pride, they can't help it. They're always like that. And guys like him have pride too, this kind of noble mysterious pride, except that — I know more than ever after him — they always get kind of stuck on themselves. They really start to think they're special or something, as soon as things get close. The way he did. And you know it's probably because of what's happened to them in the past, like they're so ashamed of it they feel like they have to take it out on you somehow. And that's when you feel the most sorry for them, because you know, you can see it in their eyes, what they're holding back; it's like they really want to reach out for once, in a way, the way they do when they do it, but they're afraid. And then you can almost forgive them for it because you know they want you — they really want you. And you can, because it was worth something to you, that time, because how often did somebody do that, how often . . . it was really worth something. It was a real human moment. You felt it. You always feel it and you know it too.

Because he really cared about me. Loved me. I know, he really wanted me, he was always telling me how much he loved me and how beautiful my hair was and everything. You're fly, he used to say, and all those other things you hear them say. And even now I can forgive him for everything except that one bad time, because I know he cared about me and I know too that I really believe in the power of people even more than the power of God sometimes. Because I've seen it.

We met just like other people meet, I guess, at lunch, in the street, in the subway, in an elevator — how do you ever meet someone? You see something you like and you start talking. And from the very first I could tell he would be good to me — really good. He spoke so well and said he'd been to college and I believed him, a college up in Massachusetts or someplace that cost twenty thousand a year or so and gave scholarships for minority excellence and what not. You could tell it was true because of the way he spoke, and he carried himself in a really special way, not like the guys in the mailroom or the messengers. (They're nice guys, they all know I like them and everything, but you can tell they're more like the ones you see more often on the street and always in the subway too. You know the kind I mean. There's just no other way to say it.) And so we would take walks and all that, only I could never invite him to my place because it was never clean enough, since I work all the time I never have enough time to clean, you know how that is . . . people might've started too although that really wouldn't be a problem because I could always say he was a friend or something and just leave it at that. And maybe they wouldn't even stare, who knows? — but anyway we always wound up going to his place that was on the edge of a kind of awful neighborhood but not right in it so you could feel kind of safe, you know, and then we always took a cab to get there which was sort of romantic, I guess, and safe too. The people around there actually seemed friendly; they always smiled at us and laughed and talked about him being on top of the world now, calling him brother and all that the way they do and slapping his hand and so on, and you could see it was like they were really proud of him for something, like he was a real star to them or whatever. And his apartment! — it was really special. It always smelled like incense, just like him; he had it filled up with all these cultural things. And he loved to read! I never saw so many books in my life — all on interesting things. You wondered how he did it. That's why more than ever I don't like to hear anybody say anything about this country and how bad it is, because it looked like he was doing pretty well, once you got inside the apartment. You wouldn't ever see *him* out there burning things.

We did talk there, sometimes, but most of the time we did other things, and I guess that was when the bad times came. It just happened so fast, that one night, I couldn't stop it. I wasn't even sure I really wanted to stop it. It's not like I had anything against him; it could have been anybody who did it. It was just that time, that time it was feeling so good, it never felt that good with anybody. God, no, not anybody else, never, always scary and sort of sick for some reason which made it feel even better in a way. You know what I mean. Because for the first time in my life ever, I mean the first time, I felt wild, I mean just free and wild and then scared and thrilled too all at the same time, and it was all so bad in a way and dirty and sick too but in a kind of good wicked secret way, because you could just let go for once, when *no one* was watching, and *give* yourself, I mean really give yourself to it. Whatever. It was like for the first time, I swear to God, I didn't care about sin then or anything, not Jesus or my family and what they'd say or anything, and it's like I swear I'm telling you the truth when I say that for once, really for once I wasn't scared of any of them, not the loud ones on the street or that mean bitch in the office or even the crazy killer one on the railroad. Because I'm telling you it was like we were having a real human moment, him and me, right there, in the dark, private, nobody else around, sort of dirty and sick like I said but good too, God, so good and all you could see were his eyes, looking at me. Like he was catching something. Holding me. Like that. And then it was like I could feel his skin next to mine and how it smelled and felt, kind of rough, and how it tasted too, really rough and smooth and black next to mine, God, like the way he felt on me really wild, it was like you couldn't break or catch that thing in him at all because whatever it was, *him*, Jesus, would kill you first, and then it was like you knew you really knew you'd never see anything like that again in this life, like that, *on fire:* out of control. In me. In me. Fucking God. Just wild. I didn't care. God forgive me, it was so much, it was so . . . But then — I didn't want to remember this, I really didn't have anything against him, it wasn't because of him — I wanted him to stop because it began to hurt, really hurt, and it was like I couldn't cry or scream or do anything. God forgive me please, because I wanted to but I didn't want to. I couldn't, I didn't want to. It was like all at once, I don't know what happened, it happened so fast, like all of a sudden he was really angry like all the rest of them, like there was something angry inside him and he wanted to kill somebody. Kill them. And I got so scared, it was like . . . That was when I wanted to get out of there, I wanted to leave, But I couldn't. Do you know what I mean? I *couldn't.* And then, God, it was like I started getting this really cold feeling, sort of cold and

almost dead like when you know one of them's going to hurt you, you
didn't do anything except maybe look at them and they want to hurt
you, cold, dead, and he wasn't saying anything but you could tell he
was angry and he knew, he *knew* I knew. It was like that *very real* angry
that makes them burn things and kill people, always with the police,
the guns, the blood, *angry* and *angry*, and then so fast even though I
was cold and so scared, God, I started to get angry too but in a different
kind of way. *Get off me you bastard,* I thought but couldn't say, *Get off
me you black bastard,* I thought but couldn't say, God forgive me, *I'd like
to kill you you black bastard kill you* — I thought but couldn't say, Jesus,
and it was like a nightmare or something, I was feeling blood everywhere, blood all over the place even though I wasn't bleeding, Jesus, it
was like there was this blood you could feel but you couldn't see hot
and sticky the way blood really is. The blood. Angry. He was burning
me with it. You're killing me, you fucking animal, you black bastard,
you're hurting me, this fucking hurts, stop it, can't you see I'm crying,
you bastard, *stop.* . . . I *hate* you. — I couldn't say that to him. He loved
me, I know he cared about me, I couldn't say all that to him. He just
got out of control. He wasn't paying attention. He didn't mean to hurt
me. He didn't even know. If he'd known he wouldn't have done it like
that. I should've said something. I should've told him. I should've. I
don't know why I didn't. I swear I don't. And then it was like I wasn't
crying — something else was crying but I wasn't. I couldn't, you know,
I was just really cold and feeling sick all of a sudden. It wasn't even like
I was scared anymore, oh no; — not scared that he might kill me because I knew he couldn't, *he* couldn't even with all the angry, yes, no,
but just there, I was kind of alone or something, how can I describe it,
it was like I was way out on top of the world and then, I don't know
how, I was way down under it, falling, and I wasn't feeling anything,
not anything at all. I couldn't feel the hurting anymore and the blood
that wasn't even there, can you explain that? — and I couldn't feel him
anymore like I couldn't see him either, and not even how it felt to be
so cold and dead sort of with him way inside me, oh my God inside
me. And still there was that horrible feeling oh God like blood you
could feel but you couldn't see. Sick. The whole time I was just lying
there wanting him to stop killing me, please stop, but then I swear
I don't know why something in me wanted him to go on killing me,
yes, don't stop you fucking bastard, because it was like for a minute or

I don't know how long both of us were sort of sick or crazy or something and when it hurt it felt sort of *right* or I don't know what, like
what I *ought* to do, what I *should* feel, *I should you black bastard* even
though I knew I really knew he wanted to stop too but he couldn't
because it felt like there was something missing somewhere, there was
something missing we should have had or I don't know what, don't
ask me please, don't ask because I couldn't tell you. I can't. No, please.
Can't. And then under him there for the first time ever it was like I
knew something I'd never known before, God, now I remember, something, I knew it. It was all there in his eyes like in the rest of them,
what they try to keep from you. I could see it, Jesus, it was so sick,
glowing fierce and so hot. Hot, glowing in the darkness. Everything so
hot. Beating, roaring. I knew it. The smell of it. And the cold. Right
there.

When we got up a little later I felt dead enough, you know, the way
you feel just dead and sore, but with him I knew something had happened. Something more than angry. I didn't want to know, God. You
shouldn't know. It's better not to. Like when there's all that blood you
can feel but you can't see, everywhere, and you're wondering, wondering what, how, *who.* . . . And then I swear it's like when you feel it like
that, a nightmare or something, I can't explain it, when you feel it
like that even though you know it's not there *right now* still you know
in a weird horrible way that it's always there. Hot. You know it, you
feel it. And when you feel it like that so hot and sticky all over you like
this nightmare or something, it won't end already, it's so horrible and
you can't get away from it, Jesus, you just want to get away from
it — when you feel it like that and see it too that's when you see them.
Just like I saw him and that sick look in his eyes all black and white,
really horrible like they were on fire or something, with all that blood.
And it's like when you see that, when you see all that, I don't know
why but I do know . . . that's when you *really* begin to hate them.

We had coffee afterward with cream and then without later because
he said that would keep him going until he got his strength back — I
guess there was something funny in that because he laughed. It was
so strange then, because I felt farther away from him, from all of them,
than I'd ever felt before and yet closer to him and the rest of them than
I'd ever felt before even though I was remembering all of it. I was still
scared, and then I was kind of dead and cold and hot and I didn't know

what was real for a little while if you know what I mean, because it was like all that anger in him was gone although it was still there somewhere, you could see it. His eyes weren't glowing anymore but just kind of tired, heavy and almost sort of sad or something when he looked at me — when he looked at me. Maybe (but I don't like to remember it, God, and I was trying not to remember it) that's when I decided to get out of there, because all at once that room we were sitting drinking coffee in and the whole apartment began to look old, small, mean and shrinking in, so dark and ugly and even creepy all of a sudden, really spooky, and I couldn't breathe that incense smell anymore because I was feeling sick kind of and falling again and still so dead, falling way down with nothing to hold on to anywhere. That's when I got my things, fast, and got up, fast, and I was beginning to get scared again even though I knew for God's sake he wouldn't hurt me, stupid, I was being so stupid, he wouldn't hurt me, all that stuff was in the past already. I knew that. But then so fast sort of it was all beginning to be like a dream again all filled up with red and those shadows I didn't want to see anymore with those weird colors in his eyes that you always see in their eyes sometimes. . . . I was up already, walking to the door, not in a funny way or anything but just quietly kind of, but I had to look back once to where he was still sitting with his hands so tight around that mug holding the black coffee. I can remember that — the tension in his hands and his eyes kind of hard and soft too, almost innocent, looking sort of like how I was feeling, just out there and really cold. And I did look at him for a little while but he never raised his head to look up at me. Then — I don't know what, I still don't know — something came racing up in me really hot and I wanted to tell him that even though I was feeling that way kind of cold and dead like his eyes and even his hands and his mouth, like that, it wasn't that bad, I wanted to tell him, he didn't have to feel ashamed for any of it, it was over, I was forgetting it! It was history already, no more, please! It's like when you're dead you don't have to think about all those things. We could just pretend, you know, that we'd never seen each other or anything. It was like we hadn't, really, and couldn't, at all. You could tell that. And then I was really out the door, leaving him there like I could feel him still sitting with his head down, remembering things maybe, remembering. . . . The guys were still out on the street, almost invisible in the darkness, laughing and smiling again this time and asking me if I was going to hang with them, and even though I was still feeling dead and cold and hot too I didn't feel afraid of them, I'd never been afraid of any of them, I thought, afraid of what? — I walked right on past them and smiled back and didn't look back. Walking not running to the subway wishing I could've found a cab but there were no cabs. Walking down into the subway like falling again down into that dark thing and *Jesus God oh God I'd never be the same again God oh God.* Angry. Not scared not of them but just wanting to get home and take a shower, to wash it all away the blood and now falling again the heat crawling up my legs

to take a shower and
walking very fast yes very fast not looking back and
is one of them behind me in the darkness is he there and will he will he: —
— not looking back. Not ever. Not once.

None of that ever happened. I'm telling myself now. Never.
Put it all behind you, I'm telling myself. It's all in the past.
It never happened.

Only one time. That time. Just once.

Once. God. Once.

PART IV

Moving On . . .

BREAKING NEW GROUND

An Area in the Cerebral Hemisphere

by Clarence Major

SHE IS NOT ABSOLUTELY anything. She is something naked, skin and thought but so hot today. Because the walls are pressed. The release for the electric lock downstairs. Incidentally, a man in the building across the alley had watched. Her naked movements ate candy from a heart-shaped box. Finally it becomes clear: she is behind fieldglasses.

Smelling like yards of flesh red flowers. She entered and climbed her second stage of privacy. Wrapped a thick silk nightgown around. Much to the disappointment. An old high school friend who liked laughing. Came toward blue bell bottom pants and blouse to match. These little thoughts that slide back down narrow, worn paths. To match other thoughts.

Girl, her best friend once said, you need to get a elevator for this fucking building.

Come on in and close the.

It's just too hot — I got my fan going but.

The friend lit a cigarette and sat on the sounds of her own voice. Motion. And made a blowing sound.

Say. Who were those people out on the sidewalk?

Grown men and they never go anywhere.

They were arguing together like kids.

I'm scared of them.

I think I heard your name mentioned, the friend said.

Did they say anything worth anything.

They might have beyond me.

See that picture of flowers they gave it.

Really.

The friend went over read the card attached to it and said why didn't they give you real flowers.

Laughter caused the first young woman to hit her own chest with a small hand. Turned darker and eyes closed tears fumbled in the fieldglasses watching her.

She went to see her mother and said tell me about my father, I don't know said the mother I told you all I know. Were just standing there with their backs to each other.

I don't even know why you two divorced.

I told you he wanted to treat me like a kid.

You mean — what did he do.

Everything I nothing.

Mother, said the young woman with tears, this is the first time in many weeks, I ask you again, be honest. Tell me.

I'm telling you all I know.

She was in no mood for this and the radio gave them B. B. King and that little baby next door was teething screaming. And mother's couch was eaten by what might easily have been taxicabs with hooks on them. Anything can happen. (In any case, swift traffic was known to move through her living room.)

Who got the divorce you or him.

We separated then later he.

Never heard any more from.

Last I heard he moved to. Then somebody said he was in. And had come into a lot of money.

I wonder.

The mother left the lowrent room and stuck her hands into soapy water to try to dream and not hear. The daughter though took the conversation into the kitchen where the traffic noise was also loud. But it was really no good to go on like this mother would not open.

She jumped into a yellow cab and was shot away into the traffic with the sounds of screaming children in playgrounds on both sides.

Had come into a lot of money, huh. All these details add up she'd ask her best friend's advice. A pack of Salem's fell on the motion floor. *I'm scared of them I think I heard your name.* The traffic, however, at the friend's place.

They smoked a joint while trying to understand the strangeness of it all. Natural processes informed by instances that snag the spirit and strangle the hope of many ways. Much in the way of the probable when no clue comes. A small child does it unconsciously but adults like these must try harder and then only rarely it works. So talking with the friend is nothing new and at best not even a careful way to go crazy for fun. To be quiet or face danger are two other matters. But did she want her father or his money or his. You know what I think?

She felt she must be crazy or the moment was a mistake and she was not really involved in it — perhaps not even live. Let us see. Then really she had no idea why she got up or felt scared. Let's see. She had wet the bed and was warm and cold. Her own pee. At first it might be painful but there were sounds in other parts of the building. The people fucking next door the woman screams and the old couple upstairs fighting again, gin heads. And who was the man in the hallway talking at this hour? Can't you see how all these tidbits add up to a mistake. But maybe not.

Maybe she was alive and not dreaming. A little girl sitting on side the bed somewhere in dark room listening carefully for sounds outside. Be quiet or face danger. Seeing herself through grownup eyes or face . . .

At first it might have been without sincere meaning and the pain of just being not knowing created. Knowing who was not present. The father was not. And half way woke up grown but surely that had to be something that really happened. Not simply in a child's possession, a dream being the sounds of sex in the moaning, I mean in the morning, liquid youth wetdreams all the stuff that goes with the senses and organs.

But once sound asleep again she plunged right into sound. Delightful questions such as what makes your lips so pretty mother, your words yet so ugly with cold cheese sauce.

She looked out the window and the strange brothers were still standing on the sidewalk whispering. Might be some sort of substance or spy ring, for a delightful government that believes only in candy-sticks or mouthwash. Who knows what might be the actual point — if there is one. Dipped in blue sauce her thoughts were cheerful this morning. How was mother or friend. The men down there were all trying to talk at the same. The first time she'd seen them she'd thought. Plump fried shrimps dipped in cheese sauce, that's what I want. Did they really possess one. Just one idea, or motive. And incidentally, now she knew she was dreaming. Dreaming while she dreamed. Adventure with the playful picture of flowers. In a fine pink outfit, imagine it!

Her father was up early Sunday morning ready for. Lying awake with her large dark eyes upon him. Quietly by her young mother, the father lovingly looks down at his four-year-old . . .

  His his his his!

But why couldn't everything be that simple forever and the punishment be taken out of ups and downs. Lord had blessed them with her, the child. Enough to be. Ones own image and they understood the dances in the spirit the spirit of what happened — this new person. Or were they simply going through the motions.

Meanwhile the father dressed darkly in a suit of cold wool and punishment was in his eyes. But she knew he was kind. Could it have really been this way. Dreaming of his death she'd cried in her sleep and came. Soon to become herself again, in the morning cold kitchen trying, with stiff fingers, to make coffee. The big man was father and was good. But soon came the terror of being alone with mother. Growing up and Lord . . .

Awake with those large dark eyes. He, the father, told himself, she imagined, I understand that. Old enough to be her grandfather. Getting ready for church on Sunday morning, a preacher perhaps even God himself.

Clad in tough white suit she gyrated into restaurant and sat next to nobody. Had milk shake was teenage head filled with bubbles of pain and anxiety music and frenchfries. That was not such a warm feeling. One guy she'd gone with was now in Kentucky for the cure. Wasn't such a good memory or was the routine of school books a pleasant light in the brain. Her eyes were light and her mouth dry. Thankful for her good looks she walked with a uniqueness and even turned to acknowledge whistles. Both human and mechanical. Even the score. Two studs zipped into her once and left her angry as hell.

But these tough white suits she did not wear often and studs did not zip into her everyday. She liked herself best naked anyway though it was not an absolute hangup. With the odor of fresh flowers the stems just cut.

But those years in high school where dudes in Stetsons and Sansabelts and new cars were the In. And later the college crowd and the little income from the poverty program that sent her. Used her for an example of how smart their money could stretch and look. See, all the poor children aren't dumb nor are all the dumb students pennyless. Those were the dark days. And the boys around in a midget race for manhood! Who'd want a husband from that crowd. Each trying to get something for keeps for nothing, tight asses. All the talk shit like hay baby and pardon me and ain't dug that cat lately how you doing yourself though oh yeah he got busted that's news and maybe the cat got strung out or being a waitress after school for show money on Saturday or selling tickets in a dump theater. Often such tough young men would be very vengeful if they felt — nothing. But she felt like playing with her self, alone under the cover nights. What the answer would be to her life might be there in the wet substance. . . . Until the boss of that hole would come; often such tough young (or old) men never came. They too play with themselves, alone under the cover of night — with guns or flesh or comic books. Until their own bosses come.

So she had all this to look back on before knowing the right moment to jump into the space left her for future activity. But she certainly knew she had a future. A position of awareness, not being a waitress nor a student, without or with father's bread, she'd burn her bridges. Softly.

Her girl friend came (tho she herself did not) when they slept together that first time. They both got nice people all fucked up in their minds. They were trying to catch up with each other and talking out of their heads. I just wondered, she said. The friend said, wondered what. If the heat got to you that's what. Anything else you want to know. No, nothing else. The friend sipped something through a straw and looked crazy. Her hair was uncombed and her eyes closed for a moment.

Motherfucker, she said. Who, the friend said. Anybody. And, I'd hate to see you try to get really angry you'd probably kill somebody or yourself or — No, she answered, not me. I'm too careful, I like living too much. Too much? Well, not too much but I'm learning to roll with the tide, you know. How about your mother how is she these days. Anyway she can be I guess. You wanna know anything else? And the friend could see she was dead serious.

oh she gotta head fulla hair

by Ntozake Shange

for months allegra simply brushed her hair. she had a dream that she had such a head fulla hair that she cdnt lift her head offa her pillows. yeah. she had light blue satin pillows like the sky in manhattan the four days a year that the wind blows. blue like the horizon in curacao, so it's hard to tell the bottom of the sea from the blue reaching to the sun. she had awready had this dream where she had such a head fulla hair that yng rita hayworth wda blushed with shame. rapunsel pull her tresses back into the tower. & lady godiva give up horse back riding.

allegra altered her social life dramatically. she brushed 100 strokes in the morning. 100 strokes midday & 100 strokes before retiring. she had a busy schedule. between the local train & the express, she brushed. she brushed between telephone calls. at the disco she brushed on the slow songs. (she didnt slow dance with strangers) she brushed her hair before making love & after. she brushed her hair in taxis. while window-shopping. when she had visitors, over the kitchen table, she brushed. allegra brushed her hair while thinking abt anything. mostly she thought abt what it wd be like when she got her full heada hair. like lifting her head in the morning wd be a chore. she wd try to turn her cheek & her hair wd weight her down. she dreamed of chaka khan, chocolate from graham central station with all seven wigs, & mcdusa. allegra brushed & brushed. she used olive oil, hair food, & posner's vitamin E, but she brushed & brushed.

she soon lost contact with most of her friends. she wda lost her job, but she waz on unemployment & brushed while waiting in line for her check. she got good recommendations from her social worker: such a fastidious woman, that allegra, always brushing her hair. nothing in thr dream allegra had suggested that hair brushing, per se, had anything to do with her particular heada hair. a therapist wd say the head fulla hair had to do with something else, like a symbol of allegra's unconscious desires. but allegra had no therapist & to her dreams meant things like if you dreamed about tobias, then something happened to tobias, or he waz gonna show up. if you dreamed abt yr grandma who's dead, then you must be doing something she doesnt like or she wdnt a gone to all the trouble to leave heaven like that. if you dream something red, you shd stop.; if you dream something green, you shd keep doing it. if a blue person appears in yr dreams, that's a person who's yr true friend. that's how allegra saw her dreams.

& this head fulla hair she had in her dreams waz lavender & nappy as a three yr-old's in a apple tree. Allegra cd fry an egg & see the white of the egg spreading in the grease like her hair waz gonna spread in the air, but she waznt egg-yolk yellow/ she waz brown & the egg white wdnt be white at all/ & it wd be her actual hair/ & it wd be lavender & go on & on forever, but irregular like a rasta'man's hair. irregular, gargantuan & lavender. Nestled on the blue satin pillows/ pillows like the sky. & so she fried her eggs.

she bought daisies dyed lavender & laced-lavender tablemats & lavender nail polish. though she never admitted it, allegra believed in magic. she cd do strange things. when she felt moved, when something came over her. after a while everything around her waz lavender, fluffy & consuming, except her hair. she even found a man who was so malnourished he looked blue. allegra had all intentions of turning him lavender, but her cooking brought him back to health.

her sense of time changed. usedta be that daylight & nightime waz different. but so she cd see her head fulla hair allegra began to sleep at noon & get up at midnite. her eyes wd be so stunned from visions of herself laden in lavender nappy tufts, she stopped seeing the sky as indigo & azure/ always there was a hint of violent. lavender seepin in the air abt her. she brushed. & she brushed & her hair waz certainly healthy, but not significantly changed. allegra knew not a moment of bitterness. thru all the wrist aching & tennis elbow from brushing, she smiled. no regrets. 'je ne regrette rien' she'd sing like edith piaf. when her friends wanted her to go see tina turner or pacheco, she crooned, "sorry, i have to brush my hair."

some people send to japan for ben-wa, others to sweden for kitty porno books. allegra simply brushed her hair & smiled as if jesus had not foresworn celibacy. when she started to schedule her day or what we wd call day & jimi hendrix wd call 'lavender blue' around the different brushes she used at different hours, something happened.

allegra found ambrosia. her hair grew pomegranates & soil, rich as round the aswan. allegra woke in her bed to bananas/ avocados/ collard greens/ the Tramp's latest disco hit/ fresh croissant/ pouilly-fuisse/ ishmael reed's essays/ charlotte carter's stories/ streamed from each strand of her hair. everything in the universe that allegra needefell from her hair. but it still waznt lavender. waznt any thicker or nappier than ever before. but with the bricks that plopped from where a nine year old's top braid wd be, allegra built herself a house with running water & a bidet. she found germaine monteil bath soaps & douches in her roots. her brick house with the garden she planted in the soil that fell from her head waz bob marley's permanent address & only michael manley knew the phone number. she hadda closet full of clean bed linen & the lil girl from the castro convertible commercial opened the bed repeatedly & stayed on as a helper to brush allegra's hair. allegra waz the only person i know whose every word left a purple haze on the tip of yr tongue. when this happened she said clouds were forming & she wd have to close the windows. violet rain waz hard to remove from blue satin pillows.

BREAKING NEW GROUND

That Place

by Carolivia Herron

THE THIRD WORLD

Dañarme, a mí siempre maś que a los otros:
¡oh derrota mía, mi derrota, que a nadie
sabría communicar, que me coloca de cara
frente a los dioses que no me dispensaron
su piedad, que me exigieron apurarla hasta
el fin para saber de mí y de mis semejantes!

— Carlos Fuentes, *La Región Más
Transparente*

AFTER HER ACQUITTAL she packed her bags in the city of Washington, boarded the plane at National Airport, arrived at Aeropuerto International Benito Juárez in Mexico City, and did nothing. It is difficult to do nothing. I awake before dawn and go down to the garden, and there in the garden, before the servant has come out to sweep, before la señora begins screaming through the house, I collect red-violet petals from the bougainvillaea and set them floating in a white porcelain bowl. She fills the electric pot with water. She walks down into the garden with a white paper napkin and collects the white lily-shaped flowers that have fallen from the grapefruit tree. White with yellow-orange tongues.

On the table in the studio, centered by white flowers with yellow-orange tongues, the white napkin awaits the slow crawl of worms toward its edge. She walks up the steep half-flight of stairs to the bathroom where she fills the teapot with cold water, pours the water with old leaves through a sieve, empties the sieve into a plastic bag, steps out from the bathroom through the glass door, and taps the sieve on the stones of the terrace. It is difficult to do nothing. In the studio she tosses the worms through the window and places the grapefruit flowers in a clean olive jar to be washed.

And this is the place I was trying to get to from Washington. To see the mountains swing against the sky. When the first tremor began I thought it was the uneven table rocking back and forth — I was sitting here eating a stewed apple for breakfast. Then I noticed the wind pushing the lights that hang from the ceiling. I stood at the studio window a moment and watched the rhythmic toss of petals on the rose bushes. Red hearts rapping out time on air. And the leaves not bending, toward and away from each other, scattered, as is usual in the wind. Rather, every flower, leaf, and stem bowed toward some point west of the city. Then I noticed that my studio itself was rocking westwardly. I ran down into the garden. The mountains were swinging back and forth against the backdrop of clouds.

She is still dizzy at times. She still grasps walls and curtains and the edge of the bookcase, the table in the studio, the small waist high refrigerator. Holding on. She slips many times in a day. She drinks grapefruit flower tea. And now you ask her about Washington. How can she remember Washington? That place is so different from here that she can hardly remember it.

They have scooped a hole in the garden again this afternoon, in front of the white wrought-iron bench beside the parrot cage. The green parrots chatter and fluff for conversation as la señora crosses the garden, touches the heavy bougainvillaea and steps under the stone archway — the grapefruit tree stretching across the arch to touch the bougainvillaea — and la señora turns in the sunlit patio beyond the archway, pink flowers in her white robe gleam out as she passes the servant rooms and walks into the house. From the ivy covered terrace I look down. The naked, pregnant black woman drops heavily on her knees. Then I see her ease her belly into the hole they have scooped for her. She stretches out to be whipped. The white soles of her feet southward and toward the sky. The white palms of her hands northward and toward the earth.

The overseer stands with his left shoe by her right hip. In his right hand the handle of the whip slants downward. Threads of the whip hang loosely in his fingers, or brush against the grass. He gazes at the wings of her backbone through the skin.

The owner leans against the arch. Behind him I see her father, a skull of black ash. His child is being whipped with passion, diligence, exactitude — the owner reaches for the whip and continues to strike blood into the black flesh. I stand on the terrace with my hands on the vines, and then I notice that you are beside me. Pointing the scene out to me, showing me, telling me, Yes, yes, yes — that is your ancient father, and that, your ancient mother. He will kill her, and will take their son, his inheritance, and return eastward to the Mediterranean. From their son you are descended in the line of your fathers.

She sits in the late afternoon sun of La Plaza Hidalgo and reads *Jane Eyre* in Spanish. I'm always thirsty. I don't like boiled water. I don't like mineral water. I'm thirsty. No matter what I drink there is always something left over unquenched. Minerals or sugar or salt or acid. Something is always left over, something I long to balance or dilute with a drink of water.

Slices of poignant lime ooze untouched beside the place of rich alambre tacos. She has given up. A young man slices leaves of meat and cheese from the upright rotisserie, flourishes them through the air. Red tomatoes, white onions, green chile. Callalilies, wrought-iron benches, hedges. La Plaza Hidalgo in the late afternoon sun — and in the center, the eagle reptante. Her strength scutters loose with the rats beneath the paving stones, free.

She lies on the couch in the studio and listens to la señora screaming at the servant who has not fed the parrots the choicest morsels of fruit. La señora, who for the sake of those who lay beneath the rubble, never thought to buy a shovel, in this city whose god drinks hearts rather than grapes. Lord of Anáhuac, Duende de Anáhuac, you have blighted as good a woman as ever came to you. She lies on the couch in the studio.

She is dizzy. She can't walk. Everything is uneven. She can't see. The midday heat whitens the corners of her brain, whitens the green leaves, her will collapses within tropical blankness, her body untangles, softens, and she finds the thought there, quietly, in the center of her brain. I am grappling with anguish, I am fighting for my life. I am in a bitter struggle for the life of my immortal soul.

Every act, every awakening is a successively weaker act of defiance.

The paints are under the bed. The canvas is behind the dresser. She has forgotten why she came. Go to another land and steal fire with which to paint your city, your people, your nation. Gather up the living soul of little black Pip from the ocean of exile, that frantic lunatic soul carried down alive to the abyss, gather him up in your hands and bring him back to the light of day.

As a black Saint Peter. Pip as the child judge at the moment in which you step up to him and he recognizes you, his eyes widened in understanding, and you see how much he longs to love you, to smile at you, to welcome you, while soft creases of unexpected sorrow touch either side of his mouth. Which never opens. No. You are excluded. You look into that young black wise face, and understand, and turn away sorrowing. That face, that scene, painted upon the landscape of Washington. She was to have recorded it, to have painted it, to have made something of it. Think of it, imagine — imagine what it would have meant to have done what I set out to do! But I have ridden the wind to get here and do nothing.

Just as the fevered heads that preceded her into the world have at times rested their heat against cold stone, just so she grips the edge of the roof above her, pulls her body toward it, and rests her cheeks against the cool wall of the terrace. There she is even now stepping upon the roof. And the red comet, the morning star, the last slither of moon urging itself to the east, and the innocent unsuspecting sun appear as portentous to her as once the eagle and serpent to Aztecs. Foundation of a city that shook itself down upon its people. Annihilation. The Middle Passage. Fifteen million Africans rising from the sea each night in front of the draped partition that separates her bedroom from the studio. She awakes heartbroken, incapable of understanding her sorrow. It is as if I had heard for the first time that the black peoples of Africa were enslaved by the white peoples of Europe. In this new world, our land, before it could get started, it was paradise lost, already lost.

The fickle mountain. It meant nothing in its turning and tumbling. Indifferent to life and work. The artist whose paintings exploded with the building looks on as volunteers cast away carvings by a woman who ate a last meal of menstrual blood under eight stories of dust. The fickle mountain. There was to have been more time. There was not enough time. She had no time.

When the glow from grapefruit flower tea wears off, I drink wine. I am casting my life away. I want to cast it away. Only the servant from Oaxaca was with her in the garden when the walls swung toward each other and touched. And later it was the wine that made her cry, Blacken me, blacken me, but please don't fall, don't fall down any more. As if to be angry at the earth were to be angry at genealogy, she sang in drunken whispers, Carry me black to old Virginny, carry me black, black. As if to be pure were to be free, chanting. Bin a yankee whore since these goddamn rebels slept this nigger-white baby outa me. As if, what never has been, as if to be utterly black were to escape from pain, Sandy, at first they called me Sandy, but I didn't mean to be Sandy, blacken me and forgive me, forgive me. I have loved their works. I have loved the art of the nations that enslaved my mothers. Shaking. Standing on shaky ground. Trembling. The earth. Still clapping pieces of ground against each other, holding together a world.

It was defeat. Finally it was defeat. She of whom it was foretold that she would climb the ladder of Anansi, the African spider god, she who had been named gazelle of the stars by her people, she who had imagined the coming of Africa to the city of Washington as the judgment of Saint Pip, now lies in another country in a grapefruit flower dream, lies so far from the light, each breath a whimper, she plunges down and does not arise, coming upon the damp soul of black little Pip, at the bottom of the world, and there, in that extremity, she realizes that she has plunged down not to save that live soul from the abyss, but to strangle it, kill it once and for all, her eyes glaze over at the vision of her fingers around his throat. She is panting and stammering in a bed fouled with vomit, in Mexico City, where the bright precious god of the flower war bends over her tenderly, dreamily, to kiss her softly between her heaving breasts, and drink, drink, she is panting terrified — How have I come to this? When did I choose this? It didn't begin like this. It began with an argument, I'm sure I was arguing with someone because I did not want to be born. But something snapped in the conversation, and finally I was convinced — or did I decide to come for my own reasons, on my own account? Or was there a voice that subverted me? I couldn't see anything, I was walking along in the dark with this buzzing, whispering thing walking beside trying to talk me into something. And I didn't want to at all. how well I remember I didn't want to, but finally I knew that I would do it and the next thing I knew I was lying in the nursery at Freedman's Hospital in Washington, D.C. I didn't want to stay.

And now, all I want to know is did I kill him? Did I really kill him? My black brother. I would give anything to know that I did not kill him.

THE SECOND WORLD

Hell shall unfold,
To entertain you two, her widest Gates,
And send forth all her kings

— John Milton, *Paradise Lost*
IV: 381–383

I felt the rough elbow around my neck, the hand under my dress, the knee kicking my back, my side, my hip, my butt — toward the open door of the car. I saw the checkered shirt on the brown arms, neck, shoulders of the hands that exposed me. I heard the wild whispering voice, Pussy, pussy, got me some good pussy. I tasted the filth of the undershorts that gagged me. I smelled the stink of the penis that entered me.

I huddled into the corner of the room clinging to the rags of my clothes, as he smacked my face, my breasts, my butt. I fell to the floor as he jabbed his knee into my ribs. I cried mute, and tears and snot ran down on the undershorts in my mouth. I ached and could not cry out as he jabbed the sharp point of his shoe again and again into my side, again. I lay flat on the floor on my stomach, exhausted, arms spread up and out, exhausted, not moving, as he beat me with his fists.

I kneeled, leaning on my lower arms and elbows, while he took off the remainder of my clothes behind with a belt. I lay on my back spread-eagle, while he took off the remainder of my clothes in front. I burned in the bruises of the sores he had given me as his urine dripped over me. I obeyed him and shook my head yes when he asked if I wanted to be beaten again. I ate the only food he gave me when he removed the gag from my mouth, food spit from his mouth or easing slowly against my face from his butt.

I lay naked on the floor before him. I opened my legs wide and high at his command. I kept my eyes where I was ordered to keep them, on the high brown penis pumping erect up from the brown man erect up between my lifted legs. I lay wide open unflinching. I endured that he should enter me many times, the names he called me, the dry pain in my gut, the weariness of the thighs that I dared not lower, I endured.

I struggled against the ropes that tied my wrists to my ankles. I shivered in my nakedness against the bare wooden floor. I kept my knees open even in sleep that he might see me and enter me. I cleaned his penis with my tongue. I kissed him in the place from which he gave me my food.

I held on.

I dreamed of the brown penis that entered me. I awoke to his thumping laughter. I begged him not to use the belt against my open, exposed sex any more, not to beat me any more between my legs. I grieved. I stretched my breasts toward him, hoping to pacify him, to please him, that he would not hurt me so much any more, it hurt so much.

I turned the parts of my body that they might be in the places where he wanted them, to be whipped. I winced against the splinters of the floor away from the whip that struck me. I bled from all the soft places and hard places of my body. I lay there whimpering. I asked what I was ordered to ask, that I might stay with him forever, that he might keep me forever, beating me, whipping me, tying me, fucking me, forever.

I kneeled on my raw elbows, knees, that he might enter me from behind. I did not speak. I drank his urine. I knew that the search for me had been given up. I felt nothing.

I crawled in front of him when he shoved me from the floor of the living room to chain me to the wall of the bedroom. I stooped in the corner, using the space the chain gave me to relieve my bowels, my bladder, my uterus. I ate his shit from the spoon he placed in my mouth. I slept leaning against the hard wooden side of a table while chained to the wall. I got used to it.

I held on.

I turned my hips toward him when he walked into the room. I hunched over with open legs to increase his pleasure. I begged for the favor of his sexual attention. I made vulgar motions with my lower body to please him. I lifted my leg, my hip, to ease his access.

I held on.

I twisted off a three inch piece of metal from the empty bed frame. I was sweet to him with my voice, sweet, sweet, pretty man, until he unchained me to love me. I clasped his neck in my hands and held on and cut one side of his neck and stuck my finger into the hole. I flipped my forefinger against a tube I found in his neck, he coughed, I pressed the sharp edge of my thumb nail through the tube, he stopped screaming. I waited, I held on until he lay very quiet, oh so very quiet, upon the floor, and blue, he looked so blue and quiet.

THE FIRST WORLD

Thou Sun, said I, faire light,
And thou enlight'nd Earth, so fresh and gay,
Ye Hills and Dales, ye Rivers, Woods, and Plaines,
And ye that lie and move, fair Creatures, tell,
Tell, if he saw, how came I thus, how here?
Not of my self; by some great Maker then,
In goodness and in power pre-eminent;
Tell me, how may I know him, how adore,
From whom I have that thus I move and live,
And feel that I am happier than I know.

— John Milton, *Paradise Lost*
VIII: 273–282

Quietness

I wonder why it's so quiet in here. And my mother is quiet too. Look how quiet she is standing there in the middle of the room with her mouth wide open and her eyes squinched shut and her hands up in the air. She's twisting and turning and falling down and not making a sound. And the cradle is very quiet and the blanket is on the floor. Over there in the corner. It's my baby brother and he's all colored blue. All blue and still. And so quiet.

And my father comes in now, running by me fast and he catches my mother and holds her so that she won't fall down. But I wonder why nobody says anything. Why is it so quiet?

My baby brother is so beautiful now and his arm is smooth and blue and cold. I wonder why he pushed the blanket on the floor. Is somebody calling me? Yes? That's my name. Are you calling me? Yes, that's me? I'm Brenda Antonia Johnson. Yes, I live here with Mommy and Daddy and my baby brother.

It's very quiet today isn't it? I was in the living room trying to see if I can read. But I can't. When I'm four years old I'm going to nursery school. Do you live in my tree? Or up in the air? Or way over there above the water on the other side of the playground? I like it up here with you. We can see a long way can't we? You can't see? But I can see. I can see the playground and the water and everything. Can you see things when I tell you about them? Is that why you came and called at the window? You want to know about that place down there where I live.

I don't know very much. I'm only a little girl. But look. Can you see me there in the window looking out at you? You make a round circle of light on the screen and I'm going to sing a song to you right through the middle. Can you understand it? It's a rain song. You never heard of rain before? Well I can tell you how rain is down there if you want. But right now I'm going with Grandma. I didn't know Grandma was coming to see me but she just came into the bedroom suddenly. She's going to take me to her house.

The air outside is cool and leaves are falling off the trees and my grandmother's hand is very cold as we walk down the street. Can you see me there walking along beside my grandmother? I keep bending forward and looking up at her face. It's because my grandmother's face is wet. Can you see? Do you think she's crying?

I thought so. Yes. Down here it isn't happy is it? Those ladies over there want to talk to my grandmother. Can you hear them?

Is the baby gone then? We heard your daughter-in-law screaming two blocks away. Ain't it a shame?

And now can you see? Their faces are wet too. But my grandmother and I keep walking and now in the cab we're warm. Do you feel how nice and warm it is?

Lavender

Red flowers yellow flowers orange flowers pink flowers purple flowers white flowers green leaves with edges that scratch my hand and green grass and trees over there then I walk up the other side of the white flowers first then purple flowers pink flowers orange flowers yellow flowers red flowers and all with green leaves — I cross the other lawn and sit on the bench beside my mother and look across the grass just like my mother looks across the grass.

Sunny and bright and warm, can you see? And now I'm going to count to a hundred 1, 2, 3, 4, 5, and when I reach a hundred, 6, 7, 8, 9, 10, 11, 12, 13, 14, 15, 16 I'll think of a new word for what I see, 17, 18, 19, 20, 21, 22, 23, 24, 25 sometimes I want to run on the grass, 26, 27, 28, but it isn't 29, 30, it isn't happy to run here, 31, 32, 33, 34, 35, 36, 37, 38, 39, 40, 41 Do you ever run in the air up here? 42, 43, 44, 45, 46, 47, but you don't have grass do you? 48, 49, 50, 51, 52, You know my mother . . . 53, 54, 55, 56, 57, Can you see my mother? 58, 59, 60, 61, 62, 63, 64, 65, My mother never says any-thing, 66, 67, 68, 69, 70, 71, my mother likes to look at grass. 72, 73, 74, 75, 76, 77, 78, I don't have far to go now, 79, 80, 81 and after I think of a new word, 82, 83, 84, 85, 86, I'm going to walk down the path again, 87, 88, 89, 90, between those flowers and back to the bench 91, 92, 93, 94, 95, 96, 97, 98, ninety-niiinnnne — a hundred! And my new word is — is "glorious" for that tall fountain way over there by the building with the angel blowing a trumpet.

Can you see it? So bright and shining splashing down down like my rain song, see? How pretty it is over there. My mother never looks at it but I look at it every day every time we come. And now I'm going to walk back between the flowers, first the red flowers . . . then yellow . . . orange . . . pink . . . purple . . . but do you know what this one is? The man who lives in the building next to the fountain told me that this flower is a lilac and the color is a hard word. The color is lavender. Yes. Can you see?

Look down at me now. Do you see me reaching my hand out to touch the lilac? A smell comes from it into the air and I breathe it inside me. Can you smell that? That's a fragrance. A fragrance of lavender lilac. And down in that place where I live there are lots of fragrances.

But notice now, the coolness of the air and the quiet sounds of the birds are soft and feathery and wispy and you can hear the man who lives beside the fountain walking over here and I can look high, high to the top of the building and pretend that I live up there, right there with the angel. I'm pretending I can walk around and touch the trum-pet and everything.

Pretending? Pretending is a strange thing. Or maybe it's what you're doing right now when you look out of my eyes. My eyes are joined together with you. But pretend for me is different. Down in that place where I live I can pretend in my head all by myself, I don't have to join with anyone. You're pretending now because I'm here with you, because while I'm living down in that place I'm also up here talking to you. But back in that place I can pretend all by myself in my head any time I want. I can be in one place and let my eyes see another, yet I'm still in the same place with my eyes and everything. Yes, I know. It's magic.

Back in that place there's magic.

Ma'am, I know it ain't none of my business but do your husband know you bringin' this little girl out here everyday and sittin' in a graveyard. A graveyard ain't no place to be bringin' this little girl, so don't you bring her out here no more. If you bring her out here one more time I'm gonna call your husband.

Redface

Now look where we are. My grandfather works the ferris wheel at Glen Echo Amusement Park. Can you see? I'm sitting beside him while the ferris wheel turns. The air is too hot and full. Flies and bees buzz soft under the platform, and the sun shines bright on the building. They sell popcorn and cotton candy and pizza and frozen custard and up-stairs there's a restaurant with umbrella tables on the patio and tables behind the windows and the sun shines on the windows bright, and can you see way over there? The sun is so bright on the shining cars. But my grandfather and I sit together under a tree with dark green leaves. Can you smell the heavy leaves. And there are specks and dust in the air.

I watch my grandfather's hands as he pulls the levers sending the happy beautiful children up and around and over the air and down. I look at the children. I pretend that I can go high in the air, as high as the top of the ferris wheel.

But look. My grandfather winks. He's whispering and smiling.

Come on quick and take a ride.

Now you see me running quickly under the ferris wheel and I sit on the slatted wood of the bench and rock back and forth as my grand-father closes the safety bar. You can see my hands holding the wood. And there I go up and around where I look over the trees and squinch my eyes and see to the end of the world.

But it stops too soon. My grandfather is quiet as he opens the safety bar and when I look up there is a redface man standing in front.

You know we don't allow no coloreds to ride in this park. What you think you doing?

... she's my granddaughter. ...

This little girl? Well, what's your name?

Brenda Antonia Johnson.

Oh, is that so? Are you a smart girl? Do you know when's your birthday?

June 24, 1947.

And where do you live?

3758 Hayes Street, N.E., Washington 19, D.C.

And what's your phone number?

Adams 2-4858

What's today's date?

August 17, 1953.

And what country do we live in?

The United States of America.

And who's the president of our country?

President Dwight David Eisenhower.

And what's the capital city of our country?

Washington, D.C.

He smiles at me, can you see? And now he laughs.

So you one of thuh smart ones, hunh? A cute, smart little colored girl. It's good to know ya'll got some smart ones. Well here, I'll give you this, and today I'll let you ride in the park — but only today — you a smart one. I ain't seen no little colored girl smart as you.

And now he's walking away from us and can you feel that fire in my hand? I lift my hand toward my grandfather.

I don't want to hold this. It hurts.

Can you see how softly my grandfather takes the two silver coins from my hand? He tosses them into the speckled air shining and turning they fall into the dark leaves of the bush beside the ferris wheel. Now my grandfather holds my hand between his hands.

Look. The air is warm and the sky is clear and bright in the sun and you can see me in my blue and white dress running, can you see how lovely everything is as I run down the gravel path to the Merry-Go-Round? Running in my brown and white saddle oxford shoes that are running, running down the path.

D. C. Transit

They crucified that little baby who was born at Christmas. He's already a man and yesterday they crucified him. Tomorrow he's going to come alive again but I don't care. I don't think they should have crucified him in the first place.

The elevator takes a long time because the Monument is so tall. Wait. Let's go to the window after the others are through. And step up on the box. It's clear outside. Do you see the cars and buses? They don't look like toys. And the people don't look like ants. Everything looks real.

The castle is beautiful, dark red, and quiet. Someone is living in the tower. The echo of my shoes clacking against the floor runs down the hallway and up the stairs. Who lives in the tower? An old woman. Or a little girl. Where have they buried the old king? Here it is. Now I remember. In this quiet room.

There are so many things in this next building. Arts and Industries. The costumes hang in glass cages. They shine with gold cloth and jewels but they are old and have holes. There is a music box and a button outside to push, and the music plays. Everything in here is old. An old train. An old sewing machine. Bright polished silver swords hanging on the wall.

Look at the ceiling. It's made of swirls and curls and that old wooden fan is turning. The carriages and cars are back here. Against the wall there are popcorn machines and mirrors with fuzzy gold.

Come here where the stairway curves down from the ceiling empty and cool. Smell the palm trees in the pots beside me. The stairs are made of marble. The palm trees are tall and I step in between and wait. Nobody knows. Nobody comes down the stairs.

Tell me the difference between faeries and angels. Do faeries tear curtains like that angel did yesterday? The veil of the temple was rent. Will everyone be good now that Jesus is dead?

Artch — hives. Ark — hives. Artch — hives. Ark — hives. You say it different from how it looks. We're not going home. WHAT IS PAST IS PROLOGUE. What does prologue mean? Athena lives in there. We're taking a different bus because we're going somewhere else.

This is the Shakespeare Library. The baby boy in that picture will grow up and make stories. Those are passions and graces around him. They're not faeries or angels. These ropes are smooth and soft. Maroon.

But look at this picture over here. That's a real faerie whose name is Ariel and she wants to fly out of the picture and play.

Bra — ssss — eee — ears, brassicres, brassieres. What does that mean? When I grow up I'm going to know everything. Eighth and H. We're going home now. My mother said I can't know everything. So I'm going to know one thing completely. Tomorrow God is going to make Jesus come back alive and I'm the angel at the tomb. I don't want to. They shouldn't crucify that little baby in the first place. I don't want to ever crucify any one.

Safety Cavalier

Yes, it is far away isn't it? The dust is so pale and dry there, and the light has so many shapes. I know it is strange for you. And when you finally go there, if you ever go, you will have to travel a long way.

Look at the back of my elementary school auditorium. It's warm where I'm sitting in a row with other children. We hook the heels of our shoes on the wooden bars under our seats and the cludding is like pale dust.

On the stage a redface man is talking. He's asking if someone will come up to be a Safety Cavalier. And listen to the teachers whispering my name as they move back through the auditorium.

Brenda. Where's Brenda? She should go up.

Can you hear them whispering? And now Mrs. Holloway lifts me from the chair. Mrs. Dedmon pats my shoulder. The children look at me as I walk down the center aisle and onto the stage to talk to Safety Officer Dick Mansfield.

He is asking questions.

What is your name?

And what is your birthday?

And where do you live?

And who's our president living right here in Washington?

Now you can see him smiling.

And do you want to be a Safety Cavalier?

I walk to the front of the stage and stand. Now I am singing.

> We're Safety Cavaliers.
> We use our eyes and ears.
> We look both ways, we watch our steps.
> We're Safety Cavaliers.

And now I sing it again and the children sing with me softly.

> *We're Safety Cavaliers.*
> *We use our eyes and ears.*
> *We look both ways, we watch our steps.*
> *We're Safety Cavaliers.*

And now the children and the teachers, Mrs. Holloway and Mrs. Dedmon and Mrs. Reed, the principal, and Safety Officer Dick Mansfield on the stage behind me are all singing with me as we sing louder and louder.

> *We're Safety Cavaliers.*
> *We use our eyes and ears.*
> *We look both ways, we watch our steps.*
> *We're Safety Cavaliers.*

And now Safety Officer Dick Mansfield gives me a badge and a belt and a baton and can you hear the children clapping for me? they are leaving the auditorium and Mrs. Dedmon is there with me, leading me down from the stage. She gives me an apple, and Mrs. Holloway tells me I can play on the playground, so now I'm outside entwined along the cool metal bars of the guard rail between the playground and the auditorium. I didn't ask Safety Officer Dick Mansfield my question. They always ask me questions. Whenever I ask my question nobody knows the answer.

Angels and Faeries

Let's go with me down the end away from those apartments where I live up there, down here where the trees are close together with thick leaves and the Anacostia River curves around by the Potomac Electric Power Company and the schools there on the hill. Spingarn Senior High School and Phelps Vocational School and Browne Junior High School and Charles Young Elementary School and the Langston Library is over there too.

Can you see that mountain on the other side of the water? How still it is. I am sad. Sad? Sadness is what you feel inside me. Yes. Sadness is that air in my chest that breathes out of me slowly. Is it happy for you to live up here in the sky? And to come down here sometimes and play with me? And talk?

Now I turn away from the river and walk back through the woods to the lawn and the playground. There's Miss Hopkins going into her apartment. Can you hear that noise? The children are teasing Miss Hopkins.

> *Miss Hopkins is a bull dagger!*
> *Miss Hopkins is a bull dagger!*
> *Miss Hopkins is a bull dagger!*
> *Miss Hopkins is a bull dagger!*

I like Miss Hopkins. I walk across the playground and down along the green park to her apartment and up the steps to her door.

Hello, Brenda.

Let's go in. It's shadowy in here. Can you see the room? It's dark and cool with all the pretty things Miss Hopkins keeps in the tall wooden cabinets. Her carpet is soft under my shoes. Can you feel it? And look at the red and gray pattern of it. With swirls. I'm happy sitting here.

Miss Hopkins, can you tell me the difference between faeries and angels? No one will tell me the difference. Do you think they are kin to each other?

Maybe faeries are not as tall as angels, but faeries are interesting aren't they? They point to strange places don't they? Sometimes I think faeries are in the rainbow I see in the morning, Miss Hopkins, when I look toward the water that's behind the trees down the end.

And Miss Hopkins, why do you think the tree in front of my apartment is so crooked? The trees in front of the other apartments are straight and short and bushy with round tops and their branches reach out to the sides. But mine is tall and thin and the trunk is crooked and the branches reach up to the sky slanted.

And Miss Hopkins, don't you think that even if it's an angel that lives high above the trees and pulls them to heaven, even if it's an angel, don't you think my angel is a faerie because she saw something else in the sky and went toward it and bent away from the other angels, and pulled my string crooked. And that's why my tree is bent?

And now you see me standing at the low table, holding a beautiful piece of carved glass that Miss Hopkins brought from Germany — I look at the pattern. Miss Hopkins kneels beside me and one of her hands holds me by my waist in front and softly, gently from behind, Miss Hopkins strokes my leg with her other hand and my thigh and up warm, warm, tender and warm between my legs — can you feel Miss Hopkins rubbing me softly? I look into the carved glass in my hands and I tremble. I hold the glass against my chest until I'm so warm where Miss Hopkins touches me. I open my legs wider and lean against Miss Hopkins, leaning my head against her shoulder and neck. Until now happiness fills up inside me. Can you feel how happy it is? And Miss Hopkins is holding me tight. Very tight.

Shower

I ache. You want to know about that place. You want to go there. You want to be born. You want to know what will happen. You don't understand aching.

Look. I'm tossing a ring of keys into the air and each time they hit against each other they chime, and at each chime — can you tell? — I pretend that it's an angel running up the path toward me as I come down the hill from under the trees on my way to junior high school.

I'm taking a shower in gym class. Can you feel the water trying to pierce my skin? And do you feel that strange feeling? It's because I ache.

I'm looking at the white soap on the girl over there. Aren't her breasts small and round and brown? I want to talk with her and touch her. Do you think she's an angel? Maybe tomorrow morning she will run up the path when I come down the hill. The water hurts my skin, it tries to pierce me. That's why I lean back away from the water. But look at the pretty white soap moving down on her brown skin under her arms and down her legs.

The pretty brown girl rinses off the soap and leaves the shower and I want to be an angel in heaven walking down a golden street and holding hands with another angel who's smiling at me. She doesn't want me to look at her.

Stop. You stop looking at me like that. Stop it.

She doesn't want to take a shower any more. She doesn't want me to look at her. I want to live in a tree with my arms soft leaves and when little girls walk under my tree I'll brush my leaves against them and they won't know it's me.

I'm on my way home from school walking back up the hill. I like the sound of keys when I throw them in the air and they chime together.

Party

The pleats on the pink skirt I wear to the party open to show lime green. And I'm wearing my mother's string of white pearls, you can feel my fingers touching them. Round and smooth. My blouse is lime green. I have white shoes and gloves.

My mother and father think I should go to this party. I'm afraid of it. Afraid? Afraid is to pretend something sad instead of something happy. It's dark at the party and all the faces are dark. Eyes look around trying to see. I can't see. And can you smell those fragrances? Cologne and sweat and talcum. It stinks.

A boy is dancing with me close and hot. He hunches his back over me and squeezes me down against his hips. I'm suffocating. Can you feel that against my thigh? I feel it through his pants and through my skirt. It's his penis and it's hard and he's rubbing it back and forth because he wants to.

It's too hot here at the party and that's why I go to the punch bowl to get a cup of pineapple and ginger ale with ice. But the boy comes to the punch bowl too. He sticks his hand into the pocket of my lime green blouse and squeezes my left breast and takes his hand out again fast. I stop drinking punch, can you feel that emptiness in my throat? And now I'm drinking punch again. I'm afraid. I'm supposed to do something or feel something but I don't know what it is.

Supposed? Supposed is when someone gives you a task to do and you don't want to do it but still someone gives it to you. Up here you don't understand supposed because each of you here chose your own task, each of you chose to try to be born in that place. No one chose it for you. And you have gathered up here to experience my life because my life shows you where you want to go. But the people in that place have chosen tasks for me that I don't want. These tasks are the acts I'm supposed to do there. This is what supposed means. And this is why all the girls are laughing at me as we stand beside the punch bowl.

Girl, what's wrong with you? I would have slapped that nigger's face if he had done that to me. Ain't you got no pride? His head still be spinnin' if he done that to me.

I want the girls to stop laughing at me and I want to kiss them. The pretty girls with their pretty eyes.

The party is almost over. The boy comes into the room and turns on the bright light. He puts a naked rubber doll baby backside up in the middle of the floor. Can you see the hole cut into the rubber between the doll's legs? He calls his pet dog.

Here Avalon, Avalon. Come fuck baby. Baby say my pussy's hot and ready. Come on Avalon, give baby some cock.

Now you see the fuzzy white dog Avalon hunch over the rubber doll and he sticks his penis into the hole between the doll's legs. He thrusts his penis into the hole again and again and everyone is laughing.

How intense you are as you look through my eyes and watch the dog stick his penis into the doll. There is a beautiful light in you as you lean through me to listen. It is because you have already imagined your future. Imagined? To imagine is to pretend with your whole self rather than just with your mind. You have imagined that you will be born there, in that place.

The Boy

I'm in the hallway at senior high school talking with the boy and I ask him if he will let me sit my vagina on his penis because I read that it feels good and I want to know if it's true. He answers me, yes.

It's night. Can you feel how cool it is and sweet with flowers as we ride to Fort Dupont Park and into the parking lot? Don't you think the night is beautiful? We get out and look for a place and he sits on a park bench with his back against the table and he unzips his pants and reaches into his undershorts and pulls out his penis. And I reach under my skirt and pull my underpants down and off and step over the bench to sit down on his lap facing him. I'm trying to sit down on his penis. But the opening to my vagina is too small and when I push and sit down hard it hurts and I scream. I jump up and fall backwards on the ground. I tell the boy, I won't do that any more, it hurts.

I get up from the ground and turn around and run back to the car and the boy comes and drives me home.

It's Monday morning and I walk to class through the corridor where the boys are standing and look, those are my underpants hanging by a thumbnail tack with my name printed on them in big letters and can you hear all the boys laughing at me as I walk past?

University

It is autumn. And the students are angry. Can you see the effigy catch fire? The flames flash against dark, dark eyes. The rope around his neck. University president. Papier-mâché and white-washed black paint. Choking. Smoke. Clogging the windows of Douglass Hall. A black man leaps up on the box, grabs the megaphone, and demands that all black sisters subjugate themselves to their men. A white man from the *Washington Post* lies where they tossed him, with his broken camera and his broken arm, crushed against the steps of Locke Hall. A white woman with stringy blond-brown hair leaps with both arms into the effigy tree demanding to be sacrificed for the cause. But I sit in philosophy class in Douglass Hall. Can you see me there? Metaphysics.

The flames rise from the effigy to move along the branch. Black smoke bundles upward through the open classroom window. The students in the room, save one, all panic, grab up papers and books, knock into chairs escaping, scream, depart quickly. The professor stops her lecture a moment and gazes after the students. Tall black woman. Then her brown eyes meet the brown eyes remaining. My eyes. Black woman. Yes. I'm still sitting there looking up at her. Waiting.

Hesitation.

Spinoza.

She glances toward the window, the smoke. Her fingers are on the handle of the window. She pulls it shut and locks it and then turns to me.

Or if not Spinoza, then certainly Aristotle.

Screams batter the side of the building. They are cursing each other's souls to hell. Somebody snickers close to the wall. The fire lifts. The University police arrive.

It was by accident of course that the branch of metaphysics received its name. It was the book following physics when Aristotle's works were catalogued, but through a propitious coincidence . . .

The fire consumes the scene behind her, engulfing the tree and blotting out for a moment the intricate crevices of Miner Teacher's College, echoing the far strip of sunset.

Not physics, but metaphysics.

Her slender fingers in the half-opened volume. The perturbed earnestness in her appeal to me, what is it she wants of me? What? What am I being asked to do? Who am I?

... such that the nature of ultimate reality, regardless of intellectual laziness, of productivity that is mere intelligential automatonism — evokes an inescapable human confrontation with extremity.

A long enflamed branch falls carrying others with it. I jump in my seat but she holds my eyes with her eyes. Brown eyes.

Not physics, but metaphysics.

But the tree is burning down to the ground.

Through the agency of metaphysics.

In the silence my silent question — my teacher, can you tell me who I am?

The gazelle of the stars. She speaks until the end of the hour. To me alone. You are the gazelle of the stars, but you do not yet know it. It will be a long time before you know it.

I pack my books and papers and leave. She sits at the desk with her head in her hands.

Genesis

Washington, D.C.

A black woman. I have imagined her as my descendant, and for this reason I have desired no child of my body and have wished that I had not been born.

She stands halfway between the Folger Library and East Capitol Street, her left foot lifted up for the next step.

There is thick white dust in the air.

The town houses across the street, especially at the end closest to the Supreme Court Building, are somewhat unkempt, and without curtains, as if they had been allowed to run down for several years. Or perhaps they are deserted. It is difficult to be sure. And should you focus on a particular feature of a house — say the stone sill under an upper window — looking for a sign of decay so inescapable that it would be evidence of ancient abandonment, the whitish dust defeats your eyes. You give up with a shrug. And perhaps it is only the late afternoon mist — Washington has always been a humid city.

She looks to her left down East Capitol Street, toward the Capitol. It must be a day of late spring, the grass lawn in front of the Folger and the leaves on the trees that border the Library of Congress, have a youthful shimmer in the light. Perhaps those are tall banners decorating the north wall of the Folger behind her, heavy dark parallel gashes filled with blinding white dust. It is difficult to see clearly. She is the only sign of life on the street.

Only one corner of the Supreme Court Building is clear, still standing, the remainder is blurred by the dust, a pure white powder, like talcum or chalk or fibrous asbestos. Or the angle of sun in the mist. Her eyes are focused on the Capitol Building, which is partially hidden by the glimmer of intervening trees. The sky is pale white far above the horizon, a high rain cloud passing over. And then a stroke of baby blue sky fingering toward the high dome, heaped marble glistening in that shattered light — with her foot still in the air she bends and looks. From your angle you can see the tension in her back and shoulders, all her energy has rushed into vision as she tries to see if the Capitol Building is still there. But such a puff of dust dazzles all that space, it is difficult to be sure. It is hard to see.

You see it there in front of you in the gallery, my painting, stark pastel against the thick weave of the canvas. "That Place," my project for my Fine Arts degree from the University. I am here to receive the award, a fellowship to any third world country. I choose Mexico.

THE LAST WORLD

Greatly instructed I shall hence depart
Greatly in peace of thought, and have my fill
Of knowledge, what this Vessel can contain;
Beyond which was my folly to aspire.

— John Milton, *Paradise Lost*
XII: 557–560

We are the gods.

It will come to you when your body has been utterly ruined by disease, when the putrid black bile has drained down from your heart into the toilet, seven times, ten times, twelve times in an hour, and you lie there weakened, and weakened again, each flushed stinking pool of black water carries half your strength to feed the roots of a city of exile. Bitter bread. You lie depleted of everything except the amoebae that

nibble the black walls of your gut and lift you again and again to release filth and blood into the sewers of a land that is not your land.
This is the moment it will come to you. The people of your own land
will lift their heads, and call to you, and look for you, and not find you
who leans from your bed to vomit into the green plastic bucket. That
is when your muse will arrive, fifteen million sea rotted bodies, one at
a time, each offering a cup of sea water to drink. Drink that salt and
know at last that you have descended into hell. That you have found
your people at last. This is the moment in which you must rise and
place the canvas against the wall. With each cup each ancestor will
lean into the canvas, as you drink, each cup. And this shall be the sign
unto you that the moment is upon you. There will be no water. It is
many years since the lake burned away and left a thick jelly which now
will tremble softly, quietly, clacking the buildings together and dropping them in dust. There will be no water to drink. You will long for a
drink of water that could wash the taste of vomit from your throat.
There will be no water to wash clothes with. You will wince power-
lessly away from the black stains in your underpants. There will be
no water for washing out the green plastic bucket. You will sprinkle a
layer of dry soap powder over the drying rot. Then you will know that
you have been called, and you have been chosen, and you have been
ordained even now as we speak together, here at the foundation of the
world. You will be too weak to move, so weak that there will be no
more pain. That will be the moment, remember it well. Rise up then,
and fulfill the promise we lay upon you in this moment.

But she answered saying, I do not want to be born.

We give to you the loom of Anansi, spinner of the thread, that
weaves the web, which is the ladder to heaven, oh black widow who
will lose so many of your people. Gazelle of the stars your name as
you climb that ladder with your living body from the earth. But there
will be other names for you. Imagining their heavens without you
they will call you black nigger slavedaughter, looking up into the
sky they will ask what's a black nigger slavedaughter doing at the top
of heaven, a slave and a descendant of slaves, servant of servants, your
father's children, yes, the white children of your fathers shall make you
the keeper of the vineyards, but your own vineyard, remember that I
told you, your own vineyard shall you not keep, and the penis of every
man, whether he be darkness or whether he be light, shall be raised

against you, black and beautiful, yes, as the tents of Kedar, as the curtains of Solomon, black, beautiful, and fucked. But do not refuse to be born into that place, do not refuse to reascend in your living body with the vision to answer this vision, gazelle of the stars, great black angel, be born, go live this life, and return.

But she turned herself away saying I want no part of these visions, neither the loom nor the ladder. I do not want to be born.

You have a city in the world and I have heard you crying throughout that city seeking your home. They have wearied of your crying. That place is the place you love. It is a great and beautiful city and will lift its hands to tear the limbs from your body and plant them at the three corners of the diamond and in the River. Stop crying so much. You must learn to stop crying. Perhaps you think you were to have found someone. That song about a beloved somewhere to find is a mistake. I am telling you now before it even begins. I see your hands beating against a wall. I see you naked, tied hand and foot, flat on your back beneath the grin of the rapist. You are crying. You believe that the thing you most feared has come upon you. It has not. You lie there thinking you have given up. You have not. Stop crying and listen. There is no beloved. There is just a job you have to do. Do you think we care about your being raped? I know I don't care. I care about the job and whether it gets done. We are not sending you there to be happy, we are sending you there to work. Look at the scene we have prepared for you. You are looking down on the Potomac River and that place which is cut off by a creek and on one side of the creek the faces are black and on the other side the faces are white. Now I'm going to tell you your job. Your job is to stand in that creek where it meets the Potomac and sing. I'm serious. Stand there in the mud and pollution and undertow and sing. I can tell you there are a lot worse things to have to do. That's the only way we can get the information we need. We need information. And anyway it's your job. You should be happy to be chosen by the gods. We all have a job to do, you like everyone else. Did you expect to be the only one exempt? I need information. Lots more information. All these hungry heads are waiting for me just outside the door. What am I going to feed them? You should practice singing. Be born, find that creek, and sing.

But she turned away her head and her eyes in anger saying, I do not want to be born.

For a long time I have wanted to ask you who you are, and now you have come to me asking this same question about yourself. Look at the desert — scrub brushes and grit. It is a perfect place, is it not? when you long to discover your own mind. I come here often. And you? What do you plan to do? We have not given you much time to decide. So you come to me for comfort and advice. Will you have a cup of tea as we walk? Perhaps we do not need the information you could bring us back from that place, but we certainly desire it. I desire it. Indeed I have been considering little else for this past while. I tell you this frankly, and yet I'm also capable of considering it from your point of view. I have been looking at you for quite a while now. Yes, as you may know, I have been warned and chided by the others for favoring you. Yes, the mica and obsidian in the yellow stone make an amazing pattern. This is not the place to come if you are afraid of your own mind. Would you prefer to sit and watch the light? I'm not afraid of what will happen, that is if you decide not to go. But my greater concern is the meaning of it. I understand nothing. I have only determined that your birth will have a special and personal significance for me, me to the exclusion of the others, although of course it will have a significance for us all. I suppose you don't remember anything prior to the beginning of this argument. No? And yet I'm sure I spoke to you once in the assembly. Can you remember? They were all laughing at you then. But even I don't remember very well. I know I didn't laugh. Are you certain that you have never called to me? that you have never visited me through a secret window or a dream? I want to know who you are. You have disturbed my peace. And already you are preparing to go. But why can you not stand still a moment and let me look at you? And yet why should I detain you, as I have no answers. I hope that you will have mercy on me, and that we will meet again, and that you will be born, and that you will tell me your name.

But with great sadness she turned away from her saying, You do not understand, my teacher. I came to you so that you would tell me who I am. I had wanted to stay here with you forever, to be with you forever, but I do not want to be born.

So you come with me at last to see the streets of your dark city. This is the Eastern Branch of the Anacostia River as it flows under East Capitol Street. And here it is further north where you shall know it best. Here is the marsh where the children will be smothered in quicksand.

Over here, on firmer ground, is the place of the murders, the police chase, suicide. When you have become a child you will play here. You will stand and look out over the water and talk to us. But come with me down into the large cement basement workroom of one of the apartments where you shall live. Look at the children crowded around the walls, three rows thick, four, six, ten, their black and brown and yellow faces squirming above and around each other — curiosity and suspense and fear. Most of them have paid a nickel apiece to watch the eight-year-old female child — no, it is not you, this is not what you have to fear — slowly pull up her dress. You did not pay a nickel, you think it is shameful, you have refused to go, you sit on the porch of your apartment alone with a copy of *A Child's Garden of Verses* on your lap when all the other children have gone to see Penelope pull down her pants. They have been whispering about it all week. Friday afternoon, right after school, Penelope is going to pull up her dress and pull down her pants. A nickel apiece. And bright pretty little girls and boys are paying up. You look up from the poetry. Your young eyes are sad and tormented. You know the truth. You want to see Penelope pull up her dress and pull down her pants. You want to see her do it. The lawns are quiet as you walk across, and up the stairs, and down to the basement with the book under your arm. The child guards are busy looking to stop you or to ask for a nickel. And then you see Penelope in the middle of the room, a wide space around her, stiff terrified hands holding her skirt up around her waist. A yellow girl. Puny legs between the white pants and the dirty socks. But you see only her face. Terror. The eyes glaze over and refuse to focus on the maniacal faces screaming, Pull down your pants! Pull down your pants! Pull down your pants! Her face is like your face. Her eyes are like your eyes. Her color is like your color. You stop breathing for a moment. No, Penelope, don't pull down your pants! Screamed out, and you turn and run up the stairs and out over the lawn clutching the book with both hands, running home. And a few minutes after, through all the doors and windows of that basement, one hundred children come running. You stand at the third floor window of your apartment and watch them run. This is your land, your country, your city, your people. By these images you will know that place when you come to it.

But she turned away lightly from that scene and looked into their eyes saying, You presume too much when you assume that I shall be born into the world. You have shown me nothing that calls me away. There is nothing on earth that I want, and what they would have from me I shall not give. I have no desire to be born.

I await you by the sea. When all of these events are over, whether or not you take up our challenge. Whether or not you give up. I will be walking here, waiting, waiting for you. Did you think there was no one among the gods who loves you? But I love you. You do not remember when we first walked here in the beginning, and here we first imagined you, and we agreed that we would work together to accomplish the task we have been deciding upon for so long. You separated from me to travel these spheres, gathering the indications, comprehending the task. Now you repudiate it. You want to be free. Let it be as you will. And yet, though it may take many defeats, many incarnations, this thing must be at last. I will wait as long as it takes. I will wait here for you by the sea, beyond the corridor that will incarnate you, the vestibule of heaven.

The corridor of the future is long, is it perhaps infinite?

It will first appear to you, the future, as a mild passage into a narrow room, a vestibule with a bright window at the far end reflecting the variations of light. The walls on either side of the room are covered by bookcases whose shelves are filled with volumes. The upper rows are hidden beneath multicolored maps that hang loose from the ceiling. Yes, the future first appearing to you as a mild passage into a narrow room, you will consider it a storage place of rustling curiosities and superfluous study. You finger the maps and lift them one after another slowly, their colors pass your eyes. You scan the titles of the irrelevant volumes, because slowly it has pleased you long waiting, choosing and beginning late, late in eternity.

Infinite. Infinite because finally you choose a volume, after you select a comfortable chair upholstered in burgundy cloth woven into brocade diamonds by pink and green garlands, a chair with wide wooden arms and a sturdy frame, an old-fashioned Morris chair with an adjustable wrought-iron rod wedged in the mechanism supporting the back, after you walk again beside the shelves and reach at last for a volume that is to solace your premonitions, there at the end of eternity, before your fingers touch the engraved letters along the spine, you are distracted because the window opens there on your right, opens without reference to the metal grooves along the bottom for lifting it. Somehow there is a vertical split down the central column of window panes, and the split passes down through all four rows of glass and wood, and the wall itself opens, and you step to the open space and stand on the edge alone.

Yes, infinite because there at last your window opens on desire, your desire. Finally you will recognize an uncanny desire within yourself. A terrible yearning — for what? What? Human life. It is human life you yearn for. And human life, when compared with the rustling maps, the engraved volumes, the burgundy-colored chair; human life, with its forking paths, its flagrant impossibilities, its stubbornness, its arbitrary goals, its biased repudiations, its ingratitude; human life, unlike heaven and the vestibule of heaven; human life, unlike eternity, is infinite.

And she cried in her earnestness saying, I do not want to be born, I do not, I do not. Why will you place the burden of this memory upon me? I do not want to be born. You don't give me any peace, you give no peace. How can I complete what you ask of me? Why should I go for you? I shall not live in that place for you. I shall never be born into the world.

Will you not stand still and let me look at you? Stand still. Lie still and let me touch you. Gazelle of the stars, stay one moment while I love you. And when morning comes, and you hide upward into day, beloved, for one moment I will hold your face in my hands, one moment before you dress yourself and ascend — let me hold you as you flame away in my hands. Let me love you. Let me touch you — oh let me love you. Lie with me a moment, speak with me a moment, so many centuries of desire, reaching through so many ages and never touching, never, why have you never let me touch you? Why have you never let me love you? Let this be the moment. Let this be the night. Lie still with me a moment. Unveil yourself for me. Undress your body not turning away. And lie with me my woman while I roll you in my river and give you that long moment you have desired since the foundation of the world.

But she did not. She did not undress herself veil after veil. She did not lay herself down. She did not receive from her hands what she had never received, no not from gods, women, or men. She turned away

from the touch of the hands that would have loved her into life saying
I do not want to be born, and she stepped upon the ladder of Anansi
and turned her face upward to darkness, to return to the stars.

But the woman who loves her calls to her again saying, Come back.
Why? I'm going to take you to bed and make love to you and put my
penis inside you. But I have to return to the stars. You don't need to
return to the stars you need to come here to me. And when she comes
to the door of their house they take her hand and lead her toward the
stairs. At the foot of the stairs she stops.

Why are we going upstairs?

I'm taking you to bed upstairs. I'm going to make love to you and
put my penis inside you. They go up the stairs holding her hand and
she follows. And halfway up she is trembling so much that she cannot
lift her legs. He turns back to her surprised. His brown eyes widening,
softening.

And are you so afraid? Is that what it is? I'm going to make love to
you but I'm not going to hurt you. He steps back down beside her
and places one arm, his right arm, around her waist in the front, and
places his left hand gently and completely between her legs in the back,
and whispering in her ear, I'm going to put my penis inside you. I'm
going to take you to bed and make love to you. But I won't hurt you.
And he helps her up the stairs with his arm and his hand, she trembling against him and fluttering afraid and he walks her into the bedroom. He takes her clothes from her body. He leads her to the bed and
guides her under the sheet. He stands by the bed and undresses himself.
He pulls the sheet back and places her body to receive him — her
hands beside her head on either side, her legs open — he kneels between them at first and touches her body to comfort her, and he is
speaking.

It's because of your songs that you must receive me. You sent us
those songs, and now I'm going to put my penis inside you.

So he lifts her hips in his hands and places her thighs around his
waist, and stretches himself out above her, coming closer, and puts his
penis inside her vagina and pushes it all the way in, slow, how slowly,
and she touches her legs around his body and holds him, and touches
his back with her fingers. And he pushes himself in and out of her
many times and calls her gazelle of the stars.

But at the end of eternity she lies there, inert, in the strength of all her unredeemed aboriginal repudiation, a still-born high-yellow black child, sandy yellow-brown eyelids closed over darkening blue eyes, nappy blond hair, given up on, cast aside, scrunched into the incubator in the corner of the delivery room of Freedman's Hospital of Howard University of Washington, D.C., that place, back-slapped, ankle-hung, shook, thumped, tossed, stung with smacks, pierced with needles, twisted, turned and oxygenized to no avail, at the end of eternity, long-awaited, dream-foretold, and now failed of all promise, when suddenly, for no discernible reason, she breathed in.

Finis May 12, 1986, Puerto Escondido, Oaxaca, México

LAUNCHING THE FUTURE

New York Day Women

by Edwidge Danticat

TODAY, walking down the street, I see my mother. She is strolling with a happy gait, her body thrust toward the DON'T WALK sign and the yellow taxicabs that make forty-five-degree turns on the corner of Madison and Fifty-seventh Street.

I have never seen her in this kind of neighborhood, peering into Chanel and Tiffany's and gawking at the jewels glowing in the Bulgari windows. My mother never shops outside of Brooklyn. She has never seen the advertising office where I work. She is afraid to take the subway, where you may meet those young black militant street preachers who curse black women for straightening their hair.

Yet, here she is, my mother, who I left at home that morning in her bathrobe, with pieces of newspapers twisted like rollers in her hair. My mother, who accuses me of random offenses as I dash out of the house.

Would you get up and give an old lady like me your subway seat? In this state of mind, I bet you don't even give up your seat to a pregnant lady.

My mother, who is often right about that. Sometimes I get up and give my seat. Other times, I don't. It all depends on how pregnant the woman is and whether or not she is with her boyfriend or husband and whether or not *he* is sitting down.

As my mother stands in front of Carnegie Hall, one taxi driver yells to another, "What do you think this is, a dance floor?"

My mother waits patiently for this dispute to be settled before crossing the street.

In Haiti when you get hit by a car, the owner of the car gets out and kicks you for getting blood on his bumper.

My mother who laughs when she says this and shows a large gap in her mouth where she lost three more molars to the dentist last week. My mother, who at fifty-nine, says dentures are okay.

You can take them out when they bother you. I'll like them. I'll like them fine.

Will it feel empty when Papa kisses you?

Oh no, he doesn't kiss me that way anymore.

My mother, who watches the lottery drawing every night on channel 11 without ever having played the numbers.

A third of that money is all I would need. We would pay the mortgage, and your father could stop driving that taxicab all over Brooklyn.

I follow my mother, mesmerized by the many possibilities of her journey. Even in a flowered dress, she is lost in a sea of pinstripes and gray suits, high heels and elegant short skirts, Reebok sneakers, dashing from building to building.

My mother, who won't go out to dinner with anyone.

If they want to eat with me, let them come to my house, even if I boil water and give it to them.

My mother, who talks to herself when she peels the skin off poultry.

Fat, you know, and cholesterol. Fat and cholesterol killed your aunt Hermine.

My mother, who makes jam with dried grapefruit peel and then puts in cinnamon bark that I always think is cockroaches in the jam. My mother, whom I have always bought household appliances for, on her birthday. A nice rice cooker, a blender.

I trail the red orchids in her dress and the heavy faux leather bag on her shoulders. Realizing the ferocious pace of my pursuit, I stop against a wall to rest. My mother keeps on walking as though she owns the sidewalk under her feet.

As she heads toward the Plaza Hotel, a bicycle messenger swings so close to her that I want to dash forward and rescue her, but she stands dead in her tracks and lets him ride around her and then goes on.

My mother stops at a corner hot-dog stand and asks for something. The vendor hands her a can of soda that she slips into her bag. She stops by another vendor selling sundresses for seven dollars each. I can tell that she is looking at an African print dress, contemplating my size. I think to myself, Please Ma, don't buy it. It would be just another thing I would bury in the garage or give to Goodwill.

Why should we give to Goodwill when there are so many people back home who need clothes? We save our clothes for the relatives in Haiti.

Twenty years we have been saving all kinds of things for the relatives in Haiti. I need the place in the garage for an exercise bike.

You are pretty enough to be a stewardess. Only dogs like bones.

This mother of mine, she stops at another hot-dog vendor's and buys a frankfurter that she eats on the street. I never knew that she ate frankfurters. With her blood pressure, she shouldn't eat anything with sodium. She has to be careful with her heart, this day woman.

I cannot just swallow salt. Salt is heavier than a hundred bags of shame.

She is slowing her pace, and now I am too close. If she turns around, she might see me. I let her walk into the park before I start to follow again.

My mother walks toward the sandbox in the middle of the park. There a woman is waiting with a child. The woman is wearing a leotard with biker's shorts and has small weights in her hands. The woman kisses the child good-bye and surrenders him to my mother, then she bolts off, running on the cemented stretches in the park.

The child given to my mother has frizzy blond hair. His hand slips into hers easily, like he's known her for a long time. When he raises his face to look at my mother, it is as though he is looking at the sky.

My mother gives this child the soda that she bought from the vendor on the street corner. The child's face lights up as she puts in a straw in the can for him. This seems to be a conspiracy just between the two of them.

My mother and the child sit and watch the other children play in the sandbox. The child pulls out a comic book from a knapsack with Big Bird on the back. My mother peers into his comic book. My mother, who taught herself to read as a little girl in Haiti from the books that her brothers brought home from school.

My mother, who has now lost six of her seven sisters in Ville Rose and has never had the strength to return for their funerals.

Many graves to kiss when I go back. Many graves to kiss.

She throws away the empty soda can when the child is done with it. I wait and watch from a corner until the woman in the leotard and biker's shorts returns, sweaty and breathless, an hour later. My mother gives the woman back her child and strolls farther into the park.

I turn around and start to walk out of the park before my mother can see me. My lunch hour is long since gone. I have to hurry back to work. I walk through a cluster of joggers, then race to a *Sweden Tours* bus. I stand behind the bus and take a peek at my mother in the park. She is standing in a circle, chatting with a group of women who are taking other people's children on an afternoon outing. They look like a Third World Parent-Teacher Association meeting.

I quickly jump into a cab heading back to the office. Would Ma have said hello had she been the one to see me first?

As the cab races away from the park, it occurs to me that perhaps one day I would chase an old woman down a street by mistake and that old woman would be somebody else's mother, who I would have mistaken for mine.

Day women come out when nobody expects them.

Tonight on the subway, I will get up and give my seat to a pregnant woman or a lady about Ma's age.

My mother, who stuffs thimbles in her mouth and then blows up her cheeks like Dizzy Gillespie while sewing yet another Raggedy Ann doll that she names Suzette after me.

I will have all these little Suzettes in case you never have any babies, which looks more and more like it is going to happen.

My mother who had me when she was thirty-three — *l'âge du Christ* — at the age that Christ died on the cross.

That's a blessing, believe you me, even if American doctors say by that time you can make retarded babies.

My mother, who sews lace collars on my company softball T-shirts when she does my laundry.

Why, you can't you look like a lady playing softball?

My mother, who never went to any of my Parent-Teacher Association meetings when I was in school.

You're so good anyway. What are they going to tell me? I don't want to make you ashamed of this day woman. Shame is heavier than a hundred bags of salt.

BIOGRAPHIES

Maya Angelou is the author of several volumes of poetry and autobiography, most notably *I Know Why the Caged Bird Sings*. She is Reynolds Professor at Wake Forest University and resides in North Carolina.

James Baldwin wrote novels, plays, and numerous essays as well as a collection of short stories, *Going to Meet the Man*. Raised in Harlem, he spent much of his adult life in France and died in November 1987.

Toni Cade Bambara is the author of two collections of short stories, *Gorilla, My Love* and *The Sea Birds Are Still Alive*, as well as a novel, *The Salt Eaters*. The editor of *The Black Woman: An Anthology*, she resides in Philadelphia.

Edwidge Danticat is the author of *Krik? Krak!*, a collection of short stories, and *Breath, Eyes, Memory*, a novel. Born in Haiti, she came to the United States when she was twelve. She lives in Brooklyn, New York.

Samuel Delany, a Nebula Award winner, published the first of his many science-fiction novels at age twenty. His stories are collected in *Driftglass/Starshards*. He lives in Amherst, Massachusetts, where he is a professor of comparative literature at the University of Massachusetts.

Alexis DeVeaux is the author of *Spirits in the Street*, a novel, children's books, and several plays. She lives in Buffalo, New York.

Rita Dove was the poet laureate of the United States. Recipient of the Pulitzer Prize for her poetry collection, *Thomas and Beulah*, she is the author of *Fifth Sunday*, a collection of short stories. She lives in Virginia and is a professor at the University of Virginia, Charlottesville.

Ralph Ellison spent much of his life in New York City. A member of the American Academy of Arts and Letters and winner of the National Book Award for *Invisible Man*, an American classic, he died in 1994.

Carolyn Ferrell lives in New York City. Her story "Proper Library" also appears in *The Best American Short Stories 1994*. She is the author of an upcoming collection of short fiction, *Surprised by Joy and Other Stories*, to be published by Houghton Mifflin.

Thomas Glave has been published in *Muleteeth*, *Callaloo*, and *Gay Community News*, among other journals. He lives in New York City.

Jewelle Gomez is the author of *The Gilda Stories*, a novel for which she won the 1992 Lamda Book Award for Lesbian Fiction and Lesbian Science Fiction, and a collection of poetry, *Oral Tradition*, published by Firebrand Books. A resident of New York City for twenty years, she now lives in San Francisco.

Howard Gordon is the author of the short story collection *The African in Me*. He lives in Syracuse, New York.

Sam Greenlee, a native Chicagoan, is the author of *The Spook Who Sat by the Door*, and other works of fiction and poetry.

Carolivia Herron is the author of *Thereafter Johnnie* and edited *Selected Works of Angelina Weld Grimke*. She lives outside Boston.

Kelvin Christopher James is the author of *Jumping Ship*, a collection of short stories, and a novel, *Secrets*. He lives in Harlem.

Charles Johnson won the National Book Award for his novel *Middle Passage* and is the author of a collection of short stories, *The Sorcerer's Apprentice*. He lives in Seattle, where he is a professor at the University of Washington.

Edward P. Jones is the author of *Lost in the City*, a collection of short stories. In 1994, he won a Lannon Award for fiction. He resides in Arlington, Virginia.

Randall Kenan is the author of the short story collection *Let the Dead Bury Their Dead* and *Visitation of Spirits*, a novel. He lives in New York City.

Jamaica Kincaid is the author of a collection of short stories, *At the Bottom of the River*, and other works of fiction and nonfiction. She lives in Vermont.

Andrea Lee received the Jean Stein Award from the American Institute of Arts and Letters for her first book, *Russian Journal*. She is the author of a novel, *Sarah Phillips*, and lives in Europe.

Helen Elaine Lee had her first novel, *The Serpent's Gift*, published in 1994. Her story "Silences" appears in the novel. She lives in Washington, D.C.

Clarence Major is the author of several novels and volumes of poetry. He edited *Calling the Wind: 20th Century African American Short Stories* and resides in California, where he is the director of the Creative Writing Program at the University of California at Davis.

Colleen McElroy is the author of two collections of short fiction, *Jesus and Fat Tuesday and Other Short Stories* and *Driving under the Cardboard Pines*, and several volumes of poetry. A professor of English and creative writing at the University of Washington, she lives in Seattle.

Terry McMillan is the author of three novels, including *Waiting to Exhale*. She edited *Breaking Ice: An Anthology of Contemporary African-American Fiction* and lives in California.

James Alan McPherson won the 1978 Pulitzer Prize for fiction. He is the author of two collections of short stories, *Hue and Cry* and *Elbow Room*, and is a professor at the University of Iowa, where he makes his home.

Jess Mowry won the PEN Oakland/Josephine Miles Award for his first book, *Rats in the Trees*, a collection of stories. He lives in Oakland, California.

Gloria Naylor won the National Book Award for her first novel, *The Women of Brewster Place*. Her latest novel, *Bailey's Cafe*, was adapted for the stage and saw its world premier at the Hartford Stage Company in 1994. She lives in New York.

Diane Oliver died tragically in a car accident at the age of twenty-three. She was a graduate of the University of North Carolina, Greensboro, and the Writers Workshop at the University of Iowa. Her story "Neighbors" was included in *Prize Stories 1967: The O. Henry Awards* and has been frequently anthologized.

Ann Petry is the author of the short story collection *Miss Muriel and Other Stories*, and three novels, including *The Street*. She lives in Old Saybrook, Connecticut.

Jewell Parker Rhodes is the author of *Voodoo Dreams*, a novel. She lives in Arizona.

Ntozake Shange is the author of three novels, several volumes of poetry, and the choreoplay *for colored girls who have considered suicide/when the rainbow is enuf.* "oh she gotta head fulla hair" became a part of *Spell #7: A Play with Music*. She lives in Philadelphia.

Joyce Carol Thomas won the National Book Award for *Marked by Fire*, her first novel. She is a professor at the University of Tennessee and resides in Tennessee and California.

Alice Walker received the Pulitzer Prize and the National Book Award for her novel *The Color Purple*. She is the author of two collections of short stories, *You Can't Keep a Good Woman Down* and *In Love & Trouble* as well as several novels and volumes of poetry. She lives in California.

Michael Weaver is the author of five volumes of poetry, including *Timber and Prayer*. A graduate of Brown University's Creative Writing Program, he lives in Philadelphia.

John Edgar Wideman, Rhodes scholar, is the author of several novels and two memoirs, *Brothers and Keepers* and *Fatheralong*. His short fiction has been collected in *The Stories of John Edgar Wideman*. He teaches at the University of Massachusetts and lives in Amherst, Massachusetts.

Sherley Anne Williams is the author of a novel, *Dessa Rose*, two volumes of poetry, and the critical work *Give Birth to Brightness: A Thematic Study in Neo-Black Literature*. She is a professor at the University of California, San Diego, and resides in California.

Shay Youngblood, author of *Big Mama Stories*, is a graduate of Brown University's Creative Writing Program. She lives in Providence, Rhode Island.

The editor is grateful for permission to include the following previously copyrighted material:

Maya Angelou. "Steady Going Up" from *10 Times Black*. Copyright © 1972 by Maya Angelou. Reprinted by permission of The Helen Brann Agency, Inc.

James Baldwin. "Tell Me How Long the Train's Been Gone." Copyright © 1968 by James Baldwin. Reprinted by permission of the James Baldwin Estate and Michael Joseph Ltd.

Toni Cade Bambara. "The Lesson" from *Gorilla, My Love*. Copyright © 1972 by Toni Cade Bambara. Reprinted by permission of Random House, Inc. and The Women's Press Ltd.

Edwidge Danticat. "New York Day Women" from *Krik? Krak!* Copyright © 1995 by Edwidge Danticat. Reprinted by permission of Soho Press, Inc.

Samuel R. Delany. "The Tale of Gorgik." Copyright © 1979 by Samuel R. Delany. Reprinted by permission of the author and his agent, Henry Morrison, Inc.

Alexis DeVeaux. "Remember Him a Outlaw" from *Midnight Birds*. Copyright © 1972 by Alexis DeVeaux. Reprinted by permission of Marie Brown Associates.

Rita Dove. "Second-Hand Man" from *Fifth Sunday: Short Stories by Rita Dove, Callaloo Fiction Series*. Copyright © 1985 by Rita Dove. Reprinted by permission of the author.

Ralph Ellison. "Backwacking, a Plea to the Senator" from *Massachusetts Review, 18*. Copyright © 1977 by Ralph Ellison. Reprinted by permission of the William Morris Agency, Inc. on behalf of the author.

Carolyn Ferrell. "Proper Library." Copyright © 1993 by Carolyn Ferrell. Reprinted by permission of the Charlotte Sheedy Agency.

Thomas Glave. "— And Love Them?" Copyright © 1993 by Thomas Glave. Reprinted by permission of the author.

Jewelle Gomez. "Louisiana: 1850" from *The Gilda Stories*. Copyright © 1991 by Jewelle Gomez. Reprinted by permission of Firebrand Books.

Howard Gordon. "After Dreaming of President Johnson" from *The African in Me*. Copyright © 1992 by Howard Gordon. Reprinted by permission of the author.

Sam Greenlee. "Blues for Little Prez" from *Black World*. Copyright © 1973 by Sam Greenlee. Reprinted by permission of Lawrence Jordan Literary Agency.

Carolivia Herron. "That Place" from *Callaloo, Vol. 10, No. 3*. Copyright © 1987 by Carolivia Herron. Reprinted by permission of Marie Brown Associates.

Kelvin Christopher James. "Transaction" from *Jumping Ship and Other Stories*. Copyright © 1990 by Kelvin Christopher James. Reprinted by permission of Villard Books, a division of Random House, Inc. and the Robert Lantz/Joy Harris Agency.

Charles Johnson. "China" from *Sorcerer's Apprentice*. Copyright © 1983, 1986 by Charles Johnson. Reprinted by permission of Simon & Schuster and Georges Borchardt, Inc.

Edward P. Jones. "Lost in the City" from *Lost in the City*. Copyright © 1992 by Edward P. Jones. Reprinted by permission of William Morrow & Co. and Janklow & Nesbit Associates.

Randall Kenan. "Run, Mourner, Run" from *Let the Dead Bury Their Dead*. Copyright © 1992 by Randall Kenan. Reprinted by permission of Harcourt Brace & Company and Little, Brown and Company (U.K.) Ltd.

Jamaica Kincaid. "Blackness" from *At the Bottom of the River*. Copyright © 1983 by Jamaica Kincaid. Reprinted by permission of Farrar, Straus & Giroux, Inc. and Sanford J. Greenberger Associates.